□

ONE ACROSS, TWO DOWN
THE FACE OF TRESPASS
MAKE DEATH LOVE ME

□

□

ONE ACROSS, TWO DOWN
THE FACE OF TRESPASS
MAKE DEATH LOVE ME

□

RUTH RENDELL

QUALITY PAPERBACK BOOK CLUB
NEW YORK

□

ONE ACROSS, TWO DOWN

For my son

Come into the garden, Maud,
For the black bat, sight, has flown,
Come into the garden, Maud,
I am here at the gate alone.

ALFRED, LORD TENNYSON

1. Blank Puzzle

1

Vera Manning was very tired. She was too tired even to answer her mother back when Maud told her to hurry up with getting the tea.

"There's no need to sulk," said Maud.

"I'm not sulking, Mother. I'm tired."

"Of course you are. That goes without saying. Anyone can see you're worn out with that job of yours. Now if Stanley had the gumption to get himself a good position and brought a decent wage home you wouldn't have to work. I never heard of such a thing, a woman of your age, coming up to the change, on her feet all day in a dry-cleaner's. I've said it before and I'll say it again, if Stanley was a man at all . . ."

"All right, Mother," said Vera. "Let's give it a rest, shall we?"

But Maud, who scarcely ever stopped talking when there was anyone to listen to her and who talked to herself when she was alone, got out of her chair and, taking her stick, limped after Vera into the kitchen. Perching herself with some difficulty—she was a large heavily-built woman—on a stool, she surveyed the room with a distaste which was partly sincere and partly assumed for her daughter's benefit. It was clean but shabby, unchanged since the days when people expected to see a ganglion of water pipes protruding all over the walls and a dresser and built-in plaster copper requisite fitments. Presently, when the scornful glance had set the scene for fresh propaganda, Maud drew a deep breath and began again.

"I've scraped and saved all my life just so that there'd be something for you when I'm gone. D'you know what Ethel Carpenter said to me? Maud, she said, why don't you give it to Vee while she's young enough to enjoy it?"

Her back to Maud, Vera was cutting meat pie in slices and shelling hard-boiled eggs. "It's a funny thing, Mother," she said, "the way I'm an old woman one minute and a young one the next, whichever happens to suit your book."

Maud ignored this. "Why don't you give it to Vee now, she said. Oh no, I said. Oh no, it wouldn't be giving it to her, I said, it'd be giving it to that no-good husband of hers. If he got his hands on my money, I said, he'd never do another hand's turn as long as he lived."

"Move over a bit, would you, Mother? I can't get at the kettle."

Shifting an inch or two, Maud patted her thick grey curls with a lady's idle white hand. "No," she said, "while I've got breath in my body my savings are staying where they are, invested in good stock. That way maybe Stanley'll come to his senses. When you have a nervous breakdown, and that's the way you're heading, my girl, maybe he'll pull his socks up and get a job fit for a man, not a teenager. That's the way I see it and that's what I said to Ethel in my last letter."

"Would you like to sit up now, Mother? It's ready."

Vera helped her mother into a chair at the dining room table and hooked her stick over the back of it. Maud tucked a napkin into the neckline of her blue silk dress and helped herself to a plateful of pork pie, eggs, green salad and mashed potato. Before starting on it, she swallowed two white tablets and washed them down with strong sweet tea. Then she lifted her knife and fork with a sigh of sensual pleasure. Maud enjoyed her food. The only time she was silent was when she was eating or asleep. As she was starting on her second piece of pie, the back door slammed and her son-in-law came in.

Stanley Manning nodded to his wife and gave a sort of grunt. His mother-in-law, who had temporarily stopped eating to fix him with a cold condemning eye, he ignored. The first thing he did after throwing his coat over the back of a chair was to turn on the television.

"Had a good day?" said Vera.

"Been up to my eyes in it since nine this morning." Stanley sat down, facing the television, and waited for Vera to pour him a cup of tea. "I'm whacked out, I can tell you. It's no joke being out in the open all day long in weather like this. To tell you the truth, I don't know how long I can keep on with it."

Maud sniffed. "Ethel Carpenter didn't believe me when I told

her what you did for a living, if you can call it a living. A
petrol pump attendant! She said that's what her landlady's son
does in his holidays from college. Eighteen he is, just a student
doing it for pin money."

"Ethel Carpenter can keep her nose out of my business, the old
bag."

"Don't you use language like that about my friend!"

"Oh, pack it up, do," said Vera. "I thought you were going
to watch the film."

If Stanley and Maud were in accord over one thing it was
their fondness for old films and now, having exchanged venomous
glances, they settled down among the tea things to watch Jeanette
MacDonald in *The Girl of the Golden West*. Vera, a little revived with two hot cups of tea, sighed thankfully and began
clearing the table. Altercation would break out again, she knew,
at eight o'clock when Stanley's favourite quiz programme con-
flicted with Maud's favourite serial. She dreaded Tuesday and
Thursday evenings. Of course it was only natural that Stanley,
with his passion for puzzles, should want to watch the quizzes
that took place on those nights, and natural too that Maud, in
common with five million other middle-aged and elderly women,
should long for the next development in the complicated lives of
the residents of "Augusta Alley." But why couldn't they come
to an amicable arrangement like reasonable people? Because
they weren't reasonable people, she thought, as she began the
washing up. For her part, she couldn't care less about the television and sometimes she hoped the cathode ray tube would
break or a valve go or something. Certainly the way things were,
they wouldn't be able to afford to get it seen to.

Jeanette MacDonald was singing "Ave Maria" when she got
back into the living room and Maud was accompanying her in
a sentimental cracked soprano. Vera prayed for the song to end
before Stanley did something violent like bringing Maud's stick
down on the table with a thunderous crash, as he had done
only the week before. But this time he contented himself with
low mutterings and Vera leant her head against a cushion and
closed her eyes.

Four years Mother's been here, she thought, four long years of
unbroken hell. Why had she been so stupid and so impulsive as
to agree to it in the first place? It wasn't as if Maud was ill or

even really disabled. She'd made a marvellous recovery from that
stroke. There was nothing wrong with her but for a weakness in
the left leg and a little quirk to her mouth. She was as capable
of looking after herself as any woman of seventy-four. But it was
no good harking back now. The thing was done, Maud's house
sold and all her furniture, and she and Stanley had got her till
the day she died.

Maud's petulant angry wail started her out of her half-doze
and made her sit up with a jerk.

"What are you turning over to I.T.V. for? I've been looking
forward to my 'Augusta Alley' all day. We don't want that
kids' stuff, a lot of schoolkids answering silly questions."

"Who pays the licence, I'd like to know?" said Stanley.

"I pay my share. Every week I turn my pension over to Vee.
Ten shillings is the most I ever keep for my bits and pieces."

Stanley made no reply. He moved his chair closer to the set and
got out pencil and paper.

"All day long I was looking forward to my serial," said Maud.

"Never mind, Mother," said Vera, trying to infuse a little
cheerfulness into her tired voice. "Why don't you watch 'Oak
Valley Farm' in the afternoons when we're at work? That's a
nice serial, all about country people."

"I have my sleep in the afternoons, that's why not. I'm not
upsetting my routine."

Maud lapsed into a moody silence, but if she wasn't to be
allowed to watch her programme she had no intention of allowing
Stanley uninterrupted enjoyment of his. After about five minutes,
during which Stanley scribbled excitedly on his pad, she began
tapping her stick rhythmically against the fender. It sounded as if
she was trying to work out the timing of a hymn tune. "Dear
Lord and Father of Mankind," Vera thought it was, and presently Maud confirmed this by humming the melody very softly.

Stanley stood it for about thirty seconds and then he said,
"Shut up, will you?"

Maud gave a lugubrious sigh. "They played that hymn at your
grandfather's funeral, Vera."

"I don't care if they played it at Queen Victoria's bloody
wedding," said Stanley. "We don't want to hear it now, so do
as I say and shut up. There, now you've made me miss the score."

"I'm sure I'm very sorry," said Maud with heavy sarcasm. "I know you don't want me here, Stanley, you've made that very plain. You'd do anything to get rid of me, wouldn't you? Grease the stairs or give me an overdose?"

"Maybe I would at that. There's many a true word spoken in jest."

"You hear what he says, Vera? You heard him say it."

"He doesn't mean it, Mother."

"Just because I'm old and helpless and sometimes I hark back to the old days when I was happy."

Stanley leapt to his feet and the pencil bounced on to the floor.

"Will you shut up or do I have to make you?"

"Don't you raise your voice to me, Stanley Manning!" Maud, satisfied that she had ruined Stanley's quiz, rose and, turning to Vera with great dignity, said in the voice of one mortally wounded, "I shall go to bed now, Vera, and leave you and your husband in peace. Perhaps it wouldn't be expecting too much if I was to ask you to make me my Horlick's and bring it up when I'm in bed?"

"Of course I will, Mother. I always do."

"There's no need to say 'always' like that. I'd rather go without than have it done in a grudging spirit."

Maud wandered round the room, picking up her knitting from one chair, her glasses from another, her book from the sideboard. She could have got all these things by walking behind Stanley, but she didn't. She walked between him and the television set.

"Mustn't forget my glass of water," she said, and added as if she was boasting of some highly laudable principle, as salutary to the body as it was demanding of strength of character. "I've slept with a glass of water beside my bed ever since I was a little mite. Never missed once. I couldn't sleep without my glass of water."

She fetched it herself, leaving a little trail of drips from the overfull glass behind her. They heard her stick tapping against the treads as she mounted the stairs.

Stanley switched off the television and, without a word to his wife, opened the *Second Bumper Book of Advanced Crosswords*. Like an overworked animal, worn out with repetitive tedious labour, her mind empty of everything but the desire for sleep, Vera stared at him in silence. Then she went into the kitchen, made the Horlick's and carried it upstairs.

Sixty-one, Lanchester Road, Croughton, in the northern suburbs of London, was a two-storied red brick house, at the end of a terrace, and built in 1906. There was a large back garden, and between the living room bay and the front fence a strip of grass five feet by fifteen.

The hall was a passage with a mosaic floor of red and white tiles, and downstairs there were two living rooms and a tiny kitchen, as well as an outside lavatory and a cupboard for coal. The stairs ran straight up without a bend to a landing from which opened four doors, one to the bathroom and three to the bedrooms. The smallest of these was big enough to accommodate only a single bed, dressing table and curtained-off area for clothes. Vera called it the spare room.

She and Stanley shared the large double bedroom at the front of the house and Maud slept in the back. She was sitting up in bed, the picture of health in her hand-knitted angora bedjacket. But for the thirty or so metal curlers clipped into her hair, she might well have entered for and won a glamorous grandmother contest.

Perhaps the bottles and jars of patent and prescribed medicaments on the bedside table had something to do with the preservation, indeed the rejuvenation, of her mother, Vera thought, as she handed Maud the mug of Horlick's. There were enough of them. Anti-coagulants, diuretics, tranquillizers, sleep inducers and vitamin concentrates.

"Thank you, dear. My electric blanket won't come on. It needs servicing."

Turning away from her draggled and exhausted reflection in Maud's dressing table mirror, Vera said she would see to it tomorrow.

"That's right, and while you do you can ask them to look at my radio. And get me another ounce of this pink wool, will you?" Maud sipped her Horlick's. "Sit down, Vee. I want to talk to you where *he* can't hear."

"Can't it wait till tomorrow, Mother?"

"No, it can't. Tomorrow might be too late. Did you hear what he said to me about doing me in if he had the chance?"

"Oh Mother, you don't really think he meant it?"

Maud said calmly, "Stanley hates me. Not that it isn't mutual. Now you listen to what I've got to say."

Vera knew what was coming. She heard it with slight variations once or twice a week. "I'm not leaving Stan, and that's that. I've told you over and over again. I'm not leaving him."

Maud finished her Horlick's and said in a cajoling tone, "Just think what a life we could have together, Vee, you and me. I've got money enough for both of us. I'm telling you in confidence, I'm a wealthy woman by anyone's standards. You wouldn't have to go to work, you wouldn't have to lift a finger. We'd have a nice new house. I saw in the paper they're building some lovely bungalows out Chigwell way. I could buy one of them bungalows outright."

"If you want to give me some of your money, Mother, you can give it to me. I shan't argue. God knows, there's plenty we need in this house."

"Stanley Manning isn't getting a penny of my money," said Maud. She took her teeth out and placed them in a glass; then she gave Vera a gummy wheedling smile. "You're all I've got, Vee. What's mine is yours, you know that. You don't want to share it with him. What's he ever done for you? He's a crook and a jail-bird."

Vera controlled herself with difficulty.

"Stanley has been to prison once and once only, Mother, as you very well know. And that was when he was eighteen. It's downright cruel calling him a jailbird."

"He may have been to prison just the once, but how many times would he have been back there if all those people he works for hadn't been soft as butter? You know as well as I do he's been sacked twice for helping himself out of the till."

Getting to her feet, Vera said, "I'm tired, Mother, I want to go to bed and I'm not staying here if all you can do is abuse my husband."

"Ah, Vee . . ." Maud put out a hand and managed to make her wrist quiver as she did so. "Vee, don't be cross with me. I had such high hopes for you and look at you now, a poor old drudge tied to a man who doesn't care whether you live or die. It's true, Vee, you know it is." Vera let her hand rest limply in her mother's and Maud squeezed it tenderly. "We could have a lovely house, dear. We'd have fitted carpets and central heating and a woman in to clean every day. You're still young. You could learn to drive and I'd buy you a car. We could go for holidays. We could go abroad if you like."

"I married Stanley," said Vera, "and you always taught me marriage is for keeps."

"Vee, I've never told you how much I've got. If I tell you, you won't tell Stanley, will you?" Vera didn't say anything, and Maud, though seventy-four and for many years married herself, hadn't yet learnt that it is no good telling secrets to a married person if you want them to remain secrets. For, no matter how shaky the marriage and how incompatible the partners, a wife will always confide other people's confessions in her husband and a husband in his wife. "My money's mounted up through the years. I've got twenty thousand pounds in the bank, Vera. What d'you think of that?"

Vera felt the colour drain out of her face. It was a shock. Never in her wildest dreams had she supposed her mother to have half that amount, and she was sure it had never occurred to Stanley either.

"It's a lot of money," she said quietly.

"Now don't you tell him. If he knew what I was worth he'd start thinking up ways to get rid of me."

"Please, Mother, don't start that all over again. If anyone heard you they'd think you were going daft in the head. They would."

"Well, they can't hear me. I'll say good night now, dear. We'll talk about it again tomorrow."

"Good night, Mother," said Vera.

She didn't think any more about what her mother had said on the lines of taking her away from Stanley. She had heard it all before. Nor was she very much concerned that Maud suspected Stanley of murderous inclinations. Her mother was old and the old get strange ideas into their heads. It was silly and fantastic but it wasn't worth worrying about.

But she did wonder what Stanley would say when—and that

would have to be when she was less tired—she told him how much
money Maud had in the bank. Twenty thousand! It was a fortune. Still thinking about it, and thinking how even one-twentieth
part of it would improve the house and make her lot so much
lighter, Vera stripped off her clothes and rolled exhausted into
bed.

2

Maud was an old woman with dangerously high blood pressure
and one cerebral thrombosis behind her, but she wasn't affected
in her mind. The ideas she had that her son-in-law might kill
her if he got the chance weren't the fruit of senile maunderings
but notions of human behaviour formed by Maud in her im-
pressionable teens.

She had gone into service at the age of fourteen and much
of the talk in the kitchen and the servants' hall had dealt with
unscrupulous persons whom her fellow servants suspected of
murder or the intention of murder for gain. Cook often insisted
that the valet in the big house across the square would poison his
master as soon as the time was ripe merely for the sake of the
hundred pounds promised to him in the old man's will, while the
butler countered this with horrible tales of greedy heirs in the
great families that had employed him. Maud listened to all this
with the same receptive ear and the same gullibility as she listened
to the vicar's sermons on Sundays.

It seemed that from the butler down to the tweeny, no servant
was without a relative who at some time or another had not considered popping arsenic in a rich aunt's tea. A favourite phrase
in the servants' hall, on the lines of Eliza Doolittle's statement,
was:

"It's my belief the old man done her in."

And it was Maud's sincere belief that Stanley Manning would
do her in if he got the chance. Enlightening Vera as to the extent
of her fortune had been a temptation she hadn't been able to

resist, but when she awoke on the following morning she
wondered if she had been unwise. Vera would very likely tell
Stanley and there was nothing she, Maud, could do about it.

Nothing, that is, to silence Vera. Much could perhaps be
done to show Stanley that, though he might kill her, he wouldn't
profit from his iniquities. With these things uppermost in her
mind, Maud ate the breakfast Vera brought to her in bed and
when her daughter and son-in-law had left for work, got up,
dressed and left the house. With the aid of her stick she walked
the half-mile to the bus stop and went down into town to consult a solicitor whose name she had found in Stanley's trade
directory. She could easily have bought her own wool and seen
to the servicing of her electric blanket at the same time and
saved Vera's feet, but she didn't see why she should put herself
out for Vera when the silly girl was being so obstinate.

Back in the house by twelve Maud ate heartily of the cold
ham, salad, bread and butter and apple crumble pie Vera had
left her for her lunch and then she settled down to write her
weekly letter to her best friend, Ethel Carpenter. Like most of
the letters she had written to Ethel since she came to live in
Lanchester Road, it dealt largely with the idleness, ill manners,
bad temper and general uselessness of Stanley Manning.

There was no one, Maud thought, whom she could trust like
she could trust Ethel. Even Vera, blindly devoted to that good-
for-nothing, couldn't be relied on like Ethel who had no husband, no children and no axe to grind. Poor Ethel had only
her landlady, owner of the house in Brixton where she occupied
one room, and Maud herself.

Ah, you valued a friend when you'd been through what she
and Ethel had been through together, thought Maud as she
laid down her pen. How long ago was it they'd first met?
Fifty-four years? Fifty-five? No, it was just fifty-four. She was
twenty and the under housemaid and Ethel, little, innocent
seventeen-year-old Ethel, the kitchen maid at that sharp-tongued
cook's beck and call.

Maud was walking out with George Kinaway, the chauffeur,
and they were going to get married as soon as their ship came
in. She had always been a saver, had Maud, and whether the ship
came in or not they'd have enough to get married on by the

time she was thirty. Meanwhile there were those delicious quiet walks with George on Clapham Common on Sundays and the' little garnet engagement ring she wore round her neck on a bit of ribbon, for it wouldn't have done at all to have it on her finger when she did out the grates.

She had George and something to look forward to but Ethel had nothing. No one knew Ethel even had a follower of her own or had ever spoken to a man, bar George and the butler, until her trouble came on her and Madam turned her out of the house in disgrace. Ethel's aunt took her in and everyone treated her like dirt except Maud and George. They weren't above going to see her at the aunt's house on their evenings off, and when the child came it was George who persuaded the aunt to bring it up and George who contributed a few shillings every week to its maintenance.

"Though we can ill afford it," said Maud. "Now if she'd only stop being a little fool and tell me who the father is . . ."

"She'll never do that," said George. "She's too proud."

"Well, they do say that pride goeth before a fall and Ethel's taken her fall all right. It's our duty to stick by her. We must never lose touch with Ethel, dear."

"If you say so, dear," said George, and he got Madam to take Ethel back just as if she were a good girl without a stain on her character.

Those were hard days, Maud thought, leaning back her head and closing her eyes. Twelve pounds a year she got until the Great War came and made people buck up their ideas. Even when the master raised her wages it was hard going to get a home together and in the end it was George's good looks and nice manners that gave them their start. Not that there had ever been anything wrong between him and Madam—the very idea!—but when she died George was in her will, and with the two hundred and fifty he got and what Maud had saved they'd bought a nice little business down by the Oval.

Ethel always came to them for her holidays and when Vera was born Ethel was her godmother. It was the least she could do for Ethel, Maud confided in George, seeing that she'd been deprived of her own daughter and wasn't likely ever to get a husband of her own, second-hand goods as she was.

What with George's charm and Maud's hard work the shop prospered and soon they could think themselves comfortably off. Vera was sent to a very select private school and when she left at the late (almost unheard-of) age of sixteen, Maud wouldn't let her get a job or serve in the shop. Her daughter was going to be a lady and in time she'd marry a nice gentlemanly man, a bank clerk or someone in business—Maud never told people her husband kept a shop. She always said he was "in business"—and have a house of her own. Meanwhile she gave Vera all the money she wanted within reason for clothes and once a year they all went down to Brayminster-on-Sea—dear old Bray, as they called it—and stayed at a very genteel boarding-house with a view of the sea. Sometimes Ethel went with them and she was just as pleased as they when her goddaughter found favour in the sight of the boarding-house keeper's nephew, James Horton.

James had the very job Maud envisaged as most desirable in a son-in-law. He worked in the Brayminster branch of Barclay's Bank, and when during the winter months he occasionally came up to London and took Vera on the river or to the theatre matinée, Maud smiled on him and began discussing with George what they could do for the young couple when they fixed the day. A deposit on a house and two hundred for furniture was Ethel Carpenter's recommendation and Maud thought this not unreasonable.

Four years older than Vera, James had been a petty officer in the Royal Navy during the war. He had a nice little sum on deposit at the bank, was a dutiful son and churchgoer. Nothing could be more suitable.

Maud had old-fashioned ideas and thought young people should only be allowed to know each other if they had been properly introduced or if their parents were old friends. It was with horror, therefore, that she learned from Mrs. Campbell, the wife of the fishmonger down the road, that Vera had been seen about in the company of the young barman at the Coach and Horses whom, Mrs. Campbell alleged, she had met at a dance.

It was all George's fault, Maud told Ethel. If she had had her way, Vera would never have been allowed to go to that dance. She had tried to put her foot down but for once George had asserted himself and said there was no harm in Vera going with a

girl friend and what could be more respectable than the Young
Conservatives' annual ball?

"I'm sure I don't know what James will say when he hears about
it," Maud said to Vera.

"I don't care what he says. I'm sick of James, he's so boring. Always on about going to bed early and getting up early and saving
money and keeping oneself to oneself. Stanley says you're only
young once and you might as well enjoy yourself. He says
money's there to spend."

"I daresay he does when it's someone else's. A barman! My
daughter sneaking out with a barman!" Although she sometimes
permitted George to enjoy a quiet pint in the Bunch of Grapes
with Mr. Campbell on Friday nights, Maud had never in her life
set foot in a public house. "Anyway, it's got to stop, Vee. You
can tell him your mother and father won't allow it."

"I'm twenty-two," said Vera, who, though her father's daughter in looks and generally in temperament, had inherited a
spark of her mother's spirit. "You can't stop me. You're always on
about me getting married but how can I get married when I
never meet any men? Girls can't meet men when they don't
go out to work."

"You met James," said Maud.

Afterwards she wasn't sure which was the worst moment of
her life, the time when Mrs. Campbell told her Stanley Manning
had served two years for robbery with violence or the time when
Vera said she was in love with Stanley and wanted to marry
him.

"Don't you dare talk of marrying that criminal!" Maud
screamed. "You'll marry him over my dead body. I'll kill myself
first. I'll put my head in the gas oven. And I'll see to it you won't
get a penny of my money."

The trouble was she couldn't stop Vera meeting him. For a
time nothing more was said about marriage or even an engagement but Vera and Stanley went on seeing each other and Maud
nearly worried herself into a nervous breakdown. For the life
of her, she couldn't see what Vera saw in him.

In all her life she had only known one man she could fancy
sharing her bed with and by this yardstick she measured all men.
George Kinaway was six feet tall with classic Anglo-Saxon good

looks apart from his weak chin, while Stanley was a little man, no taller than Vera. His hair was already thinning and always looked greasy. He had a nut-brown face that Maud prophesied would wrinkle early and shifty black eyes that never looked straight at you. Well aware of who wore the trousers in the Kinaway household, he smiled ingratiatingly at Maud if ever he met her in the street, greeting her with an oily, "Good morning, Mrs. Kinaway, lovely morning," and shaking his head sadly when she marched past him in cold silence.

She wouldn't have him in the shop or the flat above it and she consoled herself in the knowledge that Stanley worked in his bar every evening. The main disadvantage of Vera not having a job was that she was at liberty to meet Stanley during the day, and barmen work peculiar hours, being free for most of the morning and half the afternoon. But Maud thought that "anything wrong," by which she meant sexual intercourse, only ever took place between ten and midnight—this belief was based on her own experience, although in her case she regarded it as right and proper —and it was during those two hours that Stanley was most busily occupied. It was with horror and near-incredulity, therefore, that she learnt from a weeping Vera that she was over two months pregnant.

"Poor Ethel all over again," sobbed Maud. "That such a disgraceful thing should happen to my own child!"

But foolish and wicked as Vera had been, she mustn't be allowed to suffer as Ethel had suffered. Vera should have her husband and her house and a decent home for her baby. Vera should be married.

Instead of the big wedding Maud had dreamed of, Vera and Stanley were married quietly with only a dozen close relatives and friends as guests and they went straight off home to the little terraced house in Lanchester Road, Croughton. There was little Maud could do to humiliate Stanley but she had seen to it that when she and George put up the money for the house, the deeds were in Vera's name and Stanley was made to understand that every penny must be paid back.

They had been married three weeks when Vera had a miscarriage.

"Oh my God," said Maud at the hospital bedside, "why ever

were we so hasty? Your father said we should wait a bit and he was right."

"What do you mean?"

"Three weeks we should have waited . . ."

"I've lost my baby," said Vera, sitting up in bed, "and now you'd like to take my husband away from me."

When she was well again, Vera took a job for the first time in her life to pay back the money she owed her parents. For Maud was adamant. She didn't mind giving Vera a cheque now and then to buy herself a dress or taking her out and giving her a slap-up lunch, but Stanley Manning wasn't getting his hooks on her money. He must pull up his socks, make a decent living and then Maud would think again. . . .

As soon as she realised this would never happen, she set out to get Vera away from him, a plan which was far more tenable now she actually lived in the same house with her daughter. She pursued it in two ways: by showing her how difficult her present life was, making it even more difficult and maintaining an atmosphere of strife: and by holding out the inducements of an alternative existence, a life of ease and peace and plenty.

So far she had met with little success. Vera had always been stubborn. Her mother's daughter, Maud thought lovingly. The little bribes and the enticing pictures she had painted of life without Stanley hadn't made a chink in Vera's armour. Never mind. The time had come to put the squeeze on. It hadn't escaped Maud's notice that Vera had turned quite pale at the mention of that twenty thousand pounds. She'd be thinking about that now while she stood in that dreadful place, shoving re-texed, moth-proofed coats into polythene bags. And tonight Maud would play her trump card.

Thinking about it and the effect it would have made her sigh contentedly as she laid her head back against the pillows and switched on the second bar on the electric fire with her good foot. Vera would realise that she meant business and Stanley . . . Well, Stanley would see it was useless getting any ideas about helping his mother-in-law out of this world.

Funny, really. Stanley wanted to get rid of her and she meant to get rid of Stanley. But she was going to get in first. She had him by the short hairs. Maud smiled, closed her eyes and fell at once into deep sleep.

3

Of the fifty motorists who pulled in for petrol at the Superjuce garage that day only five got service from Stanley. He didn't even hear the hooters and the shouts of the half-dozen out of the other forty-five who bothered to wait. He sat with his back to them in his little glass booth, dreaming of the twenty thousand pounds Maud had in the bank and which Vera had told him about at breakfast.

When George Kinaway had died, Stanley had waited excitedly for the contents of the will to be made known to him. He could hardly believe his ears when Vera told him there was no will, for everything had been in her mother's name. Impatient like most people of his kind, he prepared for another long bitter wait and his temper grew sourer.

The tobacconist's had been given up and Maud had retired to luxury in a small but sumptuous detached house at Eltham. Stanley never went there—he wasn't invited—and he showed small sympathy when Vera, lunched and cosseted by her mother, returned home from a day at Eltham full of anecdotes about Maud's high blood pressure. Through the years this was Stanley's only consolation and, being a man of more than average intelligence who could have excelled at any of several well-paid careers if he had only put his mind to it (if he had had a chance, was the way he put it), he set out to study the whole subject of blood pressure and hardening of the arteries. At that time he was working as a factory night watchman. No one ever tried to break into the factory which was on its last legs and contained nothing worth stealing, so Stanley whiled away the long hours very pleasantly in reading medical books he got out of the public library.

It was therefore no surprise to him when he arrived home one morning to be greeted by Vera with the news that her mother had had a cerebral thrombosis.

While pulling long faces and being unusually kind to his wife, Stanley began calculating his inheritance. There ought to be at least eight thousand from the sale of Maud's house as well as a tidy sum in the bank. The first thing he'd buy would be a large car just to put the neighbours' noses out of joint.

Then Maud got better.

Stanley, hope springing eternal, agreed that she should come and live with them in Lanchester Road. The extra work, after all, would fall on Vera and if the eight thousand didn't immediately fall into his lap, there was bound to be a share-out. No one, in Stanley's view, parked themselves on a relative without paying their way, and if Maud was sticky, he would drop her a gentle but unmistakable hint.

Two days after she arrived, Maud explained her intentions. With the exception of ten shillings a week, her whole pension would be handed over to Vera but her capital remained where it was, comfortably invested.

"I never heard such a diabolical bloody liberty," said Stanley.

"Her pension pays for her food, Stan."

"And what about her lodgings? What about the work she makes?"

"She's my mother," said Vera.

The time had come to put that phrase into the past tense. Not murder, of course, not actual murder. Since he had knocked that old woman on the head and taken her handbag when he was eighteen, Stanley had never laid violent hands on anyone and when he read of murder in the newspapers he was as shocked as Vera and as vociferous as Maud in demanding the return of the death penalty. As in the case of that shot police constable, for instance, P. C. Chappell, who had died trying to stop thugs breaking into Croughton Post Office last month. No, murder was something he wouldn't even consider. An accident was what he had in mind. Some short of carelessness with the gas or a mix-up over all those pills and tablets Maud took.

A scheme for gassing Maud taking shape in his mind, Stanley walked into the house whistling cheerfully. He didn't kiss Vera but he said hallo to her and patted her shoulder as he went to switch on television.

Thinking now of her days as numbered, Stanley had been

prepared to unbend a little with Maud. But as soon as he saw her, sitting up straight at the table and already on her second helping of eggs and chips, her face red with determination and ill temper, he girded himself for battle.

"Had a busy day, Ma?"

"Busier than yours, I daresay," said Maud. "I had a chat over the fence with Mrs. Blackmore this afternoon and she said her husband went to get his petrol at your garage but he couldn't get no service. He could see you, though, and he reckoned you were asleep."

Stanley glared at her. "I don't want you gossiping over the fence any more, is that clear? Walking all over my garden and trampling down the plants."

"It's not your garden, it's Vera's."

She could scarcely have said anything more irritating to Stanley. Brought up in the country, on the borders of Essex and Suffolk where his father had a small holding, he had loved gardening all his life and he called it his only relaxation, forgetting for the time his crosswords and his medical books. But this passion of his was out of character—gardening is generally associated with the mild, the civilised and the law-abiding—and Maud refused to take it seriously. She liked to think of Stanley as among the outcast, the utterly lost, while gardening was one of the pastimes she had respected all her life. So she would watch him tending his heather garden or watering his gladioli and then, when he came in to wash his hands, tell him not to forget that the garden, along with the rest of the property, was Vera's and Vera could sell it over his head whenever the fancy took her.

Now, pleased that her retort had needled Stanley, she turned to Vera and asked if she had remembered to get her skein of wool.

"It went right out of my head, Mother. I *am* sorry."

"That puts paid to my knitting for tonight then," said Maud sourly. "If I'd known I'd have got it myself when I was in town."

"What were you doing in town?"

"I went," said Maud, shouting above the television, "to see my solicitor."

"Since when have you had a solicitor?" said Stanley.

"Since this morning, Mr. Clever. A poor old widow in my

position needs a solicitor to protect her. He was very nice to me, I can tell you, a real gentleman. Great comfort he gave me. I told him, I'll be able to sleep in my bed now."

"I don't know what you're on about," said Stanley uneasily and he added, "for God's sake someone turn that T.V. down," as if Vera or her mother and not he had switched it on. "That's better. Now we can hear ourselves speak. Right, what's all this about?"

"My will. I made my will this morning and I got the solicitor to put it the way I want it. If Vera and me were living alone it'd be a different thing. All I've got is coming to her, I don't know how many times I've told you. But you listen, this is what I've done. If I die of a stroke you get the lot but if I die of anything else it all goes to Ethel Carpenter. And now you know."

Vera dropped her fork. "I don't know at all, Mother. I don't know what any of that's supposed to mean."

"It's clear enough," said Maud. "So just you think about it."

She gave them a grim smile, and hobbling rapidly to the television, turned up the volume.

"That," said Stanley in bed that night, "is the biggest bloody-insult I've ever had said to me. Insinuating I'd put her out of the way! I reckon she's going cracked."

"If it's true," said Vera.

"It doesn't matter a damn whether it's *true*. Maybe she went and maybe she didn't, and maybe the solicitor put that in and maybe he never did. Whichever way you like to look at it, she's got us by the short hairs."

"No, she hasn't, love. It's not as if we'd have dreamt of harming her. Of course she'll die of a stroke. What hurts is that Mother should even think of such a thing."

"And if she doesn't die of a stroke, what then?"

"I don't believe any solicitor'd put that in a will." Vera sighed heavily and turned over. "I must go to sleep now. I'm dead tired."

On the whole, Stanley thought Vera was right and no solicitor would have agreed to Maud's condition. It probably wasn't legal. But if Maud said it was and there was no one with the knowledge to argue. . . .

Vera worked all day Saturdays and Stanley and Maud were left alone together. On fine Saturdays Stanley spent hours in the garden and when it rained he went to the pictures.

March had been mild and the almond tree was already in flower. Daffodils were in bud but the ericas in his heather garden were just past their prime. It was time to nourish them with a bale of peat, for the soil of Croughton was London clay. Stanley fetched a new sackful from the shed, scattered peat around the established plants and dug a trench. This would be filled with peat for the new plants he had ordered.

Although he objected to Maud's gossiping over the fence with Mrs. Blackmore at number 59 or Mrs. Macdonald at number 63, Stanley wasn't averse to breaking off from his digging for an occasional chat. Today, when Mrs. Blackmore came out to peg a couple of shirts on her line, he would have liked nothing better than to have catalogued, as was his usual habit, Maud's latest solecisms and insults, but this would no longer do. He must establish himself in his neighbour's estimation as a tolerant and even affectionate son-in-law.

"She's all right," he said in answer to Mrs. Blackmore's enquiry. "As well as can be expected."

"I always say to John, Mrs. Kinaway's wonderful really when you think what she's been through."

Mrs. Blackmore was a tiny birdlike woman who always wore her dyed blonde hair tied up in two bunches like a little girl, although in other respects she seemed resigned to middle age. Her eyes were sharp and bright and she had the disconcerting habit of staring hard into the eyes of anyone with whom she happened to be talking. Stanley met those eyes boldly now, doing his best not to blink.

"You can't help admiring her," he said with a little smiling shake of his head.

"I know you really feel that." Mrs. Blackmore was somewhat taken aback and temporarily her eyes wavered. "Has she seen the doctor lately?"

"Old Dr. Blake retired and she won't have anything to do with the new one. She says he's too young."

"Dr. Moxley? He's thirty-five if he's a day. Still, I daresay that seems young to her."

"You have to respect their funny ways, the old folks," said Stanley piously. Their eyes engaged in a hard tug-of-war which Stanley won. Mrs. Blackmore dropped her gaze and, muttering something about getting the lunch, went into her house.

Stanley's own meal was of necessity a cold one. He and Maud ate it in silence and afterwards, while Stanley sat down with the *Daily Telegraph* crossword, his mother-in-law prepared to have her rest.

When she was alone she simply sat in an armchair and dozed with her head against one of the wings, but on Saturdays with Stanley in the room, she made a considerable fuss. First she gathered up every available cushion, making a point of pulling out of one behind Stanley's head, and arranged them very slowly all over the head and foot of the sofa. Then she made her way upstairs, tapping her stick and humming, to return with an armful of blankets. The weight of the blankets made her breath laboured and she gave vent to groans. At last, having taken off her glasses and her shoes, she heaved herself up on to the sofa, pulled the blankets over her and lay gasping.

Her son-in-law took absolutely no notice of any of this. He filled in his crossword, smiling sometimes at the ingenuity of the man who had set it, and occasionally mouthing the words of a clue. When Maud could stand his indifference no longer, she said acidly:

"In my young days a gentleman took pride in helping an old lady."

"I'm no gentleman," said Stanley. "You have to have money to be a gentleman."

"Oh, no, you don't. Gentlemen are born, let me tell you. You'd be uncouth no matter what money you'd got."

"You could do with being a bit more couth yourself," said Stanley, and having triumphantly silenced his mother-in-law, he filled in 28 across which completed his puzzle.

Maud closed her eyes and set her mouth in a grim line. Doodling on the edge of his paper, Stanley watched her speculatively until those crinkled compressed lips relaxed, the hand which gripped the blanket went limp, and he knew she was asleep. Then, folding his paper, he tiptoed out of the room and made his way to Maud's bedroom.

She had evidently spent the greater part of the morning writing to Ethel Carpenter, for the finished letter lay exposed on her bed-side table. Stanley sat down on the edge of the bed to read it.

He had always suspected that he and his doings formed one of the favourite topics of the old women's discussions, but he had never supposed that Maud would devote three and a half sides of paper to nothing but a denigration of his character. He was outraged and he was also bitterly hurt. It was a favour he was doing Maud, after all, letting her live in his house, and the in-gratitude implicit in this letter made his blood boil.

Frowning angrily, he read through what Maud had to say about his laziness and his ill manners. She had even had the effrontery to tell Ethel that he had borrowed a fiver from Vera the day before which, Maud declared, he intended to put on a horse for the National. This had been Stanley's purpose but now he told himself he had wanted it to buy more peat and young heather plants. The old bitch! The evil-tongued old bitch! What was this next bit?

"Of course poor Vee will never see her money again," Maud had written. "He will see to that. She works like a slave but she wouldn't have a rag for her back, bar what I give her. Still, it is only a matter of time now before I shall get her away from him. She is too loyal to say yes mother I'll come, knowing no doubt what a scene *he* would make and perhaps even strike her. I wouldn't put anything past him, my dear. The other day I told her I would buy her whatever she liked to name on condition she would leave him and the tears came into her poor eyes. It went to my heart, I can tell you, seeing my only child in distress. But I tell myself I am being cruel only to be kind and she will thank me on her bended knees when she is rid of him at last and living with me in the lovely house I mean to buy her. I have got my eye on one I saw in an advertisement in the Sunday paper, a lovely place just built in Chigwell, and when Vee has her after-noon off I am thinking of hiring a car to take us both out to look at it. Without *him* of course. . . ."

Stanley nearly tore the letter up, he was so angry. Until then he had had no idea of Maud's plans, for Vera had been afraid to tell him about them, although he had guessed there was some-thing afoot. If I'd only got money, he raged, I'd sue the old bitch for what-d'you-call-it?—enticement. That's what I'd do, have her

up in court for trying to take a man's lawful wife away from
him.

He sat staring moodily at the letter, suddenly aware of the
great danger he was in. Without Vera, he had no hope of ever
getting his hands on that twenty thousand. It would be the
breadline for him all the rest of his life while Vera lived in
luxury. My God, he thought, even the house, the very roof over
his head, belonged to her. And what a beanfeast those two would
have, hired cars, perhaps even a car of their own, a modern
house in snooty Chigwell, clothes, holidays, every convenience.
The whole idea was unbearable to contemplate and suddenly he
was seized with the urgency of what he must do and reminded
too of his original purpose in coming up to Maud's room.

Leaving the letter as he had found it, he turned his attention to
the three containers of pills which stood under the bedlamp.
Those pale blue capsules were sleep-inducing; they didn't interest him. Next came the yellow vitamin things which, Stanley
was sure, were responsible for Maud's abundant vitality and kept
her tongue in sprightly working order. Nevertheless, he wouldn't
mess about with them. These were the ones he wanted, the
tiny anti-coagulant tablets called Mollanoid of which Maud took
six a day and which, Stanley supposed, kept her blood from
clotting as it coursed through those brittle arteries. He took one
from the carton and folded it inside his handkerchief.

She was still asleep when he came downstairs and, generously,
he would have let her have her rest without interruption on any
other Saturday. But now, with the memory of the libellous letter
uppermost in his mind, he switched on the television for "Sports
Round-Up" and took a bitter pleasure in seeing her jerk awake.

Stanley wasn't allowed to leave his glass booth between nine
and five, although he often did so and for this truancy had several
times been threatened with the sack. But the chemist on the other
side of the street would be closed when he knocked off and he
couldn't afford to wait until the following Saturday before buying
the substitute tablets he required.

He waited until one o'clock, the slackest time of the day, and
then he sneaked across the road. But instead of one of the girls
being behind the counter, the pharmacist himself was on duty
and showed such an interest in all this fumbling among the

bottles and boxes that Stanley thought it wiser to try Boot's, although it was a quarter of a mile away.

There he found all the goods on display on self-service stands and he was able to study a variety of white pills without being observed. All the aspirin and codeine and phenacetin tablets were too big and the only thing he could find approximating in size to Maud's anti-coagulants were a saccharine compound for the use of slimmers.

These he thought would do. The tablets looked exactly like the one he had appropriated. He tried a single tablet on his tongue and it was very sweet, but Maud always swallowed her tablets down quickly in a sweet drink and very likely the taste would be disguised.

"D'you mind not eating the goods before you've paid for them?" said a girl assistant pertly.

"If you're accusing me of stealing I want to see the manager."

"All right, all right. There's no need to shout. That'll be five and six, please."

"And bloody daylight robbery," said Stanley. But he bought the phial of Shu-go-Sub and ran all the way back to the garage.

Three cars were drawn up by the pumps and Stanley's boss, holding the petrol nozzle delicately and furiously as far as possible from the lapels of his immaculate suit, was doing his best to serve the first customer. Stanley went into his booth and watched him through the glass. Presently, when the cars had gone, his boss marched into the booth, rubbing his oily hands.

"I've had about as much of this as I can stand, Manning," he said. "God knows how much custom we'd have lost if some enterprising motorist hadn't phoned me to ask what the hell was going on. I said I wouldn't tell you again and I won't. You can have your cards and get out on Friday."

"It'll be a pleasure," said Stanley. "I was going, anyway, before this dump goes bust."

The loss of his job didn't particularly dismay him. He was used to losing jobs and he enjoyed the freedom of several weeks out of work, during which he would draw ample untaxed unemployment benefit. Telling Vera, though, was something he didn't much look forward to and he was determined to prevent Maud finding out. That would be nice, something to cheer a man up, having his misfortunes shouted over the garden fences and sent winging in choice virulent phrases down over the river to Ethel Carpenter in Brixton.

But perhaps Maud wouldn't be able to gossip or write letters much longer. Stanley fingered the phial in his pocket. She often said it was only her tablets that kept her alive and maybe it wouldn't be more than a few days when her system reacted violently to a concentration of saccharine instead of its usual anti-coagulant intake.

Stanley walked home slowly, stopping outside the Jaguar show-rooms to eye speculatively a dark red E-type.

4

"These tablets," said Maud, "have a very funny taste. Sweetish. You're sure they made up the prescription right, Vee?"

"It's your regular prescription, Mother. The one old Dr. Blake wrote out before he retired. I took it to the chemist like I always do." Vera picked up the carton and looked at it just to make sure Maud wasn't taking vitamins or diuretics by mistake. No, it was the Mollanoid all right. *Mrs. M. Kinaway*, the label said, *two to be taken three times a day*, and there was the little smear the chemist's thumb had made because he hadn't waited for the ink to dry before handing it to her. "If you've got any doubts," she said, "why don't you let me make you an appointment with Dr. Moxley? They say he's ever so nice."

"I don't want him. I don't want young boys messing me about." Maud sipped her breakfast tea and swallowed her second tablet. "I daresay I've made the tea too sweet, that's what it is. Anyway, they're not doing me any harm, whatever's in them. To tell you the truth, I feel better than I have done for months, not so tired. There's the postman now. Run down like a good girl and see if there's anything from your auntie Ethel."

The telephone bill and a letter with the Brixton postmark. Vera decided she wouldn't open the bill until she got home. All right, that was being an ostrich, but why not? Ostriches might stick their faces in the sand but they did all right, galloping about in Australia or wherever it was and they didn't get old before their time. I wouldn't mind being an ostrich or anything, come to that, thought Vera as long as it was a change from being me.

She grabbed her coat from the hook in the hall and trailed up the stairs again, buttoning it as she went. Maud was up, sitting on the side of her bed buffing her fingernails with a silver-backed polisher.

"It's only ten to," said Maud. "You can spare the time to hear what Auntie Ethel has to say. You never know what news she's got."

What news did she ever have? Vera didn't want to chance being late just to hear that Ethel Carpenter's cyclamen had got five flowers on it or her landlady's little niece had the measles. But she waited just the same, tapping her feet impatiently. Anything to keep the peace, she thought, anything to put Mother in a good mood.

"What d'you think?" said Maud. "Auntie Ethel's going to move. She's giving up her room and getting one near here. Listen to this: 'I heard of a nice room going in Green Lanes just half a mile from you, dear, and popped over to see it on Saturday.' Why didn't she call, I wonder? Oh, here it is, she says—yes, she says, 'I would have looked you up but I remembered you always have your rest in the afternoon and it seemed a shame to disturb you.' Ethel always was considerate."

"I must go, Mother."

"Wait just one minute . . . 'I wouldn't want to come when Vee was out and you say she works Saturdays.' Et cetera, et cetera . . . Oh, listen, Vee. 'My landlady has got a student to take my room from April 10th, a Friday, and as she has been so good to me and I don't want to put her out, and Mrs. Paterson in Green Lanes can't take me till the Monday, I was wondering if Vee could put me up for that weekend. It would be such a treat to see you and Vee and have a nice long chat about old times. . . .' I'll write back and say yes, shall I?"

"I don't know, Mother." Vera sighed and gave a hopeless shrug. "What will Stanley say? I wouldn't want you and Auntie Ethel getting at him all the time."

"It's your house," said Maud.

"That sort of thing now. That's the very thing I mean. I'll have to think about it. I must *go*."

"I'll have to let her know soon," Maud called after her. "You put your foot down. Stanley'll have to lump it."

He was bound to have heard that, she thought, lying in bed in the next room as he no doubt was. The prospect of the ensuing battle excited her and she felt a surge of well-being comparable to that she used to feel long ago on Sunday mornings when she was looking forward to her weekly walk with George.

It was wrong, of course, to *enjoy* quarrelling. George would have told her to keep the peace at any price. But George had never lived in the same house as Stanley Manning and if he had he would have approved of her tactics. He would have seen the importance of rescuing Vera.

Maud went over to the dressing table and took her framed photograph of George out of a drawer. The slight sentimentality which the sight of it aroused in her was mixed with that exasperation she had so often felt for her husband when he was alive. Without a doubt she missed him, and if he could have been resurrected, would have welcomed him back but still she had to admit that in some ways he had been a drag on her, too weak, too scrupulous and much too inclined to let things drift. Ethel now was a different person altogether. Ethel had had to fight for things all her life, just as she had.

Maud put the photograph away. Nothing could have pleased her more than the news contained in the letter. With Ethel just down the road, and very likely popping in every day, the conquest of Vera would be accomplished in a matter of weeks. Ethel had such a grasp on things, such bustling strength. She would talk to Vera and when Vera saw that an outsider, an uninvolved observer, agreed with her mother, she would surrender and bow to circumstances with all George's resignation.

Stanley would be left alone. It made Maud almost chuckle aloud to think of him dependent only on what he could earn for himself, cooking his own meals and sinking into the squalor which Maud felt was his natural habitat. Not that he would be allowed to occupy this house. He must find himself a room somewhere. But all that could be gone into once Vera was out of his influence. And then perhaps they could settle Ethel in here. Life

had treated Ethel badly and it would be such a joy to give her a
home of her own at last and see her smiling, maybe even weeping, with gratitude. Maud's heart swelled, full of the pleasure of
philanthropy.

The unemployment benefit which the Labour Exchange paid
out to Stanley was a good deal in excess of the sum he had
mentioned to Vera. He needed the surplus for himself, for he
was spending a fortune on Shu-go-Sub as well as a fair amount on
almost daily visits to the pictures to get out of Maud's way.
Hoping to see a considerable decline in her health by this time,
he was bitterly disappointed to notice that rather than enfeebled,
she seemed actually stronger, more vital looking and younger
than before he had begun emptying Shu-go-Sub tubes into the
Mollanoid carton. If only she would exert herself more, go for
walks or carry heavy weights. Letter writing wasn't likely to raise
her blood pressure.

Entering the house that evening after a pleasant three hours
watching a double horror bill, he was sure there was something
going on. Those two were hatching a plot between them, perhaps
the very thing he most dreaded, the enticement of Vera. They had
stopped talking the minute he walked in the back door and Vera
looked as if she had been crying.

"I've been tramping the streets since one," he said, "looking
for work."

"Work's not easy to come by when you've no qualifications,"
said Maud. "Can't they find you anything down at the Labour?"

Stanley took the cup of tea Vera handed him and shook his
head gloomily.

"Something will turn up, dear."

"Doesn't matter to him one way or the other, does it?" said
Maud. "He's got someone to keep him. Have you given Vee that
money you owe her?"

Since he had been substituting saccharine for Maud's tablets,
Stanley had moderated his attitude to her, calling her "Ma" and
giving in over the television programmes, much as it went against
the grain. But now his self-control snapped.

"You mind your own business, Maud Kinaway. That's a private
matter between me and my wife."

"What concerns Vera concerns me. That's her money that she

earned. Haven't you ever heard of the Married Women's Property Act? Eighteen seventy-something that went through Parliament. More than a hundred years a woman's had a right to her own money."

"I suppose you were sitting in the Ladies' Gallery when it was passed," said Stanley.

The blood rushed into Maud's face. "Are you going to sit there and let him speak to me like that, Vera?"

Vera wasn't sitting at all, but scuttling between the living room and the kitchen with plates of sausages and mashed potato. "I'm so used," she said not quite truthfully, "to hearing you two bicker that it goes right over my head. Come and sit down, do. We want to be finished and cleared away before 'Augusta Alley' comes on."

Prickly and resentful, Maud and Stanley sat down. Neither of them had done a stroke of work all day and their stored-up energy showed in their eyes and the zest with which they both fell on their food. Vera picked at a sausage and left half her mashed potato. It was no good, she hadn't any appetite these days and she began to wonder if Maud hadn't been right when she said she was heading for a nervous breakdown. Sleep didn't refresh her and she was as tired in the mornings as when she went to bed. Having Auntie Ethel here for a long weekend wouldn't help either, as Maud would want a great fuss made over her best friend's entertainment, a clean cloth on the table every day, homemade cakes and then, of course, there would be the spare room to get ready.

Maud must have read her thoughts or else she hadn't been thinking of anything else all day, for she said as she spooned up a second helping of potato, "Have you told Stanley yet?"

"I haven't had a chance, have I? I only got in half an hour ago."

"Told me what?" said Stanley.

Maud swallowed two tablets and made a face. "We're having my friend Ethel Carpenter to stay here."

"You what?" Stanley was much relieved, in fact, to hear that was all it was, for he had expected an announcement of Vera's imminent departure. But now that the greater evil was at least temporarily postponed, the lesser seemed outrageous and he got

up, flinging back his chair, and drawing himself up to his full
height of five feet five.

"Only for two or three days," said Vera.

"*Only.* Only two or three days. Here am I, up to my neck in
trouble, no job, no peace in my own home, and you tell me I've
got to have that old cow. . . ."

"Don't you dare! Don't you dare use that foul language in my
presence!" Maud was on her feet as well now, clutching her stick.
"Ethel's coming here and that's that. Vera and me, we've made
up our minds. And you can't stop us. Vera could have you evicted
tomorrow if she liked, turned out in the street with just the
clothes you stand up in."

"And I," said Stanley, thrusting his face close up to hers,
"could have you put in an old folks' home. I don't have to have
you here, nobody can make me."

"Criminal!" Maud shouted. "Jailbird! Pig!"

"Two can play at that game, Maud Kinaway. Mean old hag!
Poisonous bitch!"

"Lazy no-good wastrel!"

Watching them from the end of the table, Vera thought that
any minute they would come to blows. She felt quite calm. If
they did strike each other, if they killed each other, she thought
she would feel just the same, just as enervated, disembodied and
empty of everything but a cold despair. With a dignity neither
of them had ever seen in her before, she got up and said in the
steady emotionless voice of a High Court judge:

"Be quiet and sit down." They stopped and turned to look
at her. "Thank you. It's quite a change for either of you to do
anything I ask. Now I've got something to say to you. Either you
learn to live together like decent people . . ." Maud tapped her
stick. "Shut up, Mother. As I said, either you behave yourselves
in future or I'm going." Vera turned away from the flash of
triumph in Maud's eyes. "No, Mother, not with you, and not
off somewhere with Stanley either. I shall go away by myself.
This house doesn't mean a thing to me. I can earn my own
living. God knows, I've had to do it long enough. So there you
are. One more row and I pack my bags. I mean it."

"You wouldn't walk out on me, Vee?" Stanley whined.

"Oh, yes, I would. You don't love me. If I hadn't got a wage
coming in and—and what I'll get from Mother one day, I

wouldn't see you for dust. And you don't love me either, Mother. You just love power and playing God and being possessive. All your life you've got your own way but for the once, and you can't bear it that once somebody beat you at your own game."

Vera paused for breath and stared into the two flabbergasted faces. "Yes, I've shaken you both, haven't I? Well, don't forget what I said. One more row and off I go. And another thing. We'll have Auntie Ethel here but not because you want her, Mother. Because I do. She's my godmother and I'm fond of her, and as you're always pointing out, *this is my house*. Now we'll have the television on. 'Augusta Alley,' and you can watch it in peace, Mother. Stanley won't disturb you. He knows I mean what I say."

After that she went out into the kitchen and, although she had won and silenced them, although they were now sitting sullenly in front of the screen, she laid her head on the table and began to sob. Her strength wasn't like Maud's, constant, implacable, insensitive, but intermittent and brief as her father's had been. She doubted whether she had enough of it to make good her threat.

Presently, when she had stopped crying, she washed the tea things and went upstairs. There, in front of her dressing table, she had a good hard look at herself in the glass. Crying hadn't helped. Of course, her face wasn't usually as blotchy and patched with red, but the wrinkles were always there and the brown bruise shadows under her eyes, and the coarse white hairs among the sandy ones, dull pepper-coloured hair that had once been red-gold.

It was understandable that Stanley no longer loved her, that he only kissed her now during the act of love and sometimes not even then. There came into her mind the memory of those afternoons they had spent in the country, London's country of commons and heaths, before they were married and when she had conceived the child that died before it could be born. It seemed like another life, and the man and the woman who had ached for each other and had clung together gasping in the long grass under the trees, other people.

Strange how important passion was to the young. Beside it, suitability and prudence and security went for nothing. How she and Stanley had laughed at James Horton with his bank account and his church membership and his modest ambition. He'd be a bank manager now, she thought, living in a fine house and married to a handsome woman in her early forties, while she and Stanley . . . She had wasted her life. If James saw her now he wouldn't even recognise her. Miserably she stared at her own worn and undesirable reflection.

Downstairs, Maud and Stanley watched "Augusta Alley," the old woman with a triumph that showed on her face in a perpetual smug smile, her son-in-law impassively, biding his time.

5

Everyone has his escape, his panacea, drugs, drink, tobacco or, more cheaply and innocently, the steady and almost mechanical habit of reading light fiction. Stanley liked a drink and a smoke when he could afford them and he had always been a reader, but the true and constant consolation of his life came from doing crossword puzzles.

Almost every paperback issue of crossword books as well as the fuller and fatter annuals reposed in his bedroom bookcase along with a much-thumbed copy of *Chambers' Twentieth Century Dictionary*. But the white squares in these books had long been filled in and, in any case, the solving of these problems afforded him less pleasure than completing a fresh puzzle each day, one which arrived virgin white on the back page of the *Daily Telegraph* and which, if the answers eluded him, could only be solved by waiting, sometimes almost breathlessly, for the following morning's issue.

He had been doing the *Telegraph* puzzle every day for twenty years and now there was no longer any question of not finishing it. He always finished it and always got it right. Once, some years back, he had found it necessary, like most crossword enthusiasts, to abandon the puzzle when it was half complete and take it up some hours later to find that the elusive clues had clarified during the interim. But even this small frustration had passed away. He would sit down with the paper—he never bothered to read the news—and generally every clue had been solved twenty minutes later. Then an immense satisfaction bathed Stanley. Self-esteem washed away his pressing problems, every worry was buried, sublimated in those interlocking words.

It was no sorrow to him that his wife and his mother-in-law showed not the slightest interest in this hobby of his. He preferred it that way. Nothing can be more irksome, more maddening, to the amateur of crosswords than the well-meaning idiot who, anxious to show off his etymological knowledge, demands from his armchair to be told how many letters in fifteen down or what makes you think four across is yelp and not bark.

Stanley had never forgotten George Kinaway's efforts in this direction, his feebly hearty, "Haven't you finished that puzzle yet?" and his groping determination to supply straightforward answers to clues whose fascination lay in their almost lunatic subtlety. How explain to such a fool as he that "One who is willing" (nine letters, five blanks, T, three blanks) is obviously Testatrix and not Volunteer? Or that "One way or the other, he is tops in the Moslem world" (three letters) is the palindrome Aga and not Bey?

No, those women knew their limitations. They thought it was a silly kid's game—or said they did because it was all Greek to them—but at least they didn't interfere. And these days Stanley needed his puzzles more than ever. The one high spot in his day was the half-hour, perhaps at lunch time, perhaps in the evening, when he could escape from his worries, and suddenly far away from Vera and her mother, lose himself in the intricacies or words and plays upon words.

The rest of the time, God knew, he had trouble enough. He saw very clearly that matters had come to a head, to a straight battle between Maud and himself. On his side he had youth, comparative youth, at any rate, but he couldn't see that he had much else. The dice were heavily loaded in Maud's favour. She wanted to get Vera away from him and it was hard to see how, in time, she could fail. Stanley couldn't understand how she hadn't already succeeded. If he had been in Vera's place, if his mother had come to him with bribes and offers of money and ease, he would have been off like a shot. Stanley felt quite sick when he thought of his fate if Maud were allowed to

win. Why, the chances were that pair of bitches wouldn't even
let him keep this house.

And now Maud had an ally rushing to her support. If that
letter he had read was a typical example of the sort of effusions
Maud sent weekly to Ethel Carpenter, her friend would arrive
armed against him. He shuddered when he thought of Ethel
taking Vera aside, whispering to her in corners, putting Maud's
case far more forcefully than Maud could herself, because Ethel
would appear as a detached observer, an impartial outsider, seeing
the pros and cons without emotional involvement. There was
nothing he could do about it. Ethel would come, put in three
days' forceful persuasion, and if that wasn't enough to do the
trick, would be just around the corner, dropping in two or three
times a week, ready with arguments, wearing away Vera's opposition until, at last, beaten down by the pair of them, she would
give in.

There was nothing he could do about it—except get rid of
Maud first.

But the failure of the Shu-go-Sub had shaken Stanley badly.
He read and re-read all his medical books and when he had
digested every word reached the conclusion that there are basically
no rules as to the incidence of stroke. Maud had had one: she
might have another tomorrow; she might never have another.
Worry could induce one, but on the other hand, it might not.
And what worries did Maud have? Anti-coagulants might prevent
one. Ease and quiet might prevent one. No one could say for
sure that the absence of anti-coagulants and a life of anxiety
would cause one. Stanley reflected disgustedly that what doctors
didn't know about cerebral thromboses would fill more volumes
than their knowledge. They couldn't even tell you when one
was going to occur.

Then there was the question of the will. Stanley was almost
certain that Maud couldn't have got any solicitor to agree to that
condition. Why, she might quite accidentally fall under a bus. In
that case was Vera not to inherit? No, it was an impossible, lunatic
condition, but how was he to find out for sure whether or not
it had been made? Of course, there was nothing to stop him
walking into any solicitor's office and asking straight out. And
then, if Maud died, accidentally or by his hand, you could be
damn sure the first thing to happen would be that solicitor shoot-

ing his mouth off to the police. Clever Maud, Maud with the balance swinging down and throbbing heavily in her favour.

If only he could think of something. It was April now and in a week's time Ethel Carpenter would be here. Once let her arrive and he could say good-bye to everything he had ever hoped for, and look forward to a miserable poverty-stricken old age.

Meanwhile, Stanley continued to substitute Shu-go-Sub for Mollanoid, destroying the anti-coagulants as Vera fetched them on prescription from the chemist and dropping the saccharine into the labelled bottle while Maud was asleep. But it was a forlorn hope. Without his crossword puzzles, he sometimes thought he would go utterly to pieces.

"We can't let your auntie Ethel sleep in that room as it is," Maud said. "We'll have to get a new bedspread for one thing, and some sheets and towels."

"Well, don't look at me, Mother," said Vera. "I've just had the phone bill to pay."

"I wasn't intending you to pay for them, dear," Maud said hastily. "You get them and I'll give you a cheque." She smiled ingratiatingly at her daughter and stirred herself to help clear the table. The last thing she wanted at the moment was to antagonise Vera. Suppose she had really meant what she said and would be wicked enough to run away and leave her with Stanley? She would have to cook Stanley's meals and wait on him. "We'd better both have new dresses, too. When you have your afternoon off we'll go down to Lucette's and choose something really smart."

"Anyone would think it was the Queen coming," said Stanley.

Maud ignored him. "I'm getting quite excited. I think I'll have that girl in to give me a home perm and you must have your hair set in your lunch hour. And we'll need some flowers for Auntie's room. Auntie Ethel loves flowers."

She settled down contentedly with her knitting, repeating silently the words she had written to Ethel Carpenter that morning. ". . . You mustn't be too upset by the state of this house, dear. It's a poor old place and a crying shame that Vee should have had to live in it so long but we shall soon see some changes. When I see you I'll show you some of the details of new houses estate agents have sent me. The one I have my eye on has a fully fitted Wrighton kitchen and luxury sunken bath. Quite

a change from the old days!! And I've been wondering if you
would like to move in here. Of course, I would have it painted
throughout for you and a sink unit put in. We can talk about
it when you come. I know I can rely on you to help me in
bringing Vee round to my point of view. . . ." Maud smiled and
saw that Stanley had caught her smile. He frowned blackly. If
only he knew!

"Time for 'Augusta Alley,'" she said confidently.

Stanley didn't say a word. He threw down his completed puzzle,
flung open the french windows and went out into the darkening
garden.

"We've got some old tab coming here," said Stanley to Mr.
Blackmore. "Pal of my ma-in-law's. They couldn't make more fuss
if it was royalty."

"I daresay Mrs. Kinaway doesn't see all that many people."
Blackmore stuck his ladder against the house wall and mounted
it, carrying with him brush and paint pot.

"Excitement's no good to her." Stanley stuck his fork in the
soil. "Going on the way she is she'll have another one of those
strokes."

"I sincerely hope not."

"Hmm," said Stanley and he turned away to concentrate on
his trench. He had ordered a fresh bale of peat and it ought to
arrive in a day or two. The next thing was to wheedle the money
for some of that new variety of majenta heather out of Vera. If
she had any. God knew how much she and the old girl together
had blued on entertaining Ethel Carpenter.

For once, however, she'd done some of the work herself. Light
work, of course, the kind of thing the ladies who had employed
her wouldn't have been above undertaking. Stanley drew in his
breath in an angry hiss when he looked at his ruined display
of daffodils, every other one snapped off, not even cut, to make a
fancy flower arrangement in Ethel Carpenter's bedroom.

The room itself had been transformed. Anxious about the sudden dissipation of his inheritance, Stanley had looked on gloomily
while Maud wrote out cheques, one for Lucette's where her
dress and Vera's had come from, one for all the special food they
had to get in and another for the draper's who had sent up a
pair of lemon nylon sheets, two matching frilled pillowcases and

a pair of black and lemon towels. But it was Vera, of course, who
had washed all the paintwork and turned the mattress and
starched the little lace mats Maud wanted to see on Ethel's dressing table.

The depredations of his daffodil bed so depressed Stanley that
he gave up gardening at eleven and trailed despondently into the
house. He didn't go into the dining room. Maud was in there,
having her hair permed by the dispirited young housewife who
went out hairdressing to help make ends meet. The door was shut
but didn't prevent a nasty smell of ammonia and rotten eggs
from seeping into the rest of the house.

The second post had come, the one that brought local or
near-local letters. A fortnight before Stanley had written to the
editor of a national newspaper offering his services as a crossword puzzle setter, a job which he felt would really suit him and
give outlet to his creative talents. But the editor hadn't replied
and Stanley had almost given up hope. He picked up the letters
from the mat and contemplated them gloomily. Nothing for him
as usual. Just the gas bill and a long envelope addressed to Maud.

It wasn't stuck down. Stanley took it into the kitchen and
wondered who could be writing to Maud and typing the address.
Possibly her solicitor.

From the other side of the thin dividing wall he heard
Maud say, "If that's the last curler in, dear, why don't you pop
into the kitchen and make us a nice cup of coffee?" He grabbed
the letter and took it upstairs.

In the privacy of his bedroom, his crossword annuals around
him, he slid the single folded sheet out of the envelope. It wasn't
from a solicitor. It wasn't a letter as such at all. Growing suddenly
cold, Stanley read:

64, Rosebank Close, Chigwell, Essex.

This desirable bungalow property, freehold and overlooking the
Green Belt, is moderately priced at £7,600, and comprises a
magnificent through lounge with York stone fireplace, two double
bedrooms, luxurious air conditioned kitchen with waste dis-
posal unit, spacious bathroom and separate W.C. Details are as
follows: . . .

Stanley didn't read the details. He had seen enough. Maud
must be very confident if she had reached the stage of actually

approaching estate agents. Like the commander of an army, she had decided on her strategy and was marching ahead, overthrowing everything that obstructed her path. While he . . . He and his poor forces were falling back on every hand, their weapons impotent, their pathetic outflanking movement ineffective. Soon he would be driven into what sanctuary he could find for himself. And it wasn't going to be any St. Helena but a furnished room or even—horror of horrors!—a working man's hostel.

Here, at least, was one desirable property she would never get her hands on. Stanley put a match to the paper and burnt it in the grate. But destroying it afforded him small pleasure. It was about as satisfying as burning the dispatch that tells the defeated general the battle is over, his forces scattered and capitulation inevitable. As in such a case, another dispatch will come. The destruction of the news does nothing to impair the fact of defeat.

He went downstairs and indulged himself in the only comfort left to him. But the crossword puzzle was completed in fifteen minutes and Stanley found that these days he was no longer able to derive his old pleasure from digesting and appreciating the clues after they were solved, from chuckling silently over such witty efforts as: "Nutcracker Suite"—Tchaikovsky's interpretation of shelling, or "Wisdom Tooth"—Root cause of biting wit? Nevertheless he repeated them slowly to himself and the very repetition of the words soothed him. He rested his elbows on the kitchen table and whispered over and over again: "Underwear for barristers"—briefs. "Does this book tell of a terrible Tsar at Plymouth?"—Ivanhoe. A pity they didn't put two in every day instead of only one, he thought with a sigh. Maybe he'd write to them and suggest it. But what would be the use? They wouldn't answer. Nothing went his way these days.

The hairdresser girl was off now. He heard the front door close. Maud came out into the kitchen, her iron-grey hair in large fat curls all over her head. The curls reminded Stanley of those cushion-shaped pot scourers one buys in packets. They had the same hard, metallic and durable look. But he said nothing, only gave her a dismal stare.

Since Vera's threatening outburst they had been wary of each other in the evenings, distant rather than polite, scarcely ever provocative. But during the day war had been maintained with as much vitriol as ever and Stanley expected her to pull the paper away from him with some such accompanying insult as: "Why don't you take your lazy self out somewhere?" But Maud merely said, "She's made a nice job of my hair, hasn't she? I wouldn't want Ethel to think I'd let myself go."

Half a dozen apt and rude retorts came to Stanley's lips. He was deciding which one of them would have the most stinging effect, bring the blood rushing to Maud's face and spark off a bitter interchange, when, staring sourly at her, he saw it would be of no use. Maud hadn't made that innocent remark about her hair because she was weakening or softening with age or because it was a nice sunny day. She wasn't trying to establish a truce. She had spoken as she had because warfare was no longer necessary. Why bother to swat a fly when you have only to open a window and drive it outside? She had won and she knew it.

Speechless, Stanley watched her open the larder door and view with a blank, perhaps very faintly amused expression, the cold pie Vera had left for their lunch.

6

When Stanley was out of work, it was unusual for either him or Maud to appear downstairs before nine-thirty in the morning. Indeed, Maud often remained in her room until eleven, manicuring her nails, tidying her dressing table and her shelf of medicaments, writing another instalment of her weekly letter to Ethel Carpenter. But on Friday, April the tenth, the morning of Ethel's arrival—E-Day, as Stanley called it bitterly—both astonished Vera by appearing at the breakfast table.

Each had awakened early, Stanley because the gloom and actual dread occasioned by the imminence of Ethel's coming had made dozing in bed impossible, and Maud because she was too excited to sleep.

Taking her place at the table and filling her plate liberally with cornflakes, Maud thought how wonderfully and suddenly those two had begun to dance to her piping. It was a good fortnight since Stanley had spoken an insolent word to her. Defeat was implicit in every line of his body, hunched up as it was, elbows on the table, dull eyes staring disconsolately out into the garden. And as for Vera . . . Maud had hardly been able to stop herself from shouting with triumph at Vera's face when she had seen all those new towels and sheets arrive at the house, her wistful wonder at the blue and white spotted dress, a model, Maud had made her buy. One word from Auntie Ethel and she would yield utterly. Of course she would; it wasn't human nature to do otherwise.

"One egg or two, Mother?" Vera called from the kitchen.

Maud sighed with satisfaction. Her quick ears noted that Vera's voice had lost that querulous, martyred tone which used to annoy her so much. It was now reserved for Stanley.

"Two, please, dear." Maud swallowed her two tablets, washing them down with a big gulp of tea. Really strong and sweet it was, the way she liked it. Sugar was what she needed to keep her strength up for the long day ahead, sugar and plenty of protein.

Vera bustled in with the plate of eggs and bacon, stopping to saw off a thick slice of bread for Maud. Stanley sipped his tea slowly like an invalid.

"Try and get home early, won't you, Vee?"

"I'll see if I can make it by five. You said Auntie Ethel wouldn't be here till five, didn't you?"

Maud nodded complacently.

She went to work with a will as soon as Vera had gone, scouring the thin carpets with Vera's old vacuum cleaner, waxing the hall floor and lastly preparing the feast which was to gladden Ethel's heart. It was years since she had done a stroke of housework and in former days she would rather have seen the place turn into a slum about her than let Stanley Manning see her lift a duster. But now it no longer mattered. Stanley wandered about from room to room, watching her and saying nothing. Maud didn't care. She hummed her favourite old hymn tunes under her breath as she worked ("Lead Us, Heavenly Father, Lead Us" and "Love Divine, All Loves Excelling"), just as she used to do all those years ago in the big house before the master and mistress were up.

They had lunch at twelve.

"I'll clear away and do the dishes," she said when they had finished their cold rice pudding. "It wouldn't do to have Ethel come and find the place in a mess."

"I don't know why you and Vee can't act more nautral."

"Cleanliness," said Maud, taking advantage of Vera's absence to have a prohibited dig at him, "*is* natural to some people." She rushed around, wiping surfaces, her limp hardly noticeable. "I shall put on my new dress and get myself all ready and then I'll have a lay-down on my bed."

"What's wrong with the couch in there?" Stanley cocked a thumb towards the dining room.

"That room is all tidied up ready for tea, and I can't go in the lounge on account of that's where we're going to receive Ethel."

"My God," said Stanley.

"Please don't blaspheme." She waited for the spirited rejoinder and when it didn't come, said sharply, "And you needn't go messing the place up. We don't want them crossword puzzles of yours laying about."

Stanley rose to that one but only with a shadow of his former verve. "You needn't worry about me. I'm going to take my lazy no-good self out. Maybe you'd like me to stay away the whole weekend." Maud sniffed. She rinsed her hands, dried them and moved majestically towards the door. Stanley tried a feeble parting shot. "Mind you don't oversleep. God knows what would happen if *Miss* Carpenter had to hang about waiting on the step."

"I'm a very light sleeper," Maud said gaily. "The least little thing wakes me."

Life wasn't going to be worth living for the next few days. Those women would be screaming at him morning, noon and night to wipe his feet and wash his hands and run around after Ethel Carpenter till he couldn't call his soul his own. She would go, of course, on Sunday or Monday, but only round the corner to Green Lanes, and how many times a week would he find her back here again, her feet under his table?

That in itself was a sufficiently gloomy prospect, Stanley thought, leaning forward on the table, his head in his hands. He could at a pinch put up with that, but one day he'd walk in from the pictures or from work—he'd have to get a job if only to get out of this house—to find the lot of them gone and a note on the table with a Chigwell phone number on it and a short sharp request for him to find other accommodation.

Once let Ethel arrive and the eventual outcome was inevitable. Stanley glanced up at the old kitchen clock. Half-past one. Three and a half hours and she would be here.

He wandered into the dining room to find himself a more comfortable chair but it was chilly in there and the excessive neatness had about it an almost funeral air. The laid and spread table was covered by a second cloth, as white as snow. Indeed, the whole arrangement, stiff and frigid-looking, gave the impression of a hillocky landscape blanketed by crisp fresh snow. Stanley approached the table and lifted the cloth, then pulled it away entirely.

In the centre of the table stood a pillar of red salmon, still keeping the cylindrical shape of the can from which it had come, and surrounded by circles of cucumber and radishes cut to look like flowers. This dish was flanked by one of beetroot swimming in vinegar, another of potato salad and a third of cole slaw. Three cut loaves of different varieties awaited Maud's attention when her guest arrived. The butter, standing in two glass dishes, had been cut about and decorated with a fork. Next Stanley saw a cold roast chicken with a large canned tongue beside it, and on the perimeter of the table three large cakes, two iced and bound with paper frills and one Dundee. Chocolate biscuits and ginger nuts had been arranged in patterns on a doily and there were half a dozen little glass dishes containing fish paste, honey, lemon curd and three kinds of jam.

All that fuss, Stanley thought, for an old woman who was no better than a common servant. Sausages or fish fingers were good enough for him. So this was the way they meant to live once they'd got all their sneaking underhand plans fixed up? He dropped the cloth back and wondered what to do with himself for the rest of the afternoon. He couldn't go out, except into the garden, for he hadn't a penny to bless himself with.

Then he remembered he'd seen Vera drop some loose change into the pocket of her raincoat the night before. She hadn't worn that coat this morning because the early part of the day had been bright and summery. Stanley went upstairs and opened his wife's wardrobe. Hoping for a windfall of five bob or so which would take him to the pictures, he felt in the pockets, but both were empty. He swore softly.

It had begun to rain, a light drizzle. Vera would get wet and serve her damn well right. Five past two. The whole grey empty afternoon stretched before him with an old women's tea party at the end of it. Might as well be dead, he thought, throwing himself on the bed.

He lay there, his hands behind his head, miserably contemplating the cracked and pock-marked ceiling which a fly traversed with slow determination like a single astronaut crossing the bleak surface of the moon. The *Telegraph* was on the bedside table where he had left it that morning, and he picked it up. He didn't intend to do the puzzle—that he was saving to alleviate the deeper gloom of the coming evening—but looked instead at the deaths' column which ran parallel to the crossword clues.

How different his life would be if between the announcements of the departure of Keyes, Harold, and Konrad, Franz Wilhelm, there appeared Kinaway, Maud, beloved wife of the late George Kinaway and dear mother of Vera. . . . He scanned the column unhappily. Talk about threescore years and ten being man's allotted span! Why, to find a man or woman dying in their late eighties was commonplace, and Stanley counted three well over ninety. Maud might easily live another twenty years. In twenty years' time he'd be sixty-five. God, it didn't bear thinking of. . . .

Stanley was aroused from this dismal reverie by the front doorbell ringing. Only the girl come to read the gas meter, he supposed. Let her ring. By now Maud was snoring so loudly that he could hear her through the wall. So much for all that rubbish about being a light sleeper and hearing every sound.

She had overtired herself with all that unaccustomed work. A tiny shred of hope returned as Stanley wondered if the work and the excitement had perhaps been too much for her. All that polishing and bending down and reaching up . . .

The bell rang again.

It could be his new bale of peat arriving. Stanley got off the bed. The rain had stopped. He poked his head out of the window and, seeing no seedsman's van parked in the street, was about to withdraw it when a stout figure backed out on to the path from under the overhanging canopy of the porch.

Stanley hadn't seen Ethel Carpenter since his wedding but he had no doubt that this was she. The frizzy hair under the scarlet felt helmet she wore was greyish white now instead of greyish brown but otherwise she seemed unchanged.

She waved her umbrella at him and called out, "It's Stanley, isn't it? I thought for a minute there was nobody in."

Stanley made no reply to this. He banged down the window, cursing. His first thought was to go into the next room and shake Maud till she woke up, but that would put Maud into a furious temper, which she would assuage by abusing him violently in the presence of this fat old woman in the red hat. Better perhaps to let Ethel Carpenter in himself. Two or three hours' chatting alone with her was Stanley's idea of hell on earth, but on the other hand he might use the time profitably to put in some propaganda work.

On his way down, he peered in at Maud but she was still snoring with her mouth open. He trailed downstairs and opened the front door.

"I thought you were never coming," said Ethel.

"Bit early, aren't you? We didn't expect you till five."

"My landlady's new lodger came in a bit before time, so I thought I might as well be on my way. I know Maud'll be sleeping, so you needn't wake her up. Well, aren't you going to ask me in?"

Stanley shrugged. This old woman had an even more shrewish and shrill manner than Maud and he could see he was in for a fine time. Ethel Carpenter trotted past him into the hall, leaving her two suitcases on the doorstep. Treating me like a bloody porter, thought Stanley, going to pick them up. God, they weighed a ton! What had she got in them? Gold bars?

"Heavy, aren't they? I reckon I've nearly broke my back lugging them all the way from the station. I'm not supposed to carry weights, not with my blood pressure, but seeing as you haven't got no car and couldn't put yourself out to meet me, I didn't have much option."

Stanley dumped the cases on the gleaming mosaic floor. "I was going to meet you," he lied. "Only you were coming at five."

"Well, we needn't have a ding-dong about it. By all accounts, you're fond of a row. There, I'm coming over dizzy again. The room's just going round and round."

Ethel Capenter put one hand up to her head and made her way somewhat less briskly than before into the seldom used front room Vera and Maud called the lounge.

"I had a couple of dizzy spells on my way here," she said, adding proudly, "my blood pressure was two hundred and fifty last time I saw my doctor."

Another one, thought Stanley. Another one moaning about something no one could prove and using it to get out of doing a hand's turn. For his part, he was beginning to believe, despite all his reading, that there was no such thing as blood pressure.

"Don't you want to take your things off?" he said gloomily. Get her upstairs and maybe Maud would wake up. He saw that any anti-Maud propaganda he might have in mind would fall on stony ground. "D'you want to see your room?"

"May as well." Ethel took her hand from her head and shook herself. "The giddiness has passed off. Well, that's a relief. I'll have my cases up at the same time. Lead on, Macduff."

Stanley struggled up the stairs after her. Anybody would think by the weight of them that she was coming for a fortnight. Maybe she was. . . . Christ, he thought.

In the spare room Ethel took off her hat and coat and laid them on the bed. Then she unpinned her scarf to stand revealed in a wool dress of brilliant kingfisher blue. She was about Maud's build but fatter and much redder in the face. She surveyed the room and sniffed the daffodils.

"I've been to this house before," she said. "There, you didn't know that, did you? I came with Maud and George when they were thinking of buying it for Vee." Stanley clenched his teeth at this reminder, certainly intentionally made, of the true ownership of the house. "I thought you'd have bettered yourself by now."

"What's wrong with it? It suits me."

"Tastes differ, I daresay." Ethel patted her hair. "I'll just have a peep at Maud and then we'll go down again, shall we? We don't want to wake her up."

Grimly resigning himself to fate, Stanley said, "You won't wake her. It'd take a bomb falling to wake *her*. She always sleeps her three hours out."

A sentimental smile on her face, Ethel gazed at her friend.

Then, closing the door, she resumed a more truculent and severe expression.

"That's no way to talk about Vee's mother. Everything you've got you owe to her. I knew you'd be here when I came, being as you're on the dole, and I thought we might have a little talk, you and me."

"You did, did you? What about?"

"I don't want to stand about on the landing. The giddiness is coming over me again. We'll go downstairs."

"It strikes me," said Stanley, "you'd be better lying down if you feel queer. I've got to go out, anyway. I've got things to see to."

Once in the lounge she sank heavily into a chair and lay back in silence, her breath coming in rough gasps. Stanley watched her, convinced she was putting on a show for his benefit. No doubt, she thought she'd get a cup of tea out of him this way.

Presently she sighed and, opening her large black handbag, took out a lace handkerchief with which she dabbed at her face. For the time being she seemed to have forgotten her plan to take him to task, for when she spoke her voice was mild and shaky and her attention caught by a framed photograph of Vera and Stanley which stood on the marble mantelpiece. It had been taken at their wedding and Vera, deriving no pleasure from looking at it, usually kept it in a drawer. But Maud, determined to brighten up this gloomy room, had got it out again along with a pair of green glass vases, a Toby jug and a statuette of a nude maiden, all of which were wedding presents.

"I've got that picture myself," said Ethel. "It stands by my bed. Or stood, I should say, seeing that it's packed in the trunk I'm having sent on with all my other little bits."

"Sent on to Green Lanes?" asked Stanley hopefully.

"That's it. Fifty-two Green Lanes, to Mrs. Paterson's." She stared at the picture. "No, I don't reckon that's the same as my one. My one's got the bridesmaids in, if I remember rightly. Let's have a closer look."

As soon as she got to her feet she became dizzy again. Although it went against the grain with him, Stanley got up to give her his arm. But Ethel made a little movement of independence, a gesture of waving him away. She took a step forward, and as she did so, her face contorted and she gave a hollow groan, an almost animal sound, the like of which Stanley had never heard before from a human being.

This time he started forward, both arms outstretched, but Ethel Carpenter, groaning again, staggered and fell heavily to the floor before he could catch her.

"My Christ," said Stanley, dropping to his knees.

He took her wrist and felt for a pulse. The hand sank limply into his. Then he tried her heart. Her eyes were wide open and staring. Stanley got up. He had no doubt at all that she was dead.

It was twenty-five to three.

Stanley's first thought was to go for Mrs. Blackmore. He knocked at the front door of number 59 but there was no one in. There was no need to knock at Mrs. Macdonald's. Underneath the figures 63 a note had been pinned: "Gone to shops. Back 3:30." The street was deserted.

Back in the house a thought struck him. Who but he knew that Ethel Carpenter had ever arrived? And immediately this idea was followed by another, terrible, daring, wonderful and audacious.

Maud would sleep till four at least. He looked dispassionately at the body of Ethel Carpenter, speculatively, calculatingly, without pity. There was no doubt she had died of a stroke. She had overdone it. Her blood pressure had been dangerously high and carrying those cases three quarters of a mile had been the last straw. It was cruelly unfair. No one profited by her death, no one would be a scrap the happier, while Maud who had so much to leave behind her . . .

And of a stroke too, the one death Maud had to have if he was ever going to get his hands on that twenty thousand. Why couldn't it have been Maud lying there? Stanley clenched his hands. Why not do it? Why not? He had a good hour and a half.

Suppose it didn't work out? Suppose they rumbled him? There wasn't much they could do to him if one of them, Maud or Vera or some nosy neighbour, came in while he was in the middle of his arrangements. They might put him inside for a bit. But a couple of months in jail was better than the life he lived. And if it came off, if the hour and a half went well, he'd be rich and free and happy!

In his last term at school, when he was fifteen, Stanley had taken part in the school play. None of the boys had understood what it was all about; nor, come to that, had the audience. Stanley had forgotten all about it until now when some lines from it came back to him, returning not just as rubbish he had had to learn by heart, regardless of their meaning, but as highly significant advice, relevant to his own dilemma.

> *There is a tide in the affairs of men*
> *Which, taken at the flood, leads on to fortune.*
> *Omitted, all the voyage of their lives*
> *Is bound in shallows and in miseries.*
> *On such a full sea are we now afloat,*
> *And we must take the current while it serves*
> *Or lose our ventures.*

If ever a man was afloat on a full sea it was Stanley Manning. These iambic pentameters, hitherto meaningless, had come into his mind as a direct command. If he had been a religious man, he would have thought them from God.

The telephone was in the lounge where Ethel Carpenter lay. He ran upstairs two at a time to make sure Maud was still asleep and then he shut himself in the lounge, drew a deep breath and dialled the number of Dr. Moxley's surgery. Ten to one the doctor wouldn't be in and they'd tell him to phone for an ambulance and then it would all be over.

But Dr. Moxley was in, his last afternoon patient just gone. So far, so good, thought Stanley, trembling. The receptionist put him through and presently the doctor spoke.

"I'll come now before I make any of my other calls. Mr. Manning, you said? Sixty-one Lanchester Road? Who is it you think has died?"

"My mother-in-law," said Stanley firmly. "My wife's mother, Mrs. Maud Kinaway."

2. Across

7

When he put the phone down Stanley was shaking all over. He'd have to take the next step before the doctor came and his courage almost failed him. There was a half bottle of brandy, nearly full, in the sideboard and Stanley, sick and shivering, got it out and drank deep. It wouldn't matter if Dr. Moxley smelt it on his breath as it was only natural for a man to want a drink when his mother-in-law had fallen down dead in front of him.

Vee would have to see the body, *a* body. That meant he'd have to be careful about how he did it. God, he *couldn't* do it! He hadn't the strength, his hands weren't steady enough to swat a fly, let alone . . . But if Maud were to come down while the doctor was there . . .

Stanley drank some more brandy and wiped his mouth. He went out into the dark still passage and listened. Maud's snores throbbed through the house with the regularity of a great heart beating. Stanley's own had begun to pound.

The doorbell rang and he nearly fainted from the shock.

Dr. Moxley couldn't have got there already. It wasn't humanly possible. Christ, suppose it was Vee forgotten her key? He staggered to the door. This way he'd have a stroke himself. . . .

"Afternoon, sir. One bale of peat as ordered."

It was in a green plastic sack. Stanley looked from it to the man and back again, speechless with relief.

"You all right, mate? You look a bit under the weather."

"I'm all right," Stanley mumbled.

"Well, you know best. It's all paid for. Shall I shove it in your shed?"

"I'll do that. Thanks very much."

Dragging the sack through the side entrance, Stanley heard Mrs. Blackmore pass along the other side of the fence. He ducked his head. When he heard her door slam he tipped the peat out on to the shed floor and covered it with the empty sack.

Seeing two other people circumstanced very much like himself, the delivery man who lived, he knew, in a poky council flat, and Mrs. Blackmore, a tired drudge with a chronic inability to manage on her housekeeping, brought Stanley back to reality and hard fact. He must do it now, vacillate no longer. If he had been as familiar with *Hamlet* as he was with *Julius Caesar*, he would have told himself that his earlier hesitation, his moment of scruples, was only the native hue of resolution sicklied o'er with the pale cast of thought.

He closed the front door behind him and mounted the stairs, holding his hands clenched in front of him. Maud was quiet now. God, suppose she was up, dressed, ready to come down . . . ? Outside her door he knelt down and looked through the keyhole. She was still asleep.

It seemed to Stanley that never in his life had he been aware of such silence, the traffic in the street lulled, no birds singing, his own heart suspending its beats until the deed was done. The silence, heavy and unnatural, was like that which is said to precede an earthquake. It frightened him. He wanted to shout aloud and break it or hear, even in the distance, a human voice. He and Maud might be alone in an empty depopulated world.

The hinges of the door had been oiled a week before because Maud complained that they squeaked, and the door opened without a sound. He went to the bed and stood looking down at her. She slept like a contented child. His thoughts were so violent, so screwed to courage that he felt they must communicate themselves to her and wake her up. He drew a deep breath and put out his hands to seize the pillow from under her head.

Dr. Moxley didn't ring the bell. He used the knocker and it made a tumultuous metallic clatter through the house. Maud turned over, sighing, as if she knew she had been reprieved. For a moment, watching her, Stanley thought it was all up with him. His plan had failed. But still she slept and still her hand hung limp over the side of the bed. Holding his hand to his chest, as if he feared his lurching, actually painful, heart would burst through his rib cage, Stanley went down to admit the doctor.

He was a boyish-looking man with a shock of black hair, a stethoscope hanging round his neck.

"Where is she?"

"In here," said Stanley, his voice throaty. "I thought it better not to move her."

"Really? I'm not a policeman, you know."

Stanley didn't like that at all. He was beginning to feel sick. He shuffled into the room after the doctor, aware that his face was covered in sweat.

Dr. Moxley knelt down on the floor. He examined the body of Ethel Carpenter and felt the back of her neck.

"My mother-in-law," said Stanley, "had a stroke four years back and . . ."

"I know all that. I looked up Dr. Blake's notes before I came out. Help me to lift her on to the couch."

Together they got the body on to the couch and Dr. Moxley closed her eyes.

"Have you something to cover her with? A sheet?"

Stanley couldn't bear another moment's delay.

"Was it a stroke, Doctor?"

"Er—yes. A cerebral thrombosis. Seventy-four, wasn't she?"

Stanley nodded. Ethel Carpenter, he remembered, had been a bit younger than that, three or four years younger. But doctors couldn't tell, could they? They couldn't tell that precisely. Apparently they couldn't.

Now the doctor was doing what Stanley had longed for, getting a small pad out of his briefcase and a pen from his breast pocket.

"What about that sheet, then?"

"I'll get it," Stanley mumbled.

"While you're doing that I'll write out the death certificate for you."

The sheets were kept in the linen cupboard in the bathroom. Stanley pulled one out, but, before he could go downstairs again the sickness overcame him, accompanied by a fresh outbreak of sweat, and he vomited into the washbasin.

The first thing he saw when he came back into the lounge was Ethel Carpenter's ringless left hand dropping from the couch. Christ, she was supposed to be a married woman. . . . The doctor had his back to her and was writing busily. Stanley unfolded the sheet and draped it over the body, tucking the hand into its folds.

"That's right," said Dr. Moxley more pleasantly. "This is an unfortunate business for you, Mr. Manning. Where's your wife?"

"At work." Give me the certificate, Stanley prayed. For God's sake, give it to me and go.

"Just as well. You must tell yourselves that she'd had a long life, and certainly it was a quick and probably painless death."

"We can't any of us go on forever, can we?" said Stanley.

"Now you'll need these." Dr. Moxley handed him two sealed envelopes. "One is for the undertaker and the other you must take with you when you go to register the death. You follow all that?"

Stanley wanted to say, I'm not stupid just because I don't talk la-di-da like you, but instead he simply nodded and put the envelopes on the mantelpiece. Dr. Moxley gave a last inscrutable glance at the sheeted body and strode out, his stethoscope swinging. At the front door he stopped and said, "Oh, just one thing . . ."

His voice was terribly loud, ringing as if he were addressing an audience instead of just one man. A cold shiver ran through Stanley, for the doctor's expression was suddenly thoughtful. He looked like a man who has recalled some vital step he has omitted to take. Holding the door ajar, he said, "I didn't ask whether you wanted burial or cremation."

Was that all? Stanley hadn't thought of it either. He wished he dared ask the doctor to keep his voice down. In a tone so low that it was almost a whisper, he said, "Cremation. That was her wish. Definitely cremation." Burn Ethel, destroy her utterly, and then there could never be any questions. "Why d'you want to know?" he asked.

"In cases of cremation," said Dr. Moxley, "two doctors are required to certify death. It's the law. Leave it to me. I imagine you'll be having Wood's, the undertakers, and I'll ask my partner. . . ."

"Dr. Blake?" Stanley said before he could stop himself.

"Dr. Blake has retired from practice," said Moxley a shade coldly. He gave Stanley a penetrating look, reminiscent of Mrs. Blackmore, and then he banged out of the house, crashing the front door.

Enough to wake the dead, Stanley thought. It was a quarter to four. Time enough to get on to the undertakers when he had

hidden Ethel's body and dealt with Maud. . . . The corpse under
the sheet might get by a doctor who had never seen Maud before,
but it wouldn't get by Vera. Vera must see Maud and, needless
to say, she must see Maud dead.

He pulled back the sheet and rolled it up. Then he put his
hands under Ethel Carpenter's arms and dragged her half on to
the floor. He was a small thin man and her weight was almost too
much for him. He stood up, gasping, and his eye lighted on the
black handbag which stood beside the chair she had been sitting
in. That would have to be hidden too.

He opened the bag and a wave of something sweet and sickly
tickled his nostrils. The scent came from a half-empty packet of
violet cachous. Stanley vaguely remembered seeing these things,
sweets used as breath fresheners, in glass bottles in sweetshops
before the war when he had been a boy. Sometimes his mother
used to buy them at the village shop or when they went into
Bures for a day out. He thought they had long elapsed into
disuse along with aniseed balls and Edinburgh rock and now
their scent, assailing him unexpectedly, brought back his old home
to him, the green river Stour where he had fished for loaches and
miller's thumbs, the village between a fold in the shadow hills,
an ancient peace.

He took out a violet cachou and held it between finger and
thumb. A powerful perfume of violets and strong sugar came to
him and he held it to his nose. Seventeen he'd been when he'd
run away from them all, his parents, his brothers, the river and
the fishing. Off to make his fortune, he'd told them, sick with
envy and resentment of his two brothers, one halfway through
a good apprenticeship, the other off to college. I'll be back, he'd
said, and I'll be worth more than the lot of you. But he never
had gone back and the last time he'd seen his father was at the
Old Bailey where they'd sent for him to be present at his son's
trial.

Things were different now. That fortune had taken nearly
thirty years to make but now it was almost made. Just one more
little step to take . . . And when he'd got the money, maybe
next week, he'd go up to Bures in his car and surprise them all.
"How about a spot of fishing?" he'd say to his brother, the master
printer, and he'd bring out his shining new tackle. "Put it away,"
he'd say to his brother, the secondary school teacher, when he

felt in his pocket for a handful of silver. The envy and the resentment would be theirs then when his mother took him about to the neighbours boasting of her most successful son. . . .

Stanley put the cachou back in the packet and the vision dimmed. The only other thing of interest in the bag was a fairly thick wad of pound notes, bound with an elastic band. Ethel's savings, he supposed, money to pay her new landlady advance rent.

No need to destroy those with their dead owner.

He was counting the notes when he heard a very faint sound above him, a stair creaking. His fantasies had temporarily calmed him but now the sweat started again all over his face. He took a step backwards to stand trembling like a small animal guarding its kill in the face of a larger advancing predator.

The door opened and Maud came in, leaning on her stick.

8

Maud screamed.

She didn't stop to argue with Stanley or question him. What she saw before her told her exactly what had happened. For twenty years she had been expecting her son-in-law to repeat the violence for which he had been sent to prison. It had been an elderly woman then; it was an elderly woman now. As before. Stanley had attacked an old woman for her money but this time he had gone further and had killed her.

She raised her stick and advanced upon him. Stanley dropped the wad of notes and backed against the open piano. His hands, crashing down on the keys, struck a deep resounding chord. Maud made for his face, but Stanley ducked and the blow caught him agonisingly between his neck and his shoulder blade. He fell to his knees but staggered up again almost at once and hurled one of the green glass vases at her.

It struck the wall behind Maud's head and sent a shower of emerald slivers spraying across the room.

"I'll kill you for this!" Maud screamed. "I'll kill you with my own hands."

Stanley looked around for more missiles, edging between the couch and the piano, but before he could snatch up the second vase, Maud struck him again, this time on the top of his head, and caught him as he staggered with a series of violent blows to the body. For a moment the room went black and he saw shapes whirling against the blackness, red squares and triangles and cascading stars.

Maud would beat him to death. Horror and rage had given her an unexpected strength. Sobbing now, crouched in a corner, he turned his shoulder to receive the coming blow and as it struck him he seized the tip of the stick.

It struggled in his grasp like something alive. Stanley pulled himself up on it, hand over hand. He was stronger than she, for he was male and thirty years younger, and he pulled himself to his feet until he was face to face with Maud.

Still they didn't speak. There was nothing to say. They had said it all in those four years and now all that was left was a crystallisation of mutual loathing. It throbbed in Maud's breathless grunts and in Stanley's hiss. Once again they might have been alone in the world or outside the world, on some unpeopled unfurnished plane where there was no emotion but hatred and no instinct but self-preservation.

For each of them there was one desire, possession of the stick, and they concentrated on it in a savage, but for some moments, equal tug-of-war. Then Stanley, seeming to retreat from a very slightly advantageous position, kicked hard at Maud's shins and with a cry she let the stick fall and rattle to the floor.

Stanley picked it up and hurled it across the room. He made a leap for her throat, seizing her neck in both hands. Maud gave a hoarse gasp. As Stanley's hard fingers dug into her carotid artery, she kneed him in the groin. They both cried out simultaneously, Stanley sobbing with pain, and fell apart.

He jerked back on his heels, ready to spring again, but Maud was enfeebled without the stick she had depended on for years. Her arms flailing, she had nothing to break her fall, and as she toppled her head struck the jutting edge of the marble mantelpiece.

Stanley crept over to her on all fours and looked down, his heart drumming, at the consummation of all his wishes.

Vera didn't cry or even speak at all when he broke the news to her but her face went very white. She nodded her head, accepting, as he told her how Maud had been in the lounge, just standing by the mantelpiece and looking at the wedding photograph, when suddenly she had felt bad, touched her forehead and fallen to the floor.

"It was bound to happen sooner or later," he ended.

"I'll go up and see her," said Vera.

"As long as it won't upset you." He had expected this, after all, and provided for it. He followed her up the stairs.

Vera cried a little when she saw Maud.

"She looks very peaceful."

"I thought that myself," Stanley said eagerly. "She's at peace now, I thought."

They spoke in whispers as if Maud could hear them.

"I wish you'd rung me at the shop."

"I didn't see any point in upsetting you. It wasn't as if there was anything you could do."

"I wish I'd been here." Vera bent over and kissed Maud's cold forehead.

"Come on," said Stanley. "I'll make you a cup of tea."

He wanted to get her out of there as quickly as possible. The curtains were drawn and the room dim, only a wan filtered light playing on Maud's features and the medicine store by the bed. But let Vera shift that pillow an inch and she'd see the gash on Maud's head under the grey curls.

"I suppose I ought to watch by the bed all night."

"You what?" said Stanley, alarmed, forgetting to whisper. "I never heard such rubbish."

"It used to be the custom. Poor mother. She loved me really. She meant things for the best. The doctor said it was another stroke?"

Stanley nodded. "Come on down, Vee. You can't do any good hanging about in here."

He made a pot of tea. Vera watched him, murmuring the same things over and over again as recently bereaved people do, how unbelievable it was but really only to be expected; how we must all die but still death came as a shock; how glad she was that her mother had had a peaceful end.

"Let's go into the other room. It's cold out here."

"All right," said Stanley. As soon as she saw the table she'd remember and start asking questions, but he was ready for her. He picked up their two cups and followed her.

"My God," said Vera, opening the dining room door, "Auntie Ethel! I forgot all about Auntie Ethel." She looked at her watch and sat down heavily. "It's nearly six. She's late. She was coming at five. Not like Auntie Ethel to be late."

"I don't reckon she'll come now."

"Of course she'll come. She wrote and said definitely she was coming. Oh, Stan, I'll have to break it to her. She'll take it hard, she was ever so fond of Mother."

"Maybe she won't come."

"What's the good of saying that?" said Vera. "She's late, that's all. I couldn't eat a thing, could you?"

Stanley was famished. The mingled scents of the salmon and the chicken were working on his salivary glands and he felt sick with hunger, but he shook his head, putting on a maudlin expression.

As well as hungry, he felt utterly exhausted and he couldn't relax until he was out of danger. Vera had seen her mother and hadn't been suspicious; there was no reason why she should go into the spare room where the body of Ethel Carpenter lay under the bed, concealed by the overhanging bedspread. So far so good.

"I can't think what's happened to Auntie," said Vera fretfully. "D'you think I ought to ring her landlady in Brixton?"

"She's not on the phone."

"No, but I could get on to the café on the corner and ask them to take a message."

"I wouldn't worry," said Stanley. "You've got enough on your plate without bothering about Ethel Carpenter."

"No harm in waiting a bit longer, I suppose. What time are the undertakers coming in the morning?"

"Half ten."

"I'll have to ring Doris and say I shan't be in to work. Though God knows how they'll manage with the other girl away on holiday."

Stanley almost choked over his tea. "I can see to the undertakers, Vee. You don't want to be here when they come."

"I don't want to . . . But my own mother, Stan!"

"If you want to go in, you go in. You leave everything to me."

Further discussion was prevented by the doorbell ringing. Vera came back with Mrs. Blackmore who, though Stanley had imparted the news to no one, was by this time in full possession of the facts. Perhaps the doctor's doorstep speech had been overheard by her. Whatever her source, she had, she told Vera, already passed on what she called the "sad tidings" to Mrs. Macdonald and various other cronies in the neighbourhood. So confident was she of her intuition in matters of this kind that she had not thought it necessary to wait for confirmation. A black coat thrown hastily over her floral overall, she announced that she had come to pay her last respects to Mrs. Kinaway. In other words, she wanted to view the body.

"Only yesterday I was having such a lovely talk with her over the fence," she said. "Well, we're all cut down like flowers, aren't we?"

Distastefully eyeing Mrs. Blackmore's inquisitive rabbity face and her bunched hair, Stanley reflected that the only flower she reminded him of was the deadly nightshade. Still, better let them all come and gawp at Maud now than sneak in on her substitute at the undertakers'. A watchful guardian of his dead, ready to intercept any tender hand which might try to smooth back Maud's hair, he went upstairs with the two women.

Five minutes after Mrs. Blackmore, loudly declaring her willingness to do "anything I can, dear. Don't hesitate to ask," had gone, both Macdonalds arrived with a bunch of violets for Vera.

"Sweet violets for mourning," said Mrs. Macdonald sentimentally. Their scent reminded Stanley of Ethel Carpenter's handbag. "We don't want to see her, Mrs. Manning. We want to remember her as she was."

After that Vera and Stanley were left alone. It unnerved Stanley to realise that his wife was waiting for Ethel Carpenter but he could do nothing about that. Presently, without a word, Vera took away the cutlery that had been laid by her mother.

"You'd better eat something," she said.

At ten o'clock when Ethel Carpenter still hadn't come, she cleared the table and they went to bed. She had a last look at

Maud from the doorway but she didn't go in again. They put the light out and lay side by side, not touching, each wide awake.

Vera fell asleep first. Every nerve in Stanley's body was tingling. What was he going to do if Vera didn't go into work in the morning? He'd have to make her go out. Perhaps he could get her to go and register the death. . . . That wouldn't leave him much time for all he had to do.

Soon after midnight he too slept and immediately, or so it seemed to him, began to dream. He was walking by the river, going home, and he had walked all the way from London like a tramp, his possessions in a bundle on his back. It seemed that he had been walking for years, but he was nearly there now. Soon he would reach the point where the river described a great meander and at this point his village would come into view, the church spire first and then the trees and the houses. He could see them now and he quickened his pace. For all his apparent poverty, the pack on his back and his worn-out shoes, he knew they would be glad to see him and welcome him home with congratulations and tears of joy.

The sun was coming up, for it was very early morning, and Stanley struck across the meadow, soaking his trousers in dew up to his knees. In the village no one was up yet. But his mother would be up. She had always been an early riser. The cottage door opened when he pushed it in and he went in, calling her.

He heard her coming down the stairs and went to the foot of them, looking up. His mother came down. She had grown old and she used a stick. First he saw her legs and her skirt, for the stairs had become long and steep in his long absence, and at last her face. He started back, crying something aloud. It wasn't his mother's face, but Maud's, waxen yellow, the teeth bared, blood running from a wound in her scalp. . . .

He awoke screaming, only the screams came out as a strangled groan. It took him several minutes to re-orientate himself, to realise it had been a dream and that Maud was dead. After that he couldn't sleep again. He got up and walked about the house, looking first in on Maud and then into the spare room. The daffodils Maud had picked for Ethel gleamed whitely at him in the thin moonlight.

He went downstairs where he felt it was safe to put a light on. The house smelt of food, tinned fish and cold meats which wouldn't keep long because there was nothing to preserve them. Now that he had come to himself and the dream was fading, he was struck by a sudden anxiety that he had failed to take some important step. He had forgotten to do something but he couldn't think what that something was. He sat down and put his head in his hands.

Then he remembered. Nothing so very important after all. For the first time in twenty years he had passed a day without doing the crossword puzzle.

He found the *Daily Telegraph* and a ballpoint pen. The sight of the virgin puzzle sent a little thrill of pleasure through him. Funny how just looking at the empty puzzle frame, the exquisitely symmetrical mosaic, brought him peace and steadied his shaking hands. He must have done thousands of them, he thought. Six a week times fifty-two times twenty. God, that was six thousand, two hundred and forty puzzles, not counting all the ones in his crossword paperbacks and annuals.

Stanley picked up the pen.

One across: "Calf-love may decide one to take this German language course" (two words, six, eight). Stanley pondered only for a moment before filling in "Wiener Schnitzel." His body relaxed as if it was immersed in a warm bath and he smiled.

9

The alarm went off at seven.

Vera was out of bed and halfway to the bathroom before she remembered. She came back, wondering whether there was any point in waking Stanley, but he was awake and staring wide-eyed at the ceiling.

"I'm up now," she said. "I may as well go to work."

"I should. It'll take your mind off things."

But he couldn't be sure she really would, she dithered and hesitated so much, until he saw her actually going down the path. As soon as she was out of sight he fetched in the empty peat sack and took it upstairs. Better remove Maud's wedding ring and slip it on Ethel's finger. Funny, the way it made him feel so squeamish. He was glad he hadn't eaten the eggs and bacon Vera had offered him for breakfast.

Ethel had a ring of her own which she wore on the little finger of her right hand. His own hands shaking, Stanley pulled it off. It was an odd little ring, a thin circle of gold with two clasped hands, tiny gold hands, where there might have been a stone. Stanley put it on Maud's finger and then he bundled her body into the sack.

There was no one about in Blackmore's garden—they lay in bed till all hours on Saturdays and their bedroom was in the front. Gasping with the weight of it, Stanley dragged the sack across the narrow strip of concrete outside the back door and humped it into the shed. Next Ethel's suitcases. They were of the expanding kind and not fully expanded, although they were so heavy. Stanley opened the lighter of the two and crammed in Ethel's coat and hat and the umbrella which, to his relief, he found was of the telescopic variety. He lugged them downstairs and put them in the shed beside the sack. Nobody but he ever went to the shed, but just to be on the safe side, he shovelled peat all over the sack and the cases. Anyone going in and just giving things a cursory glance would think Stanley Manning had a ton of peat in there instead of a couple of hundredweight.

Things were going well.

By half-past nine he had got Ethel lying where Maud had been, on the back room bed, covered by a sheet. It would be a nice touch, he thought, and one likely to impress the undertakers if the corpse they came for had flowers by it so he fetched the vase of daffodils and put it among Maud's pills.

On the dot of ten the undertakers arrived, and having given Stanley a form to fill in, applying for permission to cremate, took away the body of Ethel Carpenter.

When she had registered Maud's death during her lunch hour, Vera telephoned the Brixton café next door to Ethel's former landlady.

"I'm ever so sorry to bother you. My dad was in business and

I know you're busy, but could you ask Mrs. Huntley to ring me back?"

It was ten minutes before the phone rang and when it did Vera was filling in time by placing newly cleaned blankets into polythene bags.

"I just wondered," she said to Mrs. Huntley, "if Miss Carpenter's still with you. She never turned up at our place yesterday."

"Never turned up? She left here—let's see—it would have been about twenty to one. She had her two cases with her and she left a trunk for me to send on to her new address in Green Lanes, 52, Green Lanes, Croughton. The men came for it just now."

Vera had to sit down, she felt so weak at the knees.

"Did she say anything about coming to us?"

"The last thing she said to me was, 'They won't be expecting me so early, Mrs. Huntley, but I may as well go. Mr. Manning's bound to be in,' she said, 'and I can have a chat with him.' She said she'd take it slow on account of her cases being so heavy."

"Did you say *twenty to one?*"

"Might have been a quarter to," said Mrs. Huntley.

"Then she should have been here by two!"

"Maybe she changed her mind. Maybe she went straight to Green Lanes after all."

"I suppose she must have done," said Vera.

But it wasn't like Ethel. To arrange to come to stay, arrange it by letter, putting everyone out, and then just not turn up would be a churlish way to behave. And Ethel, though sometimes sharp and malicious and difficult, wasn't churlish or unpunctual or casual at all. She belonged to the old school. Vera couldn't understand it.

At five, when things were slack and the High Street shops emptying, Vera left the cleaners in charge of Doris, her assistant, and caught the bus that went down Green Lanes.

Number 52 was a much nicer house than her own in Lanchester Road. Although semi-detached, it had a double front with imposing gables, a big front garden that was mostly elaborate rockery and a half-timbered garage. A thin middle-aged woman came to the door with a boy and a girl tagging along behind her who might have been either her children or her grandchildren.

"Won't you come in?" she said when Vera had introduced herself.

"I mustn't. My husband will worry if I'm late." Stanley had never worried in the past when she was late but he had been so nice to her since Maud died, so considerate, that the possibility didn't seem so fantastic as it might have been once. "I only wanted to know if Miss Carpenter was here."

"I'm not expecting her till Monday," said Mrs. Paterson in a breathless harassed voice. "Monday she said definitely. I couldn't cope with anything extra *now*." The hall behind her was cluttered with toys and from the depths of the house came sounds suggestive of a hungry bitch with a litter of puppies. "My daughter's had to go into hospital and left the children with me, and my dog's just whelped. . . . Really, if I'd known there was going to be all this trouble, I wouldn't have considered letting the room at all."

Vera looked at her helplessly. "I thought she must be here," she said. "She's disappeared."

"I expect she'll turn up," said Mrs. Paterson. "Well, if you won't come in, perhaps you'll excuse me while I go and get all this lot fed."

Stanley was waiting on the doorstep for her, the anxious husband she had never quite believed in even when she was boasting of his concern for her to Mrs. Paterson.

"Where have you been? I was worried about you."

Vera took off her coat. That he should have worried about her brought her such intense pleasure that it was all she could do not to throw her arms around him.

"The undertakers came," he said. "I've fixed up the cremation for Thursday. We'll have to get cracking asking all the family along. Leave getting the tea for a bit. I've got a form here I want you to sign." Completing it had been interesting but somewhat frightening as well. Stanley had not much cared for that bit where the applicant was asked if he had any reason to suspect foul play or negligence. Nor had he enjoyed telephoning Dr. Moxley to ask for the name of the second certifying doctor, although it had been a relief when Moxley had called him back to say all was done and that the other doctor was some character called Diplock. Blake's name hadn't been mentioned.

"Just sign here," he said, putting the pen into Vera's hand. Vera signed.

"Oh, Stan, you've been so marvellous in all this. I can't tell you what a comfort you've been, taking everything off my hands."

"That's O.K.," said Stanley.

"Now the only real worry I've got is Auntie Ethel." Briefly Vera told him about her phone call and her visit to Mrs. Paterson. "D'you think we ought to go to the police?"

Every scrap of colour left Stanley's face. "*Police?*"

"Stan, I'll have to. She may be lying dead somewhere."

Stanley couldn't speak properly. He cleared his throat. "The police aren't interested when women go missing."

"That's only when it's young girls, when it's women who may have gone off with men. Auntie Ethel's seventy."

"Yeah. I can see that." Stanley thought quickly, wishing he didn't have to think at all. And now, just when everything was going so well. . . . "Look, don't you do anything till Monday. Wait and see if she turns up at Mrs. Paterson's. Then if you don't hear from her we'll get on to the police. Right?"

"Right," said Vera doubtfully.

All day long John Blackmore had been stuck on a ladder outside his back door painting his house. And as soon as he had gone in for tea Vera had come home. Stanley peeped into his shed, noting that the pile of peat was just as he had left it. He locked the door and put the key in his trousers pocket. Then he went over to the heather garden where the deep trench was still unfilled. In the cool May twilight the heathers stood brilliant white against the soft chestnut-coloured peat. White heather, he thought, white heather for luck. . . .

The following day, Sunday, was bright and hot. Vera got the piece of beef topside out of the larder and sniffed it. Just on the turn again. It was always the same. Every hot weekend the Sunday joint was high before she could cook it and she had to soak it in salt water to try and take away the sweetish fetid taint.

"You'll be able to buy a fridge now," said Stanley. He could see she didn't quite know what reply to make to this. Casually he gave her arm a light pat. Tears came into Vera's eyes. "I'll just walk up the road and get myself a paper," he said. "I miss the crossword on Sundays."

It was years since he had felt so happy and light-hearted. Everything had gone perfectly. And what had he done wrong? Nothing. It would have been unpleasant if he had actually had to—well, smother Maud, but that hadn't been necessary. Maud had died through her own fault. Now all that remained to stop any awkward questions being asked was to pay a visit to Mrs. Paterson.

He jumped on the Green Lanes bus. It stopped right outside the house and within two minutes Stanley was smiling ingratiatingly at Mrs. Paterson whom he quickly summed up as a tired grandma, a busy woman who would be only too glad to have one of her problems taken off her shoulders.

"Name of Smith," he said. A dog was howling and he raised his voice to a shout. "Miss Ethel Carpenter asked me to call."

"Oh, yes?" Over her shoulder, Mrs. Paterson bellowed, "Shut the dog in the garden, Gary. I can't hear myself speak. There was a lady here," she said to Stanley, "asking after her."

"Well, it's like this. She's stopping with me. I've got this room going, you see, and she looked at it last week. Couldn't make up her mind between this place and mine."

"These old dears!" said Mrs. Paterson, clearly relieved.

"Yeah. It's good of you to take it this way. Fact is, she came round Friday afternoon and said she'd settled for my place, after all. I reckon she didn't like to tell you herself." With some reluctance, Stanley felt in his pocket for the wad of notes he had taken from Ethel's handbag. "She wouldn't want you to be out of pocket. She reckoned five quid would make it all right."

"You don't want to bother," said Mrs. Paterson, taking the notes just the same. "I'm not sorry things have turned out this way, I can tell you. Now I can let my grandson have her room."

"There'll be a trunk coming," said Stanley. "Being sent on it is. I'll call round for that." Was she going to ask for his address? She wasn't.

"You can leave that to me. I'll take it in. It was good of you to come."

"My pleasure," said Stanley.

He bought a paper from the kiosk on the corner and by the time the bus got to the top end of Lanchester Road he had done half the clues in his head. "Frank takes a well-known stage part." Candida, thought Stanley, wishing he had brought a pen with him. Marvellous, really. Whatever would they think of next? Good training for the mind, crossword puzzles. He marched up the path, whistling.

10

Throughout that Sunday John Blackmore stood on his ladder, painting the side of his house, and every time Stanley put his nose outside the back door, Blackmore acknowledged him with a wave of his brush or a remark to the effect that it was all right for some. It was still light at eight and Blackmore was still painting.

"Don't you worry about me if I'm late home tomorrow," said Vera as they went to bed. "I'm going straight round to Mrs. Paterson when I've finished work to see if Auntie Ethel's turned up."

"Sometime," said Stanley casually, "I suppose we'd better have a word with your mother's solicitor."

"That can wait until after the funeral."

"Oh, sure. Sure it can," said Stanley.

He slept well that night and when he got up Vera had gone. Everything was clean and tidy downstairs and Vera had left his breakfast on a tray as usual, cornflakes poured out for him, milk already in his teacup and water in the kettle. Blackmore's car was gone; he had left for work. Stanley felt considerable relief. He was beginning to be afraid his neighbour might be taking his summer holiday and intended to devote an unbroken fortnight to house painting.

Mrs. Blackmore's Monday wash was flapping on the line, but she was still coming and going with pegs and odds and ends of small linen, adjusting the clothes prop and disentangling sheets which had wound themselves round the line in the stiff breeze.

"Lovely drying day!"

"Uh-huh," said Stanley.

"Things are getting back to normal with you, I daresay. Mrs. Manning bearing up all right?"

Stanley nodded, trying not to look at the shed.

"Well, I'll get these last few bits out and then I'm off to my sister's."

Feeling more cheerful, Stanley pottered about the garden. He pulled a couple of groundsel plants and a sow thistle out of the rose bed but he wasn't in the mood for weeding this morning and his attention kept wandering back to the heather bed with its blanket of peat and the yawning trench in the middle of it. Mrs. Blackmore's voice made him jump.

"What are you going to put in that great hole?"

A light sweat broke out on Stanley's forehead.

"I'm going to fill it up with peat. I'm putting a whole sack of peat in there."

"That's what I said it was for," said Mrs. Blackmore. "John and me, we noticed it, you see, and John said . . ." She giggled embarrassedly and bit her lip. "Well, never mind what he said. I wondered if you were going to bury some new potatoes in a tin. They say if you do that you have them all fresh for Christmas."

"It's for peat," said Stanley doggedly. He knew what Blackmore had said all right. He could just picture the two of them gossiping and sniggering and Blackmore saying, "Maybe that's for Mrs. Kinaway, save him paying out for the funeral."

He moved over in the direction of the Macdonalds' garden. Mrs. Macdonald, whose husband had a better job than Blackmore, was hanging her wash on a metal whirl line with plastic strings. She, too, glanced up in happy anticipation of a chat but Stanley only nodded to her.

The two women began shouting amicably to one another across his intervening lawn. Stanley went back into the house and did the crossword puzzle.

In the end, by a stroke of luck, the two women set off out together. From his vantage point behind the piano in the lounge, Stanley watched Mrs. Macdonald come out of her own house with her basket on wheels and wait at Mrs. Blackmore's gate. The Blackmores' door closed with a crash and then Mrs. Blackmore, dressed for a day out in a summery pink coat and floral hat, trotted up to her friend and whispered something to her. They both looked hard at Stanley's house. Blackening my character again, he thought. He watched them move off towards the bus stop.

When they were out of sight, he went upstairs and from the bedroom that had been Maud's, scanned the surrounding gardens. Everywhere washing waved and bellied and streamed in the wind. The linen was brilliant white, whiter and tidier than the ragged clouds which tossed above the tossing lines, and all this eddying whiteness had an almost hypnotic effect on Stanley so that he felt he could stand there forever, staring himself to sleep. His limbs seemed weighted down by a great reluctance for the task ahead of him. So far everything had been done secretly and covertly. Now he must do something in the open air, publicly (although he couldn't see a soul in all those gardens who might observe him), and perhaps what he was about to do was the first truly illegal and punishable thing. But it must be done, and now before Mrs. Macdonald returned from shopping.

Both his neighbours' houses were empty. Stanley was sure of that. The Blackmores had no children and the Macdonalds' two teenagers were at school. It was unnerving, though, to have to start work with that blank bedroom window of the Macdonalds' staring down at him. Who did those Macdonalds think they were, anyway, having an extension built on the back of their house, jutting right out and overlooking his garden? He'd have had the law on them for that, infringing his right to ancient lights or whatever it was, only he'd never been able to afford a solicitor. . . . Damn that sightless, closed, uncurtained window! There's no one at home, no one at home, he assured himself as he unlocked the shed and scraped away peat with his hands.

The wind blew the light feathery stuff about, powdering Stanley's clothes and hands with brown dust. He lugged the suitcases out first and, having peeped out cautiously to make sure he was still unobserved, dragged them towards the trench and lowered them in. They took up more room than he had bargained for, leaving only about a foot to accommodate the sack which contained Maud's body.

Maud's body . . . Up till then Stanley had felt a little weary, a little mesmerized and considerably apprehensive, but he hadn't felt sick. Now a lump of nausea came up into his throat. He kicked some peat over the suitcases and breathed deeply. The nausea receded slightly.

Screwing himself to a pitch of determination, Stanley went back into the shed and grasped the neck of the sack. His fingers, slippery now with sweat, slid about on the thick green plastic. No one watching him would imagine that sack contained anything as soft and amorphous as peat. But no one *was* watching him. He was observed only by a bird which sat on the spiraea branch and by the black, pupilless eye of Macdonalds' window.

If only it was quiet . . . The thrashing linen made slapping, cracking sounds as it filled with air and the wind drove the air out of it. Stanley was surrounded by a chorus of busy disembodied noise, but the linen didn't seem disembodied to him. Rather it was as if he was attended and observed by a crowd of crackling idiots, white watchers that cackled and sniggered at each fresh move he made.

Cocooned in gleaming slippery green, Maud's body slithered and bumped over the concrete. Stanley had to drag it, for it was too heavy for him to lift. A dead weight, he thought, a dead weight. . . . He mustn't be sick.

Pushing the body into the cavity above the cases was the worst part of all. He had thought he would be able to avoid actually touching Maud, but now he couldn't. Her dead flesh felt icy and stiff through the cold damp folds of plastic. Stanley heard himself give a sob of horror. The top of the sack lay almost level with the surrounding earth. Stanley crouched over it, pressing at it with his hands. He didn't think he had the strength to get up, but he managed it at last, staggering. With heavy hands from which the sweat streamed just as if they had been dipped in water, he got his shovel and filled bucket after bucket with peat.

When the operation was completed, the resulting heap looked just what it was—a grave. He began levelling the soil which abutted on to it, pulling heather fronds and flowers above the dusty brown mass, until finally the sickness overcame him. He lay spreadeagled, face downwards on the ground and retched.

"Whatever's the matter, Mr. Manning? Are you all right?"

It sounded to Stanley as if Mrs. Macdonald must be standing right behind him. He jerked up, half-rolling on to the peat heap.

She was ten yards away, staring curiously at him from the other side of her fence, the washing on her whirl line streaming out and crackling as the metal shaft squeaked. Ghosts on a crazy roundabout, Stanley thought wildly.

"I came back from shopping and I saw you lying on the ground. Whatever came over you?"

He muttered, "Something disagreed with me. . . ." And then, his face and hands streaked with peat dust, he lurched unsteadily to his feet and staggered into the house.

When Vera came away from Mrs. Paterson's, she felt as if a load had been lifted from her shoulders. But her relief was mixed with annoyance. How could Auntie Ethel be so inconsiderate? To write to Maud promising to come for the weekend, even to fix a definite time of arrival, and then just not turn up; worse even, to take Mrs. Paterson's room only to throw her over for someone else. Well, she was very lucky, Vera thought, in encountering someone as tolerant and easy-going as Mrs. Paterson. Not many landladies would take that sort of treatment and be content with a mere five pounds as recompense. It was a pity, though, that she hadn't had the presence of mind to ask this Mr. Smith for his address.

Still, if Ethel was going to behave in this cavalier way, they were well rid of her. Let her make a fuss because no one told her Maud was dead or asked her to the funeral. How was anyone supposed to get in touch with her when she hid herself in this stupid mysterious way?

As Vera was unlatching her front gate, Mrs. Macdonald came out.

"Has your husband got over his bad turn?"

"Bad turn?"

"Oh, haven't you seen him yet? I never meant to upset you, really I didn't."

"Just tell me what's happened, Mrs. Macdonald."

"Well, nothing really. Only when I got in from the shops this morning there was poor Mr. Manning laying, actually laying, on the ground out among those heather plants of his. Been sick, he had."

"But what was it?"

"Something that disagreed with him, he said. My boy Michael was home from school with a sore throat and he said he'd been watching Mr. Manning at his gardening, watching him through the back bedroom window, and he saw him collapse."

Vera hurried indoors, expecting to see Stanley prone on the sofa, but he was sitting in a chair, intent on his crossword annual, and he had his usual healthy, though sallow, colour. Better say nothing of what she had seen. Stanley hated being spied on by the neighbours. Instead she told him of her interview with Mrs. Paterson.

"I said it'd be all right," said Stanley.

"I know, dear. I've been very silly. The best thing will be to forget all about Auntie Ethel and her nonsense. Could you eat a bit of steak?"

"Uh-huh," said Stanley, taking no further notice of her. Vera sighed. Of course he'd been under a strain, what with Mother dying like that before his eyes, but if only he would sometimes, just sometimes, speak nicely to her or thank her for what she did for him or show by a glance or a smile that he still loved her. Perhaps you couldn't expect it after twenty years. Vera ate her meal in silence. There was a lot she would have liked to discuss with her husband but you cannot have much of a conversation with a man whose face is concealed behind a large book. She cleared the table, Stanley moving impatiently but not looking up while she removed his plate, and then she went up to the room that had been Maud's.

She sat down in front of the dressing table, but before she opened the drawer where Maud had kept her papers she caught a glimpse of herself in the glass and sighed afresh at her reflection. It wasn't only lack of money but lack of time. . . . She wondered apprehensively what Stanley would say if she spoke to him of giving up her job. Then, averting her eyes, she opened the middle drawer and lifted its contents out on to the bed.

On top was a bundle of letters from Ethel Carpenter. Beneath these Maud's cheque book, her birth certificate, her marriage lines, Vera's own certificate of baptism. How painful it all was, a job that had to be done and as quickly as possible. The light was fading fast now and the room growing dim, but the papers in her hands still showed white with the last brilliant whiteness that comes before dark.

Here was a letter from a firm of solicitors: Finbow and Craig, of High street, Croughton. "Dear Madam, An appointment has been made for you with our Mr. Finbow to discuss the question of your testamentory dispositions. . . ." After the funeral, Vera decided, she too would make an appointment with Mr. Finbow.

Next, sandwiched among the papers, she found a flat jewel box full of little brooches and chains and souvenir trinkets. There was nothing she really fancied for herself—perhaps she might keep that cameo pendant with the picture of Mother and Dad inside it, and most of it could be given away to the relatives coming on Thursday.

Vera came next to Maud's red leather photograph album. On the first page was her parents' wedding picture. George tall and awkward in his hired morning coat, Maud in a knee-length dress of white crepe-de-chine, clutching his arm determinedly. Then there were photographs of herself as a baby. Maud had put captions to them all in careful copperplate: Vera aged one; Vera takes her first steps; then, when she was older, a child of five or six: Vera gets to know her auntie Ethel; Vera on the sands at Brayminster-on-Sea.

Dear old Bray! That was the heading written across the next double page. Maud had always called the seaside resort that, loving it and making it her own. Dear old Bray! On a postcard photograph, taken by a beach photographer, Ethel Carpenter in 1938 hat and Macclesfield silk dress walked along the sands, holding the hand of ten-year-old Vera. Maud wore sunglasses in the next snapshot and George had a handkerchief with knots in its four corners stuck on his balding head to protect it from the sun.

More and more snaps of Bray . . . 1946 and the war over. Vera grown up now, a pretty eighteen with long curls and a crimson mouth that looked black and shiny in the snap.

Two years later the New Look. Little cotton jacket with a peplum, long skirt with a flare at the hem. Had she really worn shoes with ankle straps and heels four inches high? James Horton holding her hand, whispering something to her in the sunshine, the bright sea behind them. James Horton. Suppose it had been he downstairs, he her husband who had been ill and on whom she had tended, would he have smiled and thanked her and held up his face for a kiss?

There were no pictures of Stanley in the album, not even

a wedding photograph. Vera closed it because it was too dark now to see any more. She bent her head and wept softly, the tears falling on to the old red leather binding.

"What are you doing up here in the dark?"

She turned as Stanley came into the room, and thinking she heard in his voice a tiny hint of tenderness or concern, she reached for his hand and held it against her cheek.

11

Standing with bowed head between George Kinaway's brother Walter and Maud's sister Louisa, Stanley watched the coffin slowly drawn away from behind the gilt screen towards the waiting fire. The vicar exhorted them to pray for the last time and while Vera wept quietly, Stanley looked down even further, studying his shoes.

"Nothing from Ethel Carpenter, I see," said Aunt Louisa when they were outside the paved courtyard looking at the flowers. "I must say I expected to see her here. These are from Uncle Tom and me, Stanley. Wreaths are so dear these days and they all go to waste, don't they? So we thought a sheath would be nice."

"Sheaf," said Stanley coldly. It was just like those Macdonalds to send an enormous great cross of lilies. Done on purpose to make the relatives' flowers look mean, he had no doubt.

They got into the hired cars and went back to Lanchester Road. It was all Stanley could do to keep his temper at the sight of Mrs. Blackmore getting stuck into the sherry and the ham sandwiches. They hadn't even had the decency to send flowers either. With a long pious face he brushed off Mrs. Blackmore's attempts to find out how much Maud had left but as soon as they had all gone he telephoned Finbow and Craig.

"It seems a bit soon," said Vera when he told her an appointment had been made for the following day.

"Tomorrow or next week, what's the odds?"

"I'll be glad to get it over. It was a nice funeral."

"Lovely," said Stanley with sincerity. He couldn't, in fact, recall any clan gathering he had ever enjoyed so much. If only he hadn't got to solve the problem of collecting that trunk . . .

"You know, love," Vera said, "it's years since we had a holiday. When we've got everything settled, why don't we go down to dear old Bray for a week?"

"You go," said Stanley. "I've got business to see to."

"You mean you've got a job?"

"Something in the offing."

Stanley looked away coldly. He didn't care for that wistful encouraging look Vera had given him. A job indeed. She couldn't think big, that was her trouble. He poured himself the dregs of the sherry and began to think about Pilbeam.

In telling his wife he had a job in the offing Stanley hadn't been strictly truthful. It was not in the offing, it was in the bag but it was also nothing to be proud of. He had only taken it because it allowed him more or less unrestricted use of a van.

A florist in Croughton Old Village wanted a driver and delivery man and on the day before the funeral Stanley had walked down to the old village, the vestigial remains of a hamlet that had been there before London spread across the green fields, applied for the job and was told to start on the following Monday.

Delighted with the way things were working out for him, he wandered across the village green and, sitting down on the steps of the war memorial (*Dulce et decorum est pro patria mori*), lit a cigarette.

There is perhaps no more pleasant occupation for a man whose expectations have almost come to fruition as that of speculating what he will do with the money when he gets it. His thoughts toyed happily with visions of cars, clothes, abundant liquor and the general appurtenances of making a splash, but Stanley was under no illusion that he could live for the rest of his life on twenty thousand pounds. He was too big a man now to consider working for anyone else, unless it was as a setter of crossword puzzles. That might come later as a sideline. First, he thought, he would rather like to go into business and what he saw before him as he crossed the road and stepped on to the pavement gave him the idea that it might be profitable and consistent with his new dignity as a man of private means to keep a shop. After all, dreary old George Kinaway had made a good thing out of it, a very good thing, and what George Kinaway could do he could do standing on his head.

In front of him was a row of shops with crazily sagging Tudor gables above them and a row of aged trees to give them an old-world expensive look. There was a chi-chi-looking art place with abstract paintings in its window, a dolly girl's boutique, a treasure house of Indian jewellery and between this and a place selling old books a vacant shop, its door boarded up and a notice over its window: *These desirable premises to let.*

Standing with his nose pressed against the dirty fingermarked glass of the shop window was a short stout man. Still whistling, Stanley too stopped and stared inside at a dim dusty interior cluttered with cardboard boxes. The other man gave a heavy sigh.

"Lovely day," said Stanley cheerfully.

"Is it?" His companion turned to face him and Stanley saw a snub-nosed baby face topped by sparse colourless hair. He was smoking a cigarette he had obviously rolled himself and as he raised his hand to his mouth Stanley noticed that the top of the forefinger was missing and this finger ended in a blob of calloused flesh instead of a nail. It reminded him of a chipolata sausage. "All right for some, I daresay." Stanley grinned. "What's with you, friend? Won the pools, have you?"

"As good as," said Stanley modestly.

The other man was silent for a moment. Then he said somewhat less lugubriously, "I'm a joiner by trade, a joiner and cabinet-maker. Thirty years I've been in the trade and then the firm goes bust."

"Hard cheese."

"This place . . ." He banged on the glass. "This place could be a little gold-mine in the right hands."

"What sort of a gold-mine?" Stanley asked cautiously.

"Antiques." The other man bit off the dental with a short sharp explosion and a spot of saliva struck Stanley's cheek. "What I don't know about the antique . . ." Spit, splutter, bite . . .

"business you could write down on a postage stamp." He backed away from Stanley slightly and assumed the attitude of an orator. "It's like this," he said. "You buy up a couple of chairs, genuine Hepplewhite, say, and make—or I make—a dozen more, incorporating bits of the genuine two in each chair. D'you get the picture? Then you can sell the lot as Hepplewhite. Who's to know? It'd take a top expert, I can tell you. Or a table. An inlaid table top, circa eighteen ten—put legs on it, Bob's your uncle."

"Where d'you get the table top?"

"Knocking. Going on the knock. Up Barnet way and further out, Much Hadham and the villages. Some of those old girls have got treasure trove hidden away in their lofts."

"Who'd buy it?"

"You're joking. There's not an antique shop in Croughton as yet, but there's folks with so much lolly they don't know what to do with it. Antiques are the thing. Didn't you know? All you need is capital."

"I might be able to lay my hands on some capital," said Stanley carefully.

The snub nose wrinkled. "Come and have a drink, my old love. Name of Pilbeam, Harry Pilbeam."

"Stanley Manning."

Pilbeam bought the first round and they discussed it. When it came to Stanley's turn he excused himself, saying he had to see a man, but they arranged to meet on the following Wednesday when Stanley said he would have more idea of how the land lay.

He didn't want to waste his money on Pilbeam yet, and whisky was a diabolical price these days. Of course, he'd still got most of the money he'd taken from Ethel Carpenter's handbag but he was reluctant to break into that.

Alone in the house the morning after the funeral, he took the notes out of his pocket and looked at them. They smelt strongly of violet cachous. Compared to what was coming to him, they were a drop in the ocean. The smell slightly disquieted him and he knew the wisest thing would be to burn them but he couldn't bring himself actually to destroy money. No harm could come of keeping them for a week or so. He went upstairs and from the bedroom bookcase took out the crossword annual of 1954. Then he distributed Ethel's money evenly among its pages before replacing it in the bookcase.

At this moment, he thought, looking at the old metal alarm clock, Vera would be at the solicitor's. He had almost made up his mind to enter into partnership with Harry Pilbeam but it would be nicer if he could go to the Lockkeeper's Arms next Wednesday a rich man instead of just an heir apparent.

"Your mother's will is quite straightforward, Mrs. Manning," said Mr. Finbow. "I don't understand what you mean about a condition."

Vera didn't know how to put it. It sounded so strange. She floundered. "My mother . . . er, my mother said she'd altered her will—well, way back in March. She said her money would only come to me if— Oh, dear, it does sound so awful —if she died of a stroke and not of anything else."

Mr. Finbow's eyebrows went up at that as Vera had known they would. "There was nothing like that. Mrs. Kinaway made her will on March fourteenth and, as far as I know, that was the only will she had ever made."

"Oh, I see. She must have been—well, joking, I suppose. She really led us to believe . . . It was rather awful."

"Such a condition would have been most irregular, Mrs. Manning, and hardly legally binding." What must he think of her? Vera wondered. That Maud had gone in terror of her life while she lived with her only daughter? It was cruel of Maud to have exposed her to such embarrassment.

"Anyway, I have the will here," said Mr. Finbow. He opened a drawer in his cabinet and withdrew an envelope. "All the late Mrs. Kinaway's estate passes unconditionally to you as her sole heir. Indeed, there was no real need for her to have made a will under the circumstances, except that it avoids intestacy problems, probate and so on. Had you predeceased her, the estate was to have been divided equally between Mrs. Louisa Bliss, her sister, and a Miss Ethel Carpenter. The property amounts to—let me see—approximately twenty-two thousand pounds, at present mostly invested in stock."

"When can I . . . ?"

"Quite soon, Mrs. Manning. In a week or two. If you wish the stock to be sold, I will personally hand you a cheque.

Of course, should you require any cash at present, a hundred or two can easily be made available to you."

"No, thank you," said Vera.

"A week or two?" said Stanley thoughtfully when she got home. "Just what I thought, all plain sailing." He smiled wryly to himself when he thought how Maud had fooled them, or half-fooled them, over that condition. Not that it mattered. Taken all in all, things were working out beautifully.

12

The van was a green one, plain on one side and painted with a wreath of roses on the other. Stanley parked it at the kerb, the plain side towards Mrs. Paterson's house, and tossing the bouquets of flowers on to the van floor so that they wouldn't be visible through the window, knocked at the front door.

As soon as Mrs. Paterson opened the door, he saw the trunk behind her in the hall.

"Oh, Mr. Smith, I'd just about given you up."

"Couldn't make it before," said Stanley.

"Would you like my son-in-law to give you a hand with it?"

And see the flowers he was supposed to be delivering?

"I'll manage," said Stanley. The heavy weights he had to carry these days! He'd rupture himself at this rate.

"Here, why don't you put it on my grandson's push-chair and wheel it out."

To Stanley's relief she didn't come down the path with him as he trundled the wobbly trunk out to the van. Nor did she seem sufficiently curious about him as to ask his address or keep the door open after he had started the van.

He drove the van down the narrow cobbled lane that led from the old village into Croughton High Street and parked it half on the pavement and half in the street. Then, making sure no one was watching him, he clambered into the back of the van and contemplated Ethel Carpenter's trunk.

It was made of wood and painted black. Stanley thought it must be very old, probably the "box" Ethel had taken with her from situation to situation when she was in service. Of course, it *would* be locked. He wasn't at all anxious to dispose of it without making himself aware of its contents, so he got a hammer and a wrench out of the van's tool kit and got to work on the lock.

After about ten minutes straining and hammering the lock finally gave. Stanley lifted the lid and looked inside. On top of the winter clothes was a cardboard box made to contain writing paper. It still contained writing paper only this paper had been written on. His eyes narrowing, Stanley read the letters Maud had written to her best friend. As he had suspected, they were full of derogatory allusions to himself. Fine thing if they fell into the wrong hands. The best thing would be to burn them. Stanley rolled them up and stuffed them in his pocket.

There didn't seem much else of any interest apart from a wedding photograph of himself and Vera and one of George Kinaway. Someone had written on the back of it. *This and your ring, all I have of you.* Stanley put it in his pocket with the letters and then he looked to see if any of the clothes were marked with Ethel's name. They weren't, but rummaging among camphor-smelling wool, his hand encountered something hard and cold.

The bottom of the trunk contained several small parcels wrapped in tissue paper. The cold thing his hand had touched was the elbow of a china figurine protruding from the paper. He unwrapped it and saw a shepherdess with a crook and a black lamb. Tearing off paper excitedly, he brought to light next a carriage clock, a pot pourri bowl and a silver cream jug. With a thoughtful backward glance at the vacant shop, Stanley wrapped all these things in the *Daily Telegraph.*

The canal banks were shored up with walls of yellow brick beneath which the duller yellow water flowed sluggishly. A couple of barges waited at the lock gates and a woman was walking a corgi along the towpath. Two children were at play in the garden of the lockkeeper's house and Stanley quickly realised he had no opportunity of disposing of the trunk at present.

He drove back to the shop and gave a fictitious order to

the florist to have a bouquet of spring flowers made up for delivery to the other side of Croughton at 10 P.M. The florist grumbled a good deal but cheered up when Stanley said he would take the flowers himself. Stanley didn't want any bills sent out to people who didn't exist and he decided reluctantly to pay for the order himself with what remained of his dole money.

While he had his tea he left the van parked outside the house with the trunk still in it but he brought the newspaper parcel indoors. He hid Ethel Carpenter's treasures in the back of his wardrobe and burnt the letters and the photograph in the bedroom fire grate.

It had been raining intermittently all day but now the rain fell heavily, drumming against the windows. Vera drew the curtains, put the light on and fetched writing paper and envelopes. Then she sat down and stared helplessly at the paper. What a fool she was! All day long she'd been thinking about this holiday of hers without ever considering how to set about finding an hotel in Brayminster. How did you find out about hotels, anyway? Vera had never stayed in one.

This, she reflected miserably, was something everyone knew about, everyone but her. Her life had been hard but it had also been sheltered and now she realised that, though forty-two years old, she couldn't begin to do any of the things other people seemed to take in their stride. Suppose I had to book a restaurant for a dinner or buy theatre tickets or make a plane reservation or buy a car, she thought. I wouldn't know how to set about it. I'm like a child.

Other people had guidebooks and holiday brochures. You wrote to the address or rang them up. Vera knew she would never have the courage to telephone an hotel. Oh, it was all hopeless, she was too tired and too old to learn now.

Unless . . . of course! Why hadn't she thought of it before? She knew one boarding-house in Bray, Mrs. Horton's in Seaview Crescent.

It was more than twenty years since she had last stayed there. Mrs. Horton had seemed old to her then but probably she had really been younger than Vera was now. That meant she'd be under sixty. Certainly James wouldn't still be living with his aunt, so she needn't be afraid of running into him, of seeing his face fall at the sight of the change in her. But James would have moved far away. . . .

More at ease than she had been all day, Vera began to write her letter.

The rain had driven much of the traffic off the roads but Stanley drove on doggedly, the wheels of the van sending fountains spraying over the pavements. He kept to a snail's pace, though, for the windscreen wipers were inadequate to deal with the torrents that poured down the glass and he could hardly see.

A deluge, he thought, that's what it is. A nice word for a crossword puzzle. How would you set about making up a clue for it? "A pull in the river causes this flood?" Not bad that. "Lug in Dee," he said aloud, as if explaining to some novice. Now that would be a job he'd really like, setting crosswords, and maybe, after the business had got going and he had ample time on his hands, he would be able to get himself such a job, for money talked and influenced and opened doors. With money you could do anything.

This was just the weather he would have ordered if he'd had any choice in the matter. You'd think the end of the world was coming the way everybody was shut up indoors. He drove slowly up the approach road to the lock and saw that the windows in the lockkeeper's house were curtained. The rain, though savage enough close to, had the appearance in the distance of a thick swirling mist.

No silly old bags giving their dogs an airing tonight. Two empty barges were moored this side of the lock, their hulls rapidly filling with water. The canal had already begun to rise. Its yellow frothing waters seemed to reach up and meet the rain which crashed on to it like a quivering sheet of steel.

Stanley had never seen the canal quite like this before. Usually, at any rate by day, it was busy with barges and kids fishing and the eternal procession of dog walkers. And although it wound among fields of a sort, litter-covered waste ground really, dotted about with sick-looking trees, it was a hideous mockery of what a water-way should be. Instead of woods and unspoilt countryside, all you could see were the slummy backs of two or three converging suburbs, half-built factories and tumbled warehouses.

But tonight the rain obscured all this. No houses were discernible in clear silhouette, only lights visible in clusters and separated from each other by the black unlit masses of factory buildings. And suddenly, because of the rain and the sparse scattered lights, the whole place took on an almost rural aspect so that Stanley was again reminded strongly of his old home where, as you walked along the river bank by night, a mist rose thickly from the water and the villages could be seen as knots of light gleaming between the shallow folded hills.

A faint nostalgia took hold of him, a nostalgia that was mixed with irritation as he drove very slowly along the towpath, wincing each time his tyres sank into ruts filled with muddy water.

When he was well out of sight of the lockkeeper's house, he switched off his own feeble sidelights and drove on for a few yards in darkness, very conscious of the canal—briefly and foolishly he had thought of it for a moment as the river —lapping and gurgling to the left of him. Now if it *had* been his river, there'd be a bend here where you had to turn sharply to the left. When you got along a few yards the hills divided and you could see the village lights winking over there. Well, this wasn't the Stour but Croughton canal and now was no time for fantasies of that sort. A fine thing if he and the van went into the water with Ethel's trunk.

When he had reversed it almost to the brink, he opened the van's rear doors. Cursing the blinding rain, he clambered over the driver's seat and began to shove the trunk from behind. It slid slowly along the rubber mat. Stanley grabbed the bouquet of flowers and tossed them on to the passenger seat. Another final heave . . . He pushed, bracing his feet against the dashboard.

Suddenly the trunk shot out, bounced once on the canal wall and fell into the water with a tremendous splash. Kneeling between the open doors, Stanley started back on to his heels but the water broke against him in a huge wave, drenching him from head to foot. He swore luridly.

Great eddies wheeled away across the canal. Too wet now to bother with a raincoat, Stanley crouched on the parapet of

the wall and looked down into the depths. Then, rolling up
his soaked sleeves, he thrust his arm into the water. But he
couldn't touch the top of the trunk, although he reached down
as far as he could without actually toppling in. Right, he thought,
getting up, another job jobbed.

After she had sent the letter Vera thought she had been
rather silly. Twenty years were a long time and Mrs. Horton
would have moved away. But in the middle of the week a
letter arrived with the Brayminster postmark. When she had
allowed herself to hope at all, Vera had looked forward to a
long chatty letter full of reminiscences and news, but Mrs.
Horton wrote formally, simply saying she would be pleased
to see Mrs. Manning and would reserve a nice room for her
with a view of the sea.

The price quoted was well within Vera's means. She would
have her holiday money and the small bonus the dry-cleaners
gave their manageresses in the summer. Nor was there any need
to worry about Stanley who had settled down quite marvel-
lously in his new job and would have his own wages to live
on while she was away.

"You won't be here to collect the cheque from Finbow and
Craig," he grumbled when she told him her holiday was fixed.

"Mr. Finbow said a week or two, dear, and two weeks will
only just be up when I get back." She smiled lovingly at
him, remembering the beautiful and totally unexpected gift of
flowers he had brought her that wet night when he had had
to work late. If only he was coming with her . . .

"I'll drive you to the station in the morning if you like."

"That's sweet of you, dear."

"The week after you come back I'll have my own car."

"Whatever you like, Stan, and I'll have an automatic washer,
I think, and a fridge."

"There's no need to go mad," said Stanley coldly and he
pencilled in the word which completed his crossword, "onyx."
"Only a pound left out and with ten to come it's turned to
stone."

"I only hope you'll be all right on your own."

"I'll be fine," said Stanley.

13

Alone in the house, Stanley took stock of his life, congratulating himself on his excellent management. Nothing had gone wrong. Maud was safely buried and the heathers were beginning to flourish on her grave. Perhaps in a few months' time he'd have a garage built just on that spot. He'd need somewhere to keep his Jaguar. Ethel Carpenter was a handful of grey ashes, or rather an urnful, the mere powdery contents of a casket now reposing on the lounge mantelpiece between the wedding photograph and the nude statuette. Her trunk and clothes were at the bottom of the canal, the *objets d'art* which he had retrieved stowed in his wardrobe and waiting to be sold over the counter as soon as he and Pilbeam had opened their shop.

He had met Pilbeam as arranged and they had celebrated their new partnership in the Lockkeeper's Arms. Pilbeam had been less affable when Stanley had admitted his capital was at present tied up but Stanley thought he had been able to allay his doubts. Once Vera had returned and Finbow come up with the loot, a matter of ten days or so, he would be able to show Pilbeam concrete proof of his affluence.

Yes, things had gone admirably.

Stanley went down to the old village, told the florist that the job didn't suit him, after all, and, turning a deaf ear to the reproaches and indeed abuse which ensued, collected his week's money. He walked across the green and smoked a cigarette, sitting on the steps of the war memorial and gazed in the direction of the shop which would soon be his. His vivid imagination presented it to him not as it now was but as it would be when Gothic gilt lettering ornamented the blank space above the window, when the door was a mullioned affair with a chased brass knob, the window was full of apparently authentic collector's pieces and the interior thronged with customers all desperate to part with their money.

Life was glorious.

He went into the Lockkeeper's off-licence and bought him-self a half-bottle of whisky and six cans of beer. Then, armed with the materials for a liquid lunch, he returned home where he settled himself on the dining room sofa, a spot for four years sacrosanct and reserved to Maud.

Stanley poured himself a tumbler of whisky and raised it at the framed photograph of her mother Vera had hung on the wall. "Absent friends!" he said. He smiled and switched on the television for "Sports Round-up," recalling how in the past he had almost always had to miss it because the noise disturbed Maud's afternoon rest.

Vera only had one case and she meant to go from the station to Mrs. Horton's by bus. The bus came and it was a single-decker green one, not very different from the buses she and James used to travel in down to the sea. They hadn't changed the sea-front at all. There was the old bandstand, the pretty little pier, there the cliffs where thrift grew and the orange daisies with the long Latin name Vera could never remember.

She couldn't see a single amusement arcade or fish and chip shop but the old stall selling rock and candy floss was still there and she saw a child go up to it with a bucket and spade, a fair-haired child who might have been herself all those many years ago.

Vera got off at the bottom of Seaview Crescent, feeling she must be in a dream. It wasn't possible that progress and the current mad craze for pulling things down and putting new things up had passed Brayminster by. It wasn't possible but it had happened. It was a Saturday afternoon in summer on the South Coast and there was no canned music, no screaming mobs, no coach parties and no strings of exhausted donkeys carrying screaming children along the sands. Vera listened to the quiet. In the copper beech tree, which still stood in the garden of the big house on the corner, a bird was singing. She was at the seaside in the South of England in spring and the only sound was a singing bird.

She walked slowly up the street and rang the bell of Cres-cent Guest House and when Mrs. Horton herself opened the door, Vera was almost too moved to speak. Inside, the house looked just the same. Vera looked wonderingly at the beach ball and the spade a child had left by the umbrella stand, just where she had left hers.

"Brings back the past a bit, doesn't it?" said Mrs. Horton kindly. "You look all in. Would you like to go up to your room and have a lie-down?"

"I'm not tired," said Vera, smiling. "I was just thinking how nothing's changed."

"We don't like changes in Bray."

"No, but how do you avoid them? I mean, everywhere else has changed utterly since the war."

Mrs. Horton led the way upstairs. "Well, down here, you see, we like to keep ourselves to ourselves. We're a bit like Frinton in Essex. Other places want the money, but we don't care so much about that. We don't let the coach parties in and our preservation society sees to it that the place doesn't get all built up. And we've got a good council. I only hope things stay this way."

"So do I," said Vera as Mrs. Horton showed her into the room Maud and George used to share.

"Your mother was so fond of this room. How is your mother, Mrs. Manning?"

"Dead," said Vera.

"Oh dear, I'm sorry to hear that." Mrs. Horton looked searchingly at Vera and then she said, before she went downstairs, "You have had a bad time, one loss after another."

Stanley lay on the sofa all Saturday afternoon. He wasn't used to whisky and it made him sleep heavily. The phone ringing awakened him but before he could get to it it had stopped. Ten minutes later it rang again. Pilbeam. Would Stanley meet him for what he called a short snort in the Lockkeeper's Arms at eight and discuss business? Stanley said he would and had Pilbeam phoned him before?

"Not me, my old love. Maybe it was your stockbroker."

Well, suppose it had been? The solicitor, that is, to say the money had come through. But he wouldn't be working on a Saturday, would he? Stanley considered calling the number of Finbow and Craig but then thought better of it. Early days yet.

He opened a can of beans for his tea and he was making

himself a piece of toast to go with them when the phone rang again. Vera, he supposed, to tell him she'd arrived safely just as if he'd be worrying himself in case the train had crashed.

He gave the number and it was a girl's voice he heard.

"Mr. Manning? Mr. Stanley Manning?"

Finbow's secretary. Bound to be. "Speaking," Stanley said smoothly.

"You won't know me, Mr. Manning. My name's Caroline Snow. I was given your phone number by a Mrs. Huntley."

Mrs. Huntley? Mrs. Huntley? Where had he heard that name before? In some unpleasant connection, he was sure. Stanley felt a very faint disquiet, nothing amounting to a shiver, but a kind of sense of coming events casting their shadows before them. He cleared his throat. "What were you wanting?"

"Well, to talk to you or your wife, actually. I'm making some enquiries about a Miss Ethel Carpenter."

Stanley lowered himself gingerly into the chair Ethel Carpenter had occupied a few minutes before her death. His mind was curiously blank and he found himself temporarily quite unable to speak.

The girl's voice said, "Could I come over and see you? Would you be very kind and let me come tomorrow evening?"

A faint squeak that Stanley hardly recognised as coming from himself said, "No, but . . . look, what exactly . . . ?"

"Then, may I come at eight? That's marvellous. I'll be over at eight and I'll explain everything. Thank you so much."

"Look, don't ring off. I mean, could you give me some idea . . . ?" The phone clicked and went dead in his hand.

He found that he was trembling very much as he had done when, sitting in this very chair, he had held the receiver in his hand after Dr. Moxley had promised to come. Then he had been at the height, the very zenith of his troubles, but now they were all over. Or were they? He found that the palms of his hands were sweating and he wiped them on the knees of his trousers.

This was trouble from the least expected quarter. The beauty of making use of Ethel Carpenter in his plan had been her solitary state, her lack of any friends in the world but Maud and the extreme unlikelihood of anyone ever enquiring about her. This was the last thing he had anticipated. He went back into the dining room and finished off the whisky, but he had no appetite for his beans and he dropped the can into the pedal bin.

The whisky comforted him a little but it also made him feel slightly sick. Suppose that girl had been a policewoman? Unlikely. She had sounded young, nervous and eager. Who the hell could she be, this Caroline Snow? She didn't sound more than twenty-five, if that. Not one of Mrs. Huntley's friends or she wouldn't have said "a Mrs. Huntley" like that. Some child, now grown up, whose family Ethel had worked for? That would be it. He wished he had bothered to listen when Maud had told all those interminable stories about where Ethel had worked and whom she had worked for and the names of their kids. But he hadn't and it was too late now. Still, the more he thought about it the more likely it appeared that this was who she was, some upper-class little madam looking up her old nanny. In London on holiday from the provinces, no doubt, and taking it into her head to go and be patronising to the family retainer. Mrs. Huntley would simply have told her the Mannings were Ethel's friends and their house the best place to root her out. In that case, why hadn't Mrs. Huntley sent her along to Green Lanes?

There would be, no doubt, a perfectly simple explanation. Feeling a good deal better, Stanley decided to tell her Ethel was lodging with some people called Smith but that he didn't know where they lived. A girl like that, spoilt and used to having everything done for her, would soon get fed-up. He belched loudly, looked around for his crossword and then remembered he had already done it.

Still rather queasy, Stanley made his way down to the Lockkeeper's Arms at eight o'clock. He took a single pound note with him for, since Vera wasn't about to borrow from, he'd have to make his pay last him a week.

Pilbeam was already there and he looked as if he had been drinking steadily for several hours. The whisky he was putting away had put him in an aggressive, prickly mood.

"Your round, I think," he said to Stanley. Evidently he had a long memory. Reluctantly Stanley bought two double whiskies.

"Well, old man, when can I expect the first instalment?"

"The what?" said Stanley, his mind still on Caroline Snow.

"Don't give me that," said Pilbeam loudly. "You heard. The first instalment of this capital of yours we hear so much about."

"There's been a hold-up at my solicitor's."

"Well, you'd better get twisting your solicitor's arm, then, hadn't you?"

"It's coming. A week or two and we'll be able to get started."

"O.K. But just remember I'm an impatient man. I've got the lease and I had to touch the missus for the lolly. She'll want it back and quick, make no mistake about that."

"I won't," said Stanley feebly, and then more firmly, "your round, I reckon."

"We'll drink to a glorious future," said Pilbeam more amiably and he fetched two more whiskies.

"By the way," said Stanley, remembering Caroline Snow who might be a policewoman and might have a search warrant or something, "by the way, I've got a few bits to show you, pieces we might flog."

"That's my boy. What sort of bits?"

"A carriage clock and some china stuff."

"Where are they?"

"Back at my place."

"I tell you what," said Pilbeam. "Why don't you and me go back there now and give the stuff the once over? Your wife there, is she?"

"My wife's away."

"No kidding? You nip round the Off, Stan old boy, and get us a bottle of Haig and we'll make an evening of it."

Stanley had to tell him he hadn't got any money and Pilbeam, his bad temper returning, said in a very nasty tone that he'd buy it just this once but Stanley would have to stump up his share when they got to Lanchester Road.

Still in an ill humour, Pilbeam hardly spoke until they were inside the house and then he said he wasn't impressed by Stanley's domestic arrangements.

"Don't do yourself very well, do you?" Pilbeam looked scornfully at the worn carpet and Vera's framed photographs. "No wonder you've capital. You haven't spent much on this place."

"I'll get the stuff I told you about. It's upstairs."

"You do that, old man. And while you're about it, I'll relieve you of twenty-six and nine."

"That's upstairs too," Stanley muttered.

There was no help for it. He'd have to use a couple of
Ethel's notes. Stanley opened the crossword annual for 1954
and took two from between the pages. Then he got the parcels out of his wardrobe and went back to Pilbeam who was
already drinking whisky from one of Vera's sherry glasses.

"Funny pong they've got about them," he said, sniffing the
notes. "Where've you kept them? In a tin of talcum powder?
Right old miser you are, Stan." He pocketed the notes but
he didn't produce any change.

"Are you going to have a dekko at these, then?"

Pilbeam examined the shepherdess, the bowl, the jug and
the clock, sniffed and pronounced them saleable but of no great
value. Then he put his feet up on the sofa and, without
waiting for an invitation, told Stanley the story of his life.

It made an interesting narrative, full as it was of accounts
of Pilbeam's brushes with the law, his escapades with women
and the fortunes he had nearly made. But Stanley found his
attention wandering constantly back to Caroline Snow. Who
was she? What was she going to ask him? Would she come
alone? Stanley drank for comfort until his head was thick and
fuddled and when Pilbeam reached a point in his story where
he had nearly married an heiress old enough to be his mother,
he nodded off into a jumpy stupor.

The last thing he remembered that night was Pilbeam getting up, pocketing the three-quarters empty bottle and saying,
"I'll give you a ring in a day or two."

"No good," Stanley murmured thickly, "before next week."

"You leave that to me, Stan old boy. I'll twist your arm
so as you know how to twist your stockbroker's."

It was noon the next day before Stanley came down after
a night spent stretched on his bed, fully clothed. Pilbeam had
left all Ethel's property behind, but he had taken the bottle
and Stanley's change.

Unused to heavy drinking, Stanley had a blinding headache.
He felt as if there was someone standing inside his head, press-

ing with all his force against the bony walls of his prison in a splitting effort to get out.

The sight of food made him give a slow, painful retch. Tentatively, he peeled the paper from the joint of beef Vera had left him and which he had forgotten to leave, soaking in salt water, on the tiled larder shelf the night before. It was on the turn, not exactly high but too far gone to eat when you felt as queasy as he did. He tipped it into the bin to join the beans. Well, he didn't feel up to eating anything, anyway. Instead he took two aspirins and wandered out into the garden.

Suddenly, for the first time since he got up, he was aware that it was a very hot day, blindingly, oppressively hot for late April, the kind of day that makes weather records and gives rise to newspaper articles about people fainting from the heat and the tar melting on the roads. The garden was virtually without shade. Never a sun worshipper, Stanley gave a malevolent glare over the fence to where the Macdonalds sat, eating their Sunday lunch under a striped awning. Some people didn't know what to do with their money, he thought, eyeing their new garden furniture with scorn and Mrs. Macdonald's bikini with disgust. She was forty-five if she was a day and she ought to know better, she with a son of fifteen. The boy, who was wearing nothing but a pair of swimming trunks, glared back at Stanley and Stanley went indoors.

The dining room, shut up since the night before, its french windows beaten on by the sun since seven, was as hot as a furnace and it stank of Pilbeam's cigars. Stanley retched again and staggered into the cooler kitchen. He might have taken a chair out on to the concrete into the shade by the back door but he didn't want to be overlooked by John Blackmore who, still painting his house, was perched on his ladder.

Presently he made himself a cup of tea and took it upstairs. He lay on the rumpled bed, sweating profusely, but he couldn't relax. In seven hours' time he was going to have to deal with Caroline Snow.

His feelings about the coming interview were considerably less sanguine than they had been on the previous evening. It was difficult to understand how a few words on the telephone and the revelation of certain aspects of Pilbeam's character could have drawn so sudden and so dark a cloud across his happiness. Only hours, not years, had passed since he had sat without a care in the world on the steps of the war memorial.

At last he fell into an uneasy sleep and dreamed that he could hear Maud snoring through the wall. It was only the Blackmores' lawn mower, he discovered when he awoke, but the notion that his subconscious was translating commonplace sounds into aural hallucinations of his late mother-in-law upset him. That was the first dream he had had of her since the night of her death.

The sun had moved round to the front of the house and penetrated the thick curtains, suffusing the bedroom with hot glowing light. All Stanley's clothes seemed to be sticking to him. When it was nearly six he got up and put on a clean shirt. He went downstairs and re-wrapped Ethel's bowl and jug and clock and china and pushed them inside the sideboard.

He hadn't had a thing to eat all day but the very thought of food made him queasy again. Maybe he'd go out, go for a bus ride or see what was on at the pictures. Then Caroline Snow would find an empty house and serve her right. But Stanley knew he wouldn't go. To postpone for another day or even days finding out who Caroline Snow was and what she wanted would be unbearable.

At half-past seven he found he had started to pace up and down. It was cooler now but not very much and he kept the french windows shut. The Macdonalds were still outside, still laughing and playing with a beach ball and exchanging badinage with John Blackmore on his ladder as if, because they hadn't a care in the world, they thought no one else should have either. Stanley forced himself to sit down. A muscle in the corner of his mouth had started to twitch and jump.

Suppose she brought her husband with her? Or Mrs. Huntley or—God forbid—a policeman? She'd be at the station by now, he thought, looking at his watch, just about to catch the bus up. Ten minutes and she'd be here. Stanley went upstairs and looked out of all the windows which gave on to the street. It was deserted, but for one brave spirit washing his car down. That'll be me in a week or two, Stanley told himself for comfort, me with my Jaguar and my van parked side by side.

By that time Caroline Snow would be in the past, a bad dream. . . .

What could they do to him, anyway? What could anyone do? Ethel Carpenter was a handful of ashes in an urn and he'd yet to learn any clever sod could analyse ashes and find out whose they were. In any case, he hadn't laid a finger on her. Was it his fault she'd fallen down dead in his lounge? He'd given her a damn' good funeral, far better than she'd have had if that Mrs. Huntley had found her dead in her own room. Really, he'd done her a service. Very dignified that cremation had been and in the best of taste. The way he worried you'd think he was a murderer or something.

Five past eight. Stanley found that his heart had begun to grow very gradually lighter as the crucial hour passed by. He went downstairs and opened the french windows. The Macdonalds were packing up their furniture and their stupid toys. Stanley felt almost sufficiently well and relaxed to mow the lawn. He muttered something in reply to Blackmore's greeting and got the mower out of the shed. Up and down the lawn twice, the shorn grass spraying into the box. Perhaps it would be just as well to pop indoors and check she hadn't turned up, after all.

Stanley ran quite lightly up the stairs, leaving a trail of grass cuttings behind him. His bedroom windows showed him a deserted street. Even the car washer had finished and gone in. A beautiful, calm evening. Not normally a man to derive peace and tranquillity from communing with nature, Stanley now felt that nothing bad could happen on such a serene and tender night. The sky was a cloudless pastel violet, the shadows long and still. How beautiful his lawn would look when close-cut, its edges trimmed with the long shears.

Almost placid now, he returned to it.

The mower cut smoothly in long clean sweeps and Stanley worked evenly and methodically, for he liked his lawn to have a neat ribbed look like a piece of corded velvet or a very expert sample of knitting. The heather garden was in shadow now, sleeping under its quilt of peat and mowings. Up and down, up and down . . . Twenty-five past eight. What a fool he had been to get into a state!

He came down towards the house, pushing the machine. What the hell was Blackmore up to, making signs to him?

"There's someone at your door, mate."

Stanley's mouth dried.

"What?"

"A young lady ringing your door bell."

"O.K., O.K.," said Stanley. His palms were running with sweat. He wiped them on his trousers and went into the dining room. The whole house seemed to reverberate with the vibration of the bell. Momentarily, Stanley put his damp hands over his ears. Why shouldn't he just go upstairs and keep his ears covered until she had gone? But Blackmore had seen her, Blackmore would tell her where he was. . . .

"Oh, Christ!" Stanley moaned. "All right, all right," he said, "I'm coming."

The ringing stopped. He opened the door.

"Mr. Manning? Oh, good evening. I'm Caroline Snow. I'm so sorry I'm late. I had a job finding your house."

Stanley gaped at her. For a moment his terror had left him. It wasn't fear which made him speechless. He had seen such creatures as she before, of course, seen them on television in the Miss World contests or on the covers of the magazines Vera sometimes bought, even sometimes seen near copies of them driving up to the pumps at the Superjuce garage. But no one like this had ever until now rung the bell at 61, Lanchester Road.

"Isn't it hot? May I come in? Oh, thank you so much. I'm afraid I'm being a terrible nuisance."

"That's all right," Stanley mumbled.

He followed her into the dining room. Even from behind she looked nearly as good as from in front. Her long pale blonde hair covered her shoulders in a thick gold veil. Stanley didn't think he had ever seen such a straight back or such legs, legs which were so long and smooth and exquisite that it was almost painful to look at them.

When she was in the room and had turned to face him he wondered how he could ever have thought her back view was as nice. Her skin was tanned a smooth, even and satiny brown, much darker than her hair. Swedish or something, Stanley thought feebly. His eyes met sea-green eyes, as cool and calm as

northern waters, and a wave of perfume floated over him so that
he felt slightly faint.

"Can I get you a cup of tea?" he said.

"That would be great."

He went into the kitchen and put the kettle on. It wasn't
just the beauty of that face that had made him stare at her.
He stared because he felt it wasn't entirely unfamiliar to him.
Somewhere he had seen it, or a face very like it though somehow
changed and spoiled, in the recent past. In a film? In the
paper? He couldn't remember.

"First I'd better explain," said Caroline Snow when he went
back to her, "why I've come."

"Well, I did wonder," said Stanley.

"Naturally, you did. But I didn't feel I could talk about
something so—well, personal and private on the phone. Did you
know your kettle's boiling?"

Stanley got up and went out to turn it off. He meant to go
on being tactful and polite but when he came back he found
himself blurting out involuntarily, "Who are you?"

She smiled. "Yes, well, that's the embarrassing part. I may as
well tell you and get it over. I'm Ethel Carpenter's granddaughter."

14

"You can't be," Stanley said. "She wasn't ever married."

"I know, but she had a baby at seventeen just the same."

Stanley, who had held his mouth open ever since Caroline
Snow's revelation, now closed it, swallowing some air. At last
he said, "Now you mention it, I did know. My wife must have
told me."

Caroline Snow said, "I think I'd better tell you the whole
story."

"O.K.," said Stanley, resigning himself. Having got so far,
he'd better know the worst. "I'll get the tea." Her granddaughter,

he thought miserably as he poured on the boiling water. Almost as bad as a policewoman.

She smiled at him. Stanley thought she looked less pretty when she smiled, for her teeth were uneven. She also looked much more like Ethel Carpenter and now Stanley knew whose face hers had reminded him of.

"Let's have it, then," he said.

"My people live in Gloucester," Caroline Snow began, "but I'm at training college in London. I'm training to be a teacher and I'm in my second year. Well, we had to do a special study this term, Greek myths or genealogy, and I chose genealogy." Stanley looked at her suspiciously. He knew quite well what genealogy was, for his passion for crossword puzzles had given him a large vocabulary and, in any case, he was fond of words. But he couldn't see what genealogy had to do with teaching kids to read and write and he wondered if Caroline Snow was lying. "Honestly, I'd have chosen the myths if I'd known what I was letting myself in for. Our lecturer wanted us all to make family trees, one for the paternal side and another for the maternal. You do follow what I mean?"

"Of course I do," said Stanley, offended. "I'm not ignorant."

"I didn't mean that. Only it's a bit complicated. Well, doing Dad's tree was easy because all his people came from a village outside Gloucester and I got hold of the parish records and everything. I got that all finished by half-term. Then I came to Mummy's. She was very shy about it, didn't want to give me any help at all, which isn't a bit like Mummy. She's a marvellous person, absolutely terrific. You'd adore her."

"I daresay," said Stanley. When was she going to come to the point? The last thing he wanted was to hear about marvellous adorable Mummy whom he was sure he'd loathe at sight.

Caroline Snow crossed her long legs and lit a cigarette. Gimlet-eyed, Stanley watched the packet returned to her handbag with mounting rage. "Anyway, to cut a long story short, I rather nagged Mummy about it all and then she told me. She said she was illegitimate. I'd always understood her parents were dead and that's why she'd been brought up in an orphanage, but she said she'd just told me that. The truth is her mother's still alive and she never knew who her father was. Well, at last I got it all out of her.

"Her mother was Ethel Carpenter, a housemaid who'd had her when she was only seventeen. My mother was brought up by Ethel's aunt until she was seven and then the aunt got married and the new uncle sent Mummy to this orphanage. Wasn't it awful? Mummy never saw her own mother and for years the only member of her family she did see was a cousin who came to visit her. He was Ethel's cousin actually and he was very kind to Mummy.

"Well, Mummy had brains, thank goodness, and went to training college—the same one as I'm at actually—and when she was teaching in a school in Gloucester she met Dad and married him and they lived happily ever after. It's rather a terrible story, though, isn't it?"

"Yeah." Stanley watched her stub out her cigarette. "I don't see where you come into it," he said.

"I've had my grandmother on my conscience," said Caroline Snow. "I felt so bad about her, you see. Mummy's never wanted to meet her. I suppose she thought it would be too heartbreaking for both of them. But now I've come so far I've just got to find her. Think what it would mean to her, Mr. Manning, a poor lonely old woman suddenly finding she'd got a whole family of her own."

Stanley could well understand Mummy's feelings, although most of his sympathy went to Mr. Snow. That'd be a fine thing, he thought, having the good luck to marry an orphan and then getting an old mother-in-law thrust on you when you were middle-aged. Probably have to part out with money for her too. If I were in his shoes, Stanley said to himself, I'd smack that girl's bottom for her. Interfering little bitch of a do-gooder.

"I'd give the whole idea up if I were you," he said aloud. "It stands to reason, if she'd wanted a family she'd have hunted all you lot up long ago." It was, he thought, a good line to take, charitable to the unfortunate Mr. Snow as well as opening up a let-out for himself. He warmed to it. "She won't want to be reminded of her past, will she? The disgrace and all? Oh, no, you give it up. I reckon your dad'd say the same. It's always a mistake, stirring things up. Let sleeping dogs lie is what I say."

"I'm afraid I disagree with you," Caroline Snow said stiffly. "You must read the papers. You know what a terrible problem we have in this country with our old people, how lonely some of them are and how friendless. I'd never forgive myself if I gave up now." She smiled, giving him an indulgent look. "Anyway, you don't really mean it. Mrs. Huntley told me you'd had your own mother-in-law living with you for years and having to be looked after. You didn't abandon her now, did you? And now she's dead you've got nothing to reproach yourself with. Well, I don't want to reproach myself either."

This little speech temporarily took Stanley's breath away. He gaped at her, frowning. Her zeal and her innocence were beyond his understanding. He cleared his throat. "How did you get on to Mrs. Huntley?"

Serene again, Caroline Snow said, "The cousin who used to visit Mummy in the orphanage is still alive, although he's a very old man. I went to see him first and he said he'd lost touch with my grandmother but he knew her last place had been with some people called Kilbride. I found them and they told me she had a room with a Mrs. Huntley."

"And she put you on to us?"

"Well, she said you'd know where my grandmother was, on account of she and Mrs. Kinaway being such close friends. And she said my grandmother had been coming to stay here with you but she'd changed her mind and now she's got lodgings in Croughton with a Mrs. Paterson but she'd forgotten the address. I thought—I thought if you could just give me that address I'd go round now and introduce myself and . . . Oh, I feel so nervous and excited! I'm quite sick with nerves. Just imagine, Mr. Manning, what she'll think when she sees me. I'm going to tell her she'll never be alone again. We've got quite a big house in Gloucester and I want Daddy to turn the attics into a flat for her. I want to take her home myself and show her her new home and just see her face."

I'd like to see Daddy's, thought Stanley. Poor sod. It was one thing for this silly little piece, arranging people's lives for them. She wouldn't be there to listen to Ethel banging on the floor with her stick and demanding meals at all hours and monopolising the T.V., she'd be living it up in London at her college. That poor devil, he thought with indignation. It was his, Stanley's, duty to prevent anything like that happening, his bounden duty. . . . He was so outraged that for a moment he had forgotten the impossibility of Snow's house ever being invaded by a mother-in-law. Then, suddenly, he remembered. Ethel was dead, all that remained of her some fifteen feet away from them in an urn on the mantelpiece. It didn't matter where Caroline Snow went or where she looked, for Ethel had vanished from the face of the earth.

"Mrs. Paterson's address is 52, Green Lanes," he said, "but I don't think you'll find her there. My wife said she'd found somewhere new."

Caroline Snow wrote down the address. "Thank you so much," she said fervently. "I'm sure I'll be able to trace her now. But wasn't it odd her telling Mrs. Huntley she was coming here and then suddenly changing her mind?"

Stanley frowned. "When you've had as much experience of old people as I have," he said with feeling, "you won't be surprised by any of the funny things they do."

She got up, first looking at him in rather a woe-begone way, her ardour perhaps a little dampened, and then eyed herself critically in the mirror. "I wonder if I look at all like her? I'm the image of Mummy and Mummy's supposed to look like her."

"Yeah, you do a bit," said Stanley.

Caroline Snow swung round to face him. "Then, you do know her? You have seen her?"

Stanley could have bitten his tongue out.

"She was at my wedding," he muttered.

"Oh, I see." She picked up her bag and Stanley saw her to the door. "I'll let you know how I get on," she said.

From his bedroom window Stanley watched her hurrying along in the direction of Green Lanes. Somewhere he had once read that most of the things one has worried about have never happened. How true that was! When the girl had disappeared from view he finished mowing the lawn in the half-light, whistling an old tune which he later realised had been Tennyson's "Maud."

Vera was enjoying her holiday. She had met some nice people, a married couple about her own age and who were also staying at Mrs. Horton's. They insisted on taking her about with them in their car, along the coast to Beachey Head and inland to Arundel Castle, and they laughed and asked Vera if she thought they were on their honeymoon when she demurred and suggested she was intruding. They wanted her to share their table but Vera wouldn't do that. She ate alone, sitting in the window and watching holidaymakers coming up from the beach, and she enjoyed her food, relishing every scrap because she hadn't had to cook it herself.

There was only one thing that troubled her and that was that neither her new friends, the Goodwins, nor Mrs. Horton had once asked about Stanley, where he was and why he hadn't come with her. Vera felt rather piqued. She couldn't help thinking that in the early days of her marriage when Maud had still come to Bray for holidays, she had poisoned Mrs. Horton's mind against Stanley. I shan't mention him, if that's the way they want it, Vera said to herself. She felt no pressing need to talk about him. Now he was far away, she found she hardly thought about him and this made her so guilty that she sent him a postcard every day.

At a loss to know how to amuse herself one wet afternoon, Mrs. Goodwin took Vera up to her bedroom where she washed and set her hair, made up her face, and, while Vera was waiting for the set to dry, turned the hem of Vera's blue and white spotted dress up two inches.

"You've got very nice legs. Why not show them off?"

"At my age?" said Vera.

"Life begins at forty, my dear. You'll look ten years younger, anyway, when I've finished with you."

Vera did. She stared in wonderment and unease at her new self, at the bouffant golden-brown hair, the pale blue eyelids and the pink mouth Mrs. Goodwin had created with a lip-brush. The dress barely reached her knees. Feeling half-naked, she went down to dinner and hid herself in her alcove away from the other diners.

She was waiting for Mrs. Horton's maid to bring her second course, when a man came into the dining room and wandered about, evidently looking for someone. Vera watched his reflection in the window. She was so busy staring at this that she nearly jumped out of her skin when a hand touched her shoulder. She turned and looked upwards, flushing slightly.

He was a stranger, quite unfamiliar to her, a man of fifty perhaps with a rather haggard face, fair hair gone pepper and salt, a long lean man with an anxious, even forbidding, look. Vera half-rose. She must have done something wrong. Forgotten to pay for her deck chair perhaps. . . .

"I'm sorry . . ." she hesitated, stammering. "What—er . . . ?"

He smiled at her and it made him look much younger. "Hallo, Vee."

"I don't think . . . I don't know you, do I?"

"You used to know me. I know I've changed. You haven't, not very much. I'd have recognised you anywhere. May I sit down?"

"Oh, yes, of course."

He pulled up a chair, offered her a cigarette. Vera shook her head.

"My aunt told me you were here. I meant to come yesterday but, I don't know . . . I suppose I was shy. It's been so long. How are you?"

Confidence suddenly came to Vera and a poise she didn't know she possessed.

"I'm very well, thank you, James. It's good to see you."

"Oh, Vee, you don't know how glad I am to see you," said James Horton.

15

Gradually, as the week went on, Stanley's small panic receded. For the first few evenings he sat close to the phone, the crossword puzzle on his knees, expecting a call from Caroline Snow. But no call came. In fact nothing came from the world outside at all but daily postcards from Vera. She wrote that she was having a wonderful time, meeting new people, going out and about with them every day. Stanley felt very bitter towards her and resentful.

As soon as she got back she could go down to that Finbow and get Maud's money out of him. It was downright diabolical, solicitors hanging on to other people's rightful inheritances for weeks on end.

"How's your head, Stan?" said Pilbeam when he phoned on Thursday.

"There's nothing wrong with my head," said Stanley.

"Bet there was Sunday morning. One sniff of a barmaid's apron and you're out like a light."

"I told you," said Stanley, "it was no good ringing me this week. I'll have the money on Tuesday like I said."

"You never did, in point of fact, me old love. But let it pass. Tuesday, you said?"

"That's a promise."

"I sure am glad to hear that, Stan. I've been out knocking today—got a lend of a van—and some of the things I've picked up'll make your hair curl." It was a funny thing about Pilbeam, Stanley thought. The mere sound of the man's voice brought him vividly before one, snub nose, sausage-like finger and all. "How about a sniftah in the Lockkeeper's tomorrow night, so as I can get a clearer picture of the state of your finances?"

Stanley was obliged to agree. Pilbeam would get a clear picture of his finances all right when he turned up in the Lockkeeper's with all he had left of last Friday's pay, ten bob.

The whole Macdonald family and the two Blackmores were outside the Macdonalds' gate, admiring Fred Macdonald's new car, when Stanley left the house to keep his appointment. He would have marched past them without a word but the Macdonald boy, Michael, barred his way, holding both arms outstretched.

"Look what my dad's just brought home, Mr. Manning."

"Very nice," said Stanley, but still they wouldn't let him get away. Macdonald got out of the car and invited Stanley to take his place and examine the arrangements for the automatic gear change. Unable to think of an excuse, Stanley got sulkily into the car and contemplated the control panel.

"No more wearing my left foot out on the clutch in a traffic jam," said Macdonald jubilantly. "Comfortable, isn't she? I've only got one complaint. When I sink into that I'll fall asleep behind the wheel."

The women were nattering nineteen to the dozen, scuttling around the car and pointing out the mirror-like gloss on its bodywork, the vast capacity of its boot and the workmanship of its chrome. Mrs. Macdonald was swollen with pride. Wait till they see my Jag, Stanley thought, after this tin can. Then they'll laugh on the other side of their faces.

"The mirror adjusts at the touch of a finger," said Macdonald, thrusting his head through the window.

Stanley put it to the test. He moved the mirror an inch down and glanced into it. Then he stared harder, going hot all over. From the High Street end of Lanchester Road Caroline Snow was walking along the pavement in the direction of his house. She wore large round sunglasses with mauve lenses and a skirt several inches shorter than the one she had worn on Sunday. Stanley looked down, twiddling knobs and pulling small levers. One of these operated the windscreen washers and a fountain of water gushed across the glass.

"Here, here," said Mrs. Macdonald. "Mind what you're doing. I shall have to get a leather to that." She frowned spitefully at Stanley and pulled the car door open. "Anyway, you're wanted. There's someone come to call on you."

Stanley got out very slowly, not looking behind him. Macdonald slapped him on the shoulder. "When the cat's away the mice will play, eh, old man? Very good taste you've got, if I may say so."

"I don't know what you're talking about," Stanley muttered. Six faces confronted him, the children's inquisitive, the women's indignant, the men's frankly prurient. John Blackmore gave a crooked grin and then he slowly winked. "Excuse me," Stanley said. "Got to go in."

He scuttled up the path to where Caroline Snow stood waiting for him on the doorstep. Behind him he heard Mrs. Blackmore say, "Well, really! How disgusting."

"I just had to come and see you again, Mr. Manning. I do hope it's not inconvenient?"

The air in the house smelt stale. Stanley flung open the french windows. The girl followed him.

"Perhaps we could sit in the garden? It's so hot, isn't it? And your garden's lovely."

"I haven't got time for any sitting about," said Stanley hurriedly. He looked at his watch. "I've got an appointment at half-past six."

"I've really come to you," the girl said, taking no notice of all this, "because—well, you were very kind to me on Sunday and you're really the only responsible man I can talk to. You see, I've relied on Daddy all my life but Daddy's such a long way away."

Let me be your father, Stanley thought eagerly, forgetting for the moment all about his date with Pilbeam. "What exactly d'you want me to do, Miss Snow?"

"I went to see Mrs. Paterson," Caroline Snow said earnestly, "and she said Miss—er, my grandmother had got a room with a Mr. Smith but she doesn't know his address. Now college comes down on Tuesday and I have to go home so I wondered . . . My grandmother's bound to come and see you and your wife sometime, isn't she? I thought if you'd be kind enough to tell her about me if she does and—well, write to me, I could look her up when I get back to London."

"Yeah, I could do that," Stanley said slowly. Of course he could. He could tell her he'd seen Ethel and Ethel had moved again or even that Ethel didn't want to make contact with her relatives. Suddenly he was inspired. Making his voice sound as confident as he could and infusing into a hint of the paternal, he said, "Why don't you ask your father's advice? Have you told him anything of all this?"

"Well, no . . . As far as Mummy and he know, I just wanted my grandmother's name for this family tree."

Wonderful. Just what he'd hoped for. He could just imagine Snow's horror when he heard of this search for his mother-in-law and his relief when he learned she wasn't to be found. "Your dad's a man of experience. He'll know what's the best thing to do." He will, Stanley thought, if he's in his right mind. "He might feel rather hurt if you went over his head like this. She is his mother-in-law after all. He might not . . ."

"Oh, but Daddy's a marvellous person. He's got a terrific social conscience. He couldn't bear to think . . ."

"Can you be quite sure of that, Miss Snow?" Stanley leaned earnestly towards her. "Certainly your father'll want to know all the details you've told me, but isn't it likely he'll want to do any further investigating himself? Besides, he and your mother may feel your grandmother's got a right to privacy, if that's what she wants and it seems she does want it. No, he wouldn't

like it at all if you put people's backs up and got the police on
a wild goose chase."

"I wonder if you're right?" Caroline Snow looked nearly convinced. "You've put things in a different perspective for me,
Mr. Manning. Actually, I've just remembered something. Once,
years ago when I was quite young a gipsy came to our door when
Mummy was out and I gave her some clothes and made her
a cup of tea and when Daddy heard about it he was *furious*.
He said the state should look after people like that. He'd got
quite enough supporting his own family."

The man with the terrific social conscience! Stanley almost
laughed aloud.

"Of course, it's not really a parallel case, but it does make me
think I ought to ask Daddy before I go any further." She got
up and held out her hand. "You've really been very kind, Mr.
Manning. I'm sure you've given me the right advice. I won't do
another thing before I've asked Daddy." She held out her hand.
"I'm afraid I've made you late for your appointment."

"Better late than never," Stanley said cheerfully. "I'll walk
with you. It's on my way."

They left the house together. John Blackmore, who was trim-
ming his hedge, favoured Stanley with another wink. Stanley
talked about the weather and the car he was going to buy and
the business he was going into to take the girl's mind off Ethel
Carpenter.

"I wonder now why I got this idea something terrible might
have happened to her? I suppose it was because Mrs. Huntley
said she was carrying fifty pounds on her."

"She'll be living it up on that without a care in the world,"
Stanley said reassuringly.

Caroline Snow smiled at him and in that smile he saw Ethel
grinning up at him and waving her umbrella. She gave him
the address of her father's house and they parted cordially.

That, Stanley thought, was the last he would ever see or hear
of her. He walked to the Lockkeeper's because he couldn't afford
the bus fare. The little shop was still boarded up but the agent's
placard had been taken away.

Pilbeam wasn't alone but surrounded by a circle of friends, all
of whom seemed extravagantly big men. He didn't introduce

any of them to Stanley but moved away from them without a word. For some indefinable reason this made Stanley uneasy.

Without asking Pilbeam's preferences—he knew them—Stanley bought two halves of bitter and, floundering in a mass of prevarication, set about giving his new partner a picture of his finances.

Pilbeam said only, "Next week, me old love. First thing next week."

Some of Vera's ideas about James Horton had been right and some wrong. He was manager of Barclay's Brayminster branch; he was well-off, for he had inherited money both from his father and his uncle; he did live in a nice house. But he wasn't married to a woman in her handsome early forties and he hadn't a family of teenage children. His wife had died of cancer five years before, leaving him with one son, now at university.

"A lonely life, James," Vera said on her last evening as she and James sat in the cocktail lounge of the Metropole hotel.

"It gets lonely sometimes."

"You never thought of marrying again?"

"Not until lately," said James. "You know, Vee, you haven't told me a thing about yourself. We've been out together every night—oh, mostly with the Goodwins, I know—but all the time I've seemed to do nothing but talk of my life and I haven't given you a chance to tell me about yours. I'm afraid I've been very self-centred."

"Oh, no. I've been so interested."

"I suppose it's living alone that makes one want to talk. But your life must have been as lonely as mine."

"What makes you say that?" Vera looked at him, puzzled.

"Aren't we almost in the same boat, Vee? I a widower and you a widow, you childless and I . . ."

"James," Vera said loudly, "whatever made you think I was a widow?"

He turned rather pale and stammered, "But my aunt said . . . You came down here alone and you never . . ."

"I'm afraid Mrs. Horton's got it wrong. I'm not a widow. My husband just couldn't get time off from work. Oh dear, now I begin to see a lot of things I didn't understand."

"You mean you live with your husband? You and your husband . . ."

"Of course. I'm going home to him tomorrow."

"I see," said James Horton. "I've been rather foolish and obtuse."

16

All Vera's cards were on the mantelpiece but not displayed. They were tucked in a stack behind a vase. Stanley hadn't asked her if she had enjoyed herself and she was very hurt.

"How's the job?" she asked quietly.

"I've resigned, if you must know. I'm going into the antique business. There's pots of money to be made out of antiques and we're taking a shop in the old village. Me and my partner, that is."

"Your partner?" said Vera. "What partner? Who is he, Stan? Where did you meet him?"

Vera looked so aghast that it would hardly have made matters worse to tell her he had met Pilbeam in the street and founded the partnership in a pub. But Stanley was one of those men who never tell their wives the truth if a lie will serve instead. "He was put in touch by a mutual friend," he said vaguely. "A client of mine at the Superjuce gave him my name." He knew Vera wouldn't believe him but at the moment he hardly cared. He shifted his eyes sullenly. Two hours before she came home he had telephoned Finbow and Craig only to be told by a secretary that Mr. Finbow had a matter he wanted to discuss urgently with Mrs. Manning and a letter on the subject would reach her on Monday morning. Another hold-up. God knew what Pilbeam would say if the money wasn't forthcoming in the Lockkeeper's on Tuesday night.

Vera said astutely, "Has this man got any capital?"

"Be your age," said Stanley. "He's rolling. Would I get involved with him if he hadn't?"

"I don't know what you'd do, Stan. But I reckon you're a child when it comes to business. I know more about business than you do. Promise me you won't do anything silly."

Stanley didn't answer her. He couldn't get that letter out of his mind and the more he thought about it the more he felt the tiny muscles around his eyes twitching. On Sunday night he slept badly, being visited by troubling dreams of Maud. In one of them he and she were discussing the contents of her will and Maud told him she hadn't finished with him yet, that Mr. Finbow's letter would be concerned with a clause in that will designed to upset any business schemes he might have.

He was therefore less indignant than he might otherwise have been when Vera brought him a cup of tea and read aloud to him.

Dear Mrs. Manning,

With regard to your inheritance from the late Mrs. Maud Kinaway, I have been in touch with the firm of stockbrokers acting for the late Mrs. Kinaway. Owing to the recent fall in the stock market, I feel it my duty to inform you that I consider it inadvisable to sell the stock in which your late mother's monies are invested, at the present time. I am, however, reliably advised that the market is once more rising and that it would be expedient to retain these stocks for a further few weeks.

No doubt, you will wish to discuss this whole question with me as soon as posible. I should like to stress that should you desire this stock to be sold forthwith, I will naturally proceed to instruct your late mother's stockbroker accordingly. Perhaps you could arrange to call at my office early this week.

I remain,

Yours sincerely,

CHARLES H. FINBOW.

"I just hope he's on the level," Stanley said gloomily, "and not playing ducks and drakes with our money. You can tell him to sell that stock right away."

"Don't be silly, dear," Vera said mildly. "Mr. Finbow's only acting in our interests. He means that if he sold those shares now he'd get hundreds less than if we waited a few weeks."

Stanley sat up, choking over his tea. "You what? We've got to have that money. God knows, we've waited long enough." He felt quite sick with horror. Imagine Pilbeam's face if he was asked to wait weeks. The whole enterprise would go up the spout. "You'll go there today," he spluttered, "in your lunch hour and I'm coming with you."

"I can't, Stan. Doris is off and I can't get away for lunch."

"If you won't, Vee, I will." Stanley threw back the covers. "I'll go down there alone and get that money if I have to knock his teeth in."

"I'll see what I can do," Vera sighed.

Alone in the house, Stanley paced up and down, sweating. In the pub on Friday he had confidently promised Pilbeam money to buy a van, money for decorating and furnishing the shop and enough ready cash to stock it. Finbow would have to cough up. His eye fluttered painfully and to calm himself he sat down and did the crossword puzzle.

He was just filling in 26 across "Last Post" eight letters, four and four, "Ultimate mail before leaving the field" when the doorbell rang on a sharp peremptory note.

Stanley never answered a doorbell naturally and innocently as other people do. He always debated whether it was wise to answer it at all. Now he crept into the front room and peeped through the curtains. Pilbeam stood on the doorstep with a large heavily built man who looked no more than twenty-eight and who was recognisable as one of those henchmen who had moved silently away from Pilbeam in the pub on Friday.

Stanley let the curtain fall, but not before Pilbeam's eyes had met his. There was no help for it. The door would have to be answered. He opened it and Pilbeam put his foot inside and on to the mat like a pushing salesman.

He didn't introduce his companion. Stanley didn't expect him to. They all knew why the friend had come. There was no need for hypocritical formalities.

"I told you Tuesday," Stanley said.

"I know, old man, but what's a day one way or the other? We all realise the big lolly's coming tomorrow. What I want is fifty on account now."

They came in. Stanley couldn't stop them.

"I haven't got fifty," he said, very conscious of the friend's size and youth.

"Thirty, then," said Pilbeam. "It's in your own interest, Stan.

Me and my mate have got our eye on a couple of *famille rose* vases. It'd be a sin to let them go."

"I'll see," said Stanley feebly. The friend's mammoth shoulder was nudging his. "Sit down. Make yourselves at home. The money's upstairs."

He scuttled up the stairs and made for the bookcase. Leafing thirty notes from the pages of the crossword annual, he became aware of a step behind him and then that Pilbeam was standing in the doorway, watching the operation with interest and a certain bewilderment.

"So that's your little safe deposit, is it? By gum, it stinks of violets."

Speechless, Stanley handed over the thirty pounds. There were now only thirteen notes left in the annual.

"This is my husband," Vera said when they were admitted to Mr. Finbow's office. It wasn't an introduction she had often had to make. She and Stanley hadn't lived in a world where many introductions were called for. But whenever she had to say those words she was conscious of a little creeping feeling of shame, a feeling which was even more intense today as she glanced at Stanley and noticed the belligerent set of his chin and the calculating suspicious gleam in his eye. "He wanted to come with me."

"How do you do, Mr. Manning?" said Mr. Finbow. "Won't you both sit down? Now then, I think my letter explained the situation, but if you'd like any further details I'd be glad to give them."

Stanley said, "We would. That's why we're here."

Mr. Finbow raised his eyebrows slightly and turned his attention pointedly in Vera's direction. "The position is this, Mrs. Manning. The money your late mother bequeathed to you is principally invested in two stocks, Euro-American Tobacco and Universal Incorporated Tin. Both very sound investments, as safe, if I may say so, as houses. You are, however, no doubt aware of the effect on the stock market of the recent Arab-Israel crisis."

He paused, perhaps for some comprehending response from Vera. But Vera, although vaguely aware that there had been a lot on television about the Middle East during recent weeks, had been too involved with personal crises to pay much attention, and she could only give a rather helpless nod.

"I am told," said Mr. Finbow, "that to sell at this juncture would result in a loss of several hundred pounds, owing to the considerable fall in prices."

Vera nodded again. "But these—er, investments, they'll get back to what they were before?"

"I am assured they will. You see, Mrs. Manning, the two companies I've mentioned are vast world-wide concerns which generally maintain their shares at a steady level. There's absolutely no question of any long-term deterioration in their value. The point is that the current price is temporarily unsatisfactory. In other words, any knowledgeable person would tell you it would be unwise to sell at present. But wait, say, six weeks and we should see a considerable improvement in . . ."

"Six weeks?" Stanley interrupted. "What about the interest? What's happening to all that?"

"As I have just explained," the solicitor said less patiently, "the price is currently reduced. The price of each individual share is lowered but your wife's income is unaltered as there has been no change in the dividend policies of the companies."

"O.K., O.K.," said Stanley. "So you say. But how do we know there won't be more of these crises? You can keep us hanging on like this month after month. It's our money you're playing with."

"I *beg* your pardon?"

"Well, isn't it? My wife told you to sell. Weeks ago that was. And now, because you've been hanging about, there's not so much money there as what you said at first. Seems plain enough to me."

Mr. Finbow got up out of his chair and turning his back on Stanley, addressed Vera in a cold courteous voice, "If you're dissatisfied, Mrs. Manning, perhaps you would prefer to find another firm of solicitors to act for you?"

Red with shame, afraid to look at Stanley, Vera stammered, "Oh, no. No, you mustn't think that. I don't think my husband quite . . ."

"I understand all right," said Stanley, not at all put out. "Not that at any of that matters a damn. We said we wanted you to sell and we do. You can sell the lot right now, this afternoon. It's our money and that's what we want. Right?"

For a moment Mr. Finbow looked as if he would have a seizure. Then he said very icily, "I am not a stall-holder in a street market. I am a solicitor and senior partner in a firm of unblemished reputation. Never—never have I been spoken to in those terms before in my own office." Momentarily he closed his eyes as if in pain. Stiffly, he addressed Vera, "May I have your instructions, Mrs. Manning?"

Vera looked down. Her hands were trembling in her lap. "I'm sorry, Mr. Finbow. Really, I'm very sorry." She raised her eyes miserably. "Of course, you must do whatever's best. We're not in actual need of the money. It's just—just that there were one or two things . . ."

Mr. Finbow said quickly and slightly more sympathetically, "There are several insurance policies also which matured at your mother's death. If it was a question of, say, five hundred pounds, I will be happy to give you a cheque for that immediately."

"Five hundred pounds would do very nicely," said Vera more happily. She waited, her head turned away from Stanley, while Mr. Finbow drew the cheque. "And please don't do anything about selling those shares until you and the stockbroker think it's right."

"Very well," said Mr. Finbow, shaking hands with her and behaving as if Stanley wasn't there. "May I say I think you've been very wise, Mrs. Manning? Good afternoon."

"Oh, Stan, how could you?" Vera said as they went downstairs. "I don't know what Mr. Finbow must have thought of you."

"Blow that for a lark. He can think what he likes, pompous old bastard. Now, if you'll just write your name on the back of that cheque I'll take it along to Barclay's and open an account. Here'll do, on that table. You'd better get back to the shop or you'll be late."

Vera stopped, but she didn't open her handbag. "I don't have to be back till two. I thought I'd miss lunch today and go and look at some fridges in the Electricity Board."

"Good idea. Get cracking, then." Stanley held out his hand expectantly.

"When I said 'look at,' I meant buy. You know I've been

longing to get a fridge. I can't buy one without any money and I shan't have any money till I get a cheque book. We'll both go to the bank first. Don't you think it would be nicer to have a joint account?"

"Nicer," in Stanley's mind, was hardly the word. He saw, however, that under the circumstances it was inevitable and they entered the Croughton branch of Barclay's together.

The manager wasn't in the least like James Horton to look at, being short and stout, but he reminded Vera of James perhaps because, like James, he was a manager of another branch of James's bank. She hadn't thought much about James since her return but now he returned vividly to her mind, a gentle, courteous and thoughtful man, and she couldn't help contrasting his civilised behaviour with Stanley's conduct at Finbow and Craig.

"There you are, Mrs. Manning," said the chief clerk, bending over the manager's desk. "Your cheque book, and Mr. Manning's too. And a paying-in book for each of you. Naturally, we'll send you cheque books with your names printed on them as soon as they come through."

The manager showed them to the door.

"That," said Stanley, "is what I call a gentleman."

He had deciphered the last clue in the crossword puzzle ("Golden Spaniel"—"The marksman's 9—carat companion") when Vera came in, pink with excitement.

"I've bought it, dear, a lovely refrigerator with a place to keep salads. And, oh, I know it's very extravagant but I've bought an automatic washer, too. They're sending both of them up tomorrow."

"What did all that lot cost?" said Stanley, replacing the cap on his pen.

"Just on a hundred. Having all that money went to my head, I suppose. But I've made up my mind, I shan't touch another penny until the rest comes through from Mr. Finbow."

"It's your money," said Stanley graciously. "It's you your mum left it to, after all."

"You mustn't say that, darling. It's ours. I want you to buy yourself a new suit and any little thing you fancy. You've got your own cheque book now."

Stanley put his hand in his pocket and fingered it, the crisp green book, hard and as yet untouched in its plastic folder. Very generous of Vee really, to look as it in that light, giving him *carte blanche* as it were. He would have dipped lavishly into the account, anyway, but it was nice getting permission first.

The washing machine and the refrigerator arrived at nine-thirty the following day. Stanley was still in bed and getting up to let the men in put him in a bad temper. Then he reflected that it was Tuesday, a good day for him in two ways. He was going to keep Pilbeam happy and Caroline Snow was off to Gloucester. At one o'clock he put the wireless on for the news, thinking wistfully how one problem would be off his mind forever if the Paddington-Gloucester train crashed. It was amazing what a lot of trains did crash these days. Rail travel was getting as dangerous as going in aircraft. But the news was all about the negotiations taking place to quieten down the Middle Eastern ferment and trains weren't mentioned.

Vera was too occupied playing with her new kitchen toys to enquire closely into his reasons for going out at a quarter to eight. He told her casually that he had a business appointment without adding that it was to take place in a pub, a venue which rather detracted from the respectable air with which Stanley wanted his new venture inbued.

Pilbeam was already there. He always was already there.

"Sorry about yesterday's little *contretemps*, Stan, but needs must when the devil drives. I got the vases and some *very* pleasing Georgian silver. Time you came down to the shop and looked over the loot. Now, about this van. A mate of mine's offered me a smart little job. It's ours tomorrow if we fancy it and only two hundred and fifty quid."

"I reckon I can find that," Stanley said.

"Well, I should hope so, old man. After your promises, I really should hope so. I've the wife to pay back, you know, and if we're off to Barnet in our van tomorrow . . ."

"Leave it to me," said Stanley.

They bought the van in the morning. Stanley gave Pilbeam's friend a cheque for it and drew another to cash. The van wasn't his idea of a smart little job, being battered about the bumpers and chipped on the bodywork, but it started first go and carried them as far as Croughton old village.

Pilbeam didn't say much on the journey and Stanley supposed he was sulking. But when he pulled up outside the shop he realised he'd been wrong. Far from sulking, Pilbeam had been silent from suppressed excitement and now, as he got out, he said proudly, "Well, old man, what d'you think? Surprise, surprise, eh? You can see I haven't been idle."

Stanley could hardly believe his eyes. When he'd last seen the shop the bow window had been cracked and dirty and the doorway boarded up. Now the window was repaired and every pane highly polished, affording a delectable view of treasures within. Above it, expertly lettered in gilt, was the name *The Old Village Shop*, and there was more gilt lettering on the door, a glass and wrought iron affair with a curly brass handle.

Pilbeam unlocked it and let him in.

Inside, the walls were papered in a Regency stripe and the floor was carpeted in dark red. On an oval table stood a pair of candelabra and a big glass rose bowl. Wide-eyed, Stanley tiptoed about, looking at hunting prints and Crown Derby plates and unidentifiable pieces of bric-a-brac. What he saw cheered him enormously, for he had begun to lose faith in Pilbeam. The man's arrival on the previous day to extort money from him by violence if necessary had shaken him, and the knocked-about old van had been almost the last straw. Now, gazing around him at polished wood and gleaming china, he felt his faith renewed.

"Who did all this decorating, then?" he asked.

"Couple of mates of mine." Pilbeam seemed to have dozens of friends. "I got them to do a rush job as a special favour. Like it?"

"It's grand," said Stanley.

"I told them to send the bill to you. That all right?"

"Oh, sure," Stanley said less comfortably. "About what sort of—er, figure will it be?"

"Say fifty, old man. About fifty. That won't break you, eh? Then there's the carpet. Lovely drop of Wilton that is, as you can see. But I don't reckon you'll get the bill for that before the autumn. Open up tomorrow, shall we?"

"Why not?"

They celebrated with a drink at the Lockkeeper's Arms and then they took the van up north into the villages of Hertfordshire. At the houses they called on Pilbeam did the talking. He seemed to like best the shabbier among the ancient houses and those occupied by a lone middle-aged or elderly woman whose husband was away at work.

His method was to ask this housewife if she had any old china or silver and mostly she had. While she was up in the loft turning it out, Pilbeam had a quick glance round at her furnishings, and when she came down again he bought everything she showed him, paying good prices until she was bemused by the sudden influx of cash given in exchange for what she thought of as rubbish. Just as they were leaving Pilbeam would offer her ten or twenty pounds for the piece he had had his eye on all the time, a wing chair or a writing desk, and in her greed and delight she usually agreed to his offer. Pilbeam took the attitude that he didn't really want this particular piece, he was doing her a favour in taking it off her hands.

"I'll give you twenty, lady," he would say, "but it'll cost me the same again to do it up, then I can sell it for forty-five. You see, I'm being completely honest with you. I'm in this for a profit."

"But I could have it done up and make the profit myself."

"I said it'd cost *me* twenty to do it up. That's not the price a cabinet-maker'd charge you. More like thirty or forty."

"Well, *you* know," the woman would say. "I'm sick of it, anyway. I'm glad of the chance to get rid of it. The last lot of stuff I cleared out I had to pay them to take it away."

The cash for these transactions came out of Stanley's pocket.

"It's not falling on stony ground, old boy," said Pilbeam. "Now, if you could just let me have twenty-five for the wife, we'll call it a day, shall we?"

Stanley had to write a cheque for Mrs. Pilbeam. He had no cash left. "Just make it to H. Pilbeam," said her husband. "Hilda's her name, the old battleaxe."

Well, he'd got through the four hundred remaining in the bank all right, Stanley thought. The decorators would have to wait. Still, he wouldn't have to part out with any more for a bit and Vera had said she wouldn't touch another penny. In any case, by the end of the week, he'd take his first money out of the business.

The next day he took Ethel Carpenter's ornaments with him down to the Old Village Shop and arranged them tastefully on the oval table.

17

It was no good Stanley going out with the van. He wouldn't know, as Pilbeam put it, a Meissen vase from a baby's chamber-pot, so while his partner plundered drawing rooms, Stanley stayed behind to mind the shop. The price of everything was marked on its base or one of its legs and Pilbeam said not to drop at all, not to haggle. They could take it or leave it.

They left it. Stanley made only one sale on his first day and that was a silver teaspoon, sold to a putative godmother for fifteen bob. He went home rather crestfallen to find a tight-lipped red-eyed Vera who answered him in monosyllables when he told her about his day.

"What got into you?"

"You know very well what's got into me."

"No, I don't. You were all right this morning." Surely she couldn't have found out about the money he'd had? His cheque book was safe in his own pocket. "I'm not a thought reader."

Vera sat down, picked at her food and burst into tears.

"For God's sake!" said Stanley. "What's wrong with you?"

"You are. You're what's wrong with me, you having your girls in this house while I was away." She lifted to him red eyes full of bitter reproach. "How could you, Stan?"

"Girls?" said Stanley. "What the hell are you on about? I never had any girls here. You must be round the twist."

"Well, girl, then. One girl, if that makes it any better. The whole neighbourhood's talking about it. They're all laughing at me, the lot of them. They always say the wife's the last to know, don't they?"

Caroline Snow. Damn her, she was a jinx, an evil genius if ever there was one. Trouble after trouble she was making for him.

"I suppose Mrs. Macdonald told you," he said.

"As a matter of fact, it was Mrs. Blackmore, but they all know. They're all talking about it. How this tall blonde girl came here on Sunday, the day after you'd got me out of the way, and then how she was back again on the Friday. Stayed for hours, Mrs. Blackmore said, and she saw you go off down the road together."

"I can explain," said Stanley classically. "She's—she's a girl me and my partner are thinking of taking on to do the books. I had to interview her, didn't I?"

"I don't know. But if that's true, why did you say no one came here when I was away. Those were your words, not mine, I didn't ask you. Nobody came here, you said."

"I forgot."

"Nobody ever comes here," Vera said wearily. "We haven't got any friends, or hadn't you noticed? Nobody but the neighbours come in here for years on end, but that girl came and you forgot to tell me. You *forgot*. How d'you think I feel? What am I supposed to think?"

"You ought to believe me," said Stanley. "Me, not the neighbours, bloody gossiping mob. I'm telling you the truth, Vee."

"Are you? You wouldn't know the truth if you saw it, Stan. Lies or truth, it's all the same to you. Suppose I ring up this Pilbeam, this partner of yours, and ask him if you're engaging a girl to do your books?"

"He's not on the phone," Stanley muttered. Christ, he'd have to prime Pilbeam in the morning just in case she made good her threat. "I reckon you ought to trust me, Vee."

"Why? Have you ever given me any reason to trust you the whole of our married life?"

That night Vera slept in the bed she had got ready for Ethel Carpenter.

As the weeks went on the shop did better. Because their funds were exhausted Pilbeam served in the shop on Thursday

and Friday and his presence made a difference to their sales.
Stanley could see he was a good and relentless salesman with
a fine line in persuasive talk. He sold the oval table and the
four chairs which each had a fragment of Hepplewhite concealed
about them as genuine unblemished Hepplewhite to a woman
who claimed her house was furnished throughout with Swedish
white wood, and the candelabra as a present for a teenage
tear-away. Pilbeam said he could sell central heating to tribes-
men in equatorial Africa and Stanley believed him. But when
he asked for his cut out of their week's takings, Pilbeam said
they mustn't touch a penny for a long time yet. All their
cash was needed for buying in.

Stanley went home empty-handed.

His relations with Vera had improved but they weren't re-
stored to normal. Feeling relaxed and happier one evening, he'd
rested his arm lightly round her shoulders while she was
standing by the cooker, but she'd flinched away from him as if
his arm were red hot.

"Isn't it time we let bygones be bygones?" he said.

"Do you swear that girl was nothing to you, just a girl
after a job? Will you swear you never touched her?"

"I can't stand the sight of her," Stanley said truthfully, and
after that Vera was nicer to him, asking about the business
and planning what they'd do with the money when it came,
but sometimes when they were watching television or he was
at work on a crossword, he'd look up and catch her staring
at him in a strange way. Then she would drop her eyes in
silence.

She was beginning to look forward to the arrival of the
money now and while Stanley did the *Telegraph* puzzle she
begged the city page from him and studied the markets, well-
satisfied that from day to day Euro-American Tobacco and
International Tin showed a steady improvement. Maud would
have wanted her to have the money, she thought, wanted her
above all to have the things that money would buy. She had
had one of those snapshots of Maud enlarged and hung on
the dining room wall and now when she looked at it she often
reflected how sensible and perceptive Maud had been, seeing
Stanley from the first for what he was. Money wouldn't improve her daughter's marriage, Maud had always known that,

but it would make her life as an individual rather than as a wife easier. It was something to be miserable in comfort.

It was nice now to sit at the table while Stanley was engrossed in his puzzle and write out cheques for the gas bill and the electricity instead of having to empty one of the tins she kept in the kitchen dresser and take the money all in coins down to the showrooms. Marvellous just to write eight pounds, nine and three and sign it without having to wonder whether you couldn't make it less next time by turning the light out every time you left a room. . . .

That week Stanley took ten pounds home with him.

"It could be five times that, me old love," said Pilbeam, "only we need all the capital we've got for fresh stock. The fact is we're hamstrung till you cough up."

And Stanley, who had been doubtful about his partner right up until the time the shop opened, now saw that every forecast Pilbeam had made was true. He *did* know what he was talking about; he *was* an expert in the antique business. The whole thing was the gold-mine he had promised, a quarry of rich ores which could only be dug out and converted into coin when a sizeable capital sum was invested in it. The terrible thing was that his capital, his own legitimate capital was invested elsewhere in footling tin and tobacco, untouchable until Finbow gave the word.

His nerves were in a bad way. His hands didn't shake and he no longer had those attacks of sick fainting but something even more upsetting had happened to him. The twitch in his eye had become permanent.

The twitching had come on again when Vera had questioned him about the girl's visits. Then it had been in the muscles of his right eye. His eyelid jumped up and down especially when he was tired. Stanley went into the public library and looked up his symptoms in the medical dictionary he had first consulted when he had had designs on Maud. The dictionary said the twitching was commonly known as "live flesh" and was brought about by tiredness and worry but usually stopped after a short time. If it didn't it might be more serious, an early sign, in fact, of some disease of the central nervous system.

What, anyway, was a short time? Hours, days, weeks? There

was no sign of this twitch abating and he'd had it for a fortnight now. The only time it stopped was when he was doing
a crossword. The trouble with that as therapy was that he could
now do the puzzle in ten minutes. Perhaps a better idea would
be to begin at the other end, as it were, and make up crosswords
himself.

Two or three years before he had tried doing this but there
was no peace with Maud always there in the evenings and he
had given it up. Now it was different. Sitting in the shop,
whiling away time between customers, he sketched out crossword frames on the pad Pilbeam and he used for their bills.
Sometimes Pilbeam was out on the knock, sometimes tapping
away in the little workshop at the back. His eye was obedient
and still while he invented clues and slotted in the words,
for the task was a challenge to his mental powers. It preoccupied him, often to the exclusion of all else, and he found
himself devoting whole hours together to the problem of finding
a word to fit blank, R, O, G, blank, blank, S, blank, blank,
before finally coming up with prognosis.

It was becoming something of an obsession, but Stanley
knew it would go, just as the twitching would go, when the
money came. Then he'd attend to the shop with real vigour,
knowing that Pilbeam wouldn't appear from the back every
few minutes to make nasty cracks about people who couldn't
honour their obligations. Meanwhile, his crosswords were harmless enough and they kept his mind off the money and his
eye from twitching.

Nearly a month had passed after opening the joint account
when a letter came for Vera from the bank. Stanley had already gone to work, muttering under his breath E, blank, G,
H, blank, and quite unable as he had been for three days
now to find a word to fit this five letter puzzle. He passed
the postman but he was too involved with this apparently in-
soluble cypher even to suppose he might at last be bringing
news from Finbow and Craig.

The envelope was addressed to Mr. and Mrs. Manning and
Vera hesitated before opening it on her own but at last she
did and a shiver of disbelief ran through her.

Dear Mr. and Mrs. Manning,

I am sorry to have to inform you that your joint current account is overdrawn to the sum of £35. I feel sure that you will wish to rectify this matter as soon as possible and am confident of receiving a remittance to cover the outstanding amount within the next few days.

Yours sincerely,
ARTHUR FRAZER (Manager).

But it couldn't be! She had only drawn cheques for the refrigerator and the washer and to pay the fuel bills. The account stood at five hundred pounds when opened and there ought to be at least three hundred and seventy there now. She had told Stanley to buy himself a suit, but he hadn't. Could it be a mistake? Oh, it must be. Did banks make mistakes? Everyone did sometimes, so banks must too.

Again Vera was aware of her ignorance of so many of those matters the average person takes in his stride. Perhaps she had written one of those cheques wrongly, put in an extra nought. But wouldn't the gas or the electricity people be honest about it? Or would they just hang on to what they'd got like Stanley had once when a greengrocer had handed him change for a fiver and not the single pound note he'd given him?

Worse than that, could the bank prosecute her? Somewhere she remembered hearing that it was an offence, actually against the law, to write cheques that couldn't be honoured. If only there was someone she could turn to, someone she could ask.

Maud would have known. Vera looked desperately at the photograph of her mother on the wall. Maud had been a good businesswoman, a marvellous manager, as sharp as any accountant, but Maud was dead. There was only Doris at the shop or Mrs. Blackmore or Mrs. Macdonald. Vera didn't want any of those women knowing her business. It was bad enough their discussing her married life among themselves and Stanley's deceit.

She didn't know anyone else, unless . . . Well, why not? James had said he was her friend. "Don't let's lose touch now, Vera," he'd said. Of course, that was before she'd told him her husband was alive and living with her, and they *had* lost touch. Not a word had passed between them since she came back from Bray.

But if she didn't ask James, what was she going to do? Lose

three hundred and seventy pounds? More than that, because she was overdrawn by another thirty-five.

Almost distraught, Vera telephoned the dry-cleaner's and told Doris she wouldn't be in. She didn't feel well, she said truthfully. There was no point in hesitating any longer, pacing up and down and re-reading that letter. Vera got out her address book and then she dialled the long string of numbers that would put her directly through to Brayminster.

The bank wasn't open yet and James was free. He seemed very pleased to hear Vera's voice, not sad or disillusioned as he had been at their last encounter.

"You're not putting me out at all, Vee. Of course, I'll give you any advice I can."

Rather haltingly and with many apologies for troubling him, Vera explained.

"I see. What does your husband say?"

It had never occurred to Vera to get in touch with Stanley. "I haven't told him yet."

There was a short silence at the other end of the line. Then James said, "It's a joint account, you say?"

"Yes, but Stanley doesn't need money. He's in business, he's doing well."

Why did James suddenly sound so sympathetic, so gentle?

"I really think you should speak to your husband, Vee. But I'll tell you what I'll do. I've met Mr. Frazer once or twice and I'll give him a ring now and say you're a friend of mine and that you'll be in to see him at eleven. Will that be all right? You'll have time to get in touch with your husband first."

"You're awfully kind, James."

"I'd do anything for you, Vee. You know that. Would you like me to lend you thirty-five pounds just to tide you over?"

"I couldn't think of it," Vera said vehemently. "No, please, I didn't want to speak to you for that."

"You're welcome if you need it. Now, Vee, don't *worry*. The bank has honoured these cheques so there's no question of their being returned to drawer or anything of that sort. Mr. Frazer will be quite understanding. Just ask him to give you a statement and show you the cheques that have passed through your account. D'you understand?"

"Yes, of course."

"Good. Nobody is going to lecture you or threaten you in any way. I suppose as a bank mamager I shouldn't say this, but thousands upon thousands of people are overdrawn every month and they don't even turn a hair. I only wish they would. Get in touch with me tomorrow, will you?"

"I wouldn't think of it," said Vera.

James said calmly, "Then I'll phone you. Yes, I will. It's been lovely talking to you, Vee. Give me that pleasure again tomorrow."

Vera felt a good deal better and very pleased that she had plucked up the courage to talk to James. But she wouldn't be able to see Stanley before she went into the bank. He had told her he'd be out in the van till noon.

She made up her face carefully in the way Mrs. Goodwin had taught her and put on the blue and white spotted dress. By five to eleven she was in a waiting room at the bank and after a few minutes Mr. Frazer himself put his head round the door and invited her into his office. His manner was quite pleasant and cordial.

"I had a call from your friend, Mr. Horton," he said. "But you mustn't ever be afraid to come and see me, Mrs. Manning."

Vera blushed hotly. What a fool they must both think her!

"Perhaps you'd like to see your statement," said Mr. Frazer.

While it was being fetched he chatted easily about the weather and about Brayminster where he had once spent a holiday. Vera could only answer him in monosyllables. She felt anything but at ease. The bank had a serious air about it and she suddenly wondered if she was on the threshold of something immensely serious in a personal sense to herself.

The statement was brought in by a girl clerk. Mr. Frazer sent her away and then he passed the statement with its batch of cheques enclosed over to Vera. He lit a cigarette but Vera shook her head when he offered one to her.

It was the first time she had ever seen a bank statement and she didn't understand it. Bewildered, she picked up the top cheque, expecting to find it as incomprehensible as the statement, and then she saw her own handwriting. It was the one she had sent to the Gas Board. I suppose they pay it into their bank, she thought, and the money's marked to their credit there and then it somehow gets to my bank and they subtract the money from what I've got. Straightforward, really.

Back to the statement. The Gas Board had their money all right but only because the bank had paid, not because she had the money. She hadn't had any money before she'd written that cheque. She blushed again.

Here was her cheque for the refrigerator and the washer and another one to the electricity people. Vera turned up the last but one. She drew in her breath sharply. Verity Vehicles, she read, two hundred and fifty pounds, £250.0.0, Stanley G. Manning. There was one more. To cash, £150. Stanley G. Manning.

"My husband," she stammered. "I'd forgotten . . . He did say . . . Oh, dear, I'm so sorry. . . ."

"Well, we like to think we don't make many mistakes, Mrs. Manning."

"I'm the one who made the mistake," Vera said and the words suddenly meant far more than just an apology for extravagance. "I'll try to pay it back—well, next week. I don't know how but I'll try."

"My dear Mrs. Manning, we're not bloodsuckers. You mustn't be so upset. As long as you've managed to straighten matters out by the end of the month . . ."

"You're very kind," said Vera. Everyone was very kind, very understanding, bending over backwards to help her because —because they pitied her so. And, of course, they knew what had happened. James had guessed from the start. Mr. Frazer had seen through her clumsy little covering up tactics. They all knew she was married to a man she couldn't trust an inch.

As soon as he saw Vera's face, Stanley realised he was in trouble again. This time he wasn't going to put up with being ignored, more or less sent to Coventry. He flung his coat over the back of a chair, scowled at Maud's picture on the wall— she might as well be still alive for all the good her death had done him—and said:

"I suppose those bloody interfering women have been giving you a few more details about my so-called girl friend."

"I haven't seen Mrs. Blackmore or Mrs. Macdonald today."

"What is it, then?"

Vera poured herself a cup of tea and sipped it in silence. Silence, thought Stanley. "Permission is possibly quiet." Anagram on "licence" . . . God, he'd have to control himself, not keep seeing every word as part of a crossword puzzle. For the first time in their married life Vera had helped herself to a cup of tea without pouring one for him.

"What's up with you?" he said, his nerves on edge.

Vera turned round. She looked old and ugly, deep shadows ringing her eyes, deep lines scored from nose to mouth. "I may as well have it out," she said. "I've been to the bank this morning. I had a letter from the manager."

"Oh, that."

"Yes, that. Is that all you can say?"

"Look Vee, you said I could have some of the money. You said, buy yourself anything you want."

"I said a suit or any little thing you wanted. I didn't say draw out four hundred pounds. Stan, I don't mind you having the money. But couldn't you have told me? You wanted it for the business, didn't you? Couldn't you have just said? Did you have to make me look a fool in front of the bank manager and nearly worry myself to death?"

"You said you wouldn't write any more cheques. How was I to know you'd start paying bills?" Why was she staring at him like that? Her eyes were fixed on him so that he had to look away.

"What's wrong with your eye?" she said coldly.

"Nothing. The muscles keep jumping, that's all. It's my nerves."

Silence again. Then Vera said, "We can't go on like this, can we? God knows, I didn't want Mother to die, but when she was dead, I thought—I thought things would be better. I thought we'd have a proper marriage like other people. It hasn't worked that way, has it?"

"I don't know what you're on about," said Stanley, edging his way into the dining room. He sat down on the sofa and began doodling on a sheet of paper. Vera followed him. "Look, I'm sorry about the money, but there's no need to make a song and dance about it. I can easily get it back out of the business."

"Can you, Stan? We haven't seen much out of the business yet, have we? Come to that, I don't even know there is a business. You haven't taken me to the shop or introduced me to Mr. Pilbeam or . . ."

"Do me a favour," said Stanley huffily. His eye was opening and shutting like an umbrella. "Can't you take my word for it?"

Vera laughed. "Take your word? Stan, you can't be serious. I can't take your word for anything. You just say the first thing that comes into your head. Truth or lies, it's all the same to you. I don't think you know the difference any more. And Stan, I can't bear it. I can't bear to be left in the dark and humiliated and deceived just because doing that to me is easier for you than telling the truth. I'd—I'd rather be dead or not with you."

Stanley hadn't paid much attention to all this. Vera's remark about his eye had affected him more than all her analysis of his shortcomings. Drawing a crossword puzzle frame and inserting a couple of words, he had heard nothing since then but her last sentence. It leapt at him like a red warning light.

Alarmed, he said, "What d'you mean, not with me?"

"When people reach the stage we've reached, they separate, don't they?"

"Now, look, Vee, don't you talk like that. You're my wife. And all this—well, it's six of one and half a dozen of the other. If I keep you in the dark it's on account of the way you nag me. A man can't stand nagging." Can't stand, either, having no control over his own face. Stanley covered up his eye and felt the lid jerk against his hand. "You're my wife, like I said, and have been for twenty years. There's a good time coming, Vee, I promise you. We'll both be in clover by the end of the year and . . ."

She stared at him even harder.

"Do you love me?"

What a question! What a thing to ask a man when he was tired and worried and maybe on the verge of Parkinson's Disease. "Of course I do," Stanley muttered.

Her face softened and she took his hand. Stanley dropped his pencil reluctantly and laid his other hand on her shoulder. His eye was aching. For a long time Vera said nothing. She held his hand tightly and then, without letting it go, sat down beside him. Stanley fidgeted nervously.

"We'll have to make a fresh start," Vera said suddenly.

He sighed with relief. A fresh start. "Beginning with a new

jump"? Surreptitiously he felt among the cushions for his pencil. That S could be the S in business, the word going down. "After public transport I'm on a Scottish loch. . . ."

"Yes, we'll have to start again," Vera said. "We'll both have to make an effort, Stan, but that won't be so hard now we've got all this money coming to us."

Stanley smiled at her, his eye quite normal.

"We'll sell this house and buy a new one and we'll scrap all this old furniture. Mother would have liked to see us in a modern house." That "us," Stanley thought, was a mere courtesy. Maud would have liked to see *him* in a modern concentration camp. "And we'll have proper holidays together and a car. I'll promise never to nag you again if you'll promise to be open with me. But I have to trust you, Stan. You do see that?"

"I'll never tell another lie to you, Vee, as long as I live."

She stared at him, wishing she could believe what he said, that at last he was being sincere. Stanley returned her gaze glassily. He had thought of his word. E, blank G H blank. Eight, of course, the only English word surely to fit that particular combination. And all day long he'd been wondering if he could alter the H to O—change the word across from phone to Poona—and make 18 down ergot. Triumphantly Stanley wrote in "eight" and beside it, "One over it is too many drinks."

18

The bill came in from the decorators and someone had written across the top of it: "Prompt settlement will be appreciated." They would have to take their appreciation elsewhere. Stanley didn't at all appreciate the demand for £175, instead of the fifty Pilbeam had spoken of so confidently. Vera and he, making their fresh start, sat side by side on the sofa, studying the market. Euro-American Tobacco had dropped a couple of points overnight. Stanley's eye fluttered lightly, then began a rhythmic blinking.

"You want to put some more money into the business, don't you, Stan? I only hope it'll be safe."

"You said you wouldn't nag me," said Stanley. He reached for the sheet of paper on which he was composing a larger and more ambitious crossword. Nag would fit into that three-letter space, he thought. Nag, nag, nag. How about, "The horse may pester?" Yes, that would do. Nag meant "horse" and "pester" . . .

"I don't mean to nag. But have you formed a sort of company or a partnership? Have you had it done legally, Stan?"

"I trust my partner and he trusts me," said Stanley. "Pity I can't say the same for my wife." He printed in "nag" and then tacked "wife" on to the W in "window." Wife: "If in two compass points find a spouse." Vera was looking at his eye now, although the twitching had stopped.

"Don't you think you ought to see the doctor about that tic you've got?" she said.

James was as good as his word. He phoned Vera at home and, getting no reply, phoned the cleaner's.

"Well, Vee, I said he wouldn't eat you, didn't I? What was it all about, a simple mistake on someone's part?"

"My husband forgot to tell me he'd written rather a large cheque." Loyally, Vera lied, "He's put it all back out of his business."

"That's fine." James didn't sound as if he thought it was fine at all. He sounded as if he didn't believe her, a notion which was confirmed when he said, "Vee, if you're ever worried about anything, you'll get in touch with me, won't you?"

"I've got Stanley," Vera said.

"Yes, of course. I hadn't forgotten. But there might be a time when . . . Good-bye, Vera. Take care of yourself."

It was time she did, Vera thought, time she took care of herself. Really, it was ridiculous for a woman in her financial position, or prospective financial position, to keep on working in a cleaner's. She handed a customer two newly cleaned pairs of trousers and then she sat down to write her resignation as manageress of the Croughton Laundry.

Thursday. Her afternoon off. Vera left the shop at one and called in at the nearest estate agent. He would be pleased to handle the selling of her house, he said. What kind of figure had she thought of asking? Vera hadn't thought about it at all, but the estate agent knew the type of house and suggested four thousand, five hundred pounds. He promised to come to Lanchester Road during the afternoon and look the place over.

Vera made herself some scrambled eggs for lunch and finished up the chocolate mousse they could now keep overnight because they had the refrigerator. It was unlikely the estate agent would get there before three and that would give her an hour to make things look a bit shipshape upstairs.

Before the house was sold she'd have to make an effort and clear out Maud's room properly, all those clothes that Aunt Louisa didn't want, all those papers and the bottles and jars whose contents had kept Maud alive for four years.

After the funeral Vera had shut them up in one of the dressing table drawers. She opened it now and contemplated Maud's various medicines, anti-coagulants, diuretics, mineral salts, vitamins, sleeping tablets and tranquillizers. I wonder if the chemist would take them back? Vera thought. It seemed a wicked waste just to throw them away.

Now for the clothes. She was packing them into an old bolster case when the doorbell rang. Vera was expecting the estate agent and she was surprised to see a young woman on the doorstep.

"Good afternoon. I'm collecting for the Chappell Fund."

Vera thought she said "chapel fund" and was about to say she was Church of England when she remembered the young policeman who had been shot during the Croughton Post Office raid. She opened her purse.

"Thank you so much. Actually, we're trying to get a thousand pounds collected privately for Mrs. Chappell and some of us are getting up a few stalls at the Police Sports next week. If you do happen to have . . ."

"Would you like some cast-off clothing?" Vera asked. "My mother died recently and all her clothes were good. Nobody wants them now and I'd be glad if you'd take them off me."

The young woman looked delighted, so Vera went upstairs, fetched the bolster and handed it to her.

"These were your mother's, you say?"

"That's right. I've no use for them, really."

"Thank you very much. You've been a great help."

The only thing that worried him now was the money. Once get his hands on that and life would be serene. It was obvious he was never going to hear another word from Caroline Snow.

Relishing the picture, Stanley imagined her bursting into her home in Gloucester and pouring out the whole story to Snow, tired, poor devil, after a hard day's work toiling to keep women in luxury. Probably Snow was watching the box or even doing a crossword. In his mind's eye, Stanley saw the man's face fall when he heard how he was expected first to find a mother-in-law he had never before considered as a serious menace and then welcome her to his hearth and home.

"We must find her, mustn't we, Daddy? You're so marvellous in a crisis. I knew you'd know what to do."

Stanley chuckled at this piece of silent mimicry. And what would Snow say?

"You leave it to me, darling." Soothing tone, brain sorting it all out like a computer. "I'd like to talk it over with your mother when we're alone."

Shift to scene with marvellous Mummy, tête-à-tête, lights dimmed, Caroline off somewhere with dog or boy friend.

"She's such an impetuous child, dear."

"Yes, I know. But I can't destroy her faith in me, can I?"

"She adores you so, darling. I must say for my part, I don't exactly relish a reunion with a mother I haven't seen for forty years."

"There's no question of that. Nothing would induce me to pal up with the old lady and have her here. Good heavens, I'm not a glutton for punishment. . . ."

"Why not just say you've got in touch with the police, dear? Say they're making enquiries. Caroline will have forgotten the whole thing when she's been home a week."

"Of course she will. You're so marvellous, darling."

Stanley laughed uproariously at this invented cameo of the set-up and dialogue *chez* Snow. He could almost see them sitting there among their refined middle-class G-plan furniture. It was a pity he had to keep it to himself and couldn't tell anyone about it. He wiped his eyes and when he had stopped laughing his eye began to twitch ferociously.

He was trying to hold the eyelid steady, seeing if he could control it by an effort of will, when Pilbeam walked into the shop, holding a plastic bag full of horse brasses.

You want to get that eye of yours seen to, old man. I had an aunt with the same trouble, St. Vitus's Dance."

"What happened to her?"

Pilbeam tipped the horse brasses on to the floor and sat down. "She got to jerking all over. It was embarrassing being with her." He scratched his nose with the nailless finger. "Why don't you go and see the quack? I can cope here."

The group practice whose list he was on held an afternoon surgery three times a week. His worry over getting his hands on his inheritance had long since driven any apprehension over the part he had played in Maud's death from Stanley's mind so, after waiting forty minutes, he walked more or less serenely into the surgery where Dr. Moxley sat behind his desk.

"What seems to be the trouble?"

The swine might take the trouble to look at me, Stanley thought sourly. He explained about his eye and as he spoke it fluttered obligingly.

"They call it 'live flesh.'"

"They do, do they? And who might 'they' be?"

"A medical book."

"Oh, dear, I wish you lay people wouldn't be always poking about in medical books. You only frighten yourselves. I suppose you thought you'd got muscular dystrophy."

"Well, have I?"

"I shouldn't think so," said Dr. Moxley, laughing breezily. "Been worrying about something, have you?"

"I've got a lot on my mind, yes."

"Stop worrying, then, and your twitch'll stop." Just like that, Stanley thought indignantly. As if telling someone not to worry would stop them. Bloody doctors, they were all the same. He took the prescription for a sedative and was halfway to the door when Dr. Moxley said, "How's your wife? Getting over Mrs. Kinaway's death all right?"

What business was it of his? Stanley muttered something about Vera being all right. The doctor, a past master, Stanley thought, at switching moods, smiled and said genially, "I ran into old Dr. Blake the other day. He was quite upset to hear Mrs. Kinaway had died. Surprised, too. He said he'd seen her in the street only a couple of days before and she looked very fit."

Stanley was speechless. The scare over Caroline Snow, now past, had been bad enough. The last thing he had anticipated was that questions might be asked at this late date about Maud. Why, it was weeks and weeks . . .

"He couldn't understand Mrs. Kinaway having another stroke when she was on Mollanoid." Moxley gave an innocent yet somehow sinister smile. "Still, these things happen. Dr. Blake's very conscientious. I advised him not to give it another thought."

Stanley walked out in a daze. Who would have thought Maud's old doctor would still be hanging about the neighbourhood? Probably it meant nothing. He had enough troubles without bothering about that.

To get his prescription made up Stanley went in to the same chemist he had been to when buying Shu-go-Sub and suddenly he remembered that two and a half tubes of saccharine tablets still remained in Maud's Mollanoid cartons. The first thing he'd do when he got home was get hold of those tablets and burn them just in case Moxley and the conscientious Blake were planning to make a swoop on the house and investigate.

"What's happened to all your mother's stuff," he asked Vera.

"All gone. I've been having a turn-out. The estate agent said we could get a better price if the place was smartened up so I thought I'd do some decorating."

Decorating was a dirty word to Stanley. Sourly he watched Vera come down the steps, wipe her brush and put the lid on the distemper tin. Distemper was a good word for a puzzle and he couldn't remember ever doing one in which it had been used. Distemper: "Paint prescribed for the dog's disease." Very good.

"You've thrown everything out?" he asked casually.

"Everything but her clothes. Someone came round collecting for the police."

Stanley felt the sweat break out on his upper lip. "The *what*?"

"Whatever's the matter? You're jerking all over."

Stanley clenched his hands. Even they were jumping. He couldn't speak.

"Well, not the police really, dear." Vera was sorry she had put it that way. Stanley had always been afraid of the police. "They were collecting for that policeman's widow, Mrs. Chappell, and they were so pleased when I gave them Mother's clothes. Stan, dear, let me make you a cup of tea. You're overwrought, you're worrying about your eye. Come along. You can do your crossword while I'm making the tea."

"I've done it."

"Then make one up. You know you like doing that."

Still jumping and shivering, Stanley tried to sketch a crossword frame. He wrote in "distemper" and then "policewoman" going down from the P. Perhaps the woman had come on an innocent errand; perhaps Moxley had meant nothing sinister. But suppose instead that Moxley had dropped a hint or two to the police and they had sent this woman round because . . . What could they find out from Maud's clothes? Perhaps there was some substance present in a person's sweat when they had high blood pressure or when they were taking saccharine or weren't taking Mollanoid. For all Stanley knew, Moxley might be an expert in forensics. He wrote "forensics" in, going down from the R in distemper.

They might go round all the chemists and find that a man answering his description had bought a lot of saccharine. . . . Then they'd dig Maud up. The gash on her head might be gone by now. They'd analyse the contents of her stomach and find Shu-go-Sub, masses of it. But no Mollanoid. Maud hadn't taken any since early March.

His eye winked, half-blinding him, so that he couldn't see the words he had printed across the white squares.

3. Down

19

It was high summer now, a fine, beautiful summer. Hot day succeeded hot day and this sameness was reflected in the Mannings' life. Nothing changed for the better or—Stanley comforted himself—for the worse either. The police showed no further interest in him and he hadn't been back to Dr. Moxley, although his eye still twitched. He couldn't stop worrying about the money.

Letters went back and forth between Vera and Mr. Finbow but there was no hint in anything the solicitor wrote that it would now be prudent to sell those tin and tobacco shares. Vera refused firmly though kindly to sell them against Mr. Finbow's advice or to ask for another advance, even though Stanley had shown her the reminder which had come from Pilbeam's decorators with "please settle outstanding payment at once" scrawled across it. Pilbeam made Stanley's life a misery with his nagging about the shop's need for more capital.

A "For Sale" board had been put up outside the house. No one came to view it. It lacked, the agent told Vera, certain amenities which these days were indispensable.

"We might have a garage built," said Vera. "Only it would mean sacrificing your heather garden."

"Doesn't matter," said Stanley. A garage would keep Maud hidden forever. On the other hand, how much unearthing would the builders have to do to lay foundations?

"I'll see about it, then, and I'll carry on with my decorating. We ought to get an offer soon. The agent says sales are booming."

"Dare say it to the goose in front of the vase for a big bang. . . ."

"What did you say, dear?"

"A clue in my crossword. Booming. Dare say it to . . . Oh, never mind."

"You don't seem to think about anything but crosswords these days," said Vera.

It was true. Puzzles, inventing them and solving them, had become an obsession with him. He even did them secretly in the shop while Pilbeam was out, so that when his partner came back his head was full of floating words and puns and anagrams, and when Pilbeam started afresh on his demands, as he did every day, he could turn a vague, half-deaf ear.

"Remember that old bag we flogged the Georgian table to?" Pilbeam would say. "She wants to do her whole flat over in period. With me working day and night and you coming up with the cash to buy in, we could make five hundred on this deal alone." Or, "We're hamstrung, Stan. It makes me weep the opportunities we're missing." And always he ended up with, "We've got to have that money. Now, Stan, not in the sweet by-and-by."

Stanley was too much in awe of Pilbeam to do more than placate him with soothing promises. He saved his rage for Vera.

"I tell you, I've got to have that money for the business. It's ours but we can't touch it. We're as poor now as when your bloody old mother was still alive. The business'll go bust if I don't have the money. Can't you get that into your head?"

Vera flinched away from him, afraid of his greed and the wild light in his eyes. His face twitched dreadfully when he was angry. But she was most frightened when instead of answering her properly he replied with some meaningless conundrum.

One day towards the end of July Vera started work on the small spare bedroom and as she was turning out she came upon Maud's collection of pills which she had put in here while she was painting her mother's room. It seemed wasteful to discard them all, especially as one of the little plastic cartons hadn't been opened and the other was only half empty. There would be no harm in asking the chemist about them while she was out shopping.

As she left the house she encountered the builders bringing in bags of cement and a concrete mixer.

"No need to wait in for us, lady," said the foreman. "We shan't make a start on your garage till next week what with this strike at the brickworks. You won't mind us leaving our gear in readiness, will you?"

Vera said she wouldn't. She went straight into the chemist and asked if it would be all right to return the carton of tablets as none of them had been used.

The pharmacist smiled. "Sorry, madam, we don't do that. We advise our customers to throw away all unused drugs. To be on the safe side, you see." He removed the cap and looked at the contents of the carton.

"They're called Mollanoid, I believe."

Pharmacists, like doctors, prefer lay people to be in utter ignorance of such esoteric matters. This one was no exception. He frowned at Vera. Then he took out a single tablet, looked closely at it and said:

"What makes you think these tablets are Mollanoid?"

Vera said rather tartly, "You made up the doctor's prescription and you wrote Mollanoid on the label. My mother always took Mollanoid for her blood pressure."

"Certainly I made up the prescription and *wrote* the label, but these are not the tablets I put in the carton. Mollanoid is what we call an anti-coagulant; in other words it helps prevent the formation of clots in the bloodstream. As I say, these tablets aren't Mollanoid."

"What are they, then?"

The pharmacist sniffed the tablet he was holding and put it to his tongue. "Some compound of saccharine, I imagine."

"*Saccharine?*"

"The stuff slimmers use to sweeten tea and coffee," the pharmacist said in the tone of one addressing a retarded child.

Vera shrugged. Rather confused and puzzled, she finished her shopping. Was it possible that the pharmacist himself had made a mistake in his dispensing and the carton had always contained saccharine? It seemed unlikely but more probable than that Maud had been secretly taking saccharine. If that had been the case, what had she done with the Mollanoid? Certainly she wouldn't have stopped taking them. She depended on them utterly as a lifeline and often said that but for them she would have had a second stroke.

Choosing a cheap but pretty wallpaper and deciding on a colour scheme distracted Vera's mind but, for all that, she decided to mention the matter to Stanley when he came in. He was rather late and as soon as Vera saw him she knew he was in no °tate to be interested in other people's medical problems.

"My eye's killing me," he said.

For the first time in their married life he left his dinner, lamb chops, chips and peas, untouched, and Vera, who formerly would have been anxious and solicitous, hardened her heart. If she told him to go to the doctor again he would only snap at her. She couldn't talk to him, they had no real communication any more. Often these days days she thought of James Horton who was sympathetic and gentle and with whom it was possible to have conversation.

"What's the matter with you now?" she asked at last, trying to keep her tone patient.

"Nothing," said Stanley. "Nothing. Leave me alone."

His eye blinked and squeezed shut as if fingers inside his head were squeezing it. The something that was doing the squeezing seemed to laugh at him and at the success of its tricks which he couldn't combat. But that something must be himself, mustn't it? God, he thought, he'd go off his rocker at this rate.

Vera was watching him like a hawk. He couldn't tell her that he was trembling and twitching and off his food because he was terribly frightened, because something had happened that day to reduce him to a far worse state than he had been in when the Chappell Fund woman had called or even when he had first seen Maud fall to her death. His teeth were chattering with fear and he ground them tightly together as if he had lockjaw.

That afternoon, while he was out in the van, a policeman had called at the Old Village Shop.

He had been to Hatfield to relieve an old woman of an eighteenth-century commode for approximately a fifth of its true value, and driving back had tried to calm his pulsating eye by finishing off an imaginary crossword. Stanley could now invent and complete crosswords in his head just as some people can play chess without a board. He drove the van into the yard at the back of the shop, murmuring under his breath, Purchase: "An almost pure hunt for this buy," when he saw a uniformed policeman leave the shop and cross to a waiting car. His eye moved like a pump, jerked and closed.

"What was that copper doing in here?" he asked Pilbeam in a strangled thin voice.

"Just checking on the stock, old man." Pilbeam stroked the side of his nose with the nailless sausage-like finger. He often did this but now Stanley couldn't bear to see it. It made him feel sick. "They often do that," Pilbeam said. "In case we're harbouring stolen goods in all innocence."

"They've never done it before. Did they ask for me?"

"You, old boy? Why would he ask for you?" Pilbeam smiled blandly. Stanley was sure he was lying. He was always up to something when he stared you candidly in the eye like that. "Been a good day, me old love. I reckon we can each take ten quid home with us tonight."

"I see that china and silver of mine went."

"A lady from Texas, she had them. Crazy about anything English, she was. I reckon she'd have paid anything I'd asked." Pilbeam laid his hand on Stanley's sleeve, the finger stump just touching the bare skin at the wrist. His eyes weren't frank and friendly any more. "I promised my old woman I'd pay her back next week. Money, Stan, loot, lolly. My patience, as the old ex-fuhrer put it, is getting exhausted."

Stanley wanted to ask him more about the policeman's visit but he didn't dare. He desperately wanted to believe Pilbeam. Surely if the policeman had wanted to talk to him he would have called at Lanchester Road. Perhaps he had called and found no one in.

If he'd been right and somehow or other they'd analysed Maud's clothes, if Moxley had been shooting his mouth off, if Vera had boasted to all the neighbours about the garage they were going to have built . . . Suppose, all these weeks, the police and the doctors had been building up a case against him from hints and hearsay. . . . He was afraid to go home, but he had nowhere else to go. All the evening he could sense Vera had something she wanted to tell him but was too sulky or too subtle to come out with it. Maybe the police had been getting at her too.

He couldn't sleep that night. Every muscle was twitching now and the remedy seemed almost worse than the disease. He began to wish he'd never done a crossword in his life, so compulsive was this need to keep inventing clues, to slot words across, fit others down. All that night and Saturday night he had a chequer board pattern in front of his eyes.

He felt he was on the edge of a nervous collapse.

Vera couldn't stay in the same bed with him when he twitched like that. He slept on Sunday night, from sheer exhaustion, she guessed, and his whole body rippled galvanically in sleep. In the small hours she made tea but she didn't wake him. Instead she took her own tea into the spare room.

She switched on the light, stepped over paint pots and got into the spare bed. As soon as she saw Maud's pills all her bewilderment of the morning came back to her. She reached for the half-empty carton of Mollanoid, the ones Maud had been taking right up to her death, and removed the lid.

I wonder, she thought, if Mother planned to stop taking sugar because Dr. Blake told her she should lose weight? Perhaps she had bought saccharine and had used a Mollanoid carton to keep it in.

It was beginning to get light. Vera could hear a thrush singing in the Blackmores' laburnum. The meaningless and not really musical trill depressed her. She felt very cold and she pulled the bed covers up to her chin.

But as she prepared to settle down and snatch a couple of hours' sleep, her eye fell once more on the carton she had opened. Mollanoid. Of course they were Mollanoid. They looked exactly like the tablets Maud had been taking three times a day, every day, for four years. But they also looked exactly like the ones she had taken to the chemist on the previous morning. Again Vera sat up.

Maud hadn't touched those, hadn't taken a single one of them. These, on the other hand, were three-quarters used, and the carton which contained them had stood by Maud's plate at her last breakfast. Vera knew that. In the increasing light she noticed the smear on the label the chemist had made, handing her the carton before the ink had quite dried. And casting her mind back to that breakfast—would she ever forget it or forget Maud's elation?—she recalled her mother's taking two of the tablets just after spooning sugar plentifully into her tea.

Her heart began to pound. Slowly, as if she were a forensic

expert about to test poison at some risk to himself, she picked out one of the tablets and rested it on her tongue.

For a moment there was no taste. Vera's heart quietened. Then, because she had to know, she pressed the tip of her tongue with the tablet on it against the roof of her mouth. Immediately a rich sickly sweetness spread across the surface of her tongue and seeped between her teeth.

She spat the tablet into her saucer and then lay face downwards, numb and very cold.

It was ten when Stanley woke up. He stared at the clock and was out of bed and half across the room before he remembered. This was the day he was going to the doctor's. He'd told Pilbeam he wouldn't be in before lunch.

Just thinking the word doctor started his eye twitching again. He cursed, put on his dressing gown and went into Maud's room to see if the builders had started work yet. It was imperative to keep an eye on them in case they got too enthusiastic and began digging the earth they were to cover. But the garden was empty and the concrete mixer idle.

It wasn't like Vera not to bring him a cup of tea. Perhaps she hadn't wanted to disturb him. Poor old Vee. She wasn't much to look at any more and, God knew, she'd always been as dull as ditch-water, but a man could do worse.

No breakfast tray either. Come to that, no Vera. The house stank of paint. Stanley felt the beginnings of a headache. He'd missed Moxley's morning surgery but there was another one at two and he'd go to that. Everywhere was tidy and clean. Obviously, Vera had cleaned the place and gone out shopping.

He mooched back to the kitchen, his eye opening and shutting in a series of painful winks. She hadn't even left the cornflakes out for him. He got the packet out of the larder, poured out a dishful and looked around for the *Telegraph*. Might as well do the puzzle. There was no question any more whether he could do it or not or even whether he could do it at a single sitting. The only amusement it still afforded Stanley was seeing if he could beat his record of seven minutes.

The newspaper was folded up, lying on top of the refrigerator. Stanley picked it up and saw that underneath it was a letter poking half out of its envelope. The envelope was addressed to

Vera but that had never deterred him before and it didn't deter him now. He pulled it out with shaking fingers and read it.

The money had come through.

Mr. Finbow would expect Vera at her earliest convenience and would hand her a cheque.

Stanley rubbed his eyes. Not because they were twitching but because tears were running down his face.

20

Years and years he had waited for this moment. Ever since he'd first set eyes on Maud and heard how well-heeled she was, he'd dreamed of today, now or long ago, now or in time to come, the shining hour with it would all be his. Twenty-two thousand pounds.

His eye hadn't twitched once since he had read that letter. He also now saw clearly that in imputing sinister motives to a harmless housewife collecting for a sale and a policeman on routine duty he had been letting his imagination run away with him. Money cured all ills, mental and physical. No doctors for him. Instead he would take a bus down to the old village.

Pilbeam was in the shop, polishing a brass warming pan. "You're early," he said morosely. "What did the quack say?"

Stanley sat down on the piecrust table. He felt like a tycoon. Laconically he said, "I've got a thousand quid for you. I may as well write a cheque for the decorators at the same time and you can give it to them. There'll be loads more next week if we need it. We're laughing now, boy. No more worries. No more struggling on a shoestring."

"You won't regret it, Stan. I'll promise you you won't regret it. My God, we knew what we were doing when we started this little lark!" Pilbeam slapped him on the back and pocketed the cheques. "Now, I'll tell you what. We'll go down the Lockkeeper's and we'll split a bottle of scotch and then I'll treat you to a slap-up lunch."

Not quite half a bottle, but four double whiskies on an empty stomach, followed by a heavy meal of steak, fried potatoes, french beans, carrots, mushrooms, raspberry pie and cream, sent Stanley reeling towards Lanchester Road at half-past two. He badly wanted to burst into song as he made his way unsteadily along the respectable streets of dull little villas, but to be arrested on this glorious golden day, one of the happiest days of his life, would be a disastrous anti-climax.

The sky which, when he first got up, had been overcast had cleared while they were in the Globe and now it was very hot. One of the hottest days of the year, Stanley thought, immensely gratified that the weather matched his mood. He passed the Jaguar showrooms and wondered whether it would be possible to buy a car that very afternoon. That scarlet Mark Ten, for instance. He didn't see why not. It wasn't as if he was after some little mass-produced job like Macdonald's tin can which lesser mortals, miserable wage-earners, had to wait months for. He must sober up. Have a cup of tea perhaps and then he'd buy the car and take Vera for a ride in it. Maybe they'd go out Epping Forest way and have a meal in a country pub.

These pleasant fancies sliding across the surface of his fuddled brain, he marched into the kitchen and called, "Vera, where are you?" There was no answer. Sulking, he thought, because I didn't hang about to tell her what the doctor said. Doctor! The last thing he needed.

He could hear her moving about upstairs. Probably she was toiling away painting that bedroom. Well, she'd have to buck her ideas up, expand her horizons. People with his sort of money didn't do their own decorating. He moved carefully into the hall. Better on the whole not to let her see he'd been drinking.

He called her name again and this time he heard a door close and her face appear over the banisters. For a woman who had just come into twenty-two thousand pounds, she didn't look very happy.

"I thought you'd gone in to work," she said.

"The doctor said I was to take the day off. Come down here. I want to talk to you."

He heard her say something that sounded like, "I want to talk to you, too," and then she came slowly down the stairs. She was wearing the blue and white spotted dress and she hadn't

any paint on her hands. A sudden slight chill took the edge off
his joy. What a moody, difficult woman she was! Just like her to
find something to nag about on this day of days. He knew she
was going to nag. He could see it in the droop of her mouth and
her cold eyes.

"Did you get the money?" he said heartily. "I couldn't help
seeing old Finbow's letter. At last, eh?"

She was going to say she hadn't got it. She'd asked Finbow to
hang on to it, re-invest it, something diabolical. Christ, she
couldn't have!

"You *did* get the money?"

He'd never heard quite that tone in her voice before, that
chilling despair. "Oh yes, I got it."

"And paid it into the bank? What's up, then, love? Isn't this
what we've been waiting for, planning for?"

"Don't call me love," said Vera. "I'm not your love. You mean
you've been planning for, don't you? But you haven't planned
quite well enough. You should have disposed of your saccharine
tablets after you'd killed my mother."

Momentarily Stanley thought that this couldn't be real. He'd
drunk too much and passed out and that bloody awful puzzle
dream was starting again. But we always know when we are
awake that we cannot be dreaming even though when actually
dreaming we feel all this may be real, and Stanley, after the
first sensation of nightmare unreality, had no need to pinch
himself. Vera *had* said what she'd said. They were in the kitchen
at 61, Lanchester Road and both were wide awake. She *had* said
it, but he asked her to repeat it just the same.

"What did you say?"

"You said for two pins you'd kill her and she said you would
and, God forgive me, I didn't believe either of you. Not until I
found what was in those medicine cartons."

There is a great difference between anticipating the worst,
dreading, dreaming and living in imagination through the worst,
and the worst itself. Stanley had visualised this happening, or
something like this, over and over again, although usually his
accuser had been a doctor or a policeman, but he found that all
these preparations and rehearsals did nothing to mitigate the
shock of the reality. He felt as if he had been hit on the head by

something heavy enough to half-stun but not heavy enough to bring blissful unconsciousness.

In a feeble trembling voice he said what he had planned to say when "they" started asking, "I didn't kill her, Vee. Just taking saccharine didn't kill her."

"She died of a stroke, didn't she? *Didn't she?* Isn't that what she had while I was out? You know it is. Dr. Moxley came and said she'd died of a stroke."

"She'd have had that stroke, anyway," Stanley muttered.

"How do you know? Have you got medical degrees? You know very well you wanted her to die, so you took away her tablets and put saccharine in the carton and she died. You murdered her. You murdered her just as much as if you'd shot her."

Vera went out of the kitchen and slammed the door behind her. Alone, Stanley felt his heart pounding against his ribs. Why hadn't he had the sense to burn those bloody saccharines after Maud had died? And how had Vera found out? That hardly mattered now. He put his head into the sink and drank straight from the cold water tap. Then he went upstairs.

She was in their bedroom, throwing clothes into a couple of suitcases. He fumbled in his mind, trying to find the words. At last he said, "You wouldn't go to the police about this, would you, Vee?"

She didn't answer. Her hands went on folding mechanically, slipping sheets of paper between the clothes, tucking in a pair of rolled-up stockings. He stared at her stupidly and suddenly the meaning of what she was doing came home to him.

"Are you off somewhere, then?"

She nodded. There were little beads of sweat on her upper lip. It was a very hot day.

Stanley managed a hint of sarcastic bravado. "May I ask where?"

"I'll tell you whether you ask or not." Vera marched into the bathroom and came back with her sponge-bag. "I'm leaving you," she said. "It's all over for us, Stanley. It was over years ago really. I could take you treating me like a servant and having that girl here and living off my money, but I can't stay with a man who murdered my mother."

"*I did not murder your mother*," he shouted. "I never murdered anyone. Anyone'd think you liked having her here. Christ, you wanted her out of the way as much as I did."

"She was my mother," Vera said. "I loved her in spite of her faults. I couldn't live with you, Stanley, even if I managed to forget what you've done. You see, I can't stand you near me. Not now. Not any more. After what I found out last night, you make me feel sick just being in the same room with me. You're really wicked, you're evil. No, please don't come near me." She moved away as he came towards her and he could see that she was trembling. "Mother always wanted me to leave you and now I'm going to. Funny, isn't it? It was what she wanted and now she's getting what she wanted but not until after she's dead. I suppose you could say she's won at last."

Stanley's head was splitting. "Don't be so stupid," he said.

"You've always thought me stupid, haven't you? I know I'm not brainy, but I can read, and once I read somewhere that people mustn't be allowed to profit from their crimes. I can't think of anything worse than letting you have any of Mother's money when it was you that killed her. So I'm sorry, I didn't mean to lead you on and then let you down. Up till this morning I meant the money to be yours as much as mine, more yours than mine if you wanted it. But I've hardened myself now." Vera closed the lid of one of the suitcases and looked at him. "Mother left it to me and I'm keeping it."

"You can't!" Stanley shouted, one triumph left to him. "You can't keep it. That bank account's a joint account. I can draw the lot out tomorrow if I like and, by God, I will!"

Vera said quietly, "I didn't pay it into the joint account. That account was more or less closed, anyway, thanks to you overdrawing on it. I opened a new one this morning, a private account for me only."

21

Vera picked up the cases and carried them downstairs. Stanley remained sitting on the bed, the hot sun striking the back of his neck through the closed windows. Again he was aware of a sense of unreality, of nightmare. Nightmare. He said the word over and over to himself. Nightmare, nightmare, nightmare . . . "Nasty dream of a nocturnal charger"? Christ, not that again!

His left eye had begun opening and shutting involuntarily, tic, tic, tic. Stanley swore and clenched his hands. He listened. She was moving about downstairs. She hadn't gone yet. He'd have to talk to her, make her see reason.

She was standing in front of the dining room mirror, applying lipstick.

It is hard to say nice things to someone you hate. Stanley hated Vera at that moment far more than he had ever hated Maud. But the things had to be said. Most men will say anything for twenty-two thousand pounds.

"You've been the only woman in my life, Vee. Twenty years I've been devoted to you. I've taken everything for your sake, your parents insulting me and then your mother moving in here. I'm a middle-aged man now. I'll go to pieces without you."

"No, you won't. You've always been in pieces. Having me here never made you pull yourself together yet. God knows, I tried and now I'm sick of trying."

He began to plead. He would have gone down on his knees but he was afraid she'd walk away and leave him there on all-fours like an animal. "Vee," he said, pulling at her sleeve, "Vee, you know I'm making a go of this business, but I have to have a bit of capital." It was the wrong thing to say. He could tell that from the look on her face, the contempt. Like a really distraught husband, he moaned at her, "Vee, you're all I've got in the world."

"Let's call a spade a spade," said Vera. "My money's all you've got in the world." She pulled on a pair of navy-blue gloves and sat down on an upright chair as if she were waiting for something or someone. "I've thought about that," she said. "I've thought and thought about it all. And I've decided it wouldn't be right to leave you without anything." She gave a heavy sigh. "You're so hopeless, Stan. Everything you touch turns out a mess except crosswords puzzles. You're never held a job down yet and you won't hold this one. But I wouldn't like to think of you penniless and without a roof over your head, so I'm going to let you have this house. You can keep it or sell it, do what you like. If you're silly to sell it and hand the money over to that Pilbeam—well, that's your business."

"Christ," said Stanley, "thanks for bloody nothing." She was going to give him this house! She was taking everything that was his and leaving him this end-of-a-terrace slum. And suddenly what she was doing and that she meant it came fully home to him. Vee, his wife, the one person he was sure he could keep under his thumb and manipulate and get round and persuade that black was white, Vee was selling him down the river. He said wildly, "You don't think I'm going to let you get away with it, do you? Let you go just like that?"

"You haven't got much choice," Vera said quietly, and suddenly there was a sharp knock on the door. "That'll be the driver of the car I've hired."

She bent down to pick up her cases. Stupefied, Stanley would have liked to kill her. As she lifted her face, he struck her hard with the flat of his hand, first on one cheek, then the other. She made a whimpering sound and tears began to flow over the marks his hand had made but she didn't speak to him again.

After the car had gone he wept too. He walked about the room, crying, and then he sat down and pounded the sofa arm with his fists. He wanted to scream and break things but he was afraid the neighbours would hear him.

Crying had exacerbated the twitch in his left eye. It continued to water and pulsate after he had stopped crying. He tried holding the lid still in two fingers but it went on moving in spite of this as if it wasn't part of his body at all but a trapped fluttering insect with a life of its own.

He had lost the money. *He had lost it, all of it.* And now, his face working terrifyingly and uncontrollably, he realised amid the turmoil of his thoughts that for almost the whole of his adult life the acquiring of that money had been his goal, its possession the dawning of a golden age. At first he had thought of it in terms of only a thousand or two, then eight or nine, finally twenty with a bonus of two added. But always it had been there, a half-concealed, yet shimmering crock at the end of a rainbow. To possess it he had stayed with Vera, put up with Maud and, he told himself, never bothered to carve out a career. He had wasted his life.

He thought of it all but not calmly and panic kept returning by fits and starts, making him catch his breath in loud rasping gasps. At last he knew the true meaning of living in the present. Everything behind him was waste and bitterness while ahead there was nothing. Worse than nothing, for now that Vera knew of his attempt on Maud's life and the police had somehow been alerted, now that Pilbeam would have to know that all his vaunted capital amounted to just the roof over his head, how could he even contemplate the passing of another hour, another minute?

He stared at the clock, watching, though not of course, actually seeing, the hands move. That was what his life had been, a slow, indiscernible disintegration towards the present utter collapse. And each moment, apparently leaving the situation unchanged, was in reality leading him inexorably towards the end, something which, though inconceivable, must be even worse than present horror.

A little death would make the unbearable present pass. With jumping twitching hand, he felt in his pocket. Eight pounds remained out of the ten he brought home on Friday. The pubs wouldn't yet be open but the wine shop in the High Street would. He staggered into the kitchen and rinsed his face at the sink.

Outside it was even hotter than indoors but the feel of fresh air made him flinch. Walking was difficult. He moved like an old man or like one who had been confined to bed after a bad illness. There were only a few people about and none of them took any notice of him and yet he felt that the streets were full of eyes, unseen spies watching his every movement. In the wine shop it was all he could do to find his voice. Speaking to another human being, an ordinary reasonably contented person, was grotesque. His voice came out high and weak and he couldn't keep his hands from his face as if, by continually wiping it, smoothing the muscles, he could still those convulsive movements.

The assistant, however, was accustomed to alcoholics. His own face was perfectly smooth and controlled as he took the five pounds from Stanley for two bottles of Teacher's and another pound for cigarettes.

Back at the house he drank a tumblerful of the whisky, but without enjoying it. Instead of making him feel euphoric, it merely deadened feeling. He took one of the bottles and a packet of cigarettes upstairs with him and lay on the bed, wishing in a blurred, fuddled way that it was winter and not nearly midsummer so that the dark might come early. Stanley found he didn't like the light. It was too revealing.

Words came unbidden into his mind and he lay on his back splitting them and anagramming them and evolving clues. He found he was saying the words and the clues out loud, slurring them in a thick voice. But the twitch, temporarily, was gone. He went on talking to himself for some time, occasionally reaching for the bottle and then growing irritable because the drink was making him forget how to spell and lose the thread of words in black spirals which had begun to twist before his eyes.

A whole night of deep sleep, total oblivion, was what he needed, but instead he awoke at nine with a headache that was like an iron hand clamped above his eyebrows. It was still light.

The dream he had just had was still vividly with him. It hadn't been what one would call a nasty dream, not in the sense of being actually frightening or painful, and yet it belonged nevertheless in the category of the worst kind of dreams a human being can have. When we are unhappy we are not made more so by nightmares of that unhappiness; our misery is rather intensified when we dream of that happy time which preceded it and of people, now hateful or antagonistic, behaving towards us with their former affability.

Such had been Stanley's recent experience. He had dreamed he was back in the Old Village Shop distributing largesse to Pilbeam and had seen again Pilbeam's joy. Now, wide awake, he realised that four hours before, thinking he had reached the depths, he had underestimated his situation. Not only had he been robbed of his expectations and left penniless; he had also given his partner a cheque for a thousand pounds and another, to be handed to the decorator, for one hundred and seventy-five. Both those cheques would bounce, for the money was all Vera's, stashed away in a private account.

There seemed no reason to get up. He might as well lie there till lunchtime. Somewhere he could hear water running, or thought he could. The night had been so full of dreams, dream visions and dream sounds that it was hard to sort out imagination from reality.

He had forgotten to wind the clock and its hands pointed to ten past six. It must be hours later than that. Pilbeam would wonder why he hadn't come in but Stanley was afraid to telephone Pilbeam.

His head was tender and throbbing all over. At the moment he wasn't twitching and he didn't dare think about it in case thinking started it up again. He lay staring at the ceiling and wondering whether there was any point in going down to fetch the *Telegraph*, when a sharp bang at the front door jolted him into sitting up and cursing. Immediately he thought of the police, then of Pilbeam. Could it be his partner, come already to say the cheques were no good?

He rolled out of bed and looked through the crack in the curtains, but from there he couldn't see under the porch canopy. Although there was no lorry in the street, it occurred to him that his visitor might be one of the builders. Whoever it was knocked again.

His mouth tasted foul. He slid his feet into his shoes and went downstairs without lacing them. Then he opened the door cautiously. His caller was Mrs. Blackmore.

"I didn't get you out if bed, then?" Presumably she inferred this from the fact that he was still wearing his day clothes, although these were rumpled and creased. "I just popped in to tell you the pipe from your tank's overflowing."

"O.K. Thanks." He didn't want to talk to her and he began to close the door.

She was back on the path by now but she turned and said, "I saw Mrs. Manning go off yesterday."

Stanley glowered at her.

"She looked proper upset, I thought. The tears was streaming down her face. Have you had another death in your family?"

"No, we haven't."

"I thought you must have. I said to John, whatever's happened to upset Mrs. Manning like that?"

He opened the door wider. "If you must know she's left me, walked out on me. I slapped her face for her and that's why she'd turned on the waterworks."

That wives sometimes leave their husbands and husbands strike their wives was no news to Mrs. Blackmore. Speculating about such occurrences had for years formed the main subject of her garden fence chats, but no protagonist in one of these domestic dramas had ever before spoken to her of his role so baldly and with such barefaced effrontery. Rendered speechless, she stared at him.

"That," said Stanley, "will give you something to sharpen your fangs on when you get nattering with old mother Macdonald."

"How dare you speak to me like that!"

"Dare? Oh, I dare all right." Savouring every luscious word, Stanley let fly at her a string of choice epithets, finishing with, "Lazy, fat-arsed bitch!"

"We'll see," said Mrs. Blackmore, "what my husband has to say about this. He's years younger than you, you creep, and he hasn't ruined his health boozing. Ugh, I can smell it on your breath from here."

"You would, the length of your nose," said Stanley and he banged the door so hard that a piece of plaster fell off the ceiling. The battle had done him good. He hadn't had a real ding-dong like that with anyone since Maud died.

Maud . . . Better not think about her or he'd be back on the bottle. He wouldn't, he'd never think of her again unless—unless the police made him. His eye was still twitching but he was getting used to it, "adapting" himself, as some quack of Moxley's ilk would put it. One thing, the police hadn't come yet. Would they search the house before they started on the garden? Stanley decided that probably they would. Not that there was anything for them to find, as Vera was sure to have taken that carton of Shu-go-Sub away with her. Might as well check, though . . .

He went into the room where Vera had spent her last night in Lanchester Road. The carton with the little smear on its label was still beside the bed. Stanley could hardly believe his eyes. What a fool Vera was! Without that no one could prove a thing. The police wouldn't even get a warrant to dig up the garden.

Stanley took the cap off the carton and flushed the tablets down the lavatory. Then he ran the basin and the bath taps. Often this simple manoeuvre had the effect of freeing the jammed ballcock and making it rise as it should do as the water came in from the main. He listened. The outfall pipe had stopped overflowing.

The phone bell made him jump, but he didn't consider not answering it. Letting it ring and then wondering for hours afterwards who it had been would be far worse. He picked up the receiver. It was Pilbeam and Stanley swallowed hard, feeling cold again.

But Pilbeam didn't sound angry. "Still under the weather, old boy?" he asked.

"I feel rotten," Stanley mumbled.

"Bit of a hypochondriac you are, me old love. You don't want to dwell on these things. Still, I'm easy. Take the rest of the week off, if you like. I'll pop round to see you sometime, shall I?"

"O.K.," Stanley said. He didn't want Pilbeam popping round but there was nothing he could do about it.

Just the same, the call had put new heart into him, that and his discovery and destruction of the tablets. Maybe those cheques wouldn't bounce. That man, Frazer, the bank manager, was a good guy, a real gentleman. He mightn't like it but surely he'd pay up. What was a mere £1,175. to him? Probably that private account business was just a polite sop to silly women like Vera. He and she were still man and wife, after all. Frazer had seen them together and given them a cheque book each. Those two cheques would come in and Frazer wouldn't think twice about them. He'd pay up and then perhaps he'd write to Stanley and caution him not to be too free with writing cheques. Absurd, really, how low he'd let himself get yesterday. Panic and shock, he supposed. Very likely Vera would come back, asking for his forgiveness.

There was someone knocking at the door again. John Blackmore, come to do battle on his wife's behalf. The fool ought to know better, ought to thank his stars someone with more guts than he had had put his wife in her place at last.

Stanley had no intention of answering the door. He listened calmly to the repeated hammering on the knocker and then he watched Blackmore return to his own house. When he went downstairs again he found a scribbled note on the mat:

"You have got it coming to you using language like that to my wife. You came from a slum and are turning this street into one. Don't think you can get away with insulting women.

J. BLACKMORE."

This note made Stanley laugh quite a lot. Slum indeed! His father's cottage was no slum. He thought once more of the green East Anglian countryside, but no longer of going back there as a conquering hero. Go back, yes, but as the prodigal son, to home and peace and forgiving love. . . .

Through the kitchen window he could see that water was again beginning to stream from the outfall pipe. It looked as if he would have to go up into the loft. Vera had always seen to things of this kind but Stanley had acquired, mostly from her accounts, a smattering of the basic principles of plumbing. He fetched the steps from where she had left them, mounted them and pushed up the trap-door. It was dusty up there and pitch dark. He went back for a torch.

This was the first time he had ever been in the loft and he was surprised to find it so big, so quiet and so dark. Vera had said you must stand on the cross-beams and not between them in case you put your foot through the plaster, and Stanley did this, encountering on his way to the tank, the skeleton of a dead bird lying in its own feathers. It must have come in under the eaves and been unable to find its way out. Stanley wondered how long it had been there and how long it took for newly dead flesh to rot away and leave only bones behind.

He lifted off the tarpaulin which covered the tank and plunged his arm into the water. The ball on the end of its hinged arm was some nine inches down. He raised it and heard the cocks close with a soft thump.

Having washed his hands in a dribble of water—he didn't want the ballcock to stick again—he fetched the paper and took it back to bed with him to do the crossword. As if he were a real invalid, he slept most of the day away and during the afternoon, dozing lightly, he several times thought he heard someone at the door. But he didn't go down to answer it and when he finally left the bedroom at half-past six there was no one about and the builders' equipment hadn't been moved. By now he was light-headed with hunger so he ate some bread and jam. This place, he thought, is more like Victoria station in the rush hour than a private house. There was someone at the door again. Blackmore. He'd heard a car draw up. Adrenalin poured into Stanley's blood. If he wanted a fight he could have it. But first better make sure it was Blackmore.

Once more he stationed himself at the window, one eye to the division between the curtains. There was a car there all right but it wasn't Blackmore's old jalopy. Stanley waited, gazing down. The man retreated from the porch. He was tall and dark and in his middle thirties. Stanley didn't know him but he had seen him about, mostly going in and out of Croughton police station.

Christ, he thought, Vera hasn't wasted much time.

Stanley prayed the policeman would go back to his car but instead he made for the side entrance, going out of his watcher's line of vision. Quaking, Stanley crept into Maud's room. From there he watched the policeman walk slowly round the lawn. He by-passed the heather garden but stopped in front of the cement mixer. Then he walked round it, rather as a man may walk round an isolated statue in an exhibition, looking it up and down with a thoughtful and puzzled expression. Then he gave his attention to the cement sacks, one of which he kicked so that the paper ripped and a thin stream of grey dust trickled out.

Back in his own bedroom, Stanley stood as still as he could, which wasn't very still as his whole body was twitching and quivering with fear. It was a job to bring the front garden into focus, particularly as his eyelids weren't under control. At last he got a blurred image of the policeman going back to his car. But instead of getting into it, he unlatched the Blackmores' gate and walked up their path.

Stanley had reached a stage of fear when no stimulant could help him. If he drank whisky he knew he would throw it up. His thoughts raced incoherently. The Blackmores would pass on everything they knew of his relations with Maud. Mrs. Macdonald would tell of finding him prone on the earth after filling in the trench he'd prepared in advance. Flushing away those tablets wouldn't help him, for there had been at least one other carton, now no doubt handed over to the police by Vera. That would be enough for them to get a warrant and dig and find Maud, bones maybe among her outer coverings like the bird in the loft.

The loft! He could hide in the loft. It wouldn't matter then if they broke down the doors to get in. He'd be safe up there. The steps were still where he had left them under the trap-door. Cigarettes in one pocket, bottle in the other, he went up the steps and hoisted himself on to a beam. Then, looking down, he knew it wouldn't work. Even if he closed the trap, they'd see the steps.

Unless he could pull the steps up after him.

Stanley lay down flat, bracing his feet against the galvanised wall of the tank. At first, when he grasped the steps, he thought he'd never do it, but he thought of the policeman and renewed fear brought strength. Dragging them straight up was no use. He'd have to use a sort of lever principle. Who was it said, Give me something to stand on and a long enough pole and I will move the earth? Well, he was only trying to move a pair of steps. Use the edge of the trap as a fulcrum, ease them slowly towards him, then pull them down to rest on the joists. Careful . . . Mustn't make a mark on the plaster. He felt as if his lungs would burst and he grunted thickly. But it was done.

When he was shut in he kept his torch on for a while but he didn't need light and he found he could listen better in the dark. With the extinction of light he felt something that was almost peace. There was no sound but a tiny lapping in the tank.

Sitting there in the dark, he felt the twitches beginning again like spirit fingers plucking at his eyelids, his knee, and delicately with the gentleness of a caress, across the skin of his belly. Stanley found that he was crying. He only knew it because the fingers holding his cigarette encountered tears.

He wiped them away on his sleeve and then, although he couldn't see them, he spoke silently the name of every object in the loft: joists, beams, bottle, matches, stepladder, storage tank. Clues formed themselves expertly. "Storage tank," eleven letters, seven and four. "It holds water but rots up with age on the armoured vehicle." "Stepladder": "Snake spelt wrong at first for a means of climbing."

Oh God, he thought, he must be going mad, sitting in the dark in a loft, setting clues for puzzles that would never be solved, and he rested his cheek against the cold metal in despair.

4. Last Word

22

When Stanley came down from the loft the whole neighbourhood was asleep, not a light showing anywhere. He rolled into his unmade bed, certain he wouldn't sleep, but he did and very heavily until past nine in the morning. Fumbling his way downstairs, still in his soiled and sweaty clothes, he found a letter on the front door mat.

It was from Vera and headed with the address of that boarding-house at Brayminster.

> Stanley,
>
> After what you did you will probably think I have changed my mind about the house. Don't worry, you can still have it. I promise you can and I am putting it in writing as I don't suppose you would take my word. I am staying here until I find somewhere else to live. Please don't try to find me. I have been told I could ask for police protection if you did and then get a court order. I never want to see you again.
>
> VERA.

Cursing, Stanley screwed it up. It more or less proved she'd been to the police, the bitch. Who else would have told her about getting court orders? Better keep the letter, though. Carefully he smoothed out the creases. Once he got out of this mess, he'd sell the house all right. Get four thousand for it and put the lot in the business. Maybe in the long run he'd make as much money that way as if he'd had Maud's money and when he did he'd take care Vera got to know about it.

After another meal of bread and jam, he had a bath and put on clean clothes, and as he had foreseen, the pipe started overflowing again. By this time he had become an expert in getting quickly in and out of the loft and he could manage it without getting too dirty. Stanley passed a reasonably serene day, lying on the sofa, gently sipping whisky and drawing, on the plain side of a sheet of wallpaper, an enormous crossword, eighteen inches square.

Pilbeam came round about eight. Having first checked that this wasn't another representative of the law, set on his trail by Vera, Stanley let his friend in. Together they finished the whisky.

"You look a bit rough, old man." Pilbeam studied him with the disinterested and unsympathetic curiosity of a biologist looking at a liver fluke through a microscope. "You've lost weight. That must be trying, that eye."

"The doctor," Stanley said, "says it'll just past off."

"Or you'll pass on, eh?" Pilbeam laughed uproariously at his joke. "Not before we've made our packet, I trust."

Stanley thought quickly. "Would you have any objection if I took a bit of time off? I'm thinking of going away, maybe down to the South Coast to join my wife."

"Why not?" said Pilbeam. "I may go away myself. We can close the shop for a week or two. One way of whetting our customers' appetites. Well, I must be on my way. All right if I have twenty of your classy fags off you? I haven't got a bean on me but we're more or less one flesh, aren't we, like it says in the marriage service?"

Pilbeam laughed loudly all the way up the path.

The cheque was all right, then. He'd given it to Pilbeam on Monday and today was Thursday, so it must be all right. And in the morning he would go away. Not to Vera but to his mother and father. I'm going home, Stanley thought. Even if I have to hitch all the way, even if I arrive penniless on the doorstep, I'm going home. But he cried himself to sleep, weeping weakly into the dirty pillow.

Early on Friday morning, when Vera was told that she was urgently needed at Croughton police station, she went to catch the first train but Mrs. Horton had alerted James and he was waiting for her with his car. They reached Croughton by ten-thirty.

Pilbeam had already been with the police for two hours by then.

She passed him coming out as she was taken into the superintendent's office but neither knew the other. There were a great many people coming and going whom Vera didn't know but whom she suspected were connected with the case against her husband. She avoided Mrs. Blackmore's sharp eye and the curious fascinated gaze of young Michael Macdonald. The superintendent questioned her closely for an hour before he let her go back to James and weep in his arms.

Stanley awoke with a splitting headache. Another hot day. Still, better to stand by the roadside in sweltering heat than pouring rain. His reflection in the mirror showed him a seedy, nearly elderly man with a pronounced and very apparent tic. Maybe his appearance would arouse pity in the heart of those arrogant bastards of motorists from whom he hoped to cadge lifts.

He bundled up a spare pair of trousers and the two clean shirts he had left and stuffed them into a suitcase. It was nearly noon. God, how deeply he slept these days! He was sitting on the bed, combing his hair, when he heard a car draw up. Blackmore home for lunch. Without getting up, he shifted along the bed and put his eye to the crack between the curtains.

All the blood receded from the muscles of his face. He crushed the comb in his hands and a bunch of teeth came off into his palm. A police car was parked outside. As well as the man who had been there before, there were three others. One of them opened the boot and took out a couple of spades. The others marched up the path towards his front door.

Stanley climbed up the steps, clutching his suitcase. At the moment his hand touched the trap-door he heard his callers hammer on the front door. He gave a violent shiver. Almost as soon as the hammering stopped the door bell rang. Someone was keeping his finger on the button. Stanley clambered through the square aperture, lay across the joists and hauled on the steps. Afterwards he didn't know how he'd managed to lever the steps up without dropping them to ricochet over the banisters, or how he lifted them at all, his whole body was jumping so violently. But he did lift them and, almost by a miracle, succeeded in laying them soundlessly down beside him. He wiped his hands on his trousers to avoid making marks on the outer surface of the door, and then he dropped it into its frame.

When it was done he rolled on to his back and lay in the dark, murmuring over and over, "Oh, Christ, Christ, Christ . . ."

Stanley pressed his ear to a very thin crack, more a join than a crack, between the boards of the door and listened. Yes, he could hear something now, the sound of someone forcing open the back door. He heard the lock give and footsteps in the kitchen. How much of his movements could they hear? Would even the most minute shifting on the old joists send a great reverberation to those on the ground floor?

They were coming up the stairs.

The wood creaked under his ear and then someone spoke.

"I reckon he's gone, Ted. Pilbeam said he'd do a bunk and Pilbeam wouldn't lie to us. We've got too much on him."

Judas, thought Stanley, bloody double-crossing Judas with his "me old love" and his Stan this and Stan that. Footsteps moved across the landing. Into the bathroom, Stanley thought. Ted's voice said: "They've started digging, sir. There's quite a crowd in the Macdonalds' garden. Shall I put up screens?"

"They'd have to be sky-hooks, wouldn't they?"

They stopped talking and Stanley heard "Sir"—an inspector? A chief inspector? A superintendent?—moving about in the bedrooms. Ted went downstairs.

So they knew now. Stanley held his body as still as he could, clenching his hands. They knew. Vera had told them and Blake had put his spoke in and somehow or other Moxley had supported them. In a minute they would scrape away the peat and find Maud's body.

No one would hear him now if he struck a match. They weren't looking for him, anyway, they had said so, but searching the house for evidence of how he had killed Maud. Without getting up, he felt for the box, took out a match and struck it in front of his face. The flame sent strange long shadows like clasping and unclasping fingers rippling across the beams and up into the roof. He looked at his watch. He thought that hours and hours had passed but it was only twelve-thirty. Would they go away when they had found what they had come to find, or would they leave a man in the house? He could do nothing about it but continue to lie between the joists, walled in by wood as if he were already in his own coffin.

Stanley had no idea how much time passed before "Sir" and his assistants returned to the landing. Again it seemed like many hours. His limbs ached and every few seconds sharp burning pains stabbed his knees, his shoulders and the joints of his arms. He wanted to scream and scream to let the fear out of him, for he was like a man possessed of a devil which could only be released in a scream. He clasped his hand over his mouth to stop the screaming devil leaving him and tearing down through the floor to those below.

Someone slammed the back door.

Feet, many feet, tramping up the stairs, sent vibrations through his body. There was about eight feet, he thought, between the landing floor and ceiling and he was perhaps a foot above the ceiling. That meant "Sir's" head might be only three feet away from his. He pressed his mouth against raw splintery wood to muffle his ragged gasping breath.

"Thirteen quid in pound notes, sir," someone said. "They were between the pages of this annual."

For a second the words were meaningless. They were nothing like those he had expected. Why didn't they speak of Maud? Maud, Maud, he mouthed into the wood. She must be lying down there now amid the ruins of his garden, bones in her own feathers.

"Sir's" voice broke up the fantasy and Stanley felt his body stiffen. "They smell of violets like the inside of that handbag."

"And the thirty Harry Pilbeam handed over to us, sir."

"Yes. I never thought I'd say, thank God for Harry Pilbeam. But he knows which side his bread is buttered, that lad. Shop his own wife for a quid if she hadn't divorced him ten years back. When I told him we were on to his little game, faking antiques and selling them for the genuine article, he couldn't wait to get back in good with us by passing over the carriage clock and that piece of china."

Someone laughed.

"I must say it's given me some satisfaction to know that he conned Manning properly. The moron's actually handed Pilbeam —Pilbeam, I ask you!—nearly two thousand quid all told. God knows where he got it from."

"What had Pilbeam in mind, d'you know?"

"Bleed him for as much as he could get and then do a bunk's my guess."

Silence fell. Stanley lay as still as a corpse, letting the words flow and pass over him. He didn't understand. What were they doing there? What were they hoping for? They had dug but they hadn't found Maud. Why not? A tiny thrill of hope touched him. Was it possible that they hadn't been looking for Maud at all but for stolen goods, something that Pilbeam had put them on to?

From a long way away a voice came. Unidentifiable, the words a jumble of sound. They were in Maud's room now, now moving back to the landing. The muzzy sound cleared into distinguishable words like a picture coming into focus.

"That'll have been the mother-in-law's room, Ted."

"What's happened to her, then? Gone off with the wife?"

"No, no. The old woman's dead. Died of a stroke round about the time Manning . . ."

Again the voices swam away into a jumble and the footfalls receded. Stanley had been holding his breath. Now he let it out carefully. His heart was hammering. It was true, they hadn't found Maud. They hadn't found anything but a handful of pound notes. He was hiding in vain. They only wanted to question him about Pilbeam. And he'd tell them, everything they wanted to hear and more besides. An eye for an eye . . . Revenge on Pilbeam would be sweet indeed. They had nothing on him, nothing. By a miracle they had guessed nothing, found nothing, and they thought Maud had died a natural death.

He moved his right hand and brought it in silence across to the handle on the inside of the trap-door. The cramped fingers closed over the handle and then Stanley hesitated. If he came down now they'd think he had something to hide. Better let them go, let them leave the house, then come down and tell them what they wanted of his own volition. "Sir" and his assistants were directly underneath him again now and someone was descending the stairs. They were leaving. Once more Stanley held his breath.

More than anything in the world now he wanted one of them to speak the words that would tell him he was free, cleared of any suspicion, just a fool who had allowed himself to be taken for a ride by a con man. The briefest sentence would do it. "We only need Manning for a witness" or "I reckon Manning's paid enough already for trusting Pilbeam." They must say it. He could almost hear them saying it.

The footsteps went down the stairs.

Ted said, "I suppose we'll have to get Mrs. Huntley for the identification, sir," and "Sir" said softly and slowly, "There's not much doubt, though, that this is the body of Miss Ethel Carpenter."

23

"You poor dear," said Mrs. Huntley. In the police station waiting room she moved her chair closer to Vera's and touched her hand. "It's far worse for you than any of us."

"At least I didn't have to identify her. That must have been awful."

Mrs. Huntley shuddered. "But for the little ring, I wouldn't have known her. She'd been in the ground for—oh, I can't bear to speak of it."

"He—my own husband—he killed her for fifty pounds. They found the wound on her head where he struck her. If there's any comfort for me at all, it's that Mother never knew. I'll tell you something I won't ever tell anyone else. . . ." Vera paused, thinking that there was one other person she might tell, one person to whom in time she might tell everything. "I thought," she said softly, "I thought he'd killed Mother for her money, but now I know that was wrong. There's a mystery there that'll never be cleared up. You see, if he'd killed Mother, he wouldn't have needed that fifty pounds. Thank God, Mother never knew anything about it."

"There were a good many things poor Mrs. Kinaway never knew," said Mrs. Huntley thoughtfully. "Like who was the father of Miss Carpenter's child. She told me one day when she was feeling low. You know now, don't you?"

"I guessed. I guessed as soon as I saw that girl this morning. She must be my niece. If Mother had ever met that girl, and she would have if . . ." Vera half-rose as Caroline Snow came into the room. In spite of the shock of it all and the horror, she smiled, gazing at the face which might have been her own twenty years ago.

"This is my father," said Caroline Snow. "He helped me. He went to the police when we couldn't find her. Daddy is absolutely marvellous. He promised that when we found her she could come and live with us, but we didn't find her. Well, not until . . ."

The man's eyes met Vera's. He looked kind, patient, capable of great endurance. He was her brother-in-law. She had a whole family now.

"I'm sorry, I'm sorry," was all she could say.

"It wasn't your fault." George Snow's blue eyes flashed. "Mrs. Manning, you're all alone. Come and stay with us. Please say you will."

"One day I'd like to," said Vera. "One day when this is all past and gone." And meet my sister, she thought. "But I have somewhere to go to, somewhere and someone."

The police wouldn't let her go yet. They questioned her and questioned her as to where Stanley might be but Vera couldn't help them. She could only shake her head helplessly. There were so many people in the police station, so many faces, Mrs. Paterson, Mrs. Macdonald and her son, an important key witness, Mrs. Blackmore, the man who delivered peat, and they all reminded her of that old unhappy life in Lanchester Road. She wanted only one person and at last they let her go out to the car where he was waiting for her.

"One day," he said, echoing her own words, "when this is all past and gone, you'll get a divorce and . . ."

"Oh, James, you know I will. It's what I want more than anything in the world."

Stanley stayed in the loft until his watch told him it was ten o'clock. He used his last match to see the time, but it was pain rather than the loss of light that drove him down. His body ached intolerably in every joint and he would have come down in any circumstances, even if, he told himself, the house had still been full of policemen.

Very clearly now he saw the trap he had made for himself. He had murdered no one but the body he had hidden had died by violence; by burying Ethel's cases and Ethel's ring with it, by using Ethel's money, he had irrevocably branded himself as a killer and a thief. There was his record too, the record which showed he was capable of such an act. No use now to ask for an examination of the real body of Ethel. By his own desire that body was reduced to ashes, a fine soft powder, delicate and evanescent, far more elusive of analysis than the cobwebby dust which now clung to his clothes and his skin.

Standing on the landing in the shadowy gloom of the summer night, Stanley tried to brush this dust off his clothes until the air was filled with soot-smelling clouds. He wanted to cleanse himself of it entirely, for he felt that it was Ethel who clung to him, enveloping him in ashy vapour. For months Maud had haunted him, appearing in dreams, but Maud was gone now for ever. He seemed to feel Ethel standing beside him as she had stood on the day of her death, listening to Maud's snores, about to admonish him as she was admonishing him now. He shivered and whimpered in the dusk, brushing Ethel off him, wiping her off his face with shaking hands.

His own body had a smell of death about it. Afraid to use water and set the pipe overflowing again, he made his way down the stairs. His limbs were gradually losing their stiffness and their pain. Life was returning to them and with it fear. He had to get away.

The house was full of creaks and whispers. In the dark Stanley bumped into furniture, knocking the telephone off its hook so that it buzzed at him and made him whimper abuse at it. Ethel was in here too, the very essence of Ethel, waiting quietly for him on the mantelpiece. The room was full of greenish sickly light from the single street lamp outside. He took hold of the urn in fingers which shook and twitched and threw it on to the floor so that grey powdery Ethel streamed across the carpet. And then he had to go, run, escape, leave the house and Ethel in possession of it.

Nobody followed him. No one had been waiting for him. He ran, his heart pounding, until he was far from Lanchester Road, across the High Street and into the hinterland of winding, criss-crossing roads where everyone went to bed early and nearly all the lights were out. Then he had to stop running, stand and hold his aching chest until he could breathe normally again.

Just to be out of that house, to be free of it and not pursued, brought him a tiny shred of something like hope. If he could get hold of some money and some means of transport . . . Then he could go home to Bures and his river. They wouldn't look for him there because Vera would tell them how he didn't get on with his parents and had run away and never wrote. He leant against a wall, bracing himself, trying to get his thoughts into some sort of coherent order, trying to make his brain work realistically, calmly. I'm going home, he said, going home, and then, shuffling at first, then moving faster, he turned his steps in the direction of the old village.

The shop was in utter darkness. Steadier and saner now that he was doing something purposeful, Stanley made his way round the back, checked that the van was there and unlocked the back door. Thank God, he said to himself, he always carried the shop key and the van key in his jacket pocket. In his absence, Pilbeam had got rid of nearly all their stock, and apart from a few hideous and probably unsaleable pieces, the place was empty. Pale light from a metal-bracketed antique street lamp filtered waterily across a huge mahogany table and lay in pools on the floor.

A couple of cars passed in the street and one stopped outside, but it wasn't a police car. Stanley looked at it vaguely across the shadows and the flowing citron-coloured light and then he opened the till. It contained twenty pounds in notes and just short of another five in silver. He was transferring them to his pocket when he heard footsteps coming round the back. There was nothing to hide behind but a pair of maroon velvet curtains Pilbeam called portieres and which he had rigged up on one of the walls. For a moment Stanley's body refused to obey him, he was so frightened and so dreadfully weary of being frightened and hunted, but at last somehow he got behind the curtains and flattened himself against the wall.

The back door opened and he heard Pilbeam's voice.

"That's funny, me old love, I could have sworn I locked that door."

"Did you leave anything in the till?"

"You must be half-cut, Dave. That's what we've come for, isn't it? Should be near enough thirty quid."

Stanley trembled. He couldn't see anything but he felt their presence in the room where he was. Who was Dave? The huge man Pilbeam had brought round with him to Lanchester Road? He heard the till open with a squeak like an untuned violin string. Pilbeam said, "Christ, it's empty!"

"Manning," said Dave.

"How could it be? They'll have him behind bars."

Dave said, "You think?" and ripped aside the left-hand portiere. Leadenly, Stanley lifted his head and looked at them. "Turn out your pockets," Dave said sharply.

A little courage returned to Stanley. There is always a little left in reserve right up to the end.

"Why the hell should I?" he said in a thin high voice. "I've a right to it after what he's had out of me."

Dave's shadow was black and elongated, the shadow of a gorilla with pendulous hands. He didn't move.

Pilbeam said, "Oh, no, Stan, old man. You haven't got a right to nothing. You never had nothing, did you? It's easy giving away what's not your own."

Stanley edged behind the table. Nobody stopped him. "What's that supposed to mean?" he said.

"Cheques that bounce, Stan, that's what it means. I don't think you've ever been properly introduced to my friend, Dave. Let me do the honours. This is Stan, my partner, Dave old boy. Dave, Stan, is the—er, managing director of the firm that did our decorating."

Stanley's mouth went dry. He cleared his throat but still he had no voice.

"What d'you expect me to do?" Dave said. "Shake hands with him? Shake hands with that dirty little murderer?"

"You can shake hands with him in a minute," said Pilbeam. "I promise you you shall and I will too. First I'd like to tell my friend Stanley that both his cheques, mine and Dave's, came back yesterday marked Returned to Drawer. Now I might overlook a thing like that, old man, being as we're old mates, but Dave . . . Well, Dave's different. He doesn't like sweating his guts out and then being made a monkey of."

Stanley's voice came out as a squeak, then grew more powerful. "You shopped me," he said. "You bleeding copper's nark. You did dirt on me behind by back. Nothing but lies you've told me. You haven't got a wife, haven't had a wife for ten years. You . . ."

His voice faltered. Pilbeam was looking at him almost gently, his eyes mild, his mouth twitching at the corners. Even his voice was indulgent, kindly, when he said, "Let's shake hands with him now, Dave, shall we?"

Stanley ducked, then overturned the table with a crash so that it made a barricade between him and the other two men. Dave kicked it, planting his foot in the centre of its glossy top. It skidded back until its legs struck the wall and Stanley was penned in a wooden cage.

They came for him, one on each side. Stanley thought of how he had fought with Maud, centuries, aeons ago. He felt behind him for a vase or something metal to throw but all the shelves had been emptied. He cringed, arms over his head. Dave pulled him out, holding him by a handful of his jacket.

When he was in the middle of the shop, Dave held him, locking his arms, and as he kicked and wriggled, Pilbeam caught him under the jaw with his fist. Stanley sobbed and kicked out. For that he got a kick on the shin from Dave, a kick which made him scream and stagger.

In wordless dance, the three men edged round the overturned table, Stanley hoping for a chance to grab its legs and send the heavy mass of wood toppling to crush Dave's feet. But he was limping and shafts of pain travelled from his shin up through his body. When he was back against the wall again he cringed back cunningly to make them think he was done for, and as Pilbeam advanced slowly upon him, Stanley twisted suddenly and grabbed the velvet portieres. There was a scrunch of wood as the rail which held them came apart from the wall. Stanley hurled the heavy mass at his assailants and for a moment they were enveloped in velvet.

Right at the back of the shop now, within feet of the door, Stanley found a weapon, a nine-inch-long monkey wrench Pilbeam had left under the till counter. As Dave emerged, struggling and cursing, Stanley threw the wrench as hard as he could. It missed Dave's head and struck him in the chest, just beneath the collar bone. Dave howled with pain. He flung himself on Stanley as Stanley reached the door and was struggling with the handle.

For perhaps fifteen seconds the two men grappled together. Dave was much taller than Stanley but he was impeded by the pain in his chest and even then Stanley might have got away but for the intervention of Pilbeam who, creeping along the floor, suddenly grabbed Stanley's legs from behind and threw him face downwards.

Dave picked him up, held him while Pilbeam pummelled his face and then, holding him by the shoulders, banged his head repetitively against the wall. Stanley's knees sagged and he dropped, groaning, into the pile of velvet.

When he came to he thought he had gone blind. One of his eyes refused to open at all, and with the other he could see only implacable blackness. He put his hand up to his face and it came away wet. With blood or with tears? He didn't know because he couldn't see. His fingers tasted salty.

Then gradually something took vague dark shape before him. It was the table, set up on its legs again. Stanley sobbed with relief because he wasn't blind. The place was so dark only because the street lamp had gone out.

The velvet he was lying on was soft and warm, a tender gentle nest like a woman's lap. He wanted to bury himself in it, wrap it round his tired body and all the hundred places that ached and throbbed. But he couldn't do that because he was going home. The green Stour was waiting for him, the fields that were silver with horse beans and emerald with sugar beet.

He sat up in the darkness. The place he was in seemed to be a sort of shop without any goods for sale. What was he doing there? Why had he come and where from? He couldn't remember. He knew only that he had passed through a time of great terror and pain and violence.

Had he always trembled and jumped like this, as if he had an incurable disease? It didn't matter much now. The beckoning of the river was more urgent than anything. He must get to the river and lie on its banks and wash away the tears and the blood.

Vaguely he thought that someone was after him but he didn't know who his pursuers were. Attendants in a hospital perhaps? He had run away from a hospital and fallen among thieves. When he stood up he rocked badly and walking was difficult. But he persevered, shuffling, his arms outstretched to fumble his way along by feel. Outside somewhere he thought there was a car and it was his car because he had an ignition key in his pocket. He found the car—in fact, he bumped into it—and opened the door with his key.

When he was sitting in the car he switched on the light and looked at his face in the mirror. It was black and bruised and there was dried blood on it. Over his left eye was a cut and under the cut the eye jerked open and shut.

"My name is George Carpenter," he said to the stranger in the mirror, "and I live at . . ." He couldn't remember where he lived. Then he tried to recall something—anything—out of the past, but all he could see were women's faces, angry and threatening, swimming up out of darkness. Everything else had gone. No, not quite . . . His own identity, he hadn't lost that. His name was George Carpenter and he had been a setter of crossword puzzles, but he had become very ill and had had to give it up. The illness was in his brain or his nerves and that was why he twitched so much.

An unhappy life, a life of terrible frustration. The details of it had gone beyond recall. He didn't want to remember them. When he was a boy he had been happy, fishing in the river for miller's thumbs and loaches. The miller's thumbs had faces like coelacanths. They were fish left over from another age when there were no men in the world. Stanley found he liked to think of that time; it eased the pressure in his head.

Loach was a funny name. Useful if you were setting a puzzle and had to fit a word into "l" blank "a" blank "h." "Loach: For this fish the Chinese pronounces another." He turned the ignition key and started the van.

Stanley had been driving for so long that by now he drove quite mechanically, as if the van were not something he had to operate but an extension of his own body. He had no more need to think about driving than he had to think about walking when he moved across a room. The streets he drove through seemed familiar but still he couldn't place them. On the bridge by the lockkeeper's house he stopped and looked down into the canal. He wasn't far from home then, for here was the Stour, lying limpid between its green willows, his green river, cold and deep and rich with fish. It wasn't green now but black and ripple-free, a metallic gleam on its flat surface.

Soon the dawn would come and then the river would go bright as if its green came, not from the awakening sky, but from some hidden inner source of colour. And people would appear from those black unlighted houses, whose outlines he could just see cutting into the horizon, and walk in the fields as the morning mist rose and spread and pearled the grass.

There was a white police car on the other side of the bridge, a stationary car with its headlights full on but trained away from him. A speed trap, he thought, although there were no cars but his to trap. They must be waiting for someone, some runaway villain they were hunting.

They would have no chance to trap him, for he wasn't going their way. He was going to take the towpath and drive slowly along it until the dawn came and then, when the river became a dazzling green, lie on the bank and bathe his hurt face in the water.

The surface of the path was hard and bumpy like ridged rock. Each time the van shuddered a spasm of fresh pain made him wince. Soon he would stop and rest. The dawn was coming up ahead of him, the black sky shredding apart to disclose the thin pale colour behind it. Bures and the Constable villages lay before him. He could see the shape of them now in a crenellated horizon.

Stanley switched off his lights, and in the distance he saw another car following him. They must be coming, he thought, to warn him off the river. Someone had fishing rights here and he'd be poaching. When had he ever cared for anyone else's rights?

They wouldn't be able to see him now his lights were off. He knew his river better than they did. Every bend in it, every willow on its banks was as familiar to him as a solved crossword.

Once he was home and safe he'd start doing crosswords again, bigger and better ones, he'd be the world's champion crossword puzzler. Even now, weak and trembling as he was, he could still make up puzzles. He found he had forgotten the words that made up his own name, but that didn't matter, not while he had his skill, his art. "Undertake the fishing gear": "Tackle." "Sport a leg in fruity surroundings": "Fishing." "Undertake . . ." Stanley shivered. There was some reason why he couldn't find a clue for that word, that ugly word which had dealings with death. He drove faster, the van's suspension groaning, but his mind was calmer, he was almost happy. Words were the meaning of existence, the panacea for all agony.

"Panacea": "Cure is a utensil with a twisted card." "Agony": "The non-Jew mixes with an atrocious pain." He could do it as well as ever.

There was a bend ahead at this point. Very soon the bank veered to the left, following the river's meander, and when you could see his village, just a black blot it would be on the grey fields, you had to brake and turn to the nearside. "Meander"— a beautiful word. "I and a small hesitation combine to make the river twist." Or better perhaps, "Dear men," (anag. seven letters) or, how about "Though mean and red, the river has a curve in it?"

Stanley's body ached and his eyes glazed with weariness. He was afraid he might fall asleep at the wheel, so he shook himself and forced his eyes to stare hard ahead. Then, suddenly, he saw his village. It was floating in grey mist, peaceful, beckoning. Now, at this point, the river meandered.

"The winding river," he heard himself whisper, anagramming, "is a dream need." He groaned aloud with pain and longing and then he pulled the wheel feebly to follow the way the path should go.

The van slid and sagged, running out of control, but gradually and slowly. Stanley's hands slipped weakly from the wheel. It was all right now, he was home. No more running, no more driving. He was home, cruising gently downhill to where his village loomed in front of him.

And the dawn was coming, rising bright and green and many-coloured like a rainbow, pouring in through the van's open windows with a vast crunching roar. Stanley wondered why he was screaming, fighting against the wet dawn, when he was home at last.

The police car screeched to a halt on the canal bank. Two men got out, running, slamming doors behind them, but by the time they reached the shored-up edge the water was almost calm again with nothing to show where the van had gone down but dull yellow ripples spreading outwards in wide concentric rings. The dawn showed muddy red over the warehouses and the first few drops of rain began to fall.

□

THE FACE OF TRESPASS

I have peace to weigh your worth, now all is over,
　　But if to praise or blame you, cannot say.
For, who decries the loved, decries the lover;
　　Yet what man lauds the thing he's thrown away?

Be you, in truth, this dull, slight, cloudy naught,
　　The more fool I, so great a fool to adore;
But if you're that high goddess once I thought,
　　The more your godhead is, I lose the more.

Dear fool, pity the fool who thought you clever!
　　Dear wisdom, do not mock the fool that missed you!
Most fair,—the blind has lost your face for ever!
　　Most foul,—how could I see you while I kissed you?

So . . . the poor love of fools and blind I've proved you,
For, foul or lovely, 'twas a fool that loved you.

Rupert Brooke

BEFORE

The new Member of Parliament finished his after-dinner speech and sat down. He was not, of course, unaccustomed to public speaking but the applause of these men who had been his school fellows brought him a slightly emotional embarrassment. Accepting the cigar which the chairman of the Feversham Old Boys' Society was offering him covered for a moment this disturbance of his poise and by the time it was lit for him he was once more at ease.

"Did I do all right, Francis?" he said to the chairman.

"You were absolutely splendid. No platitudes, no dirty stories. Such a change to hear a crusader against social outrage! It almost seems a pity we don't have capital punishment any more so that you could abolish it."

"I hope I wasn't a prig," said the new Member quietly.

"My dear Andrew, you left-wingers always are, but don't let it worry you. Now do you want another brandy or would you like to —er, circulate?"

Andrew Laud refused the brandy and made his way to one of the tables where his former housemaster sat. But before he reached it someone tapped him on the shoulder and said, "Congratulations, Andy, on the speech and your success in the by-election."

"Jeff Denman," said the M.P. after a moment's thought. "Thank God for someone I know. I thought I was going to be stuck with old Scrimgeour there and that foul fellow, Francis Croy. How are you? What are you doing these days?"

Jeff grinned. "I'm fine. Now that I'm knocking thirty my family are getting over the disgrace of my driving a van for a living, so if you ever feel like moving house to live among your constituents I'll be happy to oblige."

"I might at that. Come and have a drink? You know, everyone here seems so *young*. I can't see a soul I know. I thought Malcolm Warriner might be here or that bloke David Something I used to have those fierce arguments with at the debating society."

"Mal's in Japan," said Jeff as they went up to the bar. "He'd be one of your constituents, as a matter of fact, if he were at home. Which brings me to one who isn't here but *is* a Waltham Forest constituent. Remember Gray Lanceton?"

The Member, to whose back this had been addressed, turned and emerged from the crush with two halves of lager in his hands. "He'd have been a year behind us. Tall dark bloke? Wasn't there a bit of a fuss when his mother remarried and he threatened suicide? I heard he'd written a novel."

"*The Wine of Astonishment*," said Jeff. "It was obviously auto-biographical, about a sort of hippie Oedipus. He shared my flat in Notting Hill with me and Sally for a bit but he didn't write anything more and when he started to feel the pinch he took Mal's place for somewhere to live rent-free. There was some sort of messy love affair too, I gather."

"He's living in my constituency?"

Jeff smiled. "You said 'my constituency' like a bridegroom saying 'my wife,' with shyness and great pride."

"I know. For weeks I've been thinking, suppose I lose the election and still have to come and talk to you a lot? What a fool I'd have felt. Does he like living there?"

"He says the Forest gets him down. I've been out there and I was surprised that there are such remote rural corners left only fifteen miles out of London. It's a weatherboard cottage he lives in at the bottom of a forest road called Pocket Lane."

"I think I know it," said the M.P., and reflectively, "I wonder if he voted for me?"

"I'd be very much surprised if Gray even knew there was a by-election, let alone voted. I don't know what's happened to him but he's turned into a sort of hermit and he doesn't write any more. In a way, he's one of those people you've committed your-self to help, the misfits, you know, the lost."

"I should have to wait till he asked for that help."

"No doubt you'll have enough on your plate without Gray Lanceton. I see Scrimgeour bearing down on us with the head-master in tow. Shall I melt away?"

"Oh, God, I suppose so. I'll give you a ring, Jeff, and maybe you'll come and have a meal with me at the House?"

The Member set down his glass and composed his features into that earnest and slightly fatuous expression which, generally reserved for babes in arms and the senile, seemed to do equally well for those pedagogues who had once awed him into terrified submission.

CHAPTER 1

It was sometime in early May, round about the fifth. Gray was never sure of the date. He had no calendar, he never bought a paper and he'd sold his radio. When he wanted to know the date he asked the milkman. The milkman always came on the dot of twelve, although he had no difficulty about knowing the time because he still had the watch she'd given him. He'd sold a lot of things but he wasn't going to sell that.

"What day is it?"

"Tuesday," said the milkman, handing over a pint of homogenised. "Tuesday, May the fourth, and a lovely day. Makes you feel glad to be alive." He aimed a kick at the young bracken shoots, hundreds of them all tightly curled like pale green question marks. "You want to get them ferns out of your garden, plant annuals. Nasturtiums'd do well there and they grow like weeds."

"Might as well keep the weeds."

"Them ferns'd get me down, but we can't all be the same, can we? Be a funny old world if we were."

"It's a funny old world now."

The milkman, who was easily amused, roared with laughter. "I don't know, you are a scream, Mr. L. Well, I must be off down the long long road that has no turning. See you."

"See you," said Gray.

The forest trees, which came very close up to the garden, weren't yet in full leaf but a green sheen hung over them, and this bright veil made a dazzlement against the sky. It was prematurely, freakishly hot. Gleaming in the sunshine, the beech trunks were the colour of sealskin. A good metaphor that, he thought, and thought too how once when he was a writer he would have noted it down for future use. Maybe some day, when he'd got himself

together and got some money and rid himself finally of her and
. . . Better not think of it now.

He'd only just got up. Leaving the front door open to let some
warmth and fresh air into the dank interior, he carried the milk
into the kitchen and put the kettle on. The kitchen was small and
very dirty with a slightly sunken floor of stone flags covered with
a piece of linoleum curling at its edges like a slice of stale bread.
All around him, as he waited for the kettle to boil, were those
kitchen appointments which had been the latest mod cons in
1890 or thereabouts, an earthenware sink, a disused range, an
enamel bathtub with a wooden cover on it. The kettle took a long
time to boil because it was coated with burnt-on grime and the
gas burner wasn't very clean either. Inside the oven it was even
worse. When he opened the oven door a black cavern yawned at
him. A good many times last winter, sitting in front of the
lighted oven in the Windsor chair, sitting in front of the black
cave with the gold-tipped blue flames quivering in its heart, he'd
been tempted to put out the flames, lay his head within that open
door and wait. Just wait for death—"Do something foolish," as
Isabel would put it.

He wouldn't do it now. The time for that was past. He would
no more kill himself over her than he would over his mother and
Honoré, and the time would come when he'd think of her as
he did of them—with irritable indifference. Not yet, though.
Memories of her were still in the forefront of his mind, lying down
with him at night, meeting him when he first woke, clinging to
him through the long empty days. He drugged them down with
cups of tea and library books but they were a long way from being
exorcised.

The kettle boiled and he made the tea, poured milk over a
couple of Weetabix and sat down to eat his breakfast on the bath
counter. The sun was high, the kitchen stuffy because the window
hadn't been opened for about a hundred years. Motes of dust
dancing in it turned the beam of sunshine into a solid shaft that
burned his neck and shoulders. He ate his breakfast in the destruction that wasteth at noonday.

This was her most usual time for phoning—this and, of course,
Thursday evenings. While he'd adjusted more or less to not seeing her, he still couldn't manage the problem of the phone. He

was neurotic about the phone, *more* neurotic, that is, than he was about other things. He didn't want to talk to her at all but at the same time he passionately wanted to talk to her. He was afraid she'd phone but he knew she wouldn't. When the tension of wanting and not wanting got too bad he took the receiver off. The phone lived in the horrible little parlour Isabel referred to as the "lounge." He thought of it as "living" there rather than standing or just being because, although for days on end it never rang, it seemed alive to him when he looked at it, vibrant, almost trembling with life. And when he took the receiver off on Thursday evenings, it seemed baulked, frustrated, peevish at being immobilised, its mouth and ears hanging useless from the dangling lead. He only went into the "lounge" to answer the phone—he couldn't afford actually to make calls—and sometimes he left the receiver off for days.

Finishing his breakfast and pouring himself a second cup of tea, he wondered if it was still off. He opened the "lounge" door to check. It was on. Saturday or Sunday he must have replaced it, turning the phone to stare at him like a squat, smug little Buddha. His memory had got very bad since the winter. Like an old man, he could remember the past but not the immediately recent past; like an old man, he forgot the date and the things he had to do. Not that there were many of those. He did almost nothing.

He opened the window on to the greening sunlit forest and drank his tea, sitting in an armchair covered with some early, perhaps the very earliest, prototype of plastic, a brown shiny fabric worn down to its cloth base at the arms and on the seat. There was only one other armchair. Between the two chairs was a low table, its legs made of moulded iron, its top burned by cigarettes from the days when he'd been able to afford cigarettes and marked with white rings from the base of the hot teapot. A stained Turkey rug, so thin that it wrinkled and rucked when he walked on it, lay in the middle of the floor. Apart from these, the only furnishings were Mal's golf clubs resting against the wall under the phone shelf and the paraffin heater on which she'd broken the perfume bottle and which, throughout the winter, had mingled her scent, evocative and agonising, with the reek of its oil each time it was lighted.

He pushed away the thought. He finished his tea, wishing he

had a cigarette or, preferably, a whole packet of twenty king-size. Almost hidden by the golf bag under which he'd concealed it, he could see the grey cover of his typewriter. It wouldn't be true to say he hadn't used it since he came to this cottage Mal called the hovel. He'd used it for a purpose he liked thinking about even less than he liked thinking about her, although the two were one and inextricably linked. To think of one was to think of the other. Better dwell instead on Francis's party, on getting away from this hole to London if only for a weekend, to meeting there some girl who would replace her—"with eyes as wise but kindlier and lips as soft but true, and I daresay she will do." To getting money together too, and finding a room, to sloughing off this dragging depression, this nothingness, even to writing again . . .

The phone gave the nasty little prefatory click it always made some ten seconds before it actually rang. Ten seconds were quite long enough for him to think in, to hope it was going to ring and at the same time to hope the click wasn't from the phone at all but from the worm-eaten floorboards or something outside the window. He still jumped when it rang. He hadn't learned how to control that, although he had managed to regard his reaction very much as a convalescent regards the headaches and tremors he still has. They will pass. His reason and his doctor have told him so, and meanwhile they must be borne as the inevitable aftermath of a long illness.

Of course it wasn't she. The voice wasn't husky and slow but squeaky. Isabel.

"You do sound tired, dear. I hope you're eating properly. I just rang to find out how things are."

"Just the same," he said.

"Working hard?"

He didn't answer that one. She knew he hadn't done a day's work, an hour's, for three years, they all knew it. He was a bad liar. But even if he lied and said he was working, that didn't help. They only asked brightly when "it" was coming out and what was it about and said how marvellous. If he told the truth and said he wasn't, they told him never to say die and would he like them to try and help get him a job. So he said nothing.

"Are you still there, dear?" said Isabel. "Oh, good. I thought they'd cut us off. I had a lovely letter from Honoré this morning.

He's really wonderful with your mother, isn't he? It always seems so much worse somehow, a man having to care for an invalid."

"Don't see why."

"You would if you had to do it, Gray. It's been a great blessing for you your mother having got married again and to such a wonderful man. Imagine if you had the looking after of her."

That was almost funny. He could scarcely look after himself. "Isn't that a bit hypothetical, Isabel? She married Honoré when I was fifteen. You might as well say, imagine if my father had lived or I hadn't been born or mother'd never had thrombosis."

As always when the conversation became what Isabel called "deep," she switched the subject. "What d'you think? I'm going to Australia."

"That's nice. What for?"

"My friend Molly that I used to have my typing bureau with, she lives in Melbourne now and she wrote and asked me. I thought I might as well go before I get past it. I've fixed on the beginning of the first week in June."

"I don't suppose I'll see you before you go," Gray said hopefully.

"Well, dear, I might drop in if I have a spare moment. It's so lovely and peaceful where you are. You don't know how I envy you." Gray gritted his teeth. Isabel lived in a flat over shops in a busy Kensington street. Maybe . . . "I always enjoy a quiet afternoon in your garden. Or wilderness," she added cheerfully, "as I should call it."

"Your flat will be empty, then?"

"Not a bit of it! The decorators are moving in to do a mammoth conversion job."

He wished he hadn't asked, for Isabel now began to describe, with a plethora of adjectives, precisely what alterations, electrifications, and plumbing work were to be undertaken in her absence. At least, he thought, laying the receiver down carefully on the shelf, it kept her off nagging him or harking back to the days when his life had looked promising. She hadn't questioned him about his finances or asked him if he'd had his hair cut. Making sure that the blether issuing distantly from the phone was still happily going on, he eyed himself in the Victorian mirror, a square of glass that looked as if it had just been breathed on or, possibly, spat on. The young Rasputin, he thought. Between shoulder-length hair and uneven beard—he'd stopped shaving at Christmas —his eyes looked melancholy, his skin marked with spots, the result presumably of a diet that would have reduced anyone less healthy to scurvy.

The mirrored face bore little resemblance to the photograph on the back jacket of *The Wine of Astonishment*. That had looked rather like a latter-day Rupert Brooke. From Brooke to Rasputin in five months, he thought, and then he picked up the phone again to catch the breathless tail end of Isabel's sentence.

" . . . and double glazing in every single one of my rooms, Gray dear."

"I can't wait to see it. D'you mind if I say goodbye now, Isabel? I have to go out."

She never liked being cut short, would have gone on for hours. "Oh, all right, but I was just going to tell you . . ."

Hollowly through the phone he heard her dog barking. That would fetch her. "Goodbye, Isabel," he said firmly. With a sigh of relief when she had finally rung off, he put his library books into a carrier bag and set off for Waltham Abbey.

Drawing a cheque to cash was the traumatic highspot of his week. For half a year he'd been living on the royalties he'd received the previous November, a miserable two hundred and fifty, drawing at the rate of four pounds a week. But that didn't take into account the gas and electricity bills he'd paid and Christmas expenses at Francis's. There couldn't be much left. Probably he was overdrawn already and that was why he waited, tense and uncomfortable by the bank counter, for the cashier to get up and, having flashed him a look of contempt, depart into some nether regions to consult with higher authority.

This had never happened and it didn't happen now. The cheque was stamped and four pound notes handed over. Gray spent one of them at the supermarket on bread and margarine and cans of glutinous meat and pasta mixtures. Then he went into the library.

On first coming to the hovel, he'd determined, as people do when retiring temporarily from the world, to read all those books he'd never had time for: Gibbon and Carlyle, Mommsen's

History of Rome and Motley's *Rise of the Dutch Republic*. But at
first there had been no time, for she had occupied all his thoughts,
and then when she'd gone, when he'd driven her away, he'd fallen
back on the anaesthesia of old and well-loved favourites. *Gone
With the Wind* would just about be readable again after four
months' abstinence, he thought, so he got that out along with Dr.
James's ghost stories. Next week it would probably be *Jane Eyre*,
Sherlock Holmes, and Dr. Thorndyke.

The librarian girl was new. She gave him the sort of look that
indicated she liked unwashed bearded men who had nothing
better to do than loaf around libraries. Gray hazarded a return of
the look but failed in mid-glance. It was no use. It never was. Her
hands were stubby, the nails bitten. She had a ridge of fat round
her waist and, while he was among the shelves, he had heard her
strident laugh. Her lips were soft but she wouldn't do.

The books and the cans were heavy to carry and he had a long
way to go back. Pocket Lane was a deep hole through the forest,
a long tunnel to nowhere. The signpost at this end said
LONDON 15, a fact which still amazed him. He was in the
depths of the country but the heart of London was only fifteen
miles distant. And it was quieter than the country proper, for here
no men worked in the fields, no tractors passed and no sheep were
pastured. A bright still silence, broken only by the twitter of birds,
surrounded him. He wondered that people actually lived here
from choice, voluntarily bought houses here, paid rates, *liked* it.
Swinging his carrier bag, he passed the first of these houses, the
Willises' farm—so-called, although they farmed nothing—with
its exquisite lawns and florist's shop borders, tulips in red and gold
uniforms standing in precise rows as if on parade. Next came
Miss Platt's cottage, smart brother of the hovel, showing what
fresh paint and care could do for weatherboard; lastly, before the
rutted clay began and the forest closed in, the shuttered withdrawn abode of Mr. Tringham. No one came out to talk to him,
no curtain moved. They might all have died. Who would know?
Sometimes he wondered how long it would be before they found
him if he were to die. Well, there was always the milkman . . .

The hawthorn hedges, fresh green and pearled with buds, ended
at the end of the metalled road, and tall trees crowded in upon
Pocket Lane. Nothing but bracken and brambles was strong enough

to grow under the shade of those trees, in the leaf-mould crusted clay their roots had deprived of nourishment. Just at this point she had always parked her car, sliding it under the overhanging branches away from the eyes of those most incurious neighbours. How frightened she had always been of spies, of watchers existing only in her imagination yet waiting, she was sure, to relay her movements back to Tiny. No one had ever known. For all the evidence there was of their meetings, their love, none of it might ever have happened. The lush grass of spring had grown over the impress of her car tyres, and the fragile branches which had been broken by that car's passage were healed now and in leaf.

He had only to lift the phone and ask her and she'd come back to him. He wouldn't think of that. He'd think of *Gone With the Wind* and making a cup of tea and what to have for supper. It would be better to think about phoning her after six o'clock when, on account of Tiny, it would be impossible to do so, not now when it was practicable.

They said bracken made a comfortable bed and they were right. He lay on the springy green shoots reading, occasionally going into the hovel for fresh tea, until the sun had gone and the sky behind those interlaced branches was a tender melted gold. The birds and their whispered song disappeared before the sun and the silence grew profound. A squirrel slid down a branch onto the verge where it began to chew through the stem of a small doomed sapling. Gray had long ago got over thinking he was mad because he talked to squirrels and birds and sometimes even to trees. He didn't care whether he was mad or not. It hardly seemed important.

"I bet," he said to the squirrel, "you wouldn't mess about drinking tea or, in your case, eating plants, if you knew there was a beautiful lady squirrel panting for you not four miles away. You'd go right off and pick up the phone. You're not messed in your mind like humans and you wouldn't let a lot of half-baked principles get between you and the best lay in Metropolitan Essex. Especially if the lady squirrel had a whole treeful of luscious nuts stored away, now would you?"

The squirrel froze, its jaws clamped round the stem. Then it leapt up the trunk of an enormous beech. Gray didn't go near the phone. He immersed himself in the Old South until it grew too dark to read and too cold to lie any longer on the ground. The sky above him was indigo now but in the southwest over London a glowing plum-red. He stood by the gate as he always did at this hour on fine evenings, looking at the muted blaze of London.

Presently he went into the house and opened a can of spaghetti. At night the sleeping wood seemed to stir in its slumber and embrace the hovel entirely in great leafy arms. Gray sat in the Windsor chair in the kitchen under the naked light bulb, dozing, thinking, in spite of himself, of her, finally reading almost a third of *Gone With the Wind* until he fell asleep. A mouse running over his foot awakened him and he went upstairs to bed in the silent close blackness.

It had been a typical day, varying only in that it had been warm and sunny from the hundred and fifty or so that had preceded it.

CHAPTER 2

The post office, Gray thought, ought really to pay him a fee for causing them so little trouble. It couldn't be above once a week that the postman had to make the long trek down Pocket Lane to the hovel and then he brought only bills and Honoré's weekly letter. That had come on the previous Thursday in company with the gas bill, a demand for nine pounds which Gray didn't want to pay until he was more certain of his financial position. He'd be a whole lot more certain when he received from his publishers his royalty statement, currently due. It must be, he reflected, somewhere about May the twelfth or thirteenth now and surely that statement would arrive any day.

Meanwhile, he ought to write to Honoré before he did his shopping. *M. Honoré Duval, Petit Trianon*—God, he could never write that without squirming—*Bajon*, followed by the number that signified the department, *France*. He did the envelope first while he thought of what to say, always a difficult task. Two cups of tea had been drunk before he started. *Cher Honoré, Je suis très content de recevoir votre lettre de jeudi dernier, y inclus les nouvelles de maman* . . . His French was bad but no worse than Honoré's English. If his stepfather insisted on writing in a language of whose grammar and syntax he was abysmally ignorant—just, Gray was sure, to annoy—he would get as good, or as bad, as he gave. A few remarks on the weather followed. What else was there to say? Ah, yes, Isabel. *Imaginez-vous, Isabel va visiter Australie pour un mois de vacances* . . . *Donnez mes bons voeux à maman, votre* Gray.

That would shut him up for a bit. Gray took *Gone With the Wind* and the ghost stories and set off for the town where he posted his letter, bought half a pound of tea, a giant packet of Weetabix (this week's cheap offer) and two cans of Swedish meatballs. *Jane Eyre* was out and they'd only got one copy. He glowered

at the fat girl, feeling ridiculously disappointed, almost paranoid.
Didn't they realise he was one of their best customers? If Char-
lotte Brontë were still alive she'd be short of income through their
incompetence. He took out *The Man in the Iron Mask* and the
first of the Herries Chronicles, cast a glance of dislike at the grey
pile of the Abbey, and walked gloomily back along Pocket Lane.
A cigarette would have done a lot to mitigate the misery of these
walks. Perhaps he could give up milk, cut down his tea, and use
the resulting savings to buy forty cigarettes a week. Of course it
was all absurd, this life. He could easily do something about it.
Well, not *easily* but he could do something. Get a labouring job,
for instance, or train as a G.P.O. telephonist. Half the telephon-
ists in London were failed authors, broken lovers, unappreciated
poets, intellectuals *manqué*. Only a little energy was needed, a
scrap of drive . . .

The sun was unseasonably hot and, because of the humidity in
this wooded place, unpleasant. In the shadowy gaps between the
bushes gnats buzzed in clouds. Sparrows chattered, bathing in dust
pockets in the dry clay of the path, and occasionally a
jay screamed. The lane was sylvan, unspoilt countryside really, but
it had something about it of a dusty room. And no matter what
time of the year it was, the dead leaves lay everywhere, brown on
the surface, falling to dust and decomposition below.

It was Friday, pay day, so the milkman was late, trundling back
along the ruts, his work done.

"Lovely day, Mr. L. Makes you feel glad to be alive. May I
trouble you for forty-two pee?"

Gray paid him, leaving himself with one, eighty, to last till he
went to the bank next week.

"That's a couple of great books you've got there," said the milkman. "Studying, are you? Doing one of them external degrees?"

"The University of Waltham Holy Cross," said Gray.

"University of Waltham Holy Cross! You are a scream. I must
tell the wife that one. Don't you want to know what day it is?"

"Sure. You're my calendar."

"Well, it's Friday, May the fourteenth, and I reckon you need
reminding you've got a date. There's a car parked outside your
place, one of them Mini's, red one. You expecting some beautiful bird?"

Isabel. "My fairy godmother," said Gray glumly.

"Best of luck, Cinderella. See you."

"See you—and thanks."

Bloody Isabel. What did she want? Now he'd have to find something to give her for her tea. You couldn't give a sixty-two-year-old Kensington lady ravioli or Weetabix at three in the afternoon. It was some months since he'd possessed a bit of cake. And she was bound to have brought that dog of hers, that Dido. Gray didn't at all dislike Isabel's Labrador bitch—in fact, he preferred her to her owner—but his godmother had a nasty way of forgetting to bring anything for the dog's evening meal and of raiding his meagre store of corned beef.

He found her sitting in the Mini's passenger seat, the door open. The Labrador was digging a hole among the bracken, snapping sometimes at the flies. Isabel was smoking a king-size cigarette.

"There you are at last, dear. I poked around the back a bit but you hadn't left a window open so I couldn't get in."

"Hallo, Isabel. Hallo, Dido. When you've dug that lot up you can get planting nasturtiums like the milkman said."

Isabel gave him rather a funny look. "Sometimes I think you're alone too much, dear."

"Could be," said Gray. Dido came up to him, got up on her hind legs and licked his face, putting her large, clay-filled paws around his neck. He thought she had a beautiful face, much nicer than most human faces—except one, always except one. Her nose was shrimp-pink and ice-cold. She had deep brown eyes—kind eyes, Gray thought, which was a funny thing to think about a dog. "I'll go and make us some tea." Dido, who was intelligent in matters of food, wagged her long frondy tail.

Isabel followed him. She pretended not to see the dirty plates or the flies and fixed her eyes on Gray instead.

"I won't ask you why you don't have your hair cut," she said, laughing merrily and sitting on the back step which she first dusted with her handkerchief.

"Good." Gray put the kettle on.

"No, but really, dear, you're not a teenager any more. Your hair's down on your shoulders."

"Since you're not going to ask me why I don't have it cut," said

Gray, "we may as well talk about something else. I'm afraid I don't have any cake. There's bread." He considered. "And Stork."

"Oh, but I brought a cake." Isabel creaked to her feet and loped off towards the car. A small fat woman, she wore turquoise trousers and a red sweater. Gray thought she looked like one of Honoré's garden gnomes. When she came back she was smoking a fresh cigarette. "I won't offer you one. I remember you said you'd given it up."

Experience should have taught him the cake wouldn't be the large homemade Dundee, marzipanned and iced, which he had been hungrily envisaging. He took the bakewell tart out of its packet. It was already in a foil case so he didn't bother with a plate. The dog walked in and shoved her nose between his hand and the bath cover.

"Now, darling, don't be tiresome." Isabel always called her dogs darling, reserving this endearment for canines exclusively. "Perhaps we could go into your lounge. I do like to sit down properly to my tea."

The phone was still off the hook from the night before. Tiny went to his masonic thing on Thursday nights and if she was going to phone, Thursday evening was the most likely time. Maybe she'd tried. Maybe she often tried on Thursday nights. He put the receiver back on the Buddha's knees, wondering what he'd say or do if she phoned now while Isabel was there. He fancied that today he could smell a faint breath of *Amorce dangereuse*, brought out perhaps by the warmth. Isabel watched him dealing with the phone. She preserved a tactful, heavily curious silence that was scarcely more endurable than her questions. She had armed herself, he noticed, with a box of tissues as might someone suffering from a heavy cold. Isabel didn't have a cold. She dusted the seat of her armchair with one tissue, spread another on her lap and asked him finally how he was getting on.

Gray had given up placating the old. It necessitated too many lies, too much elaborate subterfuge. Life might have been easier if he had deceived Isabel and Honoré into believing he was actually writing another novel, that the place was filthy because he couldn't get a cleaning woman, that he lived in Pocket Lane because he liked it. But he told himself that the approval of people he didn't himself approve of wasn't worth having so, accordingly, he replied that he wasn't, in the accepted meaning of the phrase, getting on at all.

"What a pity that is, dear. You were such a lovely little boy and you used to have such marvellous school reports. And when you got your degree your mother and I had such high hopes of you. I don't want to say anything to hurt you, but if anyone had asked me to predict your future in those days, I'd have said you'd be at the top of the tree by now."

"You won't hurt me," said Gray truthfully.

"And then you wrote that book. Not that I liked it myself. I don't care for books without a proper story. But all the people who know about these things forecast a wonderful career for you. And, oh, Gray dear, what has it come to?"

"Pocket Lane and Swedish meatballs," said Gray, blessing Dido for causing a diversion by sweeping her tongue across his plate.

"Take your face off the table, darling. Cake isn't good for doggies." Isabel lit a fresh cigarette and inhaled dizzily. "What you need," she said, "is some outside interest, something to take you out of yourself."

"Like what?"

"Well, that's really why I've come. No, I must be honest. I've come to ask you a favour but it would be very good for you as well. You'd admit you need something to do?"

"I'm not taking a job, Isabel. Not your sort of job, anyway. I can't be a clerk or a salesman or a market researcher, so can we get that clear from the start?"

"My dear, it's nothing like that. This isn't *paid*. It isn't a job in that sense. I only want you to do something for *me*. I may as well come straight to the point. What I want you to do is look after Dido for me while I'm in Australia."

Gray said nothing. He was watching a fly which was either eating, or laying eggs on, a lump of icing that had fallen onto the rug. Dido was looking at it too, her eyes going round in wild circles when the fly rose sluggishly from the crumb and drifted about in front of her nose.

"You see, dear, I've never left her since she was a puppy and she's five now. I couldn't put her in kennels. She'd fret and I shouldn't enjoy myself knowing she was fretting."

London, Kensington, just to get away, and so easily. "You mean, look after her in your flat?"

"No, dear. I told you I was having builders in. Look after her here, of course. She loves it here and your not having a job means she wouldn't be left alone. You could take her out for lovely walks."

It wouldn't be too bad, he supposed. He liked Dido better than he liked most people. And Isabel would provide her food with possibly a little extra in the shape of actual money.

"How long for?"

"Just four weeks. I go on Monday, June the seventh. My aircraft leaves Heathrow at three-thirty. What I thought was I could bring Dido to you on the Sunday evening."

"Sunday, the sixth?"

"That's right."

"Sorry, Isabel," said Gray firmly. "Not possible. You'll have to find someone else."

He wasn't going to give up Francis's party, especially for Isabel. Francis's party was the only thing he had to look forward to, the only thing that kept him going, he thought sometimes. He'd planned ahead for it, deciding to go up on the Sunday morning, wander round the Park, look at the street vendors in the Bayswater Road and arrive at Francis's by about four. That would mean helping to get food ready and hump crates of booze, but he didn't mind that, particularly as it would get him into Francis's good books and secure him the offer for a bed for the night. Well, not the night but the period of from five in the morning till he woke up somewhere around noon. He had had fantasies about this party, real people to talk to, unlimited drink and cigarettes, the new girls, one of whom might be the one to make him forget and with whom he might even share that bed or couch or carpet or patch of floor. The idea of sacrificing this for anything less than severe illness or his mother's dying or something equally seismic made him feel almost sick.

"Sorry, but I'm doing something that Sunday."

"Doing what? You never do anything."

Gray hesitated. It was one thing to resolve not to placate the old, quite another to stick this system out. He could tell Isabel he'd be dining with his publishers but that was improbable on a Sunday night and, knowing he hadn't published anything for three years, she was unlikely to believe it. Again he decided on the truth.

"I'm going to a party."

"On a *Sunday*? Oh, Gray dear, I do find that strange. Unless you're going to see someone there you might—well, who might give you a helping hand?"

"Very possibly," said Gray, thinking of the imaginary girl. Not wanting to be jesuitical, he added, "This party's just for pleasure, no strings. But I want to go. I'm sorry, Isabel, I see you think it's selfish and maybe immoral—yes, you do—but I can't help that. I'm not putting off this party for you or Dido or anyone."

"All right, dear, don't. I can manage to bring Dido the next morning. I can bring her at twelve and go on from here to the airport."

Christ, he thought, that was persistence for you. No wonder she'd made a fortune bludgeoning executives into employing her illiterate little typing pool rejects.

"Isabel," he said patiently, "this is not going to be a cocktail party where nice middle-aged fuddy-duddies eat twiglets and drink martinis from six till eight. This is going to be more in the nature of an all-night orgy. I shan't get to bed till five or six and, naturally, I shan't want to leap up again at nine to get back here and receive you and your dog."

"You're very frank!" Isabel tossed her head and coughed in a futile effort to prevent his seeing how deeply she had blushed. "I should have thought a little natural shame about carryings-on of that kind wouldn't be out of place. You might have had the decency to think up some excuse."

They didn't even want you to be truthful. They knew you liked sex and liquor—in fact, they thought you liked them a hell of a lot more than you did—but you were supposed to put up some Victorian pretence that a simple Westbourne Grove rave-up was really a conference at the Hyde Park Hotel.

"Can I have one of your cigarettes?"

"Of course you can. I would have offered, only I thought you'd given it up. Now, dear, why shouldn't I bring Dido here at twelve and just put her in the house—shut her in the kitchen, say, till you get home?"

"O.K., you can do that." There was evidently no escape. "I'll be back around three. I suppose she'll be all right for three hours?"

"Of course she will. I'll leave her some water and I'll leave you enough tins and money for fresh meat to last you out." Isabel went off into a long string of instructions for Dido's proper care while the dog, unobserved by her owner, though not by Gray, removed the remains of the bakewell tart from the table. "Now what about a key?"

When he first came to the hovel there had been three keys. One he carried about with him, one hung on a nail above the kitchen sink, and the third—probably she had thrown it away by now, along with anything else she had to remember him by. Gray went out and fetched the spare key.

"I'll shut her in the kitchen because, though she's very clean *normally*, she might have a little accident if she's alone in a strange place."

Gray said that little accidents would make small difference to the general grot in the hovel, but he agreed to this, telling Isabel the kitchen window didn't open.

"That won't matter for three hours, as long as you make a fuss of her when you come in and take her for a nice walk. I'll put the key back on the hook, shall I?"

Gray nodded. While Isabel wiped her mouth and brushed her lap with fresh tissues, he put out his hand to the dog who gambolled over at once, licked his fingers and sat down beside him, leaning her soft golden weight against his knees. He let his arm fall over her as it might encircle a woman's shoulders. The warmth of flesh, of blood pulsing, was a strange sensation to him, new in a way. This wasn't human flesh and blood; there was no infinity of mind under that shapely skull. But the very touch of warmth and the pressure of what seemed like real affection, brought him a sudden sharp pain, brought home to him the agony of his loneliness. And at that moment he was terribly near to tears for loss, for unconquerable apathy, for waste, and for his own feeble self.

But it was in his normal voice that he said, "We'll be all right, won't we, Dido, my old love? We'll get on fine."

Dido lifted her head and licked his face.

CHAPTER 3

At some sleepy hour, about eight perhaps, he heard a letter flop on to the front door mat. It couldn't be another one from Honoré, not yet. The electricity bill—too small to distress his bank account —was paid; the final demand for the gas wasn't due yet surely. It must be that royalty statement at last. And about time too. Not that it would announce some huge windfall, but if it was only a hundred, only fifty . . . Just a tiny bit of capital like that would give him the incentive to get away from here, find a room in London, take a job working a bar or washing up till he got himself together to write again.

The bedroom was filled with pale light, moving as wind tossed the beech branches. He lay there, thinking about London, about Notting Hill, Ladbroke Grove switchbacking up to Kensal Green, people in the streets all night. No branches, no clay, no leaves crepitating and rustling wherever you walked, no more vast blank days. Although he didn't expect to sleep again, he dozed off into a dream—not of London, as might have been expected, but of her. In the weeks following their separation he had dreamed of her every night, had been afraid to sleep because of those dreams, and they still came often, once or twice a week. Now she was in the room with him, this very room, the wind blowing her hair that was neither red nor gold nor brown but a fox fur blend of all three. And her eyes, the colour of smoky crystal, were on him.

She said, holding out a little hand the rings shackled, "We'll talk about it. There's no harm in just talking."

"There's no point either."

She didn't listen to his reply. Perhaps he hadn't made it aloud. Who knows in dreams? "It's been done before," she said. "Lots of people in our sort of situation have done it. You'll say they got caught." He said nothing, only gazed into those eyes. "You'll say that, but we don't know about all the ones who didn't get caught. They're the kind we'll be."

"We?" he said. "The kind we'll be?"

"Yes, darling, yes, Gray . . ." Closer now, her hair blown against his skin. He put out his arms to hold her, but her flesh was hot and that flying hair flames. He shrank, pushing away the fire, crying out as he surfaced from the dream, "I couldn't do it, I couldn't kill a fly . . . !"

There was no staying in bed after that. Shivering from the effect of her presence—for is a dream woman less a presence than a real one?—he got up and pulled on jeans and faded T-shirt. Gradually his body stopped shaking. Reality splashed back in hard light and loneliness and the dull hopeless safety of being without her. He looked at his watch. Half-past eleven. He wondered what day it was.

Almost the first thing he saw when he got downstairs was a cow's face, white and gingery-brown, looking at him through the kitchen window. He opened the back door and went out into the patch of stinging nettles, birch saplings and hawthorn that was supposed to be a garden. It was full of cows milling about under the sagging greyish washing he'd left hanging on the line since Sunday. The Forest wasn't fenced and farmers could let their cattle wander about as they pleased which was a cause of misery and frustration to the garden-proud. Gray approached the cows, patting several of them on their noses which had much the same feel as Dido's, and addressing them aloud on the virtues of anarchy and contempt for property. Then he remembered the letter, the royalty statement, and he went in to fetch it. But before he picked it up, the stamp on the envelope—that bloody affected Marianne strewing flowers or whatever—told him he'd been wrong.

"My dear son . . ." Gray was used to that by now but it still made him wince. "My dear son, I try to telephone to you Thursday last evening but the line is occupied and again Friday and the line still occupied. How gay the life you have with many friends! You must not be unquiet but mummy is again not well and the doctor Villon say she have an other attack of paralyse. There is much work here for me who is habituate to be just a poor infirmier and work all day and night making care of your mummy.

"Now it will be good if you come. Not today I mean but be

ready to come if mummy is not so well. For that when you must come I will talk to you with the telephone to tell you now is the time you must come my son. You will say you have no money to pay the train or the avion company but I will send you the money not in a letter as that is against law which I will not but to your bank that is Midland in Waltham Abbey as you have said where you can take it when you must come. Arrangements for this I make. Yes you say this is funny. Honoré pay money to me when he is caring so for his little saved money but old Honoré know the duty of a son for his mummy and for this he break the rule of sending no money to a son who work not at all and make arrangement for the bank to have thirty pounds of money.

"Do not be unquiet. Doctor Villon say the good God take mummy not yet and no need to send to Father Normand but tell you who is her one son and child. Be calm my boy. Your loving papa Honoré Duval. P.S. I have borrowed to the mayor the french traduction of your book you have gave me and he read when he has leisure. You will like to have the critique of a man of reason what the mayor is. H.D."

Gray knew that the Mayor of Bajon's sole claim to literary judgment was the fact of his great-aunt's having been maid to a cousin of Baudelaire. He screwed the letter up and threw it behind the bath. Honoré knew perfectly well he could read French without difficulty but he insisted on writing in the horrible diningroom English he had picked up while a waiter in Chaumont. Gray didn't suppose his mother's life was really in danger and he wasn't prepared to rely on the word of Dr. Villon, another one of Honoré's cronies along with the mayor at Bajon's local, the Écu d'Or.

He wouldn't go so far as to say he didn't care whether his mother lived or died, and he certainly intended to fly over to France if she were really on her deathbed, but he hadn't much feeling for her left. It would be false to say that he loved her. It had been a great shock to him when, touring through France with Isabel, his mother had fallen in with—Gray wasn't prepared to say fallen in love with—one of the waiters at the Chaumont Hotel. He had been fifteen, his mother forty-nine and Honoré probably about forty-two. Honoré even now never revealed his true age, making out he was a poor old man on whom the duties of nursing weighed heavily. They had got married very quickly after that, Honoré being well aware, Gray knew, that his betrothed owned the car she was travelling in as well as, far more important, a fairly large house on Wimbledon Common. Whatever its effects on the bride's relatives, the marriage had apparently worked out wisely and well. The Wimbledon house had been sold and Honoré had built a bungalow in his native village of Bajon-sur-Lone, where they had lived ever since. Mme. Duval had become a Catholic on her marriage, another departure which Gray found hard to forgive. He had no religion himself, largely due to his mother's having taught him agnosticism from his cradle. All that had gone when she remarried. Now she had the priest to tea and put ashes on her forehead on *mercredi des Cendres*, or had done when she had been well enough. The first stroke had hit her four years before. Gray had gone over then, paying his own fare out of money earned by selling short stories, and again when she had the next one, relying this time on part of the handsome advance on his novel. Sometimes he wondered how he was going to make it when the *attaque de paralyse* struck again, perhaps fatally. Now he knew. Honoré would stump up.

Honoré *had* stumped up. It was quite pleasant to think of the money being there, waiting for him, making his own waiting for that statement less fraught with worry. He mixed some packet curry with water, heated it in a saucepan and ate it on the front doorstep while watching the cows who had begun to wander off in search of richer pastures than Mal's nettle bed. At twelve sharp the milkman arrived.

"I've got my own dairy," said Gray, who sometimes felt obliged to live up to his reputation as an entertainer. "You'd better watch out or you'll find yourself redundant."

"Got your own dairy? You're a real comedian, you are. Them cows is all bullocks, or hadn't you noticed?"

"I'm just a simple Londoner and proud of it."

"Well, it takes all sorts to make a world. Wouldn't do if we was all the same. Just for the record, it's Thursday, May the twentieth."

"Thanks," said Gray. "See you."

"See you," said the milkman.

Gray did a mammoth wash-up, his first for four or five days, read the last chapter of *Rogue Herries* and set off down the lane. Rain had fallen at the beginning of the week and the clay was soggy, churned up by the hooves of the twenty or so bullocks who had left behind them steaming pats of dung from which rose a sour scent. He caught up with them outside the gate to the farm. He didn't know much about Willis except that he had a hatchet-faced wife and a red Jaguar. But cows live on farms; these cows evidently wanted to get into this farm; obviously it was the place for them. He opened the gate, a fancy affair of cartwheels stuck between bars, and watched the cows canter clumsily in the way cows have, up the gravel drive and across Mr. Willis's lawn. This was a sheet of glistening green velvet onto which a sprinkler scattered a fine cascade of water drops. He leant against the gatepost, interested by the cows and amused at their antics.

Three of them began immediately to devour tulips, stalks, and vermilion blooms sprouting from their jaws in a way that Gray thought rather delightful and reminiscent of some Disney cartoon. The others jostled each other about the lawn and one began to make its way round the back of the house. He was just moving off again, shifting his books to his other arm, when a bedroom window of the farmhouse was flung open and a voice screamed at him:

"Did you open that gate?"

The hatchet-faced Mrs. Willis.

"Yes. They wanted to come in. Aren't they yours?"

"*Ours?* When did we ever keep cattle? Can't you see what you've done, you stupid man? Look what you've done."

Gray looked. The exquisite moist turf was mashed by the indentations of some eighty cloven feet.

"I'm sorry, but it's only grass. It'll heal up or whatever the right term is."

"Heal up!" yelled Mrs. Willis, leaning out and shaking her arms at him. "Are you mad? D'you know what it's cost my husband to get his lawn like that? Years and years of labour and hundreds of pounds. You ought to be made to pay for what you've done, you—you long-haired layabout. I'll see to it my husband makes you pay if he has to take you to court."

"Oh, piss off," said Gray over his shoulder.

Screeches of reproach, threats of retribution and of shocked disgust at his language pursued him down the lane. He felt rather cross and shaken, a state of mind which wasn't improved by finding, when he got to the bank five minutes before they closed that he had just two pounds, forty-five pence in his account. This he drew out, remembering Honoré's thirty which should arrive any day. It wouldn't do, however, to splash out on any fancy tins. He returned *Rogue Herries* and *The Man in the Iron Mask* and took out *Anthony Absolute*, *The Prisoner of Zenda*, and *No Orchids for Miss Blandish*, all in paperback treated with the sort of fortifying process the library went in for. They were light to carry and on the one day he didn't need a lift he got one. He had just entered Pocket Lane when Miss Platt's car pulled up beside him.

"I'm so glad I saw you, Mr. Lanceton, because I want to ask you if you'll come to my little party on Tuesday fortnight."

Gray got into the car. "Your what?" he said. He hadn't meant to be rude, for he liked what he knew of Miss Platt, but the idea of anyone of seventy giving a party and out here was so novel as to be shocking.

"Just a few friends and neighbours in for drinks and a sandwich at about seven on June the eighth. I'm moving, you see. I've sold the house and I'm moving out on the ninth."

Gray muttered something about being sorry to hear that. They passed the farm which the cows had now left. Mrs. Willis was on the lawn, prodding at the broken turf with a rake.

"Yes, I sold it the same day I advertised it. Really, I thought the price the agent told me to ask was quite ridiculous—fifteen thousand pounds for a cottage! Can you imagine?—but the man who's bought it didn't turn a hair."

"It's a lot of money," Gray said. He could hardly believe it. Miss Platt's place was just like the hovel, only smartened up a bit. Fifteen thousand . . .

"House prices have trebled around here in the past few years. The Forest can't be built on, you see, and yet it's so near London. I've bought the flat above my sister's in West Hampstead because she's really getting past looking after herself. But it seems dreadful after this lovely spot, doesn't it?"

"I wouldn't say that," said Gray sincerely. "You'll have a great time."

"Let's hope so. But you will come?"

"I'd like to." A thought struck him. "Will the Willises be there?"

"I haven't asked them. Are they particular friends of yours?"

"I think Mrs. Willis is my particular enemy. I let the cows into her garden."

Miss Platt laughed. "Oh, dear, you must be unpopular. No, there'll just be me and my sister and Mr. Tringham and a few friends from Waltham Abbey. Do you often hear from Malcolm Warriner?"

Gray said he'd had a postcard with a picture of Fujiyama at Easter, thanked Miss Platt for the lift and got out. He made a pot of tea and sat in the kitchen reading *The Prisoner of Zenda* and eating slices of bread and Stork. The wind had risen, blowing the clouds and making the place quite dark, though it was still early. He lit the oven and opened it to give him some warmth.

It wasn't till the phone started ringing that he remembered the milkman had said it was Thursday, the night he always took the receiver off. His watch said ten past seven. Tiny would have been off to his masonic thing an hour ago. Every Thursday night she tried to get him, but she'd never been able to because the receiver was always off. It wasn't off tonight and she was succeeding. Of course it was she. She would speak to him, he would speak to her, and in half an hour she would be here. He moved towards the "lounge," the phone, not rushing but walking slowly and deliberately as a man may walk to an inevitable, hated, yet desired, fate. His heart was thudding, it actually hurt. She was in that phone like a genie in a lamp, waiting to be released by his touch, to flow into and fill the room, red-gold, crystal green, *Amorce dangereuse*.

He was so certain it was she that he didn't say hallo or give Mal's number but said what he'd always said when he knew it was she phoning, "Hi," miserably, resignedly, longingly, in a very low voice.

"Gray?" said Francis. "I want to speak to Graham Lanceton."

Relief? Despair? Gray hardly knew what he felt unless it were the beginning of a coronary. "This is me, you fool. Who did you think it was? D'you think I keep a staff?"

"It didn't sound like you."

"Well, it was. It is."

"Really, this is getting ridiculous. You sound as if you're messing your mind properly out in that dump. Look, I'm phoning about this party. Could you possibly come up on the Saturday?"

Ten minutes before he'd have been excited at the very idea. "Yes, if you like," he said.

"I've got to meet this aged relative at Victoria on the Saturday morning and I want someone to be here when the blokes come to fix up some rather fancy electric wiring I'm having done for the party. A sort of blink arrangement that has quite an alarming psychedelic effect."

"I'll be there. I can get to you by ten." His heart had stopped pounding. As he put the phone down, he felt limp, sick. He sat in the brown plastic armchair, in the dusk, and stared at the silent secretive phone, the detached self-confident phone that had snapped shut its organs like a sea anemone, and squatted on its seat, not returning his gaze but withdrawn now as if it were asleep.

Christ, but he mustn't start investing the thing with a personality. That was real neurosis. That could lead to only one end, to a ward in a mental hospital and E.C.T. or something. Better anything than that. Better dial her number now, talk to her, establish once and for all that there was never again to be any contact between them.

But they'd established that at Christmas, hadn't they?

"If you phone me, I'll put the receiver down."

"We'll see about that," she'd said. "You wouldn't have the will power."

"Don't try me then. I've told you till I'm sick of it, if you can't leave off getting at me about that obsession of yours, it's no use any more. And you can't obviously."

"I do what I want. I always do what I want."

"All right, but I don't have to do what you want. Goodbye. Go away now, please. We shan't see each other again."

"You're bloody right there," she'd said.

So it had been a pact, hadn't it? I've loved you faithfully and well two years or a bit less, it wasn't a success . . . If it had been a pact, why did he hope and fear? Why did he take the receiver off? Because she'd been right and if she phoned he wouldn't have the will power to resist. Because he knew confidently, proudly, that five months separation wouldn't be long enough to stop her loving him. But, as a woman, maybe she wouldn't risk the humiliation of phoning him and being repulsed. He could phone her . . .

Tiny wouldn't be home before eleven. She was alone there, he alone here. It was all ridiculous. He was making himself ill, ruining his life. He jerked out of the chair and stood over the phone.

Five-O-eight . . . He dialled that bit fast but paused before going on with the rest of the number, the four digit bit. Then he dialled it more slowly, dialled three of the numbers. He inserted his finger in the nine hole, let it linger there, trembling, pulled it out with a soft "Oh, Christ" and banged the side of his hand down on the receiver rest. The receiver dropped, swinging, knocking against the golf clubs.

It wasn't any good. For one evening, maybe for a whole week, he'd have her in peace, but it would start again, the nagging, the one topic of conversation that filled the spaces between lovemaking. And he couldn't keep on stalling the way he'd stalled last summer and last autumn because in the end he'd have to tell her he couldn't do it. He'd have to say, as he'd said at Christmas, that if it was doing that or not seeing her he'd choose not seeing her.

He went out of the front door and stood among the bracken the cows had flattened into a prickly mattress. Black branches whipped against a sky of rushing cloud. Over there, behind him, lay Loughton, Little Cornwall, Combe Park. It was ironic, he thought wearily, that he was longing for her and she for him, that only four miles separated them, that the phone would link them in a second; that neither had qualms about betraying Tiny or revulsion for adultery, but they could never meet again because she wouldn't stop demanding what he wouldn't do, and he couldn't, under any circumstances, agree to do it.

CHAPTER 4

He didn't sleep much that night. Probably this was due to his not following his usual sleep-inducing method, the writer's resource, of telling himself a story as soon as he laid his head on the pillow. Instead, he did what he'd done those sleepless nights of January, thought about her and their first meeting.

Yet he'd hardly intended to get on to it. He lay there, examining the curious results of haphazard chance, how some tiny alteration of purpose or a word spoken by a friend, a delay or a small change in the day's routine, may ineluctably dictate the course of a life. Such had happened when his mother and Isabel, awakened in the small hours by the phone ringing—a wrong number, of course—and unable to sleep again, had set off earlier than they'd intended and reached Dover in time to catch the first boat. Because of this they were down as far as Chaumont by the evening, although they shouldn't really have been there till the next night when Honoré would have been off duty. Who had made that phone call? What careless unthinking arbiter had misdialled at four in the morning and so made a marriage and changed a nationality?

In his own case, he knew his arbiter's identity. Jeff had helped himself to the last twenty sheets of typing paper—for what? To make out some removals bill? Some list of household goods?—and he'd had to go out to Ryman's and get a fresh ream. The branch in Notting Hill were out of stock. Why hadn't he walked across the Park to the branch in Kensington High Street? Because the 88 bus had stopped at the red light. At that moment the traffic lights had turned red, the bus had stopped and he had got on it. So was it the light that had made his fate, or the buyer who hadn't got the paper in, or Jeff, or the householder who had to have a list of tables and chairs made before he could move? Useless to go on.

You could get back to Adam that way, back and back, trying to learn who spun, who held the scissors and who cut the thread.

The 88 took him down Oxford Street and he'd gone to Ryman's in Bond Street. He'd always felt good with a fresh ream of paper under his arm. It wasn't daunting but a challenge, that virgin pack he would fill with richness. And because he'd been dwelling on this, looking down and not where he was going, he'd crashed into her before he even saw her face, cannoned right into the girl who was walking towards him, so that her parcels tumbled on to the pavement and her scent bottle broke against a shop window ledge.

He could smell it now, the same smell that had lingered so long in the hovel. It rose in a hot heady cloud, steaming on the crisp January air.

"Can't you look where you're going?"

"The same applies to you," he'd said, not very politely, and then, softening because she was beautiful, "I'm sorry about your perfume."

"So you bloody should be. The least you can do is buy me another bottle."

He shrugged. "O.K. Where do we get it?" He thought she'd refuse then, say it didn't matter. The impression he had of her as they stood close together, picking up parcels, was that she wasn't at all badly off. A red fox coat, the same colour as her hair, cream leather boots—at least thirty quids' worth—rings bulging through the fine leather gloves.

"In here," she'd said.

He didn't mind. At that time, though not rich, he was richer than he'd ever been before or since. He followed her into the hot crowded store, holding his small square packet of paper.

"What's it called, that stuff of yours?"

They were at a vast series of cosmetic counters.

"*Amorce dangereuse.*"

It cost him nearly six pounds. The price was so ridiculous, her childlike simple acceptance of it so straightforward—she smiled happily, dabbed some of it on his wrist as well as on her own—that he burst out laughing. But he stopped laughing abruptly when she brought her face close to his, laid a hand on his arm and said, whispering, "D'you know what it means, the name of that perfume?"

"Dangerous bait, dangerous allure."

"Yes. Rather apt."

"Come on. I'll buy you a coffee or a drink or something."

"I can't. I have to go. Get me a taxi."

He hadn't much liked being commanded but he hailed a taxi and gave the driver some address in the City she'd told him. While he was holding the door open for her, holding it rather ironically because she took so much for granted, took and tempted and withdrew, she almost floored him with a farewell remark thrown casually over her shoulder.

"Tomorrow, seven, New Quebec Street. O.K.?"

Certainly it was O.K. It was fantastic, also absurd. The taxi moved off, lost itself in the traffic. His hand smelt of *Amorce dangereuse*. Tomorrow, seven, New Quebec Street. He didn't know where New Quebec Street was but he'd find it and he'd be there. An adventure wouldn't do him any harm.

Had he really thought of it like that before it had begun, as an adventure? He remembered that he had and also that it would very likely come to nothing. Arrangements like that which gave the parties thirty hours to think in so often came to nothing . . . But that was how it had happened. Jeff had pinched the last of his paper and, godlike, sent him to Bond Street and to her. Jeff had ruined him, kind Jeff who wouldn't hurt a fly. By rights then, Jeff ought to save him, though no one, of course, could do that except himself.

For he had been ruined. The ream had been started on but only about a hundred of the sheets used up. How can you complete a novel whose purpose is to explore the intricacies of love as you know them when halfway through you find your whole conception has been wrong? When you find that the idea of love on which you based it is vapid and false because you've discovered its true meaning?

Dreaming of her, thinking about her, all night, he was purged of her by the morning. But he knew this wasn't a full catharsis. Possessing him again, his succubus would come to him again in the day and the next night.

A strong furious gale howled about the hovel. No post had come

for days. Pushing her firmly out of a mind that felt excoriated, he
began worrying about his royalty statement. Why hadn't it come?
The last one had arrived early in November, stating the income
he'd made up to the previous June, and he'd had the cheque by
the end of the month. By now, well by now, he ought to have had
the statement for his earnings from June till December. *Maybe
there wasn't anything to come.* In the days when the cheques
had been for several hundreds he'd never considered whether
they'd bother to tell him if there wasn't any money to pay out.
Perhaps they didn't. Perhaps their accountants or cashiers or
whatever just went heartlessly through a list of names and when
they came to him, said, "Oh, Graham Lanceton? Nothing for
him. We can forget him."

He hunted out the November statement which he kept in a
strongbox in the spare bedroom. There was a phone number on
the top of it, the number of their accounts department which was
somewhere out in Surrey, miles from the London office. Gray
knew that any responsible practical author would simply dial that
number, ask to speak to someone in authority and enquire what
the hell had happened to his money. He wasn't keen on doing this.
He didn't feel he could take, at this period of his life, after the
night he'd spent, the brusque voice of some accountant living on a
safe three thousand a year telling him his coffers were empty. What
he'd do, he decided, was wait one more week and if it still hadn't
come he'd phone Peter Marshall. Peter was his own editor and
a very nice bloke who'd been charming and hospitable when *The
Wine of Astonishment* was born into a waiting world and still
charming and kind, though wistful, when it was clear *The Wine of
Astonishment* was to have no siblings. Of course, he'd ask if Gray
was writing anything and remind him they had the first option on
any full-length work of fiction he might produce, but he wouldn't
nag or be unpleasant. He'd promise very kindly and reassuringly
to look into the matter for him and maybe ask him to lunch.

This decision made, he examined his larder. It was obvious that
even he couldn't exist until the end of the month on two cans of
mincemeat, a packet of raspberry jelly, and the rock-hard end
of a Vienna loaf. Money must be acquired. He thought vaguely of
touching Francis (fairly hopeless), of the Social Security (if he
was going to do that he'd pack up and do it in London), of selling

his watch to the shop near the Abbey which was already in possession of his lighter. He didn't want to part with that watch. The only thing would be to use Honoré's money or part of it. The sheer awfulness of using money sent to one for the reaching of one's mother's deathbed chilled him, but he told himself not to be stupid. Presumably, even Honoré wouldn't want him to starve.

It had begun to rain, was now pouring with rain. He put on Mal's oilskins which hung in the cellar and trudged off through the rain to the bank. There he drew out ten pounds which he meant to spend very sparingly indeed, reducing himself if necessary to a diet of milk, bread, and cheese till the cheque came. He had stuffed the money into a pocket of the oilskins and when he fished in it for a pound he brought out with it a crumpled sheet of paper. Reading it, Gray could hardly believe his eyes. It was nearly six months since he'd worn these oilskins—generally he stayed in when it rained—and he must have shoved the letter from his publishers' contracts manager into this pocket sometime in December. It was dated just before Christmas—Oh, Drusilla, that Christmas!—and it informed him that the Yugoslavian serial rights of *The Wine of Astonishment* had been sold for fifty pounds. A measly sum, but money. He must be going to get a cheque, they hadn't forgotten him. Right, he wasn't going to stint himself. He bought fresh meat, frozen vegetables, bread, real butter, and forty cigarettes, one of which he lit as soon as he was outside the shop.

It made him feel a bit faint. Apart from the one he'd had off Isabel, it was the first he'd smoked since the autumn when he'd always helped himself out of her packets of king-sized.

"I'll have to give it up," he'd said then. "It gets on my conscience, Tiny keeping me in fags, because that's what it amounts to."

"It needn't be that way."

"Don't start. Let's have one day of rest."

"You mentioned him. You brought Tiny up."

There had been no talk of Tiny that first time, no ridiculous diminutive bandied between them, only the hint of a husband somewhere in the background.

"Mrs. Harvey Janus? My God, if I were Mr. Harvey Janus I wouldn't be too happy about this, but since I'm not . . ."

Waiting for her in New Quebec Street, in the complex that lies behind Marble Arch, he hadn't even known her name. She was late and he'd begun to think she wasn't coming. The taxi drew up at twenty past seven when he was on the point of giving up, of realising that it wasn't any use wondering where he was going to take her, whether they were going to walk about or go into a pub or what. A hand was thrust out of the window, beckoning him. She sat in the middle of the seat, dressed in white trousers, a fur jacket, a huge black hat and huge black sunglasses. Sunglasses in January . . .

"Hi. Get in."

He looked at the driver who was staring deadpan in front of him.

"Come on, get in." She tapped on the glass. "The Oranmore Hotel, Sussex Gardens. You don't know it? Can't say I'm surprised. Keep going down Sussex Gardens, it's nearly halfway down on the right."

To say he was flabbergasted was an understatement. He got in, raising his eyebrows at her, and then closed the glass panel between them and the driver. "You might put me in the picture."

"Oh, isn't the picture clear? There's an old girl and her husband keep this place. You just register when we get there, and she'll say you want to pay now, don't you, in case you're leaving early in the morning."

"Well, well." He couldn't get over the speed of it, the lack of preamble. "We don't have to leave too early in the morning, do we?"

"We have to leave at nine thirty tonight, ducky. Just two hours we've got. She'll tell us to leave the key on the dressing table when we go. For God's sake, you don't know much about it, do you?"

"My women usually have flats or rooms."

"Well, I'm a married lady and just for your information I'm supposed to be at my yoga class." She giggled and in that giggle he heard a note of childlike triumph. "It's not everyone I'd sacrifice my yoga class for."

"I'll do my best to make it worth your while."

The Oranmore turned out to be an early nineteenth century house that had probably once been a brothel. It had its name in blue neon over the front door, but both the o's were blacked out.

He registered as Mr. and Mrs. Browne—not so much because the name is common as through association with the title of a peerage —and was given a key for number three. The old woman behaved exactly as had been predicted.

On the stairs Gray said, "Do you have a first name, Mrs. Browne?"

"It's Drusilla," she said.

He unlocked the door. The room was small with twin beds, Junk City furniture, a washbasin, a gas ring. Drusilla pulled down the window blind.

"Drusilla what?" he said, going up to her, putting his hands on her waist. It was a very narrow fragile waist and when he touched it she thrust her pelvis forward. "Drusilla what?"

"Janus. Mrs. Harvey Janus."

"My God, if I were Mr. Harvey Janus I shouldn't be too happy about this, but since I'm not . . ." He unfastened the fur jacket. Underneath it she was naked. He had expected that somehow. Already he was beginning to assess her, the kind of things, daring, provocative, direct, she would do. But he gasped just the same and stepped back, looking at her.

She began to laugh. She took off her hat, the knot of pearl strings from her neck, the jacket, sure, he thought, that she had the situation under control, that it was going to be her way. But he'd had enough of her running things.

"Shut up," he said. He picked her up, lifting her bodily, and she stopped laughing, but her lips remained parted and her moonstone eyes grew very wide. "That's better. Two hours, I think you said?"

She had hardly spoken again for those two hours. That time she hadn't told him anything about herself, hadn't asked his name till they were downstairs again, passing the old woman who, playing her part, had wished them a pleasant evening and reminded them not to forget their key. He took her to the tube at Marble Arch and at the entrance, between the newspaper vendors, she said, "Next Thursday? Same time? Same place?"

"Kiss?"

"You've got an oral fixation," she said but she put up her lips which were thin, delicate, unpainted.

He'd bought a packet of cigarettes, lit one and begun to walk all the way back to Notting Hill. How had that cigarette tasted? He couldn't remember. The one he was inhaling on now was ash-flavoured, a hot rasping smoke. He threw it away among the bracken, half hoping it would start a fire and the whole of lonely silent Pocket Lane go up in flames.

That day he hadn't even seen the milkman and he didn't see anyone else to talk to throughout the weekend. No trippers, no picnickers, penetrated so far down the lane. Only old Mr. Tringham passed the hovel, taking his Saturday-evening walk, apparently his only walk of the week. Gray saw him from the window, strolling slowly, reading from a small black book as he walked, but he didn't lift his head or glance to either side of him.

The phone, still off its hook, hung dumb.

CHAPTER 5

In the middle of the week he got the final demand from the Gas
Board and, by the same post, a card from Mal: *Coming home
August. Not to worry. We can share the hovel till you find another place.* Mal wouldn't like it if he came back to find they'd cut
off the gas, which they'd certainly do if the bill wasn't paid by the
weekend. No royalty statement had arrived.

Friday morning and as bitterly cold as November. He'd saved
one cigarette and he lit it as he dialled his publishers' London
number.

"Mr. Marshall is out for the day," said the girl they'd put him on
to. "Can I help?"

"Not really. I'll phone him on Monday."

"Mr. Marshall starts his holiday on Monday, Mr. Lanceton."

That, then, was that. For the rest of the day he debated whether
to phone the Surrey department but by half-past five he still
hadn't done so and then it was too late. He decided to write to
them instead, a good idea which he couldn't understand not having thought of before. When he'd finished the letter and its carbon
copy, he sat with his fingers resting on the typewriter keys, thinking about the last time he'd used the machine. The ribbon was
nearly worn clean. He'd worn the ribbon out writing those letters
to Tiny. The absurdity, the grotesquerie, of that business made
him wince. How had he ever been such a fool as to let her persuade him so far, to type those dreadful letters with her standing
over him? He'd better make sure he remembered that next time
he was tempted into phoning her.

The phone was on its hook but it had a passive look as if it were
asleep. It hadn't made a sound since it had opened its mouth more
than a week ago to let Francis speak through it, and he hadn't
again contemplated ringing that Loughton number. He took his

letter and stuck it on the hall window sill. Tomorrow he'd buy a
stamp for it.

Saturday was bath day. Until he came to the hovel he'd hardly
ever passed a day without a bath. Now he understood why the
poor smell and he saw how insensitive are those bathroom owners
who won't sympathise with the dirty because washing is free and
soap cheap. When you wanted a bath at the hovel you had to heat
water up in two saucepans and a bucket and then you didn't get
enough hot to cover your knees. Back in the days when he was
Drusilla's lover he went through this ritual quite often or stood
up at the sink and washed himself all over in cold water. You
needed an incentive to do that. After the parting there wasn't
much incentive. The milkman never got very close to him and he
was past caring what the librarian thought, so these days he had
a bath on Saturday and washed his hair in the bath. Then he used
the same water to wash his jeans and T-shirt.

All the week he used the bath as a repository for dirty sheets,
chucking them on to the floor as a sort of absorbent mat when
he was actually in the water. He hadn't been to the launderette
for ages and they were getting mildewed. He washed his hair and
was just rinsing it, dipping it into the scummy water, when the
phone belched out its warning click. Ten seconds later it began
to ring. It couldn't be Drusilla, who went shopping with Tiny on
Saturdays, so he let it ring till he was out of the bath and wrapped
in a grey towel.

Cursing, leaving footprints on the stone hall floor, he went
into the "lounge" and picked up the phone. Honoré.

"I disarrange you, I think, my son."

For once, his choice of a word was apt. Gray gathered the damp
folds around him, forgetting to talk French in the slight anxiety
the call had caused.

"How's Mother?"

"That is for why I call. Mother goes better now so I say, I call
to Gray-arm and give him these good news so he is no more
unquiet."

Wants his money back, more like, thought Gray. "*Que vous êtes
gentil, Honoré. Entendez, votre argent est arrivé dans la banque.
Il paraît que je n'en aurai besoin, mais . . .*"

Trust Honoré to interrupt before he'd reached the point of asking whether he could keep the money a little longer.

"Like you say, Gray-arm, you need my money no more and old Honoré know you so well." Gray could see the brown finger wagging, the avaricious knowing smile. "Ah, so well! Better for you and me you send him back, hein? Before you spend him for wine and women."

"This call," said Gray, whose French wasn't adequate for what he wanted to say, "is going to cost you a lot."

"Very sure, so I say goodbye. You send him back today and I get you again if Mummy go less good."

"Right, but don't phone next weekend as I'll be at Francis Croy's place. *Vous comprenez?*"

Honoré said he understood very well and rang off. Gray ran the water out of the bath. It was evident his mother wasn't dying and the money wasn't going to be needed for any trip to France, but it was absurd Honoré wanting it back at once. What difference could it make to him whether he got it now or in, say, a fortnight? Didn't he own his own house and car, all bought out of Gray's father's life assurance? Now he knew his mother wasn't dying, Gray allowed himself to dwell on a usually forbidden subject— her will. Under that, he and Honoré were to have equal shares. When she died . . . No, he'd let himself sink into enough deep dishonour without that. She wasn't going to die for years and when she did he'd have a flat of his own in London and a string of successful novels behind him.

Because it had begun to rain, he draped his wet clothes over a line he put up in the "lounge" and read *Anthony Absolute* dejectedly till the milkman came. The lane had turned bright yellow in the wet, the colour of gamboge in a paintbox, and the wheels of the can were plastered with it.

"Lovely weather for ducks. Pity we're not ducks."

Gray said savagely, "God, how I hate this place."

"Don't be like that, Mr. L. There's some as likes it."

"Where do you live?"

"Walthamstow," said the milkman stoically.

"I wish I lived in Walthamstow. Beats me how anyone can live out here from choice."

"The Forest's very desirable residentially like. Some of them big houses Loughton way are fetching prices you wouldn't believe. Real high-class suburbia, they are."

"Christ," said Gray feelingly. He didn't like to see the milkman look so bewildered and crestfallen, and to know he'd been the cause of it. But his words had gone in like a knife teasing an already open wound.

"Where do you live?" he'd said, drawing one finger down the smooth white body, white as lily petals, blue-veined. "I don't know anything about you."

"Loughton."

"Where's that, for God's sake?"

She made a face, turning her shoulder, giggling. "Real high-class suburbia. You keep going forever down the Central Line."

"D'you like that?"

"I have to live where Tiny lives, don't I?"

"*Tiny?*"

"It's just a nickname, everyone calls him that." She put up her arms, holding him, saying, "I like you a lot, Mr. Browne. Let's keep this going a bit longer, shall we?"

"Not in this dump. Can't I come to your suburb?"

"And have all my neighbours dropping hints to Tiny at bridge parties?"

"Then you'll have to come to Tranmere Villas. Will you mind other people being in the flat?"

"You know," she said, "I think I'll like it."

His eyebrows went up. "That doesn't quite go with the Loughton housewife bit."

"Damn you, I married him when I was eighteen, that's six years ago. I didn't know then. I didn't know a thing."

"You don't have to stay with him."

"I have to stay," she said. "God, who asked you to criticise my life style, Mr. Justice Browne? That's not what I miss my yoga class for. That's not what I strip off for. If you don't want it I'll soon find someone who does."

Toughness, sophistication, hung on her like a call girl's see-through dress on an ingenue. For that's what she was, an ingenue, a green girl, a late starter and he was only her second lover. She didn't admit she knew the Oranmore because she'd been there with her first, or New Quebec Street because she'd once bought a vase in the pottery shop. She didn't admit it but he was a writer and he could tell. He could tell she got that smart wisecracking talk of hers out of books, bought her Harrods clothes because she'd seen them advertised in magazines at the hairdresser's, her hard brittle manner out of films seen at Essex Odeons. He wanted to find the little girl that existed somewhere underneath it all and she wanted equally hard to stop him knowing the little girl was there.

When he met her at the station he knew at once she'd never been to Notting Hill before. If he hadn't stopped her she'd have crossed the street to the Campden Hill side. No one else seeing her would have guessed the underlying naivety from her appearance, the long purple dress, the silver chains, the purple paint on her mouth, for her face was made up that night. He took her to the flat and it was he, not she, who was put off by the bedroom door being accidentally opened and as quickly closed again. So he took her for a walk up through the drab, exotic, decaying streets of North Kensington, into little pubs with red plush and gilded saloon bars. They saw a sad skeletal boy giving himself a fix in a telephone box. She didn't find it sad; her eyes were greedy for what she called life and she made out so well that he almost forgot how innocent she was.

"That cinema," he said, "they smoke in there. The air hangs blue with it."

"They what? Everyone smokes in cinemas."

"I meant pot, Drusilla."

The little girl turned on him furiously. "Damn you! I can't help not knowing. I want to know. I want to be free to know things and you—you bloody laugh at me. I want to go home."

And then he had really laughed at her, poor little child in adult's clothes, who wanted both to be free and to be safe at home; little sheltered girl, protected all her life. Tantalised by innocence that should have, but didn't, go hand in hand with prudery, thinking only of the delight she gave him, he hadn't considered the full significance of a child in a grown-up body. He hadn't thought then what it must mean—to have an adult's subtlety, command of language and sensual capacity without an adult's humanity.

"I didn't know you owned a house," Gray said when Mal dropped in at Tranmere Villas one night, a fortnight before he left for Japan.

"It's just a hovel, no hot water, no mod cons. I had a Premium Bond come up about five years ago and someone said property was the thing, so I bought this place. I go to it sometimes at weekends."

"Where is it, for God's sake?"

"Epping Forest, near Waltham Abbey. I was born near there. I mention it because I was wondering if you'd like to take it on while I'm away."

"Me? I'm a Londoner. It's not my scene."

"It's just the place for you to write your masterpiece. Isolated, dead quiet. I wouldn't want rent. But I do want someone to see it doesn't fall into rack and ruin."

"Sorry. You've come to the wrong shop."

"Maybe the right shop," said Mal, "would be an estate agent's. I'd better try and sell it. I'll get hold of an agent in Enfield or Loughton."

"*Loughton?*"

"It's four miles from there. D'you know it?"

"In a sort of way I do."

So he'd agreed to take care of the hovel because it was only four miles from Loughton . . .

"A funny sort of lane east of Waltham Abbey?" said Drusilla when he told her.

" 'The beds i' the East are soft.' "

"Beds, floor, stairs, kitchen table, it's all the same to me, ducky. I expect I could pop over quite often."

The beds were no longer soft. There is no bed so hard as the one deserted by one's lover. For her sake he had come here and now she was gone there was no longer anything to keep him but poverty.

He paid the gas bill, went to the library (*The Sun Is My Un-*

doing, The Green Hat, King Solomon's Mines) but forgot to buy a stamp. Well, he'd buy one on Monday, post the letter, and as soon as the money came—as soon as there was a definite prospect of the money—he'd shake the dust of this place off his feet for ever.

Mr. Tringham went by at six thirty, reading his book. He too could become like that one day, Gray thought, a hermit who has grown to love his solitude and who jealously preserves it. He must get away.

CHAPTER 6

He finally posted the letter on Wednesday. By that time he had just seven pounds of Honoré's money left and he'd have to save that for incidental expenses in London. There were bound to be plenty. Francis would expect a bottle and some cigarettes and probably a meal out. By Monday he'd be skint but by Monday the statement and the cheque would have arrived. He'd allow himself a week at the hovel to clean it up a bit—get some of those stains off the bedroom haircord, for instance—and then he'd ask Jeff to cart his stuff away the following weekend. Francis, if handled right, might just possibly agree to put him up for a week or two. A happier state of affairs, of course, would be to meet some girl at the party who had a room of her own and who liked him enough to shack up with him. He'd have to like her enough too and that would be the trouble. Drusilla had spoilt other women for him.

"After me," she'd said, "other women'll be like cold mutton."

"You got that out of a book. Sounds like Maugham."

"So what? It's true."

"Maybe. And what will other blokes be like for you?"

"You scared I might go back to Ian?"

Ian was his predecessor, a sportsman, tennis coach or something, the man who'd introduced her to the amenities of the Oranmore. Gray couldn't play her game of pretending not to care. He was beginning to care quite a lot.

"Yes, I'm scared of losing you, Dru."

At first she'd scoffed at the hovel. She'd gone all over it, laughing incredulously, amazed that there was no bathroom, no indoor loo. But he'd let her know it wasn't the thing these days to be snobbish about material things. She learned fast and soon she was as slapdash about the place as he, using saucers for ashtrays and putting her teacup on the floor.

"Who cleans your place?" he'd asked.

"A woman comes in every day," she said, but still he didn't understand quite how rich she was.

The first time she came to the hovel he walked back down the lane with her to where she'd left her car. A Mini, he expected it to be, and when he saw the E-type, he said, "Come off it. You're joking."

"Am I? Look, the key fits."

"Who does it really belong to? Tiny?"

"It's mine. Tiny gave it me for my last birthday."

"God, he must be rolling in it. What does he do?"

"Property," she said. "Directorships. He's got his finger in a lot of very lucrative pies."

And then he knew she'd been telling the truth when she said her dress came from Dior, that the rings she took off when they made love were platinum and diamonds. Tiny wasn't just well-off, making ends meet comfortably on five thousand a year. He was rich by anyone's standards, what even rich people call rich. But it had never occurred to Gray to try and get his hands on some of it. In fact, he avoided the subject of her wealth, careful not to let any of it rub off on him via her. It seemed ugly that he who had stolen—at least, temporarily—Tiny's wife, should be enriched even in a small way by Tiny's money.

She'd read his book and liked it but she never nagged him about writing anything else. That was one of the things he liked about her. She wasn't moralistic. No "You ought to work, think of your future, settle down," from her. Preaching had no place in her nature. She was a hedonist, enjoying herself, taking from whoever was prepared to give, but giving of herself amply in return. It was because she gave so much, all her body, all her thoughts, reserving nothing, confessing to him with a child's simplicity every need and emotion which most girls would have kept hidden, that it became not a matter of liking her any more, but of love. He knew he was in love with her when one day she didn't phone and he spent the day thinking she was dead or gone back to Ian, the night lying wakeful until the next day she did phone and the world was transformed for him.

She'd come to him in the mornings, in the afternoons, but Thursday had been their evening together. Thursday was the one evening she could be sure of being free of Tiny, and no Thursday ever passed without his thinking of her alone, perhaps taking her own receiver off as he was doing now. He stood looking at the deadened instrument for some time, just standing there and looking at it. Alexander Graham Bell had a lot to answer for. There was something sinister, frightening, dreadful, about a telephone. It seemed to him as if all the magic which in ancient times had manifested itself in divination, in strange communions across land and ocean, in soul-binding spells, conjurations, fetishes that could kill by the power of fright, were now condensed and concentrated into the compact black body of this instrument. A night of sleep might depend on it, days of happiness; its ring could break a life or raise hilarity, wake the near-dead, bring to the tense body utter relaxation. And its power was inescapable. While you possessed one of its allotropes—or it possessed you—you were constantly subject to it, for though you might disarm it as he had just done, it wasn't really gagged. It always retained its ultimate secret weapon, the braying howl, the long-drawn-out crescendo cry of an encaged but still dangerous animal, which was its last resort. Hadn't she once put the howlers on him when, by chance—no leaving the receiver off deliberately in those days—he'd replaced it imperfectly?

"Playing hard to get, lovey? You can't get away from me as easily as that."

But he had got away and into his miserable high-principled freedom, though not easily, not easily—how long would it take before it got easier? He slammed the door shut on the muck and dust and the immobilised phone and went upstairs to look out some gear to wear at Francis's party. His one decent pair of trousers, his one good jacket, were rolled up in the bottom of the bedroom cupboard where he'd slung them after that London weekend with Drusilla. He took out the cream silk shirt, dirty and creased, *Amorce dangereuse* breathing from its creases as he unfolded it. In the darkening bedroom with its low ceiling, rain pattering overhead on the slates, he knelt on the haircord, on the tea stains, and pressed the silk against his face, smelling her smell.

"Shall I wear your shirt to go out in? Do I look good?"

"You look great," he'd said. Fox-gold hair cloaking the cream silk, blood-red fingernails like jewels scattered on it, her naked breasts swelling out the thin, almost transparent stuff. "What am I supposed to wear? Your blouse?"

"I'll buy you another shirt, ducky."

"Not with Tiny's money, you won't."

Tiny had gone on a business trip to Spain. That was how they'd managed the weekend. Until then he'd never had a whole night with her. He'd wanted Cornwall but she'd insisted on London, the Oranmore.

"I want to go to way-out places and do decadent things. I want to explore vice."

"Doriana Gray," he said.

"Damn you, you don't understand. You've been free to do what you like for ten years. I had my father keeping me down and I went straight from him to Tiny. There's always been someone bloody looking after me. I can't go out without publishing where I'm going or making up lies. I'll have to phone Madrid in a minute to keep him quiet. You don't know what it's like never to do *anything.*"

"Darling," he'd said very tenderly, "they're nothing, these things, when you're used to them. They're boring, they're ordinary. Imagine the people who think living in your place and having your clothes and your car and your holidays the acme of sophistication. But to you it's all—ordinary."

She took no notice of him. "I want to go to awful places and smoke pot and see live shows and blue films."

Christ, he'd thought, she was so *young.* That's what he'd thought then, that it was all bravado, and they'd quarrelled because his London wasn't the London she said she wanted; because he wouldn't take her round Soho or to the drag ball she'd seen advertised, but to little cinemas with mid-'30s kitsch décor, Edwardian pubs, the Orangery in Kensington Gardens, the Mercury Theatre, the mewses, and the canal at Little Venice. But she'd enjoyed it, after all, making him laugh with her shrewd comments and her flashes of surprising sensitivity. When the weekend was over and he back at the hovel, he'd missed her with a real aching agony and it wasn't just laziness that made him not wash out the shirt. He kept it unwashed for the scent that imbued it, knowing even then when their affair was a year old and almost at its zenith that the time would come when he'd need objects to evoke memory, objects in which life is petrified, more present (as he'd read somewhere) than in any of its actual moments.

Well, the time had come, the time to remember and the time to wash away memories. He took the clothes downstairs, washed the shirt and went down into the cellar. He hadn't got an electric iron but there was an old flatiron in the cellar, left there by the occupant before Mal.

The cellar steps were steep, leading about fifteen feet into the bowels of the Forest. It was a brick-walled, stone-flagged chamber where he kept his paraffin and where former owners had left a broken bike, an antique sewing machine, ancient suitcases and stacks of damp yellowish newspapers. The iron was among these newspapers along with the thing Gray thought was called a trivet. He took it up to the kitchen and put it on the gas.

Now that he'd made up his mind to leave the hovel, he no longer had to pretend to himself that this kitchen where he'd spent the greater part of two years was less horrible and squalid than it was. In all that time he'd never really cleaned it and the condensation of cooking and gas fumes had run unchecked, unwiped, down the pea-green painted walls. The sink was scored all over with brown cracks and under it was a ganglion of grime-coated pipes, hung with dirty cloths. An unshaded bulb, hanging from the veined and cobwebby ceiling, illuminated the place dully, showing up the cigarette burns and the tea stains on the line. Mal had asked him to see it didn't go to rack and ruin, so it was only fair to Mal to clean it up. Next week he'd have a real spring clean.

It was pitch-dark outside, soundless but for the faint pattering of rain. He got up out of the Windsor chair and spread his velvet trousers on top of the bath cover. He'd never handled the flatiron before, only electric irons with insulated handles. Of course he knew very well you needed a kettle holder or an old sock or something before you got hold of a hot iron bar, but he'd acted instinctively, without thought. The pain was violent, scarlet, roaring. He dropped the iron with a shout, cursing, clutching his burnt hand and falling back into the chair.

When he looked at his hand there was a bright red weal across the palm. And the pain travelled up his wrist, his arm, a pain that was almost a noise in the silence. After a while he got up and held his hand under the cold tap. The shock was so great that it brought tears to his eyes, and when he'd turned off the tap and dried his hand, the tears didn't stop. He began to cry in earnest, abandoning himself to a storm of weeping, sobbing against his folded arms. He knew he wasn't crying because he'd burnt his hand, though that had caused the first tears. Full release had never come to him before, the release of all that pent-up pain. He was crying now for Drusilla, for obsession unconquered, for loneliness and squalor and waste.

His hand was stiff and painful. It felt enormous, a lump of raw flesh hanging from the end of his arm. He hung it outside the bed, the sour sweat-smelling sheets, and lay, tossing and turning, until the birds started their dawn song and pale grey waterish light came through the faded curtains. Then at last he slept, falling at once into a dream of Tiny.

He'd never seen Drusilla's husband and she'd never described him to him. She hadn't needed to. He knew very well what a forty-year-old rich property dealer would look like, a man whose facetious parents or envious school fellows had called Tiny because even as a child he'd been huge and gross. A vast man with thinning black hair, who drank hard, smoked heavily, was vulgar, taciturn, and jealous.

"What does he talk about? What do you do when you're alone together?"

She giggled. "He's a man, isn't he? What d'you think we do?"

"Drusilla, I don't mean that." (Too painful to think of, imagine, then or now). "What have you got in common?"

"We have the neighbours in for drinks. We go shopping on Saturdays. He's got his old mum that we go and see once a week after the shopping, and that's a right drag. As a matter of fact, he collects old coins."

"Oh, *darling!*"

"It's not my bloody fault. He's got his car, it's a red Bentley, and we go out in that to eating places with his dreary middle-aged mates."

Tiny was in that car, the red Bentley he'd never seen, when he dreamed about him. He was standing by the side of the road, one of the Forest roads that converge at the Wake Arms, when the Bentley came up the A.11. Tiny was at the wheel. He knew it was Tiny, the man in the car was so big and so flashily dressed. Besides, one does know these things in dreams. The car screamed to a slower speed, slower than the eighty it had been doing, and then Tiny roared on but not round the roundabout. He careered over the grass mound in the middle of it, the car leaping and jerking until it bounded into the air and crashed, bursting into flames among the scattering, hooting traffic that was coming the other way.

Gray crept forward along with the other people who crowded round the burning car. The car was burning, Tiny was burning, a living torch. But he was still conscious, still aware. He lifted his charred, flame-licked face and shouted at Gray, "Murderer! Murderer!"

Gray tried to stop him, thrusting his hand over that red-hot mouth that was a glowing cinder now, crushing the words away, plunging his fingers into a cavern of fire. He woke up, thrashing about on the bed, staring at his hand which bore on its palm the mark of Tiny's burning lips.

CHAPTER 7

A long oval blister crossed his palm from forefinger to wrist. He lay in bed most of Thursday, sleeping intermittently, waking to stare obsessively at his injured hand. His hand was branded, and it seemed to him, because of that vivid terrible dream, that the burn was Tiny's way of punishing him.

When at last he got up it was early evening, Thursday evening. He took the phone receiver off carefully, holding it between thumb and forefinger. In the cloudy spotted mirror his face looked cadaverous, the eye sockets like hollow bruises. A line from some half-forgotten play, Shakespeare probably, came to him and, staring at his face and the burnt hand which had gone up to shield it, he whispered it aloud, Let me know my trespass by its own visage. Let me know my trespass . . . He had trespassed against Tiny, against her perhaps, most violently against himself.

He slept heavily that night, sliding from dream to dream without any return to consciousness, and in the morning his hand was still throbbing, pulsating like an overtaxed heart. The bandage he made from strips torn off a sheet didn't help much, and he had to make tea and iron the shirt and trousers with his left hand. There was a small hole in the trousers just below the right knee, a hole Drusilla had made, brushing against him with her cigarette, but it would just have to stay there as darning was now beyond him.

"I can't mend it," she'd said. "I wouldn't know how."

"What d'you do when your own things need mending?"

"Throw them away. Do I look as if I wore mended clothes?"

"I can't throw them away, Dru. I can't afford to."

She did something very rare with her. She kissed him. She brought her delicate lips that really were like the petals of some flower, an orchid perhaps, up to his face and kissed him on the corner of his mouth. It was a very tender gesture, and something in him, something that had been mocked by her too often to be anything but wary at tenderness, made him say, "Careful, Drusilla, you'll be loving me next."

"Damn you! What do I care if you bloody starve? I'd give you money, only you won't take it."

"Not Tiny's, I won't."

The trousers had never been mended and nor had his watch which had stopped the same week and refused to go again. On the Thursday night when they'd made love in the hovel, had walked in the forest in the moonlight and at last were sitting in the "lounge" in front of the fire they'd made, she gave him a new watch, the one he now wore, the one he'd never sell no matter what.

"It's beautiful and I love you, but I can't take it."

"Tiny didn't pay for it. My dad gave me a cheque for my birthday."

"Coals to Newcastle, that must have been."

"Maybe, but these coals aren't tainted. Don't you like it?"

"I love it. It makes me feel like a kept man but I love it."

Moonstone eyes, the colour of transparent cloud through which the blue sky shows; white skin, blue-veined at the temples; hair like the pale hot flames that warmed them.

"I'd like you to be a kept man. I'd like Tiny to die so that we could have all that loot for us."

"What, marry me, d'you mean?" The thought had never before crossed his mind.

"To hell with marriage! Don't talk about it." She shuddered, speaking of marriage as some people speak of cancer. "You don't want to get married, do you?"

"I'd like to live with you, Dru, be with you all the time. Marriage or not, I shouldn't mind."

"The house alone'd fetch a fortune. He's got hundreds of thousands in the bank and shares and whatever. Be nice if he had a coronary, wouldn't it?"

"Not for him," he said.

The watch she'd given him just ten months before the end of it all told him now it was twelve noon. But it was Friday so the milkman wouldn't get there till nearly three. He went down into

Waltham Abbey, returned the library books but took out no fresh ones, and at the bank drew out seven pounds, thus emptying his account. On the way back he met the milkman who gave him a lift to the hovel on his van.

"Going to be a scorcher tomorrow, I reckon," said the milkman. "If you're out when I come I'll pop the milk in the shade, shall I?"

"I shan't want any milk till Monday, thanks. Come to think of it, I shan't want any more milk ever. I'm moving out next week." That would spur his going. He could always buy milk when he went into Waltham Abbey for the few days that remained to him of next week. "Getting out of here for good," he said.

The milkman looked quite upset. "Well, it'll make my work lighter. I shan't have to come all the way down here. But I'll miss you, Mr. L. No matter how low I felt, I could always count on you to cheer me up."

One of the Pagliacci, Gray thought, one of the sad clowns. All the time he'd been so wretched the milkman had seen him as a lighthearted joker. He'd have liked to have achieved just one last mild wisecrack—very little wit was ever needed—but he couldn't manage it. "Yes, well, we've had a good laugh, haven't we, one way and another?"

"It's what makes the world go round," said the milkman. "Er—you won't mind me pointing out you owe me forty-two pee?"

Gray paid him.

"When are you going?"

"Tomorrow, but I'll be back again for a few days."

The milkman gave him his change and then, unexpectedly, held out his hand. Gray had to take it and have his own blistered hand shaken agonisingly. "See you, then."

"See you," said Gray, though the chances were he'd never see the milkman again.

He had nothing to read and his burnt hand kept him from starting on the spring clean. Instead, he passed the rest of that hot day sorting through his papers, some of which were in the strongbox, the rest in an untidy heap on top of the disused range. It wasn't a task calculated to cheer him. Among the pile on the range, he found four old royalty statements, each one showing a smaller amount than its predecessor, a demand for back tax he hadn't paid, and—most troubling of all—a dozen drafts of, or attempts at, letters to Tiny.

Rereading them made him feel a little sick. They were only pieces of paper, creased, soiled, thumb-marked, some bearing no more than two or three lines of typed words, but the motive behind them had been destructive. They had been designed to lure a man to that holocaust, realised, as it happened, only in dreams of fire.

Each one was dated, and the whole series spanned a period from June to December. Although he'd never really intended that any one of them should be sent, although he'd typed them only to humour her, he felt that he was looking at a side of himself which he didn't know at all, at a cruel and subtle alter ego which lay buried deep under the layers of idleness, talent, humanity, and saneness, but was nevertheless real. Why hadn't he burned them long ago? At any rate, he'd burn them now.

In a space that was clear of nettles down by the back fence he made a little fire and fed it with the letters. A thin spire of smoke, sequinned with red sparks, rose into the night air. It was all over and dead in five minutes.

He'd never before seen the Forest in its golden cloak of morning mist, it was so rare for him to be up this early. The squirrel was sitting where the fire had been.

"You can move in if you like," Gray said. "Be my guest. You can keep your nuts in the cellar."

He bathed and put on a T-shirt and the velvet trousers, hoping the hole didn't show. The silk shirt was to be saved for Sunday night and he packed it into his bag along with his toothbrush and a sweater. There was no point in going into the "lounge" before he left or changing the filthy sheets, but he washed the dishes with his left hand and left them to drain. By nine he was on his way to the station at Waltham Cross.

The tube didn't come out this way. You had to catch a train that went from Harlow (or somewhere equally remote) to Liverpool Street. The powers that be, he often thought, had been singularly narrow in their attitude to the travel requirements of the residents of Pocket Lane and its environs. It was possible to go to London or Enfield or places no one would want to go to in Hertfordshire, extremely difficult to get to Loughton or anywhere in that direction except by car or on foot. The only time he'd been to Loughton he'd walked to the Wake Arms and caught the 20 bus that came from Epping.

"I can't think why you want to see my place," she'd said, "but you can if you want. You could come on Thursday evening. Just this once though, mind. If the neighbours see you I'll say you came selling encyclopaedias. They think I have it off with the tradesmen, anyway."

"I hope you'll have it off with this tradesman."

"Well, you know me," she said.

Did he? The Thursday they'd chosen was in early spring when the trees of the Forest weren't yet in leaf but hazed all over with the golden-brown of their buds, when the flowers were on the blackthorn but the holly berries still scarlet. He caught the bus to one of the fringe-of-the-forest ponds, a water-filled gravel pit, overlooked by the large houses that sprang up in this district on every bit of land they'd let you build on. Everywhere there were trees, so that in summer the houses would seem to stand in the Forest itself. It would be, he'd decided, in such a one that she lived, a four-bedroomed Tudor-style villa.

She'd drawn him a little plan and told him which way to go. The sun had gone but it would be an hour yet before it was dark. He walked along a road on one side of which open green land, dotted with bushes, fell away into a valley. Beyond this valley the Forest rose in blue-black waves. On the other side were old cottages of weatherboard and slate like the hovel, new houses, a pub. They called the district he was approaching, the part where she lived, Little Cornwall, because it was exceptionally hilly and from its hills, she'd said, you could look down into Loughton which lay in a basin below, and then on and on over Metropolitan Essex, over the "nice" suburbs, the distant docks, and see sometimes the light shining on the Thames.

It was too dark for that by the time he'd reached the top of the hill. Lights were coming out everywhere over the blue spread of land. He turned off along Wintry Hill and found himself in a lane—gates in high fences, trees overhanging, long drives disappearing into shrubberies and leading to distant hidden houses.

The Forest hung behind them, densely black against a primrose sky. And he felt that this was very different from the area around the pond. This was grandeur, magnificence and, in a way, awesome. Her house (Tiny's house) was called Combe Park, a name which she'd got haughty and self-conscious about when she'd mentioned it and which he'd laughed at as absurdly pretentious.

But it wasn't pretentious. He came to the end of the lane to face wrought-iron gates which stood open. The name COMBE PARK was lettered on these gates and he saw at once that it hadn't been bestowed with the intention to impress on some detached three-bedroomed affair. The grounds were enormous, comprising lawns and flowerbeds and an orchard which was a mass of daffodils, a pond as large as a small lake and ringed with rockeries on which cypresses, twice as tall as a man, were dwarfed by overhanging willows and cedars. The neighbours would have needed periscopes as well as binoculars to see the house through those tree screens. Not that the house itself wasn't large. He saw an enormous box, flat-roofed and balconied, part of white stucco, part cedar-boarded, with a kind of glass sun lounge on its roof and a York stone terrace spreading away from front door and plate-glass picture windows. The terrace was set about with white metal furniture and evergreens in marble urns.

At first he'd thought it couldn't be hers, that he couldn't know (let alone, love) anyone that affluent. But this was Combe Park all right. The triple (quadruple? quintuple?) garage, a large house in itself, had its doors wide open and inside he could see the E-type, reduced to Mini scale by the vastness of its shelter. There was no red Bentley to keep it company but, just the same, he didn't move from the position he'd taken up and in which he felt frozen outside the gate. He didn't want to go in, he wasn't going in. He forgot then that it was he who'd invited himself, who'd insisted, and thought only of his poverty, her wealth, and that if he set foot on that drive and began to walk up it under her eye, he'd feel like the village boy sent for by the squire's lady. And he might start getting greedy too. He might start thinking of that coronary she'd wished on Tiny.

So he'd walked back to the bus stop, caught the bus after half an hour's wait, walked back to Pocket Lane, and before he'd been in the house five minutes the phone started.

"Damn you! I saw you at the gate and I came down to open the door and you'd bloody gone. Were you scared?"

"Only of your money, Drusilla."

"God," she'd said, drawling then, the little girl voice submerged in the lady-who-picks-up-men voice. "It could all be yours if he had a heart attack or a car crash. Yours and mine. Wouldn't that be super?"

"That's just pointless fantasy," he'd said.

He got on at Liverpool Street tube station and out at Bayswater. Queensway, very lively with its clothes shops and fruit shops, Whiteley's cupola, the interesting trendy people, cheered him up. And the weather was perfect, the bright blue sky giving Porchester Hall an almost classical look to his London-starved eyes.

Francis lived in one of those old streets of Victorian houses, each one separate and each one different, each in its garden of very old London shrubs and town flowers that seem faded to pale pinks and golds by dust and hard light, which lie to the north of Westbourne Grove. Francis's flat was the conservatory of one of these houses, a red and blue crystal palace partitioned off into two rooms with bathroom and kitchen added.

He opened the crimson glass door to Gray and said, "Hallo, you're late. Just as well I don't have to meet my aunt after all. We can get on with moving the furniture. This is Charmian."

Gray said, "Hi," and wished he hadn't because Hi was what he said to Drusilla. Charmian, who in any case, was probably booked for Francis, wasn't the girl to rid him of Drusilla, being plump, snub-nosed, and ungainly. She had a lot of jolly fair curls and she wore a very short skirt which showed her fat thighs. While she looked on, sitting cross-legged on a windowsill and eating a banana, Gray helped Francis move the enormous Victorian sideboard and tallboy from the living room into the bedroom, and moved beds out to make divans for exhausted, lecherous or stoned guests. His hand was thickly bandaged but it throbbed, sending shafts of pain up his arm.

Francis said discouragingly, "I tried to phone you to tell you not to bother to come till tomorrow but your line's always engaged. I suppose you leave the receiver off. What are you scared of? Your creditors?"

Charmian laughed shrilly. The receiver was still off, Gray realised. It had been off since Thursday evening.

Presently the men arrived to fix up the winking lights. They took hours about it, drinking very inferior tea made by Charmian with tea bags. Gray wondered when they were going to get a meal, as both Francis and the girl had said they were on diets. At last the men went and the three of them went down to the Redan where Francis and Charmian drank orange juice in accordance with their diets and Gray drank beer. It was nearly six o'clock.

"I hope you've got some money on you. I've left mine in my other jacket."

Gray said he had. He thought Francis lucky to possess another jacket. "When you've had that orange juice, maybe you'll go back and fetch it and then we can eat somewhere."

"Well, actually, Charmian and I are dining with some people we don't know very well. I only mention that about our not knowing them to show we can't exactly take a stranger with us."

"Not very well," said Charmian. She had been staring fixedly at Gray for some minutes and now she launched suddenly into a lecture. "I read your book. Francis lent it to me. I think it's terrible your not writing anything else. I mean, not doing any work at all. I know it's nothing to do with me . . ."

"No, it isn't."

"Steady, now," said Francis.

The girl took no notice of either of them. "You live in that dreadful place like a sort of country hippy and you're just not together. You're all spaced out. I mean, you leave your phone off for days and when you're with people half the time you're not, if you know what I mean. You're off on a sort of trip of your own. No one would *believe* you'd written *The Wine of Astonishment.*"

Gray shrugged. "I'm going to eat and then I'm going to the pictures," he said. "Have a good time with the people you don't know."

Of course she was quite right, he thought, as he went off on his own to find a cheap Chinese restaurant. It wasn't her business and she was a stupid boring girl, but she was right. He'd have to do something and quick.

The people who sat at the tables around him and something she'd said about a trip were reawakening memories he'd thought London would help to exorcise. He sucked a sugar loaf from the paper-thin china bowl in front of him. It was only a sugar loaf. It wouldn't distort reality any more than he could distort it himself . . .

Drusilla in spring, Drusilla before the letters started—"You know a lot of weird freaky people, don't you?" she'd said. "All that Westbourne Grove-Portobello Road lot?"

"I know some."

"Gray, could you get hold of some LSD?"

He was so unused to hearing it called by those initials that, although decimal coinage had been in for a year and more, he said, "Money? How?"

"Oh, God, I don't mean money. I mean acid. Could you get us some acid?"

CHAPTER 8

First the Classic Cinema in Praed Street where he saw an old Swedish film full of pale Strindbergian people in Grimms Fairy Tale forests, and then, for the night was warm and clear, he walked southwards across Sussex Gardens.

The Oranmore wasn't there any more. Or, rather, it was there but it had been painted glistening white and a new name, this time in veridian neon, stuck up above the portico: THE GRAND EUROPA. Combe Park hadn't been a pretentious name but this was. A large German tourist coach was parked outside, disgorging what looked like the Heidelberg Community Centre ladies' package tour. The ladies, large and tired, all wearing hats, drifted with bewilderment through the front door, driven by brisk polyglot couriers. Gray wondered if the old woman would give them each a key and tell them to leave it on the dressing table because she knew they'd want to leave early in the morning. He felt sorry for the German ladies, told, no doubt, that they'd be staying in the heart of trendy London, in a quaint period hotel within walking distance of Oxford Street and the Park, and then landing up at the Oranmore. It didn't, after all, hold for any of them his own memories of lost splendour.

A young porter came down the steps to help them; behind him a bright young woman. It seemed as if the old people had gone, along with the old name. He turned down the Edgware Road, a great ache inside him, a hungry longing to hear her voice just once more.

The letters slid into a dark curtained recess of his memory. In the light exposed parts, as bright as this blazingly lit street, all the joy she'd brought him seemed to shine. If he could have her without demands, without complications! It was impossible—yet to hear her voice just once?

Suppose he were to phone her now? It was nearly midnight.
She'd be in one of the beds in the room she shared with Tiny,
the room that overlooked those black waves of forest. Tiny would
be there too, asleep possibly; possibly sitting up reading one of
those books he was so fond of, memoirs of some tycoon or retired general, and she'd be reading a novel. Although he'd never
been in the bedroom, he could see them, the gross bloated man,
curly black hair showing at the open neck of red and black silk
pyjamas, the slim girl in white frills, her fiery hair loose, and
around them all the lush appointments of a rich man's bedroom,
white pile rugs, white brocade curtains, Pompadour furniture,
ivory and gold. Between them, the white, silent, threatening
phone.

He could phone her but not speak to her. That way he'd hear
her voice. When she didn't know who was calling, when it wasn't
someone to say "Hi" to, she just said "Yes?" with cool indifference. She'd say "Yes?" and when there wasn't any reply, "Who the
hell *is* that?" But he couldn't phone her now, not at midnight.

He walked down past the Odeon Cinema to Marble Arch. The
last of the queue was going in for the midnight movie. There were
still a lot of people about. He knew he was going to have to phone
her. It was as if it was too late to go back, though he'd done nothing, taken no decisive step, only thought. He went into Marble
Arch tube station and into a phone booth. For two pence he
could buy her voice, a word or two, whole sentences if he was
lucky and got a bargain. His heart was thudding and his hands
were wet with sweat. Suppose someone else answered? Suppose
they'd moved? They could be on holiday, taking the first of those
two or three annual holidays which in the past had brought him
postcards and loneliness. With a sweaty hand he lifted the receiver and placed a finger in the five slot on the dial.

Five-O-eight, then all the four digits including the final nine.
He leant against the wall, the receiver cold as ice against his
branded palm. I am a little mad, he thought, I'm breaking
down . . . They might have gone out with those friends to a
roadhouse, they might . . . He heard the whistling peep-peep
that told him he was through and, trembling, he pressed in his
coin. It fell through the machinery with a hollow crash.

"Yes?"

Not Tiny, not some newcomer, but she. The single mono-syllable was repeated impatiently. "Yes?"

He'd resolved not to speak to her but he needed no resolve. He couldn't speak, though he breathed like one of those men who phone women in the night to frighten them. She wasn't easily frightened.

"Who the hell's that?"

He listened, not as if she were speaking to him—as indeed she wasn't—but as though this were a tape someone was playing to him.

"Listen," she said, "whoever you are, some bloody joker, you've had your kick, you pervert, so just piss off!"

The phone went down with a crack like a gunshot. He lit a cigarette with shaking fingers. Well, he'd had what he wanted, her voice, the last of her to remember. She'd never speak to him again and he'd be able to remember forever her parting words, the positively last appearance of the prima donna—piss off, you pervert. He went back into the street, swaying like a drunk.

It was about ten in the morning when Francis appeared by his bed with an unexpected cup of tea. Francis had slept in the bedroom, Gray on one of the beds that had been moved into the main room where the sun now penetrated in red, blue, and golden rays through the glass and made dancing blobs on the floor.

"I owe you an apology for that carry-on in the pub yesterday. Charmian's a wonderful girl but she is impulsive."

"That's all right."

"I Spoke to Her About It," said Francis rather pompously. "After all, what you'd take from an old mate like me doesn't come too well from someone you've just met. But she's a marvellous girl, isn't she?"

Gray smiled neutrally. "Are you and she . . . ?"

"We aren't yet having a sexual relationship, if that's what you mean. Charmian views these things very seriously. Time will tell, of course. It might be as well for me to consider marriage quite soon."

"Quite soon?" said Gray, alarmed at possible interference with his plans. "You and Charmian mean to marry quite soon?"

"My God, no. It may not even be with Charmian. It's just that I think marriage should be the next big event I plan for in my life."

Gray drank his tea. Now was the moment and he'd better seize it. "Francis, I want to come back to London."

"Of course you do. I've been telling you for ages."

"I'll get paid quite soon and when I do—well, could I come here for a bit while I look for a room?"

"Here? With me?"

"It wouldn't be for more than a month or two."

Francis looked rather sour. "It'll be very inconvenient. I'd have to have help with the rent. This place costs me eighteen a week, you know."

There'd be at least fifty when the cheque came . . . "I'd go halves."

Maybe it was his guilt over the lecture he'd exposed Gray to the night before that made Francis put aside his usual scepticism when his friend mentioned making monetary contributions to anything. "Well, I suppose so," he said ungraciously. "Let's say you'll stay six weeks. When d'you want to come? Charmian and I are going down to Devon to her people tomorrow for a few days. How about next Saturday?"

"Saturday," said Gray, "would suit me fine."

After he'd had a bath—in a proper bathroom with hot water coming out of a tap—he walked over to Tranmere Villas. Jeff was still in bed and it was the tenant of Gray's old room, the room where just once he'd made love to Drusilla, who admitted him to the flat.

"Sally out?" he said when Jeff appeared, sleepy, gloomy, and myopic without his glasses.

"She's left me. Walked out a few weeks back."

"God, I'm sorry." He knew how it felt. "You'd been together a long time."

"Five years. She met this bloke and went off with him to the Isle of Mull."

"I *am* sorry."

Jeff made coffee and they talked about Sally, the bloke, loneliness, the Isle of Mull, a man they'd been at school with who was now Gray's M.P. and then about various people they'd known in the old days, all of whom seemed to have gone off to remote places. Gray told his friend about the move.

"Yes, I could shift your stuff on Saturday. There isn't much of it, is there?"

"Some books, a typewriter, clothes."

"Say midafternoon, then? If you change your plans you can give me a ring. By the way, there's a letter here for you, came about a month back just when Sally went. It looked like a bill so what with Sally and everything, I never got around to sending it on. I know I should have done but I was in a hell of a mess. Thank God, I'm getting myself together again now."

Gray wished he could do the same. He took the envelope, knowing what it was before he opened it. How could he forget so much that was important when he remembered everything that was past and dead and useless? She'd left him and he'd gone to London for Christmas with Francis, resolving then never to go back to the hovel, never to set foot within ten miles of her. And he'd written to his publishers asking them to send the next statement to Tranmere Villas because that was the one address he could be sure of being permanent. How could he have forgotten? Because he'd felt so hopeless and disorientated that he'd drifted back to Pocket Lane, fleeing from the tough members of his tribe like a wounded animal seeking the shelter of its lair?

He slit open the envelope. *The Wine of Astonishment*: Sales, home, £5; 75% sales, French, £3.50; 75% sales, Italian, £6.26. Total, £14.76.

"Since you're not doing anything," said Charmian, "you can give me a hand with the food. We're not having a real lunch, just picking at bits from this lot." "This lot" was a heap of lettuces, tomatoes, plastic wrapped cheese, envelopes of sliced meat and French loaves. "Unless you feel like treating us to a meal."

"Now then, lovey," said Francis.

Gray wasn't annoyed with her. He was too shattered by the royalty statement to feel anything much. On the way to Jeff's he'd bought a bottle of Spanish Chablis for the party and now he'd got just two pounds of the seven left.

"There's plenty of food here," said Francis kindly. "My God, there goes the phone again."

The phone had been ringing ever since Gray got back. People couldn't come or wanted to know if they could bring friends or couldn't remember where Francis lived.

"So you're moving in here," said Charmian, vigorously washing tomatoes.

Gray shrugged. Was he? "Only for a few weeks."

"My mother invited a friend for the weekend once and she stayed three years. You're very neurotic, aren't you? I notice you jump every time the phone rings."

Gray cut himself a piece of cheese. He was just thinking what a snorter of a letter he'd write them about those Yugoslavian rights when Francis came back into the kitchen, his expression concerned, rather embarrassed. He came up to Gray and laid a hand on his shoulder.

"It's your stepfather. Apparently, your mother's very ill. Will you go and talk to him?"

Gray went into the living room. Honoré's broken English rushed excitedly at him out of the receiver. "My son, I try to find you at your house but always the telephone is occupy, so I re-member me you go to the house of Francis and I find the num-ber—Oh, the difficulty of finding him!"

"What is it, Honoré?" said Gray in English.

"It is Mummy. She die, I think."

"You mean, she's *dead?*"

"No, no, *pas du tout*. She have a grand *paralyse* and the doctor Villon he is with her now and he say she die very soon, tomorrow, he don't know. He wish her go to the hospital in Jency but I say no, no, not while old Honoré have breath and force to take care of her. You come, *hein?* You come today?"

"All right," said Gray, a hollow feeling at the pit of his stomach. "Yes, sure I'll come."

"You have the money, you carry him with you? I give you suf-ficient money to go with the plane for Paris and then the bus for Bajon. So you fly with him this day from Eetreau and I see you tonight at Le Petit Trianon."

"I'll come straightaway. I'll go home and get my passport and then I'll come."

He walked back into the kitchen. The others were sitting at the table, silent, wearing long faces as suitable to the occasion.

"I say, I'm awfully sorry about your mum," said Charmian gruffly.

"Yes, well, of course," said Francis. "I mean, if there's anything we can do . . ."

There was something he could do but Gray postponed asking him for a few minutes. He knew very well that people who make this offer at times of bereavement or threatened bereavement seldom intend to do anything beyond producing sympathy and a drink.

"I'll have to miss the party. I'd better go now if I've got to get to the hovel before going to the airport."

"Let me give you a drink," said Francis.

The whisky, on a more or less empty stomach, gave Gray courage. "There is one thing you could do," he said.

Francis didn't ask him what it was. He sighed slightly. "I suppose you haven't got the money for your fare."

"All I've got between me and the dole is about two quid."

Charmian said, but not unkindly, "Oh, God."

"How much would it be?"

"Look, Francis, I'm expecting a cheque any day. It'll only be a short-term loan. I know I've got money coming because I've sold some Yugoslavian rights."

"You can't get money out of Communist countries," said Charmian briskly. "Writers never can. My mother's got a friend who's a *very famous* writer and he says publishers have to pay so much tax or something that they just leave the money in banks in places behind the Iron Curtain."

It was like a jet of cold water hitting him in the face. It didn't occur to him to doubt what she said. He remembered now hearing remarks very like hers from Peter Marshall at one of those convivial lunches, only Peter had added, "If you do sell in Yugoslavia, say, we'll leave the money in our account in Belgrade and maybe you can have a holiday there sometime and spend it." Pity Honoré didn't live in Belgrade . . .

"Christ, I'm in a hell of a mess."

Francis said again, "How much would it be?"

"About thirty-five pounds."

"Gray, you mustn't think I'm not sympathetic, but how the hell d'you think I'm going to lay my hands on thirty-five quid on a Sunday? I don't have more than five in the flat. Have you got any money, lovey?"

"About two, fifty," said Charmian. Having apparently decided that the period of empathetic grieving was over, she had resumed her eating of ham and lettuce.

"I suppose I'll have to go down to the tobacconist and see if he'll cash me a cheque."

Gray phoned the airport and was told there was a flight at eight thirty. He felt stunned. What was going to happen when he got back from France? When the cheque came he'd have about sixteen pounds but he'd owe thirty-five to Francis, and then there was going to be the business of giving Francis another nine pounds a week to share this bloody greenhouse. Oblivious of the girl, he put his head in his hands and closed his eyes . . .

Inevitably, he began to think how different his situation would have been if he'd agreed to what Drusilla had required of him a year ago. Of course he'd still be going to Bajon, that and that only would be the same. But he wouldn't have been dependant on other people's charity, despised by this girl, the object of Francis's contempt, always worried out of his wits over money . . .

A touch on his shoulder jerked him out of this reverie. "Bear up," said Francis. "I've got you the thirty-five."

"Thanks. I'm very grateful, Francis."

"I don't want to press you at a time like this but the thing is it doesn't leave me much to spare, and what with these few days in Devon and the rent and everything, if you could see your way . . . ?"

Gray nodded. It seemed pointless to make promises about quick repayment. He wouldn't be able to put conviction into his voice and Francis wouldn't believe him if he did.

"Have a good party."

"We'll drink to you," said Francis. "Absent friends."

Charmian lifted her head and managed a half-hearted farewell smile. And Francis's own expression was indulgent but impatient too. They'd both be glad to get rid of him. The red glass door closed with a relieved bang before he was halfway down the path.

If he'd done what she'd asked, he thought, he'd be in a taxi now, proceeding from his luxury flat to a first-class seat in an air-craft, his pigskin luggage up there beside the driver, his pockets full of money. He'd be like Tiny who, she'd once said, always carried huge sums about on him, ready to pay cash for what he wanted. And in Bajon the chambermaids would be preparing for him the best bedroom with private bath at the Écu d'Or. Above all, he'd have been free from worry.

It seemed to him as he waited for his train that all his troubles had come upon him because he hadn't done what she'd asked and conspired with her to kill her husband.

CHAPTER 9

Although he'd been preoccupied with thoughts of money throughout that long journey, it wasn't until he was back at the hovel that
he remembered his mother's will. Under it, he was to inherit half
her property. Well, he wouldn't dwell on that, it was too base.
Pushing away the thought with all its attractions and all its attendant guilt, he packed some clothes, put his royalty statement
into the strongbox and got out his passport. There didn't seem
any point in locking the strongbox, so he just closed the lid, leaving the key in. Was there anything else he had to do before leaving for France, apart from putting the phone back on the hook?
He did this, but at the back of his mind there remained something
else. What? Not put Jeff off. He'd be back by next Saturday, and
Francis would take him in all right when he knew he was heir to
half his mother's money. No, this was some engagement, some
duty . . . Suddenly he remembered—Miss Platt's party. On his
way back down the lane he'd call on Miss Platt and tell her he
wouldn't be able to go.

Seen from the gate, the hovel looked as if it hadn't been inhabited for years. Its weatherboard soaked by seasons of rain,
scaled and bleached by sun to the texture of an oyster shell. It lay
deep in its nest of bracken, a decaying shack behind whose windows hung faded and tattered cotton curtains. Silver birches,
beeches with trunks as grey as steel, encroached upon it as if trying to conceal its decrepitude. It had a lost abandoned look as of
a piece of rubbish thrown into the heart of the Forest along with
the rest of the trippers' litter. But it was worth fifteen thousand
pounds. Miss Platt had said so. If Mal were to put it up for sale,
he'd get rid of it that same day for this huge, this unbelievable,
sum.

He found the lucky vendor in her front garden, cutting early roses.

"Aren't we having a lovely warm spell, Mr. Lanceton? It makes me more sorry than ever I have to leave."

Gray said, "I'm afraid I shan't be able to come to your party. I've got to go to France. My mother lives there and she's dangerously ill."

"Oh, dear, I *am* sorry. Is there anything I can do?" Miss Platt put down her scissors. "Would you like me to keep an eye on The White Cottage?"

But for the letters to Tiny, Gray might have forgotten this was the hovel's real name. "No, thanks. I haven't anything worth pinching."

"Just as you like but it wouldn't be any trouble and I'm sure Mr. Tringham would take over from me. I do hope you'll find your mother better. There's no one like one's mother, is there? And worse for a man, I feel."

As he went down the lane, past the Willises' churned-up lawn, past the new estate and out into the High Beech Road, he thought about what she'd said. "There's no one like one's mother" . . . Since Honoré's phone call, he'd thought a lot about money, about Drusilla and money, about his mother's money, but he hadn't really thought about his mother herself at all. Did he care for her? Did it matter to him at all whether she lived or died? In his mind he had two mothers, two separate and distinct women, the woman who had rejected her son, her country, and her friends for an ugly little French waiter, and the woman who, since her first husband's death, had kept a home for her son, loving him, welcoming his friends. It was of this woman—lost to him, dead for fourteen years—that Gray tried to think now. She had been a friend and companion rather than a parent and he had mourned her with the bitter bewilderment of a fifteen-year-old, unable to understand—he understood now all right—the power of an obsessive passion. Understanding doesn't make for love, only for indifferent forgiveness.

He'd mourned her then. But, because she wasn't really two women but only one, he couldn't grieve now for the broken creature who was dying at last, not his but Honoré's, the property of Honoré and of France.

Flying to Paris was nothing to Tiny, no more than driving down to Loughton High Road. He flew to America, Hong Kong, Australia; to Copenhagen for lunch and back home for dinner. Once, Gray remembered now, he'd flown to Paris for the weekend . . .

"You'll be able to come and stay with me at the hovel. We can have the whole weekend together, Dru," he'd said.

"Yes, and it'll give us a chance to take the acid."

"I thought you'd forgotten all about that."

"How little you know me. I never forget anything. You can get some, can't you? You said you could. I hope you weren't just bragging to impress."

"I know a bloke who can get me some acid, yes."

"But you're going to be all moralistic and bloody upstage about it? Damn you, you make me sick! What's the harm? It's not addictive, it's anti-addictive. I know all about it."

From reading pop paperbacks, he'd thought, with sections entitled *The Weed* and *Club des Haschischins* and *A New Perception*. "Look, Dru, I just happen to believe it's wrong to use a drug like LSD just for playing, for sensation-seeking. It's quite another thing when it's used in psychotherapy and under supervision."

"Have you ever taken it?"

"Yes, once, about four years ago."

"Christ, that's marvellous! You're like one of those crappy old saints who went to orgies every night until they were about forty and then turned on everybody else and told them sex was sin just because they'd got past it themselves. *God!*"

"It wasn't a nice experience. It may be for some people but it wasn't for me."

"Why shouldn't I try it? Why you and not me? I've never done anything. You're always stopping me when I want to have experiences. I shan't come here at all if you won't get the acid. I'll go to Paris with Tiny and, my God, won't I live it up while he's at his stupid old seminar. I'll pick up the first guy that makes a pass at me." She leaned towards him then, wheedling, "Gray, we could take it together. They say it makes sex wonderful. Wouldn't you like that, me even more wonderful than I am?"

Of course he'd got the acid. There was very little he wouldn't have done for her except that one thing. But he wasn't going to take it himself. That was dangerous. One to take it, one to be there and watch, to supervise and, if necessary, to restrain. For, although the stable personality may react no more than to see distortions (or realities?) and experience a heightening of certain senses, the unstable may become violent, manic, wild. Drusilla, whatever she was, however much he might love her, was hardly stable.

It was early May, just over a year ago, the east wind sharp and chill. On the Saturday morning they had gone into his bedroom and he'd given her the acid while the wind howled around the hovel and, up above them somewhere, Tiny's plane flew away to France. Massive Tiny in his eighty-guinea suit leaned back in his first-class lushly cushioned seat, taking his double Scotch from the air hostess, opening his *Financial Times*, reading, having no idea, no idea at all, of what was taking place those thousands of feet below him. Serene, innocent Tiny, who had never for a moment suspected . . .

"*And many a man there is, even at this present,*
Now while I speak this, holds his wife by th'arm,
That little thinks she has been sluiced in's absence,
And his pond fished by his next neighbour,
By Sir Smile, his neighbour . . ."

Gray felt a shiver run through him. It was ugly when put like that, for he had been Tiny's neighbour, in the geographical as well as the ethical sense, had even pointed out the fact in the first of those letters. He'd been Sir Smile, Tiny's neighbour, who had fished his pond in his absence—how coarse and clinical was that Jacobean imagery!—and had scarcely considered the man as a person except when it came to drawing the line at the farthest limit.

Well, it was past now, and he and Tiny, the sparer and the

spared, perhaps both betrayed in their absence by a neighbour, that smiling tennis player . . .

Gray blocked off his memories. Beneath him now he could see the lights of Paris. He fastened his seat belt, put out his cigarette and braced himself for further ordeals ahead.

The aircraft was late and the one available bus took him only as far as Jency, ten miles from Bajon, but he thumbed an illegal hitch the rest of the way. The only lights still on in Bajon were those of the Écu d'Or, haunt of Honoré, the mayor, and M. Reville, the glass manufacturer. Honoré, however, would hardly be there now. Gray looked at his watch, striking a match to do so, and saw it was close on midnight. Strange to think that at this time twenty-four hours before he'd been in Marble Arch tube station phoning Drusilla.

He went past the clump of chestnut trees, past the house called Les Marrons and down the little side road which would, after the bungalows, finally peter out as miserably as Pocket Lane itself into fields, woods, and the farm named Les Fonds. Honoré's was the fourth bungalow. A light was on in a front room. By this light Gray could see the sheet of green concrete spread over and crushing every growing thing that might have protruded its head, the plastic-lined pond, and around the pond, the brightly coloured circus of gnomes, frogs fishing, coy naked infants, lions with yellow staring eyes and fat ducks, which was Honoré's great pride. Mercifully, the light was too dim to show the alternating pink and green bricks of which the bungalow was built.

Not for the first time Gray reflected on this extraordinary anomaly in the French nation, that they who have contributed more to the world's art in music, in literature, in painting, than perhaps any other race and have been the acknowledged arbiters of taste, should also possess a bourgeoisie that exhibits the worst taste on earth. He marvelled that the French who produced Gabriel and Le Nôtre should also have produced Honoré Duval, and then he went up to the door and rang the bell.

Honoré came running to answer his ring.

"Ah, my son, at last you come!" Honoré embraced him, kissing him on both cheeks. He smelt, as usual, very powerfully of garlic.

"You have a good fly? Don't be unquiet now, *ce n'est pas fini*. She lives. She sleeps. You see her, no?"

"In a minute, Honoré. Is there anything to eat?"

"I cook for you," said Honoré enthusiastically. It was a fervour, Gray knew, which would soon wane and be replaced by wily suspiciousness. "I make the omelette."

"I only want a bit of bread and cheese."

"What, when I not see you three, four years? You think I am that bad father? Come now to the kitchen and I cook."

Gray wished he hadn't mentioned food. Honoré, though French and an ex-waiter, one who had moved for two-thirds of his life among French *haute cuisine* and in the ambience of its tradition, was an appalling cook. Aware that French cooking depends for much of its excellence on the subtle use of herbs, he overdid the rosemary and basil to an inedible degree. He also knew that cream plays an important part in most dishes but he was too mean to use cream at all. This would have been less unbearable if he had cooked egg and chips or plain stews but these he scorned. It must be the time-honoured French dishes or nothing, those traditional marvellous delicacies which the world venerates and copies—only with the cream and wine left out and packet herbs thrust in by spoonfuls.

"Extinguish, please," said Honoré as Gray followed him tiredly into the kitchen. This was Honoré's way of telling him to put the light out. Every light had to be put out when one left a room to keep the electricity bills down. Gray extinguished and sat down in one of the bright blue chairs with scarlet and blue plastic seat. It was very quiet, nearly as quiet as in the hovel.

In the middle of the kitchen table was a pink plastic geranium in a white plastic urn and there were plastic flowers all over the windowsill. The wall clock was of orange glass with chrome hands and the wall plates which ringed it showed châteaux in relief and glorious Technicolour. All the tints of a tropic bird were in that kitchen and every surface was spotless, bathed in the rosy radiance of a pink strip light.

Honoré, who had tied an apron round himself, began beating eggs and throwing in pinches of dried parsley and dried chives until the mixture turned a dull green. Cooking demanded concentration and a reverend silence and neither man spoke for a while. Gray eyed his stepfather thoughtfully.

He was a thin spare man, rather under middle height, with brown skin and hair which had been black but now was grizzled. His thin lips were permanently, even when relaxed, curled up into a sickle-shaped smile, but the small black eyes remained shrewd and cool. He looked what he was, a French peasant, but he looked more so; he looked like a French peasant in a farce written by an Englishman.

Gray had never been able to fathom what his mother had seen in him but now, after three years' separation, he began to understand. Perhaps this was because he was older or perhaps it was because he had only in those years really known the power of sex. To a woman like his mother, sheltered, refined even, this dark and certainly vital little man with his sharp eyes and his calculating smile, might have been what Drusilla had been to him, Gray, the embodiment of sex. He always reminded Gray of one of those onion sellers from whom his mother used to buy when they called at the house on Wimbledon Common. Could it be that Enid Lanceton, outwardly cool and civilised, had been so drawn to these small brown men with onion strings hanging from their bicycles, that she longed to find one for herself? Well, she'd found him, Gray thought, looking at Honoré, his plastic flowers and his curtains patterned with yellow pots and pans, and she'd paid very dearly for her find.

"*Voilà!*" said Honoré, slapping the omelette down on a green and red checked plate. "Come now, eat her quick, or she grow cold."

Gray ate her quick. The omelette looked like a cabbage leaf fried in thin batter but it tasted like a compost heap and he gobbled it down as fast as he could, hoping in this way to avoid those pauses in eating in which the full flavour might make itself felt. There was a faint sound in the bungalow which reminded him of the regular whirr, rising and falling, of a piece of machinery. He couldn't think what it was but it was the only sound apart from the clatter Honoré was making at the sink.

"Now for some good French coffee."

Good coffee was the last thing one got at Le Petit Trianon. Honoré scorned instant which all his neighbours now used but his avarice jibbed at making fresh coffee each time it was needed. So once a week he boiled up a saucepanful of water, coffee, and chicory, and this mixture, salt and bitter, was heated up and served till the last drop was gone. Gray's stomach, which digested Swedish meatballs, ravioli, and canned beef olives with impunity, revolted at Honoré's coffee.

"No, thanks. I shan't be able to sleep. I'll go in and see Mother now."

Her bedroom—their bedroom—was the only room she had managed to keep unscathed from her husband's taste. The walls were white, the furniture plain walnut, the carpet and covers sea-blue. On the wall above the bed hung a painted and gilded icon of a Virgin and Child.

The dying woman lay on her back, her hands outside the counterpane. She was snoring stertorously, and now Gray knew what was the dolorous, regular sound he had heard. It had been machinery, the machinery of Enid Duval's respiration. He approached the bed and looked down at the gaunt, blank face. He had thought of her as two women but now he saw that there were three, his mother, Honoré's wife, both absorbed in this third and last.

Honoré said, "Kiss her, my son. Embrace her."

Gray took no notice of him. He lifted one of the hands and held it. It was very cold. His mother didn't stir or change the rhythm of her breathing.

"Enid, here is Gray-arm. Here is your boy at last."

"Oh, leave it," said Gray. "What's the point?"

His English deserting him, Honoré burst into an excited Gallic tirade. Gray caught only the gist of it, that Anglo-Saxons had no proper feelings.

"I'm going to bed. Good night."

Honoré shrugged. "Good night, my son. You find your room O.K., *hein?* All day I run up and down, the work is never done, but I make time for arranging clean drapes for you."

Used to Honoré's curious and direct rendering of French terms into English, Gray knew this meant he had put clean sheets on the bed. He went into "his" room which Honoré had furnished as suitable for the son of the house. It was mainly blue—blue for a boy—magenta roses on the blue carpet, yellow daffodils on the blue curtains. The one picture, replacing a *pietà* Gray had once told his stepfather he loathed, showed Madame Roland in a blue gown standing on the steps of a red and silver guillotine and uttering, according to the caption beneath, *O Liberté, que de crimes on commis en ton nom!*

The truth of this was evident. Many crimes were committed in the name of liberty, his mother's marriage for instance. For liberty Drusilla had contemplated a crime far more horrible. Gray thought he would probably stay awake dwelling on this but the bed was so comfortable—the best thing about Le Petit Trianon, the most comfortable bed he ever slept in, vastly superior to the one at the hovel or Francis's or the one by the window at the Oranmore—that he fell asleep almost immediately.

CHAPTER 10

He was awakened at seven by a racket so furious that at first he thought his mother must have died in the night and Honoré had summoned the whole village to view her. Surely no one could make so much noise getting breakfast for three people. Then, under the cacophony, as it were, he heard the rhythm of her snoring and understood that Honoré, who never seemed tired, was using this method of indicating it was time to get up. He rolled over and, though he couldn't get back to sleep, lay there defiantly till eight when the door flew open and a vacuum cleaner charged in.

"Early to bed and early to rise," said Honoré merrily, "make him wealthy, healthy, and wise. There, I know the English proverb."

Gray noticed he'd put "wealthy" first. Typical. "I didn't get to bed early. Can I have a bath?"

At Le Petit Trianon you couldn't count on there being hot water. A bathroom there was with fishes on the tiles and a furry peach-coloured cover on the lavatory seat; a large immersion heater there was also, but Honoré kept this switched off, washing up from heated kettles. If you wanted a bath you had to book it some hours or even days in advance.

"Later," said Honoré. In very colloquial French, he went on to say something about electricity bills, the folly of too much bathing and—incredibly, Gray thought—that he had no time at present to turn on the heater.

"Sorry, I didn't get that."

"Aha!" His stepfather wagged a finger at him while energetically vacuuming the room. "I think you don't know French like you say. Now you are here you practise him. Breakfast waits. Come."

Gray got up and washed in water from a saucepan. The cheap cheese-coloured soap Honoré provided stung his hand so that he almost cried out. In another saucepan was coffee, on the table half a *baguette*. The custom of the French is to buy these bread sticks freshly each morning but Honoré never did this. He couldn't bear to throw anything away and old *baguettes* lingered till they were finished up, even though by then they looked and tasted like petrified loofahs.

After Dr. Villon had called and pronounced no change in his patient, Gray went down to the village to get fresh bread. Bajon hadn't altered much since his last visit. The Écu d'Or was still in need of painting, the brown-grey farm buildings still slumbered like heavy old animals behind brown-grey walls. The four shops in the postwar parade, wine shop, baker, butcher, and general store-post office, were still under the same management. He walked to the end of the village street to see if the bra advertisement was still there. It was, a huge poster on a hoarding showing two rounded mountains encased in lace, and the words, *Desirée*, Votre *Soutien-gorge*. He retraced his steps, went past Honoré's turning, past two new shops, past a hairdresser ambitiously called *Jeanne Moreau, Coiffeur des Dames*, and came to the road sign, *Nids de poules*. When he'd first come to Bajon he'd thought this really meant there were hens' nests in the road, not just potholes, but Honoré had corrected him, laughing with merry derision.

The day passed slowly and the slumbrous heat continued. Gray found some of the books his mother had brought with her from Wimbledon and settled down in the back garden to read *The Constant Nymph*. The back garden was a lawn ten metres by eight on which Honoré had erected three strange objects, each being a tripod of green-painted poles surmounted by a plaster face. Three chains hung from the poles bearing a kind of urn or bucket filled with marigolds. Gray couldn't get used to these elaborate and hideous devices, designed with such care and trouble to display such small clusters of flowers, but the sun was warm and this a way of passing the time.

At about eight Honoré said that a poor old man who was on his feet from morning till night, worn out as cook, nurse and general manager, deserved a little relaxation in the evenings. Gray, he was sure, would stay with Enid while he went to the Écu for a *fine*.

Several neighbours had called during the day to offer their services as sitters but Honoré had refused them, saying Gray would like to remain with his mummy.

Enid maintained her regular unbroken snoring while Gray sat beside her. He finished *The Constant Nymph* and began on *The Blue Lagoon*. Honoré came in at eleven, smelling of brandy and with a message from the mayor that he longed to meet the author of *Le Vin d'Étonnement*.

In the morning Father Normand appeared, a stout and gloomy black figure whom Honoré treated as if he were at least an archbishop. He was closeted for a long time with Gray's mother, only leaving the bedroom on the arrival of Dr. Villon. Neither priest nor doctor spoke to Gray. They had no English and Honoré had assured them that Gray had no French. The week-old chicory concoction was served and the two elderly men drank it with apparent pleasure, complimenting Honoré on his selfless devotion to his wife and pointing out to him (Father Normand) that he would find his reward in heaven, and (Dr. Villon) that he would find it on earth in the shape of Le Petit Trianon and Enid's savings. Since Gray wasn't supposed to be able to understand a word of this, they spoke freely in front of him of Enid's imminent death and Honoré's good fortune in having married, if not for money, where money was.

Gray wouldn't have put it past him to help Enid towards her end if she lingered on much longer. He showed no grief, only a faint unease at the mention of money. The priest and the doctor praised him for his stoical front, but Gray didn't think it was stoicism. Honoré's eyes flashed with something like loathing when he was feeding Enid or sponging her face, and when he thought Gray wasn't looking.

How many husbands and wives were capable of murder in certain circumstances? A good many, maybe. Gray had hardly thought of Drusilla since he'd arrived in France. There was nothing here to evoke her. He hadn't been to France since becoming her lover so he hadn't even the memory of remembering her while there. Nor had she ever been near the place. She and Tiny holidayed in St. Tropez and St. Moritz—those patron saints of tourism—or further and more exotically afield. But he thought of her now. When he considered spouses as murderers, he could hardly fail to think of Drusilla.

When had she first mentioned it? In March? In April? No, because she hadn't taken the acid till May . . .

It took about half an hour to work. Then she began to tell him what she saw, the old beamed bedroom vastly widened and elongated so that it seemed to have the dimensions of a baronial hall. The clouds outside the window became purple and vast, rolling and huge as she had never seen clouds before. She'd got up to look more closely at them, distressed because the window wasn't a hundred feet away but only two yards.

She was wearing an amethyst ring, its stone a chunk of rough crystal, and she described it to him as a range of mountains full of caves. She said she could see little people walking in and out of the caves. He wouldn't make love—it seemed wrong to him, unnatural—and she didn't seem to mind, so they went downstairs and he cooked her lunch. The food frightened her. She saw the vegetables in the soup as sea creatures writhing in a pool. After that she sat still for a long time, not telling him any more until at last she said:

"I don't like it. It's bending my mind."

"Of course. What did you expect?"

"I don't feel sexy. I've got no sex any more. Suppose it doesn't come back?"

"It will. The effects will wear off quite soon and then you'll sleep."

"What would happen if I drove the car?"

"For God's sake, you'd crash! Your sense of distance would be all messed up."

"I want to try. Just in the lane."

He had to hold her back by force. He'd known something like that might happen but he hadn't realised she was so strong. She struggled, striking him, kicking at his legs. But in the end he got the car key away from her, and when she was calmer they went out for a walk.

They walked in the forest and saw some people riding ponies. Drusilla said they were a troop of cavalry and their faces were all cruel, cruel and sad. He sat down with her under a tree but the birds frightened her. She said they were trying to get at her and peck her to pieces. Early in the evening she'd fallen asleep, waking once to tell him she'd dreamed of birds attacking Tiny's aircraft and pecking holes in it till Tiny fell out. One of the birds was herself, a harpy with feathers and a tail but with a woman's breasts and face and long flowing hair.

"I can't understand people taking that for *fun,*" she said when she left for home the next night. "Why the hell did you give it to me?"

"Because you nagged me into it. I wish I hadn't."

Many times he'd wished he hadn't, for that wasn't the end of the nagging but only the beginning. That was when it had begun. But it didn't matter now, it was all the same now . . .

"Raise yourself, my son. You are having a dream?"

Honoré spoke jovially but with a hint of reproof. He expected young people—especially young people without means of support —to leap to their feet whenever their seniors entered or left a room. Dr. Villon and Father Normand were leaving, lost in admiration apparently of Honoré's linguistic ability. Gray said *au revoir* politely but remained where he was. Out in the hall he could hear Honoré waving away their compliments with the explanation that anyone who had been for years in a managerial situation in the international hotel business was bound to have several languages at his tongue's end.

After the evening meal—canned lobster bisque with canned prawns and bits of white fish in it that Honoré called *bouillabaisse* —he went for a walk down the road as far as Les Fonds. There were nearly as many gnats and flies as in Pocket Lane. In fact, the place reminded him of Pocket Lane except for the persistent baying of the farmer's chained dog. Gray knew that French country people like to keep their dogs chained. Presumably the animals get used to it, presumably this one would be let loose at night. But for some reason the sight and sound disquieted him deeply. He didn't know the reason. He couldn't think why this thin captive sheepdog, straining at its chain, barking steadily, hollowly and in vain, awakened in him a kind of chilly dread.

When he got back Honoré was spruce in dark jacket, dark cravat and beret, ready for his *fine.*

"Give my love to the mayor."

"Tomorrow he come here to call. He speak good English—not

so good as me, but good. You must stand when he come in, Gray-arm, as is respectable from a young boy to an old man of honour and reason. Now I leave you to give Mummy her coffee."

Gray hated doing this, hated supporting Enid, who smelt and who dribbled, on one arm while with the other hand he had to force between her shaking lips the obscene feeding cup with its spout. But he couldn't protest. She was his mother. Those were the lips that had said—long, long ago—"How lovely to have you home again, darling," those the hands that had held his face when she kissed him goodbye, sewn the marking tags on his school clothes, brought him tea when he awoke late in the holidays.

As he fed her the hot milk with a trace of coffee in it, watching perhaps a quarter of the quantity go down her throat while the rest slopped onto the coverlet, he thought she was weaker than she had been on the previous evening, her eyes more glazed and distant, her flesh even less pliant. She didn't know him. Probably she thought he was someone Honoré had got in from the village. And he didn't know her. She wasn't the mother he'd loved or the mother he'd hated, but just an old Frenchwoman for whom he felt nothing but repulsion and pity.

The relationship between mother and son is the most complete that can exist between human beings. Who had said that? Freud, he thought. And perhaps the most easily destroyed? She and Honoré and life itself had destroyed it and now it was too late.

He took away the cup and laid her down on the pillows. Her head lolled to one side and she began to snore again, but unevenly, breathily. He'd never seen anyone die but, whatever Honoré or the doctor might say, whatever false alarms, reassurances, anti-climaxes, there had been in the past, he knew she was dying now. Tomorrow or the next day she would die.

He sat by her bed and finished *The Blue Lagoon*, relieved when Honoré came back and she was still alive.

All the next day, Wednesday, Enid went on dying. Even Honoré knew it now. He and Dr. Villon sat in the kitchen, drinking coffee, waiting. Honoré kept saying something which Gray interpreted as meaning he wouldn't wish it prolonged, and he was reminded of Theobald Pontifex in *The Way of All Flesh* who had used those words when his own unloved wife lay on her death-bed. Gray found *The Way of All Flesh* among his mother's books and began to read it, although it was a far cry from his usual reading matter, being a great novel and such as he used to prefer.

Father Normand came in and administered Extreme Unction. He left without taking coffee. Perhaps yesterday's dose had been too much for him or else he thought it a frivolous drink and unsuitable to the occasion. The mayor didn't come. By now the whole village knew that Enid was really dying at last. They hadn't loved her. How could they love a foreigner and an English-woman? But they all loved Honoré who had been born among them and who, when rich, had returned humbly to live in the village of his birth.

That night Honoré didn't go to the Écu, though Enid slept a little more peacefully. He vacuumed the whole house again, made more green omelettes and finally switched on the heater for Gray's bath. Wrapped in a dragon-decorated dressing gown belonging to his stepfather, Gray came out of the bathroom at about eleven, hoping to escape to bed. But Honoré intercepted him in the hall.

"Now we have the chat, I think. We have no time till now for the chat, *hein?*"

"Just as you like."

"I like, Gray-arm," said Honoré, adding as Gray followed him into the living room. "Extinguish, please."

Gray turned off the hall light behind him. His stepfather lit a Disque Bleu and recorked the brandy bottle from which he had been drinking while Gray was in the bath.

"Sit down, my son. Now, Gray-arm, you know of—how do you say?—Mummy's legs?"

Gray stared at him, then understood. For one grotesque moment he'd thought Honoré was referring to Enid's lower limbs, the French for legacy having eluded him.

"Yes," he said warily.

"Half for you and half for me, yes?"

"I'd rather not talk about it. She's not dead yet."

"But, Gray-arm, I do not talk of it, I talk of you. I am unquiet only for what become of you without money."

"I shan't be without money after . . . Well, we won't discuss it."

Honoré drew deeply on his cigarette. He seemed to ponder, looking sly and not altogether at ease. Suddenly he said loudly and rapidly, "It is necessary for you only to write more books. This you can do, for you have talent. I know this, I, Honoré Duval. Just a poor old waiter, you say, but a Frenchman, however, and all the French, they *know*." He banged his concave chest. "It is in-built, come in the birth."

"Inborn," said Gray, "though I doubt that." He'd often noticed how Honoré was a poor old waiter when he wanted something and an international manager when out to impress.

"So you write more books, come rich and undependant again, *hein?*"

"Maybe," said Gray, wondering where all this was leading and determined to let it lead nowhere. "I'd rather not talk about any of this. I'm going to bed in a minute."

"O.K., O.K., we talk of this at other time. But I tell you it is bad, bad, to hope for money come from anywhere but what one works. This is the only good money for a man."

People who live in glass houses shouldn't throw stones, thought Gray. "We were going to talk of something else."

"O.K., very good. We talk of England. Only once I visit England, very cold, very rainy. But I make many friends. All Mummy's friends love me. So now you tell me, how goes Mrs. Palmer and Mrs. 'Arcoort, and Mrs. Ouarrinaire?"

Resignedly, Gray told him that while the first two ladies were no longer within the circle of his acquaintance, Mal's mother was, as far as he knew, still well and happy in Wimbledon. Honoré nodded sagely, his composure recovered. He stubbed out his cigarette and lit another.

"And how," he said, "goes the good Isabel?"

CHAPTER 11

Gray too had been lighting a cigarette. He'd taken the match from Honoré and held it downwards to steady the flame. Now he let it fall into the ashtray and took the cigarette from his lips.

"Isabel?" he said.

"You look unquiet, Gray-arm, like you see the phantom. Perhaps you have too much hot water in your bath. Take a blanket from your bed or you will be enrheumed."

Gray said automatically, the words having no meaning or sense for him, "I'm not cold."

Honoré shrugged at the folly of the young who never take advice. Speaking French, he began to extol Isabel, praising her English strength of character, her intrepidity as a spinster *d'un certain age* in going by herself to Australia.

Getting up stiffly, Gray said, "I'm going to bed."

"In the centre of our chat? I see. O.K., Gray-arm, do as please yourself. Manners make man. Another English proverb. Strange that these English proverbs make nonsense to English persons."

Gray went out and banged the door, ignoring Honoré's command to extinguish the hall light. He shut himself in his room and sat on the bed, his body really cold now and convulsed with gooseflesh.

Isabel. Christ, how had he come to forget about Isabel? And he'd only just forgotten. He'd almost remembered as he was leaving the hovel. He'd known there was something to remember and he'd thought it was Miss Platt's party. As if it mattered a damn whether he went to her party or not. All the time it was Isabel. Shades of memory had flitted across his mind, making him faintly cold and sick, as when he'd walked down to the farmyard at Les Fonds. Was it possible he'd made another mistake, got the wrong weekend?

In the kitchen there was an old copy of *Le Soir*, Friday's. He went out there and found it lining the scarlet pedal bin. *Vendredi, le quatre juin*, and there the photograph of the floods in some remote antipodean city that had certainly been last Friday's main news. If Friday was the fourth, today, the following Wednesday, was June the ninth, and Monday had been the seventh. Anyway, it was pointless checking. Isabel's day was the day he'd been due back from Francis's party.

He slumped down at the table, pressing his hands so hard against his head that the burnt palm began to throb again. What the hell was he going to do, trapped here in Bajon, without money, with his mother dying?

He tried to think coolly and reasonably about what must have happened. At midday on Monday, June the seventh, Isabel must have driven down Pocket Lane in her Mini. She'd have let herself into the hovel with the key he'd given her, opened the kitchen door, left on the bath cover a dozen or so cans of meat, placed on the floor a small pan of water and, after kisses and farewells, gentle pats and promises to return after not too long a time, left Dido, the Labrador bitch, alone and waiting.

Gray will be back soon, she'd have said. Gray will take care of you. Be a good dog and sleep till he comes. And then she'd hung the key up on the hook, shut the kitchen door and driven to Heathrow, to an aircraft, to Australia . . .

It was unthinkable, but it must have happened. What was there to have stopped it happening? Isabel knew she'd find an empty house, closed-up, neglected, shabby. That was how she'd expect to find it. He'd left nothing to indicate he'd gone to France, told no one but Miss Platt who, even if she'd been in her garden, wouldn't know Isabel, still less accost a stranger to gossip about her neighbours.

The dog, that was the important thing. Dido, the dog with the lovely face and what he'd thought of as kind eyes. God, they wouldn't be kind now, not after she'd been locked in that hole without food and only about half a pint of water for more than two days, but wild and terrified. There was food beside her, food ironically encased in metal which even the most persistent fangs and claws couldn't reach. At this moment those fangs and claws would be tearing at the bolted back door, the larder door, the cellar door, until in exhaustion she took refuge in baying, roaring with far more need and agony than the farmer's chained dog.

There was no one to hear her. No one would come down the lane till Mr. Tringham passed on Saturday evening . . . Gray got up and went back to the living room where Honoré was still sitting, the brandy bottle once more uncorked.

"Honoré, can I use the phone?"

This was a request far more momentous than merely asking for a bath. Honoré used the phone to speak to his stepson perhaps three times a year on matters of urgency and, almost as rarely, to summon Dr. Villon. It stood in his and Enid's bedroom, between their beds. Actually getting one's hands on it was more difficult than obtaining the use of the phone trolley in a crowded hospital.

Having cast upon him a look of reproachful astonishment, Honoré said in elementary slow French that the phone was in Enid's room, that to disturb Enid would be a sin, that it was ten minutes to midnight and, lastly, that he had thought Gray was asleep.

"It's urgent," said Gray, but without explanation.

Honoré wasn't going to let him get away with that. Whom did he wish to phone and why? Answering his own question, he suggested it must be a woman with whom Gray had made a date he now realised he couldn't keep. In a way this was true, but Gray didn't say so. Honoré proceeded to tell him, firstly, that calls to England were of a cost *formidable* and, secondly, that any woman one could phone at midnight couldn't be virtuous and the relationship he supposed Gray was having with her must therefore be immoral. He, Honoré Duval, wouldn't give his support to immorality, especially at midnight.

Gray thought, not for the first time, how absurd it is that the French whom the English think of as sexy and raffish should in fact be morally strict while believing the English sexy and depraved. "This," he said, trying to keep his patience, "is something I've forgotten to do in the rush of coming here, something to do with Isabel."

"Isabel," said Honore, "has gone to Australia. Now go to your bed, Gray-arm, and tomorrow we see, *hein?*"

Gray saw it was useless. Whom could he phone, anyway? In his panic, he hadn't thought of that. At this hour there wasn't anyone he could phone and he told himself, still feeling sick and cold, that there was nothing to be done till the morning.

He couldn't sleep. He tossed from side to side, sometimes getting up and going to the window until the dawn came and the chained dog began to bark. Gray flung himself face-downwards on the bed. A doze that was more dream than sleep came to him at about five, the dream he often had in which Drusilla was telling him she wanted to marry him.

"Will you ask Tiny to divorce you?" he'd said as he was saying now in the dream.

"How can I? He wouldn't, anyway."

"If you left him and stayed away for five years he'd have to whether he wanted to or not."

"*Five years?* Where'll we be in five years? Who's going to keep me? You?"

"We'd both have to work. They talk about unemployment, but there's plenty of work if you don't mind what you do."

Her white hands, beringed, that had never done heavier work than put flowers in a vase, whisk cream, wash silk . . . She stared at him, her thin pink mouth curling.

"Gray, I can't live without money. I've always had it. I've always had everything I wanted. I can't imagine what life'd be if I couldn't just walk into a shop and buy something when I wanted it."

"Then we go on as we are."

"He might die," she said. "If he dies it'll all be mine. It's in his will, I've seen it. He's got hundreds of thousands in shares, not a million but hundreds of thousands."

"So what? It's his. What'd you do with it if it were yours, anyway?"

"Give it to you," she said simply.

"That's not my tough little Dru talking."

"Damn you! Damn you! I *would*."

"What can I do about it? Kill him for you?"

"Yes," she said.

He lurched awake, bathed in sweat, muttering, "I couldn't kill anyone, anything. I couldn't kill a fly, a wasp . . ." and then he remembered. He couldn't kill anything but he was now, at this moment, killing a dog. With that thought came simultaneously a tremendous relief, a knowledge, sudden and satisfying, that it was all right, that Isabel wouldn't have left Dido there after all. Because she'd have met the milkman. She was coming at twelve and she was always punctual; the milkman too was always punctual and came at twelve, except on Fridays when he was later. The milkman knew he was away and would have told Isabel. She'd have been very cross and put out but she wouldn't have left the dog.

He fell at once into a profound and dreamless sleep from which he was awakened at about eight by the pompous measured tones of Dr. Villon. The snoring was no longer audible. Gray got up and dressed quickly, rather ashamed to be so relieved and happy when his mother was dying and perhaps now dead.

Enid wasn't dead. A spark of life clung to that otherwise lifeless body, showing itself in the faint rise and fall of her chest under the bedclothes. He did what Honoré had urged him to do but what he wouldn't do in his stepfather's presence, kissed her gently on the sunken yellowish cheek. Then he went into the kitchen where Honoré was repeating to the doctor that he wouldn't wish it prolonged.

"*Bonjour,*" said Gray. "*Je crois qu'il fera chaud aujourd'hui.*"

The doctor took this to indicate Gray's having received a miraculous gift of tongues and burst into a long disquisition on the weather, the harvest, tourism, the state of French roads, and the imminence of drought. Gray said, "Excuse me, I'm going out to get some fresh bread."

His stepfather smiled sadly. "He does not understand, *mon vieux*. You are wasting your breath."

Bajon lay baked in hard white sunlight. The road was dusty, showing in the distance under the bra advertisement (*Desirée. Votre Soutien-gorge*) shivering mirages above the potholes. He bought two bread sticks and turned back, passing a milkman on a cart. This milkman wore a black T-shirt and a black beret but, in spite of his Gallic air, he had something of the look of Gray's own milkman, and this impression was enhanced when he raised one hand and called out, "*Bonjour, monsieur!*"

Gray waved back. He'd never see his own milkman again and he'd miss him more than anyone else in Pocket Lane. It had been rather nice and touching the way his milkman had shaken hands with him when they'd said goodbye and . . .

God! He'd forgotten that. Of course Isabel wouldn't have seen the milkman because he wasn't calling any more. Gray had paid him and said goodbye. And he wouldn't even be down that end of the lane. He'd said that was the one good thing about losing Gray's custom, not having to go all the way down the lane again. Oh, *God*. He'd snatched those few hours of sleep on the strength of utter illusion. Things were just as they'd been last night, only worse. Dido *was* in the hovel and now—it was half-past nine—she'd been there for nearly seventy hours.

He felt almost faint, standing there in the heat, the *baguettes* under his arm, at the enormity of it. He wanted to run away and hide somewhere, hide himself for years on the other side of the earth. But it was ridiculous thinking like that. He had to stay and he had to phone someone and *now*.

But who? Miss Platt, obviously. She lived nearest. She was a nice kindly woman who probably loved animals but wasn't one of those censorious old bags who'd relish lecturing him on his cruelty and then broadcasting it about. And she was practical, self-reliant. She wouldn't be afraid of the dog who had by now very likely lost all her gentleness in fear and hunger. Why had he been such a fool as to stop Miss Platt when she'd offered to keep an eye on the hovel? If only he'd agreed none of this would have happened. Useless thinking of that now. The only thing to think of was somehow getting hold of Miss Platt's number.

"How pale is your face!" said Honoré when he put the bread down on the kitchen table. "It's the shock," he said in French to Dr. Villon. "He mustn't be ill. What will become of me if I have two *malades* on my hands?"

"I'd like the phone, Honoré, please."

"Ah, to telephone the bad lady, I think."

"This lady is seventy years old and lives next door to me in England. I want her to see to something at my house."

"*Mais le télèphone se trouve dans la chambre de Mme. Duval!*" exclaimed Dr. Villon who had picked up one word of this.

Gray said he knew the telephone found itself in the room of his mother but the lead on it was long and could be taken out into the hall. Muttering about *formidable* expense, Honoré fetched the phone and stuck it on the hall floor. Gray was getting directory enquiries when he remembered that Miss Platt wouldn't be there. Today was Thursday and she'd moved.

He mustn't despair over a thing like that. There were other people. Francis, for instance. Francis wouldn't like it but he'd do it. Anyone but a monster would do it. No, on second thoughts, Francis couldn't because he'd gone to Devon with Charmian. Jeff, then. Jeff had the van to get him there fast. Good. After a long delay, Gray heard the distant burr-burr of the phone ringing in Tranmere Villas. Jeff was the perfect person to ask, not censorious or thick either, not the kind to want a string of explanations or to make a fuss about breaking in. Whoever went would have to do that as he, Gray, had one key, the other was on the hook, and the third . . .

When he'd heard twenty burr-burrs and got no answer, he gave up. No use wasting time. Jeff must be out with the van. Who else was there? Hundreds of people, David, Sally, Liam, Bob . . . David would be at work and God knew where he worked; Sally had gone to Mull; Liam was among the dozens of friends Jeff said had left London; Bob would be at a lecture. There was always Mrs. Warriner. He'd heard of her from Mal but not actually seen her for three years. He couldn't bring himself to phone a sixty-year-old Wimbledon lady who had no car and ask her to make a twenty-mile journey.

Back to Pocket Lane, review the scene there. Pity he hadn't chatted up the library girl or got to know some of the people on the estate. Mr. Tringham had no phone. That left the Willises. His courage almost failed him, but there was no help for it. A quickly flashing picture of Dido collapsed on the floor, her swollen tongue extended from bared teeth, and he was asking the operator to find him Mrs. Willis's number.

"Oueeleece," repeated the operator. Surely there could hardly be a more difficult name for a Frenchwoman to get her tongue round. "Will you please spell that?"

Gray spelt it. Burr-burr, burr-burr . . . She was going to be out too or on holiday. The whole world was away. He slumped on to the floor and put his hand up to his damp forehead. Click, and she answered.

"Pocket Farm."

"I have a call from Bajon-sur-Lone, France."

"Yes, all right. Who is that?"

"Mrs. Willis? This is Graham Lanceton."

"*Who?*"

"Graham Lanceton. I'm afraid we had a bit of a disagreement when last we met. I live at the White Cottage and the thing is . . ."

"Are you the person who had the nerve to let the cows into my garden? Are you the man who insulted me with some of the vilest language I ever heard in my . . . ?"

"Yes, yes, I'm extremely sorry about that. Please don't ring off."

But she did. With a shrill, "You must be mad!" she crashed down the receiver. Gray cursed and kicked the phone. He went back to Honoré and the doctor and poured himself a cup of coffee. Honoré gave him a sideways smile.

"So? You succeed?"

"No." He longed to tell someone about it, to have the views of someone else, even someone as hopelessly unsuitable as his stepfather. Honoré was narrow and bourgeois, but the bourgeois often know what to do in emergencies. Sitting down, he told Honoré what had happened and how he had failed.

Utter mystification clouded Honoré's face. For a moment he was stupefied, silent. Then he translated everything Gray had said for the benefit of the doctor. Rapidly and incomprehensibly they discussed the matter for a while, shaking their heads, shrugging and waving their hands about. Finally Honoré said in English, "Your mummy die and you are unquiet for a dog?"

"I've told you."

"For a *dog!*" Honoré threw up his hands, cackled, said to Dr. Villon in slower and readily understandable French, "I know it is a cliché to say so but the English are all mad. I who married one am forced to admit it. They are mad and they love animals more than people."

"I shall go and attend my patient," said Dr. Villon, casting upon Gray a frown of contempt.

Gray returned to the hall. All warmth had passed from his body and he was shivering. He must rescue the dog and he must phone someone to effect this rescue for him. There was only one person left.

She was the obvious person and, strangely, the best fitted for the job. She wouldn't hesitate or be afraid. She had a key. She lived near enough to be there in a quarter of an hour.

It was a Thursday. On a Thursday they had first become lovers and on a Thursday they had parted. Thursday had always been their day, Thor's day, the day of the most powerful of the gods.

He sat on the floor, not touching the phone, not yet, but confronting it, facing it as if for a duel he knew it would win. It was immobile, expectant, complacent, waiting for him to yield to it. And, though silent, it seemed to be saying, I am the magic, the saviour, the breaker of hearts, the go-between of lovers, the god that will give life to a dog and draw you back to bondage.

CHAPTER 12

A stream of sunshine poured through the frosted glass of the front door, almost blinding him. In such bright, early summer light she'd stood that morning in the hovel kitchen where Dido now was. She was so beautiful and the light so brilliant that the dazzlement of both had hurt his eyes. Wide-eyed, undisturbed by the sunlight because it was behind her, she'd said, "Yes, why not? Why not kill him?"

"You're joking. You're not serious."

"Aren't I? I've even worked out how to do it. You'll get him here and give him some acid like you gave me, only he won't know. Give it to him in tea. And then when he leaves—you'll have to time that carefully—he'll crash. He'll go over the top of the Wake roundabout."

"Apart from the fact that I wouldn't, it's absurd. It's so old-hat, freaking people out with acid for a joke."

"Damn you, it's not a joke! It'd work."

He'd laughed as one laughs with embarrassment at other people's fantasies, and said with a shrug, shifting out of the light into sane cool shadow, "You do it, then, if that's the kind of thing you fancy. He's your bloke. You give him acid and let him crash his car in Loughton High Road, only don't expect me to get it for you."

"Gray . . ." The hand in his, the thin scented lips against his neck, his ear, "Gray, let's talk about it. As a joke, if you like, but let's *see* if it could be done. We'll pretend we're the sort of unhappy wife and her lover you read about in murder books. Mrs. Thompson and Bywaters or Mrs. Bravo and her old doctor. Let's just talk, Gray."

He jerked to his feet and out of the blazing light as his mother's own old doctor came out of the sickroom. Dr. Villon threw up his hands, sighed, and went into the kitchen. Gray squatted down again, took off the phone receiver and immediately replaced it. He couldn't talk to her. How could he even have considered it? There must be other people, there must be someone . . . But he'd been through all that before and there wasn't.

The only thing to do was to put the whole thing into cold practical terms, to forget all those dreams he'd had of her and those total recall reconstructions, and tell himself plainly what had happened and what he was doing. Well, he'd had a love affair and a very satisfying one, much as most people do sometime in their lives. It had ended because the two of them weren't really compatible. But there wasn't any reason why they couldn't still be friends, was there? If he was going to go through life being afraid of meeting every woman he'd had any sort of relationship with, it was a poor look-out. It was ridiculous to get neurotic over talking to an old friend.

An old friend? *Drusilla?* No more of that . . . He could sit here all day arguing with himself and all the time the dog was in there, starving, maybe going mad. Once more he'd talk to her, just once. In some ways it might actually do him good to talk to her. Very probably hearing her voice—talking to him, not like that Marble Arch one-sided thing—and hearing the stupid ignorant things she'd say would cure him of her once and for all.

With a half-smile, blasé, a little rueful (the rake giving his discarded mistress a ring for old times' sake) he picked up the receiver and dialled her number. He dialled the code and the seven digits. It was all so simple. His hand was trembling which was rather absurd. He cleared his throat, listening to the number ringing, once, twice, three times . . .

"Yes?"

His heart turned over. He put his hand to it as if, stupidly, he could steady its turbulence through ribs and flesh. And now the temptation to do what he'd done on Saturday night, to breathe only, to listen and not to speak, was nearly overpowering. He closed his eyes and saw the sunshine as a scarlet lake, burning, split by meteors.

"Yes?"

Again he cleared his throat which felt bone dry yet choked with phlegm.

"Drusilla." That one word was all he could manage but it was enough. Enough to cause utter deep silence, broken at last by her sigh, a long rough sound like a fingernail drawing across silk.

"You took your time," she said slowly, enunciating each word with great care; then briskly, shockingly, and in her old way, "What d'you want?"

"Dru, I . . ." Where was the rake, the casual caller-up of old girl friends? Gray made a grab at this errant Don Juan who had never really been an alter ego, tried to speak with his voice, "How are you? How have you been all these months?"

"All right. I'm always all right. You didn't ring me up to ask that."

Don Juan said, "No, I rang you as an old friend."

"An old what? You've got a nerve!"

"Dru . . ." Firmly now, remembering nothing but the dog, "I'm ringing you to ask you to do me a favour."

"Why should I? You never did me any."

"Please listen, Dru. I know I've no right to ask anything of you. I wouldn't do this if it wasn't—terribly urgent. There's no one else I can ask." It was easy after all, easy after the first initial shock. "I'm in France. My mother's—well, dying." And then he told her about it, as he'd told Honoré but more succinctly.

A sort of soft vibrant moan came down the line. For a moment he thought she was crying, not at the pathos of the story, but for them, for what they'd lost. There came a gasp and he knew she was laughing.

"What a fool you are! You make a mess of everything."

"But you will go there, won't you?"

A pause. A gust of smothered laughter. He was talking to her quite ordinarily and pleasantly and she was laughing also quite ordinarily and pleasantly. It was hard to believe.

"I'll go," she said. "Haven't much choice, have I? What am I supposed to do with it when I get it out?"

"Could you get her to a vet?"

"I don't know any bloody vets. Oh, I'll find one. I think you've lost your mind."

"Quite possibly. Dru, could you—will you call me back at this number? I can't call you because my stepfather freaks out if I keep using the phone."

"I'll phone you. Tonight sometime. I'm not surprised about your stepfather. You haven't any money, that's your trouble, and when people haven't any money other people treat them like children. It's a rule of life."

"Dru . . . ?"

"Yes?"

"Nothing," he said. "You'll call me back?"

"Didn't I say I would?" The phone went down hard. He hadn't had a chance even to say goodbye. She never said it. Not once could he remember her ever saying the word goodbye. He scrambled to his feet, went into the bathroom and was sick down the loo.

Enid was snoring irregularly. Otherwise the house was silent. Gray lay on his bed in the blue room whose closed curtains couldn't shut out the blaze of noon. Mme. Roland remarked to him scornfully, aloof in the face of the scaffold, "O Liberty, what crimes are committed in thy name!"

Well, he'd done it and it hadn't been too bad. The sickness was only natural after the release of so much tension. He'd spoken to his discarded mistress and the dog would be rescued. Cool and practical, he was becoming almost what Honoré or Isabel would call a mature grown-up person. Well, well. *C'est le premier pas qui coûte:* as Honoré might say, and he'd got over the first step which counted. No harm would be done at this juncture, however, in reminding himself by another one of those reconstructions of the ugliness he'd escaped and the pitfall there still might be.

"Suppose we were serious," he'd said, "I don't see how we'd get him here."

"That's easy. You write him a letter."

"What sort of letter? 'Dear Tiny, if you'll pop over one afternoon, I'd like to give you some acid to make you crash your car. Yours truly, G. Lanceton.'"

"Don't be so bloody stupid. He collects coins, doesn't he? He's always advertising for coins in some rag called *Numismatists' News*. Get the typewriter, go on."

So he'd got the typewriter to humour her.

"Now I'll dictate. Put your address and the date, June the sixth."

She'd looked over his shoulder, her hair against his face. "Now write, 'Dear Sir, As a fellow numismatist . . .' No, that won't do. 'Dear Sir, in reply to your advertisement . . .' Sometimes he advertises in *The Times*. Oh, God, get a fresh bit of paper."

How many attempts had they made before they got the letter that satisfied her? Three? Four? At last, the final, perfect one. "Dear Sir, in reply to your advertisement in *The Times*, I think I have just what you are looking for. Since my home is not far from yours, would you care to come over and see it? Four o'clock on Saturday would be a suitable time. Yours faithfully . . ."

"And how am I supposed to sign it?"

"Better not put your real name."

He signed it Francis Duval. She folded it up and made him type the envelope: *Harvey Janus Esq., Combe Park, Wintry Hill, Loughton, Essex.*

His indulgent smile growing rather stiff, rather sick, he'd said, "I don't have any old coins, Dru."

"I'll give you one. He's got lots of worthless coins he keeps in a box, things he thought were valuable when he first started collecting. I'll give you a Roman denier."

"Then he'd know I wasn't serious."

"Of course. So what? He'll think you just don't know. He'll say that's not what he wants and you'll say you're sorry but now he's here can you give him a cup of tea?"

"Dru, I'm getting a bit tired of this game."

O, Liberty, what crimes . . . The doorbell was ringing. Gray got off the bed because no one was answering it. There was a note on the hall table: *Depart to village for shopping. Make care of Mummy. Honoré.* He opened the door. A stout elderly man in a grey suit and grey Homburg stood there. Gray recognised the mayor whom Honoré on some previous occasion had pointed out to him across the street.

"*Entrez, monsieur, je vous en prie.*"

The mayor said in English which was very beautifully pronounced, very nearly perfect, "Mr. Graham Lanceton? I saw your stepfather in the village and he told me it would be convenient to call. How is your poor mother?"

Gray said there was no change. He showed the mayor into the living room. After what Honoré had said, the mayor's command of English struck him almost dumb. But that was typical of Honoré who, with unbounded arrogance, had probably convinced himself he was the superior linguist. Sensing his astonishment, the mayor said, with a smile; "Many years ago I spent a year in your country. I was attached to a company in Manchester. A beautiful city."

Gray had heard otherwise but he didn't say so. "I believe you—er, wanted to give me your views on my book." Might as well get it over at once.

"I should not presume, Mr. Lanceton. I am not a literary critic. I enjoyed your novel. It recalled to me happy memories of Manchester."

Since *The Wine of Astonishment* was set exclusively in Notting Hill, Gray couldn't quite understand this but he was relieved to be spared the criticism. The mayor sat silent, smiling, apparently perfectly at ease.

Gray said, "Would you care for some coffee?"

"I thank you, no. If there were perhaps some tea?"

If only there were! No packet of tea had ever found its way into Le Petit Trianon. "I'm afraid not."

"It is of no importance. It was not for coffee or tea or the discussion of contemporary literature that I came."

Why had he come, then? The mayor sat in easeful silence for quite a minute. Then he leant forward and said slowly, "Your stepfather is a gentleman of great vitality. Ebullience is, I think, the word."

"Well, it's *a* word."

"A man of impulse and one who, I think I may say, is inclined somewhat to our national vice, common among our peasantry of —shall I name it?—avarice. What matters one small vice among so many virtues?"

The mayor's English grew more expert and semantically involved with every sentence. It recalled to Gray the speech of solicitors in Victorian novels. He listened, puzzled but fascinated.

"A desire too to acquire something for nothing or almost nothing, a need to cast bread upon the waters and harvest whole loaves."

"I'm afraid I don't follow you, monsieur."

"Ah, perhaps not. I will abandon metaphor, I will make a long story short. You expect, I understand, when something happens to your mother—this English euphemism I find so tactful, so gentle—to be her heir?"

Taken aback, Gray said, "I shall inherit half, yes."

"But half of what, Mr. Lanceton? Listen, if you will be so good. Let me explain. Half of what your poor mother leaves when she passes on—you see, I know you English do not care for the strict cold expression—half will be, to put it bluntly, half of this bungalow!"

Gray stared. "I don't understand. My mother had a good deal of money invested when she remarried and . . ."

" 'Had,' " interrupted the mayor urbanely, "is the operative word. Let me be quite open and aboveboard with you. M. Duval reinvested this money, speculated, if you will. There was a mine, I believe, a railway to be built that, alas, was not built. You may imagine."

Gray imagined. He knew nothing about the stock market except what everyone knows, that it is easier to lose there than to gain. But he didn't feel at all sick or angry or even very disappointed. How had he believed there would ever be any real money from any source for him?

"So you see, Mr. Lanceton," said the Victorian solicitor, "that were you to claim your inheritance, as you would be within your rights to do, you would only deprive an ageing man of the very roof over his head. This, I am sure, you would not do."

"No," said Gray rather sadly, "no, I wouldn't do that."

"Good. Excellent." The mayor got up, still smiling. "I was sure my words would be effectual. We speak," he added with a slight pedantic laugh, "the same language."

"How will he live?" asked Gray, shaking hands.

"He had the forethought, poor gentleman, to purchase a small annuity."

He would. "Goodbye," said Gray.

"I will not be so optimistic as to wish your mother recovered health, Mr. Lanceton, but say only that we must hope her suffering will not be prolonged."

They must have arranged to meet somewhere and chew over the results of the interview, for when Honoré returned with his full shopping bag, he was truly, to use the mayor's word, in an ebullient mood. He actually embraced Gray.

"My son, my boy! How goes the bad lady? You make contact with her? And the poor animal?"

Gray said, with a sense of unreality, that everything was all right now.

"Then I make the lunch. *Croque Monsieur* for us today."

"No, I'll do it." Even this simple, though grandly named, dish wasn't safe in the hands of Honoré who would be sure to add herbs and garlic to the cheese. "You go and sit with Mother."

Poor Honoré. Poor, indeed. Slicing up cheese, Gray reflected on the strange calm he felt, the lightness of heart even. Honoré while rich had been hateful to him, a kind of King to his Hamlet. For Honoré poor he had a fellow feeling. The bath water watching, the shouts of Extinguish, please! the phone fanaticism—weren't they, after all, only the sort of economies he too was forced to practise? It amused him to think of those two, Honoré and the mayor, screwing up their courage to tell him the truth, afraid of his righteous anger. But it hadn't angered him at all. Probably he'd have done the same in Honoré's place, blued all his money on a bubble and then sent some braver deputy to confess it to his judge.

No, he wasn't angry. But he was a bit ashamed of himself for mentally accusing Honoré of wanting to make away with his wife. Not every marriage partner was a Drusilla.

"Drusilla," he'd said, "I've had enough of this. It's as stupid as mooning over what you'd do if you won the pools."

"No, it isn't. You can't fix the pools. You can fix this. Just let me post that letter. I've still got it."

"It's out of date."

"Write another, then. What's the date? July the first. 'Dear Sir, In reply to your advertisement . . .'"

"I'm going out. I'm going for a walk. It's no fun being with you if all you can do is play this stupid game."

"It's not a game, it's serious."

"All right," he'd said. "So it's serious. Once and for all, will you listen to me? Leaving morality out of it, it wouldn't work. Probably he wouldn't die. He'd feel strange, see distortions and park the car. He'd ask the first motorist he saw to go to the police and the first person they'd come to'd be me."

"You don't know him. He always drives very fast. He wouldn't be able to stop in time. And they wouldn't know about you because I'd get hold of the letter and burn it."

"Burn it now," he'd said.

He shook himself and looked at Honoré who sat at the opposite side of the table, eating toasted cheese. His eyes were bright and darting but not, Gray suddenly realised, the malicious eyes of a potential killer. Honoré lacked the intelligence to be wicked. And Gray realised too that all the time he'd been at Le Petit Trianon he hadn't done a thing to help until today when he'd made the lunch. Honoré had done it all and, on the whole, done it well.

"Why don't you go out for a bit?" he said. "You need a change. Take your car."

The Citroën was hardly ever used. It lived in the garage under a nylon cover, coming out once a week to be polished. But Gray understood that now too.

"Where will I go?"

"See a friend. Go to the cinema. I don't know."

Honoré threw up his hands, smiled his monkey smile. "I don't know too, Gray-arm."

So they sat together in Enid's room, waiting for her to die. Gray read *The Way of All Flesh* intermittently. He held his mother's hand, feeling very calm, very tranquil. His mother was dying but he no longer had any reason to hope for her death. He had no money to keep him from working, to lull him into idle security. The dog would be safe now. Drusilla would phone him soon, he'd thank her and they'd say their last dignified goodbyes. Even she would say goodbye. It was wonderful to feel so free, to know that no crimes need be committed to secure liberty.

The evening was close as if a storm threatened—not tonight perhaps or tomorrow but soon. Honoré had gone to the Écu, assured by Gray that this would be good for him, that no useful purpose could be served by his staying with Enid.

Gray, who had been at peace since noon, as if his physical sickness had provided a more than physical catharsis, began to feel a gradual mounting of tension. He had meant to sit outside among the gnomes or the tripods. Provided he left the doors open, he'd hear the phone when it rang, for he'd placed it on the hall floor near the kitchen door. But, although he went into the garden, he couldn't concentrate on the last chapters of his book.

It was Thursday and Tiny went to his Masons on Thursdays at about six. She could have phoned him then. Why hadn't she? He told himself that it was only the dog's fate that was worrying him. He was concerned only for the dog and for Isabel. Drusilla was what he'd called her that morning, a discarded mistress, interesting only as an old friend might be when doing him a favour.

It was Thursday. Very likely she still turned her Thursday evenings to good account, possibly with what's-his-name, the tennis guy, Ian Something. Perhaps she was with him now and wouldn't phone till he'd gone. Gray pondered this idea, found it particularly unpleasant and went back into the house. The farmer's dog had stopped barking. No doubt it had been let off its lead. It was almost too dark to make out the shape of the phone which, doglike, was also attached to a lead, a wire stretched through the crack in the door.

Ten o'clock. He looked in on his mother who had ceased to snore, who lay on her back with her mouth open. Suppose Drusilla didn't phone? Suppose, in order to be revenged on him, she'd promised to see about the dog and then deliberately done nothing? He could phone her. If he was going to he'd better be quick, for another half hour and it would be too late for safety. But she'd phone him. She never changed her mind and she always did what she undertook.

He stood over the phone, directing his will on it, telling it to ring, ring. He clenched his fists, tensed his muscles, said to it, "Ring, damn you. Ring, you bastard!"

It obeyed him immediately and rang.

CHAPTER 13

When he had coped with the stream of idiomatic French which issued from the receiver, when he had told M. Reville, the glass manufacturer, that his mother remained the same and that Honoré had gone to the Écu, he uncorked the brandy bottle and drank some. Honoré was getting everything else, after all. He oughtn't to grudge him a drop of brandy.

If she didn't phone he wouldn't be able to sleep. That was ridiculous, though, because if she hadn't been to the hovel Dido would be dead by now and all further worry pointless. He had some more brandy and put the bottle away. He wished he knew exactly what he was worrying about. Honoré was out and he could easily phone her. There was a good half hour before danger time and Tiny got home. He'd phoned her before, twice if you counted the Marble Arch time, and it was the first step that counted.

Surely he wasn't still afraid of getting involved with her again? Or maybe afraid of *not* getting involved with her? Remember what she is, he told himself, remember what she wanted you to do . . .

" 'Dear Sir, In reply to your advertisement . . . !' Put the date. It's November the twenty-first. Oh, come on, Gray. Get up then and I'll do it. Any fool can type, I suppose. My God, it's freezing in here. When he's dead and we're together all the time we'll never be cold again. We'll have a flat in Kensington and if the central heating doesn't go up to eighty we'll have it all taken out and new in."

"We aren't going to be together all the time and you know it. We're going to go on like this till one of us gets tired of the other."

"What's that supposed to mean? I didn't see any signs of tiredness upstairs just now."

He'd turned away, warming his hands at the oil heater, looking wearily at the window scummed with frost, the skeletal trees beyond, rooted in pools of water thinly crusted with ice. Round her shoulders she'd slung the red fox, coarser and brighter than her hair.

"There's more to life than sex," he said.

"Like what? Like living in a frozen slum? Like brooding about the books you don't write and the money you can't make? I'm going to do this letter and by the spring—March, say—we can be living together with all his money in a joint account. God, but my fingers are too cold to type. You do it."

"Dru, you said just now you didn't see any signs of tiredness. All right, I'm not tired of sex. I don't think I'd ever get tired of sex with you. But I'm sick and tired to my soul of you ballsing on about killing your husband. It's grotesque."

She'd crashed her hands down on the keys so that they tangled and stuck together. Her eyes were white fire.

"D'you mean me? D'you mean I'm grotesque?"

"I didn't say that but—yes, you're grotesque and stupid and a bit mad when you talk of making that poor bloke crash his car."

"Damn you! Damn you!" He'd had to hold her off, seize her hands and force them behind her to stop her long nails tearing at his face. She'd crumpled and softened, the fur falling from her shoulders, leaving her vulnerable in the thin clinging dress that was so unsuitable for the hovel. And then, of course, the inevitable. Because this was Drusilla who, naked, warm, and sinuous under the piled blankets, was anything but grotesque, anything but stupid . . .

The tape that was playing in his brain switched off sharply. Stop, stop, remember the bad times. Forget that the bad times always ended in good times until that last time. Twenty past ten. She wasn't going to phone. That bloody thing, straining on the end of its wire leash, wasn't going to ring again tonight.

He was halfway back to the cupboard where the brandy was when the bell brayed at him. He jumped, and the jump was so galvanic that it actually pained him. Then he was on the phone at a leap, crouched over it, gasping out, "Yes, Dru, yes?"

"Hi," she said.

The coolness of her voice chilled memories, blew away longing and dreading. "What happened?" he said. "Did you find her?"

"I found her." There was a long pause. "God, Gray," she said with an almost refined distaste, quite unlike her, "God, how *could* you?"

"Is she dead?" He sat on the floor, resting his head against the wall.

"No. She was alive—just."

He exhaled on a long sigh. "What happened?" he said again.

"I took some milk and chicken with me. I was a bit scared to open the kitchen door but I needn't have been, she was too weak to move. God, the stink and the muck in there! She'd got up on the sink and plastered the window with her muck and saliva—the lot."

"Oh, Dru . . ." His head had begun to bang. It was the brandy partly, and partly the shock, though he ought to have been relieved. This was the best that could have happened.

She said harshly, "Someone ought to lock you up in a cell for three days without food or water and see how you'd like it. Why didn't you phone the police, anyway?"

Why hadn't he? It was the obvious thing. "I never thought of it."

"You haven't phoned them today?"

"No, of course not."

"You just left it to me? Typical. D'you want to hear the rest? I carried her out to the car and, Christ, was she heavy. In the car I gave her some milk but she couldn't take the chicken. Then I got her to this vet."

"Which vet?"

"A guy in Leytonstone."

"*Leytonstone?* Why on earth . . . ?"

"Because I was going up to town."

"I see," he said. She always left her car in the car park at Leytonstone tube station when she was going to London. But to have gone today? It seemed heartless, too casual. And why had she gone? To buy clothes? To—meet someone? "You went to London?"

"Why not? It's not my dog, as I hastened to tell the vet. I didn't want him thinking I'd do a thing like that. You'd better have his address and see him as soon as you get back. It's twenty-one George Street. Got that?"

"Yes. Thanks. I'm very very grateful, Dru. I ought to have phoned the police, of course. I ought . . ." He broke off, fumbling in his mind for suitable words to end the conversation. She'd done the favour he'd asked of her and now was the time for those dignified goodbyes. Thanks, no hard feelings, maybe we'll meet again someday, and meanwhile thanks . . . "Well, Dru, maybe after all this trauma we'll be able to meet one of these days and—well, you know what I mean. I'll never forget what you—I mean I'll never . . ."

"After I got back from town," she said as if he hadn't spoken, "I went in and cleaned up a bit for you."

"You did what?" He remembered once having told her that the only brush she ever lifted was the one she used for mascara. And now she, those white hands of hers, had cleaned up his filthy kitchen. He could hardly believe it. "Why did you do that?"

"Why did I get the dog? Why do I do anything for you? Don't you know yet?"

Goodbye, Drusilla. Good night, sweet lady, good night. Say it, say it, Don Juan hissed at him. A tremor rose in his throat, choking him, taking away the power of speech. He rested his cheek against the wall to cool his blood-heated face.

"You don't know, do you?" Her voice was very soft now. "You don't think about my feelings. I'm O.K. when you want someone to get you out of a mess, that's all. As far as you're concerned, the rest is over and done with."

"And you know why," he whispered, "it had to be over and done with." Clinging to a shred of sanity, he said, "We had to split up. I couldn't take it."

"That? I've given all that up. It would never have worked. I see that now." She paused and said in a very low childlike voice, almost as if reluctantly, "I tried to phone you a lot of times."

His heart was pounding. "On Thursday nights?"

"Of course."

"I left the receiver off."

"Oh, you fool," she sighed. "You hopeless fool. I wanted to tell you back in January I'd given all that up. God, I was so lonely. I wanted to talk to you so much. The line was always engaged, always engaged. I thought . . . Never mind."

"Why didn't you come to me?"

"And find you with another girl?"

"There's been no other girl, there's been no one. I was alone too."

"Then we've been a pair of hopeless fools, haven't we? Frightened of each other when all the time we really . . . Oh, what's the use? You're in France and I'm here and Tiny'll be in in a minute. We'd better stop this before we say too much."

His voice returned to him powerfully and he almost shouted at her. "Too much? How could we say too much? Don't you see we've been apart all this time over a stupid misunderstanding? We've tortured ourselves over nothing . . ."

"I've got to ring off. I can hear Tiny's car."

"Don't ring off, please. Please. No, you must. Of course you must. Listen, I'll phone you in the morning. I'll phone you at nine as soon as he's gone. God, Dru, I'm so happy . . ."

A sighing whisper cut him short. "Tomorrow, then," and the phone slid delicately into silence. In the dark warm hall he sat on the floor, cradling the receiver in his hands, hearing still an echo or a memory of her voice. His heart quietened, his body relaxed like a taut spring set free to uncoil, and as happiness, pure joy, swamped him he wanted to dance and shout, run outside and sing, embrace the tripods, yell to the whole of sleeping Bajon that his love had come back to him.

Instead of doing that, he got to his feet and went into his mother's room. Enid lay on her back, breathing shallowly, her eyes closed. Once, when he'd had nothing much to tell, he'd been able to tell her everything, and she'd listened and understood. If she were aware now, conscious, would she understand? Wouldn't her own experience of passion give her empathy?

He bent over her. He said, "Mother, I'm so happy. Everything has come right for me."

Her lids moved. The wrinkled black-stained hoods lifted and half-showed her eyes. In his euphoric state, he fancied he saw recognition there, comprehension even, and in that moment he loved

her again, forgiving her entirely. He took her face in his hands and
pressed his lips against the corner of her mouth, kissing her as
he hadn't kissed her since he was a little boy.

Mme. Roland gave him a cynical glare and he turned her picture
to the wall. He didn't want her shouting her predecapitation
liberty nonsense at him any more. He knew all about liberty, he'd
had enough of it in the past six months. He'd taken his liberty
to avoid committing a crime and now he thought he'd committed
a crime against himself and Drusilla. Let Mme. Roland make what
she liked of that with her histrionic *salon* philosophy.

He got into bed naked because of the heat. How long was he
going to have to stay here? Days? Weeks? If only he'd got money
he could fly home and see her and then come back again. That
wasn't possible—but to wait here on and on while she was in England longing for him as he was longing for her? It was a pity, he
thought, that uncomplicated joy lasts so short a time, that it must
always give way rapidly to practicalities and plans. In the morning
when he phoned her they'd have to start making plans. In the
morning, too, he'd phone Jeff and tell him not to come on Saturday. Maybe he wouldn't be moving now, after all.

In a couple of weeks time, perhaps less, she'd be visiting him at
the hovel again just like she used to before Christmas. And they'd
discuss the dead months with laughter at their own folly, reducing
Christmas as they looked back on it to a row not much bigger than
any of their rows, a momentary frown on the face of love.

In the hot stuffy bedroom where no wind lifted the curtains at
the open window, where the air was warm and dry at midnight, it
was hard to imagine snow. But snow had come before Christmas,
and on the night before the Eve, Drusilla, the red fox lady, had
pelted him with snowballs, screaming, laughing, as they walked in
the frozen forest. He caught her in his arms and, mouth to mouth,
the snow crystals melting on warm lips, they'd fallen to make love
in the drifts under the sealskin branches of the beech trees.

That was a good memory, one to hold on to now, one he
wouldn't have dared recall till now when she was back with him.
But the quarrel that came after? How many times had he played
that tape over and over, following as it did their final act of love?

The last time, he'd thought, the last time. Now it wasn't going to be the last time. It would even cease to be associated with the quarrel, and the quarrel itself would fade down one of the alleys which debouch from the avenue of time.

He turned over, spread-eagled under the crumpled sheet. A Thursday, of course. Exactly twenty-four weeks ago tonight. No Christmas decorations at the hovel, for Christmas was to be spent in London with Francis. But the present she'd given him on the bath cover in the kitchen, the present of a silver chain on which hung a silver Hand of Fortune (since sold) and all around it the red and gold wrappings he'd torn off in his love and gratitude. He'd drawn out a ridiculous amount, far more than he could afford, to buy her *Amorce dangereuse* and she'd laughed with delight, spraying it on her red fur, although she could have bought gallons of the stuff herself and not noticed.

Into the hovel to take her perfume before driving back to Combe Park. He'd worn the chain to go out in the forest and it had fallen icy against his chest, but now, under his shirt and Arran, it was warm with his body warmth. Tiny, of course, had paid for it. Her father didn't send her a cheque more than once a year.

"So what?" she'd said, and that had been the beginning. No, for it had begun long before, but just the beginning of the final quarrel, of the end. "I'm entitled to some of what he makes, I suppose? You could look on it as wages. Don't I keep house for him and cook and sleep with him? He only pays me two thousand a year and I'm cheap at the price."

"*Two thousand?*" One year he'd managed to make almost that himself, but never before and never after.

"Ah, come on, Gray. Five pounds for a silver neck thing? It's only an advance, anyway. It'll all be yours soon."

"Don't start that again, Dru. Please don't."

Don't start that, he warned himself, reaching out for the glass of water he'd put by the bed. Why remember that quarrel now? She'd given it all up, she'd said so. He'd never hear her say those things again.

"Look, Gray, you sit down and listen to me. You never thought that was a game I was playing. You were as serious as me, only you haven't got as much guts as I have."

"Please don't come the Lady Macbeth bit, Drusilla."

"Well, he did it in the end, didn't he? And so will you. We'll do another letter and you can buy the acid while you're up in town."

" 'Up in town.' You sound like the chairman of the Women's Institute off for her annual shopping spree."

She was more sensitive to this kind of insult than any other, but she took no notice. "I'll give you the money."

"Thanks. The poor bastard's going to pay for his own poison, is he? I like that. It reminds one of the Borgias. A judge'll make a lot of that—'The unfortunate Harvey Janus, murdered by his wife and her lover with a hallucinogen purchased out of his own money.' Charming."

In her red fur, waterdrops gleaming on its spikes, she sat down at the typewriter to compose another letter. The oil heater on, blue flame, incandescent; snow falling thickly, silently, against the dirty windowpane.

"Dru, will you give up this idea now? Will you promise me never to mention it again?"

"No. I'm doing it for you. You'll thank me afterwards. You'll be grateful to me all the rest of your life."

The watch she'd given him showing ten past ten; the Hand of Fortune she'd given him warm against his breastbone; melted snow lying on the floor in pools.

"It's no good, Gray. I'll never give this up."

"Will you give me up?"

She was folding the letter, sliding it into an envelope. "What's that supposed to mean?"

"That I can't go on like this. It doesn't matter what we're doing, what we're talking about. With you all roads lead to killing Tiny."

"You can put a stop to that by killing him."

"No, there's another way." He didn't look at her. "I can put a stop to it by not seeing you."

"Are you trying to say you're tired of me?"

"No, I can't imagine any man being tired of you. I'm tired of *this*. I've had it, Drusilla. As it is, I'll never be able to look back on what we had, you and me, without this poisoning it all."

"You're just a spineless coward!"

"That's true. I'm too much of a coward to kill anyone and too much of a coward to stay being your lover. You're too much for me. I hate it ending like this but I knew it would. I've known it for weeks. I shan't see you again, Dru."

"Christ, you bastard! I hate you. That's what I think of your filthy Christmas present!" The flagon broke against the heater, glass flying, scented steam rising. "I was going to make you rich. I was going to give you everything you wanted."

He felt sick. The perfume made him feel sick.

"Goodbye, Drusilla. It was nice—once. It was the best I ever had."

"You bloody liar! You ungrateful, bloody liar!"

Goodbye, Drusilla, good night, sweet lady, good night, good night . . .

"Good night, Drusilla," he said aloud. "Good night, my love. I'll talk to you in the morning."

He fell at once into a dream. He was with Tiny in the fast red car. There wasn't much room for him because Tiny was so huge, filling up his own seat and half the passenger seat, and he was driving fast, zigzagging the car from side to side of the forest road. Gray tried to make him slow down but no voice came when he tried to speak. He couldn't speak and when he put his fingers to his tongue, he found it—Oh, horrible!—divided and forked like a snake's tongue, dumb, speechless, unhuman. Then the green hillock of the roundabout was upon them, green but capped with snow, and Tiny was going over it. The red car and Tiny were going over the mountain and he, Gray, was going with them. He too was trapped in the hurtling burning car, the fire engulfing him as he struggled to get out. And now someone was hammering on the roof of the car, not a rescuer but she. Drusilla was pounding on the roof of the red Bentley to make sure that both of them were dead . . .

He gasped, "Don't, don't . . . I've had enough. I want you to give me up," and then, as the dream and the flames and the snow faded, as French smell and light and stuffiness burst back, "What . . . ? Who is it? What is it?"

Broad daylight in the bedroom and someone knocking on the door. He wrapped himself in the twisted sheet. He staggered to the door and opened it. Honoré stood outside in the dragon dressing gown, his face yellow and drawn.

"What . . . ?"

"*C'est fini.*"

"I don't . . . I was asleep."

"*C'est fini. Elle est morte.*"

"She can't be dead," he said stupidly. "It can't be finished, it's only just beginning . . ." And then he knew that Honoré meant his mother, that Enid Duval had died at last.

CHAPTER 14

In a thin high voice, Honoré said, "You come and see her?"

"All right. If you like."

The yellowness had gone from Enid's skin and death had erased most of the lines. Already she looked waxen, her open eyes glazed blue china.

"You ought to close her eyes," Gray began, and then he looked at Honoré who stood at the opposite side of the bed, dulled, silent, tears falling weakly down his cheeks. "Honoré, are you all right?"

Honoré said nothing. He fell across the bed and took the dead woman in his arms. He lay there and clung to her, making soft animal moans.

"Honoré . . ."

Gray lifted him up gently and helped him into the living room. His stepfather huddled into an armchair, shaking, his head turned against the lapel of his dressing gown. Gray gave him brandy but Honoré choked on it, sobbing. "What shall I do?" he said in French. "What will become of me?"

And then Gray saw that he'd been wrong, that his stepfather had loved her. The love hadn't been all on his mother's side but had been reciprocated to the full. Not a cynical purchase but true love. And that hatred, that disgust, he'd seen in Honoré's eyes while feeding her? Wasn't that what any man would feel? Disgust not for her but for life, for the world in which such things happened, in which the woman he loved became a helpless dribbling animal. He had loved her. He wasn't a caricature, a sick joke, but a man with a man's feelings. Gray forgot that he'd resented Honoré, hated him. He felt a great surge of guilt for misunderstanding, for laughing and despising. He forgot too, just for a moment, that he wasn't Honoré's son and—although he'd never before held a man so—he took Honoré in his arms and pressed him close against himself and forgot everything but Honoré's grief.

"My son, my son, what shall I do without her? I knew she was dying, I knew she must die, but death . . ."

"I know. I understand."

"I loved her so. I never loved any woman like her."

"I know you loved her, Honoré."

Gray made coffee and phoned the doctor and then, when it was nine and the Marseille shop where she worked would be open, he phoned Honoré's sister. Mme. Derain agreed to come. Trilling r's, swallowed vowels assaulted Gray along a crackly line, but he gathered that she'd come by Monday when she'd made arrangements with her employer.

The day was going to be close and oppressive but cooler, the sun veiled by cloud. The doctor came, then Father Normand, then an old woman, a very French little old woman looking like something out of Zola, whose job was to lay Enid Duval out. Gray, who had always been treated in this house as if he were a recalcitrant fifteen-year-old, fixed in Honoré's estimation at the age he'd been when Honoré had first met him, now found himself forced to take charge. It was he who received the mayor and M. and Mme. Reville, he who interviewed undertakers, prepared meals, answered the phone. Broken, weeping intermittently, Honoré lay on the sofa, calling to him sometimes, begging him not to leave him. His English, of which he had been so proud and which he had used as a means of defying his stepson and demonstrating his authority, deserted him. He spoke only French. And now, using his native tongue exclusively, he ceased to be a farce Frenchman. He was the dignified bereaved who commanded respect. To Gray his stepfather appeared quite different and he realised he had never known him.

"You will stay with me, my son? Now she is gone you are all I have."

"You'll have your sister, Honoré."

"Oh, my sister! Forty years have passed since we lived in the same house. What is my sister to me? I want you to stay, Gray-arm. Why not? Stay here where you have a home."

"I'll stay till after the funeral," Gray promised.

He was surprised at the intensity of his own grief. Even last night, when he'd loved his mother again and fully forgiven her, he'd thought that her death, when it came, wouldn't touch him. But he was weighed down, as he busied himself with the hundred and one things that needed doing, by a quite irrational feeling. He realised that during all those years there had existed at the back of his mind a hope that one day he'd be able to have it all out with her. He'd put his case and she hers, they'd explain to each other, and in those explanations their pain would be resolved. Now she was dead and he mourned her because that day could never come. He could never tell her now how she'd hurt him and she could never tell him why.

Drusilla seemed very far away. He hadn't forgotten to phone her but only deferred it. Later in the day, when all these people had gone, when the phone had stopped ringing and he'd finished the letters to England that Honoré had asked him to write, then . . .

"Mrs. 'Arcoort and Mrs. Ouarrinaire, and our dear Isabel."

"Isabel's in Australia, Honoré. I'll be back in England before she is."

"Change your mind. Stay here with me."

"I can't, but I'll stay while you need me."

He took his letters to the post. It had begun to rain. The great *camions* travelling along the road to Jency splashed muddy water against his legs. The funeral had been fixed for Monday, so he could go home on Tuesday and maybe see Drusilla that same night. It was getting a bit late to phone her now, nearly half-past five, and the weekend was coming. Maybe it would be better to delay phoning her till Monday morning—she'd understand when she knew about his mother. But would she? Wasn't the real reason for his not phoning her a fear that he couldn't take the sharp comment he was likely to get? The "So she's popped off at last" or "Has she left you anything?" He couldn't quite take that now, not even though it came from his Dru that he loved, his Dru who had changed and was going to be his forever.

He heard the phone bell before he was inside the house. Another local sympathiser probably. Honoré wasn't in any fit state to answer it. He went quickly into the room where the phone was, not looking at the empty bed whose blue cover was drawn taut and straight over a bare mattress. The window was open to blow in rain and blow out the smell of death. He picked up the receiver.

"Hi."

"Dru?" he said, as if it could be anyone else. "Dru, is that you?"

"You didn't phone," she said in a voice that seemed to contain a world of desolation.

"No." He knew his tone sounded clipped but he couldn't help it. He was bracing himself for the unkind retort. "No, I couldn't," he said. "Dru, my mother died this morning."

Not an unkind retort but silence. Then, as if she had received a shock, almost as if the dead woman had been someone she had known and loved, she said, "Oh, *no!*"

He was moved, warmed, by the consternation in her voice. All day, strangely when they were on the point of renewing their love affair, she had been more removed from him, less present, than at any time since Christmas. She'd been—he confessed it to himself now—almost a burden, an extra problem to cope with. But that appalled "Oh, *no!*" which seemed to contain more feeling and more sympathy than any long speech of condolence, touched his heart and brought a tremor to his voice.

"I'm afraid so, Dru. My stepfather's taken it very hard and I . . ."

She wailed, "You won't be able to come home now!" She sounded sick, despairing. "I can tell by your voice, you're going to stay for the funeral!"

It was wonderful, of course, to be wanted, to know she needed him so much. But he'd have felt happier if her sympathy had been pure and simple, without strings. Yet for her to be sympathetic at all . . .

"I must, Dru darling," he said. "Try to understand. Honoré needs me till his sister comes. I've promised to stay till Tuesday."

"But *I* need you," she cried, the imperious child whose wishes must always be paramount.

"God, and don't I need you? But we've waited six months. We can wait four more days. You must see this changes things."

Please God, let her not be difficult about it, not now. Let her not make a scene *now*. His happiness at rediscovering her couldn't take storms just yet. He felt he needed to carry that happiness undisturbed, unalloyed, through the next few days like a talisman;

to have it there as a quiet place to retreat to when the sadness of bereavement grew sharp and the practical tasks exasperating. He listened to her ominous silence that seemed charged with protest, petulance, resentment.

"Dru, don't ask me to break my promise."

He dreaded the phone going down, the angry crash as she hung up on him. But there was no crash, no stormy outburst, and when she broke the silence her voice had grown hard with the chill of Thursday morning.

"I'm afraid," she said, "I'll have to. I haven't told you why I phoned yet."

"Did we ever need a reason?"

"No, but this time there happens to be one. This vet wants to see you."

"Vet?" he said obtusely.

"Yes, *vet*. Remember?"

Dido. He hadn't forgotten Dido but somehow he'd thought that now she'd been rescued from the hovel and fed and given attention, everything would be all right.

"Why does he want to see me?"

"I phoned him today to check up. He says the dog's got something wrong with her liver, something bad, and she's in a very bad way. He has to talk to the owner or someone taking the place of the owner before he operates on her. Gray, you can't just leave all this to me. Don't you see, you have to take the responsibility?"

Gray sat down heavily on Honoré's bed. He was remembering Dido as he'd last seen her, so vigorous, so vital, rippling with health. There was something sickeningly ugly in the idea that he'd destroyed all that by his lack of responsibility.

"How can she have something wrong with her liver?" he said. "I mean, malnutrition, I could understand that. But something wrong with her liver? What can I do about it? How can I help by coming home?"

"He wants to see you tomorrow," she persisted. "Gray, I said you'd come. I didn't see why not. It isn't very far just to come to London. Tiny often flies to Paris and back in a day."

"Dru, don't you see how fantastic it is? You can tell him to go

ahead and operate, do anything to save the dog's life. I'll pay.
I'll manage to borrow the money somehow and I'll pay."

"You'll do that but you won't come home and see to it yourself? Not even if I promise to meet you at the hovel afterwards?"

His hand closed hard on the receiver and a long thrill that was
almost pain passed through his body. But it was impossible . . .
"I don't have the money to go in for this jet set flying about. All
I have is about three quid."

"I'll pay your fare. No, don't say you won't take Tiny's money.
It won't be his. I've sold my amethyst ring. And Tiny didn't give
it to me, my father did."

"Dru, I don't know what . . ."

"I told the vet you'd be there at about three. Go and ask your
stepfather if it'll be all right to leave him for a day. I'll hold on."

Dry-mouthed, he laid the receiver on the pillow and went into
the living room. "Honoré, I've got to go home tomorrow. I'll go
in the morning and be back by night."

A bitter but very non-farcical argument ensued. Why did he
have to go? Where was the money to come from? What would
Honoré do on his own? Finally, why didn't Gray get a job, settle
down (preferably in France) marry and forget about mad, bad
Englishwomen who loved animals more than people?

"I promise I'll be back by midnight and I'll stay till after the
funeral. Your friends will be with you. I'll ask Mme. Reville to
come to you for the whole day."

Gray left him, feeling sick because Honoré was crying again.
He picked up the phone.

"All right, Dru, I'll come."

"I knew you would! Oh God, I can't believe it. I'm going to see
you tomorrow. I'm going to see you!"

"I've got to see this vet first and that won't be pleasant. You'd
better tell me the set-up."

"You've got the address. Just go there and talk to him at three."

"And when and where do I see you?"

"If it were only a weekday," she said, "I could come to the airport. That's not possible on a Saturday. Tiny's going to look at
some house he wants to buy for his mother in the afternoon. I'll
get out of that and I'll see you at the hovel at five. O.K.?"

"Can't you—can't you meet me at the vet's?"

"I'll try, but don't count on it. I should be able to drive you back to Heathrow."

"But we will have . . ." He couldn't frame what he wanted to say in the right words, the words that would make her understand. "We will have a little time together?"

She'd understood. She gave an excited chuckle. "You know me," she said.

"Ah, Dru, I love you! I'd go a thousand miles to be with you. Say you love me and that everything that's happened doesn't matter any more."

He held his breath, listening to her silence. A long long silence. He could hear her breathing shallowly as he'd breathed that night he rang her from Marble Arch. Suddenly, coolly and steadily, she spoke:

"I love you. I've decided, if you still want me, I'll leave Tiny and come and live with you."

"My darling . . ."

"We'll talk about it tomorrow," she said.

Bang, the phone went down and he was left holding the emptiness, savouring the fulness, hardly daring to believe she'd said what she'd said. But she had, she had. And he was going to see her tomorrow.

At the end of the long lane she'd be waiting for him. He'd run the length of it. He'd let himself in by the front door and the scent of her would meet him, *Amorce dangereuse*. And she'd come out to him, her arms outstretched, her hair like a bell of gold, her white hand bare of the ring she'd sold to fetch him back to her . . .

Honoré had stopped crying but he looked very sad. "I have been thinking, you must take the car. *Si, si, j'insiste.* It is the quickest way to fetch you back soon."

"Thank you, Honoré, it's kind of you."

"But you must remember that in France we drive on the *correct* side of the road and . . ."

"I'll take great care of your car."

"*Seigneur!* It is not of the car that I am thinking but of you, my son, you who are all I have left."

Gray smiled, touched his shoulder. Yes, he must stop seeing the worst in everyone, attributing to people self-seeking motives. He must try to understand the power of love. Drusilla would have killed for love, was leaving Tiny for love just as he was abandoning Honoré for love. Oh Love, what crimes are committed in thy name . . .

"Let us have a little glass of *cognac*," said Honoré.

CHAPTER 15

The plane got to Heathrow at one fifteen. Gray bought a London A–Z Guide, leaving himself with just enough money for his tube fare to Leytonstone and his train fare to Waltham Abbey. By ten to three he was at Leytonstone station, one of those pallid, desertlike, and arid halts that abound on the outer reaches of the tube lines, and had walked round the curving tunnel into the street.

Drusilla had said nothing about a chance of meeting him there and he didn't expect her, but he couldn't help eyeing the cars parked by the kerb in the faint hope that the E-type might be among them. Of course it wasn't there. He thought of how often her feet must tread this very spot where he now was, how often she must come to this tunnel entrance on her way to London, and then he began to walk down the long street of biggish late Victorian houses, his A–Z in his hand.

Taking the back doubles that filled the area between the road where the station was and the last farflung finger of Epping Forest, he found George Street, a curving, respectable-looking terrace, which lay under the shadow of an enormous Gothic hospital. Number twenty-one bore no brass plate or anything else to indicate that a vet occupied it, but he went up the steps and rang the bell. Expecting that at any minute the door would open and an aggressive middle-aged man in a white coat, his pockets bristling with syringes and steel combs, would fall upon him with threats of the R.S.P.C.A. and certain prosecution, Gray mentally rehearsed his defence. But when the door did open—after he'd rung twice more—no mingled smells of dog and disinfectant rolled out, no veterinary veteran was waiting to excoriate him with his tongue. Instead, a smell of baking cakes and a girl holding a baby.

"I've an appointment with the vet at three o'clock."

"What vet?" said the girl.

"Isn't there a vet has his . . ." What did they call it? ". . . his surgery here?"

"You want the place up the road. It's on this side. I don't know the number. You'll see the name up."

Surely Drusilla had said twenty-one? But maybe she hadn't. He hadn't, after all, written it down. Perhaps she'd said forty-nine which was, in fact, the number of the house on which the vet's nameplate was. He was quite used to forgetting things and he no longer really wondered at his forgetfulness. His lapses were all due, he thought, to psychological blocks, defences put up by his unconscious, and these would soon go away now. The really important things he never forgot. Nothing could have made him forget his date with Drusilla at five.

The doggy smell was here all right, a thick animal reek. Finding the door on the latch, he'd walked in without ringing and was standing in the waiting room, contemplating the copies of *The Field* and *Our Dogs* and wondering what the correct procedure was, when a woman in a khaki smock came in to ask what he wanted.

"Mr. Greenberg doesn't have a surgery on Saturday afternoons," she said curtly. "We're only open for clipping and stripping."

Distant squeaks and grunts, coming from the upper regions, testified that these operations were at present being performed.

"My name is Lanceton," he said, pausing to allow for the expression of hatred and disgust which would cross her face when she realised she was in the presence of an animal torturer. "My dog—well, a dog I was looking after—you've got it here." Her face didn't change. She simply stared. "A yellow Labrador called Dido. She was brought to Mr.—er, Greenberg last Thursday."

"Brought here? We don't board dogs."

"No, but she was ill. She was left here. She was going to have an operation."

"I will check," said Khaki Smock.

She came back after quite a long time, more than five minutes. "We've no records of what you say happened. What time on Thursday?"

"Around lunchtime."

Khaki Smock said triumphantly, "Mr. Greenberg wasn't here after twelve on Thursday."

"Could you phone him or something?"

"Well, I could. It's very inconvenient. It won't be any use. He wasn't here."

"Please," said Gray firmly.

He sat down and leafed through *The Field*. Twenty-five past three. He'd have to get out of here in five minutes if he was going to make it to the hovel by five. He could hear her phoning in another room. Was it possible he'd got the name of the street wrong as well as the number? She came back at last, looking exasperated.

"Mr. Greenberg knows nothing about it."

He had to accept that. He went back into the street, utterly at a loss. The E-Type wasn't there. Drusilla hadn't managed to come and meet him. Or was she, at this moment, waiting somewhere else for him, parked outside another vet's in another street? There must be dozens of vets in Leytonstone. Well, not dozens but several. As he walked down the street the way he'd come he had the sensation of being in a dream, one of those nightmares in which one is already late for an urgent meeting or rendezvous, but everything goes wrong. Transport is irregular or delayed, people antagonistic, addresses mistaken and simply-reached goals hideously elusive.

The obvious thing was to try and get Drusilla on the phone. Tiny would be out house-hunting and maybe she'd be there and alone. He dialled her number but no one answered, so he looked through the yellow page directory for veterinary surgeons. Immediately he saw the mistake he'd made, a mistake possible only when two suburban and contiguous townships have closely similar names. Greenberg was a vet at 49 George Street, Leytonstone; Cherwell a vet at 21 George Street, Leyton. Dido was in Leyton, not Leyton*stone*.

Twenty to four. Well, he'd come over for the sake of the dog, hadn't he? That was the real purpose of his trip, and it was no good giving up just because time was getting on. Yet even now, if he gave up now, he wouldn't get to the hovel before five fifteen. He was aware of that pressure, engendering panic, which affects us when we know we shall be late for an all-important, longed-for appointment. The air seems to swim, the ground drag at our feet, people and inanimate things conspire to detain us.

He opened his A–Z. George Street, Leyton, looked miles away, almost in Hackney Marshes. He didn't know how to get there but he knew it would take at least half an hour. That wasn't to be thought of, out of the question when Drusilla would already be dressing for him, scenting herself, watching the clock. Instead, he dialled Cherwell's number. Nothing happened, no one replied. Vets, obviously, didn't work this late on Saturdays.

But the dog . . . Surely this Cherwell guy would act on his own initiative? Surely, if an operation were necessary, he'd operate with or without consent? All he, Gray, could do was phone him from France first thing on Monday morning. And now put all this vet business behind him, waste no more time on it, but get to Liverpool Street fast.

There must be, he thought, a quicker way of making this trans-forest journey of seven or eight miles than by going all the way back into London and out again via sprawling northern suburbs. There must be buses, if only he knew their routes and their stops. If he'd had money he could have phoned for a mini-cab. As it was, he had just enough for his train fare.

The tube seemed to go exceptionally slow and he had to wait fifteen minutes for a train to Waltham Cross. By the time it came and he was in the carriage his watch, which he had kept checking with station clocks to make sure it wasn't fast, showed twenty-five minutes to five.

Only once had she ever been late for a date with him and that had been that first time in New Quebec Street. She wouldn't be late now. By now she'd have been waiting half an hour for him, growing bewildered perhaps, distressed, as she paced the rooms, running to the window, opening the front door to look up the lane. Then, when he hadn't come and still he hadn't come, she'd say, I won't look, I'll go away and count a hundred and by then he'll have come. Or she'd go upstairs where she couldn't see the lane and scrutinise herself again in the mirror, once more comb her flying fiery hair, touch more scent to her throat, run her hands lightly, in sensuous anticipation, over the body she'd prepared for him. Count another hundred, go slowly down the stairs, walk to the window, lift the curtain, close her eyes. When I open my eyes I shall see him coming . . .

At half-past five he was at the Waltham Abbey end of the lane. There had been an accident on the corner and the police signs were still up, the police cars still there. In the middle of the road black skid marks met and converged on a heap of sand, flung down perhaps to cover blood and horror. He didn't stop to look or enquire but quickened his pace, telling himself that a man of his age ought to be able to run two miles in twenty minutes.

He ran on the hard flat surface of the metalled road, avoiding the soggy grass verges. Pocket Lane had never seemed so long, and the twists and turns in it, the long straight stretches, with which he was so familiar, seemed multiplied as if the lane were made of elastic which some hostile giant had stretched out to frustrate him. The blood pounded in his head and his throat was parched by the time he came to the point where the tarmac petered out into clay.

Under the trees where the E-Type should have been was a big dark green Mercedes. So she'd changed her car. Tiny had bought her a new one. Gray was exhausted with running but the sight of her car brought him a new impetus and he raced on, his trousers covered with yellow mud. The rain that had fallen on the other side of the Channel had fallen here too, and in the deep ruts the clay was almost liquid. This last stretch of the lane—how short it had always seemed on those nights when he had walked her back to her car! Had it really been as long as this, hundreds of yards long surely? But he could see the hovel now, the pallid hulk of it, white as the overcast sky. The gate was open, swinging slightly in the faint breeze that set all those millions of leaves trembling. He stopped for a moment at the gate to get his breath. The sweat stood on his face and he was gasping, but he'd made it, he'd done it in just under twenty minutes.

He unlocked the front door, calling before he was inside, "Dru, Dru, I'm sorry I'm so late. I ran all the way from the station." The door swung to and clicked shut. "Dru, are you upstairs?"

There was no sound, no answer, but he thought he could smell her scent, *Amorce dangereuse*. For a second he was sure he smelt it, and then it was gone, lost in the hovel smells of dust and slowly rotting wood. Breathing more evenly now, he dumped his case and shed his jacket on to the floor. The "lounge" was empty and so was the kitchen. Of course she'd be upstairs, in bed even, waiting for him. That would be like her, to tease him, to wait for him silently, giggling under the bedclothes, and then, when he came into the bedroom, break into a gale of laughter.

He ran up the staircase two at a time. The bedroom door was shut. He knew he'd left it open—he always did—and his heart began to drum. Outside the door he hesitated, not from shyness or fear or doubt, but to let himself feel fully the excitement and the joy he'd been suppressing all day. Now, when he'd reached his goal at last, he could yield to these emotions. He could stand here for ten seconds, his eyes closed, rejoicing that they were together again; stand on the threshold of their reunion, savour it and what it would mean to the full, then open the door.

Opening his eyes, he pushed the door softly, not speaking.

The bed was empty, the dirty sheets flung back as he'd left them, a cup half full of cold tea dregs on the bedside table as he'd left it, as he'd left it . . . The breeze fluttered the strips of rag that served as curtains and swayed a dust-hung cobweb. A hollowness where that full-pounding heart had been, he surveyed the empty room, unable to believe.

The spare room was empty too. He went downstairs and out into the garden where the bracken now grew as high as a man and where little weeds already greened the ash patch of his fire. No sun shone out of the white sky. There was no sound but the muted twitter of songless birds. A gust of wind ruffled the bracken tops and rustled away into the Forest.

But she must be here, her car was here. Perhaps she'd got tired of waiting and gone for a walk. He called her name once more and then he walked back down the lane, splashing through the yellow mud.

The car was still there, still empty. He went up to it and looked through its windows. On the back seat was a copy of the *Financial Times* and, lying on top of it, a spectacles case. Drusilla wouldn't have those things in her car. She wouldn't have a black leather head-rest for her passenger or a pair of very masculine-looking string-backed driving gloves on the dashboard shelf.

It wasn't her car. She hadn't come.

"You won't come? Not even if I promise to meet you at the hovel afterwards?"

That's what she'd said.

"Oh, God, I can't believe it. I'm going to see you tomorrow. I'm going to see you!"

He resisted a temptation to kick the car, the innocent inanimate thing that had nothing to do with her but probably belonged to some bird-watcher or archaeologist. Dragging his feet, his head bent, he didn't see Mr. Tringham until the old man was almost upon him and they had nearly collided.

"Look where you're going, young man!"

Gray would have gone on without making any answer but Mr. Tringham, who was for once not carrying a book and who had apparently come out of his cottage especially to talk to him, said rather accusingly, "You've been in France."

"Yes."

"There was a man in your garden earlier on. Little short chap, walking round the place, looking up at the windows. Thought you ought to know. He could have been trying to break in."

What did he care who broke in? What did it matter to him who'd been there if she hadn't? "I couldn't care less," he said.

"Hmm. I went out for my walk early, thinking it might rain later. There was this rough-looking long-haired chap sitting under a tree and this other one in your garden. I'd have called the police only I haven't got a telephone."

"I know," Gray said bitterly.

"Hmm. You young people take these things very lightly, I must say. Personally, I think we should use your phone—or Mr. Warriner's, I should say—and get on to the police now."

Gray said with irritable savagery, "I don't want the police messing about the place. I want to be left alone."

He walked away sullenly. Mr. Tringham grunted something after him about decadence and modern youth, after the manner of Honoré. Gray slammed the hovel door shut and went into the lounge, aiming a kick at the golf clubs which fell over with a clang.

She hadn't come. He'd travelled all this way to see her, travelled hundreds of miles, run the last bit till he'd felt his lungs were bursting, and she hadn't come.

CHAPTER 16

The phone clicked, then began to ring. He lifted the receiver dully, knowing it would be she, not wanting her voice or any part of her, but the whole of her.

"Hi."

"What happened?" he said wearily.

"What happened to *you*?"

"Dru, I got here at five to six. I ran like hell. Couldn't you have waited for me? Where are you?"

"I'm at home," she said. "I just got in. Tiny said he'd be home at six and I couldn't think of an excuse for not being home too. I left it till the last moment and then I had to go. He's out in the garden now but we'd better be quick."

"Christ, Dru, you promised me. You promised you'd be here. You were going to drive me to the airport. That doesn't matter but if you could have made the time for that, surely you could have . . . I wanted you so much."

"Can't be helped. I did what I could. I should have known you're always late and you always make a mess of things. You didn't even find the vet, did you?"

"How can you know that?"

"Because I rang Mr. Cherwell myself to check if you'd been."

"So it *was* Cherwell . . . ?"

"Of course it was. Twenty-one George Street, Leyton. I told you, didn't I? It's no use, anyway. The dog's had to be destroyed."

"Oh, Dru, *no!*"

"Oh, Gray, *yes*. You couldn't have done anything if you had seen Cherwell, so it's no good worrying about it. What are you going to do now?"

"Lie down and die too, I should think. I've come all this way for nothing and I haven't got a bean. If ever anyone made a pointless journey, this is it. I haven't had anything to eat all day and I haven't got my fare back. And you ask me what I'm going to do."

"You haven't found the money, then?"

"Money? What money? I've only been here ten minutes. I'm plastered with mud and dead tired."

"My poor Gray. Never mind, I'll tell you what you're going to do. You're going to change your clothes, take the money I left you—it's in the kitchen—and get the hell out of that hole back to France. Just write the day off, don't think about it. Quick now, I can see Tiny coming back up the garden."

"*Tiny?* What the hell do we care about Tiny now? If you're joining me next week, if you're coming to live with me, what does it matter what Tiny thinks? The sooner he knows the better." He cleared his throat. "Dru, you haven't changed your mind? You are going to come to me next week?"

She sighed, a fluttery trembly sound. Her words were firm but not her voice. "I never change my mind."

"God, I feel sick when I think I've come all this way and I'm not going to see you after all. When will I see you?"

"Soon. As soon as you get back. Tuesday. I'm going to ring off now."

"No, don't. Please don't." If the receiver went down now, if she ended as she always did without a farewell . . . But she always ended like that. "Dru, please!"

For the first time she said it. "Goodbye, Gray. Goodbye."

On the bath counter he found the electricity bill, the phone bill, the cheque from his publishers—the first two cancelling out the third—a postcard from Mal and, strangely enough, one from Francis and Charmian in Lynmouth. Beside all this correspondence she'd left the money for him in an untidy heap. It seemed a small heap until he looked again, saw that the notes were all tenners and that there were ten of them. He'd expected thirty pounds and found a hundred.

There was no loving note with them. She'd left a hundred pounds in a careless heap as someone else might have left twenty pence in small change; she'd sold her amethyst ring to get him money and he felt a warm, heartbeating gratitude, but he'd have liked a letter. Just a word to tell of her love for him, her distress at not seeing him. He'd never received a letter from her in all their time together and he didn't know what her handwriting looked like.

Still, he wouldn't need handwriting, mementoes, recorded evidence of her, after next week. It was getting on for half-past six and he ought to be on his way. Change these filthy clothes first, though. He went upstairs, wondering what he could find to put on, for he'd left everything dirty just as he'd taken it off.

He hadn't looked round the bedroom at all beyond looking at the bed itself. Now he saw that his dirty jeans and shirt had been washed and actually ironed and were draped over the back of the bedroom chair with his clean Arran. She'd done that for him. She'd cleaned up his kitchen and washed his clothes. Changing quickly, he wondered if she'd done that to show him she could do it, that she wouldn't be helpless, the bewildered rich girl uprooted from luxury, when she came to him. He rolled up his clay-spattered trousers and thrust them under the bath cover. The window had been polished, the paintwork washed in places. She'd done all that for him and sold her precious ring too. He ought to be on top of the world with happiness, but disappointment at not seeing her still weighed him down. Nothing she could do for him or give him made up for the lack of her.

But once back in France, he'd phone her and ask her to be waiting for him when he got home on Tuesday night. She still had her key. The one he could see hanging over the sink must be Isabel's, left there when she'd brought Dido. Guilt for the dog's death welled up inside him. His own absentmindedness had brought that about and led him to make a mistake that almost amounted to criminality. But once Drusilla was with him all that would be changed. He'd have to plan, remember, make decisions.

Just time for a pot of milkless tea and something out of a tin before he set off back to the station. The phone was on the hook, his correspondence examined, the back door bolted. Now was there anything he ought to remember? Perhaps he'd better take that spare key with him. If the little man Mr. Tringham had seen had really been a burglar, the key was in a very vulnerable position. Break one pane of glass in the window, insert a hand and reach for the hook, and the hovel, Mal's hovel, would be anyone's to do as he liked with. Mal wouldn't be too happy to have his golf clubs pinched or any of that tatty old furniture which was, after all, all he had.

Congratulating himself on this unprecedented prudence, Gray unhooked the key and was slipping it into his pocket when he paused, surprised to see how bright and shiny it was. Surely he'd given Isabel the spare key Mal had left him? This key looked more like the one he'd had specially cut for Drusilla when she'd been visiting him so often that there was a chance she'd have to let herself in before he got back from the shops. But perhaps he hadn't given her the new one. Perhaps, in fact, she'd had the old one and the shiny key had been kept for spare. He couldn't remember at all and it didn't seem to matter.

He drank his tea and left the dirty crockery on the draining board. The hundred pounds in his pocket, the two keys, he closed the front door behind him. A thin drizzle, not much more than a mist, was falling and heavier drops plopped rhythmically from waterlogged beech leaves. He walked on the wet grass to avoid the paintbox mud.

The green car was still there. Probably it was a stolen car, abandoned in this out-of-the-way spot. Or its owner had gone on some nature ramble in the forest depths. Both the Willises were in their front garden, standing on their lawn which now looked as good as new to Gray, arguing about something or commiserating perhaps with each other over a case of mildew or leaf blight. They saw Gray and turned away very stiffly, ramrod-backed.

At the corner the police cars had gone and the sand been removed. He walked quickly on towards the station.

Over France the moon was shining. Had the sky cleared in England too and was this same moon shining down on Epping Forest and Combe Park? She and Tiny would be in bed, the gross man in his black and red pyjamas reading some company chairman's memoirs or maybe the *Financial Times*, the slender girl in white frills, reading a novel. But this Saturday night there wouldn't be a phone call from a strange man, saying nothing, breathing heavily. And she wouldn't be lonely any more but thinking about how she'd have to tell the husband in the next bed she'd be leaving him next week. Dream of me, Drusilla . . .

He drove past the last *nids de poules* sign and entered sleeping Bajon, skirting the clump of chestnut trees and the house called Les Marrons. The moon gave him enough light to see by as he covered the car once more in its protective nylon. But the hall of Le Petit Trianon was pitch dark. He felt for the light switch and stumbled over something that was standing just inside the door, a bouquet of funereal lilies in a plastic urn. Afraid that the noise might have awakened his stepfather, he pushed open the bedroom door which Honoré had left ajar.

The thin moonlight, which had transformed the gnome circus into a ghostly ballet, edged the furniture with silver and made little pale geometric patterns on the carpet. Honoré, his greyish-black hair spiky and tousled, lay curled in his own bed but facing the one where Enid had slept, one arm bridging the space between, his hand tucked under her pillow. He was deeply asleep, serene, almost smiling. Gray supposed that they had always slept like that, Honoré's hand holding Enid's, and he saw that his stepfather, reality and its awfulness alienated by dreams, made belief that she lay there still and still held his hand under her cheek.

Touched, awed by the sight, Gray thought how he and Drusilla would sleep like that but in the same bed, always together. And he dreamed of her, the most tender untroubled dreams he'd ever had of her, throughout the night until the baying of the farmer's dog awoke him at eight. Then he got up and took coffee to Honoré who was neither smiling nor serene in the mornings now and whose methodical early-to-rise habits seemed to have died with Enid's death.

Mme. Reville called and carried Honoré off to Mass. Gray had the house to himself and he was alone with the phone. What did she and Tiny do on Sundays? Searching in his mind for some recollection, some account she might have given him of their usual Sunday activities, he found only a blank. Certainly they wouldn't go to church. Did Tiny perhaps play golf or drink with some equally affluent cronies in the pub that crowned the summit of Little Cornwall? There was just a chance she might be alone, or a chance even that she'd told Tiny by now and would be glad of a call from him to back her up and give her confidence.

Without further hesitation, he dialled the number. It rang and rang but no one answered. He was trying again an hour later when Mme. Reville's car drew up outside and he had to abandon the attempt. Well, he'd said Monday and surely he could wait till Monday.

The day passed slowly. Every hour now that he was away from her seemed endless. He kept thinking of the scene which might at this moment, at any moment, be taking place at Combe Park with Drusilla declaring her intention to leave and Tiny his intention of stopping her at all costs. He might even use violence. Or he might throw her out. Still, she had her key and she could take refuge at the hovel if necessary.

Honoré lay on the sofa, reading the letters Enid had written to him during the short period between their meeting and their marriage. Weeping freely, he read bits of them aloud to Gray.

"Ah, how she loved me! But so many doubts she had, my little Enid. What of my boy, she writes here, my friends? How shall I learn to live in your world, I who speak only the French I learned in school?" Honoré sat bolt upright, pointing a finger at Gray. "I crushed all her doubts with my great love. I am master now, I said. You do as I say and I say I love you, so nothing else can matter. Ah, how she adapted herself! She was already old," he said with Gallic frankness, "but soon she speaks French like a French-woman born, makes new friends, leaves all behind to be with me. With true love, Gray-arm, it can be so."

"I'm sure it can," said Gray, thinking of Drusilla.

"Let us have a little cognac, my son." Honoré bundled up his letters and rubbed at his eyes with his sleeve. "Tomorrow I shall be better. After the funeral I shall—what is it you English say? —pull me together."

After the funeral, while the company drank wine and ate cake in the living room, Gray slipped away to phone Drusilla. She'd be waiting impatiently for his call, he thought, had possibly tried to phone him earlier while they were at the church. Very likely she'd be sitting by the phone, feeling lonely and frightened because she'd had a terrible row with Tiny and now might think, because she hadn't heard from him, that her lover had deserted her too. He dialled the code and the number and heard it start to ring.

After about six double peals the receiver was lifted.

"Combe Park."

The coarse voice with its cockney inflexion, the voice that obviously wasn't Drusilla's, almost floored him. Then he realised it must be the daily woman. He and Drusilla had always had an arrangement that if he phoned and the woman answered he was to put the phone down without speaking. But not any longer surely? That didn't apply any longer, did it?

"Combe Park," she said again. "Who's that?"

Better try again later. Better not do anything now to interfere with what might be a delicate situation. He put the receiver back very carefully and quietly as if by so doing he could make belief he hadn't called Combe Park at all, and then he went back into the room where they were all talking in hushed voices, sipping Dubonnet and nibbling at *Chamonix oranges*. Immediately the mayor took him to one side and questioned him closely as to his visit to England. Had he been able to watch a Test Match or, better still, managed a trip to Manchester? Gray answered no to both, very conscious of the glare Mme. Derain had fixed on him. Her eyes were beady like her brother's and her skin as brown, but in her case the small Duval bones were concealed under a mountain of hard fat and her features buried in dark wrinkled cushions.

"*Ici,*" she said like a notice in a shop window, "*on parle français, n'est ce pas?*"

She had taken over the management of the household. It was evident that she intended to stay, to give up her job and her flat over the Marseille fish shop, for the comparative luxury and peace of Le Petit Trianon. Even more parsimonious than Honoré, she was already making plans to take in a lodger, already talking of removing the marigolds and the tripods and growing vegetables in the back garden. And English stepsons who contributed nothing to the household expenses weren't welcome to her.

One glass of Dubonnet per head was all she allowed and then the mourners were hustled away. Gray tried to phone Drusilla again and again the daily woman answered. His third attempt, made at five thirty, the last safe moment, didn't stand a chance, for Mme. Derain actually wrested the phone from his hand. She didn't moan at him or talk of *formidable* expense but said stonily that she planned to have the apparatus disconnected as soon as possible.

He'd have to try again in the morning while she was out buying bread, he thought, but when the morning came, when Honoré was drinking coffee in the kitchen, he entered the bedroom to find her already there. Ostensibly removing signs from it which would be painful to her brother, she was in fact, Gray thought, sorting out which of Enid's clothes she could convert to her own use. Gray guessed he was the type of man who would have liked to keep his dead wife's room as a shrine, each little possession of hers treasured as a reminder of their happiness. But this wasn't Mme. Derain's way. She had allowed her brother to keep Enid's wedding ring—although suggesting it would be more prudent to sell it—and Honoré held the ring loosely in his horny brown hands. It was too small to go on any of his fingers.

"I want to give you back the money you sent me," Gray said. "Here it is, thirty pounds. I want you to have it."

Honoré expostulated, but feebly and not for long. Gray foresaw his stepfather's future life as a way of crafty deception in which money would have to be slyly wrested from his sister and windfalls concealed. This was the first of them. Honoré slipped the money into his pocket but not before he had glanced, already surreptitiously, already fearfully, towards the door.

"Stay another week, Gray-arm."

"I can't. I've got a lot of things to do. For one thing, I'm going to move."

"Ah, you will move and forget to give old Honoré your new address and he will lose you."

"I won't forget."

"You'll come back for your holidays?"

"There won't be room for me when you've got your lodger."

Gray wondered suddenly if he should tell Honoré about Drusilla, give him an expurgated version perhaps, tell him there was a girl he hoped to marry when she'd got her divorce. And that was true. One day they'd be married. He wanted it that way now, open, aboveboard for all the world to see, no more secrets. He glanced at Honoré who was eating and drinking mechanically, whose thoughts were obviously with his dead wife. No, let it remain a secret for now. But it struck him as strange that he'd even contemplated telling his stepfather, his old enemy. All those years when they might have had a happy relationship they had gone out of their way each to antagonise the other, each obstinately insisting on speaking the other's language. And now, when the relationship was ending, when it was probable—and both knew it —they would never meet again, Honoré spoke French and he English and they understood each other and something that was almost love had grown up between them.

Still, one day he might come back. He and Drusilla could have their honeymoon in France, drive through Bajon—hitch through more likely, he thought—and call and see Honoré . . .

Should he try to phone her from the village? Call at the Écu and use the phone in the bar? That way they'd be able to fix a definite time for their meeting and he could have a meal ready for her and wine when she came at last to her new home and her new life.

But it would be hard to explain this action to Honoré who seemed to have an *idée fixe* that his stepson had formed a liaison with an elderly dog breeder. Why go to all that trouble, anyway, when in three or four hours he'd be in London?

"You will miss your plane," said Mme. Derain, coming in with one of Enid's scarves over her arm, a scarf that Honoré winced at the sight of. "Come now, the bus leaves in ten minutes."

"I will drive you to Jency, my son."

"No, Honoré, you're not up to it. I'll be O.K. You stay here and rest."

"*J'insiste.* Am I not your papa? Now, you do as I say."

So the nylon cover was removed from the Citroën and Honoré drove him to Jency. There they waited, drinking coffee at a little pavement café and, when the bus came, Honoré embraced him tenderly, kissing his cheeks.

"Write to me, Gray-arm."

"Of course I will."

And Gray waved from the bus until the little figure in the dark beret, the French onion seller, the waiter, the thief of his happy adolescence, the killer of his dream, had dwindled to a black dot in the wide dusty square.

CHAPTER 17

London lay under a heavy, almost unbreathable, humidity. Like November, Gray thought, but warm. The sky was uniformly pastel grey and it seemed to have fallen to lie on roofs and tree tops like a sagging muslin bag. There was no wind, no breath of it to move a leaf or flutter a flag or lift a tress from a woman's head. The atmosphere was that of a greenhouse without its flowers.

He dialled her number from the air terminal and got no reply. Probably she was out shopping. She couldn't be expected to stay in all day just on the chance that he'd phone. At Liverpool Street he tried again and again at Waltham Cross but each time the bell rang into a void. Once, maybe twice, she could have been out shopping or in the garden—but every time? He hadn't said he'd call her but surely she'd guess he would. There was no point, though, in getting into a state about it, rushing into every phone box he saw on every stage of his journey. Better wait now till he got home.

Pocket Lane had attracted to its moist dim shelter what seemed like all the buzzing insects in Essex. Slumbrously they rose from leaf and briar, wheeled and sang. He brushed them off his face and off the carrier bag of food he'd bought at a delicatessen in Gloucester Road, cold meat and salad for their supper, and a bottle of wine. Maybe she was out because she'd done what he'd wistfully envisaged, taken refuge from Tiny at the hovel. He hadn't thought of ringing the hovel. She might be there waiting for him. But no, he wasn't going to let himself in for that one again, for the hideous Saturday nightmare of half killing himself running to her and then finding she wasn't there.

Until he was inside the house and had been upstairs he couldn't rid himself of the very real hope of it. Hope doesn't die because you tell yourself it is pointless. He dropped the food on to the iron-legged table and lifted the phone. Then, before he dialled, he saw that the golf clubs were standing up, resting once more against the wall. But he'd kicked them over and left them in a scattered heap . . . So she had been there? Five-O-eight, then the four digits. He let the bell ring twenty times and then he put the receiver back, resolving to keep calm, to be reasonable and not to try her number again for two hours.

She'd said Tuesday but she hadn't said anything about getting in touch with him before she came. And there were all sorts of explanations to account for her absence from Combe Park. She might even have gone to the airport to meet him and they had missed each other. He went out into the front garden and lay down in the bracken. It was slightly less stuffy than the house, slightly less claustrophobic. But the atmosphere, thick, still, warm, was charged with the tension characteristic of such weather. It was as if the weather itself were waiting for something to happen.

No birds sang. The only sound was that of the flies' muted buzzing as they rose and fell in their living clouds. And the trees stood utterly immobile around the hovel, their green cloaks motionless, their trunks like pillars of stone. He lay in the bracken thinking about her, crushing down each doubt as it rose, telling himself how resolute she was, how punctual, how she never changed her mind. The front door was ajar so that he would hear the phone when it rang. He lay on his side, staring through the bracken trunks, through this forest in miniature, towards the lane, so that he would see the silver body of her car when it slid into the gap between thrusting fronds and hanging leaves. Presently, because it was warm and he had lulled himself into peace, he slept.

When he awoke it was nearly half-past five but the appearance of the Forest and the light were unchanged. No car had come and the phone hadn't rung. Half-past five was the last safe time to ring her. He went slowly back into the house and dialled but still there was no answer. All day long she'd been out, for the whole of this day when she was due to leave her husband for her lover, she'd been out. Those reassuring excuses for her absence, her silence, which had lulled him to sleep began to grow faint and a kind of dread to replace them. I never change my mind, she'd said, I'll leave Tiny and come and live with you. Tuesday, she'd said, when you get back. But she'd also said goodbye. She'd never said that before. Two or three hundred times they'd talked to each other on the phone; they'd met hundreds of times, but she'd never terminated their conversations or their meetings with a true farewell. See you, take care, till tomorrow, but never goodbye . . .

But wherever she was, whatever she'd been doing all day, she'd be bound to go home in the evening. Tiny demanded her presence in the evenings except when he was out on Thursdays. Well, he'd try again at six thirty and to hell with Tiny. He'd try every half hour throughout the evening. If she hadn't come, of course. There was always the possibility she'd promised Tiny to wait till he came home before leaving.

Although he hadn't eaten since he left Le Petit Trianon, he wasn't hungry and he didn't fancy starting on the wine he'd bought. Even the idea of a cup of tea didn't attract him. He lay back in the chair, watching the inscrutable phone, chain-smoking, lighting, smoking and crushing out five cigarettes in the hour that passed.

Tiny'd have been in half an hour by now. Whatever happened, unless he was away on a business trip—and if he'd been going away she'd have said—Drusilla's husband drove the Bentley through the Combe Park gates just before six. Perhaps he'd answer the phone. So well and good. He, Gray, would say who he was, give his name and ask to speak to Drusilla, and if Tiny wanted to know why he'd tell him why, tell him the lot. The time for discretion was past. Five-O-eight . . . He must have made a mess of it, for all he got was a steady high-pitched burr. Try again. Probably his hand hadn't been very steady. Five-O-eight . . .

The bell rang, twice, three times, twenty times. Combe Park was empty, they were both out. But it wasn't possible she'd go out with her husband, the husband she was on the point of leaving, on the very day he and she were due to start their life together.

"I love you. If you still want me I'll leave Tiny and come and live with you. As soon as you get back, soon, Tuesday . . ."

He went to the window. Standing there, gazing through a web

of unmoving, pendulous branches, he thought I won't look out of the window again till I've counted a hundred. No, I'll make a cup of tea and smoke two cigarettes and count a hundred and then she'll be here. He'd do what he'd thought of her as doing while she waited for him on Saturday.

But instead of going into the kitchen, he sat down once more in the chair and, closing his eyes, began to count. It was years since he'd counted up so high, not since he was a little boy playing hide and seek. And he didn't stop when he reached a hundred, but went obsessively on, as if he were counting the days of his life or the trees of the Forest. At a thousand he stopped and opened his eyes, frightened by what was happening to his mind, to himself. It was still only seven o'clock. He lifted the phone and dialled the number that was more familiar to him than his own, making the movements that were so automatic now that he could have made them in the dark. And the bell rang as if it were echoing his counting, on and on, emptily, pointlessly, meaninglessly.

Tiny must have taken her away. She'd told Tiny and he, aghast and angry, had shut up the house and taken away his wife from the lures of a predatory young lover. To St. Tropez or St. Moritz, to the tourists' shrines where miracles took place and in the glamour of high life women forgot the life they had left behind. He dropped the receiver and pushed his hand across his eyes, his forehead. Suppose they were away for weeks, months? There seemed no way to find out where they'd gone. He couldn't very well go questioning the neighbours and he didn't know Tiny's office number or her father's address. The thought came to him horribly that if she died no one would tell him; no news of her illness, her death, could reach him, for nobody in her circle knew of his existence and no one in his knew of hers.

There was nothing he could do but wait—and hope. After all, it was still Tuesday. She hadn't said *when* on Tuesday. Perhaps she'd postponed telling Tiny till the last minute, was telling him now, and their quarrel was so intense, their emotions running so high, that they scarcely heard the phone, still less bothered to answer it. In a little while she'd have said all there was to say and then she'd fling out of the house, throw her packed cases into the car, drive furiously down the Forest roads . . .

He was seeing it all, following the phases of their quarrel, the two angry frightened people in their beautiful loveless house, when the phone, so dead and silent that he had thought it would never ring again, gave its preliminary hiccup. His heart turned over. He had the receiver to his ear before the end of the first peal and he was holding his breath, his eyes closed.

"Mr. Graham Lanceton?"

Tiny. Could it be Tiny? The voice was thick, uncultured, but very steady. "Yes," Gray said, clenching his free hand.

The voice said, "My name is Ixworth, Detective Inspector Ixworth. I should like to come over and see you if that's convenient."

The anticlimax was so great, so sickening—far worse than when he had answered Honoré's phone to M. Reville—that Gray could hardly speak. It was as hard to find words as to find, from his dry constricted throat, the voice with which to speak them. "I don't. . ." he began thinly. "Who . . . ? What. . . ?"

"Detective Inspector Ixworth, Mr. Lanceton. Shall we say nine o'clock?"

Gray didn't answer. He didn't say anything. He put the phone down and stood shivering. It was fully five minutes before he could get over the shock of simply realising it hadn't been she. Then, wiping the sweat off his forehead, he made his way towards the kitchen where at least he'd be out of the sight of that phone.

On the threshold he stopped dead. The window had been broken and forced open and the cellar door stood ajar. All his papers were now stacked in as neat a pile as a new ream of typing paper. Someone had been here and not she. Someone had broken into the house. He shook himself, trying to get a grip on reason, on normalcy. Vaguely he began to understand the reason for that policeman's phone call. The police had discovered a burglary.

Well, he had to fill in the time till she phoned or came, and he might as well look round to see if anything had been pinched. It would be something to do. His typewriter was still there, though he had a feeling it had been moved. He couldn't remember where he'd left the strongbox. Having searched the downstairs rooms, he went up to the bedrooms. Everywhere smelt musty, airless. He opened windows as he went across the landing and his own bedroom but there was no breeze to blow stale air out and fresh in.

There was no fresh air. He longed to draw into his lungs great gulps of oxygen—something to relieve this tightness in his chest. But when he put his head out of the window the thick atmosphere seemed to stick at the rim of his throat.

The strongbox wasn't in either of the bedrooms. He no longer retained much faith in his own memory, but he was certain he'd left the box somewhere in the house. What else would he have done with it? If it wasn't there, the intruder must have taken it. He searched the "lounge" again and the kitchen and then went down the cellar steps.

Someone had disturbed and turned over those mounds of rubbish and the iron was gone. Its trivet stood on a heap of damp newspapers but the iron which had burnt him, which had left a still clearly visible scar on his hand, had disappeared. He kicked some of the coal aside, mystified by this strange robbery, and saw at his feet on the moist flagstones, a spattered brown stain.

The stain looked as if it might be blood. He remembered Dido again and thought that perhaps she'd succeeded in getting into the cellar and had fallen from the steps or wounded herself against one of the oil drums or the old unusable bicycle. It was an ugly thought that made him wince and he went quickly back up the steps. The box wasn't there, anyway.

The garden was crushed now by rising mist, cottony white and oppressive, hanging immobile on nettle and fern bract. The broken window made the kitchen look more derelict than ever. He put the kettle on for tea but he went out of the kitchen while he waited for it to boil. After what had happened there, he was never going to be able to bear that kitchen for long. Dido's ghost would be behind him. He'd fancy he could hear her padding steps or the touch of her moist nose against his hand.

Shivering, he reached for the phone again and dialled carefully but fast. They said that if you dialled too slowly or left too long a pause between two of the digits, something could go wrong and you'd get the wrong number. They said a hair across the mechanism or a grain of dust . . . suppose he'd been dialling the wrong number all this time? It could happen, some Freudian slip could make it happen. He put the receiver back, lifted it again, and dialled with calculated precision, repeating the seven figures over to himself aloud. The ringing began, and yet from the first double peal he knew it would be useless. Give up now till ten. Try again at ten and at midnight. If they weren't there at midnight he'd know they were away.

He'd made a cup of tea and carried it into the "lounge"—for all his resolve, he couldn't bear to be more than a yard from that phone—when he heard the soft purr of a car. At last. At last at twenty past eight, a perfectly reasonable time, she'd come to him. The long and terrible waiting was over, and like all long and terrible waiting times would be forgotten immediately now that what he had waited for had happened. He wouldn't run to the door, he wouldn't even look out of the window. He'd wait till the bell rang and then he'd go there slowly, hoping he could maintain this calm façade even when he saw her, white and gold and vital in the closing twilight, keep his rushing emotion down until she was in his arms.

The bell rang. Gray set down his teacup. It rang again. Oh, Drusilla, at last . . . ! He opened the door. Appalled, every muscle of his body flexing into rigidity, he stared, for it was Tiny who stood there. In every imagined detail—now proved correct by the too real reality—this man was Drusilla's husband. From the black curly hair, cropped too short and crowning, with coarse contrast, a veined dusky-red face, to the gingery suede shoes, this was Tiny Janus. He wore a white raincoat, belted slackly over a belly made thick with rich living.

They eyed each other in a silence which seemed immeasurable but which probably lasted no more than a few seconds. At first Gray, by instinct rather than by thought, had supposed the man was going to strike him. But now he saw that the mouth, which had been so grim and so belligerent, was curling into an expression of mockery, too faint to be called a smile. He stepped back, losing his sense of conviction, because the words he was hearing were wrong, were the last conceivable words in these circumstances.

"I'm a bit early." A foot over the threshold, a briefcase swung. "Nothing wrong, I hope?"

Everything was wrong, everything unbalanced. "I wasn't expecting . . ." Gray began.

"But I phoned you. My name's Ixworth."

Gray held himself still, then nodded. He pulled the door wider to admit the policeman. There is a limit to how long anticlimaxes remain anticlimactic. One grows to accept them, to take them as part and parcel of nightmare. It was better, probably, that this man should be anyone but Tiny, intolerable, just the same, that his caller was anyone but Drusilla.

"Just got back from France, have you?" They had got themselves into the "lounge"—Gray hardly knew how—and Ixworth moved confidently as if he were familiar with the place.

"Yes, I was in France." He had spoken mechanically, had simply answered the question, but there must have been in his reply some note of surprise.

"We talk to friends and neighbours, Mr. Lanceton. That's our job. All part of the job of investigating this sort of thing. You went to France to see your mother before she died, isn't that it?"

"Yes."

"Your mother died on Friday and you came home on a flying visit on Saturday, going back again that same night. You must have had a very pressing reason for that trip."

"I thought," said Gray, remembering, recalling the least significant shocks of the day, "you came to talk about my house being broken into."

"Your house?" The thick black eyebrows went up. "I understood this cottage was the property of a Mr. Warriner who is at present in Japan."

Gray shrugged. "I live here. He lent it to me. Anyway, there's nothing missing." Why mention the strongbox, when to mention it would only keep the man here? "I didn't see anyone. I wasn't here."

"You were here on Saturday afternoon."

"Only for about half an hour. Nobody'd been here then. The window wasn't broken."

"We broke the window, Mr. Lanceton," said Ixworth with a slight cough. "We entered this house with a warrant yesterday and found the body of a man lying at the foot of the cellar steps.

He'd been dead for forty-eight hours. The wristwatch he was wearing had broken and the hands stopped at four fifteen."

Gray, who had been standing limply but with a kind of slack indifferent impatience, lowered himself into the brown armchair. Or, rather, the chair seemed to rise and receive him into its lumpy uneven seat. The stunning effect of what Ixworth had said blanked his mind, but into this blankness came a vision of a little man prowling round the hovel garden.

The burglar or burglars, the brown stain . . . Who were these intruders who had forced their way into his own nightmare and made, with a kind of incongruous subplot, a littler yet greater nightmare of their own?

"This man," he said, because he had to say something, "must have fallen down the steps."

"He fell, yes." Ixworth was looking at him narrowly, as if he expected so much more than Gray could give. "He fell after he'd been struck on the head with a flatiron."

Gray looked down at his right hand, at the blister which had become a cracked and yellow callus. He turned his hand downwards when he saw that Ixworth was looking at it too.

"Are you saying this man was killed here? Who was he?"

"You don't know? Come outside a minute." The policeman led him into the kitchen, as if the house were his, as if Gray had never been there before. He opened the cellar door, watching Gray. The switch for the cellar light didn't work, and it was in the thin pale glow from the kitchen that they looked down into the depths and at the brown stain.

It was strange that he should feel so threatened, so impelled to be defensive, when none of this was anything to do with him. Or was it a case of any man's death diminishes me? All he found to say was, "He fell down those steps."

"Yes."

Suddenly Gray found he didn't like the man's tone, the expectancy, the accusatory note in it. It was almost as if Ixworth were trying to tease him into some sort of admission; as if, fantastically, the police could do no more unless he confessed to some defection or omission of his own—that he hadn't, for instance, taken

proper precautions against this kind of thing or was deliberately
failing to give vital information.

"I know nothing about it. I can't even imagine why he'd come
here."

"No? You don't see any attractions in a charming little weatherboard cottage set in unspoilt woodland?"

Gray turned away, sickened at this inept description. He didn't
want to know any more, he couldn't see the point. The intruder's
identity or business were nothing to him, his death an ugliness
Ixworth seemed to use only as an excuse for curious glances and
cryptic words. And Ixworth had been so suave, so teasing, that
Gray felt a jolt shake him when, after a brief silence, the policeman spoke with a clipped brutality.

"Why did you come home on Saturday?"

"It was because of a dog," Gray said.

"A *dog?*"

"Yes. D'you think we could go back into the other room?" He
wondered why he was asking Ixworth's permission. The policeman
nodded and closed the cellar door. "I went to France, forgetting
that someone had left a dog, a yellow Labrador, shut up in my
kitchen. When I realised what I'd done, I phoned a friend from
France and got them to let the dog out and take her to a vet." Silently, Gray blessed English usage which permitted him to say
"them" instead of "her" in this context. Drusilla wouldn't thank
him for involving her in all this. "It was a stupid mistake to make."
Suddenly he saw just how stupid all this would sound to someone else. "The dog died," he went on, "but—well, before that, on
Saturday, the vet wanted to see me. He's called Cherwell and he
lives at 21 George Street, Leyton."

Ixworth wrote the address down. "You spoke to him?"

"I couldn't find him. I spoke to a woman at 49 George Street,
Leyton*stone*. That would have been just after three."

"You aren't making yourself very clear, Mr. Lanceton. Why did
you go to Leytonstone?"

"I made a mistake about that."

"You seem to make a lot of mistakes."

Gray shrugged. "It doesn't matter, does it? The point is I didn't
get here till six."

"*Six?* What were you doing all that time? Did you have a meal, meet anyone? If you left Leytonstone at half-past three, a bus or buses would have got you here in three quarters of an hour."

Gray said more sharply, "It's a long walk and I can't afford taxis. Besides, I went back into London and caught a train."

"Did you meet anyone, talk to anyone at all?"

"I don't think so. No, I didn't. When I got here I spoke to an old boy called Tringham who lives up the lane."

"We've interviewed Mr. Tringham. It was five past six when he spoke to you, so that doesn't help much."

"No?" said Gray. "Well, I can't help at all."

"You haven't, for instance, any theory of your own?"

"Well, there were two men, weren't there? There must have been. Mr. Tringham said he saw another bloke."

"Yes, he told us." Ixworth spoke casually, laconically, returning to his old manner. Once more it was as if he had ceased to take Gray seriously. "The Forest," he said, "is full of picnickers at this time of year."

"But surely you ought to find the other man?"

"I think we should, Mr. Lanceton." Ixworth got up. "Don't you worry, we shall. In the meantime, you won't go popping off to France again, will you?"

"No," said Gray, surprised. "Why should I?"

He saw the policeman to the gate. When his car lights had died away, the Forest was impenetrably black. And the moonless, starless sky was densely black except on the horizon where the lights of London stained it a dirty smoky red.

It was nearly ten o'clock. Gray made tea, and as he drank it the interview with Ixworth, irritating and humiliating rather than alarming, began to fade, becoming a distant instead of a recent memory. It seemed less real now than those dreams of his, for that which supremely mattered had returned to engulf him.

The light bulb in the "lounge," one of the last in the hovel that still worked, flickered, shone briefly with a final bold radiance, fizzed and went out. He had to dial her number in the dark but it was as he'd thought, his fingers slipped automatically into the right slots.

There was no reply, and none at midnight when he tried for the last time and Tuesday was over.

CHAPTER 18

Gray and Tiny and Drusilla were travelling together in a tourist coach along a road that led through a thick dark forest. The husband and wife sat in front and Gray behind them. She wore her cream lawn dress and on her finger the amethyst ring. Her hair was a red flower, a chrysanthemum with fiery points to its petals. He touched her shoulder and asked her how she came to be wearing the ring she'd sold but she took no notice, she couldn't hear him.

The forest thinned and opened on to a plain. He knew they were in France from the road signs, but when they came to Bajon it wasn't the Écu outside which they stopped but the Oranmore in Sussex Gardens. In one hand Tiny held the case containing his coin collection, with the other he grasped a passive and meek Drusilla, shepherding her up the steps, under the neon sign and into the hotel. He was going to follow them in but the glass doors slid closed against him and, although he beat on the glass begging to be admitted, Drusilla turned her head only once before going up the stairs. She turned her head once and said, "Goodbye, Gray. Goodbye."

After that he woke up and couldn't get to sleep again. Soft hazy sunshine filled the room. It was half-past eight. He got up and looked out of the window. The mist was still there but thin now, diaphanous, shot through with shafts of gold and veiling a blue sky.

Gradually the events of the previous day came back to him, the events and the non-events. He stretched, shivered, quite unrefreshed by his eight hours of uneasy, dream-filled sleep. He went downstairs. The kitchen was beginning to fill with leaf-filtered sunshine and for the first time it didn't smell stale. Fresh air came in with the sunlight through the broken window. Gray put the kettle on. It was strange, he thought, how, since Christmas, day had followed day without anything ever happening in a terrible monotony, and then had come a week filled with ugly violent action. Wasn't it Kafka who'd said, no matter how you lock yourself away, shut yourself up, life will come and roll in ecstasy at your feet? Well, it was hardly ecstasy, anything but. And it was very far from the kind of life and ecstasy he'd envisaged.

He couldn't see how the intruders had got in. The doors had been locked and the spare key hanging at that time over the sink. Probably the police wouldn't bother him any more now they knew he hadn't been here and couldn't assist them. Strange to remember how bitterly disappointed he'd been at not finding Drusilla here on Saturday. He was glad now, he thanked God, she hadn't been here when the men had broken in.

He'd try her number just once more and if he got no reply think of ways and means to get hold of her. Why not ask her neighbours, after all? Someone would know where she and Tiny had gone. The daily woman would come in whether they were there or not and she'd be bound to know. He dialled the number just before nine, listened this time without much disappointment and no surprise to the ringing tone, put the receiver back and made tea. While he was eating some of the bread he'd bought, spreading it with vinegar-tainted melting butter, the phone rang.

It must be she. Who else would know he was home? He gulped down a mouthful of bread and answered it.

A woman's voice, a voice he didn't begin to recognise, said, "Mr. Lanceton? Mr. Graham Lanceton?"

"Yes," he said dully.

"Oh, *hallo*, Graham! It didn't sound a bit like you. This is Eva Warriner."

Mal's mother. What did she want? "How are you, Mrs. Warriner?"

"I'm fine, my dear, but I was so distressed to hear about your mother. It was nice of you to write to me. I'd no idea she was as ill as that. We were very close in the old days, I always thought of her as one of my dearest friends. I hope she didn't suffer much?"

Gray didn't know what to say. It was a struggle to speak at all, to make a recovery from the bitterness of knowing this wasn't Drusilla. "She did for a while," he managed. "She didn't know me."

"Oh, dear, so sad for you. You said you'd be back at the beginning of the week so I just thought I'd phone and tell you how sorry I am. Oh, and I rang Isabel Clarion and told her the news too. She said she hadn't heard from you at all."

"*Isabel?*" he almost shouted. "You mean she's come back from Australia already?"

"Well, yes, Graham," said Mrs. Warriner, "she must have. She didn't mention Australia but we only talked for a couple of minutes. The builders that are doing her flat were making so much noise we couldn't hear ourselves speak."

He sat down heavily, pushing his fingers across his hot damp forehead. "I expect I'll hear from her," he said weakly.

"I'm sure you will. Isn't it wonderful Mal coming home in August?"

"Yes. Yes, it's great. Er—Mrs. Warriner, Isabel didn't say anything about . . . ? No, it doesn't matter."

"She hardly said anything, Graham." Mrs. Warriner began to reminisce about her past friendship with Enid but Gray cut her short as soon as he politely could and said goodbye. He didn't replace the receiver but left it hanging as it had so often hung in the past. That would stop Isabel for a while, at any rate, Isabel who'd stayed in Australia for barely a week. Probably she'd quarrelled with her old partner or hadn't liked the climate or something. Vaguely he remembered reading in Honoré's newspaper, on that dreadful night when he'd realised Dido was at the hovel, about floods in Australia. That would be it. Isabel had been frightened or made uncomfortable by those floods and had got on a plane as soon as she could. She'd very likely got home yesterday and today she'd want her dog back . . .

Well, he'd known he'd have to tell her sometime and it would be as well to get it over. But not today. Today he had to sort out his life and Drusilla's, find where Drusilla was and get her back. He eyed the receiver that was still swinging like a pendulum. Better make one more attempt to phone. By now the daily woman would have arrived.

Five-O-eight and then the four digits. The double burrs began. After the fifth the receiver was lifted. Gray held his breath, the fingers of his left hand curling into the palm and the nails biting the flesh. It wasn't she. Still, it was someone, a human voice coming out of that silent place at last.

"Combe Park."

"I'd like to talk to Mrs. Janus."

"Mrs. Janus is away. This is the cleaner. Who's that speaking?"

"When will she be back?"

"I'm sure I couldn't tell you. Who's that speaking?"

"A friend," Gray said. "Have Mr. and Mrs. Janus gone away on holiday?"

The woman cleared her throat. She said, "Oh, dear . . ." and "I don't know if I should . . ." and then, gruffly, "Mr. Janus passed away."

It didn't register. All it did was bring back a flashing memory of the mayor and his euphemisms, those idiomatic polished understatements. "What did you say?"

"Mr. Janus passed away."

He heard the words but they seemed to take a long while to travel to his brain, as such words do, as do any words that are the vehicles of news that is unimaginable.

"*You mean he's dead?*"

"It's not my place to talk about it. All I know is he's passed away, dead like you say, and Mrs. Janus has gone to her mum and dad."

"Dead . . ." he said and then, steadying his voice, "D'you know their address?"

"No, I don't. Who's that speaking?"

"It doesn't matter," Gray said. "Forget it."

He made his way very slowly to the window but he seemed half blind and, instead of the forest, all he saw was a blaze of sun and hollows of blue shadow. Tiny Janus is dead, said his brain. The words travelled to his lips and he spoke them aloud, wonderingly, Harvey Janus, the rich man, the ogre, is dead. Drusilla's husband is dead. The phrases, the thoughts, swelled and began to take on real meaning as the shock subsided. He began to feel them as facts. Tiny Janus, Drusilla's husband, is dead.

When had it happened? Sunday? Monday? Perhaps even on Tuesday, the day she was to join him. Now her absence was explained. Even her failure to phone was explained. Dazed but gradually coming to grips with the news, he tried to imagine what had occurred. Probably Tiny had had a coronary. Heavy fat men like Tiny, men who drank too much and lived too well, men of Tiny's age, often did have coronaries. Perhaps it had happened at his office or while he was driving the Bentley, and they had sent her a message or the police had come to her. She hadn't loved Tiny but still it would have been a shock and she would have been alone.

She'd have sent for her parents, the father she loved and the mother she never mentioned. It was hard to imagine Drusilla having a mother, Drusilla who seemed man-born. They must have carried her off to wherever they lived. He realised he didn't know their name, her maiden name, or anything about where they lived except that it was somewhere in Hertfordshire. But her failure to phone him was explained. He would just have to wait.

"Wouldn't it be nice if he died?" she'd said. "He might die. He might have a coronary or crash his car."

Well, she'd got what she wanted. Tiny was dead and Combe Park and all that money hers. He thought how she'd said that when she got it she'd give it to him, that they would share it, put it into a joint account and live happily on it forever. And he'd wanted it, if it could have been his more or less legitimately, reaching a zenith of desire for it when he'd stood outside the gates of Combe Park in the spring and seen the daffodils that seemed made of pure gold. Strange that now the impossible had happened and Tiny was dead, now it would all be his and hers, he no longer cared at all about possessing it.

He tested his feelings. No, he wasn't happy, glad that a man was dead. Of course, he had nothing to do with Tiny's death, no more than he had to do with the death of the man who had fallen down his cellar stairs, yet he felt a heavy weight descend onto his shoulders, something like despair. Was it because in his heart he'd really wanted Tiny to die? Or for some other reason he couldn't define? The two deaths seemed to merge into one and to stand between him and Drusilla like a single ghost.

His body smelt of the sweat of tension. He went back to the kitchen and began heating water for a bath. All the time he was waiting for happiness and relief to dispel his depression, but he could only think of the repeated shocks to which he'd been ex-

posed. He couldn't take any more. Another shock would send
him over the edge.

He lifted the lid of the bath cover and tugged out the tangle of
mould-smelling sheets and towels. The mud-stained trousers
he'd put in there on Saturday were gone but he didn't worry about
their disappearance. Too many strange things were happening in
his world for that. He poured the boiling water into the bathtub, chucked in a bucketful of cold. Getting into the bath, soaping
himself, he thought of Tiny dead. At the wheel of his car perhaps?
In so many dreams he'd seen Tiny crash in his car, blood and
flames pouring scarlet over the green turf. Or had he died in bed
after a drinking bout while Drusilla, unaware and dreaming of
her lover, slept a yard from him?

There were many other possibilities. But the only one that came
vividly to Gray, the only one he could see as a real picture, was of
Tiny lying crumpled at the foot of a flight of stairs.

If he went up the lane just before twelve, he might be able to
catch the milkman and buy a pint off him. Tea was the only sus-
tenance he felt he could stomach. The food in the carrier bag smelt
unpleasant, and the sight of it brought him a wave of nausea.
Downstairs the hovel seemed full of death, the intruder's, Tiny's,
the dog's, and yet the rooms gleamed with sunlight. Gray could
never remember the place so bright and airy. But he longed to
get out of it. If once he got out, would he have the courage
to come back? Or would he wander through the glades of the Forest, on and on until weariness overcame him and he lay down to
sleep or die?

The chance of her phoning seemed to have grown very remote.
Days might pass before he heard from her. He couldn't envisage
those empty days and himself passing through them, waiting,
waiting, and all the time this tension mounting until, before she
phoned, it cracked.

He went upstairs and put on the dirty shirt he'd taken off the
night before. The sound of a car engine a long way up the lane
froze him as he was combing his hair. Holding the comb poised,
utterly still, he listened for the whisper of sound to grow into the
powerful purr of a Jaguar sports. He'd passed beyond feeling joy

at her coming. All these deaths, anticlimaxes, shocks, blows to his mind had removed the possibility of delight at their coming meeting. But he would fall into her arms and cling to her in silence when she came.

It was not to be yet. The engine noise had become the thinner jerkier rattle of a small car. He went to the window and looked out. Much of the lane was obscured by bracken at ground level and by branches above, but there was a space between wide enough to make out the shape and colour of a car. The Mini, small and bright red, edged cautiously along the still sticky surface and slid to a halt.

Isabel.

His first instinct was simply to hide from her, go into the spare room, lie on the floor and hide till she went away. Inside each one of us is a frightened child trying to get out. The measure of our maturity is the extent to which we are able to keep that child quiet, confined and concealed. At that moment the child inside Gray almost broke loose from its bonds, but the man who was nearly thirty held it down, just held it down. Isabel might go away but she'd come back. If not today, tomorrow, if not tomorrow, Friday. Weak as he was, trembling now, he must face her and tell her what he'd done. No hiding, defiance, blustering, could make his act less of an outrage than it was.

She was getting out of the car. In the bright, sun-flooded segment between dark green fern and lemon-green leaves, he saw her ease her thick body in pink blouse and baby blue trousers out of the driving seat. She was wearing big sunglasses with rainbow frames. The black circles of glass levelled themselves upwards towards the window and Gray turned quickly away.

He retreated to the door, to the top of the stairs, and there he stood, trying to command himself, clenching his hands. He was still a child. For more than half his life he'd fended for himself; he'd got a good degree, written a successful book, been Drusilla's lover, but he was still a child. And more than ever he was a child with these grown-ups, with Honoré, with dead Enid, Mrs. Warriner, Isabel. Even in telling himself he wouldn't conciliate them or play things their way but be honest and himself, he was a child, for his very defiance and rebellion were as childish as obedience. In a flash he was aware of this as never before. One day, he thought, when the present and all its horrors were the past, when he'd got over or through all this, he would remember and grow up . . .

Sick, already tasting the nausea on his tongue, he went down and slowly pulled open the front door. Isabel, still at the car, bending over to take milk and groceries out of the boot, lifted her head and waved to him. He began to walk towards her.

Before he was halfway down the path, before he could fetch a word out of his dry throat, the thicket of bracken split open. It burst with a crack like tearing sacking and the big yellow dog leapt upon him, the violence of her embrace softened by the wet warmth of her tongue and the rapture in her kind eyes.

CHAPTER 19

The bright air shivered. The myriad leaves, lemony-green, silk-green, feathery, sun-filtered, serrated, swam in swirling parabolas, and the ground rose in a hard wave to meet him. He just kept his balance. He shut his eyes on the green-gold trembling brightness and thrust his fingers into warm fur, embracing the dog, holding her against his shaking body.

"Dido!" Isabel called. "Leave Gray alone, darling."

He couldn't speak. Shock stunned him. All his feeling, all thought, were crystallised into one unbelievable phrase: she is alive, the dog is alive. He drew his hands over Dido's head, the fine bones, the modelling, as a blind man passes his fingers over the face of the woman he loves.

"Are you all right, Gray? You do look peaky. I suppose you're just beginning to feel what this loss means."

"Loss?" he said.

"Your *mother*, dear. Mrs. Warriner told me last night and I made up my mind to come over first thing this morning. You ought to sit down. Just now I thought you were going to faint."

Gray had thought so too. And even now, when the first shock had passed, he seemed unable to get his bearings. Following Isabel into the house, he tried to feel his way along that other path that should have led into the reaches of his mind. But he came against a blank wall. Experience and memory had become a foreign country. Logic had gone, and lost too were the processes of thought by which one says, this happened so, therefore, this and this happened too. His mind was an empty page with one phrase written on it: the dog is alive. And now, slowly, another was being inscribed alongside it: the dog is alive, Tiny Janus is dead.

Isabel was already sitting down in the "lounge," pouring out platitudes on life, death, and resignation. Gray lowered himself carefully into the other chair as if his body, as well as his mind, must be guardedly handled. Speed, roughness, would be danger- ous, for, lying beneath the surface was a scream that might burst out. He rubbed his hands over the dog's pelt. She was real, he knew that for certain now. Perhaps she was the only real thing in a tumbling, inside-out world.

"When all's said and done," Isabel was saying, "it was a merciful release." Gray lifted his eyes to her, to this fat pink and blue blur that was his godmother, and wondered what she was talking about. "You haven't got your receiver off now, I see. Really, there's no point in having a phone if the receiver's always off, is there?"

"No point at all," he agreed politely. He was surprised that he could speak at all, let alone form sentences. He went on doing it, pointlessly, just to prove he could. "I wonder sometimes why I do have one. I really wonder. I might just as well not have one."

"There's no need," Isabel said sharply, "to be sarcastic. You've no right to be resentful, Gray. The first thing I did was try to phone you. As soon as I knew I couldn't go to Australia—I mean, when I read about the floods and Molly cabled me to say she'd literally been washed out of her home—I made up my mind there was no point in trying to go. I tried to phone you that Friday and goodness knows how many times on the Saturday, and then I gave up in sheer despair. I thought you'd realise when I didn't turn up with Dido."

"Yes," said Gray. "Oh, yes."

"Well, then. Really, it was a blessing I didn't go to Molly's. All the responsibility of getting Dido boarded would have been on your shoulders, and you had quite enough with your poor mother, I'm sure. Lie down, darling. You're just making yourself hot. I shall write to Honoré today, poor man, and tell him I've seen you and how upset you are. It cheers people up knowing others are unhappy, don't you think?"

This crass expression of *schadenfreude*, which once would have made Gray laugh, now washed over him with most of the rest of Isabel's words. While she continued to burble, he sat as still as stone, his hands no longer caressing the dog who had sunk into a somnolent heap at his feet. Memory was beginning to come back now, returning in hard thrusts of pain.

"Is she dead?" he'd asked, relying on her, utterly in her hands.

"No, she was alive—just."

His hand fell again to fumble at the dog's coat, to feel her reality. And Dido turned her head, opened her eyes and licked his hand.

"I took some milk and chicken with me. I was a bit scared to open the kitchen door but I needn't have been. She was too weak to move. Someone ought to lock you up in a cell and see how you'd like it."

Oh, Drusilla, Drusilla . . .

"It's no use, anyway, the dog's had to be destroyed."

Oh, Dru, no . . .

"Anyway, dear," said Isabel, drawing breath, "you can have your key back now. Here you are. I'll go and hang it on the hook, shall I?"

"I'll take it."

An old blackened key, twin of the one he always carried.

"And put the kettle on, Gray. I brought some milk in case you didn't have any. We'll have a cup of tea and I'll run into Waltham Abbey and get us something for our lunch. I'm sure you're not fit to take care of yourself."

Not fit . . .

"I went in and cleaned up for you," she'd said.

"Why did you do that?"

"Why do I do anything for you? Don't you know yet?"

The bright key that had been Drusilla's hung on the hook, glittering like gold in the sun. She'd left her key and said goodbye. Alone, free of Isabel for a moment, he laid his face, his forehead, against the damp cold wall and the scream came out into the stone, agonising, uncomprehending, silent.

"I love you. If you still want me I'll leave Tiny and come and live with you."

I love you . . . No, he whispered, no, no. Goodbye, Gray, goodbye. I never change my mind. Punctual, relentless, unchanging in any fixed course, she never wavered. But this . . . ? Red fur, red fox hair, perfume rising like smoke, that low throaty laugh of hers —the memories spun, crystallised into a last image of her, as hard and unyielding as the stone against his face.

"A watched pot never boils, dear," said Isabel brightly from the doorway. She peered inquisitively at his numb blind face. "There's a car pulled up at your gate. Are you expecting anyone?"

He had been so adept at optimism, at supposing with uncrushable hope that every car was hers, every phone bell ringing to bring her to him. This time he had no hope and, in realising his deep stunned hopelessness, he knew too that he was living reality. He'd never see her again. She'd left her key and said goodbye. Betraying him systematically and coldly for perhaps some purpose of revenge, she'd brought him to this climax. Without speaking, he pushed past Isabel and opened the door to Ixworth. He gazed speechlessly but without dismay or even surprise at the policeman whose coming seemed the next natural and logical step in this sequence of happenings. He didn't speak because he had nothing to say and felt now that all words would be wasted effort. Why talk when event would now, in any case, pile upon event according to the pattern she had designed for them?

Ixworth looked at the flattened bracken. "Been sunbathing?"

Gray shook his head. This, then, was what it felt like to have the mental breakdown he'd feared all those months. Not manic hysteria, not fantasy unbridled or grief too strong to bear, but this peaceful numb acceptance of fate. After the liberating silent scream, just acceptance. It was possible even to believe that in a moment he would feel almost happy . . . Gently he held the dog back to keep her from springing lovingly at Ixworth.

"*Another* yellow Labrador, Mr. Lanceton? D'you breed them?"

"It's the same dog." Gray didn't trouble to consider the implication of his words. He turned away, indifferent as to whether Ixworth followed him or not, and almost collided with Isabel who was saying in sprightly tones, "Aren't you going to introduce me?"

Grotesquely girlish, she fluttered in front of the dour inspector. Gray said, "Miss Clarion, Mr. Ixworth." He wished vaguely that they would both go away. If only they would go away and leave him with the dog. He'd lie down somewhere with kind Dido, put his arms round her, bury his face in her warm, hay-scented fur.

Ixworth ignored the introduction. "Is that your dog?"

"Yes, isn't she gorgeous? Are you fond of dogs?"

"This one seems attractive." Ixworth's eyes flickered over Gray. "Is this the animal you were supposed to be looking after?"

"I'm sure he will when I do finally go away." Isabel seemed delighted that the conversation was taking such a pleasant sociable turn. "This time my trip fell through and poor Dido didn't get her country holiday."

"I see. I rather hoped I'd find you alone, Mr. Lanceton."

Quick to warm, equally quick to take offence, Isabel tossed her head and stubbed out her cigarette fiercely. "Please don't let me intrude. The last thing I want is to be in the way. I'll run into Waltham Abbey now, Gray, and get our lunch. I wouldn't dream of keeping you from your friend."

Ixworth smiled slightly at this. He waited in patient silence till the Mini had gone.

Gray watched the car move off down the lane. Dido began to whine, her paws on the windowsill, her nose pressed against the glass. This, Gray thought, was how it must have been when Isabel left her alone here that Monday . . . Only that had never happened, had it? None of that had happened.

"None of that really happened, did it?" Ixworth was saying. "Your whole story about the dog was untrue. We know, of course, that no animal answering this one's description was ever taken to Mr. Cherwell on Thursday."

Gray pulled the dog down gently. The sun's glare hurt his eyes and he pulled the chair away from the slanting dazzling rays. "Does it matter?" he said.

"Tell me," said the policeman in a tone which was both puzzled and bantering, "what you think does matter."

Nothing much now, Gray thought. Perhaps just one or two small things, questions to which he couldn't supply the answers himself. But his brain was clearing, revealing cold facts to which he seemed to have no emotional reaction. The dog had never been there. Working onwards from that, recalling certain phrases of hers in this new context—"I never change my mind, Gray"—he began to see the pattern she had designed. He saw it without pain, dully, almost scientifically. "I thought," he said, "that Harvey Janus was a big man but then I'd never seen him, and I thought he had a Bentley still, not the Mercedes he left in the lane. Strange, I suppose they called him Tiny because he *was* tiny. Would you like some tea?"

"Not now. Right now I'd like you to go on talking."

"There was no need to drug him, of course. I see that now. It was only necessary to get him here. That was easy because he was looking for a house in the Forest to buy his mother. And easy to overpower such a small man. Anyone could have done it."

"Oh, yes?"

"She had her key then. But I don't quite see . . ." He paused, sticking at betraying her even though she'd betrayed him. "But I suppose you've talked to Mrs. Janus? Even . . ." He sighed, though there was very little feeling left to make him sigh.

"Even arrested her?" he said.

Ixworth's face changed. It hardened, grew tough like that of some cinema cop. He reached for his briefcase and opened it, taking out a sheet of paper from a thin file. The paper fluttered in the sunbeam as he held it out to Gray. The typed words danced but Gray could read them. He'd typed them himself.

His address was at the top: *The White Cottage, Pocket Lane, Waltham Abbey, Essex.* Underneath that was the date: *June the sixth.* No year. And at the foot, under those terrible words he'd thought he'd never see again: *Harvey Janus Esq., Combe Park, Wintry Hill, Loughton, Essex.*

"Have you read it?"

"Oh, yes, I've read it."

But Ixworth read it aloud to him, just the same.

"'Dear Sir, In reply to your advertisement in *The Times*, I think I have just what you are looking for. Since my home is not far from yours, would you care to come over and see it? Four o'clock on Saturday would be a suitable time. Yours faithfully, Francis Duval.'"

The letter was the first they'd written.

"Where did you find it?" Gray asked. "Here? In this house?"

"It was in his breast pocket," said Ixworth.

"It *can't* have been. It was never posted. Look, I'll try to explain . . ."

"I wish you would."

"It's very difficult to explain. Mrs. Janus . . ." He didn't wince at her name but he hesitated, searching for a form into which to fit his sentence. "Mrs. Janus," he began again, wondering why Ixworth was frowning, "will have told you we were close friends.

At one time she wanted me to . . ." How to describe what she'd
wanted to this hard-faced inscrutable judge? How make him understand where fantasy ended and reality began? ". . . to play a
trick on her husband," he said, lying awkwardly, "to get money
from him. She had no money of her own and I'm always broke."
"We are aware of the state of your finances."
"Yes, you seem to be aware of everything. I did write that letter.
I wrote a whole lot more which were never sent and I've still got
them. They're . . ."
"Yes?"
"I burnt them. I remember now. But that one must have
got . . . Why are you looking at me like that? Mrs. Janus . . ."
Ixworth took the letter and refolded it. "I thought we were
really getting somewhere, Lanceton, till you brought Mrs. Janus's
name up. Leave her out of this. She doesn't know you. She's never
heard of you either as Duval or Lanceton."

The dog moved away from him. It seemed symbolic. She lay
down and snored softly. Ixworth hadn't stopped talking. Steadily,
he was outlining details of the events of Saturday afternoon.
They were precise circumstantial details and they included his,
Gray's, arrival at the hovel just before four, his greeting of Tiny
Janus, their subsequent journey round the house and to the head
of the cellar stairs. There was nothing wrong with the account
except that it was inaccurate in every particular.
But Gray didn't deny it. He said flatly, "She doesn't know me."
"Leave her out of it. On Saturday afternoon she was playing
tennis with the man who coaches her."
"We were lovers for two years," Gray said. "She's got a key to
this house." No, that wasn't true any more . . . "Does she say she
doesn't even know me?"
"Can you produce witnesses to prove she did?"
He was silent. There was no one. Nobody had ever seen them
together so it had never happened. Their love had no more hap-
pened than the dog's death had happened. And yet . . .
Without heat or the least emotion, he said slowly, "Why would
I have killed Janus except to get his wife?"
"For gain, of course," said Ixworth. "We're not children,

Lanceton. You're not a child. Credit us with a little intelligence. He was a rich man and you're a very poor one. I'll tell you frankly we have it from the French police you didn't even gain by your mother's death."

The hundred pounds . . . Had there been more hidden in the house? "He brought the deposit with him."

"Of course. You banked on that. Mr. Janus was very unwisely in the habit of carrying large sums of money on him, and these things get around, don't they? Even without seeing it, he was pretty sure he'd want this place and he was going to secure it— with cash." Ixworth shrugged, a heavy contemptuous gesture. "My God, and it wasn't even yours to sell! I suppose you worked out the sort of price it would fetch from looking in estate agents' windows."

"I know what it's worth."

"You knew what it would *fetch*, say. And you knew a good deal about human greed and need too. We found the three thousand pounds Mr. Janus brought with him in your strongbox with a copy of *The Times* and his advertisement marked. The box was locked and the key gone, but we broke it open."

Gray said, "Oh, God," very softly and hopelessly.

"I don't know if you're interested in knowing how we got on to you. It's obvious, really. Mrs. Janus knew where her husband had gone and how much money he was carrying. She reported him missing and we found his Mercedes in the lane."

Gray nodded at the inexorability, the neatness of it. "Someone ought to shut you up in a cell," she'd said. And perhaps there was a rightness in it somewhere, a harsh justice. He felt too weak, too unarmed, to argue and he knew he never would. He must accept. In writing the letters at all, he must always have hoped for an outcome of this kind; only his higher consciousness had struggled, deceiving him. He'd hoped for Tiny's death and, caught in her net, done as much as she to bring it about. Who spun, who held the scissors, and who cut the thread? Had the traffic light made his fate, or Jeff, or the buyer who hadn't got the paper in? Who made Honoré's marriage but the night phone caller? And who had made Tiny's death but he by meeting on that winter's day Tiny's wife? Who but Sir Smile, his neighbour?

"You'll want to make a statement," Ixworth said. "Shall we go?"

Gray smiled, for blank peace had returned. "If we might just wait for Miss Clarion?"

"Put the door on the latch and leave her a note." Ixworth spoke understandingly, almost sympathetically. His eye, satisfied now, no longer mocking, glanced on the sleeping Dido. "We can—er, shut the dog up in the kitchen."

AFTER

There were only six beds in the Alexander Fleming Ward. The
Member hesitated in the doorway and then made for the one bed
around which the curtains were drawn. But before he reached it
a nurse intercepted him.

"Mr. Denman's visitors are restricted to ten minutes. He's still
in a serious condition."

Andrew Laud nodded. "I won't stay long."

The nurse lifted one of the curtains for him and he ducked
under it apprehensively, wondering what he was going to see.
A hideously scarred face? A head swathed in bandages?

Jeff Denman said, "Thank God you could come. I've been on
tenterhooks all day," and then the Member looked at him. He was
as he had always been, apart from his pallor and his hair which
had been cropped to within an inch of his head.

"How are you, Jeff?"

"I'm much better. I'll be O.K. It's a strange sensation to wake
up in the morning and find that yesterday was six months ago."

The bed was covered with newspapers which the nurse stacked
into a neat pile before swishing out through the curtains. The
Member saw his own face staring out from the top one and the
headline: M.P. ACTS IN FOREST MURDER APPEAL.

"I haven't acted very much," he said. "They've let me see Gray
a couple of times but he seems to have a kind of amnesia about
the whole thing. He either can't or won't remember. All he talks
about is getting out and starting to write again but that, of course,
unless this Appeal . . ."

Jeff interrupted him. "I haven't got amnesia, surprisingly
enough." He shifted in the bed, lifting his head painfully from
the pillow. "But first I'd better tell you how I come to be here."

"You explained that in your letter."

"I had to get the sister to write that and I couldn't get my thoughts straight. You see, when I recovered consciousness and saw the papers it was such a shock. I couldn't believe Gray had got fifteen years for murder and I dictated that letter very incoherently. I just prayed you'd take me seriously and come. Give me a drink of water, will you?"

Andrew Laud put the glass to his lips and when Jeff had drunk, said, "I've gathered that your van crashed into a lorry somewhere in Waltham Abbey on June the twelfth and you were seriously injured. As soon as I read that I knew you might have something important to tell me, but you didn't explain what you were doing there."

"My job," Jeff said. "Moving furniture, or trying to." He coughed, holding his hands to his ribs. "The Sunday before that Gray asked me to move his stuff for him on the following Saturday. He said he'd phone if anything went wrong—things are liable to go wrong for him—and when he didn't I drove over there like I promised. It was the day after I'd had that letter from you asking me to dinner. You must have wondered why I didn't accept your wife's invitation."

"Never mind that. Tell me what happened."

Jeff said slowly, but quite clearly and coherently, "I got there about three. I left the van on the metalled part of the lane because it was muddy and I thought the wheels might get stuck. When I got to the cottage there was a key in the lock and a note pinned up beside it. It was typed on Gray's typewriter—I know that typewriter—but it wasn't signed. It said something like *Have to go out for a while. Let yourself in and have a look round.* I thought it was meant for me.

"I went in, made a sort of mental note of the things he'd want me to move—which is what I thought he'd meant in the note— and sat down to wait for him. Oh, and I went all over the house. If there's any question of Gray's having been there then, I can tell you he wasn't."

"You remember everything very clearly."

"Not the accident," said Jeff, and he winced slightly. "I can't remember a thing about that. But what happened before is quite clear to me. The place was very stuffy and musty-smelling," he went on after a pause, "and when it got to be nearly four o'clock I decided to go outside again, leaving the key and the note where they were. I thought I'd sit in the garden but it was so overgrown that I went into the Forest and walked about a bit. But the point is I never went out of sight of the cottage. I was pretty fed-up with Gray by this time and I wanted to get the job over and done with as soon as he got back."

"He didn't come?"

Jeff shook his head. "I sat down under a tree. I decided to give him ten minutes and then I'd go. Well, I was sitting there when I saw two people come down the lane."

"Did you now?" The Member leaned closer towards the bed. "In a car? On foot?"

"On foot. A little short bloke of about forty and a much younger woman. They went up to the door, read the note and let themselves in. They didn't see me, I'm sure of that. I realised then that the note was meant for them, not me. And I felt very strange about that, Andy. I just didn't know what to do."

"I don't quite follow you there," said the M.P.

"I recognised the girl. I knew her. I recognised her as a former girl friend of Gray's. And I couldn't understand what she was doing there with a bloke I was somehow certain must be her husband. He *looked* like a husband. I wondered if they'd come to have some sort of a scene with Gray. No, don't interrupt, Andy. Let me tell you the rest." The sick man's voice was beginning to flag. He rested back against his pillows and gave another painful dry cough. "I can tell you precisely when and where I'd seen her before. Gray brought her back to Tranmere Villas. Sally was living with me then. Gray had forewarned her and she kept out of the way when he and this girl came in, she never even saw them. But I'd been at work, I didn't know, and I opened the door of his room without knocking as soon as I got in. There was a review of his book in the evening paper and I was so pleased I rushed in to show him. They were on the bed making love. Gray was so—well, lost, I suppose you'd say—that he didn't even know I'd come in. But she did. She looked up and smiled a sort of look-how-daring-and-clever-I-am smile. I got out as fast and quietly as I could."

Andrew Laud said over his shoulder as the curtain was drawn aside, "Just two more minutes, nurse. I promise to go in two minutes."

"Mr. Denman mustn't get excited."

"I'm the one that's getting excited, Jeff," said the Member when they were alone again. "Go back to June the twelfth now, will you?"

"Where was I? Oh, yes, sitting under that tree. After a while an old boy came along the lane, reading a book, and then the bloke I'd seen go into the cottage came out and walked around the place, looking up at the windows. I thought they were going and I waited for her to come out too. Well, the bloke went back into the house and about ten minutes later the girl came out alone. She didn't put the key back in the door and the note had gone. I thought she looked a bit shaken, Andy, and she wasn't walking very steadily. I nearly called out to her to ask if she was all right, but I didn't, though I was beginning to think the whole thing was a bit odd. She walked away into the Forest and when she'd gone I went too. I thought I'd drive down to Waltham Abbey to see if I could find Gray and tell him about it. There was a big green car parked near the van. I didn't notice the make or the number.

"It must have been about half-past four then because they tell me I had the crash at twenty to five. And that's all. Since then I've been asleep and what I've told you has been asleep with me. Christ, suppose I'd died?"

"You didn't, and you won't now. You'll have to get well fast so that you can tell all that to the Appeal Court. It's a pity you don't know who the girl was."

"But I do. Didn't I say?" Jeff was lying down now, exhausted, his face grey. But he spoke with a feeble intensity. "I'd know that face anywhere and I saw it again yesterday. There was a picture in the paper of Mrs. Drusilla Janus, or Mrs. McBride, as I suppose I should call her. The *Standard* said she got married to some tennis coach last month. You'll have to go now, Andy. Keep in touch?"

Smiling, a little dazed, the Member got up. Jeff reached out from under the bedclothes and, silently, rather formally, the two men shook hands.

□

MAKE DEATH LOVE ME

To David Blass with love

In writing this novel, I needed help on some aspects of banking and on firearms. By a lucky chance for me, John Ashard was able to advise me on both. I am very grateful to him.

THE AUTHOR

1

Three thousand pounds lay on the desk in front of him. It was in thirty wads, mostly of fivers. He had taken it out of the safe when Joyce went off for lunch and spread it out to look at it, as he had been doing most days lately. He never took out more than three thousand, though there was twice that in the safe, because he had calculated that three thousand would be just the right sum to buy him one year's freedom.

With the kind of breathless excitement many people feel about sex—or so he supposed, he never had himself—he looked at the money and turned it over and handled it. Gently he handled it, and then roughly as if it belonged to him and he had lots more. He put two wads into each of his trouser pockets and walked up and down the little office. He got out his wallet with his own two pounds in it, and put in forty and folded it again and appreciated its new thickness. After that he counted out thirty-five pounds into an imaginary hand and mouthed, thirty-three, thirty-four, thirty-five, into an imaginary face, and knew he had gone too far in fantasy with that one as he felt himself blush.

For he didn't intend to steal the money. If three thousand pounds goes missing from a subbranch in which there is only the clerk in charge (by courtesy, the manager) and a girl cashier, and the girl is there and the clerk isn't, the Anglian-Victoria Bank will not have far to look for the culprit. Loyalty to the bank didn't stop him taking it, but fear of being found out did. Anyway, he wasn't going to get away or be free, he knew that. He might be only thirty-eight, but his thirty-eight was somehow much older than other people's thirty-eights. It was too old for running away. He always stopped the fantasy when he blushed. The rush of shame told him he had overstepped the bounds, and this always happened when he had got himself playing a part in some dumb show or even actually said aloud things like, That was the deposit, I'll send you the balance of five thousand, nine hundred in the morning. He stopped and thought what a state he had got himself into and how, with this absurd indulgence, he was even now breaking one of the bank's sacred rules. For he shouldn't be able to open the safe on his own, he shouldn't know Joyce's combination and she shouldn't know his. He felt guilty most of the time in Joyce's presence because she was as honest as the day, and had only told him the B List combination (he was on the A) when he glibly told her the rule was made to be broken and no one ever thought twice about breaking it.

He heard her let herself in by the back way, and he put the money in a drawer. Joyce wouldn't go to the safe because there was five hundred pounds in her till and few customers came into the Anglian-Victoria at Childon on a Wednesday afternoon. All twelve shops closed at one and didn't open again till nine-thirty in the morning.

Joyce called him Mr. Groombridge instead of Alan. She did this because she was twenty and he was thirty-eight. The intention was not to show respect, which would never have occurred to her, but to make plain the enormous gulf of years which yawned between them. She was one of those people who see a positive achievement in being young, as if youth were a plum job which they have got hold of on their own initiative. But she was kind to her elders, in a tolerant way.

"It's lovely out, Mr. Groombridge. It's like spring."

"It is spring," said Alan.

"You know what I mean." Joyce always said that if anyone attempted to point out that she spoke in clichés. "Shall I make you a coffee?"

"No thanks, Joyce. Better open the doors. It's just on two."

The branch closed for lunch. There wasn't enough custom to warrant its staying open. Joyce unlocked the heavy oak outer door and the inner glass door, turned the sign which said *Till Closed* to the other side which said *Miss J. M. Culver*, and went back to Alan. From his office, with the door ajar, you could see anyone who came in. Joyce had very long legs and a very large bust, but otherwise was nothing special to look at. She perched on the edge of the desk and began telling Alan about the lunch she had just had with her boy friend in the Childon Arms, and what the boy friend had said and about not having enough money to get married on.

"We should have to go in with Mum, and it's not right, is it, two women in a kitchen? Their ways aren't our ways. You can't get away from the generation gap. How old were you when you got married, Mr. Groombridge?"

He would have liked to say twenty-two or even twenty-four, but he couldn't because she knew Christopher was grown up. And, God knew, he didn't want to make himself out older than he was. He told the truth, with shame. "Eighteen."

"Now I think that's too young for a man. It's one thing for a girl but the man ought to be older. There are responsibilities to be faced up to in marriage. A man isn't mature at eighteen."

"Most men are never mature."

"You know what I mean," said Joyce. The outer door

opened and she left him to his thoughts and the letter from
Mrs. Marjorie Perkins, asking for a hundred pounds to be
transferred from her deposit to her current account.

Joyce knew everyone who banked with them by his or her
name. She chatted pleasantly with Mr. Butler and then with
Mrs. Surridge. Alan opened the drawer and looked at the
three thousand pounds. He could easily live for a year on
that. He could have a room of his own and make friends of
his own and buy books and records and go to theatres and
eat when he liked and stay up all night if he wanted to. For
a year. And then? When he could hear Joyce talking to Mr.
Wolford, the Childon butcher, about inflation, and how he
must notice the difference from when he was young—he was
about thirty-five—he took the money into the little room between his office and the back door where the safe was. Both
combinations, the one he ought to know and the one he
oughtn't, were in his head. He spun the dials and the door
opened and he put the money away, along with the other
three thousand, the rest being in the tills.

There came to him, as always, a sense of loss. He couldn't
have the money, of course, it would never be his, but he felt
bereft when it was once again out of his hands. He was like
a lover whose girl has gone from his arms to her own bed.
Presently Pam phoned. She always did about this time to
ask him what time he would be home—he was invariably
home at the same time—to collect the groceries or Jillian
from school. Joyce thought it was lovely, his wife phoning
him every day "after all these years."

A few more people came into the bank. Alan went out
there and turned the sign over the other till to *Mr. A. J.
Groombridge* and took a cheque from someone he vaguely
recognised called, according to the cheque, P. Richardson.

"How would you like the money?"

"Five green ones and three portraits of the Duke of Wellington," said P. Richardson, a wag.

Alan smiled as he was expected to. He would have liked to hit him over the head with the calculating machine, and now he remembered that last time P. Richardson had been in he had replied to that question by asking for Deutschemarks.

No more shopkeepers today. They had all banked their takings and gone home. Joyce closed the doors at three-thirty, and the two of them balanced their tills and put the money back in the safe, and did all the other small meticulous tasks necessary for the honour and repute of the second smallest branch of the Anglian-Victoria in the British Isles. Joyce and he hung their coats in the cupboard in his office. Joyce put hers on and he put his on and Joyce put on more mascara, the only make-up she ever wore.

"The evenings are drawing out," said Joyce.

He parked his car in a sort of courtyard, surrounded by Suffolk flint walls, at the bank's rear. It was a pretty place with winter jasmine showing in great blazes of yellow over the top of the walls, and the bank was pretty too, being housed in a slicked-up L-shaped Tudor cottage. His car was not particularly pretty since it was a G registration Morris 1100 with a broken wing mirror he couldn't afford to replace. He lived three miles away on a ten-year-old estate of houses, and the drive down country lanes took him only a few minutes.

The estate was called Fitton's Piece after a Marian Martyr who had been burnt in a field there in 1555. The Reverend Thomas Fitton would have been beatified if he had belonged to the other side, but all he got as an unremitting Protestant was fifty red boxes named after him. The houses in the four streets which composed the estate (Tudor Way,

Martyr's Mead, Fitton Close, and—the builder ran out of inspiration—Hillcrest) had pantiled roofs and large flat windows and chimneys that were for effect, not use. All their occupants had bought their trees and shrubs from the same very conservative garden centre in Stantwich and swapped cuttings and seedlings, so that everyone had Lawson's cypress and a laburnum and a kanzan, and most people a big clump of pampas grass. This gave the place a curious look of homogeneity and, because there were no boundary fences, it looked as if the houses were not private homes but dwellings for the staff of some great demesne.

Alan had bought his house at the end of not very hilly Hillcrest on a mortgage granted by the bank. The interest on this loan was low and fixed, and when he thought about his life one of the few things he considered he had to be thankful for was that he paid two and a half per cent and not eleven like other people.

His car had to remain on the drive because the garage, described as integral and taking up half the ground floor, had been converted into a bed-sit for Pam's father. Pam came out and took the groceries. She was a pretty woman of thirty-seven who had had a job for only one year of her life and had lived in a country village for the whole of it. She wore a lot of make-up on her lips and silvery-blue stuff on her eyes. Every couple of hours she would disappear to apply a fresh layer of lipstick because when she was a girl it had been the fashion always to have shiny pink lips. On a shelf in the kitchen she kept a hand mirror and lipstick and pressed powder and a pot of eyeshadow. Her hair was permed. She wore skirts which came exactly to her knees, and her engagement ring above her wedding ring, and usually a charm bracelet. She looked about forty-five.

She asked Alan if he had had a good day, and he said he had and what about her? She said, all right, and talked about the awful cost of living while she unpacked cornflakes and tins of soup. Pam usually talked about the cost of living for about a quarter of an hour after he got home. He went out into the garden to put off seeing his father-in-law for as long as possible, and looked at the snowdrops and the little red tulips which were exquisitely beautiful at this violet hour, and they gave him a strange little pain in his heart. He yearned after them, but for what? It was as if he were in love, which he had never been. The trouble was that he had read too many books of a romantic or poetical nature, and often he wished he hadn't.

It got too cold to stay out there, so he went into the living room and sat down and read the paper. He didn't want to, but it was the sort of thing men did in the evenings. Sometimes he thought he had begotten his children because that also was the sort of thing men did in the evenings.

After a while his father-in-law came in from his bed-sit. His name was Wilfred Summitt, and Alan and Pam called him Pop, and Christopher and Jillian called him Grandpop. Alan hated him more than any human being he had ever known and hoped he would soon die, but this was unlikely as he was only sixty-six and very healthy.

Pop said, "Good evening to you," as if there were about fifteen other people there he didn't know well enough to address. Alan said hallo without looking up and Pop sat down. Presently Pop punched his fist into the back of the paper to make Alan lower it.

"You all right then, are you?" Like the Psalmist, Wilfred Summitt was given to parallelism, so he said the same thing twice more, slightly rephrasing it each time. "Doing O.K., are you? Everything hunky-dory, is it?"

"Mmm," said Alan, going back to the Stantwich *Evening Press*.

"That's good. That's what I like to hear. Anything in the paper, is there?"

Alan didn't say anything. Pop came very close and read the back page. Turning his fat body almost to right angles, he read the "Stop Press." His sight was magnificent. He said he saw there had been another one of those bank robberies, another cashier murdered, and there would be more, mark his words, up and down the country, all over the place, see if he wasn't right, and all because they knew they could get away with it on account of knowing they wouldn't get hanged.

"It's getting like Chicago, it's getting like in America," said Pop. "I used to think working in a bank was a safe job, Pam used to think it was, but it's a different story now, isn't it? Makes me nervous you working in a bank, gets on my nerves. Something could happen to you any day, any old time you could get yourself shot like that chap in Glasgow, and then what's going to happen to Pam? That's what I think to myself, what's going to happen to Pam?"

Alan said his branch was much too small for bank robbers to bother with.

"That's a comfort, that's my one consolation. I say to myself when I get nervy, I say to myself, good thing he never got promotion, good thing he never got on in his job. Better safe than sorry, is my motto, better a quiet life with your own folks than risking your neck for a big wage packet."

Alan would have liked a drink. He knew, mainly from books and television, that quite a lot of people come home to a couple of drinks before their evening meal. Drinks the Groombridges had. In the sideboard was a full bottle of whisky, an almost full bottle of gin, and a very large full bottle of Bristol Cream sherry which Christopher had bought duty-free on the way back from a package tour to Switzerland. These drinks, however, were for other people.

They were for those married couples whom the Groombridges invited in for an evening, one set at a time and
roughly once a fortnight. He wondered what Pam and Pop
would say if he got up and poured himself a huge whisky,
which was what he would have liked to do. Wondering was
pretty well as far as he ever got about anything.

Pam came in and said supper was ready. They sat down
to eat it in a corner of the kitchen that was called the dining
recess. They had liver and bacon and reconstituted potato
and brussels sprouts and queen of puddings. Christopher
came in when they were halfway through. He worked for an
estate agent who paid him as much as the Anglian-Victoria
paid his father, and he gave his mother five pounds a week
for his board and lodging. Alan thought this was ridiculous
because Christopher was always rolling in money, but when
he protested to Pam she got hysterical and said it was
wicked taking anything at all from one's children. Christopher had beautiful trendy suits for work and well-cut
trendy denim for the weekends, and several nights a week
he took the girl he said was his fiancée to a drinking club in
Stantwich called the Agape, which its patrons pronounced
Agayp.

Jillian didn't come in. Pam explained that she had stayed
at school for the dramatic society and had gone back with
Sharon for tea. This, Alan was certain, was not so. She was
somewhere with a boy. He was an observant person and
Pam was not, and from various things he had heard and noticed he knew that, though only fifteen, Jillian was not a virgin and hadn't been for some time. Of course he also knew
that as a responsible parent he ought to discuss this with
Pam and try to stop Jillian or just get her on the pill. He was
sure she was promiscuous and that the whole thing ought
not just to be ignored, but he couldn't discuss anything with
Pam. She and Pop and Jillian had only two moods, apathy

and anger. Pam would fly into a rage if he told her, and if he insisted, which he couldn't imagine doing, she would scream at Jillian and take her to a doctor to be examined for an intact hymen or pregnancy or venereal disease, or the lot for all he knew.

In spite of Christopher's arrant selfishness and bad manners, Alan liked him much better than he liked Jillian. Christopher was good-looking and successful and, besides that, he was his ally against Wilfred Summitt. If anyone could make Pop leave it would be Christopher. Having helped himself to liver, he started in on his grandfather with that savage and, in fact, indefensible teasing which he did defend on the grounds that it was "all done in fun."

"Been living it up today, have you, Grandpop? Been taking Mrs. Rogers round the boozer? You'll get yourself talked about, you will. You know what they're like round here, yak-yak-yak all day long." Pop was a teetotaller, and his acquaintance with Mrs. Rogers extended to no more than having once chatted with her in the street about the political situation, an encounter witnessed by his grandson. "She's got a husband, you know, and a copper at that," said Christopher, all smiles. "What are you going to say when he finds out you've been feeling her up behind the village hall? Officer, I had drink taken and the woman tempted me."

"You want to wash your filthy mouth out with soap," Pop shouted.

Christopher said sorrowfully, smiling no more, that it was a pity some people couldn't take a joke and he hoped he wouldn't lose his sense of humour no matter how old he got.

"Are you going to let your son insult me, Pamela?"

"I think that's quite enough, Chris," said Pam.

Pam washed the dishes and Alan dried them. It was for some reason understood that neither Christopher nor Pop should ever wash or dry dishes. They were in the living room, watching a girl rock singer on television. The volume was turned up to its fullest extent because Wilfred Summitt was slightly deaf. He hated rock and indeed all music except Vera Lynn and ballads like "Blue Room" and "Tip-toe Through the Tulips," and he said the girl was an indecent trollop who wanted her behind smacked, but when the television was on he wanted to hear it just the same. He had a large colour set of his own, brand-new, in his own room, but it was plain that tonight he intended to sit with them and watch theirs.

"The next programme's unsuitable for children, it says here," said Christopher. "Unsuitable for people in their first or second childhoods. You'd better go off beddy-byes, Grandpop."

"I'm not demeaning myself to reply to you, Pig. I'm not lowering myself."

"Only my fun," said Christopher.

When the film had begun Alan quietly opened his book. The only chance he got to read was while they were watching television because Pam and Pop said it was unsociable to read in company. The television was on every evening all the evening, so he got plenty of chances. The book was Yeats, *The Winding Stair and Other Poems*.

Jillian Groombridge hung around for nearly two hours out-side an amusement arcade in Clacton, waiting for John Pur-ford to turn up. When it got to eight and he hadn't come, she had to get the train back to Stantwich and then the Stoke Mill bus. John, who had a souped-up aged Singer, would have driven her home, and she was more annoyed at having to spend her pocket money on fares than at being stood up.

They had met only once before and that had been on the previous Sunday. Jillian had picked him up by a fruit ma-chine. She got him starting to drive her back at nine because she had to be in by half-past ten, and this made him think there wouldn't be anything doing. He was wrong. Jillian being Jillian, there was plenty doing, the whole thing in fact on the back seat of the Singer down a quiet pitch-dark coun-try lane. Afterwards he had been quite surprised and not a little discomfited to hear from her that she was the daughter of a bank manager and lived at Fitton's Piece. He said, for he was the son of a farm labourer, that she was a cut above him, and she said it was only a tin-pot little bank subbranch, the Anglian-Victoria in Childon. They kept no more than seven thousand in the safe, and there was only her dad there and a girl, and they even closed for lunch, which would show him how tin-pot it was.

John had dropped her off at Stoke Mill at the point where Tudor Way debouched from the village street, and said

maybe they could see each other again and how about
Wednesday? But when he had left her and was on his way
back to his parents' home outside Colchester, he began having second thoughts. She was pretty enough, but she was a
bit too easy for his taste, and he doubted whether she was
the seventeen she said she was. Very likely she was under
the age of consent. That amused him, that term, because if
anyone had done any consenting it was he. So when Tuesday came and his mother said, if he hadn't got anything
planned for the next evening she and his father would like
to go round to his Aunt Elsie's if he'd sit in with his little
brother, aged eight, he said yes and saw it as a let-out.

On the morning of the day he was supposed to have his
date with Jillian he drove a truckload of bookcases and
record-player tables up to London, and he was having a cup
of tea and a sandwich in a cafe off the North Circular Road
when Marty Foster came in. John hadn't seen Marty Foster
since nine years ago when they had both left their Colchester primary school, and he wouldn't have known him
under all that beard and fuzzy hair. But Marty knew him.
He sat down at his table, and with him was a tall fair-haired
guy Marty said was called Nigel.

"What's with you then," said Marty, "after all these
years?"

John said how he had this friend who was a cabinetmaker
and they had gone into business together and were doing
nicely, thank you, mustn't grumble, better than they'd
hoped, as a matter of fact. Hard work, though, it was all go,
and he'd be glad of a break next week. This motoring mag
he took was running a trip, chartering a plane and all, to
Daytona Beach for the International Motorcycle Racing,
with a sight-seeing tour to follow. Three weeks in sunny
Florida wouldn't do him any harm, he reckoned, though it
was a bit pricey.

"I should be so lucky," said Marty, and it turned out he hadn't had a job for six months, and he and Nigel were living on the Social Security. "If you can call it living," said Marty, and Nigel said, "There's no point in working, anyway. They take it all off you in tax and whatever. I guess those guys who did the bank in Glasgow got the right idea."

"Right," said Marty.

"No tax on that sort of bread," said Nigel. "No goddamned superann. and N.H.I."

John shrugged. "It wouldn't be worth going inside for," he said. "Those Glasgow blokes, they only got away with twenty thousand and there were four of them. Take that branch of the Anglian-Victoria in Childon—you know Childon, Marty—they don't keep any more than seven thou. in the safe there. If a couple of villains broke in there, they'd only get three and a half apiece *and* they'd have to deal with the manager and the girl."

"You seem to know a lot about it."

He had impressed them he knew, with his job and his comparative affluence. Now he couldn't resist impressing them further. "I know the manager's daughter, we're pretty close, as a matter of fact. Jillian Groombridge, she's called, lives in one of those modern houses at Stoke Mill."

Marty did look impressed, though Nigel didn't. Marty said, "Pity banks don't close for lunch. You take a branch like that one, and Groombridge or the girl went off to eat, well, you'd be laughing then, it'd be in the bag."

"Be your age," said Nigel. "If they left the doors open and the safe unlocked, you'd be laughing. If they said, Come in and welcome, your need is greater than ours, you'd be laughing. The point is, banks don't close for lunch."

John couldn't help laughing himself. "The Childon one does," he said, and then he thought all this had gone far enough. Speculating about what might be, and if only, and if this happened and that and the other, was a sort of disease that kept people like Marty and Nigel where they were, while not doing it had got him where he was. Better find honest work, he thought, though he didn't, of course, say this aloud. Instead he got on to asking Marty about this one and that one they had been at school with, and told Marty what news he had of their old schoolfellows, until his second cup of tea, was drunk up and it was time to start the drive back.

The hypothetical couple of villains John had referred to had been facing him across the table.

Marty Foster also was the son of an agricultural labourer. For a year after he left school he worked in a paintbrush factory. Then his mother left his father and went off with a lorry driver. Things got so uncomfortable at home that Marty too moved out and got a room in Stantwich. He got a job driving a van for a cut-price electrical-goods shop and then a job trundling trolleys full of peat and pot plants about in a garden centre. It was the same one that supplied Fitton's Piece with its pampas grass. When he was sacked from that for telling a customer who complained because the garden centre wouldn't deliver horse manure, that if he wanted his shit he could fetch it himself, he moved up to London and into a squat in Kilburn Park. While employed in packing up parcels for an Oxford Street store, he met Nigel Thaxby. By then he was renting a room with a kitchen in a back street in Cricklewood, his aim being to stop working and go on the Social Security.

Nigel Thaxby, like Marty, was twenty-one. He was the son and only child of a doctor who was in general practice in Elstree. Nigel had been to a very minor public school because his father wanted him brought up as a gentleman but didn't want to pay high fees. The staff had third-class honours or pass degrees and generally no teachers' training certificates, and the classroom furniture was blackened and broken and, in fact, straight Dotheboys Hall. In spite of living from term to term on scrag end stew and rotten potatoes and mushed peas and white bread, Nigel grew up tall and handsome. By the time excessive cramming and his father's threats and his mother's tears had squeezed him into the University of Kent, he was over six feet tall with blond hair and blue eyes and the features of Michelangelo's *David*. At Canterbury something snapped in Nigel. He did no work. He got it into his head that if he did do any work and eventually got a degree, the chances were he wouldn't get a job. And if he did get one all that would come out of it was a house like his parents' and a marriage like his parents' and a new car every four years and maybe a child to cram full of useless knowledge and pointless aspirations. So he walked out of the university before the authorities could ask his father to take him away.

Nigel came to London and lived in a sort of commune. The house had some years before been allocated by the Royal Borough of Kensington and Chelsea to a quartet of young people on the grounds that it was being used as a centre for group therapy. So it had been for some time, but the young people quarrelled with each other and split up, leaving behind various hangers-on who took the padding off the walls of the therapy room and gave up the vegetarian regime, and brought in boy friends and girl friends and sometimes children they had had by previous marriages or liaisons. There was continuous coming and going, people drifted in for a week or a month and out again, contributing to the rent or not, as the case might be. Nigel got in on it because he knew someone who lived there and who was also a reject of the University of Kent.

At first he wasn't well up in the workings of the Social Se-

curity system and he thought he had to have a job. So he
also packed up parcels. Marty Foster put him wise to a lot of
useful things, though Nigel knew he was cleverer than
Marty. One of the things Marty put him wise to was that it
was foolish to pack up parcels when one could get one's rent
paid and a bit left over for doing nothing. At the time they
met John Purford in Neasden, Marty was living in Cricklewood and Nigel was sometimes living in Cricklewood with
Marty and sometimes in the Kensington commune, and they
were both vaguely and sporadically considering a life of
crime.

"Like your friend said, it wouldn't be worth the hassle,"
said Nigel. "Not for seven grand."

"Yeah, but look at it this way, you've got to begin on a
small scale," said Marty. "It'd be a sort of way of learning.
All we got to do is rip off a vehicle. I can do that easy. I got
keys that'll fit any Ford Escort, you know that."

Nigel thought about it.

"Can you get a shooter?" he said.

"I got one." Marty enjoyed the expression of astonishment
on Nigel's face. It was seldom that he could impress him.
But he was shrewd enough to put prudence before vanity,
and he said carefully, "Even an expert wouldn't know the
difference."

"You mean it's not for real?"

"A gun's a gun, isn't it?" And Marty added with, for him,
rare philosophical insight, "It's not what it does, it's what
people'll think it'll do that matters."

Slowly Nigel nodded his head. "It can't be bad. Look, if
you're really into this, there's no grief in going up this Childon dump tomorrow and casing the joint."

Nigel had a curious manner of speech. It was the result of
careful study in an attempt to be different. His accent was

mid-Atlantic, rather like that of a commercial radio announcer. People who didn't know any better sometimes took him for an American. He had rejected, when he remembered to do so, the cultured English of his youth and adopted speech patterns which were a mixture of the slang spoken by the superannuated hippies, now hopelessly out of date, in the commune, and catch phrases picked up from old films seen on TV. Nigel wasn't at all sophisticated really, though Marty thought he was. Marty's father talked Suffolk, but his mother had been a cockney. Mostly he talked cockney himself, with the flat vowels of East Anglia creeping in, and sometimes he had the distinctive Suffolk habit of using the demonstrative pronoun "that" for "it."

Seeing that Marty was serious or "really into" an attempt on the Childon bank, Nigel went off to Elstree, making sure to choose a time when his father was in his surgery, and got a loan of twenty pounds off his mother. Mrs. Thaxby cried and said he was breaking his parents' hearts, but he persuaded her into the belief that the money was for his train fare to Newcastle where he had a job in line. An hour later— it was Thursday and the last day of February—he and Marty caught the train to Stantwich and then the bus to Childon which got them there by noon.

They began their survey by walking along the lane at the back of the Anglian-Victoria subbranch. They saw the gap in the flint walls that led to the little yard, and in the yard they saw Alan Groombridge's car. On one side of the yard was what looked like a disused barn and on the other a small apple orchard. Marty, on his own, walked round to the front. The nearest of the twelve shops was a good hundred yards away. Opposite the bank was a Methodist chapel and next to that nothing but fields. Marty went into the bank.

The girl at the till labelled Miss J. M. Culver was weighing coins into little plastic bags and chatting to the customer

about what lovely weather they were having. The other till
was opened and marked Mr. A. J. Groombridge, but though
there was no one behind it, Marty went and stood there,
looking at the little office an open door disclosed. In that
office a man was bending over the desk. Marty wondered
where the safe was. Through that office, presumably behind
that other closed door. There was no upstairs. Once there
had been, but the original ceiling had been removed and
now the inside of the steeply sloping roof could be seen,
painted white and with its beams exposed and stripped.
Marty decided he had seen as much as he was likely to and
was about to turn away, when the man in the office seemed
at last to be aware of him. He straightened up, turned
round, came out to the metal grille, and he did this without
really looking at Marty at all. Nor did he look at him when
he murmured a good morning, but kept his eyes on the
counter top. Marty had to think of something to say so he
asked for twenty five-pence pieces for a pound note, wanted
them for parking meters, he said, and Groombridge counted
them out, first pushing them across the counter in two
stacks, then thinking better of this and slipping them into a
little bag like the ones the girl had been using. Marty said
thanks and took the bag of coins and left.

He was dying for a drink and tried to get Nigel to go with
him into the Childon Arms. But Nigel wasn't having any.

"You can have a drink in Stantwich," he said. "We don't
want all the locals giving us the once-over."

So they hung about until five to one. Then Nigel went
into the bank, timing his arrival for a minute to. A middle-
aged woman came out and Nigel went in. The girl was
alone. She looked at him and spoke to him quite politely but
also indifferently, and Nigel was aware of a certain indignation, a resentment, at seeing no admiration register on her
large plain face. He said he wanted to open an account, and

the girl said the manager was just going out to lunch and would he call back at two?

She followed him to the door and locked it behind him. In the lane at the back he met Marty, who was quite excited because he had seen Alan Groombridge come out of the back door of the bank and drive away in his car.

"I reckon they go out alternate days. That means the bird'll go out tomorrow and he'll go out Monday. We'll do the job on Monday."

Nigel nodded, thinking of that girl all alone, of how easy it would be. There seemed nothing more to do. They caught the bus back to Stantwich, where Marty spent the twenty five-pences on whisky and then set about wheedling some of Mrs. Thaxby's loan out of Nigel.

Fiction had taught Alan Groombridge that there is such a thing as being in love. Some say that this, indirectly, is how everyone gets to know about it. Alan had read that it had been invented in the Middle Ages by someone called Chrétien de Troyes, and that this constituted a change in human nature.

He had never experienced it himself. And when he considered it, he didn't know anyone else who had either. Not any of those couples, the Heyshams and the Kitsons and the Maynards, who came in to drink the duty-free Bristol Cream. Not Wilfred Summitt or Constable Rogers or Mrs. Surridge or P. Richardson. He knew that because he was sure that if it was a change in human nature their natures would have been changed by it. And they had not been. They were as dull as he and as unredeemed.

With Pam there had never been any question of being in love. She was the girl he took to a couple of dances in Stantwich, and one evening took more irrevocably in a field on the way home. It was the first time for both of them. It had been quite enjoyable, though nothing special, and he hadn't intended to repeat it. In that field Christopher was conceived. Everyone took it for granted he and Pam would marry before she began to "show," and he had never thought to protest. He accepted it as his lot in life to marry Pam and have a child and keep at a steady job. Pam wanted an engagement ring, though they were never really engaged, so he bought her one with twenty-five pounds borrowed from his father.

Christopher was born, and four years later Pam said they ought to "go in for" another baby. At that time Alan had not yet begun to notice words and what they mean and how they should be used and how badly most people use them, so he had not thought that phrase funny. When he was older and had read a lot, he looked back on that time and wondered what it would be like to be married to someone who knew it was funny too and to whom he could say it as a tender ribaldry; to whom he could say as he began to make love with that purpose in view, that now he was going in for a baby. If he had said it to Pam in those circumstances she would have slapped his face.

When they had two children they never went out in the evenings. They couldn't have afforded to even if they had known anyone who would baby-sit for nothing. Wilfred Summitt's wife was alive then, but both Mr. and Mrs. Summitt believed, like Joyce, that young married people should face up to their responsibilities, which meant never enjoying themselves and never leaving their children in the care of anyone else. Alan began to read. He had never read much before he was married because his father had said it was a waste of time in someone who was going to work with figures. In his mid-twenties he joined the public library in Stantwich and read every thriller and detective story and adventure book he could lay his hands on. In this way he lived vicariously quite happily. But around his thirtieth birthday something rather peculiar happened.

He read a thriller in which a piece of poetry was quoted. Until then he had despised poetry as above his head and something which people wrote and read to "show off." But he liked this poem, which was Shakespeare's sonnet about fortune and men's eyes, and lines from it kept going round

and round in his head. The next time he went to the library
he got Shakespeare's *Sonnets* out and he liked them, which
made him read more poetry and, gradually, the greater
novels that people call (for some unapparent reason) clas-
sics, and plays and more verse, and books that critics had
written about books—and he was a lost man. For his wits
were sharpened, his powers of perception heightened, and
he became discontented with his lot. In this world there
were other things apart from Pam and the children and the
bank and the Heyshams and the Kitsons, and shopping on
Saturdays and watching television and taking a caravan in
the Isle of Wight for the summer holidays. Unless all these
authors were liars, there was an inner life and an outer experience, an infinite number of things to be seen and done, and
there was passion.

He had come late in life to the heady intoxication of literature and it had poisoned him for what he had.

It was adolescent to want to be in love, but he wanted to
be. He wanted to live on his own too, and go and look at
things and explore and discover and understand. All these
things were equally impracticable for a married man with
children and a father-in-law and a job in the Anglian-Victoria Bank. And to fall in love would be immoral, especially
if he did anything about it. Besides, there was no one to fall
in love with.

He imagined going round to the Heyshams one Saturday
morning and finding Wendy alone, and suddenly, although,
like the people in the Somerset Maugham story, they had
known and not much liked each other for years, they fell
violently in love. They were stricken with love as Lancelot
and Guinevere were for each other, or Tristan and Isolde.
He had even considered Joyce for this role. How if she were
to come into his office after they had closed, and he were to

take her in his arms and . . . He knew he couldn't. Mostly he just imagined a girl, slender with long black hair, who made an appointment to see him about an overdraft. They exchanged one glance and immediately they both knew they were irrevocably bound to each other.

It would never happen to him. It didn't seem to happen to anyone much any more. Those magazines Pam read were full of articles telling women how to have orgasms and men how to make them have them, but never was there one telling people how to find and be in love.

Sometimes he felt that the possession of the three thousand pounds would enable him, among other things, to be in love. He took it out and handled it again on Thursday, resolving that that would be the last time. He would be firm about his obsession and about that other one too. After this week there would be no more reading of Yeats and Forster and Conrad, those seducers of a man's mind, but memoirs and biography as suitable to a practical working bank manager.

Alan Groombridge wondered about and thought and fantasised about a lot of odd and unexpected things. But, apart from playing with bank notes which didn't belong to him, he only did one thing that was unconventional.

The Anglian-Victoria had no objection to its Childon staff leaving the branch at lunchtime, providing all the money was in the safe and the doors locked. But, in fact, they were never both absent at the same time. Joyce stayed in on Mondays and Thursdays when her Stephen wasn't working in Childon and there was no one with whom to go to the Childon Arms. On those days she took sandwiches to the bank with her. Alan took sandwiches with him every day because he couldn't afford to eat out. But on Monday and Thursday lunchtimes he did leave the bank, though only Joyce knew of this and even she didn't know where he went. He drove off, and in winter ate his sandwiches in the car in a lay-by, in the spring and summer in a field. He did this to secure for himself two hours a week of peace and total solitude.

That Friday, 1 March, Joyce went as usual to the Childon Arms with Stephen for a Ploughman's Lunch and a half of lager, and Alan stuck to his resolve of not taking the three thousand pounds out of the safe. Friday was their busiest day and that helped to keep temptation at bay.

The weekend began with shopping in Stantwich. He went into the library, where he got out the memoirs of a playwright (ease it off gradually) and a history book. Pam didn't bother to look at these. Years ago she had told him he was a real bookworm, and it couldn't be good for his eyes, which he needed to keep in good condition in a job like his. They had sausages and tinned peaches for lunch, just the two of them and Wilfred Summitt. Christopher never came in for lunch on Saturdays. He got up at ten, polished his car, perquisite of the estate agents, and took the seventeen-year-old trainee hairdresser he called his fiancée to London, where he spent a lot of money on gin and tonics, prawn cocktails and steak, circle seats in cinemas, long-playing records, and odds and ends like *Playboy* magazine and bottles of wine and after-shave and cassettes. Jillian sometimes came in when she had nothing better to do. This Saturday she had something better to do, though what it was she hadn't bothered to inform her parents.

In the afternoon Alan pulled weeds out of the garden, Pam turned up the hem of an evening skirt and Wilfred Summitt took a nap. The nap freshened him up, and while they were having tea, which was sardines and lettuce and bread and butter and madeira cake, he said he had seen a news flash on television and the Glasgow bank robbers had been caught.

"What we want here is the electric chair."

"Something like that," said Pam.

"What we want is the army to take over this country. See a bit of discipline then, we would. The army to take over, under the Queen of course, under Her Majesty, and some general at the head of it. Some big pot who means business. The Forces, that's the thing. We knew what discipline was when I was in the Forces." Pop always spoke of his time at Catterick Camp in the 1940s as "being in the Forces" as if he had been in the navy and air force and marines as well. "Flog 'em, is what I say. Give 'em something to remember across their backsides." He paused and swigged tea. "What's wrong with the cat?" he said, so that anyone coming in at that moment, Alan thought, would have supposed him to be enquiring after the health of the family pet.

Alan went back into the garden. Passing the window of Pop's bed-sit, he noticed that the gas fire was full on. Pop kept his gas fire on all day and, no doubt, half the night from September till May whether he was in his room or not. Pam had told him about it very politely, but he only said his circulation was bad because he had hardening of the arteries. He contributed nothing to the gas bill or the electricity bill either, and Pam said it wasn't fair to ask anything from an old man who only had his pension. Alan dared to say, How about the ten thousand he got from selling his own house? That, said Pam, was for a rainy day.

Back in the house, having put the garden tools away, he found his daughter. His reading had taught him that the young got on better with the old than with the middle-aged, but that didn't seem to be so in the case of his children and Pop. Here, as perhaps in other respects, the authors had been wrong.

Jillian ignored Pop, never speaking to him at all, and Pam, though sometimes flaring and raving at her while Jillian flared and raved back, was generally too frightened of her to reprove her when reproof was called for. On the face of it, mother and daughter had a good relationship, always chatting to each other about clothes and things they had read in magazines, and when they went shopping together they always linked arms. But there was no real communication. Jillian was a subtle little hypocrite, Alan thought, who ingratiated herself with Pam by presenting her with the kind of image Pam would think a fifteen-year-old girl ought to have. He was sure that most of the extra-domestic activities she told her mother she went in for were pure invention, but they were all of the right kind: dramatic society, dressmaking class, evenings spent with Sharon, whose mother was a teacher and who was alleged to be helping Jillian with her French homework. Jillian always got home by ten-thirty because she knew her mother thought sexual intercourse invariably took place after ten-thirty. She said she came home on the last bus, which sometimes she did, though not alone, and Alan had once seen her get off the pillion of a boy's motorbike at the end of Martyr's Mead. He wondered why she bothered with deception, for if she had confessed to what she really did Pam could have done little about it. She would only have screamed threats while Jillian screamed threats back. They were afraid of each other, and Alan thought their relationship so sick as to be sinister. Among the things he wondered about was when Jillian would get married and how much she would expect him to fork out for her wedding. Probably it would be within the next couple of years, as she would very likely get pregnant quite soon, but she would want a big white wedding with all her friends there and a dance afterwards in a discotheque.

Pop had given up speaking to her. He knew he wouldn't get an answer. He was trying to watch television, but she had got between him and the set and was sitting on the floor drying her hair with a very noisy hair dryer. Alan could bring himself to feel sorry for Pop while Jillian was in the house. Fortunately she often wasn't, for when she was she ruled them all, a selfish bad-tempered little tyrant.

"You haven't forgotten we're going to the Heyshams' for the evening, have you?" said Pam.

Alan had, but the question really meant he was to dress up. They were not invited to a meal. No one at Fitton's Piece gave dinner parties, and "for the evening" meant two glasses of sherry or whisky and water each, followed by coffee. But etiquette, presumably formulated by the women, demanded a change of costume. Dick Heysham, who was quite a nice man, wouldn't have cared at all if Alan had turned up in old trousers and a sweater and would have liked to dress that way himself, but Pam said a sports jacket must be worn and when his old one got too shabby she made him buy a new one. To make this possible, she had for weeks denied herself small luxuries, her fortnightly hairdo, her fortnightly trip to Stantwich to have lunch in a cafe with her sister, the cigarettes of which she smoked five a day, until the twenty-six pounds had been garnered. It was all horrible and stupid, an insane way to live. He resigned himself to it, as he did to most things, for the sake of peace. Yet he knew that what he got was not peace.

Jillian, unasked, said that she was going with Sharon to play Scrabble at the house of a girl called Bridget. Alan thought it very handy for her that Bridget lived in a cottage in Stoke Mill which had no phone.

"Be back by ten-thirty, won't you, dear?" said Pam.

"Of course I will. I always am."

Jillian smiled so sweetly through her hair that Pam dared to suggest she move away out of Pop's line of vision.

"Why can't he go and watch his own TV?" said Jillian.

No one answered her. Pam went off to have a bath and

came back with the long skirt on and a frilly blouse and lacquer on her hair and her lips pink and shiny. Then Alan
shaved and got into a clean shirt and the sports jacket. They
both looked much younger dressed like that, and smart and
happy. The Heyshams lived in Tudor Way so they walked
there. Something inside him cried aloud to tell her that he
was sorry, that he pitied her from his soul, poor pathetic
woman who had lived her whole life cycle by the age at
which many only just begin to think of settling down. He
couldn't do it, they had no common language. Besides, was
he not as poor and pathetic himself? What would she have
replied if he had said what he would have liked to say?
Look at us, what are we doing, dressed up like this, visiting
people we don't even care for, to talk about nothing, to tell
face-saving lies? For what, for what?

At the Heyshams' the hosts and guests divided themselves
into two groups. The men talked to each other and the
women to each other. The men talked about work, their
cars, the political situation, and the cost of living. The
women talked about their children, their houses, and the cost
of living. After they had been there about an hour Pam went
to the bathroom and came back with more lipstick on.

By ten-fifteen they were all bored stiff. But Alan and Pam
had to stay for another three quarters of an hour or the
Heyshams would think they had been bored or had quarrelled before they came out or were worried about one of
their children. At exactly two minutes to eleven Pam said:

"Whatever time is it?"

She said "whatever" because that implied it must be very
late, while a simple "What time is it?" might indicate that
for her the time was passing slowly.

"Just on eleven," said Alan.

"Good heavens, I'd no idea it was as late as that. We *must*
go."

The Cinderella Complex, its deadline shifted an hour back, operated all over Fitton's Piece. Evenings ended at eleven. Yet there was no reason why they should go home at eleven, no reason why they shouldn't stay out all night, for no one would miss them or, probably, even notice they were not there, and without harming a soul, they could have stayed in bed the following day till noon. But they left at eleven and got home at five past. Pop had gone to his bed-sit, Jillian was in the bath. Where Christopher was was anybody's guess. It was unlikely he would come in before one or two. That didn't worry Pam.

"It's different with boys," he had heard her say to Gwen Maynard. "You don't have to bother about boys in the same way. I insist on my daughter being in by half-past ten and she always is."

Jillian had left a ring of dirty soap round the bath and wet towels on the floor. She was playing punk rock in her bedroom, and Alan longed for the courage to switch the electricity off at the main. They lay in bed, the room bright with moonlight, both pretending they couldn't hear the throbbing and the thumps. At last the noise stopped because, presumably, the second side of the second LP had come to an end and Jillian had fallen asleep.

A deep silence. There came into his head, he didn't know why, a memory of that episode in Malory when Lancelot is in bed with the queen and he hears the fourteen knights come to the door.

"Madam, is there any armour in your chamber that I might cover my poor body withal?"

Would he ever have such panache? Such proud courage? Would it ever be called for? Pam's eyes were wide open. She was staring at the moonlight patterns on the ceiling. He decided he had better make love to her. He hadn't done so for a fortnight, and it was Saturday night. Down in Stoke Mill the church clock struck one. To make sure it would work, Alan fantasised hard about the black-haired girl coming into the bank to order *lire* for a holiday in Portofino. What Pam fantasised about he didn't know, but he was sure she fantasised. It gave him a funny feeling to think about that, though he didn't dare think of it now, the idea of the fantasy people in the bed, so that it wasn't really he making love with Pam but the black-haired girl making love with the man who came to read the meter. The front door banged as Christopher let himself in. His feet thumped up the stairs. Madam, is there any armour in your chamber . . . ?

His poor body finished its work and Pam sighed. It was the last time he was ever to make love to her, and had he known it he would probably have taken greater pains.

Marty Foster's room in Cricklewood was at the top of the house, three floors up. It was quite big, as such rooms go, with a kitchen opening out of it, two sash windows looking out onto the street, and a third window in the kitchen. Marty hadn't been able to open any of these windows since he had been there, but he hadn't tried very hard. He slept on a double mattress on the floor. There was also a couch in the room and a gate-leg table marked with white rings and cigarette burns, and a couple of rickety Edwardian dining chairs, and a carpet with pink roses and coffee stains on it, and brown cotton curtains at the windows. When you drew these curtains clouds of dust blew out of them like smoke. In the kitchen was a gas stove and a sink and another gate-leg table and a bookcase used as a food store. Nobody had cleaned the place for several years.

The house was semidetached, end of a terrace. An Irish girl had one of the rooms next to Marty's, the one that overlooked the side entrance, and the other had for years been occupied by a deaf old man named Green. There was a lavatory between the Irish girl's room and the head of the stairs. Half a dozen steps led down to a bathroom which the top-floor tenants shared, and then the main flight went on down to the first floor where a red-haired girl and the man she called her "fella" had a flat, and the ground floor that was inhabited by an out-all-day couple that no one ever saw. Outside the bathroom door was a pay phone.

On Saturday Marty went down to this phone and got onto
a car-hire place in South London called Relyacar Rentals,
the idea of stealing a vehicle having been abandoned. Could
they let him have a small van, say a Mini-van, at nine on
Monday morning? They could. They must have his name,
please, and would he bring his driving licence with him?
Marty gave the name on the licence he was holding in his
hand. It had been issued to one Graham Francis Coleman of
Wallington in Surrey, was valid until the year 2020, and
Marty had helped himself to it out of the pocket of a jacket
its owner had left on the rear seat of an Allegro in a cinema
car park. Marty had known it would come in useful one day.
Next he phoned the Kensington commune and asked Nigel
about money. Nigel had only about six pounds of his
mother's loan left and their Social Security *Giro*'s weren't
due till Wednesday, but he'd do his best.

Nigel had learnt the sense of always telling everyone the
same lie, so he announced to his indifferent listeners that he
was going off to Newcastle for a couple of weeks. No one
said, Have a good time, or Send us a card, or anything like
that. That wasn't their way. One of the girls said, In that
case he wouldn't mind if her Samantha had his room, would
he? Nigel saw his opportunity and said she'd pay the rent
then, wouldn't she? A listless argument ensued, the upshot
of which was that no one was violently opposed to his taking ten pounds out of the tin where they kept the rent and
light and heat money so long as he put it back by the end of
the month.

With sixteen pounds in his pocket, Nigel packed most of
his possessions into a rucksack he borrowed from Samantha's mother and a suitcase he had long ago borrowed
from his own, and set off by bus for Cricklewood. The house
where Marty lived was in a street between Chichele Road
and Cricklewood Broadway, and it had an air of slightly

down-at-heel respectability. In the summer the big spreading trees, limes and planes and chestnuts, made the place damp and shady and even rather mysterious, but now they were just naked trees that looked as if they had never been in leaf and never would be. There was a church opposite that Nigel had never seen anyone attend, and on the street corner a launderette, a paper shop, and a grocery and delicatessen store. He rang Marty's bell, which was the top one, and Marty came down to let him in.

Marty smelt of the cheap wine he had been drinking, the dregs of which with their inky sediment were in a cup on the kitchen table. Wine, or whisky when he could afford it, was his habitual daily beverage. He drank it to quench his thirst as other people drink tea or water. One of the reasons he wanted money was for the unlimited indulgence of this craving of his. Marty hated having to drink sparingly, knowing there wasn't another bottle in the kitchen waiting for him to open as soon as this one was finished.

He swallowed what remained in the cup and then brought out from under a pile of clothes on the mattress an object which he put into Nigel's hands. It was a small though heavy pistol, the barrel about six inches long. Nigel put his finger to the trigger and tried to squeeze it. The trigger moved but not much.

"Do me a favour," said Marty, "and don't point that weapon at me. Suppose it was loaded?"

"You'd have to be a right cretin, wouldn't you?" Nigel turned the gun over and looked at it. "There's German writing on the side. *Carl Walther, Modell P.P.K. Cal. 9 mm. kurz.* Then it says *Made in W. Germany.*" The temptation to hold forth was too much for him. "You can buy these things in cycle shops, I've seen them. They're called nonfiring replica guns and they use them in movies. Cost a bomb too. Where'd you get the bread for a shooter like this?"

Marty wasn't going to tell him about the insurance policy
his mother had taken out for him years ago and which had
matured. He said only, "Give it here," took the gun back,
and looked at the pair of black stockings Nigel was holding
out for his inspection.

These Nigel had found in a pile of dirty washing on the
floor of the commune bathroom. They were the property of
a girl called Sarah who sometimes wore them for sexy effect.
"Timing," said Nigel, "is of the essence. We get to the bank
just before one. We leave the van in the lane at the back.
When the polone comes to lock up, Groombridge'll be due
to split. We put the stockings over our faces and rush the
polone and lock the doors after us."

"Call her a girl, can't you? You're not a poove."

Nigel went red. The shot had gone home. He wasn't ho-
mosexual—he wasn't yet sure if he was sexual at all and he
was unhappy about it—but the real point was that Marty
had caught him out using a bit of slang which he hadn't
known was queers' cant. He said sullenly, "We get her to
open the safe and then we tie her up so she can't call the
fuzz." A thought struck him. "Did you get the gloves?"

Marty had forgotten and Nigel let him have it for that,
glad to be once more in the ascendant. "Christ," he said,
"and that finger of yours is more of a giveaway than any
goddamned prints."

Neither affronted nor hurt, Marty glanced at his right
hand and admitted with a shrug that Nigel was right. The
forefinger wasn't exactly repulsive to look at or grotesque
but it wasn't a pretty sight either. And it was uniquely
Marty's. He had sliced the top off it on an electric mower at
the garden centre—a fraction nearer and he'd have lost half
his hand, as the manager had never tired of pointing out. The
finger was now about a quarter of an inch shorter than the

one on the other hand, and the nail, when it grew again, was warped and puckered to the shape of a walnut kernel.

"Get two pairs of gloves Monday morning when you get the van," snapped Nigel, "and when you've got them go and have your hair and your beard cut off."

Marty made a fuss about that, but the fuss was really to cover his fear. The idea of making changes in his appearance brought home to him the reality of what they were about to do. He was considerably afraid and beginning to get cold feet. It didn't occur to him that Nigel might be just as afraid, and they blustered and brazened it out to each other that evening and the next day. Both were secretly aware that they had insufficiently "cased" the Childon subbranch of the Anglian-Victoria, that their only experience of robbery came from books and films, and that they knew very little about the bank's security system. But nothing would have made either of them admit it. The trouble was, they didn't like each other. Marty had befriended Nigel because he was flattered that a doctor's son who had been to college wanted to know him, and Nigel had linked up with Marty because he needed someone even weaker than himself to bully and impress. But among these thieves there was no honour. Each might have said of the other, He's my best friend and I hate him.

That weekend the thought uppermost in Nigel's mind was that he must take charge and run the show as befitted a member of the elite and a descendant of generations of army officers and medical personages, though he affected to despise those forbears of his, and show this peasant what leadership was. The thought uppermost in Marty's, apart from his growing fear, was that with his practical know-how he must astound this upper-class creep. He got a pound out of Nigel on Sunday to buy himself a bottle of Sicilian wine, and wished he had the self-control to save half for Monday morning when he would need Dutch courage.

On Sunday night Joyce Culver steamed and pressed the evening dress she intended to wear on the following evening. Alan Groombridge broke his resolution and reread *The Playboy of the Western World* while his family, with the exception of Jillian, watched a television documentary about wildlife in the Galapagos Islands. Jillian was in the cinema in Stantwich with a thirty-five-year-old cosmetics salesman who had promised to get her home by ten-thirty and who doubted, not yet knowing Jillian, that there would be anything doing on the way.

John Purford, with fifty other car and motorcycle fanatics, was taking off from Gatwick in a charter aircraft bound for New York and thence for Daytona Beach, Florida.

5

The fine weather broke during the night, and on Monday morning, 4 March, instead of frost silvering the lawns of Fitton's Piece, heavy rain was falling. It was so dark in the dining recess that at breakfast the Groombridges had to have the unearthly, morgue-style, lymph-blue strip light on. Wilfred Summitt elaborated on his idea of an army takeover with a reintroduction of capital punishment, an end to Social Security benefits, and an enforced exodus of all immigrants. Christopher, who didn't have to be at work till ten, had lit a cigarette between courses (cereal and eggs and bacon) and was sniping back at him with the constitution of his own Utopia, euthanasia for all over sixty, and a sexual free-for-all for everyone under thirty. Jillian was combing her hair over a plate of cornflakes while she and Pam argued as to whether it was possible to put blond streaks in one's hair at home, Pam averring that this was a job for a professional. They all made a lot of irritable humourless noise, and Alan wondered how he would feel if the police came into the bank at ten and told him a gas main had exploded and killed all his family five minutes after he left. Probably he would be a little sorry about Pam and Christopher.

He left the sandwiches in the car because it was his day for going out. Along with her coat, Joyce had hung an evening dress in the cupboard. It was her parents' silver wedding day, and she and Stephen were going straight from

work to a drinks party and dinner at the Toll House Hotel.
"You'll be having your silver wedding in a few years, Mr.
Groombridge," said Joyce. "What'll you give your wife? My
mother wanted a silver fox but Dad said, if you don't watch
out, my girl, all you'll get is a silver*fish*, meaning one of
those creepy-crawlies. We had to laugh. He's ever so funny,
my dad. He gave her a lovely bracelet, one of those chased
ones."

Alan couldn't imagine how one bracelet could be more
chaste than another, but he didn't ask. The bank was always
busy on a Monday morning. P. Richardson was the first customer. He asked for two portraits of Florence Nightingale
and sneered at Alan, who didn't immediately guess he
meant ten-pound notes.

Marty showed Graham Coleman's driving licence to the
girl at Relyacar Rentals in Croydon and gave his age as
twenty-four. She said she'd like a ten-pound deposit, please,
they'd settle up tomorrow when they knew what mileage
he'd done, and if he brought the van back after six would he
leave it in the square and put the keys through Relyacar's
letter box?

Marty handed over the money and said yes to everything.
The Mini-van was white and clean and, from the registration, only a year old. He drove it a few miles, parking
outside a barber's shop where he had his hair and beard cut
off and his chin and upper lip closely shaved. He hadn't really seen his own face for three years and he had forgotten
what a small chin he had and what hollow cheeks. Depila-
tion didn't improve his appearance, though the barber
insisted it did. At any rate, the Relyacar girl wouldn't know
him again. His own mother wouldn't.

There was something else he had to do or buy, but he
couldn't remember what it was, so he drove back to pick up

Nigel. He went over Battersea Bridge and up through Kensington and Kensal Rise and Willesden to Cricklewood, where Nigel was waiting for him in Chichele Road.

"Christ," said Nigel, "you look a real freak. You look like one of those Hare Krishna guys."

Marty was a good driver. He had driven for his living while Nigel's experience consisted only in taking out his father's automatic Triumph, and he had never driven a car with an ordinary manual gear shift. Nor did he know London particularly well, but that didn't stop him ordering Marty to take the North Circular Road. Marty had already decided to do so. Still, he wasn't going to be pushed around, not he, and to show off his knowledge he went by a much longer and tortuous route over Hampstead Heath and through Highgate and Tottenham and Walthamstow. Thus it was well after eleven before they were out of London and reaching Brentwood.

When they were on the Chelmsford By-pass, Nigel said, "The shooter's O.K. and you've got your stocking. We can stuff the bread in this carrier. Let's have a look at the gloves."

Marty swore. "I knew there was something."

Nigel was about to lay into him when he realised that all this time Marty had been driving the van with ungloved hands, and that he too had put his ungloved hands on the doors and the dashboard shelf and the window catches, so all he said was, "We'll have to stop in Colchester and get gloves and we'll have to wipe this vehicle over inside."

"We can't stop," said Marty. "It's half eleven now."

"We have to, you stupid bastard. It wouldn't be half eleven if you hadn't taken us all round the houses."

It is twenty-three miles from Chelmsford to Colchester, and Marty made it in twenty minutes, somewhat to the distress of the Mini-van's engine. But there is virtually no on-

street parking in Colchester, whose narrow twisty streets
evince its reputation as England's oldest recorded town.
They had to go into a multistorey car park, up to the third
level, and then hunt for Woolworth's.

When the gloves were bought, woollen ones because cash
was running short, they found they had nothing with which
to wipe the interior of the van. Neither of them had hand-
kerchiefs, so Nigel took off one of his socks. The rain, of
which there had been no sign in London, was lashing down.

"It's twenty past twelve," said Marty. "We'll never make
it. We'd better do it Wednesday instead."

"Look, little brain," Nigel shouted, "don't give me a hard
time, d'you mind? How can we do it Wednesday? What're
we going to use for bread? Just drive the bugger and don't
give me grief all the goddamned time."

The narrower roads to Childon did not admit of driving at
seventy miles an hour, but Marty, his hands in green knitted
gloves, did make it. They put the van in the lane behind the
bank, up against the flint wall. Nigel got out and came cautiously to the gap in the wall, and there he was rewarded.

A middle-aged man, thin, paunchy, with greased-down
hair, came out of the back door and got into the car that
stood on the forecourt.

Half an hour before, Mrs. Burroughs had come into the
bank with a cheque drawn on the account of a firm of solicitors for twelve thousand pounds. She didn't explain its
source but her manner was more high-handed than usual.
Alan supposed it was a legacy and advised her not to put it
in her Deposit Account but to open a new account under
the Anglian-Victoria Treasure Trove scheme which gave a
higher rate of interest. Mrs. Burroughs said offendedly that
she couldn't possibly do that without consulting her hus-

band. She would phone him at his office and come back at two.

The idea of Mrs. Burroughs, who lived in a huge house outside Childon and had a Scimitar car and a mink coat, acquiring still more wealth, depressed him so much that he broke his new rule and took the three thousand out of the safe while Joyce was busy talking about the price of beef with Mr. Wolford. Strange to think, as he often did, that it was only paper, only pictures of the Queen and a dead Prime Minister and a sort of super-nurse, but that it could do so much, buy so much, buy happiness and freedom and peace and silence. He tore one of the portraits of Florence Nightingale in half just to see what it felt like to do that, and then he had to mend it with Sellotape.

He heard Mr. Wolford go. There was no one else in the bank now and it was nearly ten to one. Joyce might easily come into his office, so he put the money into a drawer and went out to the lavatory where there was a washbasin to wash the money dirt off his hands. It looked like more rain was coming, but he'd go out just the same, maybe up to Childon Fen where the first primroses would be coming out and the windflowers.

Joyce was tidying up her till.

"Mr. Groombridge, is this all right? Mr. Wolford filled in the counterfoil and did the carbon for the bank copy. I don't know why I never saw it. Shall I give him a ring?"

Alan looked at the slip from the paying-in book. "No, that's O.K. So long as it's come out clear and it has. I'm off to lunch now, Joyce."

"Don't get wet," said Joyce. "It's going to pour. It's come over ever so black."

He wondered if she speculated as to where he went. She couldn't suppose he took the car just to the Childon Arms. But perhaps she didn't notice whether he took the car or

not. He walked out to it now, the back door locking automatically behind him, and got into the driving seat—and
remembered that the three thousand pounds was still in his
desk drawer.

She wouldn't open the drawer. But the thought of it
there, and not in the safe where it should have been, would
spoil for him all the peace and seclusion of Childon Fen.
After all, she knew his combination, if she still remembered
it, just as he knew hers. Better put it away. He went back
and into his office, pushed to but didn't quite close the door
into the bank, and softly opened the drawer.

While he was doing so, at precisely one o'clock, Joyce
came out from behind the metal grille, crossed the floor of
the bank, and came face to face with Marty Foster and
Nigel Thaxby. They were between the open oak door and
the closed glass door and each was trying to pull a black
nylon stocking over his head. They hadn't dared do this before they got into the porch, they had never rehearsed the
procedure, and the stockings were wet because the threatening rain had come in a violent cascade during their progress from the van to the bank.

Joyce didn't scream. She let out a sort of hoarse shout and
leapt for the glass door and the key that would lock it.

Nigel would have turned and run then, for the stocking
was only pulled grotesquely over his head like a cap, but
Marty dropped his stocking and charged at the door, bursting it open so that Joyce stumbled back. He seized her and
put his hand over her mouth and jammed the gun into her
side and told her to shut up or she was dead.

Nigel followed him in quite slowly. Already he was thinking, She's seen our faces, she's seen us. But he closed the oak
door behind him and locked and bolted it. He closed and
locked the glass door and walked up and stood in front of

Joyce. Marty took his hand from her mouth but kept the
gun where it was. She looked at them in silence, and her
face was very pale. She looked at them as if she were studying what they looked like.

From the office Alan Groombridge heard Joyce shout and
he heard Marty's threat. He knew at once what was happening and he remembered, on a catch of breath, that conversation with Wilfred Summitt last Wednesday. His hands
tightened on the bundle of notes, the three thousand
pounds.

The Anglian-Victoria directed its staff to put up no resist-
ance. If they could they were to depress with their feet one
of the alarm buttons. The alarms were on a direct line to
Stantwich police station where they set in motion a flashing-
light alert system. If they couldn't reach an alarm, and in
Joyce's case it was perhaps impossible, they were to comply
with the demands of the intruders. There was an alarm button under each till and another under Alan's desk. He
backed his right foot and put his heel to it, held his heel
above it, and heard a voice say:

"We know you're on your own. We saw the manager go
out."

Where had he heard that voice before, that curious and
ugly mixture of cockney and Suffolk? He was sure he had
heard it and recently. It was a very memorable voice because the combination of broad flat vowels with slurred or
dropped consonants was so unusual. Had he heard it in the
bank? Out shopping? Then the sense of the words struck
him and he edged his foot forward again. They thought he
was out, they must have seen him get into his car. Now he
could depress the alarm without their having the faintest
idea he had done so, and thereby, if he was very clever, save
three thousand of the bank's money. Maybe save all of it

once he'd remembered who that strange voice belonged to.
"Let's see what's in the tills, doll."

A different voice, with a disc jockey's intonation. He
heard the tills opened. His foot went back again, feeling for
the button embedded in the carpet. From outside there
came a clatter of coins. A thousand, give or take a little,
would be in those tills. He lifted his heel. It was all very
well, that plan of his, but suppose he did save the three
thousand, suppose he stuffed it in the clothes cupboard before they came in, how was he going to explain to the bank
that he had been able to do so?

He couldn't hear a sound from Joyce. He lowered his heel,
raised it again.

"Now the safe," the Suffolk or Suffolk-cockney voice said.

To reach it they must pass through the office. He couldn't
press the alarm, not just like that, not without thinking
things out. There was no legitimate reason why he should
have been in his office with three thousand pounds in his
hands. And he couldn't say he'd opened the safe and taken
it out when he heard them come in because he wasn't supposed to know Joyce's combination. And if he'd been able to
save three, why not six?

Any minute now and they would come into the office.
They would stuff the notes and the coins—if they bothered
with the coins—into their bag and then come straight
through here. He pulled open the door of the cupboard and
flattened himself against its back behind Joyce's evening
dress, the hem of which touched the floor. Madam, is there
any armour in your chamber that I might cover my poor
body withal . . . ?

He had scarcely pulled the door closed after him when he
heard Joyce cry out:

"Don't! Don't touch me!" And there was a clatter as of
something kicked across the floor.

Lancelot's words reminded him of the questions he had asked himself on Saturday night. Would he ever have such panache, such proud courage? Now was the time. She was only twenty. She was a girl. Never mind the bank's suspicions, never mind now what anyone thought. His first duty was to rescue Joyce or at least stand with her and support her. He fumbled through the folds of the dress to open the door. He wasn't afraid. With a vague wry amusement, he thought that he wasn't afraid because he didn't mind if they killed him, he had nothing to live for. Perhaps all his life, with its boredom, its pain, and its futility, had simply been designed to lead up to this moment, meeting death on a wet afternoon for seven thousand pounds.

He would leave the money in the cupboard—he had thrust it into the pockets of his raincoat, which hung beside Joyce's dress—and go out and face them. They wouldn't think of looking in his raincoat, and later he'd think up an explanation for the bank. If there was a later. The important thing now was to go out to them, and this might even create a diversion in which Joyce could escape.

But before he touched the door, something very curious happened. He felt into the pockets to make sure none of the notes was sticking out and against his hands the money felt alive, pulsating almost, or as if it were a chemical that reacted at the contact with flesh. Energy seemed to come from it, rays of power, that travelled, tingling, up his arms. There were sounds out there. They had got the safe open. He heard rustling noises and thumps and voices arguing, and yet he did not hear them. He was aware only of the money alive between and around his fingers. He gasped and clenched his hands, for he knew then that he could not leave the money. It was his. By his daily involvement with it, he had made it his and he could not leave it.

Someone had come into the office. The drawers of his

desk were pulled out and emptied onto the floor. He stood
rigid with his hands in the coat pockets, and the cupboard
door was flung open.

He could see nothing through the dark folds of the dress.
He held his breath. The door closed again and Joyce swore
at them. Never had he thought he would hear Joyce use that
word, but he honoured her for it. She screamed and then she
made no more sound. The only sound was the steady roar of
rain drumming on the pantiled roof, and then, after a while,
the noise of a car or van engine starting up.

He waited. One of them had come back. The strange
voice was grumbling and muttering out there, but not for
long. The back door slammed. Had they gone? He could
only be sure by coming out. Loosening his hold on the
money, he thought he would have to go out, he couldn't stay
in that cupboard for the rest of his life. And Joyce must be
somewhere out there, bound and gagged probably. He
would explain to her that when he had heard them enter the
bank he had taken as much money as he had had time to
save out of the safe. She would think him a coward, but that
didn't matter because he knew he hadn't been a coward, he
had been something else he couldn't analyse. It was a
wrench, painful almost, to withdraw his hands from his
pockets, but he did withdraw them, and he pushed open the
door and stepped out.

The desk drawers were on the floor and their contents
spilt. Joyce wasn't in the office or in the room where the safe
was. The door of the safe was open and it was empty. They
must have left her in the main part of the bank. He hesitated. He wiped his forehead, on which sweat was standing.
Something had happened to him in that cupboard, he
thought, he had gone mad, mentally he had broken down.
The idea came to him that perhaps it was the life he led

which at last had broken him. He went on being mad. He
took the money out of his coat pockets and laid it in the
safe. He went to the back door and opened it quietly, looking out at the teeming rain and his car standing in the dancing, rain-pounded puddles. Then he slammed the door quite
hard as if he had just come in, and he walked quite lightly
and innocently through to where Joyce must be lying.

She wasn't there. The tills were pulled out. He looked in
the lavatory. She wasn't there either. While he was in the
cupboard, hesitating, she must have gone off to get help.
Without her coat, which was also in the cupboard, but you
don't think of rain at a time like that. Over and over to himself he said, I was out at lunch, I came back, I didn't know
what had happened, I was out at lunch. . . .

Why had she gone instead of pressing one of the alarm
buttons? He couldn't think of a reason. The clock above the
currency-exchange rate board told him it was twenty-five
past one and the date March 4th. He had gone out to lunch,
he had come back and found the safe open, half the money
gone, Joyce gone. . . . What would be the natural thing to
do? Give the alarm, of course.

He returned to his office and searched with his foot under
the desk for the button. It was covered by an upturned
drawer. Kneeling down, he lifted up the drawer and found
under it a shoe. It was one of the blue shoes with the instep
straps Joyce had been wearing that morning. Joyce wouldn't
have gone out into the rain, gone running out without one of
her shoes. He stood still, looking at the high-heeled, very
shiny, patent-leather, dark-blue shoe.

Joyce hadn't gone for help. They had taken her with
them.

As a hostage? Or because she had seen their faces? People
like that didn't have to have a reason. Did any people have

to have a reason? Had he had one for staying in that cupboard? If he had come out they would have taken him too.

Press the button now. He had been out at lunch, had come back to find the safe open and Joyce gone. Strange that they had left three thousand pounds, but he hadn't been there, he couldn't be expected to explain it. If he had been there, they would have taken him too because he too would have seen their faces. He looked at his watch. Nearly twenty to two. Give the alarm now, and there would still be time to put up roadblocks, they couldn't have got far in twenty minutes and in this rain.

The phone began to ring.

It made him jump, but it would only be Pam. It rang and rang and still he didn't lift the receiver. The ringing brought into his mind a picture as bright and clear as something on colour television, but more real. Fitton's Piece and his house and Pam in it at the phone, Pop at the table in the dining recess, drinking tea, Jillian coming home soon, and Christopher. The television. The punk rock. The doors banging. The sports jacket, the army takeover, the gas bill. He let the phone ring and ring, and after twenty rings—he counted them—it stopped. But because it had rung, his madness had intensified and concentrated into a hard nucleus, an appalling and wonderful decision.

His mind was not capable of reasoning, of seeing flaws or hazards or discrepancies. His body worked for him, putting itself into his raincoat, stuffing the three thousand pounds into his pockets, propelling itself out into the rain and into his car. If he had been there they would have taken him with them too. He started the car, and the clear arcs made on the windscreen by the wipers showed him freedom.

6

They took Joyce with them because she had seen their faces. She had opened the safe when they told her to, though at first she said she could only work one of the dials. But when Marty put the gun in her ribs and started counting up to ten, she came out with the other combination. As soon as the lock gave, Nigel tied a stocking round her eyes, and when she cried out he tied the other one round her mouth, making her clench her teeth on it. In a drawer they found a length of clothesline Alan had bought to tie down the boot lid of his car but had never used, and with this they tied Joyce's hands and feet. Standing over her, Marty looked at Nigel and Nigel looked at him and nodded. Without a word, they picked her up and carried her to the back door.

Nigel opened it and saw the Morris 1100 in the yard. He didn't say anything. It was Marty who said, "Christ!" But the car was empty and the yard was deserted. Rain was falling in a thick cataract. Nigel rolled the plastic carrier round the money and thrust it inside his jacket.

"Where the hell's Groombridge?" whispered Marty.

Nigel shook his head. They splashed through the teaming rain, carrying Joyce out to the van, and dropped her on the floor in the back.

"Give me the gun," said Nigel. His teeth were chattering and the water was streaming out of his hair down his face.

Marty gave him the gun and got into the driver's seat with the money on his lap in the carrier bag. Nigel went

back into the bank. He stumbled through the rooms, looking
for Alan Groombridge. He meant to look for Joyce's shoe
too, but it was more than he could take, all of it was too
much, and he stumbled out again, the door slamming behind him with a noise like a gunshot.

Marty had turned the van. Nigel got in beside him and
grabbed the bag of money and Marty drove off down the
first narrow side road they came to, the windscreen wipers
sweeping off the water in jets. They were both breathing
fast and noisily.

"A sodding four grand," Marty gasped out. "All that grief
for four grand."

"For Christ's sake, shut up about it. Don't talk about it in
front of her. You don't have to talk at all. Just drive."

Down a deep lane with steep hedges. Joyce began to
drum her feet on the metal floor of the van, thud, clack,
thud, clack, because she had only one shoe on.

"Shut that racket," said Nigel, turning and pushing the
gun at her between the gap in the seats. Thud, clack, thud
. . . His fingers were wet with rain and sweat.

At that moment they came face to face, head-on, with a
red Vauxhall going towards Childon. Marty stopped just in
time and the Vauxhall stopped. The Vauxhall was being
driven by a man not much older than themselves, and he
had an older woman beside him. There was no room to pass.
Joyce began to thrash about, banging the foot with the shoe
on it, clack, clack, clack, and thumping her other foot, thud,
thud, and making choking noises.

"Christ," said Marty. "Christ!"

Nigel pushed his arm through between the seats right up
to his shoulder. He didn't dare climb over, not with those
people looking, the two enquiring faces revealed so sharply
each time the wipers arced. He was so frightened he hardly
knew what he was saying.

With the gun against her hip, he said on a tremulous hiss, "You think I wouldn't use it? You think I haven't used it? Know why I went back in there? Groombridge was there and I shot him dead."

"Sweet Jesus," said Marty.

The Vauxhall was backing now, slowly, to where the lane widened in a little bulge. Marty eased the van forward, hunched on the wheel, his face set.

"I'll kill those two in the car as well," said Nigel, beside himself with fear.

"Shut up, will you? Shut up."

Marty moved past the car with two or three inches to spare, and brought up his right hand in a shaky salute. The Vauxhall went off and Marty said, "I must have been out of my head bringing you on this. Who d'you think you are? Bonnie and Clyde?"

Nigel swore at him. This reversal of roles was unbearable, but enough to shock him out of his panic. "You realise we have to get shot of this vehicle? You realise that? Thanks to you bringing us down a goddamned six-foot-wide footpath. Because that guy'll be in Childon in ten minutes and the fuzz'll be there, and the first thing he'll do is tell them about us passing him. Won't he? Won't he? So have you got any ideas?"

"Like what?"

"Like rip off a car," said Nigel. "Like in the next five minutes. If you don't want to spend the best years of your life inside, little brain."

Mrs. Burroughs phoned her husband at his office in Stantwich and asked him if he thought it would be all right for her to put Aunt Jean's money in the Anglian-Victoria Treasure Trove scheme. He said she was to do as she liked, it was all one to him if she hadn't enough faith in him to let him invest it for her, and she was to do as she liked. So Mrs. Burroughs got into her Scimitar at two and reached the Anglian-Victoria at five past. The doors were still shut. Having money of her own and not just being dependent on her husband's money had made her feel quite important, a person to be reckoned with, and she was annoyed. She banged on the doors, but no one came and it was too wet to stand out there. She sat in the Scimitar for five minutes and when the doors still didn't open she got out again and looked through the window. The window was frosted, but on this, in clear glass, was the emblem of the Anglian-Victoria, an A and a V with vine leaves entwining them and a crown on top. Mrs. Burroughs looked through one of the arms of the V and saw the tills emptied and thrown on the floor. She drove off as fast as she could to the police house two hundred yards down the village street, feeling very excited and enjoying herself enormously.

By this time the red Vauxhall had passed through Childon on its way to Stantwich. Its driver was a young man called Peter Johns who was taking his mother to visit her sister in Stantwich General Hospital. They met a police car with its blue lamp on and its siren blaring, indeed they came closer to colliding with it than they had done with the Mini-van, and these two near misses afforded them a subject for conversation all the way to the hospital.

At ten to three the police called on Mrs. Elizabeth Culver to tell her the bank had been robbed and her daughter was missing. Mrs. Culver said it was kind of them to come and tell her so promptly, and they said they would fetch her husband, who was a factory foreman on the Stantwich industrial estate. She went upstairs and put back into her wardrobe the dress she had been going to wear that evening, and then she phoned the Toll House Hotel to tell them to cancel the arrangements for the silver wedding party. She meant to phone her sisters too and her brother and the woman who, twenty-five years before, had been her bridesmaid, but she found she was unable to do this. Her husband came in half an hour later and found her sitting on the bed, staring silently at the wardrobe, tears streaming down her face.

Pamela Groombridge was ironing Alan's shirts and intermittently discussing with her father why the phone hadn't been answered when she rang the bank at twenty to two and two o'clock and again at three. In between discussing this she was thinking about an article she had read telling you how to put coloured transfers on ceramic tiles.

Wilfred Summitt was drinking tea. He said that he expected Alan had been out for his dinner.

"He never goes out," said Pam. "You know that, you were sitting here when I was cutting his sandwiches. Anyway, that girl would be there, that Joyce."

"The phone's gone phut," said Pop. "That's what it is, the phone's out of order. It's on account of the lines being overloaded. If I had my way, only responsible ratepayers over thirty'd be allowed to have phones."

"I don't know. I think it's funny. I'll wait till half-past and then I'll try it again."

Pop said to mark his words, the phone was out of order, gone phut, kaput, which wouldn't happen if the army took over, and what was wanted was Winston Churchill to come back to life and Field Marshal Montgomery to help him, good old Monty, under the Queen of course, under Her Majesty. Or it just could be the rain, coming down cats and dogs it was, coming down like stair rods. Pam didn't answer him. She was wondering if the colour on those transfers would be permanent or if it would come off when you washed them. She would like to try them in her own bathroom, but not if

the colour came off, no thanks, that would look worse than
plain white.

The doorbell rang.

"I hope that's not Linda Kitson," said Pam. "I don't want
to have to stop and get nattering to her."

She went to the door, and the policeman and the policewoman told her the bank had been robbed and it seemed
that the robbers had taken her husband and Joyce Culver
with them.

"Oh, God, oh, God, oh, God," said Pam, and she went on
saying it and sometimes screaming it while the policeman
fetched Wendy Heysham and the policewoman made tea.
Pam knocked over the tea and took the duty-free Bristol
Cream out of the sideboard and poured a whole tumblerful
and drank it at a gulp.

They fetched Christopher from the estate agent's and
when he came in Pam was half drunk and banging her fists
on her knees and shouting, "Oh, God, oh, God." Neither the
policewoman nor Wendy Heysham could do anything with
her. Christopher gave her another tumblerful of sherry in
the hope it would shut her up, while Wilfred Summitt
marched up and down, declaiming that hanging was too
good for them, poleaxing was too good for them. After the
electric chair, the poleaxe was his favourite lethal instrument. He would poleaxe them without a trial, he would.

Pam drank the second glass of sherry and passed out.

Wiser than those who had made his escape possible, Alan
avoided the narrow lanes. He met few cars, overtook a tractor and a bus. The rain was falling too heavily for him to see
the faces of people in other vehicles, so he supposed they
would not be able to see his. There wasn't much petrol in
the tank, only about enough to get him down into north

Essex, and of course it wouldn't do to stop at a petrol station.

His body was still doing all the work, and that level of consciousness which deals only with practical matters. He couldn't yet think of what he had done, it was too enormous, and he didn't want to. He concentrated on the road and the heavy rain. At the Hadleigh turn he came out onto the A.12 and headed for Colchester. The petrol gauge showed that his fuel was getting dangerously low, but in ten minutes he was on the Colchester By-pass. He turned left at the North Hill roundabout and drove up North Hill. There was a car park off to the left here behind St. Runwald's Street. He put the car in the car park, which was unattended, took out his sandwiches, locked the car, and dropped the sandwiches in a litter bin. Now what? Once they had found his car, they would ask at the station and the booking-office clerk would remember him and remember that he had passed through alone. So he made for the bus station instead where he caught a bus to Marks Tey. There he boarded a stopping train to London. His coat, which was of the kind that is known as showerproof and anyway was very old, had let the rain right through to his suit. The money had got damp. As soon as he had got to wherever he was going, he would spread the notes out and dry them.

There were only a few other people in the long carriage, a woman with two small boys, a young man. The young man looked much the same as any other dark-haired boy of twenty with a beard, but as soon as Alan saw him he remembered where he had heard that ugly Suffolk-cockney accent before. Indeed, so great was the resemblance that he found himself glancing at the boy's hands, which lay slackly on his knees. But of course the hands were whole, there was no mutilation of the right forefinger, no distortion of the nail.

The first time he had heard that voice it had asked him

for twenty five-pence pieces for a pound note. He had pushed the coins across the counter, looked at the young bearded face, thought, Am I being offhand, discourteous, because he's *young?* So he had put the coins into a bag and for a brief instant, but long enough to register, seen the deformed finger close over it and scoop it into the palm of the hand.

Suppose he had remembered sooner, this clue the police would seize on, would it have stopped him? He thought not. And now? Now he was in it as much as the man with the beard, the strange voice, the walnut fingernail.

Some sort of meeting was in progress in the village hall at Capel St. Paul, and among the cars parked in puddles on the village green were two Ford Escorts, a yellow and a silver-blue. The fifth key that Marty tried from his bunch unlocked the yellow one, but when he switched on the ignition he found there was only about a gallon of petrol in the tank. He gave that up and tried the silver-blue one. The tenth key fitted. The pointer on the gauge showed the tank nearly full. The tank of a Ford Escort holds about six gallons, so that would be all right. He drove off quickly, correctly guessing—wasn't he a country lad himself?—that the meeting had begun at two and would go on till four.

The van he had parked fifty yards up the road. They made Joyce get out at gunpoint and get into the Ford, and Marty drove the van down a lane and left it under some bushes at the side of a wood. There was about as much chance of anyone seeing them on a wet March afternoon in Capel St. Paul as there would have been on the moon. Marty felt rather pleased with himself, his nervousness for a while allayed.

"We can't leave her tied up when we get on the A-

Twelve," he said. "There's windows in the back of this motor. Right?"

"I do have eyes," said Nigel, and he climbed over the seat and undid Joyce's hands and took the gags off her mouth and her eyes. Her face was stiff and marked with weals where the stockings had bitten into her flesh, but she swore at Nigel and she actually spat at him, something she had never in her life done to anyone before. He stuck the gun against her ribs and wiped the spittle off his cheeks.

"You wouldn't shoot me," said Joyce. "You wouldn't dare."

"You ever heard the saying that you might as well be hung for a sheep as a lamb? If we get caught we go inside for life anyway on account of we've killed Groombridge. That's murder."

"Get it, do you?" said Marty. "They couldn't do any more to us if we'd killed a hundred people, so we're not going to jib at you, are we?"

Joyce said nothing.

"What's your name?" said Nigel.

Joyce said nothing.

"O.K., Miss J. M. Culver, be like that, Jane, Jenny, or whatever. I can't introduce us," Nigel said loudly to make sure Marty got the message, "for obvious reasons."

"Mr. Groombridge's got a wife and two children," said Joyce.

"Tough tit," said Nigel. "We'd have picked a bachelor if we'd known. If you gob at me again I'll give you a bash round the face you won't forget."

They turned onto the A.12 at twenty-five past two, following the same route Alan Groombridge had taken twenty minutes before. There was little traffic, the rain was torrential, and Marty drove circumspectly, neither too fast nor too slow, entering the fast lane only to overtake. By the time the

police had set up one of their checkpoints on the Colchester
By-pass, stopping all cars and heavier vehicles, the Ford Escort was passing Witham, heading for Chelmsford.

Joyce said, "If you put me out at Chelmsford I promise I
won't say a thing. I'll hang about in Chelmsford and get
something to eat, you can give me five pounds of what
you've got there, and I won't go to the police till the evening.
I'll tell them I lost my memory."

"You've only got one shoe," said Marty.

"You can put me down outside a shoe shop. I'll tell the
police you had masks on and you blindfolded me. I'll tell
them"—the greatest disguise Joyce could think of—"you
were old!"

"Forget it," said Nigel. "You say you would but you
wouldn't. They'd get it out of you. Make up your mind to it,
you come with us."

The first of the rush traffic was leaving London as they
came into it. This time Marty got on to the North Circular
Road at Woodford, and they weren't much held up till they
came to Finchley. From there on it was crawling all the
way, and Marty, who had stood up to the ordeal better than
Nigel, now felt his nerves getting the better of him. Part of
the trouble was that in the driving mirror he kept his eye as
much on those two in the back of the car as on the traffic
behind. Of course it was all a load of rubbish about Nigel
killing that bank manager, he couldn't have done that, and
he wouldn't do anything to the girl either if she did anything to attract the attention of other drivers. It was only a
question of whether the girl knew it. She didn't seem to.
Most of the time she was hunched in the corner behind him,
her head hanging. Maybe she thought other people would
be indifferent, pass by on the other side like that bit they
taught you in Sunday school, but Marty knew that wasn't so
from the time when a woman had grabbed him and he'd
only just escaped the store detective. He began to do silly

things like cutting in and making other drivers hoot, and once he actually touched the rear bumper of the car in front with the front bumper of the Escort. Luckily for them, the car he touched had bumpers of rubber composition and its driver was easygoing, doing no more than call out of his window that there was no harm done. But it creased Marty up all the same, and by the time they got to Brent Cross his hands were jerking up and down on the steering wheel and he had stalled out twice because he couldn't control his clutch foot properly.

Still, now they were nearly home. At Staples Corner he turned down the Edgware Road, and by ten to five they were outside the house in Cricklewood, the Escort parked among the hundred or so other cars that lined the street on both sides.

Nigel didn't feel sympathy, but he could see Marty was spent, washed up. So he took the gun and pushed it into Joyce's back and made her walk in front of him with Marty by her side, his arm trailing over her shoulder like a lover's. On the stairs they met Bridey, the Irish girl who had the room next to Marty's, on her way to work as barmaid in the Rose of Killarney, but she took no notice of them beyond saying an offhand hallo. She had often seen Nigel there before and she was used to Marty bringing girls in. If he had brought a girl's corpse in, carrying it in his arms, she might have wondered about it for a few minutes, but she wouldn't have done anything, she wouldn't have gone to the police. Two of her brothers had fringe connections with the I.R.A. and she had helped overturn a car when they had carried the hunger-strike martyr's body down from the Crown to the Sacred Heart. She and her whole family avoided the police.

Marty's front door had a Yale lock on it and another, older, lock with a big iron key. They pushed Joyce into the room and Nigel turned the iron key. Marty fell on the mattress, face-downwards, but Joyce just stood, looking about her at the dirt and disorder, and bringing her hands together to clasp them over her chest.

"Next we get shot of the vehicle," said Nigel.

Marty didn't say anything. Nigel kicked at the mattress and lit the wick of the oil heater—it was very cold—and then he said it again. "We have to get shot of the car."

Marty groaned. "Who's going to find it down there?"

"The fuzz. You have to get yourself together and drive it some place and dump it. Right?"

"I'm knackered." Marty heaved himself up and pushed a pile of dirty clothes onto the floor. "I got to have a drink."

"Yeah, right, later, when we've got that car off our backs."

"Christ," said Marty, "we've got four grand in that bag and I can't have a fucking drink."

Nigel gritted his teeth at that. He couldn't understand why there hadn't been seven like that guy Purford said. But he managed, for Jane or Jenny's benefit, a mid-Atlantic drawl. "I'll drive it. You stay here with her. We'll tie her up again, put her in the kitchen. You'll go to sleep, I know you, and if she gets screeching the old git next door'll freak."

"No," said Joyce.

"Was I asking you? You do as you're told, Janey."

They got hold of Joyce and gagged her again and tied her hands behind her and tied her feet. Marty took off her shoe to stop her making noises with her feet and shut the kitchen door on her. She made noises, though not for long.

The rain had stopped and the slate-grey sky was barred with long streaks of orange. Nigel and Marty got as far away from the kitchen door as they could and talked in fierce whispers. When the traffic slackened Nigel would take the car and dispose of it. They looked longingly at Marty's radio, but they dared not switch it on.

For a couple of hours the police suspected Alan Groombridge. No one had seen the raiders enter the bank. They set up roadblocks just the same and informed the Groombridge and Culver next of kin. But they were suspicious. According to his son and his father-in-law, Groombridge never went out for lunch, and the licencee of the Childon Arms told them he had never been in there. At first they played with the possibility that he and the girl were in it together, and had gone off together in his car. The presence of Joyce's shoe made that unlikely. Besides, this theory presupposed an attachment between them which Joyce's father and Groombridge's son derided. Groombridge never went out in the evenings without his wife, and Joyce spent all hers with Stephen Hallam.

A girl so devoted to her family as Joyce would never have chosen this particular day for such an enterprise. But had Groombridge taken the money, overturned the tills, left the safe open, and abducted the girl by force? These were ideas about which a detective inspector and a sergeant hazily speculated while questioning Childon residents. They were soon to abandon them for the more dismaying truth.

By five they were back where they had started, back to a raid and a double kidnapping. A lot of things happened at five. Peter Johns, driver of the red Vauxhall, heard about it on the radio and went to the police to describe the white Mini-van with which he had nearly collided. Neither he nor

his mother could describe the driver or his companion, but
Mrs. Johns had something to contribute. As the van edged
past the Vauxhall, she thought she had heard a sound from
the back of the van like someone drumming a heel on the
floor. A single clack-clack-clack, Mrs. Johns said, as of one
shoe drumming, not two.

The next person to bring them information was the driver
of a tractor who remembered meeting a Morris 1100. The
tractor man, who had a vivid imagination, said the driver
had looked terrified and there had certainly been someone
sitting beside him, no doubt about it, and his driving had
been wild and erratic. There had been three bank robbers
then, the police concluded, two to drive the van with Joyce
in it, the third in Alan Groombridge's car, compelling him to
drive. The loss of the silver-blue Ford Escort was reported
by its owner, a Mrs. Beech.

By then Nigel Thaxby and Marty Foster and Joyce Culver
were in Cricklewood and Alan Groombridge was in the Maharajah Hotel in the Shepherds Bush Road.

Literature had taught him that there were all sorts of
cheap hotels and houses of call and disreputable lodging
places in the vicinity of Paddington Station, so he went
there first on the Metropolitan Line out of Liverpool Street.
But times had changed, the hotels were all respectable and
filled up already with foreign tourists and quite expensive.
The reception clerk in one of them recommended him to
Mr. Aziz (who happened to be his cousin) and Alan liked
the name, feeling it was right for him. It reminded him of *A
Passage to India* and seemed a good omen.

Staying in hotels had not played an important part in his
life. Five years before, when Mrs. Summitt had died, she
had left Pam two hundred pounds and they had spent it on
a proper holiday, staying at a hotel in Torquay. Luggage

they had had, especially Pam and Jillian, an immense amount of it, and he wondered about his own lack of even a suitcase. He had read that hotelkeepers are particular about that sort of thing.

The Maharajah was a tall late-nineteenth-century house built of brown brick with its name on it in blue neon, the first H and the J being missing. Yes, Mr. Aziz had a single room for the gentleman, Mr. Forster, was it? Four pounds, fifty, a night, and pay in advance if he'd be so kind. Alan need not have worried about his lack of luggage because Mr. Aziz, who was only after a fast buck, wouldn't have cared what he lacked or what he had done, so long as he paid in advance and didn't break the place up.

Alan was shown to a dirty little room on the second floor where there was no carpet or central heating or washbasin, but there was a sink with a cold tap, a gas ring and kettle and cups and saucers, and a gas fire with a slot meter. He locked himself in and emptied his bulging pockets. The sight of the money made his head swim. He closed his eyes and put his head onto his knees because he was afraid he would faint. When he opened his eyes the money was still there. It was real. He spread it out to dry it, and he hung his raincoat over the back of a chair and kicked off his wet shoes and looked at the money. Nearest to him lay the portrait of Florence Nightingale which he had torn in half and mended with Sellotape.

Outside the window the sky was like orangeade in a dirty glass. The noise was fearful, the roar and throb and grind and screeching of rush traffic going round Shepherds Bush Green and into Chiswick and up to Harlesden and over to Acton and down to Hammersmith. The house shook. He lay on the bed, tossed about like someone at the top of a tree in a gale. He would never sleep, it was impossible that he would ever sleep again. He must think now about what he

had done and why and what he was going to do next. The
madness was receding, leaving him paralysed with fear and
a sensation of being incapable of coping with anything. He
must think, he must act, he must decide. Grinding himself to
a pitch of thinking, he shut his eyes again and fell at once
into a deep sleep.

Nigel delayed till half-past six, waiting for the traffic to
ease up a bit. As far as he was concerned, when you drove a
car your right foot was for the accelerator and the brake and
your left one for nothing. He got into the Escort and started
it and it leapt forward and stalled, nearly hitting the Range
Rover in front of it because Marty had left it in bottom gear.
Nigel tried again and more or less got it right, though the
gears made horrible noises. He moved out into the traffic,
feeling sick. But there was no time for that sort of thing because it was a full-time job ramming his left foot up and
down and doing exercises with his left hand. He didn't know
where he was aiming for and it wouldn't have been much
use if he had. His knowledge of London was sparse. He
could get from Notting Hill to Oxford Street and from Notting Hill to Cricklewood on buses, and that was about all.

The traffic daunted him. He could see himself crashing
the car and having to abandon it and run, so he turned it
into a side road in Willesden and sat in it for what seemed
like hours, watching the main road until there weren't quite
so many cars and buses going past. It hadn't been hours at
all, it was still only a quarter past seven. He had some idea
where he was when he found himself careering uncertainly
down Ladbroke Grove, and after that signs for south of the
river began coming up. He would take it over one of the
bridges and dump it in South London.

He was scared stiff. He wished he had some way of knowing what was going on and how much the police had found

out. The way to have found out was from Marty's radio
which the girl would have heard, and heard too that Groombridge was alive. Luckily, he'd managed to whisper to
Marty not to switch it on. He was so thick, that one, you
never knew what he'd do next.

The manual gear shift was getting easier to handle. He
tried breathing deeply to calm himself, and up to a point it
worked. What he really ought to do was hide the car somewhere where it wouldn't be found for weeks. He knew he
was a conspicuous person, being six feet tall and with bright
fair hair and regular features, not little and dark and ordinary like Marty. People wouldn't be able to remember
Marty but they'd remember him.

He turned right out of Ladbroke Grove and drove down
Holland Park Avenue to Shepherds Bush and along the
Shepherds Bush Road, thus passing the Maharajah Hotel and
forming one of the constituents of the noise that throbbed in
Alan Groombridge's sleeping brain. On to Hammersmith and
over Putney Bridge. There were still about two gallons in the
tank. In Wandsworth he put the car down an alley which was
bounded by factory walls and where there was no one to see
him. It was a relief to get out of it, though he knew he
couldn't just leave it there. He had grabbed a handful of
notes out of the carrier. In these circumstances, Marty
would have wanted a drink, but stress had made Nigel rave-
nously hungry. There was a Greek cafe just down the
street. He went in and ordered himself a meal of kebab and
taramasalata.

He might just as easily have chosen the fish and chip
place or the Hong Kong Dragon, but he chose the Greek
cafe and it gave him an idea. Beginning on his kebab, Nigel
glanced at a poster on the cafe wall, a coloured photograph
of Heraklion. This reminded him that before he had worked
round to the subject of a loan, he had listened with half an

ear to his mother's usual gossip about her friends. This had
included the information that the Boltons were going off for
a month to Heraklion. Wherever that might be, Nigel
thought, Greece somewhere. Dr. Bolton, now retired, and
his Greek wife, whom he was supposed to (or had once
been supposed to) call Uncle Bob and Auntie Helena, lived
in a house near Epping Forest. He had been there once,
about seven years before, and now he recalled that Dr. Bolton kept his car in a garage, a sort of shed really, at the bottom of his garden. An isolated sort of place. The car would
now be in the airport car park, for his mother had said they
were going last Saturday. Would the garage be locked?
Nigel tried to remember if there had been a lock on the door
and thought there hadn't been, though he couldn't be certain after so long. If there was and he couldn't use the garage, he would push the car into one of the forest ponds.
Thinking about the Boltons brought back to him that visit
and how he, aged fourteen, had listened avidly to Dr. Bolton's account of a stolen car that had been dumped in a
pond and not found for weeks.

He left the cafe at nine and returned cautiously to the
alley. The Ford Escort was still there and no other car was.
He got quickly into the car and drove off, this time crossing
the river by Wandsworth Bridge.

It took him nearly an hour to get out to Woodford, and he
had some very bad moments when a police car seemed to be
following him after the lights at Blackhorse Road. But the
police car turned off and at last he was approaching the Boltons' house, which was down a sort of lane off the Epping
New Road. The place was as remote and lonely as he remembered it, but right outside the garage, on the miserable
little bit of pavement that dwindled away into a path a few
yards on, four men were digging a hole. They worked by the
light of lamps run from a generator in a Gas Board van

parked close by. Nigel thought he had better back the car out and pretend to be using the entrance to the lane only as a place for turning. It was only the second time he had got into reverse gear, and he bungled it, getting into first instead and nearly hitting the Gas Board van. But he tried again and managed a reasonable three-point turn, observing exultantly that there was no lock on the garage door and no padlock either. But he couldn't park on the Epping New Road itself, which was likely, he thought, to be a favourite venue for traffic-control cars.

He drove a bit further, stuck the Escort under some bushes off the Loughton Road, and went into a phone box to phone Marty.

The receiver was handed to Marty by the pale red-haired girl, who looked as if she were permanently kept shut up in the dark. She passed it to him without a word. He didn't say anything to Nigel except yes and no and all right and see you, and then he went back to do as he was told and untie Joyce.

She was cramped and cold and stiff, and for the first time her spirit was broken. She said feebly, "I want to go to the toilet."

"O.K., if you must," said Marty, not guessing or even wondering what it had cost her to lie out there for hours, controlling her bladder at all costs, hoping to die before she disgraced herself in that way.

He went out first, making sure there was no one there, and brandishing the gun. He stood on the landing while she was in the lavatory. Bridey was out, and no light showed under Mr. Green's door. He always went to bed at eight-thirty, besides being deaf as a post. Marty took Joyce back and locked the door again with the big iron key, which he pocketed. Joyce sat on the mattress, rubbing her wrists and her ankles. He would have liked a cup of coffee, would have liked one hours ago, but something in him had baulked at making coffee for himself in front of a bound and gagged girl. Nor could he make it now and keep her covered with the gun. So he fetched in a half-full bottle of milk and poured it into two cups.

"Keep your filthy milk," Joyce mumbled.

"Be like that." Marty drank his and reached for the other cup.

"No, you don't," said Joyce, and swigged hers down. "When are you going to let me go?"

"Tomorrow," said Marty.

Joyce considered this. She looked around her. "Where am I supposed to sleep?"

"How about on here with me?"

The remark and the circumstances would immediately have recalled to Alan Groombridge's mind Faulkner's *Sanctuary* or even *No Orchids for Miss Blandish*, but in fact Marty had said what he had out of bravado. Being twenty-one and healthy, he naturally fancied pretty well every girl he saw, and in a different situation he would certainly have fancied big-busted long-legged Joyce. But he had never felt less sexy in his adult life, and he had almost reached a point where, if she had touched him, he would have screamed. Every sound in the house, every creak of stair and click of door, made him think it was the police coming. The sight of the unusable radio tormented him. Joyce, however, was resolved to sell her honour dear. She summoned up her last shreds of scorn, told him he had to be joking, she was engaged to someone twice his size who'd lay him out as soon as look at him, and she'd sleep on the sofa, thanks very much. Marty let her take two of the four pillows off his bed, watched her sniff them and make a face, and grab for herself his thickest blanket.

She lay down, fully clothed, covered herself up, and turned her face to the big greasy back of the sofa. Under the blanket she eased herself out of her skirt and her jumper, but kept her blouse and her slip on. Marty sat up, holding the gun and wishing there was some wine.

"Put the light out," said Joyce.

"Who're you giving orders to? You can get stuffed."

He was rather pleased when Joyce began to cry. She was deeply ashamed of herself but she couldn't help it. She was thinking about poor Mr. Groombridge and about her mother and father not having their party, and about Stephen. It was much to her credit that she thought about herself hardly at all. But those others, poor Mum and Dad, Stephen going to announce their engagement at the Toll House that night, Mr. Groombridge's poor wife, so devoted to him and ringing him at the bank every day. Joyce sobbed loudly, giving herself over to the noblest of griefs, that which is expended for others. Marty had been pleased at first because it showed his power over her, but now he was uneasy. It upset him, he'd never liked seeing birds cry.

"You'll be O.K.," he said. "Belt up, can't you? We won't hurt you if you do what we say. Honest. Get yourself together, can't you?"

Joyce couldn't. Marty switched the light off, but the room didn't get dark, never got dark, because of the yellow lamps outside. He got into bed and put the gun under the pillow and stuffed his fingers in his ears. He felt like crying himself. What the hell was Nigel doing? Suppose he didn't come back? The room vibrated with Joyce's crying. It was worse than the traffic when the lorries and the buses went by. Then it subsided, it stopped, and there was silence. Joyce had cried herself to sleep. Marty thought the silence worse than the noise. He was terribly hungry, he craved for a

drink, and he hadn't been to bed at this hour since he was
fifteen.

At the point when he had almost decided to give up, to
get out of there and run away somewhere, leaving the
money to Joyce, there came a tapping at the door. He
jumped out of his skin and his heart gave a great lurch. But
the tap came again and with it a harsh tired whisper. It was
only Nigel, Nigel at last.

Joyce didn't stir but he kept his voice very low.

"Had to hang about till the goddamned gasmen went.
The car's in the garage. I walked to Chingford and got a
bus. Christ!"

Nigel dropped the bunch of Ford keys into the carrier bag
with the money. He found a bit of string in the kitchen and
threaded it through the big iron key and hung it round his
neck. They turned off the oil heater. They put the gun under
the pillows and got into bed. It was just after midnight, the
end of the longest day of their lives.

8

When Alan woke up he didn't know where he was. The room was full of orange light. Great God (as Lord Byron had remarked the morning after his wedding, the sun shining through his red bed curtains) I am surely in hell! Then he remembered. It all came back to him, as Joyce would have said. The time, according to his watch, was five in the morning, and the light came from streetlamps penetrating a tangerine-coloured blind which he must have pulled down on the previous evening. He had slept for eleven hours. The money, now dry and crinkly, glimmered in the golden light. Great God, I am surely in hell. . . .

He got out of bed and went into the passage and found the bathroom. There was a notice inside his bedroom door which said in strange English: *The Management take no responsibilities for valuable left in rooms at owners risks.* He put the money back in his raincoat pockets, afraid now of walking about with his pockets bulging like that. All night he had slept in his clothes, and his trousers were as crumpled as the notes, so he took them off and put them under the mattress, which was a way of pressing trousers advocated by Wilfred Summitt. He took off the rest of his clothes and got back into bed, listening to the noise outside that had begun again. The noise seemed to him symptomatic of the uproar which must be going on over his disappearance and Joyce's and the loss of the money, the whole world up in arms.

It struck him fearfully that, once Joyce was set free or rescued, she would tell the police he hadn't been in the bank when the men came. He thought about that for a while, sweating in the cold room. She would tell them, and they would begin tracing his movements from the car to the bus station, the bus to the train. He saw himself as standing out in all those crowds like a leper or a freak or—how had Kipling put it?—a mustard plaster in a coal cellar. But she might not know. It all depended on whether they had blindfolded her and also on how many of them there had been. If she had seen his car still in the yard, and then they had blindfolded her and put her in their car or van for a while before driving away . . . He clung on to that hope, and he thought guiltily of Pam and his children. In her way, Pam had been a good wife to him. It seemed to him certain that, whatever came of this, he would never live with her again, never again share a bed with her or go shopping with her to Stantwich or yield to her for the sake of peace. That was past and the bank was past. The future was liberty or the inside of a jail.

At seven he got up and, wearing his raincoat as a dressing gown, went to have a bath. The water was only lukewarm because, although he had three thousand pounds in his pockets, he hadn't got a ten-pence piece for the meter. Shivering, he put his clothes on. The trousers didn't look too bad. He packed the money as flat as he could, putting some of it into his jacket pockets, some into his trouser pockets, and the rest in the breast pocket of his jacket. It made him look fatter than he was. Mr. Aziz didn't provide breakfast or, indeed, any meals, so he went out to find a place where he could eat.

Immediately when he was in the street, he felt a craven fear. He must be a marked man, he thought, his face better known than a royal prince's or a pop star's. It didn't occur to

him then that it had never been a habit in the Groombridge
or Summitt families to sit for studio portraits or go in for ambitious amateur photography, and therefore no large recognisable image of his face could exist. By some magic or some
feat of science, it would be brought to the public view. He
slunk into a newsagent's, trying to see without being seen,
but the tall black headlines leapt at him. He stood looking at
a counter full of chocolate bars until he dared to face those
headlines again.

It was Joyce's portrait, not his own, that met his eyes,
Joyce photographed by Stephen Hallam to seem almost
beautiful. *Bank Girl Kidnap*, said one paper; another, *Manager and Girl Kidnapped in Bank Raid*. He picked up both
papers in hands that shook and proffered a pound note. The
man behind the counter asked him if he had anything
smaller. Alan shook his head, he couldn't speak.

He had forgotten about breakfast and wondered how he
could ever have thought of it. He sat on a bench on Shepherds Bush Green and forced himself to look at those
papers, though his instinct, now he had bought them, was to
throw them away and run away from them himself. But he
took a deep breath and forced his eyes onto those headlines
and that smaller type.

Before he could find a picture of himself, he had to look
on the inside pages. They had put it there, he thought, because it was such a poor likeness, useless for purposes of
identification, and adding no character to the account.
Christopher had taken the snapshot of himself and Pam and
Wilfred Summitt in the garden of the house in Hillcrest. Enlarged, and enlarged only to about an inch in depth, Alan's
face was a muzzy grinning mask. It might equally well have
been Constable Rogers or P. Richardson standing there beside the pampas grass.

The other newspaper had the same picture. Were there

any others in existence? More vague snapshots, he thought. At his wedding, that shotgun affair, gloomy with disgrace, there had been no photographers. He became aware that the paralysis of terror was easing. It was sliding from him as from a man healed and made limber again. He saw the mist and the pale sun, the grass, other people, felt the renewal of hunger and thirst. If he couldn't be recognised, identified, he had little to fear. The relief of it, the slow easing that was now quickening and acquiring a sort of excitement, drove away any desire to read any more of the newspaper accounts. He forgot Joyce, who even now might be safe, might be at home once more with only a vague memory of events. He was safe and free, and he had got what he wanted.

A cup of tea and eggs and toast increased his sense of well-being. The papers he dropped thankfully into a bin. After a few minutes' exploration, he found the tube station and got a train to Oxford Circus. Oxford Street, he knew, was the place to buy clothes. Every Englishman, no matter how sheltered the life he has led, knows that. He bought two pairs of jeans, four tee-shirts, some socks and underpants and a windcheater, two sweaters and a pair of comfortable half boots. Jeans had never been permitted him in the past, for Pam said they were only for the young, all right for Christopher but ridiculous on a man of his age. He told himself he was buying them as a disguise, but he knew it wasn't only that. It was to recapture—or to discover, for you cannot recapture what you have never had—his youth.

He came out of the shop wearing his new clothes, and this transformation was another step towards ridding him of the fear of pursuit. People, even policemen, passed him without a second glance. Next he bought a suitcase, and in a public lavatory deep below the street, he filled it with his working suit and that money-loaded raincoat.

The case was too cumbersome to carry about for long. No
ardent reader of fiction could for long be in doubt about
where temporarily to rid himself of it. He caught a train to
Charing Cross, and there deposited the case in a left-luggage locker. At last he and the money were separated.
Walking away, with only his wallet filled as he had so often
filled it during those secret indulgences in his office, he felt a
lightness in his step as if, along with the money, he had dis-
burdened himself of culpability. So he made his way up to
Trafalgar Square. He went into the National Gallery and the
National Portrait Gallery and looked at the theatres in St.
Martin's Lane and the Charing Cross Road, and had a large
lunch with wine. Tonight he would go to the theatre. In all
his life he had never really been to the theatre except once
or twice to Stantwich Rep. and to pantomimes in London
when the children were younger. He bought himself a ticket
for the front row of the stalls, row A and right in the middle,
for Marlowe's *Faustus.*

Next to the threatre was a flat agency. It reminded him
that he would need somewhere to live, he wasn't going to
stay at the Maharajah longer than he had to. But it wouldn't
be a flat. A few seconds spent studying the contents of the
agency's window told him anything of that nature would be
beyond his means. But a room at sixteen to twenty pounds a
week, that he could manage.

The girl inside gave him two addresses. One was in Maida
Vale and the other in Paddington. Before he could locate either of them, Alan had to buy himself a London guide. He
went to the Paddington address first because the room to let
there was cheaper.

The landlord came to the door with an evening paper in
his hand. Alan saw that he and Joyce were still the lead
story, and his own face was there again, magnified to a fea-
tureless blur. The sight of it revived his anxiety, but the

landlord put the paper down on a table and invited him in.

Alan would have taken the room, though it was sparsely furnished and comfortless. At any rate, it would be his to improve as he chose, and it was better than the Maharajah. The landlord too seemed happy to accept him as a tenant so long as he understood he had to pay a month's rent in advance and a deposit. Alan had got out his wallet and was preparing to sign the agreement as A. J. Forster when the landlord said:

"I take it you can let me have a bank reference?"

The blood rushed into Alan's face.

"It's usual," said the landlord. "I've got to protect myself."

"I was going to pay you in cash."

"Maybe, but I'll still want a reference. How about your employer or the people where you're living now? Haven't you got a bank?"

In the circumstances, the question held a terrible irony. Alan didn't know what to say except that he had changed his mind, and he got out of the house as fast as he could, certain the landlord thought him a criminal, as indeed he was. No one knew more than he about opening bank accounts. It was impossible for him to open one, he had no name, no address, no occupation, and no past. Suddenly he felt frightened, out there in the alien street with no identity, no possessions, and he saw his act not so much as an enormity as an incredible folly. In all those months of playing with the bank notes, he had never considered the practicalities of an existence with them illicitly in his possession. Because then it had been a dream and now it was reality.

He could go on living, he supposed, at the Maharajah. But could he? At four pounds, fifty, a night, that little hole with its sink and its gas ring was going to cost him as much as one of the flats he had seen on offer in the agency window.

He couldn't go on staying there, yet he wouldn't be able to find anywhere else because it was "usual" to ask for a bank reference.

Occasionally in the past he had received letters asking for such a reference, and his replies had been discreet, in accordance with the bank's policy of never divulging to any outsider the state of a customer's account. He had merely written that, yes, so-and-so banked at his branch of the Anglian-Victoria, and that apparently had been satisfactory. He felt sick at the thought of where his own account was—with the Childon subbranch and in a name that today was familiar to every newspaper reader.

An idea came to him of returning home. It wasn't too late to go back if he really wanted to. He could say they had taken him and had let him go. He had been blindfolded all the time, so he hadn't seen their faces or where they had taken him. The shock had been so great that he couldn't remember much, only that he had saved some of the bank's money which he had deposited in a safe place. Perhaps it would be better not to mention the money at all. Why should they suspect him if he gave himself up now?

It was a quarter past three. It was not on his watch but on a clock on a wall ahead of him that he saw the time. And beside the clock, on a sheet of frosted glass, were etched the A and the V, the vine leaves and the crown, that were the emblems of the Anglian-Victoria Bank. The Anglian-Victoria, Paddington Station Branch. Alan stood outside, wondering what would happen if he went in and told the manager who he was.

He went into the bank. Customers were waiting in a queue behind a railing until a green light came on to tell them a till was free. A tremendous impulse took hold of him to announce that he was Alan Groombridge. If he did that now, in a few days' time he would be back behind his own till, driving his car, listening to Pam talking about the cost of living, to Pop quarrelling with Christopher, reading in the evenings in his own warm house. He set his teeth and clenched his hands to stop himself yielding to that impulse, though he still stood there at the end of the queue.

Steadily the green lights came on, and one customer moved to a till, then another. Alan stayed in the queue and shifted with it as it passed a row of tables spread with green blotters. A man was sitting at one of the tables, making an entry in his paying-in book. Alan watched him, envying him his legitimate possession of it.

The time was half-past three, and the security man moved to the door to prevent any late-comer from entering. Alan began framing words in his mind, how he had lost his memory, how the sight of that emblem had recalled to him who he was. But his clothes? How could he explain his new clothes?

Looking down at those jeans brought his eyes again to the man at the table. The paying-in book was open for anyone to see that two hundred and fifty pounds was about to be paid in, though Paul Browning hadn't been so imprudent as actually to place notes or cheques on it. Alan knew he was called Paul Browning because that was the name he had just written on a cheque-book request form. And now he added under it, in the same block capitals, his address: 15 Exmoor Gardens, London N.W.2.

As a green light came up for the woman immediately in front of Alan in the queue, Paul Browning joined it to stand behind him. With a muttered "Excuse me," Alan turned and made for the door.

He had found a bank reference and an identity, and with the discovery he burned the last fragile boat that could have taken him back. The security man let him out politely.

Joyce woke up first. With sleep, her confidence and her courage had come back. The fact that the others—those two pigs, as she called them to herself—still slept on, made her despise more than fear them. Fancy sleeping like that when you'd done a bank robbery and kidnapped someone! They must want their heads tested. But while she despised them, she also felt easier with them than she would have done had they been forty or fifty. Disgusting and low as they were, they were nevertheless young, they belonged with her in the great universal club of youth.

She got up and put on her clothes. She went into the kitchen and washed her hands and face under the cold tap, a good cold splash like she always had in the mornings, though she usually had a bath first. Pity she couldn't clean her teeth. What was there to eat? No good waiting for those pigs to provide something. Like the low people they were, they had no fridge, but there was an unopened packet of back bacon on a shelf of that bookcase thing, and some eggs in a box and lots of tins of baked beans. Joyce had a good look at the bacon packet. It might be a year old, for all she knew, you never could tell with people like that. But, no. *Sell by March 15th,* it said. She put the kettle on, and Flora margarine into a frying pan, and lit all the other gas burners and the oven to warm herself up.

The misery of Mum and Dad and Stephen she had got into better perspective. She wasn't dead, was she? Stephen

would value her all the more when she turned up alive and
kicking. They were going to let her go today. She wondered
how and where, and she thought it would be rather fun telling it all to the police and maybe the newspapers.

The roaring of the gas woke Marty and he saw Joyce
wasn't on the sofa. He called out, "Christ!" and Joyce came
in to stand insolently in the doorway. There are some people
who wake up and orient themselves very quickly in the
mornings, and there are others who droop about, half asleep,
for quite a long time. Joyce belonged in the first category and Marty in the second. He groaned and fumbled for
the gun.

"For all you know," said Joyce, "I might have a couple of
detectives out here with me, waiting to arrest you."

She made a big pot of strong tea and found a packet of
extended-life milk. Nasty stuff, but better than nothing. She
heard Marty starting to get up and she kept her head
averted. He might be stark naked for all she could tell,
which was all right when it was Stephen or one of her
brothers coming out of the bathroom, but not that pig. However, he was wearing blue pants with mauve bindings, and
by the time he had come into the kitchen he had pulled on
jeans and a shirt.

"Give us a cup of tea."

"Get it yourself," said Joyce. "You can take me to the toilet first."

She was a full five minutes in there, doing it on purpose,
Marty thought. He was on tenterhooks lest Bridey came out
or old Green. But there was no one. The lavatory flushed
and Joyce walked back, not looking at him. She passed
Nigel, who was sitting on the mattress with his head in his
hands, and went straight to the sink to wash her hands. All
the bacon in the pan, two eggs, and a saucepanful of baked

beans went onto the plate she had heated for herself. She sat down at the kitchen table and began to eat.

Nigel was obliged to pour tea for both of them and start cooking more bacon. He did it clumsily because he too was a slow waker. "One of us'll have to go out," he said, "and get a paper and more food."

"And some booze, for Christ's sake," said Marty.

"How about me going?" said Joyce pertly.

"Be your age," said Nigel, and to Marty, "You can go. I'll be better keeping an eye on her."

Joyce ate fastidiously, trying not to show how famished she was. "When are you going to let me go?"

"Tomorrow," said Marty.

"You said that yesterday."

"Then he shouldn't have," snapped Nigel. "You stay here. Get it? You stay here till I'm good and ready."

Joyce had believed Marty. She felt a little terrible tremor, but she said with boldness, "If he's going out he can get me a pair of shoes."

"You what? That'd be marvellous, that would, me getting a pair of girl's shoes when they know you've lost one."

"Get her a pair of flip-flops or sandals or something. You can go to Marks in Kilburn. She'll only get a hole in her tights and then we'll have to buy goddamned tights."

"And a toothbrush," said Joyce.

Marty pointed to a pot, encrusted with blackened soap, in which reposed a toothbrush with splayed brown tufts.

"Me use that?" said Joyce indignantly. She thought of the nastiest infection she could, of one she'd seen written on the wall in the ladies' on Stantwich Station. "I'd get crabs."

Nigel couldn't help grinning at that. They ate their breakfast and Marty went off, leaving Nigel with the gun.

Joyce wasn't used to being idle, and she had never been

in such a nasty dirty place before. She announced, without asking Nigel's permission, that she intended to clean up the kitchen.

Marty would have been quite pleased. He didn't clean the kitchen himself because he was too lazy to do so, not because he disapproved of cleaning. Nigel did. He had left home partly because his parents were always cleaning something. He sat on the mattress and watched Joyce scrubbing away, and for the first time he felt some emotion towards her move in him. Until then he had thought of her as an object or a nuisance. Now what he felt was anger. He was profoundly disturbed by what she was doing, it brought up old half-forgotten feelings and unhappy scenes, and he kept the gun trained on her, although her back was turned and she couldn't see it.

About an hour later Marty tapped at the door, giving the four little raps that was their signal to each other. He threw a pair of rubber-thonged sandals onto the floor and dropped the shopping bag. His face was white and pinched.

"Where's Joyce?"

"That's her name, is it? In the kitchen, spring-cleaning. What's freaking you?"

Marty began taking a newspaper, folded small, out of his jacket pocket. "No," said Nigel. "Outside." They went out onto the landing and Nigel locked the door behind them. He spread out a copy of the same newspaper Alan Groombridge had read some hours before. "I don't get it," he said. "What does it mean? We never even saw the guy."

"D'you reckon it's some sort of trick?"

"I don't know. What would be the point? And why do they say seven thousand when there was only four?"

Marty shook his head. "Maybe the guy did see us and got scared and went off somewhere and lost his memory." He voiced a fear that had been tormenting him. "Look, what you said to the girl about killing him—that wasn't true, was it?"

Nigel looked hard at him and then at the gun. "How could it be?" he said slowly. "The trigger doesn't even move."

"Yeah, I meant—well, you could have hit him over the head, I don't know."

"I never saw him, he wasn't there. Now you tear up that paper and put the bits down the bog. She's got to go on thinking we've killed Groombridge and we've got to get out of here and get her out. Right?"

"Right," said Marty.

Joyce finished cleaning the kitchen and then she cleaned her teeth with the toothbrush Marty had bought. She had to use soap for this, and she had heard that cleaning your teeth with soap turned them yellow, but perhaps that was only if you went on doing it for a long time. And she wasn't going to be there for a long time because tomorrow they were going to let her go.

Nigel sharply refused to allow her to go down to the bathroom, so she washed herself in the kitchen with a chair pushed hard against the door. Her mother used to make a joke about this fashion of getting oneself clean, saying that one washed down as far as possible and up as far as possible, but what happened to poor possible? Thinking of Mum brought tears to Joyce's eyes, but she scrubbed them away and scrubbed poor possible so hard that it gave her a reason for crying. After that she washed for herself to wear tomorrow the least disreputable of Marty's tee-shirts from the pile on the bed. She wasn't going to confront the police and be reunited with her family in a dirty dishevelled state, not she.

Marty went out again at seven and came back with whisky and wine and Chinese takeaway for the three of

them. Joyce ate hers in the kitchen, at the table. The boys
had theirs sitting on the living-room floor. The place was
close and fuggy and smelly from the oil heater and the oven,
which had been on all day, and condensation trickled down
the inside of the windows. When she had finished eating,
Joyce walked in and looked at Nigel and Marty. The gun
was on the floor beside the plastic pack with chow mein in
it. They didn't use plates, pigs that they were, thought
Joyce.

She had never been the sort of person who avoids issues
because it is better not to know for certain. She would
rather know.

"You're going to let me go tomorrow," she said.

"Who said?" Nigel put his hand over the gun. He forgot
to be a mid-Atlantic-cum-sixties-hippy-drop-out and spoke,
to Marty's reluctant admiration, in the authoritative public
school tone of his forbears. "There's no question of your
leaving here tomorrow. You'd go straight to the police and
describe us and describe this place. We took you with us to
avoid that happening and the situation hasn't changed." He
remembered then and added, with a nasal intonation, "No
way."

"But the situation won't change," said Joyce.

"I could kill you, couldn't I? Couldn't I?" He watched her
stiffen and then very slightly recoil. It pleased him. "You be
a good girl," he said, "and do what we say and stop asking
goddamned silly questions, and I'll think of a way to work it
for the lot of us. I just need a bit of hush. Right?"

"Have a drop of scotch," said Marty, who was cheered
and made affable by about a quarter of a pint of it. Joyce
wouldn't. Nor would she accept any of the Yugoslav Ries-
ling that Nigel was drinking. If the situation hadn't changed
and wasn't going to change, she would have to think of
ways to change it. The first duty of a prisoner is to escape.

Her uncle who had been a prisoner of war always said that, though he had never succeeded in escaping from the *Stalag Luft* in which for four years he had been incarcerated. She had never thought of escaping before because she had believed they would release her, but she thought about it now.

When they had settled down for the night and the boys were asleep, Marty snoring more loudly than her father did —Joyce had formerly thought young people never snore—she got up off the sofa and tiptoed into the kitchen. Earlier in the day she had found a ballpoint pen while scraping out thick greasy dirt from under the sink, and she had left it on the draining board, not supposing then that she would have any use for it. She hadn't much faith in this pen, which had probably been there for years, perhaps before the time of the present tenant. But once she had wiped the tip of it carefully on the now clean dishcloth and scribbled a bit on the edge of a matchbox to make the ink flow, she found it wrote quite satisfactorily. Enough light came in from outside to make writing, if not reading, possible. Like Alan Groombridge, Joyce found the constant blaze of light shining in from streetlamps throughout the night very strange, but it had its uses. She sat at the table and wrote on a smoothed-out piece of the paper bag in which the sandals had been:

"They have killed Mr. Groombridge. They are keeping me in a room in London." She crossed out "London" and wrote "in this street, I do not know the name of the street or the number of the house. There are two of them. They are young, about twenty. One of them is little and dark. The first finger on his right hand has been injured. The nail is twisted. The other one is tall and fair. Please get me out. They are dangerous. They have a gun. Signed, Joyce Marilyn Culver."

Joyce thought she would wrap her message round the
piece of pumice stone from the draining board and drop it
out of the window. But she couldn't open the window,
though neither of the boys seemed to hear her struggling
with it. Never mind, the lavatory window opened and she
would throw it out of there in the morning. So for the time
being she put the note in that traditional repository favoured by all heroines in distress, her bosom. She put it into
the cleft between her breasts, and went back to the sofa.
But first she favoured her captors with a look of contempt.
If she had been in their place, she thought, she would have
insisted on staying awake while her partner slept, and only
sleeping while he stayed awake to watch. Look where getting drunk and passing out had got them! But in the yellow
light the string with the key on it showed round the dark
one's neck, and the black barrel of the gun gleamed dully
against the fair one's slack hand.

At nine she was up and washed and dressed and shaking
Marty, who woke with a blinding headache and much hung
over.

"Go away. Leave me alone," said Marty, and he buried
his face in the dirty pillow.

"If you don't get up and take me to the toilet I'll bang
and bang at that door with a chair. I'll break the window."

"Do that and you're dead," said Nigel, elbowing Marty
out of the way and fishing out the gun. He had gone to bed
fully clothed, and it was out of distaste for the smell of him
that Joyce looked in the other direction. Nigel took her out
onto the landing and leaned against the wall, seeing stars
and feeling as if an army of goblins in hobnailed boots were
forming fours inside his head. He mustn't drink like that
again, it was crazy. He wasn't hooked on the stuff like that
little brain, was he? He didn't even really like it.

Joyce had her message wrapped round the pumice stone. She stood on the lavatory seat, wishing she could see something of what lay outside and below the window, but it was only a frosted fanlight that opened and this above her head, though not above the reach of her hand. The pumice dropped, and she trembled least it make a bang which the fair one might hear when it touched the ground. She pulled the flush hard to drown any other sound.

The other one glowered at her when they were back in the room. "What d'you think you're doing, wearing my tee-shirt?"

"I've got to change my clothes, haven't I? I'm not going to stay in the same thing day after day like you lot. I was brought up to keep myself nice. You want to take all that lot round the launderette. What's the good of me cleaning the place up when it just pongs of dirty clothes?"

Neither of them answered her. Marty took the radio to the lavatory with him, but he couldn't get anything out of it except pop music. Then he went off shopping without waiting for Nigel's command. The open air comforted him. He was a country boy and used to spending most of his time outside, all his jobs but the parcel-packing one had been outdoor jobs, and even when living on the dole he had spent hours wandering about London each day and walking on Hampstead Heath. He couldn't stand being shut up, scared as he was each time he saw a policeman or a police car. Nigel, on the other hand, liked being indoors, he didn't suffer from claustrophobia. He liked dirty little rooms with shut windows where he could loaf about and dream grandiose Nietzschean dreams of himself as the Superman with many little brains and stupid women to cringe and do his bidding. The stupid woman was cleaning again, the living room this time. Let her get on with it if that was all she was fit for.

On her knees, washing the skirting board, Joyce said, "Have you thought yet? Have you thought when I'm going to get out of here?"

"Look," said Nigel, "we're looking after you O.K., aren't we? You're getting your nosh, aren't you? And you can drink as much liquor as you want, only you don't want. I know this pad isn't amazing, but it's not that bad. You aren't getting ill-treated."

"You must be joking. When are you going to let me go?"

"Can't you say anything else but when are you going to get out of here?"

"Yes," said Joyce. "What's your name?"

"Robert Redford," said Nigel, who had been told he resembled this actor in his earliest films.

"When am I going to get out of here, Robert?"

"When I'm ready, Joyce. When my friend and I see our opportunity to get ourselves safely out of the country and don't have to worry about you giving the police a lot of damaging information."

Joyce stood up. "Why don't you talk like that all the time?" she said with an ingenuous look. "It sounds ever so nice. You could have a really posh accent if you liked."

"Oh, piss off, will you?" said Nigel, losing his temper. "Just piss off and give me a bit of hush."

Joyce smiled. She had never read Dr. Edith Bone's account of how, when condemned in Hungary to seven years' solitary confinement, she never missed a chance to needle and provoke her guards, while never in the slightest degree co-operating with them. She had not read it, but she was employing the same tactics herself.

The police were told of a silver-blue Ford Escort seen on the evening of Monday, 4 March, in the Epping New Road. Their informant was one of the gang of gasmen who had been working on a faulty main outside Dr. Bolton's house, and the car he had seen had in fact been Mrs. Beech's car and its driver Nigel Thaxby. But when the police had searched Epping Forest for the car and dragged one of the gravel-pit ponds, they abandoned that line of enquiry in favour of a more hopeful one involving the departure of a silver-blue Escort from Dover by the ferry to Calais on Monday night. This car, according to witnesses, had been driven by a middle-aged man with a younger man beside him and a man and a girl in the back. The man in the back seemed to have been asleep, but might have been unconscious or drugged. No one had observed the registration plates.

Alan Groombridge's car was found in the car park in Colchester. His fingerprints were on its interior and so were those of his wife. There were several other sets of fingerprints, and these came from the hands of a Stoke Mill farm worker to whom Alan had given a lift home on the previous Tuesday. But the police didn't know this, and it didn't occur to the farm worker to tell them. By that time they had questioned Christopher and Jillian Groombridge about their friends and anyone to whom they might have talked and given information about the Childon branch of the Anglian-Victoria Bank.

At first it seemed likely that the leak had come from Christopher, he being male and the elder. But it was soon clear that Christopher had never shown the slightest interest in any of the bank's arrangements, was ignorant as to how much was kept in the safe, and hadn't those sort of friends anyway. All his friends were just like himself, law-abiding, prosperous salesmen, or belonging to fringe professions like his own, well-dressed, affluent, living at home in order the better to live it up. They regarded crime as not so much immoral as "a mug's game." As for Jillian, she made an impression on them of naïve innocence. All her time away from home, she said, had been spent with Sharon and Bridget, and Sharon and Bridget backed her up. They wouldn't, in any case, have been able to give the name of John Purford because they didn't know it. Perhaps there had been no leak, for nothing need have been divulged which local men couldn't have found out for themselves. On the other hand, the Mini-van, located soon after Mrs. Beech's complaint, had been hired in Croydon by a man with a big black beard who spoke, according to the Relyacar Rentals girl, with a North Country accent. So the police, having turned Stantwich and Colchester and quite a large area of South London upside down, turned their attention towards Humberside and Cleveland.

Wilfred Summitt and Mrs. Elizabeth Culver appeared on television, but neither put up satisfactory performances. Mrs. Culver broke down and cried as soon as the first question was put to her, and Pop, seeing this as an opportunity to air his new dogmas, launched into a manifesto which opened with an appeal for mass public executions. He went on talking for a while after he had been cut off in midsentence, not realising he was no longer on view.

Looking for somewhere to live, Alan left the suitcase in a locker at Paddington Station. At the theatre he had put it under his seat where it annoyed no one because he was sitting in the front row. He had enjoyed *Faustus*, identifying with its protagonist. He too had sold his soul for the kingdoms of the earth—and, incidentally, for three thousand pounds. See, see where Christ's blood streams in the firmament! He had felt a bit like that himself, looking at the sunset while earlier he was walking in Kensington Gardens. Would he also find his Helen to make him immortal with a kiss? At that thought he blushed in the dark theatre, and blushed again, thinking of it, as he walked from Paddington Station down towards the Bayswater Road.

Notting Hill, he had decided, must be his future place of abode, not because he had ever been there or knew anything about it, but because Wilfred Summitt said that wild horses wouldn't drag him to Notting Hill. He hadn't been there either, but he talked about it as a sort of Sodom and Gomorrah. There had been race riots there in the fifties and some more a couple of years back, which was enough to make Pop see it as a sinful slum where everyone was smashed out of their minds on hashish, and black people stuck knives in you. Alan went to two agencies in Notting Hill and was given quite a lot of hopeful-looking addresses. He went to three of them before lunch.

It was an unpleasant shock to discover that London landlords call a room ten feet by twelve, with a sink and cooker in one corner, a flatlet. He could hardly believe in the serious, let alone honest, intent behind calling two knives and two forks and two spoons from Woolworth's "fully equipped with cutlery" or an old three-piece suite in stretch nylon covers "immaculate furnishings." Having eaten his lunch in a pub—going into pubs was a lovely new experience—he bought an evening paper and a transistor radio, and read the paper sitting on a seat in Kensington Gardens. It told him that the Anglian-Victoria Bank was offering a reward of twenty thousand pounds for information leading to the arrest of the bank robbers and the safe return of himself and Joyce. A girl came and sat beside him and began feeding pigeons and sparrows with bits of stale cake. She was so much like his fantasy girl, with a long slender neck and fine delicate hands and black hair as smooth and straight as a skein of silk, that he couldn't keep from staring at her.

The second time she caught his eye, she smiled and said it was a shame the way the pigeons drove the smaller birds away and got all the best bits, but what could you do? They also had to live.

Her voice was strong and rich and assured. He felt shy of her because of her resemblance to the fantasy girl, and because of that too he was aware of an unfamiliar stirring of desire. Was she his Helen? He answered her hesitantly and then, since she had begun it, she had spoken to him first, and anyway he had a good reason for his question, he asked her if she lived nearby.

"In Pembroke Villas," she said. "I work in an antique shop, the Pembroke Market."

He said hastily, not wanting her to get the wrong idea—though would it be the wrong idea?—"I asked because I'm looking for a place to live. Just a room."

She interrupted him before he could explain how disillusioned he had been. "It's got much more difficult in the past couple of years. A good way used to be to buy the evening papers as soon as they come on the streets and phone places straightaway."

"I haven't tried that," he said, thinking of how difficult it would be, using pay phones and getting enough change, and more and more nights at the Maharajah, and thinking too how exciting and frightening it would be to live in the same house as she.

"You sometimes see ads in newsagents' windows," she said. "They have them in the window of the place next to the Market."

Was it an invitation? She had got up and was smiling encouragingly at him. For the first time he noticed how beautifully dressed she was, just the way his private black-haired girl had been dressed in those dreams of his. The cover of *Vogue*, which he had seen in Stantwich paper shops but which Pam couldn't afford to buy—coffee-coloured suede suit, long silk scarf, stitched leather gloves, and nut-brown boots as shiny as glass.

"May I walk back with you?" he said.

"Well, of course."

It was quite a long way. She talked about the difficulty of getting accommodations and told anecdotes of the experiences of friends of hers, how they had found flats by this means or that, their brushes with landlords and rent tribunals. She herself owned a floor of the house in which she lived. He gathered that her father was well-off and had bought it for her. Her easy manner put him at his ease, and he thought how wonderful it was to talk again, to have found, however briefly, a companion. Must their companionship be brief?

Outside the Pembroke Market she left him.

"If you're passing," she said, "come in and let me know how you've got on." Her smile was bold and inviting, yet not brazen. He wouldn't have cared if it had been. He thought, he was sure, she was waiting for him to ask if he could see her before that, if he could see her that evening. But paralysis overcame him. He could be wrong. How was he to know? How did one ever tell? She might simply be being helpful and friendly, and from any overture he made, turn on her heel in disgust.

So he just said, "Of course I will, you've been very kind," and watched her walk away, fancying he had seen disappointment in her face.

There were no ads for accommodations in the newsagent's window, only cards put there by people who wanted rooms or had prams and pianos and kittens for sale, and an unbelievable one from a girl offering massage and "very strict" French lessons. As he was turning away, the back of the case in which the cards were was suddenly opened inwards and a hand appeared. When he looked back, he saw that a new card had been affixed. Doubtfully—because what sort of an inhabitable room could you get for ten pounds a week?—he read it: 22 Montcalm Gardens, W.11. He looked up Montcalm Gardens in his London guide, and found that it turned off Ladbroke Grove at what he was already learning to think of as the "nice" end. A boy of about twenty was looking over his shoulder. Alan thought he too must be looking for a room, and if that was so he knew who was going to get there first. The room might be all right, it was bound to be better than the Maharajah. His legs were weary, so he did another first-time thing and, copying gestures he had seen successfully performed by others, he hailed and acquired a taxi.

The name on the card had been Engstrand and it had immediately brought to Alan's mind old man Jacob and Regina in Ibsen's *Ghosts*. One branch of the Forsyte family had lived in Ladbroke Grove. Such literary associations were pleasant to think of. He himself was like a character in a book on the threshold of adventure and perhaps of love.

In Montcalm Gardens two long terraces of tall early Victorian houses eyed each other austerely across a straight

wide roadway. The street was treeless, though thready
branches of planes could be seen at the far end of it. It had
an air of dowdy, but not at all shabby, grandeur. There were
little balconies on the houses with railings whose supports
were like the legs of Chippendale chairs, and each house
had, at the top of a flight of steps, a porch composed of
pilasters and a narrow flat roof. The first thing he noticed
about number twenty-two was how clean and sparkling its
windows were, and that inside the one nearest the porch
stood surely a hundred narcissi in a big copper bowl.

The door was opened to him by a woman he supposed
must be Mrs. Engstrand. She looked inquiringly at him, her
head a little on one side.

"I saw your advertisement . . ." he began.

"Already? I only put it in half an hour ago. I've just got
back."

"They were putting it in when I saw it."

"Well, you mustn't stand there. Do come in." Her voice
was both vague and intense, an educated voice which he
wouldn't have expected from the look of her. She wore no
make-up on her pale small face that seemed to peep out
from, to be engulfed by, a mass of thick brown curly hair.
Had she really been out, dressed like that, in denims with
frayed hems and a sweater with a hole at one elbow? She
looked about thirty, maybe more.

He went in, and she closed the door behind him. "I'm
afraid the room's in the basement," she said. "I'm telling you
that now in case you've got any sort of *thing* against base-
ments."

"I don't think so," said Alan. From what he could see of
the hall, and, through an open door, of the interior of a
room, the house was very beautifully, indeed luxuriously,
furnished. There were those things in evidence that make
for an archetype of domestic beauty: old carefully polished

furniture, precious ornaments, pictures in thin silver frames, a Chinese lacquer screen, chairs covered in wild silk, long and oval mirrors, more spring flowers in shallow bowls. And there was exquisite cleanliness. What would he be offered here for ten pounds a week? A cupboard under the stairs?

Downstairs in the basement was a kind of hall, with white walls and carpeted in red haircord. He waited to be shown the cupboard. She opened a door and he saw instead something like that which he had expected to see at the first house he had visited, before he was disillusioned.

She said, "It's big, at any rate, and it really isn't very dark. The kitchen's through there. Tenants have the use of the garden. I'm afraid anyone who took this room would have to share the bathroom with Mr. Locksley, but he's very very nice. He's got the front room."

This one was large, with french windows. One wall was hung all over with shelves, and the shelves were full of books. The furniture wasn't of the standard of upstairs, but it was good Victorian furniture, and on the floor was the same haircord as in the passage. It looked new, as if no one had ever walked on it. He looked out of the window at a lawn and daffodils and two little birch trees and a peaked black-brick wall, overgrown with ivy.

"That's the chapel of a convent. There are lots of convents round here. It's Cardinal Manning country. The Oblates of St. Charles, you know."

He said, "Like in that essay by Lytton Strachey."

"Oh, have you read *that*?" He turned round and saw that her intense birdlike little face was glowing. "Isn't it lovely?" she said. "I read it once every year. *Eminent Victorians* is up there on the top shelf. Oh, do you mind the books? They're nearly all novels, you see, and there isn't anywhere else for them because my father-in-law can't bear novels."

He was bewildered. "Why not?"

"He says that fiction causes most of our troubles because

it teaches us to fantasise and lead vicarious lives instead of coming to terms with reality. He's Ambrose Engstrand, you know."

Alan didn't know. He had never heard of Ambrose Engstrand. Did she mean he could have the room? "I can give you a bank reference," he said. "Will that do?"

"I *hate* having to ask for one at all," she said earnestly. "It seems so awfully rude. But Ambrose said I must. As far as I'm concerned, anyone who likes *Eminent Victorians* is all right. But it's Ambrose's house and I do have to do what he says."

"My name is Browning," Alan said. "Paul Browning. Fifteen, Queens Vale, Highgate—that's my present address. My bank's the Anglian-Victoria, Paddington Station Branch." He hesitated. "D'you think I could move in this week?"

"Move in today if you like." She pushed back her thick massy hair with both hands, smiled at his amazement. "I didn't mean I was really going to write to that bank. I shall just let Ambrose think I have. Caesar—that's Mr. Locksley—hasn't even got a bank. Banks don't mean anything. I've proved that because he always pays his rent on the dot, and I knew he'd be lovely because he knows all Shakespeare's sonnets by heart. Can you believe it?"

His head swimming, Alan said he was very grateful and thank you very much, and he'd move in that evening. He went back to Paddington Station and fetched the suitcase and went into a cafe to have a cup of tea. He was Paul Browning, late of Northwest Two (wherever that might be), now of Montcalm Gardens, Notting Hill. It was by this name that he would introduce himself to the black-haired girl tomorrow when he went to the Pembroke Market to tell her what had happened. Tomorrow, though, not today. Quite enough had happened today. He needed peace and quiet to collect his thoughts and make himself a design for living.

Joyce Culver's father offered his house, or the price that house would fetch when sold, for the safe return of his daughter. It was all he had.

Marty and Nigel saw it in the paper.

"What's the good of a house or the bread it'll fetch," said Nigel, "if you're inside?"

"We could make him promise not to tell the fuzz. And then he could sell the place and give us the money."

"Yeah? And just why would he do that thing once he'd got her back? Be your age."

They were talking in low voices on the landing. Joyce was in the lavatory, dropping another note out of the window, this time wrapped round the metal lid of a glass jar. Even in a normal dwelling house, and Marty's place was far from that, it is difficult to find an object which is at the same time heavy enough to drop, unbreakable, and small enough to conceal on one's person. She couldn't see where it fell. She didn't know that under the window was an area containing five dustbins, and that Brent Council refuse collectors had already thrown the pumice stone and the paper round it into the crushing machine at the back of their truck. One of the dustbin lids had blown off, and Joyce's second note dropped into the bin on top of a parcel of potato peelings deposited there by Bridey on the previous night.

"When am I going to get out of here?" said Joyce, emerging.

"Keep your voice down." Nigel was aghast, in spite of the absence of Bridey and the deafness of Mr. Green.

"When am I going to get out of here!" yelled Joyce at the top of her voice.

Marty clapped his hand over her mouth and manhandled her back into the room. She felt the gun thrust against her ribs, but she was beginning to have her doubts about the gun, she was beginning to get ideas about that.

"If you do that again," said Marty, "you can pee in a pot in the kitchen."

"Charming," said Joyce. "I suppose that's what you're used to, I suppose that's what goes on in whatever home you come from. Or pig sty, as I should call it. Got an Elsan in a hut at the end of your garden, have you? I shouldn't be at all surprised."

She held up her head and glared at him. Marty was beginning to hate her, for the shot had gone home. She had precisely described the sanitary arrangements in his father's cottage. It was Thursday, and they had been shut up in here since Monday night. Why shouldn't they just get out and leave her here? They could tie her up to the gas stove or something so she couldn't move. And then when they'd got safe away they could phone the police, make one of those anonymous calls, and tell them where she was. He thought that would work. It was Nigel, whispering out there on the landing or when Joyce was washing—she was always washing—who said it wasn't on. Where could they go, he said, where the call couldn't be traced from? Once give them this address, anyway, and they'd know who Marty was and very soon who Nigel was. They might just as well go and give themselves up now. Nigel had said he had a plan, though he didn't say what it was, and Marty thought the plan must be all hot air and Nigel didn't know what to do any more than he did.

His only consolation was that he could have an unlimited amount to drink. Yesterday he had drunk more than half a bottle of whisky and today he was going to finish it and start on the next one. He couldn't understand why Nigel had begun being nice to Joyce, buttering her up and flattering her. What was the point when it was obvious the only way was to put the fear of God into her? Nigel had got him to buy her *Woman* and *Nineteen* and made him take the sheets and pillowcases to the launderette on the corner. Nigel, who liked dirt and used to say being clean was bourgeois! He poured himself a cupful of whisky.

"You can get me some wool and some needles next time you go out," said Joyce. "I need a bit of knitting to pass the time."

"I'm not your slave."

"Do as she says," said Nigel. "Why not if it keeps her happy?"

The room was spotlessly clean. Joyce had even washed the curtains, and Nigel, with the aid of sign language and a pencil and paper, had borrowed an iron from Mr. Green so that she could iron them and iron her own freshly washed blouse. Marty thought he must be off his head, that wasn't the way to break her spirit. He glowered at her resentfully. She looked as if she were just about to set off for work in a job where one's appearance counted for a lot.

Two hours earlier she had washed her hair. She had on a crisp neat blouse and a creaseless skirt, and now she was filing her nails. That was another thing Nigel had got him to fetch in, a nail file, and he'd said something about mascara. But Marty had jibbed at that. He wasn't buying bloody silly mascara, no way.

Nigel didn't say much all that day. He was thinking. Marty made him sick with his silly ideas and the way, most

of the time, he was smashed out of his mind on whisky. He
ought to be able to see they couldn't get shot of Joyce.
Where they went she must go. Only he knew they couldn't
take her out into the street with them, couldn't steal another
car while she was with them. Yet she must be with them,
and the only way she could was if she could somehow be
made to be on their side. It was with some vague yet
definite aim of getting her on his side that Nigel had started
being nice to her. That was why he made Marty buy things
for her and praised her appearance and the cleanliness of
the place—though he hated it—and why, that evening he got
Marty to fetch in three great hunks of T-bone because Joyce
said she liked steak.

There had been robberies, he thought, in which hostages
had been so brainwashed by their captors that they had
gone over to the kidnappers' side and had even assisted in
subsequent raids. Nigel didn't want to do any Symbionese
Liberation Army stuff, he had no doctrines with which to in-
doctrinate anyone, but there must be other ways. By Friday
morning he had thought of another way.

He lay on the mattress in the yellow light that was the
same at dawn as at midnight, shifting his body away from
Marty, who snored and smelt of sweat and whisky, and
looking at the plump pale curve of Joyce's cheek and her
smooth pink eyelids closed in sleep. He got up and went
into the kitchen and looked at himself in Marty's bit of broken mirror over the sink. Beautiful blue eyes looked back at
him, a straight nose, a mobile delicately cut mouth. Any
polone'd go for me in a big way, thought Nigel, and then he
remembered he mustn't use that word and why he mustn't,
and he was flooded with fear.

Marty went out and brought back brown knitting wool
and two pairs of needles and some proper toilet soap and
toothpaste—and two more bottles of whisky. They didn't

bother to count the money or ration it or note what they had spent. Marty just grabbed a handful of notes from the carrier each time he left. He bought expensive food and things for Joyce and, in Nigel's opinion, quantities of rubbish for himself, pornography from the Adult Book Exchange and proper glasses to put his whisky in and, now he could afford to smoke again, cartons of strong king-size cigarettes. And he stayed out longer and longer each day. Skiving off his duties, leaving him to guard Joyce, thought Nigel. It maddened him to see Marty sitting there, making them all cough with the smoke from his cigarettes, and gloating over those filthy magazines. He found he was embarrassed for Joyce when Marty looked at those pictures in front of her, but he didn't know why he should be, why he should care.

Joyce scarcely noticed and didn't care at all. She had the attitude of most women to pornography, that it was disgusting and boring and its lure beyond her comprehension. She was having interesting ideas about the gun. One of them was that it wasn't loaded, and the other that it wasn't a real gun. She had written on all her notes—there was a third one tucked inside her bra—that they had killed Alan Groombridge, but now she wondered if this were true. She only had their word for it, and you couldn't believe a word they said. It might be a toy gun. She had read that robbers used toy guns because of the difficulty of getting real ones. It would be just like them to play about with a toy gun. If she could get her hands on that gun and find out that it was only a toy or not loaded, she would be free. She might not be able to unlock the door because the key was on a string round Nigel's neck, but she would be able to run when they took her to the lavatory, or break one of the windows at night and scream.

But how was she ever going to get hold of the gun? They kept it under their pillows at night, and though Marty was a heavy sleeper, Nigel wasn't. Or Robert, as she thought of him, and the dark one, as she thought of Marty. Sometimes she had awakened in the night and looked at them, and Robert had stirred and looked back at her. That was unnerving. Maybe one night, if the police didn't come and no one found her notes, Robert would get drunk too and she would have her chance. She had stopped thinking much about Mum and Dad and Stephen, for when she did so she couldn't keep from crying. And she wasn't going to cry, not even at night, not in front of them. She thought instead about the gun and ways of getting hold of it, for she had as little faith in any plan Robert might concoct as the dark one had. They would keep her there forever unless she escaped.

They ate smoked trout and Greek takeaway and cream trifle from Marks and Spencers on Friday night, and Marty drank half a bottle of Teacher's. Everything was bought ready-cooked because Marty and Nigel couldn't cook and Joyce wouldn't cook for them. Joyce sat on the sofa with her feet up to stop either of them sitting there too. She had already completed about six inches of the front of her jumper, and she knitted away resolutely.

"The fact is," she said, "you don't know what to do with me, do you? You got yourselves in a right mess when you brought me here and now you don't know how to get out of it. My God, I could rob a bank single-handed better than the two of you did. No more than a pair of babes in arms you are."

Nigel kept his temper and even smiled. He could look pleasantly little-boyish when he smiled. "Maybe you've got something there, my love. We made a mistake about that. We all make mistakes."

"I don't," said Joyce arrogantly. "If you do what's right and keep to the law and face up to your responsibilities and get steady jobs you don't make mistakes."

"Shut up!" screamed Marty. "Shut your trap, you bitch! Who d'you think you are, giving us that load of shit? You want to remember you're our prisoner."

Joyce smiled at him slowly. She made one of the few profound statements she was ever to utter.

"Oh, no," she said. "I'm not your prisoner. You're mine."

The man called Locksley came home while Alan was putting his clothes away and stowing the money in one of the drawers of a Victorian mahogany tallboy. The door of the next room closed quietly, and for about an hour there penetrated through the wall soft music of the kind Alan thought was called baroque. He liked it and was rather sorry when it stopped and Locksley went out again.

The house was quiet now, the only sound the distant one of traffic in Ladbroke Grove. This surprised him. Since his landlady had a father-in-law, she must also surely have a husband and very likely, at her age, small children. But Alan felt that he was now alone in the house, though this couldn't be so as, through the french window, he could see light from upstairs shining on the lawn. The two radiators in his room had come on at six, and it was pleasantly warm, but there didn't seem to be any hot water or anything to provide it. After looking in vain for some switch or meter, he went upstairs to find Mrs. Engstrand.

He knocked on the door of the room from which the light was coming. She opened it herself and there was no one with her. She was still wearing the jeans and the sweater, not the long evening skirt he had somehow expected.

"I'm terribly sorry. There's an immersion heater in that cupboard outside your door and you share it with Caesar. I expect he's switched it off. I must tell him to leave it on *all*

the time now you've come. I'll come down with you and
show you."

He only caught a glimpse of the interior of the room, but
that was enough. A dark carpet, straw-coloured satin curtains, silk-papered walls, Chinese porcelain, framed photographs of a handsome elderly man and an even handsomer
young one.

"Caesar's very considerate." She showed him the heater
and the switch. "He's always trying to save me money but it
really isn't necessary. I pay the bills for this part of the
house, you see, so Ambrose won't ever see them."

He didn't understand what she meant and he was too shy
to enquire. Shyness stopped him asking her in for a drink,
though he had drinks, having stocked up with brandy and
vodka and gin on his way there. The bottles looked good on
top of the tallboy. Maybe when the husband turned up,
young Engstrand, he'd invite the two of them and this
Caesar and the black-haired girl. It would give him an excuse for asking her.

That night and again in the morning he listened to his
radio. There was nothing about Joyce or himself, for no
news is not good news as far as the media are concerned. He
bought a paper in which the front page headlines were *Pay
Claim Fiasco* and *Wife-swapping Led to Murder*. Down in
the bottom left-hand corner was a paragraph about Joyce's
father offering his house for the return of his daughter. Alan
wondered what the police and the bank would do if Joyce
turned up safe and told them she had been alone in the
bank when the two men came, that there had been only two
men, and only four thousand in the safe and the tills. It was
very likely that she would tell them that. He asked himself
if, by wondering this, he meant that he didn't want her to
turn up safe. The idea was uncomfortable and disturbing, so
he put it out of his head and walked to the back of this

rather superior newsagent-cum-stationers to where there were racks of paperbacks. There was no need to buy any books as his room was like a little library, but he had long ago got into the habit of always looking at the wares in bookshops, and why break such a good habit as that?

It wasn't really coincidence that among the books on the shelf labelled Philosophy and Popular Science he came upon the name of Ambrose Engstrand. Probably the man's works were in most bookshops but he had never had occasion to notice them before.

He took down *The Glory of the Real* and read on the back of its jacket that its author was a philosopher and psychologist. He had degrees that filled up a whole line of type, had held a chair of philosophy at some northern university, and made his home, when he was not travelling, in West London. His other works included *Neo-Empiricism* and *Dream, the Opiate*.

Alan read the first page of the introduction. "In modern times, though not throughout history, the dream has been all. Think of the contexts in which we use this word. 'The girl of my dreams,' 'It was like a dream,' 'In my wildest dreams.' The real has been discarded by mankind as ugly and untenable, to be shunned and scorned in favour of a shadow land of fantasy." A few pages further on he found: "How has this come about? The cause is not hard to find. Society was not always sick, not always chasing mirages and creating chimeras. Before the advent of the novel, in roughly 1740, when vicarious living was first presented to man as a way of life, and fiction took the lid from the Pandora's Box of fantasy, man had come to terms with reality, lived it and loved it." Alan put the book back. One pound, thirty, seemed a lot to pay for it, especially as—he smiled to himself—there were a lot of novels in Montcalm Gardens he hadn't yet read.

But it was certain that he had sold his soul and run away in order to find what this Engstrand called the real, so he had better begin by going to the Pembroke Market. The black-haired girl wasn't there, she was taking the day off, and Alan didn't dare ask the man who spoke to him for the number of her house. But he learned that her name was Rose. Tomorrow he would come back and see Rose and find the courage to ask her out with him on Saturday night. Saturday night was for going out, he thought, not yet understanding that for him now every night was a Saturday.

The rest of the day he spent at the Hayward Gallery, going on a river trip to Greenwich, and at a cinema in the West End where he saw a Fassbinder film which, though intellectual and obscure, would have made Wilfred Summitt's scanty hair stand on end. There was nothing in the evening paper about Joyce, only *New Moves in Pay Claim* and *Sabena Jet Hi-jacked*. He had been in his room ten minutes when there came a knock at his door.

A man of about thirty with red hair and the kind of waxen complexion that sometimes goes with this colouring stood outside.

"Locksley. I thought I'd come and say hallo."

Alan nearly said his name was Groombridge. He remembered just in time. "Paul Browning. Come in."

The man came in and looked round. "Bit of luck for both of us," he said, "finding this place. By the way, they call me Caesar. Or I should say I call me Caesar. What they called me was Cecil. I had the name part in Julius Caesar at school and I sort of adopted it."

"Do you really know all Shakespeare's sonnets by heart?"

"Una tell you that, did she?" Caesar grinned. "I'm not clever, I've just got a good memory. She's a lovely lady, Una, but she's crazy. She told me she let you have this place because you'd read some essay about Cardinal Manning. Feel like coming up the Elgin or K.P.H. or somewhere for a slow one?"

"A slow one?" said Alan.

"Well, it won't be a quick one, will it? No point in euphemisms. We have to face the real, as Ambrose would say. D'you mind if we take Una?"

Alan said he didn't mind, but what about her husband coming home? Caesar gave him a sidelong look and said there was no fear of that, thank God. However, he came back to say she couldn't come because she had to wait in for a phone call from Djakarta, so they went to the Kensington Park Hotel on their own.

"Did you mean there isn't a husband?" said Alan when Caesar had bought them two pints of bitter. It was a strange experience for him who had never been "out with the boys" in his life or even into pubs much except with Pam on holiday. "Is she a widow?"

Caesar shook his head. "The beautiful Stewart's alive and kicking somewhere out in the West Indies with his new lady. I got it all from Annie, that's my girl friend. She used to know this Stewart when he was the heart throb of Hampstead. Una's about the loneliest person I know. She's a waif. But what's to be done? I'd do something about it myself, only I've got Annie."

"There must be unattached men about," said Alan.

"Not so many. Una's thirty-two. She's O.K. to look at but she's not amazing, is she? Most guys the right age are married or involved. She doesn't go out much, she never meets anyone. You wouldn't care to take an interest, I suppose?"

Alan blushed and hoped it didn't show in the pub's murky light. He thought of Rose, her inviting smile, her elegance, the girl of his dreams soon to come true. To turn Una down, he chose what he thought was the correct expression. "I don't find her attractive."

"Pity. The fact is, she ought to get away from Ambrose. Of course he's saved her. He's probably saved her sanity and her life, but all that dynamic personality—it's like Trilby and Svengali."

"Why does she live in his house?"

"She was married to this Stewart, who's quite something in the looks line. I've seen photos. I tell you, if I wasn't hetero up to my eyebrows, he'd turn *me* on. He and Una had a flat in Hampstead but he was always going off with other ladies. Couldn't resist them, Annie says, and they never left him alone. Una got so she couldn't stand it anymore and they split up. They had this kid, Lucy her name was. She was two. Stewart used to have her at the weekends."

"Was?" Alan interrupted. "You mean she's dead?"

"Stewart took her to his current lady's flat for the weekend. Slum, I should say. He and the lady went out for a slow one and while they were out Lucy overturned an oil heater and her nightdress caught fire."

"That's horrible."

"Yes. Una was ill for months. The beautiful Stewart took himself off after the coroner had laid into him at the inquest. He shut himself up in a cottage his mother had left him on Dartmoor. And that's where Ambrose came in. He fetched Una back here and looked after her. He was writing his *magnum opus* at the time, *Neo-Empiricism*. That's what he calls himself, a Neo-Empiricist. But he dropped that for months and gave himself over to helping her. That was three years ago. And ever since then she's lived here and kept house for him, and before he went off to Java in January he had the basement converted and redecorated and said she was to let it and have the rents for her income. He said it would teach her to assume responsibility and re-face reality."

"What happened to Stewart Engstrand?"

"He turned up after a bit, wanted Una to go back to him. But she wouldn't, and Ambrose said he'd only be retreating into a mother dream, whereas what he needed was to work experientially through the reality of his exceptional looks and his sexuality. So he worked through them by taking up with a new lady who's rich and who carried him off to her house in Trinidad. Another beer? Or would you rather have something shorter and stronger?"

"My turn," said Alan awkwardly, not knowing if this was etiquette when Caesar had invited him out. But it seemed to be, Caesar didn't demur, and Alan knew that he was learning and making friends and working experientially through the reality of what he had chosen back there in Childon with the money in his hands.

Rose was there in the Pembroke Market on Friday. She had wound her long hair about her head in coils and put on a long black dress with silver ornaments. She looked remote and mysterious and seductive. He had his speech prepared, he had been rehearsing it all the way from Montcalm Gardens.

"I said I'd come in and tell you how I got on. I found a place from looking in that window, and it's ideal. But for you I'd never have thought of looking. I'm so grateful. If you're free tomorrow night, if you're not busy or anything, I wondered if I could—well, if we could go out somewhere. You've been so kind."

She said with raised eyebrows, "You want to take me out because I was kind?"

"I didn't just mean that." She had embarrassed him, and embarrassment made his voice tremble. But he was inspired to say, afraid of his own boldness, "No one would think of you like that, no one who had seen you."

She smiled. "Ah," she said, "that's better." Her eyes de-

voured him. He turned his own away, but he seemed beyond blushing.

In as casual a manner as he could muster, he said, "Dinner perhaps and a theatre? Could I fix something and—and
phone you?"

"I'll be in the shop all day tomorrow," she said. "Do
phone anytime." It was strange and fascinating the way
those simple words seemed to imply and promise so much.
It was her voice, he supposed, and her cool poise and the
swanlike way she had of moving her head. She gave a light
throaty giggle. "Haven't you forgotten something?"

"Have I?" He was afraid all the time of committing solecisms. What had he done now?

"Your name," she said.

He told her it was Paul Browning. Some hours had passed
before he began to get cold feet, and by then he had booked
a table in a restaurant whose phone number he had got from
an advertisement in the evening paper. He stood outside a
theatre, screwing up his courage to go in and buy two stalls
for himself and Rose.

13

Like Alan Groombridge, Nigel lived in a world of dreams. The only thing he liked about Marty's magazines were the advertisements which showed young men of his own age and no better-looking posing with dark glasses on in front of Lotus sports cars, or lounging in penthouses with balloon glasses of brandy in their hands. He saw himself in such a place with Joyce as his slave, waiting on him. He would make her kneel in front of him when she brought him his food, and if it wasn't to his liking he would kick her. She would know of every crime he committed—by that time he would be the European emperor of crime—but she would keep his secrets fanatically, for she worshipped him and received his blows and his insults with a doglike devotion. They would live in Monaco, he thought, or perhaps in Rome, and there would be other women in his life, models and film stars to whom he gave the best part of his attention while Joyce stayed at home or was sent, with a flick of his fingers, to her own room. But occasionally, when he could spare the time, he would talk to her of his beginnings, remind her of how she had once defied him in a squalid little room in North London, until, with brilliant foresight, he had stooped to her and bound her to him and made her his forever. And she would kneel at his feet, thanking him for his condescension, begging for a rare touch, a precious kiss. He would laugh at that, kicking her away. Had she forgotten that once she had talked of betraying him?

Reality was shot through with doubt. His sexual experience had been very limited. At his public school he had had encounters with other boys which had been nasty, brutish, and short, though a slight improvement on masturbation. When he left he found he was very attractive to girls, but he wasn't successful with them. The better-looking they were the more they frightened him. Confronted by youth and beauty, he was paralysed. His father sent him to a psychiatrist—not, of course, because of his failure with the girls, which Dr. Thaxby knew nothing about. He sent him to find out why his son couldn't get a degree or a job like other people. The psychiatrist was unable to discover why not, and this wasn't surprising as he mostly asked Nigel questions about his feelings towards his mother. Nigel said he hated his mother, which wasn't true but he knew it was the kind of thing psychiatrists like to hear. The psychiatrist never told Nigel any of his findings or diagnosed anything, and Nigel stopped going to him after about five sessions. He had himself come to the conclusion that all he needed to make him a success and everything come right was an older and perhaps rather unattractive woman to show him the way. He found older women easier to be with than girls. They frightened him less because he could despise them and feel they must be grateful to him.

Joyce, however, wasn't an older woman. He thought she was probably younger than he. But there was no question of her looks scaring him into impotence. With her big round eyes and thick lips and nose like a small pudgy cake, she was ugly and coarse. And he despised her already. Though he affected to be contemptuous of gracious living and cut-glass and silver and well-laid tables and professional people and dinner in the evening and university degrees, his up-- bringing had left on him an ineradicable mark. He was a snob at heart. Joyce was distasteful to him because she came from the working class. But he wasn't afraid of her, and as he thought of what he would gain, freedom and escape and her silence, he became less afraid of himself.

On Saturday morning he brought in coffee, a cup for her and one for himself. Marty had stopped drinking anything but whisky and wine.

"What's that you're knitting, Joyce?"

"A jumper."

"Is there a picture of it?"

She turned the page of the magazine and showed him a coloured photograph of a beautiful but flat-chested and skeletal girl in a voluminous sweater. She didn't say anything but flicked the page over after allowing him a five-second glimpse.

"You'll look great in that," said Nigel. "You've got a super figure."

"Mmm," said Joyce. She wasn't flattered. Every boy she had ever been out with had told her that, and anyway she had known it herself since she was twelve. We long to be praised for the beauties we don't have, and Joyce had started to love Stephen when he said she had wonderful eyes.

"I want you to go out tonight," said Nigel to Marty while Joyce was in the lavatory.

"You what?"

"Leave me alone with her."

"That's brilliant, that is," said Marty. "I hang about out in the cold while you make it with the girl. No way. No way at all."

"Think about it if you know how to do that thing. Just think if that isn't the only way to get us out of here. And you don't have to hang about in the cold. You can go see a movie."

Marty did think about it, and he saw it made sense. But

he saw it grudgingly, for if anyone was going to make it with Joyce it ought to be himself. For the *machismo*, if he had known the word, rather from inclination, but still it ought to be he. Not that he had any ideas of securing Joyce's silence by such methods. He was a realist whose ideas of a sex life were a bit of fun with easy pickups until he was about thirty when he would settle down with some steady and get married and live in a semidetached. Still, if Nigel thought he could get them out that way, let Nigel get on with it. So at six he fetched them all some doner kebab and stuffed vine leaves, drank half a tumbler of neat whisky, and set off to see a film called *Sex Pots on the Boil* at a nasty little cinema down in Camden Town.

"Where's he gone?" said Joyce.

"To see his mother."

"You mean he's got a mother? Where does she live? Monkey house at the zoo?"

"Look, Joyce, I know he's not the sort of guy you've been used to. I realise that. He's not my sort either, only frankly, it's taken me a bit of living with him to see that."

"Well, you don't have to talk about him behind his back. I believe in loyalty, I do. And if you ask me, there's not much to choose between the pair of you."

They were in the kitchen. Joyce was washing up her own supper plates. Nigel and Marty hadn't used plates, but they had each used a fork and Marty one of his new glasses. Joyce considered leaving the forks and the glass dirty, but it spoiled the look of the place, so she washed them too. For the first time in his life Nigel took a tea cloth in his hands and started to dry dishes. He put the gun down on the top of the oven.

His lie about Marty's mother had given him an idea. Not that mothers, feared, despised, adored, longed for, were ever far from his thoughts, whatever he might pretend. The rea-

son he had given for Marty's going out had come naturally
and inevitably to him. An hour or so before, Marty had
brought in the evening paper and Nigel had glanced
through it while in the lavatory. *Sabena Hostage Tells of
Torture* and *New Moves in Pay Claim,* and on an inside
page a few lines about Mrs. Culver recovering in hospital
after taking an overdose of sleeping pills. Nigel dried the
glass clumsily, and with an eye to the main chance, told her
what had happened to her mother.

Joyce sat down at the table.

"You're maniacs," she said. "You don't care what you do.
It'll just about kill my dad if anything happens to her."

Using the voice he knew she liked to hear, Nigel said,
"I'm sorry, Joyce. We couldn't foresee it was going to turn
out this way. Your mother's not dead, she's going to get
better."

"No thanks to you if she does!"

He came up close to her. The heat from the open oven
was making him sweat. Joyce was on the point of crying,
squeezing up her eyes to keep the tears back. "Look," he
said, "if you want to get a message to her, like a letter, I'll
see she gets it. I can't say fairer than that, can I? You just
write that you're O.K. and we haven't harmed you and I'll
see it gets posted."

Unconsciously, Joyce quoted a favourite riposte of her
mother's. "The band played 'Believe It if You Like.'"

"I promise. I like you a lot, Joyce. I really do. I think
you're fantastic-looking."

Joyce swallowed. She cleared her throat, pressing her
hands against her chest. "Give me a bit of paper."

Nigel picked up the gun and went off to find a piece.
Apart from toilet paper out in the lavatory, there wasn't any,
so he had to tear one of the end papers off Marty's much-
thumbed copy of *Venus in Furs.* The gun went back on top

of the oven, and Nigel stood behind Joyce, putting on a tender expression in case she looked round.

She wrote, "Dear Mum, you will recognise my writing and know I am O.K. Don't worry. I will soon be home with you. Give my love to Dad." She set her teeth, grinding them together. Later she would cry, when they were asleep. "Your loving daughter, Joyce."

Nigel put his hand on her shoulder. She was going to shout at him, "Get off me!" but the gun was so near, within reach if she put out her left arm. There might be no later for crying, but a time for joy and reunion, if she could only keep her head now. She bowed forward across the table. Nigel came round her. He bent over her, put his other hand on her other shoulder so that he was almost embracing her, and said, "Joyce, love."

Slowly she lifted her face so that it wasn't far from his. She looked at his cold eyes and his mouth that was soft and parted and going slack. It wouldn't be too disgusting to kiss him, he was good-looking enough. If she had to kiss him, she would. No good making a big thing of it. As for going any further . . . Nigel brought his mouth to hers, and she reached out fast for the gun.

He shouted, "Christ, you bitch!" and punched the gun out of her hand and it went skidding across the floor. Then he fell on his knees, scrabbling for it. Retreating from him, Joyce backed against the wall, holding her arms crossed over her body. Nigel pointed the gun at her and flicked his head to indicate she was to go into the living room. She went in. She sat down heavily on the mattress, her letter in her hand.

Presently she said in a hoarse throaty voice, "May as well tear this up."

"You shouldn't have done that."

"Wouldn't you have, in my place?"

Nigel didn't answer her. He was thinking fast. It needn't spoil his plan. She had been willing enough to kiss him, she had been dying for it, he could tell that by the soppy look on her face when he'd held her shoulders. It was only natural that getting hold of the gun came first with her, self-preservation came before sex. But there could be a situation where self-preservation didn't come into it, where the last thing either of them would think of was the gun. Attempting that kiss had brought him a surge of real desire. Having her at his mercy and submitting to him and grateful to him had made him desire her.

"I won't let it make any difference," he said. "Your letter still goes."

Joyce was surprised, but she wasn't going to thank him. That soft slack look was again replacing savagery in his face.

"The thing is," he said, the polite public-school boy. "I thought you really liked me. You see, I've felt like that about you from the first."

She knew what she had to do now, or not *now* but tomorrow when the dark one next went out. It sickened her to think of it, and how she'd feel when she'd done it she couldn't imagine. Dirty, revolting, like a prostitute. Suppose she had a baby? She had been off the Pill necessarily for a week now. But she'd do it and get the gun and think of consequences later when she was home with her mother and father and Stephen. It had never crossed her mind that in all her life she'd make love with anyone but Stephen. She and Stephen would go on making love every night the way they had been doing until they got to be about forty and were too old for it. But needs must when the devil drives, like her father said. She looked up at the devil with the gun.

"What you wanted to do out there in the kitchen just now," she said, "I don't mind. Only not now. I feel funny, it was a shock."

He said, "Joyce," and started to come towards her.

"No. I said not now. Not when he might come back."

"I'll get rid of him for the whole evening tomorrow."

"Not tomorrow," said Joyce, putting off the evil day.
"Monday."

At the theatre Alan had chosen was a much-praised production of one of Shaw's comedies. He had picked it because there wouldn't be any bedroom scenes or sexy dialogue or four-letter words, which would have embarrassed him in Rose's company. But when he was at the box office he found that they only had upper-circle seats left, and he couldn't take a girl like Rose in the upper circle. All the other theatres round about seemed to be showing the kind of plays he had avoided in choosing *You Never Can Tell*, or Shakespeare, which was too heavy, or musicals, which she might not like.

And then, suddenly, he knew he couldn't face it at all. His cold feet were turning to ice. He couldn't be alone with her in a restaurant, not knowing what to order or how to order or what wine to choose. He couldn't bring her home in the dark, be alone with her in the back of a taxi, after they had seen a play in which people were naked or talked about, or even acted, sex. In the midst of his doubts, a happy thought came to him. When he had gone upstairs to ask Una Engstrand about the water heater, he had considered inviting her and Caesar Locksley in for drinks on Saturday night. Why not do that? Why not ask her and Caesar and this Annie of his for drinks in his room and ask Rose too? It was a much better idea. Rose would see the home her kindness had secured for him, he wouldn't have to be alone with her until he took her home—perhaps she had a car—and he

would have the pleasure of creating an evening so different
from those encounters with the Kitsons and the Heyshams,
what a party should be with real conversation between people who liked each other and wanted to be together. And it
would break the ice between him and Rose, it would make
their next meeting easier for him.

Would drinks be enough or ought he to get food? He
couldn't cook. He thought of lettuce and sardines and madeira cake, of liver and bacon and sausages. It was hopeless.
Drinks alone it would have to be, with some peanuts. Next
to the wineshop where he bought Bristol Cream and some
vermouth was a newsagent's. The evening paper told him—it
preceded Nigel's by twenty-four hours—that the Sabena jet
had come down in Cairo, the pay-claim negotiations had
reached deadlock, and Joyce Culver's mother had been
rushed to hospital in a coma. A cloud seemed to pass across
him, dulling his happiness and the pale wintry sun. If Mrs.
Culver died, could anyone say it was his fault? No. If he had
given the alarm and the police had chased Joyce's kidnappers, who could tell what would have happened to her?
They would have crashed the car or shot her. Everything
went to prove that it was better to take no violent action
with people like that. You had only to read what was being
done in this aircraft hi-jack business. No threats or armed
onslaughts like in that Entebbe affair where a woman had
died, but submission to the hi-jackers to be followed by
peaceful negotiation.

He met Una in the hall. He and Caesar had to use the
front door because, long ago, Ambrose had had the basement door blocked up for fear of burglars. Even he, apparently, had some reservations when it came to reality.
Una, an indefatigable housewife, was polishing a brass
lamp. She had blackened her fingers with metal polish.

"I'd love to come," she said when he told her of his party.

"How sweet of you to ask me. Caesar's gone to Annie's for the weekend. He mostly does. But I'm sure he'll bring her."

"Does she live in London then?" He had only once been away for the weekend, and that had been to a cousin of Pam's in Skegness, a visit involving days of feverish preparation.

"Harrow or somewhere like that," said Una. "Not very far. I'll ask him when he phones tonight, shall I?" She added in her strange vague complex way, "He's going to phone to find out if he's had a call from someone who knows his number and he wants to talk to but he doesn't know theirs. I'll ask him but I know he'd *love* to."

She was one of those people whose faces are transformed when they smile. She smiled now, and he thought with a little twinge of real pain for her that she was full of gaiety really, of life and fun and zest, only those qualities had been suppressed and nullified by the loathsome Stewart and the death of her child and perhaps too by the Neo-Empiricist.

"As a matter of fact," she said, "it will be very nice to drink some alcohol again. Ambrose doesn't believe in it, you know, because it distorts the consciousness. Oh dear, I don't suppose there's a wineglass in the house."

"I'll buy some glasses," said Alan. He went down to his room and put on his radio. There was nothing on the news about Mrs. Culver. Some Sabena spokesman and some government minister had said they would do nothing to endanger the lives of the hi-jacked hostages.

That night he dreamed about Joyce. Caesar Locksley asked him if he found her attractive, and the implications of that question frightened him, so he hid from her in a cupboard where there was an immersion heater and lots of bottles of sherry and piles of books by Ambrose Engstrand. It was warm in there and safe, and even when he heard Joyce screaming he didn't come out. Then he saw that the cup-

board was really, or had grown into, a large room with many
flights of stairs leading up and down and to the left and the
right. He climbed one of these staircases and at the top
found himself in a great chamber as in a mediaeval castle,
and there fourteen armed knights awaited him with drawn
swords.

The dream woke him up and kept him awake for a long
time, so that in the morning he overslept. What awakened
him then was a woman's voice calling to someone named
Paul. "Paul, Paul!" It was a few minutes before he remembered that Paul was his own name, and understood that it
must have been Una Engstrand calling him from outside his
room. He thought a tapping had preceded the uttering of
that unfamiliar name, but when he opened the door she was
no longer there.

It was after half-past nine. While he was dressing he
heard from above him the sound of the front door closing.
She had gone out. Would she mind if he used her phone?
Apparently, Caesar used it. He made himself tea and ate a
piece of bread and butter and went upstairs to phone Rose
at the Pembroke Market.

It was she who answered. "Why, hallo!" The last syllable
lingered seductively, a parabola of sound sinking to a sigh.
He told her of his alternative plan.

"I thought you were taking me out to dinner."

He found himself stammering because the voice was no
longer enticing. "I've asked these—these people. You'll like
them. There's the man in the next room to me and my—my
landlady. You'll be able to see what a nice place this is."

Very slowly, almost disbelievingly, she said, "You must be
crazy. Or mean. I'm expected to come round and have
drinks with your landlady? Thank you, but I've better
things to do with my Saturday nights."

The phone cut and the dialling tone began. He looked at
the receiver and, bewildered, was putting it back when the
front door opened and Una Engstrand came in.

"I'm sorry," he said. "I shouldn't have made a call without asking you. I'll pay for it."

"Was it to Australia?"

"No, why should it be? It was a local call."

"Then please don't bother about paying. I said Australia
because you couldn't be phoning America, they'd all be
asleep." He looked at her despairingly, understanding her no
more than he had understood Rose, yet wishing Rose could
have had this warmth, this zany openness. "Caesar didn't
phone till this morning," she said. "I knocked on your door
and called you but you were asleep. He can't come to your
party, he's going to another one with Annie. But I expect
you've got lots of other people coming, haven't you?"

"Only you," he said, "now."

"You won't want me on my own."

He didn't. He thought of phoning Rose back and renewing the invitation to dinner, but he was afraid of her scorn.
He had lost her, he would never see her again. What a mess
he had made of his first attempt at a social life! Because he
had no experience and no idea of how these people or-
ganised their lives or of what they expected, he had let himself in for an evening alone with this funny little woman
whose tragic life set her apart. His dreams of freedom and
fantasies of love had come to this—hours and hours to be
spent in the company of someone no more exciting and no
better-looking than Wendy Heysham.

Una Engstrand was looking at him wistfully, meekly
awaiting rejection. He answered her, knowing there was no
help for it.

"Of course I will," he said.

The day ahead loomed tediously. He went out and

walked around the park, now seeing clearly the cause of
Rose's resentment and wondering why he was such a fool as
not to have foreseen it. He had contemplated a love affair
with her, yet he lacked the courage to make even the first
moves. Retribution had come to him for even thinking of a
love affair while he was married to Pam. The evening paper
cheered him, for it told him that Mrs. Culver was recovering
and that submitting to the hi-jackers' demands had secured
the release of all the hostages unharmed, except one man
who alleged his neck had been burned with lighted cigarettes. Alan had lunch and went to a matinee of a comedy
about people on a desert island. His freedom, so long desired, had come to solitary walks in the rain and sitting in
theatres among coach parties of old women.

Una Engstrand came down at eight-thirty just when he
had decided she wasn't going to bother to come after all,
that she was no more enticed by this dreary tête-à-tête than
he was. She had put on a skirt and tied her hair back with a
bit of ribbon, but had otherwise made no concessions to her
appearance.

"I would like some vodka, please," she said, sitting down
primly in the middle of his sofa.

"I forgot to buy the glasses!"

"Never mind, we can use tumblers."

He poured out the vodka, put some tonic in, racked his
brains for a topic of conversation. Cars, jobs, the cost of living—instinctively he knew that was all nonsense. No free,
real person would ever talk of such things. He said abruptly,
"I saw some of your father-in-law's books in a bookshop."
That wouldn't be news to her. "What's he doing in Java?"

"I suppose Caesar told you he was in Java. He's very
sweet is Caesar, but a *dreadful* gossip. I expect he told you a
lot of other things too." She smiled at him enquiringly. He
noticed she had beautiful teeth, very white and even.

She shrugged, raised her glass, said quaintly, "Here's to you. I hope you'll be happy here." Suddenly she giggled. "He's heard there's a tribe or something in Indonesia that doesn't have any folklore or any legends or mythology and doesn't read books. I expect they *can't* read. He wants to meet them and find out if they've got beautiful free minds and understand the meaning of reality. When he comes back he's going to write a book about them. He's got the title already, *The Naked Mind,* and I'm to type it for him."

He sat down opposite her. The vodka or something was making him feel better. "You're a typist then?"

"No, I'm not. Oh dear, I'm supposed to be learning while he's away, I'm supposed to be doing a course. And I did start, but they made me have a cover over the keys and it gave me claustrophobia. Caesar says that's crazy. Can you understand it?"

Her expression was such a comical mixture of merriment and rue that Alan couldn't help himself, he burst out laughing. That made her laugh too. He realised he hadn't laughed aloud like this since he ran away from Childon, and perhaps for a long time before that. Why did he have this strange feeling that laughter with her too had fallen into disuse? Because he knew her history? Or from another, somehow telepathic cause? The thought stopped his laughter, and by infection hers, but her small flying-fox face stayed alight.

"It doesn't really matter," she said. "Ambrose thinks I'm hopeless, anyway. He'll just say he's very disappointed and that'll be that. But I mustn't keep on talking about him— Ambrose says this and Ambrose says that. It's because I'm with him so much. Tell me about you."

Until then he had had to tell remarkably few lies. Neither Rose nor Caesar had asked him about himself, and he had hardly spoken to anyone else. He had lied only about his name and address. Rather quickly and with uncertainty, he

told her he had been an accountant but had left his job. The
next bit was true, or almost. "I've left my wife. I just walked
out last weekend."

"A permanent break?" she said.

"I shall never go back!"

"And that's all you brought with you? A suitcase?"

"That's all." Involuntarily, he glanced at the tallboy
where the money was.

"Just like me," she said. "I haven't anything of my own either, only a few clothes and books. But I wouldn't need
them here. There's everything you can think of in this house
and lots of things twice over. You name something, the most
way-out thing you can think of. I bet Ambrose has got it."

"Wineglasses."

She laughed. "I asked for that."

"Before you came here," he said carefully, "you must
have had things."

The sudden sharpening of her features, as if she had
winced, distressed him. He was enjoying her company so
much—so surprisingly and wonderfully—that he dreaded
breaking the rapport between them. But she recovered herself, speaking lightly. "Stewart, that's my husband, kept the
lot. Poor dear, he needs to know he's got things even if he
can't use them. Ambrose says it's the outward sign of his in-
security and it's got to be worked through."

Alan burst out, knowing he shouldn't, "Your father-in-law
is worse than mine! He's a monster."

Again she laughed, with delight. She held out her glass.
"More, please. It's delicious. I am having a nice time. I suppose he is rather awful, but if I say so people think it's me
that is because everyone thinks he's wonderful. Except you."
She nodded sagely. "I like that."

In that moment he fell in love with her, though it was
some hours before he realised it.

Una stayed till eleven, Fitton's Piece Cinderella hour. But
she didn't ask him whatever time it was or cry out that,
Good heavens, she had no idea it was so late. After she had
gone, he tidied up the room and washed the glasses, thinking how glad he was that Caesar and his girl friend hadn't
been there. He was even more glad Rose hadn't been there.
Una had talked about the books she had read, which were
much the same as the books he had read, and he had never
before talked on this subject with anyone. There was something heady, more intoxicating than the vodka he had been
drinking, about being with someone who talked about a
character in a book or the author's style with an intensity he
had previously known to be lavished only over saving
money and the cost of living. What would Rose have talked
about? During the hours with Una, Rose had slipped back
into, been engulfed by, the fantasy image from which she
had come. He could hardly believe that he had ever met her
or that she had been real at all. But he went over and over
in his mind the things Una had said and the things he had
said to her, and he thought of things he wished he had said.
It didn't matter, there would be more times. He had made a
friend to whom he could talk.

Before he went to bed he looked at himself carefully in
the mirror. He wanted to see what sort of a man she had
seen. His hair wasn't greased down anymore, so that it
looked more like hair and less like a leather cap, and his face

was—well, not exactly brown but healthily coloured. He who had never got a tan while living in the country, had got one in a week of walking round London. His belly didn't sag quite so much. He looked thirty-eight, he thought, instead of going on for fifty. That was what she had seen. And he? He conjured her up vividly, she might still have been sitting there, her small face so vital when she laughed, her eyes so bright, the curly hair escaping from the ribbon until, by the time she left, it had massed once more about her thin cheeks. Tomorrow he'd go upstairs and find her and take her out to lunch. The idea of taking her out and ordering food and wine didn't frighten him a bit. But he was very tired now. He got into bed and fell immediately asleep.

At about three he woke up. The vodka had given him a raging thirst, so he went into the kitchen and drank a pint of water. After that it would have been natural to go back to bed and sleep till, say, seven, but he felt wide awake and entirely refreshed and tremendously happy. It was years since he had felt happy. Had he ever? When he was a child, yes, and when Jillian was born because she was the child he had wanted, and in a strange way when he was driving off with the money. But he hadn't felt like this. This feeling was quite new. He wanted to go out and rush up and down Montcalm Gardens, shouting that he was free and happy and had found the meaning of life. A great joy possessed him. Energy seemed to flow through his body and out at his fingertips. He wanted to tell someone who would understand, and he knew it was Una he wanted to tell.

So this was being in love, this was what it was like. He laughed out loud. He turned on the cold tap and ran his hands under it, he splashed cold water over his face. The room was freezing because the heating went off at eleven, but he was hot, glowing with heat and actually sweating. He fell onto the bed and pulled the sheet over him and thought about Una up there asleep somewhere in the house. Or was she awake too, thinking about him? He thought about' her for an hour, reliving their conversation and then fantasising that he and she lived together in a house like this one and were happy all the time, every minute of the day and night. The fantasy drifted off into a dream of that, a long protracted dream that broke and dissolved and began again in new aspects, until it ended in horror. It ended with his hearing Una scream. He had to run up many staircases and through many rooms to find where the screams were coming from and to find her. At last he came upon her and she was dead, burnt to death with charred bank notes lying all around her. But when he took her body in his arms and looked into her face, he saw that it was not Una he held. It was Joyce.

The cold of morning pierced through the thin sheet, and he awoke shivering, his legs numb. All the euphoria of the night was gone. He had no idea of how one went a-courting. It would be as difficult to speak of love to Una as it would have been to Rose, more difficult because he was in love with her—that was unchanged—while for Rose he had felt only the itch of lust. He was alone in the house with Una, he must be, and thinking of it terrified him. Inviting her out to lunch was impossible, making any sort of overtures to her was unthinkable. He was married, and she knew it. He had a notion, gathered more from Pam's philosophy than from novels, that if you told a woman you loved her and she didn't love you, she would slap your face. Especially if you were married and she was married. It was apparently, for no reason he could think of, in some circumstances an insult to tell a woman you loved her. He dressed and went out, thinking he would collapse or weep if he were to meet Una in the hall, but he didn't meet her.

Ex-priest Marries Stripper and *Torture "Hotly" Denied*

said the Sunday papers. They were searching potholes in
Derbyshire for the bodies of himself and Joyce. The silver-
blue Ford Escort, last observed at Dover, had turned up in
Turkey, its passengers blamelessly on their way to an
ashram in India. Alan had a cup of coffee and a sandwich,
which made him feel sick. He noticed, after quite a long
while, that it was a nice day. They were back to the kind of
weather of the week before he ran away, just like spring, as
Joyce had said. The sun on his face was warm and kind. If
he went into the park or Kensington Gardens he might meet
Rose, so he made for the nearest tube station, which was
Notting Hill, and bought a ticket to Hampstead.

Una had lived in Hampstead. He didn't remember that
until he got there. He walked about Hampstead, wondering
if she had lived in this street or that, and if she had walked
daily where he now was walking. He found the Heath by
the simple expedient of following Heath Street until he got
to it. All London lay below him, and, standing on the slope
beside the Spaniard's Road, he looked down on it as Dick
Whittington had looked down and, in the sunshine, seen the
city paved with gold.

His gold lay down there, but it was nothing to him if it
couldn't give him Una. He turned abruptly and walked in
the opposite direction, through the wood that lies between
the Spaniard's Road and North End. It wasn't much like
Childon Fen. In the woods adjacent to great cities the trees
are the same as trees in the deep wild, but at ground level
all the plants and most of the grass have been trodden away.
A sterile dusty brownness lies underfoot. The air has no moist
green sweetness. But on that sunny Sunday morning—it was
still morning, he had left so early—the wood seemed to Alan
to have a tender, bruised beauty, spring renewing it all for
further spoliation, and he knew the authors were right when
they wrote of what love does, of how it transforms and

MAKE DEATH LOVE ME

glorifies and takes the scales from the eye of the beholder.

When he emerged from the wood he had no idea where he was, but he went on walking roughly westward until he came to a large main road. Finchley Road, N.W.2, he read, and he realised he must be in Paul Browning country. Strange. Paddington was West Two, so he had supposed that Northwest Two must be nearby. It was now evident that Paul Browning banked in Paddington not because he lived but because he worked there. Alan took out his London guide, for even though he would never speak to Una again, never be alone with her again, he ought to know the location of his old home.

The street plan showed Exmoor Gardens as part of an estate of houses where the roads had been quaintly constructed in concentric circles, or really, concentric ovals. Each one was named after a range of mountains or hills in the British Isles. It seemed a long way to walk, but Alan didn't know if there was any other means of getting there, and he felt a strange compulsion to see Paul Browning's home. In the event, the walk didn't take so very long.

Most of the houses in Exmoor Gardens were mock-Tudor, but a few were of newer, plainer design, and number fifteen was one of these. It was bigger than his own house at Fitton's Piece, but otherwise it was very much like it, red brick and with picture windows and a chimney for show not use, and a clump of pampas grass in the front garden. He stood and looked at it, marvelling that by chance he should have chosen for his fictional past so near a replica of his actual past.

Paul Browning himself was cleaning his car on the garage drive. The front door was open and a child of about eight was running in and out, holding a small distressed-looking puppy on a lead. There was a seat on the opposite side of the road. It had been placed at the entrance to a footpath

which presumably linked one of those ovals to another. Alan
sat down on the seat and pretended to read his paper while
the child galloped the puppy up and down the steps. Paul
Browning gave an irritable exclamation. He threw down his
soapy cloth and went up to the door and called into the
hall:

"Alison! Don't let him do that to the dog."

There was no answer. Paul Browning caught the boy and
admonished him, but quietly and gently, and he picked the
puppy up and held it in his arms. A woman came out of the
house, blond, tallish, about thirty-five. Alan couldn't hear
what she said but the tone of her voice was protective. He
had the impression from the way she put her arm round the
boy and smiled at her husband and patted the little dog,
that she was the fierce yet tender protector of them all. He
folded his paper and got up and walked away down the
footpath.

The little scene had made him miserable. He should have
had that but he had never had it, and now it was too late to
have it with anyone. He felt ridiculously guilty too for taking this man's identity and background, a theft which had
turned out to be pointless as well as a kind of slander on
Paul Browning, who would never have left his wife. Alan
asked himself if his other theft had been equally pointless.

The path brought him out at the opposite end to that
where he had entered the oval, and his guide showed him
that he wasn't far now from Cricklewood Broadway, which
seemed to be part of the northern end of the Edgware Road.
He walked towards it through a district that rapidly grew
shabbier, that seemed as if it must inevitably run down into
squalor. Yet this never happened. Expecting squalor, he
found himself instead in an area that maintained itself well
this side of the slummy and the disreputable. The street was

wide, lined with the emporiums of car dealers, with betting shops, supermarkets, and shops whose windows displayed saris and lengths of oriental silks. On a blackboard outside a pub called the Rose of Killarney a menu was chalked up, offering steak pie and two veg or ham salad or something called a Leprechaun's Lunch. This last appeared to be bread, cheese, and pickles, but the thought of asking for it in the blackboard's terms daunted Alan so he ordered the salad and a half of bitter while he waited for it to come.

The girl behind the bar had the pale puffy face and black circles under her eyes of someone reared on potatoes in a Dublin tenement. She drew Alan's bitter and a pint for an Irishman with an accent as strong as her own, then began serving a double whisky to a thin boy with a pinched face whose carrier bag full of groceries was stuffed between Alan's stool and his own. Alan didn't know what made him look down. Perhaps it was that he was still surprised you could go shopping in London on a Sunday, or perhaps he was anxious, in his middle-class respectable way, not to seem to be touching that bag or encroaching upon it. Whatever it was, he looked down, slightly shifting his stool, and saw the boy's hand go down to take a cigarette packet and a box of matches from inside the bag. It was the right hand. The forefinger had been injured in some kind of accident and the nail was cobbled like the kernel of a walnut.

The shock of what he had seen made Alan's stomach turn with a fluttering movement. He looked sharply away, started to eat his salad as smoke from the boy's cigarette drifted across the sliced hard-boiled eggs, the vinegary lettuce. Reflected in the glass behind the bar was a smooth gaunt face, tight mouth, biggish nose. The beard could have been shaved off, the hair cut. Alan thought he would know for sure if the boy spoke. He must have spoken already to ask

for that whisky, but that was before Alan came in. He
watched him pick up the bag, and this time the finger
seemed less misshapen. It wasn't the same. The finger that
had come under the metal grille and scooped into the palm
the bag of coins he remembered as grotesquely warped and
twisted, tipped with a carapace more like a claw or a bar-
nacled shell than a human nail.

It was a kind of relief knowing they weren't the same so
that he wouldn't have to do anything about it. Do what? He
was the last person who could go to the police. The boy left
the pub and after a few minutes Alan left too, not following
him though, intending never to think of him again. He was
suddenly aware that he was tired, he must have walked
miles, and he was getting thankfully on to a south-bound
bus when he caught his last glimpse of the boy, who was
walking down a side street, walking slowly and swinging his
carrier as if he had all the time in the world and nothing to
go home for.

Alan felt himself in the same situation. For the rest of
that day and most of the next he avoided seeing Una.
Nearly all the time he kept away from Montcalm Gardens.
And he kept away too from North London, from those distant outposts of the Edgware Road where an invented past
had bizarrely met an illusion. It was obviously unwise to
visit venues, shabby districts, and down-at-heel pubs, which
suggested crime and criminals to him and where conscience
worked on his imagination. He sat in parks, rode on the tops
of buses, visited Tussaud's. But he had to go back or settle
for being a vagrant. Should he move on to somewhere else?
Should he leave London and go on to some provincial city?
For years he had longed for love, and now he had found it
he wanted lovelessness back again. He came back to his
room on Monday evening and sat on the bed, resolving that
in a minute, when he had got enough courage, he would go

upstairs and tell her he was leaving, he was going back to his wife, to Alison.

From the other side of the wall, in Caesar Locksley's room, he heard her voice.

Not what she said, just her voice. And he was consumed with jealousy. Immediately he thought Caesar had been deceiving him and she had been deceiving him, and she was even now in bed with Caesar. He began to walk up and down in a kind of frenzy. They must have heard him in there because someone came to his door and knocked. He wasn't going to answer. He stood at the window with his eyes shut and his hands clenched. The knock came again and Caesar said:

"Paul, are you O.K. in there?"

He had to go then.

"Annie and I are going to see the Chabrol film at the Gate," said Caesar. "Una as well." He winked at Alan. The wink meant, take her out of herself, get her out of this house. "Feel like coming too?"

"All right," said Alan. The relief was tremendous, which was why he had agreed. In the next thirty seconds he realised what he had agreed to, and then he couldn't think at all because he was confronting her. Nor could he look at her or speak. He heard her say:

"It *is* good to see you. I've knocked on your door about fifteen times since Saturday night to thank you and say how nice it was."

"I was out," he muttered. He looked at her then, and something inside him, apparently the whole complex labyrinth of his digestive system and his heart and his lungs, rotated full circle and slumped back into their proper niches.

"This is Annie," said Caesar.

It didn't help that the girl looked quite a lot like Pam and Jillian. The same neat, regular, very English features and

peachy skin and small blue eyes. He heard Caesar say she
was a nurse, and he could imagine that from her brisk
hearty manner, but she brought Pam back to him, her calms
and her storms. He felt trapped and ill.

They walked to the cinema. He and Una walked together,
in front of the others.

"They say," said Una, "that if two couples go out together
you can tell their social status by the way they pair off. If
they're working class the two girls walk together, if they're
middle class, husband and wife walk together, and if they're
upper class each husband walks with the other one's
wife."

"Don't make me out middle class, Una," said Caesar.

"Ah, but none of us is married to any of the others."

That made Annie talk about Stewart. She had had a letter
from someone who had met him in Port of Spain. Una didn't
seem to mind any of this and talked quite uninhibitedly to
Annie about Stewart so that the two girls drifted together in
the working-class way, a pairing which settled in advance
the seating arrangement in the cinema. Alan went in first,
then Caesar, then Annie, with Una next to her and as far as
possible from Alan. The film was in French and very subtle
as well, and he didn't bother to read the subtitles. He followed none of it. In a kind of daze he sat, feeling that he
lived from moment to moment, that there was no future and
no past, only instants precisely clicking through an infinite
present.

Afterwards, they all went for a drink in the Sun in Splendour. Caesar wanted Annie to come home with him for the
night, but Annie said Montcalm Gardens was much too far
from her hospital and she wanted her sleep, anyway. There
was a certain amount of badinage, in which Caesar and both
girls took part. Alan had never before heard sexual behaviour so freely and frivolously discussed, and he was embar-

rassed. He tried to imagine himself and Pam talking like this
with the Heyshams, but he couldn't imagine it. And he
stopped trying when it became plain that Annie was going,
and Caesar taking her home, and that this was happening
now.

Una said, after they had left, "I think Annie was one of
Stewart's ladies, though she won't admit it. I expect he 'gave
her a whirl.' That was the way he always put it when he
only took someone around for a week. Poor whirl girls, I
used to feel so sorry for them." She paused and looked at
him. "Let me buy you a drink this time."

He had an idea women never bought drinks in pubs, that
if they tried they wouldn't get served. It surprised him that
she got served, and with a smile as if it were nothing out of
the way. He couldn't finish the whisky she had brought
him. As soon as he felt it on his tongue, he knew that his
gorge would rise at a second mouthful. The landlord called
time, and he and she were out in the street alone together,
walking back to Montcalm Gardens by intricate back ways.
It wasn't dark as it would have been in the country, but
other-worldly bright with the radiance from the livid lamps.
The yellowness was not apparent in the upper air, but only
where the light lay like lacquer on the dewy surface of
metal and gilded the moist leaves of evergreens.

"The night is shiny," said Una.

"You mean shining," he corrected her stiffly.

She shook her head. "No. Shakespeare has a soldier say
that in *Antony and Cleopatra*. It's my favourite line. The
night is shiny. I know exactly what he meant, though I suppose he was talking of moonlight."

He longed for her with a yearning that made him feel
faint, but he could only say stupidly, "There's no moon tonight."

She unlocked the front door and switched on lights, and

they went together into the fragrant polished hall where the vases were filled with winter jasmine. The sight of it brought back to him the yard at the back of the bank where that same flower grew, and he passed his hand across his brow, though his forehead was hot and dry.

"You're tired," she said. "I was going to suggest making coffee, but not if you're too tired."

He didn't speak but followed her into the kitchen and sat down at the table. It was a room about four times as big as the one at Fitton's Piece. He thought how happy it would make Pam to have a kitchen like that, with two fridges and an enormous deep freeze and a cooker halfway up the wall, and a rotisserie and an infrared grill. With deft swift movements Una started the percolator and set out cups. She talked to him in her sweet vague way about Ambrose and his books, about the banishment of all Stewart's mother's novels to the basement after her death, flitted on to speak of Stewart's little house on Dartmoor, now empty and neglected. She poured the coffee. She sat down, shaking her hair into a bright curly aureole, and looked at him, waiting for him to contribute.

And then something happened to him which was not unlike that something that had happened when the phone rang in the office and he had had the money in his hands, and he knew he had to act now or never. So he said aloud and desperately, "Una," just hearing how her name sounded in his voice.

"What is it?"

"Oh, God," he said, "I'll leave, I'll go whenever you say, but I have to tell you. I've fallen in love with you. I love you so much, I can't bear it." And he swept out his arms across the table and knocked over the cup, and coffee flooded in a stream across the floor.

She gave a little sharp exclamation. Her face went crimson. She fell on her knees with a cloth in her hands and began feverishly mopping up the liquid. He ran down the basement stairs and flung himself into his room and closed the door and locked it.

Up and down the room he walked as he had done earlier. He would never sleep again or eat a meal or even *be*. A kind of rage possessed him, for in the midst of this tempest of emotion, he knew he was having now what he should have had at eighteen, what at eighteen had been denied him. He was having it this way now because he had never had it before. And was he to have it now without its fruition?

Ceasing to pace, he listened to the silence. The light was still on upstairs in the kitchen. He could see it lying in yellow squares on the dark rough lawn. Trembling, he watched the quadrangles of light, thinking that at any moment he might see her delicate profile and her massy hair silhouetted upon them. The light went out and the garden was black.

He imagined her crossing the hall and going up the wide curving staircase to her own room, angry with him perhaps, or shocked, or just glad to be rid of him. He turned off his own light, for he couldn't bear to see any part of himself. Then he unlocked his door and went out into the pitch dark, knowing he must find her before she made herself inaccessible to him now and thus forever.

There was a faint light illuminating the top of the basement stairs. She hadn't yet gone to bed. He began to climb the stairs, having no idea what he would say, thinking he might say nothing but only fall in an agony at her feet. The light from above went out. He felt for the banister ahead of him, and touched instead her extended hand at the light switch. He gasped. They couldn't see each other, but they closed together, his arms encircling her as she held him, and they stood on the stairs in the black dark, silently embraced.

Presently they went down the stairs, crab-wise, awkwardly, clinging to each other. He wouldn't let her put a light on. She opened the door of his room and drew him in, and as it closed they heard Caesar enter the house. Lights came on and Ceasar's footsteps sounded softly. Alan held Una in his arms in a breathless hush until all was silent and dark again.

Very little food was kept in stock because Marty hadn't got a fridge. The bookcase held a few tins of beans and spaghetti and soup, half a dozen eggs in a box, a packet of bacon, tea bags and a jar of instant coffee, some cheese and a wrapped loaf. They usually had bread and cheese for lunch, and every day Marty went out to buy their dinner. But when it got to five o'clock on Monday he was still fast asleep on the mattress, where he had been lying since two. Joyce was in the kitchen, washing her hair.

Nigel shook Marty awake.

"Get yourself together. We want our meal, right? And a bottle of wine. And then you're going to do like a disappearing act. Get it?"

Marty sat up, rubbing his eyes. "I don't feel too good. I got a hell of a pain in my gut."

"You're pissed, that's all. You got through a whole goddamned bottle of scotch since last night." Unconsciously, Nigel used the tones of Dr. Thaxby. "You're an alcoholic and you'll give yourself cirrhosis of the liver. That's worse than cancer. They can operate on you for cancer but not for cirrhosis. You've only got one liver. D'you know that?"

"Leave off, will you? It's not the scotch. That wouldn't give me a pain in my gut, that'd give me a pain in my head. I reckon I got one of them bugs."

"You're pissed," said Nigel. "You need some fresh air."

Marty groaned and lay down again. "I can't go out. You go."

"Christ, the whole point is to leave me alone with her."

"It'll have to be tomorrow. I'll have a good night's kip and I'll be O.K. tomorrow."

So Marty didn't go out, and they had tinned spaghetti and bacon for their supper. Joyce unbent so far as to cook it. She couldn't agree to what she'd agreed to and then refuse to cook his food. Marty stayed guarding Joyce while Nigel went down and had a bath. On the way up again, he encountered old Mr. Green in a brown wool dressing gown and carrying a towel. Mr. Green smiled at him in rather a shy way, but Nigel took no notice. He flushed Joyce's letter down the lavatory pan.

Marty was holding the gun and looking reasonably alert. "You see?" said Nigel. "There's nothing wrong with you so long as you keep off the booze."

That seemed to be true, for Marty didn't drink any more that evening and on Tuesday he felt almost normal. It was a lovely day to be out in the air. On Nigel's instructions, he bought a cold roast chicken and some prepared salad in cartons and more bread and cheese and a bottle of really good wine that cost him four pounds. He forgot to get more tea and coffee or to replenish their supply of tins, but that didn't matter since, by tomorrow, the three of them would be off somewhere, Nigel and Joyce all set for a honeymoon.

The fact was, though, that neither of them seemed very loverlike. Marty wondered what had happened between them on Saturday. Not much, he thought, but presumably enough for Nigel to be sure he was going to make it. Marty observed their behaviour. Joyce sat knitting all day, not being any nicer to Nigel than she had ever been, and Nigel didn't talk much to her or call her "sweetheart" or "love," which were the endearments he would have used in the circumstances. Maybe it was just that they fancied each other so much that they were keeping themselves under control in his presence. He hoped so, and hoped they wouldn't expect him to stay out half the night, for his stomach was hurting him again and he felt as if he had a hangover, though he hadn't touched a drop of scotch for twenty-four hours.

At just after six he went off. It was a fine clear evening, preternaturally warm for the time of year. Or so Marty supposed from the way other people weren't wearing coats, and from seeing a couple of girls walking along in thin blouses with short sleeves. He didn't feel warm himself, although he had a sweater and his leather jacket on. He stood shivering at the bus stop, waiting for the number sixteen to come and take him down to the West End.

The two in the room in Cricklewood were self-conscious with each other. Nigel put his arm round Joyce and wondered how it would be if she were thirty-seven or thirty-eight and grateful to him for being such a contrast to her dreary old husband. The fantasy helped, and so did some of Marty's whisky. Joyce said she would have some too, but to put water with it.

They took their glasses into the living room.

"Did you send my letter?" said Joyce.

"Marty took it this morning."

"So that's his name? Marty."

Nigel could have bitten his tongue out. But did it matter now?

"You'd better tell me yours, hadn't you?"

Nigel did so. Joyce thought it a nice name, but she wasn't going to say so. She had an obscure feeling that some part of herself would be saved inviolate if, even though she slept with Nigel, she continued to speak to him with cold indifference. The whisky warmed and calmed her. She had

never tasted it before. Stephen said it was gin that was the
woman's drink, and once or twice she had had a gin and
tonic with him in the Childon Arms, but never whisky.
Nigel was half-sitting on the gun. It was beside him but not
between them. She let Nigel kiss her and managed to kiss
him back.

"We may as well eat," Nigel said, and he took the gun
with him to the table. The wine would put the finishing
touch to a pleasant muzziness that was overcoming his inhi-
bitions. He liked Joyce's shyness and her ugliness. It meant
she wouldn't know whether he acquitted himself well or
badly. She ate silently, returning the pressure of his knee
under the table. But, God, she was ugly! The only good
thing about her was her hair. Her eyelashes were white—no
wonder she'd nagged him to get her mascara—and her skin
was pale and coarse and her features doughy. In Marty's
tee-shirt and pullover she looked shapeless.

He started talking to her about the things he had done,
how he had been to university and got a first-class honours
degree, but had thrown it all up because this society was
rotten, rotten to the core, he didn't want any part of it, no
way. So he had gone to live in a commune with other young
people with ideals, where they had a vegetarian diet and
made their own bread and the girls wove cloth and made
pots. It was a free sexuality commune and he had been
shared by two girls, a very young one called Samantha and
an older one, Sarah.

"Why did you rob a bank then?" said Joyce.

Nigel said it had been a gesture of defiance against this
rotten society, and they were going to use the money to start
a Raj Neesh community in Scotland.

"What's that when it's at home?"

"It's my religion. It's a marvellous Eastern religion with
no rules. You can do what you like."

"Sounds right up your street," said Joyce, but she didn't say it unpleasantly, and when she got up to put the plates on the draining board beside Marty's whisky bottles, she let Nigel run his hand down her thigh. Then she sat down closer to him and they drank up the last of the wine. By now it was dark outside, but for the light from the yellow lamps. Nigel drew the curtains, and when Joyce came through from the kitchen he put his arms round her and began kissing her violently and hungrily, pushing her head back and chewing at her face.

She had very little feeling left, just enough to know from the feel of Nigel pressed like iron up against her that it was going to happen. But she felt no panic or despair, the whisky and the wine had seen to that, and no compulsion to break a window or scream when, for the first time since she had been there, she was left quite alone and free to move. Nigel went out to the lavatory, taking the gun with him. Joyce got onto the mattress and took all her clothes off under the sheet. The third note was still inside her bra. She pushed it into one of the cups and hid the bra on the floor under her pullover. Nigel came back, closing the door on the Yale but not bothering with the other lock. He switched off the light. For a little while he stood there, surprised that the lamps outside lit the room so brightly through the threadbare curtains, as if he hadn't seen that same thing for many nights. Then he stripped off his clothes and pulled back the blankets and the sheet that covered Joyce.

Her head was slightly turned away, the exposed cheek half-covered by her long fair hair. He stared at her in amazement, for he hadn't known any real woman could look like that. Her body was without a flaw, the full breasts smooth and rounded like blown glass, her waist a fragile and slender stem, the bones and muscles of her legs and arms veiled in an extravagant silkiness of plump tissue and white skin. The yellow light lay on her like a patina of gilding, shining in a gold blaze on those roundnesses and leaving the shallow hollows sepia brown. She was like one of the nudes in Marty's magazines, only she was more superb. Nigel had never thought of those as real women, but as contrivances of the pornographer's skill, assisted by the pose and the cunning camera. He looked down on her with appalled wonder, with a sick shrinking awe, while Joyce lay motionless and splendid, her eyes closed.

At last he said, "Joyce," and lowered his body onto hers. He too shut his eyes, knowing he should have shut them before or never have pulled back that sheet. He tried to think of Samantha's mother, stringy and thin and thirty-two, of Sarah in her black stockings. With his right hand he felt for the gun, imagining how it would be if he were raping Alan Groombridge's wife at gunpoint. But the damage was done. In the last way he would have thought possible, Joyce had taken away his manhood without moving, without speaking. Now she shifted her body under his and opened her eyes and looked at him.

"I'll be O.K. in a minute," said Nigel, his teeth clenched. "I could use a drink."

He went out into the kitchen and took a swig out of the whisky bottle. He shut his eyes so that he couldn't see Joyce and tied himself round her, his arms and legs gripping her.

"You're hurting!"

"I'll be O.K. in a minute. Just give me a minute."

He rolled off her and turned on his side. His whole body felt cold and slack. He concentrated on fantasies of Joyce as his slave, and on the importance of this act which he must perform to make her so. After a while, after the minutes he had asked her to give him, he turned to her once more to look at her face. If he could just look at her face and forget that wonderful terrifying body. . . . She was asleep. Her head buried in her arms, she had fallen into a heavy drunken sleep.

Nigel would have liked to kill her then. He held the gun pressed to the back of her neck. Perhaps he would have killed her if the gun had been loaded and the trigger not stiff and immovable. But the gun, like himself, was just a copy or a replica. It was as useless as he.

He took it with him into the kitchen and closed the door. Suddenly he was visited by a childhood memory, a vision from some fifteen or sixteen years in the past. He was sitting at the table and his father was spoon-feeding him, forcibly feeding him, while his mother crawled about the floor with a cloth in her hand. His mother was mopping up food that he spilt or spat out, reaching up sometimes to wipe his face with the flannel in her other hand, while his father kept telling him he must eat or he would never grow up, never be a man. The adult Nigel bent his head over the table in Marty's kitchen, as he had bent it over that other one, and began to weep as he had wept then. It was only the thought of Marty coming back and finding him there that stilled his sobs and made him get up again, choking and cursing. Reality was unbearable, he wanted oblivion. He put the mouth of the bottle to his own mouth, closed his lips right round it, and poured a long steady stream of whisky down his throat. There was just time to get back to that mattress and stretch himself out as far as possible from Joyce before the spirit knocked him out.

Marty looked at the shops in Oxford Street, thinking of the clothes he would buy when he was free to buy them. He had never had the money to be a snappy dresser but he would like to be one, to wear tight trousers and velvet jackets and shirts with girls' faces and pop stars' names on them. A couple of passing policemen looked at him, or he fancied they looked at him, so he stopped peering in windows and walked off down Regent Street to Piccadilly Circus.

In the neighbourhood of Leicester Square he visited a couple of amusement arcades and played the fruiters, and then he wandered around Soho. He had always meant to go into one of those strip clubs, and now, when he had wads of money in his pocket, was surely the time. But the pain which had troubled him on Monday was returning. Every few minutes he was getting a twinge in the upper part of his stomach, with cramps which made him break wind and taste bile when the squeezing vice released. He couldn't go into a club and enjoy himself, feeling like that and liable to keep doubling up. It wasn't his appendix, he thought, he'd had that out when he was twelve. Withdrawal symptoms, that's what it was. Alcohol was a drug, and everyone knew that when you came off a drug you got pains and sweats and felt rotten. He should have done it gradually, not cut it off all of a sudden.

How long were those two going to take over it? Nigel hadn't said what time he was to get back, but midnight ought to be O.K. for God's sake. He hadn't eaten since breakfast, no wonder he felt so queasy. He'd best get a good steak and some chips and a couple of rolls inside him. The smell in the steak house made his throat rise, and he stumbled out, wondering what would happen if he collapsed in the street and the police picked him up with all that money in his pockets.

He'd feel safer nearer home, so he got into the Tube, which took him up to Kilburn. Luckily the thirty-two bus came along at once. Marty got on it, slumped into a downstairs seat, and lit a cigarette. The Indian conductor asked him to put it out, and Marty said to go back to the jungle and told him what he could do to himself when there. So they stopped the bus and the big black driver came round and together, to the huge glee of the other passengers, they put Marty off. He had to walk all the way up Shoot-up Hill and he didn't know how he made it.

But it was too early to go back yet, only a quarter to eleven. Whether his trouble was withdrawal symptoms or a bug, he had to have a drink, and they did say whisky settled the stomach. His father used to say it, the old git, and if anyone knew about booze he should. A couple of doubles, thought Marty, and he'd sleep like a log and wake up all right tomorrow.

The Rose of Killarney was about halfway along the Broadway. Marty walked in a bit unsteadily, wincing with pain as he passed between the tables. Bridey and the licencee were behind the bar.

"Double scotch," said Marty thickly.

Bridey said to the licencee, "This fella lives next to me. Will you listen to his manners?"

"O.K., Bridey, I'll serve him."

"In the same house he lives and can't say so much as a civil 'please.' If you ask me, he's had too much already."

Marty took no notice. He never spoke to her if he could help it, any more than he did to any of these foreigners, immigrants, Jews, spades, and whatever. He drank his scotch, belched, and asked for another.

"Sorry, son, you've had enough. You heard what the lady said."

"Lady," said Marty. "Bloody Irish slag."

It was only just eleven, but he was going home anyway. The light in his room was out. He could see that from the street where he had to sit down on a wall, he felt so sick and weak. The stairs were the last phase in his ordeal and they were the worst. Outside his door he thought he'd rather just lie down on the landing floor than go through all the hassle of waking Nigel to let him in. He peered at the keyhole but couldn't see through because the iron key was blocking it. Maybe Nigel hadn't bothered to lock it because things had gone right and there was no longer any need to. He tried the key in the Yale and the door opened.

After the darkness of the landing, the yellow light made him blink. From force of habit he locked the door and hung the string the key was on round his neck. The light lay in irregular patches on the two sleeping faces. Great, thought Marty, he's made it, we'll be out of here tomorrow. Holding his sore stomach, breathing gingerly, he curled up on the sofa and pulled the blanket over him.

Joyce hadn't been aware of his arrival. It was three or four hours later that she awoke with a banging head and a dry mouth. But she came to herself quickly and remembered what her original purpose in going to bed with Nigel had been. She looked at him with feelings of amazement and distaste, and with pity too. Joyce thought she knew all about sex, far more than her mother did, but no one had ever told her that what had happened with Nigel is so usual as to be commonplace, an inhibition that affects all men sometimes and some men quite often. She thought of virile, confident Stephen, and she decided Nigel must have some awful disease.

Both her captors were deeply asleep, Marty snoring, Nigel with his right hand tucked under the pillow. Joyce put her clothes on. Then she lay down beside Nigel and put her right hand under the pillow too, feeling the hard warm metal of the gun. Immediately her hand was gripped hard, but not, she thought, because he was aware of what she was after. Rather it was as if he needed a woman's hand to hold in his troubled sleep, as a child may do. With her left hand she slid the gun out and eased her right hand away. Nigel gave a sort of whimper but he didn't wake up.

Taking a deep breath and wishing the thudding in her head would stop, she raised the gun, pointed it at the kitchen wall, and tried to squeeze the trigger. It wouldn't move. So it was a toy, as she had hoped and lately had often supposed. She was filled with exultation. It was a toy, as you could tell really by the plasticky look of it, that handle part seemed actually made of plastic, and by the way it said *Made in W. Germany.*

Her future actions seemed simple. She wouldn't try to get the key from Marty, for the two of them could easily overpower her and might hurt her badly. But in the morning, when one of them took her to the lavatory, she would run down the stairs, yelling at the top of her voice.

She decided not to take her clothes off again in case Nigel woke up and started pawing her about. That was a horrible thought when you considered that he was ill or not really a man at all. She came back and looked at him, still sleeping Wasn't it rather peculiar to make a toy gun with a trigger that wouldn't move? The point with having a toy gun, she knew from her younger brother, was that you could press the trigger and fire caps. She wondered how you put the caps into this one. Perhaps by fiddling with that handle thing at the back? She pushed it but it wouldn't move.

Joyce carried the gun to the kitchen window where the light was brightest. In that light she spotted a funny little knob on the side of the gun, and she pushed at it tentatively with the tip of her finger. It moved easily, sliding forward towards the barrel and revealing a small red spot. Although the handle thing at the back had also moved and dropped forward, no space for the insertion of caps had been revealed. But there wouldn't be any point in putting caps in, thought Joyce, if you couldn't move the trigger. Perhaps it

was a real gun that had got broken. She raised it again, smiling to herself because she'd really been a bit of a fool, hadn't
she, letting herself be kept a prisoner for a week by two
boys with a gun that didn't work? She felt quite ashamed.

Levelling the gun at Nigel made her giggle. She enjoyed
the sensation of threatening him, even though he didn't
know it, as for days he had threatened her. They'd killed
Mr. Groombridge with that, had they? Like hell they had.
Like this, had they, squeezing a broken trigger that
wouldn't move?

Joyce squeezed it, almost wishing they were awake to see
her. There was a shattering roar. Her arm flew up, the gun
arced across the room, and the bullet tore into the rotten
wood of the window frame, lodging there, missing Nigel's
ear by an inch.

Joyce screamed.

Marty was off the sofa and Nigel off the mattress before the reverberations of the explosion had died away. Nigel seized Joyce and pulled her down on the bed, his hand over her mouth, and when she went on screaming he stuffed a pillow over her face. Marty knelt on the end of the mattress, holding his head in both hands and staring at the hole the bullet had made in the window frame. In all their heads the noise was still ringing.

"Oh, Christ," Marty moaned. "Oh, Christ."

Nigel pulled the pillow off Joyce and slapped her face with the flat of his hand and the back of his hand.

"You bitch. You stupid bitch."

She lay face-downwards, sobbing. Nigel crawled over the mattress and reached out and picked up the gun. He pulled a blanket round himself like a shawl and sat hunched up, examining the gun with wonder and astonishment. The room stank of gunpowder. Silence crept into the room, heavier and somehow louder than sound. Marty squatted, taut with fear, waiting for the feet on the stairs, the knock on the door, the sound of the phone down below being lifted, but Nigel only held and turned and looked at the gun.

The German writing on the side of it made sense now. With a thrill of excitement, he read those words again. This was a Bond gun he held in his hands, a Walther P.P.K. He didn't want to put it down even to pull on his jeans and his sweater, he didn't want ever to let it out of his hands again.

He brooded over it with joy, loving it, wondering how he could ever have supposed it a toy or a replica. It was more real than himself. It worked.

"That's quite a weapon," he said softly.

In other circumstances, Marty would have been quite amused to have fooled Nigel about the gun for so long, and elated to have received his praise. But he was frightened and he was in pain. So he only muttered, "Course it is. I wouldn't pay seventy-five quid for any old crap," and winced as a twinge in his stomach doubled him up. "Going to throw up," he groaned and made for the door.

"Just check what the scene is while you're out there," said Nigel. He was looking at the small circular red indentation the moving of the safety catch had exposed. Carefully he pushed the catch down again and that thing on the back, which had always puzzled him but which he now knew to be the hammer, dropped down. Now the trigger would hardly move. Nigel looked at Joyce and at the hole in the window frame and he sighed.

Marty vomited for some minutes. Afterwards he felt so weak and faint that he had to sit down on the lavatory seat, but at last he forced himself to get up and stagger down the stairs. His legs felt like bits of wet string. He crept down two flights of stairs, listening. The whole house seemed to be asleep, all the doors were shut and all the lights off except for a faint glimmer under the red-haired girl's front door. Marty hauled himself back up, hanging onto the banisters, his stomach rotating and squeezing.

He lurched across the room to the kitchen and took a long swig from the whisky bottle. Warm and brown and reassuring, it brought him momentary relief so that he was able to stand up properly and draw a deep breath. Nigel, hunched over Joyce, though she was immobile and spent and crying feebly, ordered him to make coffee.

"What did your last slave die of?" said Marty. "I'm sick and I'm not a bloody woman. She can make it."

"I'm not letting her out of my sight, no way," said Nigel.

So no one made any coffee, and no one went to sleep again before dawn. Once they heard the siren of a police car, but it was far away up on the North Circular. Marty lay across the foot of the mattress, holding his stomach. By the time the yellow lamps had faded to pinky-vermilion and gone out, by the time a few birds had begun to sing in the dusty planes of the churchyard, they had all fallen asleep in a spread-eagled pile, like casualties on a battlefield.

Bridey went down with a bag of empty cans and bottles before she went to work. The red-haired girl, who had been lying in wait for her, came out.

"Did you hear that funny carry-on in the night?"

"What sort of carry-on?" said Bridey cautiously.

"Well, I don't know," said the red-haired girl, "but there was something going on up the top. About half three. I woke up and I said to my fella, 'I thought I heard a shot,' I said. 'From upstairs,' I said. And then someone came down, walked all the way down and up again."

Bridey too had heard the shot, and she had heard a scream. For a moment she had thought of doing something about it, get even with that filthy-spoken bit of rubbish, that Marty. But doing something meant the police. Fetching the guards, it meant. No one in Bridey's troubled family history had ever done so treacherous a thing, not even for worthy motives of revenge.

"You were dreaming," said Bridey.

"That's what my fella said. 'You were dreaming,' he said. But I don't know. You know you sleep heavy, Bridey, and old Green's deaf as a post. I said to my fella, 'You don't reckon we ought to ring the fuzz, do you?' and he said,

'Never,' he said. 'You were dreaming.' But I don't know.
D'you reckon I ought to have rung the fuzz?"

"Never do that, my love," said Bridey. "What's in it for
you? Nothing but trouble. Never do that."

They would never get out now, Nigel thought, they
would just have to stick there. For weeks or months, he
didn't know how long, maybe until the money ran out. He
found he didn't dislike the idea. Not while he had that beautiful effective weapon. He nursed the gun as if it were a
cuddly toy or a small affectionate animal, his fear of losing it
to Marty, whose possession it was, keeping it always in his
hands. If Marty tried to take it from him, he thought he
would threaten Marty with it as he threatened Joyce, if necessary kill him. During that night, what with one thing and
another, something in Nigel that had always been fragile
and brittle had finally split. It was his sanity.

Looking at the gun, passionately admiring it, he thought
how they might have to stay in that room for years. Why
not? He liked the room, it had begun to be his home. They
would have to get things, of course. They could buy a fridge
and a TV. The men who brought them up the stairs could
be told to leave them on the landing. Joyce would do anything he said now, and there wouldn't be any more snappy
back answers from her. He could tell that from one glance
at her face. Not threats or privation or uncongenial company or separation from her family had broken her, but the
reality of the gun had. That was what it had been made for.

He would have two slaves now, for Marty looked as
shaken by what had happened as she did. One to shop and
run errands and one to cook and wait on him. He, Nigel,
wasn't broken or even shaken. He was on top of the world
and king of it.

"We need bread and tea bags and coffee," he said to Marty, "and a can of paraffin for the stove."

"Tomorrow," said Marty. "I'm sick."

"I'd be bloody sick if I boozed the way you do. While you're out you can go buy us a big fridge and a colour TV."

"Do what? You're crazy."

"Don't you call me crazy, little brain," shouted Nigel. "We've got to stay here, right? Thanks to her, we've got to stay here a long, long time. The three of us can stay here for years, I've got it all worked out. Once we've got a fridge you won't have to go out more than once a week. I don't like it, you going to the same shops over and over, shooting your mouth off to guys in shops, I know you. We'll all stay in here like I said and keep quiet and watch the TV. So you don't blue all our bread on fancy stuff, right? We go careful and we can live here two years, I've got it all worked out."

"No," Joyce whimpered. "No."

Nigel rounded on her. "Nobody's asking you, I'm telling you. If I get so much as a squeak out of you, you're dead. A bomb could go off in this place and they wouldn't hear. You know that, don't you? You've had the experience."

On Thursday morning Marty made a big effort and got as far as the corner shop. He bought a large white loaf and some cheese and two cans of beans, but he forgot the tea bags and the coffee. Carrying the paraffin would have been too much for him, he knew that, so he didn't even bother to take the can. Food didn't interest him, anyway, he couldn't keep a thing on his stomach. He had some whisky and retched. When he came back from the lavatory he said to Nigel:

"My pee's gone brown."

"So what? You've only got cystitis. You've irritated your bladder with the booze."

"I'm dead scared," said Marty. "You don't know how bad

I feel. Christ, I might die. Look at my face, my cheeks are
sort of fallen in. Look at my eyes."

Nigel didn't answer him. He sat cobbling for himself a
kind of holster made from a plastic jeans belt of Marty's and
a bit of towelling. He sewed it together with Joyce's brown
knitting wool while Joyce watched him. He needn't have
bothered, for Joyce would have died before she touched
that gun again. She had given up her knitting, she had given
up doing anything. She just sat or cringed on the sofa in a
daze. Nigel was happy. All the time he was doing mental
arithmetic, working out how much they would be able to
spend on food each week, how much on electricity and gas.
The summer was coming, he thought, so they wouldn't need
any heat. When the money ran out, he'd make Marty get a
job to keep them all.

The next day there was no paraffin left and no tea or butter or milk. The bookcase in the kitchen contained only a
spoonful of coffee in the bottom of the jar, half the cheese
Marty had bought and most of the bread, two cans of soup
and one of beans, and three eggs. The warm weather had
given place to a chilly white fog, and it was very cold in the
room. Nigel put the oven on full and lit all the burners,
angry because it would come expensive on the gas bill and
upset his calculations. But even he could see Marty was no
better, limp as a rag and dozing most of the time. He considered going out himself and leaving Marty with the gun.
Joyce wouldn't try anything, all the fight had gone out of
her. She was the way he had always wanted her to be,
cowed, submissive, trembling, dissolving into tears whenever he spoke to her. She made beans on toast for their supper without a murmur of protest while he stood over her
with the gun, and she gobbled her share up like a starving
caged animal which has had a lump of refuse thrown to it.
No, it wasn't the fear of her escaping that kept him from

going. It was the idea of having to relinquish even for ten
minutes—he could see from the kitchen window the corner
shop, open and brightly lit—the precious possession of the
gun.

That evening, while he was thinking about what kind and
what size of fridge they should buy, whether they could
afford a colour television or should settle for black and
white, Joyce spoke to him. It was the first time she had really spoken since she fired the gun.

"Nigel," she said in a small sad voice.

He looked up at her impatiently. Her hair hung lank and
her nails were dirty and she had a spot, an ugly eruption,
coming out at the corner of her mouth. Marty lay bundled
up, with all the blankets they possessed wrapped round him.
What a pair, he thought. A good thing they had him to manage them and tell them what to do.

"Yeah?" he said. "What?"

She put her hands together and bowed her head. "You
said," she whispered, "you said we could stay here for years.
Nigel, please don't keep me here, *please*. If you let me go I
won't say a word, I won't even speak. I'll pretend I've lost
my memory, I'll pretend I've lost my voice. They can't make
me speak! Please, Nigel. I'll do anything you want, but don't
keep me here."

He had won. His dream of what he might achieve with
her had come true. He smiled, raised his eyebrows, and
lightly shook his head. But he said nothing. Slowly he drew
the gun out of its holster and pointed it at her, releasing the
safety catch. Joyce rewarded him by shrinking, covering her
face with her hands, and bursting into tears. In a couple of
days, he thought, he'd have her pleading with him to be
nice to her, begging him to find her tasks to do for his comfort. He laughed then, remembering all the rudeness and in-
.sults he'd had to put up with from her. Without announcing

his intention, he switched the light off and stretched out on
the mattress beside Marty.

"You smell like a Chink meal," he said. "Sweet and sour.
Christ!"

Joyce couldn't sleep. She lay staring at the ceiling in despair. With a curious kind of intuition, for she had never
known any mad people, she sensed that Nigel was mad.
Sooner or later he would kill her and no one would ever
know, no one would hear the shot or care if they did, and
wounded perhaps, she would lie in that room till she died.
The thought of it made her cry loudly, she couldn't help
herself. She would never see her mother again or her father
and her brothers, or kiss Stephen or be held in his arms.
Nigel hissed at her to shut up and give them all a bit of
hush, so she cried quietly until the pillow was wet with tears
and, exhausted, she drifted off into dreams of home and of
sitting with Stephen in the Childon Arms and talking of
wedding plans.

Marty's anguished voice woke her. It was still dark.

"Nige," he said. He hardly ever used Nigel's name or its
ugly diminutive. "Nige, what's happening to me? I went out
to the bog and I had to crawl back on my hands and knees.
I can't hardly walk. My guts are on fire. My eyes have gone
yellow."

"First your pee, now your eyes. D'you know what the
bloody time is?"

"I went down the bathroom, I don't know how I made it.
I looked at myself in the mirror. I'm yellow all over, my
whole body's gone yellow. I'll have to go see the doc."

That woke Nigel fully. He lurched out of bed, the gun
hanging in its holster against his naked side. He stood over
Marty and gripped his shoulders.

"Are you out of your goddamned mind?"

Marty made noises like a beaten puppy. Sweat was

streaming down his face The blankets were wet with sweat, but he was shivering.

"I'll have to," he said, his teeth chattering. "I've got to do something." He met Nigel's cold glittering eyes, and they made him cry out, "You wouldn't let me die, Nige? Nige, I might die. You wouldn't let me die?"

He could hear her talking to Caesar outside the room. She must have gone out to the bathroom. He looked at his watch. Half-past seven. He was embarrassed because Caesar had seen her—dressed in what? the bedspread that he saw was missing?—and he was afraid of Caesar's censure because all his life every friend or acquaintance or relative had appeared to him in the guise of critical authority. She came back and stepped naked out of wrappings of red candlewick, and into his arms.

"What did he say to you?" Alan whispered.

" 'Good luck, my darling,' " said Una, and she giggled.

"I love you," he said. "You're the only woman I ever made love to apart from my wife."

"I don't believe it!"

"Why would I say it, then? It's nothing to be proud of."

"Well, but Paul, it is *quite* amazing."

A horrid thought struck him. "And you?"

"I never made love to any women."

"You know I don't mean that. Men."

"Oh, not so many, but more than *that*."

And a horrider one. "Not Ambrose?"

"Silly, you are. Ambrose is a celibate. He says that at his age you should have experienced all the sex you need and you must turn your energy to the life of the mind."

" 'Leave me, O Love, that reachest but to dust.' "

"Well, I don't think it does. I really think it reacheth to

much nicer things than that. You know, it wasn't just incredulity that made me say it was quite amazing."

He considered. He blushed. "Honestly?"

"Honestly. But if it's true, what you said, don't you think you need some more practice? Like now?"

That was the best week he had ever known.

He took Una to the theatre and he took her out to dinner. They hired a car. They had to hire it in her name because he was Paul Browning who had left his licence at home in Cricklewood. Driving up into Hertfordshire, they played the lovers' game of looking at houses and discussing whether this one or that one would best suit them to live in for the rest of their lives. He already knew that he wanted to live with her. The idea of even a brief separation was unthinkable. He couldn't keep his eyes off her, and the memory that he had told Caesar he didn't find her attractive was a guilty reproach, though she would never know of it. The word, anyway, was inadequate to describe the effect she had on him. He was glad now that she didn't wear make-up or dress well, for these things would have been an obscuring of herself. More than anything, he liked to watch the play of emotion in her face, that small intense face that screwed itself into deep lines of dismay or surprise, and relaxed to a child's smoothness with delight.

"Paul," she said gently, "the lights are green. We can go."

"I'm sorry. I can't keep from looking at you. I do look at the road while I'm driving."

When they got home that night and were in his room—she slept with him every night in his room—she asked him about his wife.

"What's her name?"

"Alison," he said. He had to say that because he was Paul Browning.

"That's nice. You haven't told me if you've got any children."

He thought of dead Lucy, who had never been mentioned between them. How many children had Paul Browning? In this case there could be no harm in telling the truth. "I've got two, a boy and a girl. They're more or less grown up. I was married very young." Not just to change the subject, but because a greater truth, never before realised, came suddenly to him, "I was a very bad father," he said. Of course he had been, a bad father, a bad husband, whose energies went, not into giving love, but to indulging in self-pity. "They won't miss me."

Una looked at him with a wistfulness in which there was much trepidation. "You said you wanted to live with me."

"So I do! More than anything in the world. I can't imagine life without you now."

She nodded. "You can't imagine it but you could live it. Will you tell Alison about me?"

He said lightly, because "Alison" merely conjured for him an unknown blond woman in Cricklewood, "I don't suppose so. What does it matter?"

"I think it matters if you're serious."

So he took her in his arms and told her his love for her was the most serious thing that had ever happened to him. Alison was nothing, had been nothing for years. He would support her, of course, and do everything that was honourable, but as for seeing her and talking to her, no. He piled lie upon lie and Una believed him and smiled and they were happy.

Or he would have been happy, have enjoyed unalloyed happiness, had it not been for Joyce. The man he had seen in the Rose of Killarney was certainly not the man who had asked him for twenty five-pence pieces for a pound and therefore not one of the men who had raided the bank and

kidnapped Joyce. True, they both had mutilated forefingers
on their right hands, but those mutilations were quite
different, the men were quite different. And yet the sight of
that man, or really the sight of that finger, so similar to the
other and so evocative, had reawakened all his conscience
about Joyce and all his shame. The bitterness of love unat-
tained had kept that guilt at bay, the happiness of love tri-
umphant had temporarily closed his mind to it, but it was
back now, weighing on him by day, prodding him in the
night.

"Is Joyce your daughter's name?" Una asked him.

"No. Why?"

"You kept calling that name in the night. You called,
'Joyce, it's all right, I'm here.'"

"I knew a girl called Joyce once."

"It was as if you were talking to a frightened child," said
Una.

He should have done something in the Rose of Killarney,
he thought, to make the boy speak. It would have been
quite easy. He could have asked him where the buses went
or the way to the nearest Tube station. And then when he
had heard the ordinary North London voice he would have
known for sure and wouldn't be haunted like this. He understood now why he was haunted. The sight of that finger had
brought him fear, disbelief, a need to react against it by pretending to himself that the similarity was an illusion—but it
had also brought him hope. Hope that somehow this could
open a way to redeeming himself, to vindicating himself for
what he had done in leaving Joyce to her fate.

On Friday morning he locked his door and took out
the money and counted it. He could hardly believe that he
had got through, in this short time, nearly two hundred
pounds. Without really appalling him, the discovery
brought home to him how small a sum three thousand

pounds actually was. Since finding Una, he was no longer content vaguely to envisage one crowded hour of glorious life with disgrace or death at the end of it. He had known her for a week and he wanted a lifetime with her. He would have to get a job, something that didn't need credentials or qualifications or a National Insurance card. Optimistically, not doubtfully or desperately at all, he thought of taking her away from London and working as a gardener or a decorator or even a window cleaner.

The door handle turned. "Paul?"

He thrust the money back into the drawer and went to let Una in.

"You'd locked your door." Her eyes met his in bewildered rejection, and in that look of fear, of distrust, she suddenly seemed to him to represent other women that he had disappointed, that he had failed, Pam and Joyce. Trying to think of an explanation for that locked door, he understood that here was something else which eluded explanation. But she didn't ask. "I've had a letter from Ambrose," she said. "He's coming home on Saturday week."

Alan nodded. He was rather pleased. Somehow he felt that hope for them lay with Ambrose Engstrand, though he didn't know why or in what form. Perhaps it was only that he thought of the philosopher as prepared to do anything to ensure Una's happiness.

"I don't want to be here when he comes back," Una said.

"But why not?"

"I don't know. I'm afraid—I'm afraid he'll spoil this." She moved her hand in an embracing gesture to contain her and himself and the room. "You don't know him," she said. "You don't know how he can probe and question and get hold of things that are beautiful and—well, fragile—and make them mundane. He does it because he thinks it's for the best, but I don't, not always."

"There's nothing fragile about my feeling for you."

"What's in that drawer, Paul? What were you doing that you had to lock me out?"

"Nothing," he said. "It was force of habit."

She made no acknowledgement of this. "I felt," she said, "I thought you might have things of your wife's there, of Alison's. Letters, photographs, I don't know." She gave him a look of fear. Not the kind of fear that is based on imaginings and has in it a counterweight of hope, but settled despair. "You'll go back to Alison."

"I'll never do that. Why do you say that?"

"Because you never see her. You never communicate with her."

"I don't follow that logic."

"It is logic, Paul. You'd phone her, you'd write to her, you'd go and see her, if you weren't afraid that once you'd seen her you'd go back. With me and Stewart it's different. I haven't seen him for months but he'll turn up, he always does. And we'll talk and discuss things and not care because we're indifferent. You're not indifferent to your wife. You daren't see her or hear her voice."

"D'you *want* me to see her?"

"Yes. How can I feel I'm important to you if you won't tell her about me? I'm a holiday for you, I'm an adventure you'll look back on and sentimentalise about when you're back with Alison. Isn't it true? Oh God, if you went to see her I'd go mad, I'd be sick with fear you wouldn't come back. But when you did, if you did, I'd know where we were."

He put his arms round her and kissed her. It was all nonsense to him, a fabric of chimeras based on nothing. Fleetingly he thought of Alison Browning with her husband and her little boy and her puppy and her nice house.

"I'll do anything you want," he said. "I'll write to her today."

"Ambrose," she murmured, "would be so angry with me. He'd say I'd no precedent for reasoning the way I do about you and Alison except what I'd got out of books. He'd say we should never conjecture about things we've no experience of."

"And he'd be so right!" said Alan. "I said he was a monster, but I'm not so sure. I wish you'd let me meet him."

"No."

"All right. I don't meet him and I write to Alison today, now. Will that make you happy, my darling? I'll write my letter and then we'll hire the car again and I'll take you out to Windsor for lunch."

She smiled at him, thrusting back her hair with both hands. "The lights are green and we can go?"

"Wherever you want," he said.

She left him alone to write the letter, and this time he didn't lock the door. He had nothing to hide from her because he really did write a letter beginning "Dear Alison." It gave him a curious pleasure to write Una's name and to describe her and explain that he loved her and she loved him. He even addressed the envelope to Mrs. Alison Browning, 15 Exmoor Gardens, N.W.2, in case Una should catch sight of it as he passed through the hall on his way to the post.

His pillar box was a litter bin. He tore the envelope and the letter inside it into pieces and dropped them into the bin, noticing that the last scrap to go was that on which he had written the postal district, Northwest Two. Not half a mile away from Alison's house he had seen the boy with the mutilated finger. Suppose he had asked him that question about the buses and the Tube and had got an answer and the voice answering had been Suffolk-cockney? What next?

What could he have done? Written an anonymous letter to
the police, he thought, or, better than that, made an anonymous phone call. They would have acted on that, they
wouldn't dare not to. Why hadn't he made the boy speak? It
was the obvious thing to have done and it would have been
so easy, so easy. . . .

Walking back to Montcalm Gardens and Una, he was
forced to ask himself something that made him wince. Had
he kept silent and fed his incredulity and condemned his
overactive imagination because he didn't *want* to know? Because all that talk of redemption and vindication was nonsense. He didn't want to know because he didn't want Joyce
found. Because if Joyce were found alive she would immediately tell the police he hadn't been in the bank, he hadn't
been kidnapped, and they would hunt for him and find him
and take him away from freedom and happiness and Una.

"You haven't even got a goddamned doctor," said Nigel.

But there he was wrong, for Marty had needed a doctor in the days when he had worked. Medical certificates had frequently been required for imaginary gastritis or nervous debility or depression.

"Course I have," said Marty. "Yid up Chichele." He clutched his stomach and moaned. "I got to see him and get some of them antibiotics or whatever."

Nigel wrapped a blanket round himself and padded out and lit the oven. He contemplated the bookcase: half a dozen slices of stale bread, two cans of soup and three eggs, four bottles of whisky and maybe eighty cigarettes. Having made a face to these last items, he squatted down to warm himself at the open oven. He didn't want Marty coming into contact with any form of official authority, and into this category the doctor would come. On the other hand, the doctor would reassure Marty—Nigel was sure there was nothing really wrong with him—and that ignorant peasant was just the type to start feeling better the minute anyone gave him a pill. Aspirin would cure him, Nigel thought derisively, provided it came in a bottle labelled tetracycline. He wanted Marty fit again and biddable, his link and go-between with the outside world, but he didn't want him shooting his mouth off to this doctor about not needing a medical certificate, thanks, and his mate he was sharing with who'd look after him and the girl they'd got staying with them and whatever. Above all, he didn't want this doctor remembering that last time he'd seen him Marty had sported a bushy beard like the guy who had hired the van in Croydon.

A groan from the mattress fetched him back into the living room. Joyce was sitting up, looking warily at Marty. Nigel took no notice of her. He said to Marty, not too harshly for him:

"Give it another day and keep off the booze. If your belly's still freaking you tomorrow, I reckon you'll have to go see the doctor. We'll like wait and see."

They had bread and the last of the cheese for lunch, and a tin of scotch broth and the three eggs for supper. Marty didn't eat anything, but Nigel, who wasn't usually a big eater, felt ravenous and had two of the eggs himself. The main advantage of getting Marty to the doctor would mean that he could do their shopping on his way back. A lot more cans, thought Nigel hungrily, and a couple of large loaves and milk and butter and some of that Indian takeaway, Vindaloo curry and dhal and rice and lime pickle. He wanted Marty to go to the doctor now, he was almost as keen as Marty himself had been on Thursday night.

He didn't seem keen any more when Nigel woke him at eight in the morning.

"Come on, get dressed," he said to Marty. "Have a bit of a wash too if you don't want to gas the guy."

Marty groaned and rolled over, turning up the now yellow whites of his eyes. "I don't reckon I've got the strength. I'll just lay here a bit. That'll be better in a day or two."

"Look, we said if your belly's still freaking you you'd go see the doctor, right? You get down there now and do our shopping on the way back. You can do it at the corner shops, you don't need to go down the Broadway."

Marty crawled off the mattress and into the kitchen, where he ran water over his hands and slopped a little onto

his face. The kitchen walls and floor were moving and slanting like in a crazy house at a fair. He took a swig of whisky
to steady himself and managed to struggle into his clothes. It
didn't help that Joyce, sitting up on the sofa with the blanket cocooned around her, was watching him almost with
compassion or as if she were genuinely afraid he might fall
down dead any minute.

An icy mist, thick, white, and still, greeted him when he
opened the front door. It wasn't far to Dr. Miskin's, not
more than a couple of hundred yards, but it felt more like
five miles to Marty, who clung to lampposts as he staggered
along and finally had to sit down on the stone steps of a
chapel. There he was found by a policeman on the beat.
Marty felt too ill to care about being spoken to by a policeman, and the policeman could see he was ill, not drunk.

"You're not fit to be out in this," said the policeman.

"On my way to the doc," said Marty.

"Best place for you. Here, I'll give you a hand."

So Marty Foster was conducted into Dr. Miskin's waiting
room on the kindly arm of the law.

Nigel knew Marty would be quite a long time because he
hadn't made an appointment. That sort of morning surgery—
he knew all about it from the giving if not the receiving end
—could well go on till noon, so he didn't get worried. Marty
would be back by lunchtime with some food. He was hungry and Joyce kept whimpering that she was hungry, but so
what? Nobody got malnutrition because they hadn't eaten
for twelve hours.

At one o'clock they shared the can of chicken soup, eating
it cold because it was thicker and more filling that way.
There was now no food left. Marty was fool enough, Nigel
thought, to have taken his prescription to a chemist who
closed for lunch. That would be it. He had gone to the

chemist at five to one, and now he was having to wait till
two when they opened again. Probably wouldn't even have
the sense to do the shopping in the meantime.

"Suppose he doesn't come back?" said Joyce.

"You missing him, are you? I didn't know you cared."

The mist had gone and it was a beautiful clear day, sunshine making the room quite warm. Soon they could stop
using any heat, and when the fridge came and the TV . . .
Nigel saw himself lounging on the sofa with a long glass of
martini and crushed ice in his hand, watching a film in glorious colour, while Joyce washed his clothes and polished his
shoes and grilled him a steak. Half-past two. Any time now
and that little brain would be back. If he'd had the sense to
take a couple of pills straightaway he might be fit enough to
get down to the electrical discount shop before it closed.

Nigel told himself he was standing by the window because it was nice to feel a bit of sun for a change. He
watched old Green coming back from the Broadway with
shopping in a string bag. He saw a figure turning into the
street from Chichele Road, and for a minute he thought it
was Marty, the jeans, the leather jacket, the pinched bony
face, and the cropped hair. It wasn't.

"Watching for him won't bring him," said Joyce, who was
forcing herself, rather feebly, to knit once more.

"I'm not watching for him."

"He's been gone nearly seven hours."

"So what?" Nigel shouted at her. "Is it any goddamned
business of yours? He's got things to get, hasn't he? Him and
me, we can't sit about on our arses all day."

They both jumped at the sound of the phone. Nigel said,
"You come down with me," pointing the gun, but by the
time they were out on the landing the bell had stopped. No
one had come up from the lower floors of the house. In the
heavy warm silence, Nigel propelled Joyce back into the

room and they sat down again. Past three and Marty hadn't come.

"I'm hungry," Joyce said.

"Shut up."

Nothing happened for an hour, two hours. Although Nigel had turned off the oven, the heat was growing oppressive, for the room faced west. If the police had got Marty, Nigel thought, they would have been here by now. But he couldn't still be wandering about Cricklewood with a prescription, could he? The knitting fell from Joyce's fingers, and her head went back and she dozed. With a jerk she came to herself again, and seeing that neither Nigel nor the gun were putting up any opposition, she dragged herself over to the mattress and lay down on it. She pulled the covers over her and buried her face.

Nigel stood at the window. It was half-past five and the sun was going down into a red mist. There were a lot of people about, but no Marty. Nigel felt hollow inside, and not just from hunger. He started to pace the room, looking sometimes at Joyce, hating her for sleeping, for not caring what happened. Presently he took advantage of her sleeping to go out to the lavatory.

The phone screamed at him.

He left the door wide open and ran down. Keeping the gun turned on that open door, he picked up the receiver. Pip-pip-pip, then the sound of money going in and, Christ, Marty's voice.

"What the hell goes?" Nigel hissed.

"Nige, I rung before but no one answered. Listen, I'm in hospital."

"Jesus."

"Yeah, listen. I'm really sick, Nige. I got hepa- something, something with my liver. That's why I'm all yellow."

"Hepatitis."

"That's him, hepatitis. I passed out in the doc's and they brought me here. God knows how I got it, the doctor don't know, maybe from all that takeaway. They give me the phone trolley to phone you and they want my gear brought in. They want a razor, Nige, and a *toothbrush* and I don't know what. I wouldn't tell them who you was or where and . . ."

"*You've got to get out right now.* You've got to split like this minute. Right?"

"Are you kidding? I can't bloody walk. I got to be in here a week, that's what they say, and you're to bring . . ."

"Shut up! Will you for fuck's sake shut up? You've got to get dressed and get a taxi and come right back here. Can't you get it in your thick head we've got no food?"

Pip-pip-pip.

"I haven't got no more change, Nige."

Nigel bellowed into the phone, "Get dressed and get a taxi and come home *now*. If you don't, Christ, I'll get you if it's the last . . ." The phone went dead and the dialling tone started. Nigel closed his eyes. He leant against the bathroom door. Then he trailed upstairs again. Joyce woke up, coming to herself at once as she always did.

"What's happening?"

"Marty got held up. He'll be here in an hour."

But would he? He always did what he was told, but that was when he was here in this room. Would he when he was miles away in a hospital bed? Nigel realised he didn't even know what hospital, he hadn't asked. He heard the diesel throb of a taxi from the street below several times in the next hour. Joyce washed her face and hands and looked at the empty bookcase and drank some water.

"What's happened to him? He isn't going to come, is he?"

"He'll come."

Joyce said, "He was ill. He went to the doctor's. I bet he's in hospital."

"I told you, he's coming back tonight."

When it got to ten, Nigel knew for certain that Marty wouldn't come. He came back from the window where he had been standing for an hour, and turning to look at Joyce, he found that her eyes were fixed on him. Her eyes were animal-like and full of panic. He and she were alone together now, each the prisoner of the other. He had never seen her look so frightened, but instead of gratifying him, her fear made him frightened too. He no longer wanted her as his slave, he wanted her dead, but he heard the red-haired girl on the phone and then Bridey coming in, and he only fingered the gun, keeping the safety catch on.

Sunday passed very slowly, beginning and ending in fog with hot spring sunshine in between. Nigel thought Marty would phone in the morning, would be bound to, if only to go in for more bloody silly nonsense about having a toothbrush brought in. And when he did, he, Nigel, would find out just what hospital he was in, and then he'd phone for a mini-cab and send it round to fetch Marty out. He couldn't believe that Marty would defy him.

When it got to the middle of the afternoon and Marty hadn't phoned, Nigel's stomach was roaring hunger at him. The bookcase cupboard was bare but for the four bottles of whisky and the eighty cigarettes. For the sake of the nourishment, Nigel drank some whisky in hot water, but it knocked him sideways and he was afraid to repeat the experiment in case he passed out. Most of the time he stood by the window, no longer watching for Marty but eyeing the corner shop, which he could see quite clearly and whose interior, with its delicatessen counter and rack of Greek bread and shelves and shelves of cans and jars, he could recall

from previous visits. Pointing the gun at Joyce, he forced
her to swallow some neat whisky in an attempt to render her
unconscious. She obeyed because she was so frightened of
the gun. Or, rather, her will obeyed but not her body. She
gagged and threw up and collapsed weeping on the mattress.

Nigel had been thinking, when he wasn't simply thinking
about the taste and smell and texture of food, of ways to tie
her up. He could gag her and tie her hands and feet and
then somehow anchor her to the gas stove. "Somehow" was
the word. How? In order to begin he would have to put the
gun down. Nevertheless, late in the afternoon, he tried it,
seizing her from behind and clamping his hand over her
mouth. Joyce fought him, biting and kicking, tearing herself
away from him to crouch and cower behind the sofa. Nigel
swore at her. She was only a few inches shorter than he and
probably as heavy. Without Marty's assistance, he was pow-
erless.

Bridey went out, old Green went out most days. Nigel
thought of telling one of them he was ill and getting them to
fetch him in some food. But he couldn't cover Joyce with
the gun while he was doing so. If he left Joyce she would
break the windows, if he took her with him—that didn't bear
considering. He could knock her out. Yes, and if he went at
it too heavily he'd be left with a sick girl on his hands, too
lightly and she'd come to before he got back.

The shop was so near he could easily have struck its windows if he had thrown a stone. His mouth kept filling with
saliva and he kept swallowing it down into his empty
stomach.

By Monday morning Nigel knew Marty wasn't going to
phone or come back. He didn't think he would ever come
back now. Even when they let him out of hospital he
wouldn't come back. He'd go and hide out with his mother

and forget about his share of the money and the two people he'd abandoned.

"What are we going to do for food?" Joyce said.

Nigel was forced to plead with her. It was to be the first of many times. "Look, I can get us food, if you'll guarantee not to scream or try and get out."

She looked at him stonily.

"Five minutes while I go down to the shop."

"No," said Joyce.

"Why don't you fuck off?" Nigel shouted. "Why don't you starve to death?"

Alan happened to be in the hall when the phone rang. Una was in the kitchen, getting their lunch. He picked up the phone and said, "Sorry, you've got the wrong number," when a man's voice asked if he was Lloyd's Bank. Maybe if he'd been asked if he was the Anglian-Victoria he would have said yes out of force of habit.

"Who was that on the phone?" said Una.

"Alison."

"Oh."

"She wants to see me . . ." It was the only excuse he could think of for getting himself up to Cricklewood without Una. Wherever he went she went, and he wanted it that way, only not this time. "She was quite all right, nice, in fact," he said with an effort. "I said I'd go over and see her this afternoon."

Una, who had been looking a little dismayed, the flow of her vitality checked, suddenly smiled. "I'm *so* glad, Paul. That makes me feel real. Be kind to her, won't you? Be generous. D'you know, I pity her so much, I feel for her so. I keep thinking how, if it was me, I couldn't bear to lose you."

"You never will," he said.

He had dreamed in the night of the boy with the mutilated finger. In the dream he was alone with the boy in the room at the bank where the safe was, and he was desperately trying to make him speak. He was bribing him to

speak with offers of bank notes which he removed, wad by
wad, from the safe. And the boy was taking the money,
stuffing it into his pockets and down the front of his jacket,
but all the time the boy remained silent, staring at him. At
last Alan came very close to him to see why he didn't speak,
and he saw that the boy couldn't speak, his mouth wouldn't
open, for the lips were fused together and cobbled like the
kernel of a walnut.

When he awoke and reached for Una to touch her and lie
close up against her, the dream and the guilt it carried with
it wouldn't go away. He kept telling himself that the boy in
the pub couldn't be the same as the boy who had come into
the bank and who later had robbed the bank, the coincidence would be too great. Yet when he examined this, he
saw that there wasn't so very much of a coincidence at all.
In the past three weeks he had wandered all over London.
He had been in dozens of pubs and restaurants and cafes and
bars. Nearly all the time he had been out and about, explor-
ing and observing. Very likely, if that boy was also a frequenter of pubs and eating places, sooner or later they would
have encountered each other. And if the boy turned out to
be a different boy, which was the way he wanted it to be,
which was what he longed to know for certain, there would
be no coincidence at all. It would be just that he was very
sensitive to that particular kind of deformity of a finger.
What he really wanted was for someone to tell him that the
boy was an ordinary decent citizen of Cricklewood, out
doing some emergency Sunday-morning shopping for his
wife or his mother, and when he spoke it would be with a
brogue as Irish as that barmaid's.

It was just before the phone rang that the idea came to
him of going back to the Rose of Killarney and asking the
barmaid if she knew who the boy was. Just possibly she
might know because it looked as if the boy lived locally.

Surely you wouldn't go a journey to do Sunday-morning shopping, would you, when there was bound to be a shop open in your own neighbourhood? Even if she didn't know, he would have tried, he thought. He would have done his best and not have to fail this shame and self-disgust at doing nothing because he was afraid of what might happen if Joyce were found. He should have thought of that, he told himself with bravado, before he hid and left her to her fate and escaped.

It was half-past one when he walked into the Rose of Killarney. There were about a dozen people in the saloon bar, but the boy with the distorted finger wasn't among them. All the way up in the bus Alan had been wondering if he might be, but of course he wouldn't, he'd be at work. Behind the bar was the Irish girl, looking sullen and tired. Alan asked her for a half of bitter and when it came he said hesitantly:

"I don't suppose you happen to know"—it seemed to him that she was looking at him with a kind of incredulous disgust—"the name of the young man who was in here last Sunday week?" Was it really as long ago as that? The distance in time seemed to add to the absurdity of the enquiry. "Early twenties, dark, clean-shaven," he said. He held up his own right hand, grasping the forefinger in his left. "His finger . . ." he was beginning when she interrupted him.

"You the police?"

A more self-confident man might have agreed that he was. Alan, trying to think up an excuse for wanting a stranger's name and address, disclaimed any connection with the law and thrust his hand into his pocket, seeking inspiration. All he could produce was a five-pound note, a portrait of the Duke of Wellington.

"He dropped this as he was leaving."

"You took your time about it," said the girl.

"I've been away."

She said quickly, greedily, "Sure and I'll give it him. Foster's his name, Marty Foster, I know him well."

The note was snatched from his fingers. He began to insist, "If you could just tell me . . . ?"

"Don't you trust me, then?"

He shrugged, embarrassed. Several pairs of eyes were fixed on him. He got down off his stool and went out. If the girl knew him well, spoke of him therefore as a frequenter of the pub, he couldn't be Joyce's kidnapper, could he? Alan knew he could, that all that meant nothing. But at least he had the name, Foster, Marty Foster. What he could do now was phone the police and give them Marty Foster's name and describe him. He crossed the road and went into a phone box and looked in the directory. There was no police station listed for Cricklewood. Of course he could phone Scotland Yard. A superstitious fear took hold of him that as soon as he spoke they would know at once where he was and who he was. He came hurriedly out of the phone box and began to walk away in the direction of Exmoor Gardens, towards Alison, where he was supposed to be, and looked for another phone box in a less exposed and vulnerable place.

By the time he had found it he knew he wasn't going to make that call. It was more important to him that the police shouldn't track him down than that they should be alerted to hunt for a Marty Foster who very likely had no connection at all with the Childon bank robbery. So he continued to walk aimlessly and to think. In the little shopping parade among the ovals named after mountain ranges, he went into a newsagent's and bought an evening paper. As far as he could see, there was nothing in it about Joyce. At three-fifteen he thought he might reasonably go back to Una now,

and he retraced his steps to Cricklewood Broadway to wait
for a bus going south.

The bus was approaching and he was holding out his
hand to it when he saw the girl from the Rose of Killarney.
She had come out of a side door of the pub, and crossing the
Broadway, walked off down a side street. Alan let the bus
go. He thought, maybe she'll go straight to this Foster's
home with the money, that's what I'd do, that's what any
honest person would do, and then he gave a little dry laugh
to himself at what he had said. He followed her across the
road, wishing there were more people about, not just the
two of them apparently, once the shopping place and the
bus routes were left behind. But she didn't look round. She
walked with assurance, cutting corners, crossing streets diag-
onally. Suddenly there were more shops, a launderette, a
Greek delicatessen; on the opposite side a church in a
churchyard full of plane trees, on this a row of red-brick
houses, three storeys high. The girl turned in at the gate of
one of them.

Alan hurried, but by the time he reached the gate the girl
had disappeared. He read the names above the bells and
saw that the topmost one was M. Foster. Had Foster himself
let her in? Or had it been the mother or wife with whom his
imagination had earlier invested the man with the mutilated
finger? He crossed the road and stood by the low wall of the
churchyard to wait for her. And then? Once she had left,
was he also going to ring that bell? Presumably. He hadn't
come as far as this to abandon his quest and go tamely
home.

Time passed very slowly. He pretended to read the notice
board and then really read it for something to do. He
walked up the street as far as he could go while keeping the
house in sight, and then he walked back again and as far in
the other direction. He went into the churchyard and even

examined the church, which he was sure was of no architectural merit whatsoever. Still the girl hadn't come out, though by now half an hour had gone by.

M. Foster's was the topmost bell. Did that mean he lived on the top floor? It might not mean that he occupied the whole of the top floor. For the first time Alan lifted his eyes to the third storey of the house with its three oblong windows. A young man was standing up against the glass, immobile, flaccid, somehow even from that distance and through that glass giving an impression of a kind of hopeless indolence. But he wasn't Foster. His hair was blond. Alan stopped staring at him and, making up his mind, he went back across the road and rang that bell.

Nobody came down. He rang the bell again, more insistently this time, but he felt sure it wasn't going to be answered. On an impulse he pressed the one below it, B. Flynn.

The last person he expected to see was the barmaid from the Rose of Killarney. Her appearance at the door, not in her outdoor coat but with a cup of tea in one hand and a cigarette in the other, made him feel that he had walked into one of those nightmares—familiar to him these days—in which the irrational is commonplace and identities bizarrely interchangeable.

She said nothing and he had no idea what to say. They stared at each other and as he became aware that she was frightened, that in her look was awe and fear and repulsion, she put her hand into the pocket of her trousers and pulled out the five-pound note.

"Take your money." She thrust it at him. "I've done nothing. Will you leave me alone?" Her voice trembled. "Give it him yourself if that's what you're wanting."

Alan still couldn't understand, but he questioned, "He does live here?"

"On the top, next to me. Him and his pal." She began to
retreat, rubbing her hands as if to erase the contamination
of that money from them. The cigarette hung from her
mouth.

Alan knew she thought he was the police in spite of his
denial. She thought he was a policeman playing tricks. "Listen," he said. "How does he talk? Has he got an accent?"

She threw the cigarette end into the street. "Bloody English like you," she said, and closed the door.

Una was waiting for him in the hall. The front door had
yielded under the pressure of his hand, she had left it on the
latch, presumably so that she could the more easily keep
running out to see if he were coming.

She rushed up to him. "You were so long." She sounded
breathless. "I was worried."

"It's only just gone five," he said vaguely.

"Did you have a bad time with Alison?"

He had almost forgotten who Alison was. It seemed ridiculous to him that Una should be concerned about that
happy secure woman who had nothing to do with him or
her, but he seized on what might have happened that afternoon as an excuse for his preoccupation.

"She was quite reasonable and calm and nice," he said,
and he added, not thinking this time of Paul Browning's
wife, "She thinks I shouldn't have left. She says I've ruined
her life."

Una said nothing. He followed her through the big house
to the kitchen, where she began to busy herself making tea
for him. Her flying-fox face was puckered so that the lines
on it seemed to presage the wrinkles of age. He put his arms
round her.

"What is it?"

"Did it make you unhappy, seeing Alison?"

"Not a bit. Let's forget her." He held Una tight, thinking what a bore it was, all this pretence. He was going to have to fabricate so much, interviews with solicitors, financial arrangements. Why had he ever said he was married? Una was herself married, so the question of marriage between them couldn't have arisen. It seemed to him that she must have read at least some part of his thoughts, for she moved a little aside from him and said:

"I heard from Stewart. By the second post."

She gave him the letter. It was happy and affectionate. Stewart said he had had a call from his father all about her and her new man, and why didn't she and her Paul go and live in the cottage on Dartmoor?

"Could we, please, Paul?"

"I don't know . . ."

"We could just go and see if you liked it. I could write to the woman in the village who looks after it and get her to air it and warm it, and we could be there by the weekend. Ambrose'll be home on Saturday but I'd leave the house *immaculate* for him. He won't mind my not being here, he'll be glad to be rid of me at last. Paul, can we?"

"I'll do whatever you want," he said. "You know that."

He began to drink the tea she had made him. She sat opposite him at the table, her elbows on it, her chin in her hands, her eyes sparkling with anticipation. He smiled back at her and his smile was full of tenderness, yet much as he loved being with her, much as he wanted to share his whole life with her, he wished then that he could briefly be alone. It was impossible. There would be a cruelty in broaching it, he thought, after he had supposedly been all those hours with his wife. But he longed very much for solitude in which to think about what course of action next to take.

Una began talking to him about Dartmoor and the cottage itself. It would be a good place to hide in, he thought, after he had phoned the police and they had rescued Joyce and Joyce had told them the truth about him. They would never look for him in a private house in so remote a place. But before he could phone and certainly before he could leave, he must have more information. He must know for sure that Joyce's kidnapper, the boy whose walnut-nailed finger had scooped up the change, and Marty Foster were one and the same.

"Shall we go on Friday?" said Una.

He nodded. It gave him three days.

As their eyes met across the table, his troubled, hers excited, anxious, hopeful, some twenty miles to the south of them John Purford's aircraft was touching down at Gatwick.

21

Nigel and Marty had never thought of counting the notes they had stolen. They would only have done so if the question of dividing it had come up. Soon after he awoke on the morning of Tuesday, 26 March, after he had drunk some warm water, Nigel took the money out, spread it on the kitchen table, and counted it. He didn't know how much they had spent but there was over four thousand left—four thousand and fifteen pounds, to be precise. The amount they had taken, therefore, had been somewhat in excess of what he had supposed. He divided it into two equal sums and tied up each of the resultant wads with a black stocking. Then he put them back into the bag with the bunch of Ford Escort keys.

He and Joyce had eaten nothing since the chicken soup at midday on Saturday, and not much for two days before that. Nigel was no longer hungry. Nor did he feel particularly weak or tired, only light-headed. The visions of a future in which he dominated Joyce had been replaced by even more highly coloured ones in which he had Marty at his mercy in some mediaeval torture chamber. He saw himself in a black cloak and hood, tearing out Marty's fingernails with red-hot pincers. Once he was out of there he was going to get Marty, hunt him if necessary to the ends of the earth, and then he was going to come back and finish Joyce. He didn't know whom he hated most, Joyce or Marty, but he hated them more than he hated his parents. The former had succeeded the latter as responsible for all his troubles.

Since Sunday Joyce had spent most of the time lying on the sofa. She hadn't washed or combed her hair or cleaned her teeth. Dust lay everywhere once more and the bed linen smelt sour. Once she had understood that Marty wasn't coming back, that she was alone with Nigel, that there wasn't going to be anything to eat, she had retreated into a zombielike apathy, a kind of fugue, from which she was briefly aroused only by the ringing of the doorbell on Monday afternoon. She had wanted to know who it was and had tried to get to the window, but Nigel had caught her and thrown her back, his hand over her mouth. And then they had both faintly heard a bell ringing in the next room and Bridey going downstairs, and she had known to her despair what Nigel had known to his relief, that it had only been some salesman or canvasser at the door.

On the following morning it was nearly twelve before she dragged herself to the kitchen and, having drunk a cup of water, leant back against the sink, her face going white. When she drank water she could always feel the shock of it, teasingly trickling down, tracing its whole passage through her intestines. She hadn't looked directly at Nigel, much less spoken to him, since Monday morning, for whenever she allowed her eyes to meet his it only brought on a spasm of hysterical crying. Twice a day perhaps she would go limply towards the door, and Nigel would take this as a signal to escort her to the lavatory. She was weak and broken, a butt for Nigel's occasional violence. She believed that everything had been destroyed in her, for she no longer thought with longing or anguish of Stephen or her parents, or of escape or of keeping herself decent and nice. Aeons seemed to have passed since she had been defiant and bold. She was starving to death, as Nigel had told her to, and she supposed—for this was all she thought of now—that she would grow weaker and weaker and less and less conscious of herself and her surroundings until finally she did die. She walked to the door and waited there until Nigel slouched over to take her outside.

When they were both back in the room, Nigel spoke to her. He spoke her name. She made no answer. He didn't use her name again, it was almost painful to him to bring it out, but said:

"We can't stay here. You said once, you said if we let you go you wouldn't talk to the police."

Stress and starvation had taken from Nigel's speech that disc-jockey drawl and those eclectic idioms, and tones of public school and university reasserted themselves. Joyce wondered vaguely at the voice, which was beautiful and like someone in a serious play on the television, but she hardly took in the sense of the words. Nigel repeated them and went on:

"If you meant that, straight up, we can get out of here." He looked at her hard, his eyes glittering. "I'll give you two thousand," he said, "to get out of here and go and stop in a hotel for two weeks. Give me two weeks to get out of the country, get clear away. Then you can go home and squeal all you want."

Joyce absorbed what he had said. She sat in silence, nervously fingering her chin where a patch of acne had developed. After a while she said, "What about him? What about Marty?"

"Who's Marty?" shouted Nigel.

It was hard for Joyce to speak. When she spoke her mouth filled with saliva and she felt sick, but she did her best.

"What's the good of two thousand to me? I couldn't spend it. I couldn't tell my fiancé. It'd be like Monopoly money, it'd be just paper."

"You can save it up, can't you? Buy shares with it." Memories of his father's advice, often derided in the commune, came back to Nigel. "Buy goddamned bloody National Savings."

Joyce began to cry. The tears trickled slowly down her face. "It's not just that. I couldn't take the bank's money. How could I?" She wept, hanging her head. "I'd be as bad as you."

With a gasp of rage, Nigel came at her, slapping her face hard, and Joyce fell down on the mattress, shaking with sobs. He turned away from her and went into the kitchen, where the money was in the carrier bag. The bunch of car keys was there too, but Nigel had forgotten all about the silver-blue Ford Escort he had hidden in Dr. Bolton's garage twenty-two days before.

While still in Crete, Dr. and Mrs. Bolton had received a telegram announcing that Dr. Bolton's mother had died. Old Mrs. Bolton had been ninety-two and bedridden, but nevertheless when one's mother dies, whatever the circumstances, one can hardly remain abroad enjoying oneself. Dr. Bolton found the Ford Escort before he had even taken the suitcases out of his own car. He unpacked one of these in order to retrieve from where it was wrapped round his sandals the relevant copy of the *Daily Telegraph*. Having checked that his memory wasn't tricking him, he phoned the police.

They were with him in half an hour. Dr. and Mrs. Bolton were asked to make a list of all the people who knew they had no lock on their garage and also knew they were to be away on holiday.

"Our friends," said Dr. Bolton, "are not the kind of people who rob banks."

"I don't doubt that," said the detective inspector, "but your friends may know people who know people who are less respectable than they are, or have children who have friends who are not respectable at all."

Dr. Bolton was obliged to agree that this was possible. The list was a very long one and the Thaxbys were added by Mrs. Bolton only as an afterthought and not until the Thursday morning. She couldn't remember whether or not she had told Mrs. Thaxby. In this case, said the detective inspector, it wasn't a matter of when in doubt leave out, but when in doubt be on the safe side. Mrs. Bolton said it was laughable, the Thaxbys of all people. Maybe they had children? said the inspector. Well, one boy, a very nice intelligent responsible sort of young man who was at present a student at the University of Kent.

Which went to show that Nigel's mother had not been strictly honest when recounting her son's activities to her friends.

A few hours after Mrs. Bolton had given this vital piece of information to the police, John Purford at last got in touch with them. It wasn't that he was afraid or stalling, but simply that he didn't know the Childon bank robbery had ever taken place. The event had almost slipped his mother's mind. After all, it had been more than three weeks ago, the manager and the girl were sure to be dead, it was a tragedy, God knows, but life has to go on. This was what she said in defence when John saw a little paragraph in the paper about the car being found. He told his partner the whole thing, including the business in the back of the car with Jillian Groombridge. He said it must all be in his head, mustn't it? He had been at school with Marty Foster.

"That's no argument," said the partner. "There were folks must have been at school with Hitler, come to that."

"You think I ought to tell the police?"

"Sure you ought. What have you got to lose? I'll come

with you if you want. They won't eat you. They'll be all over you, nice as pie."

In fact, the police were not particularly nice to John Purford. They thanked him for coming to them, they appreciated that he was able precisely to point out on a street plan the cafe where he had met Marty Foster and Nigel Something, but they scolded him soundly for giving away information of that kind and asked him, to his horror, if he knew the age of Jillian Groombridge.

They seized upon the fairly unusual Christian name of Nigel. A couple on Dr. Bolton's list had a son called Nigel. The police went to Elstree. Dr. and Mrs. Thaxby said their son was in Newcastle. They gave the police the address of the Kensington commune, and there Samantha's mother was interviewed. She also said Nigel was in Newcastle. Marty Foster's father didn't know where his son was, hadn't set eyes on him for two years and didn't want to. The police found Mrs. Foster, who was living with her lover and her lover's three children in a council house in Hemel Hempstead. She hadn't seen Marty for several months, but when she had last seen him he had been on the dole. Immediately the police set about tracing Marty Foster's address through the files of the Ministry of Social Security.

Nigel got his passport out of the rucksack and read it. Mr. N. L. Thaxby; born 15.1.58; occupation, student; height, six feet; eyes, blue. The passport had only been used twice, Nigel not being one of those enterprising and adventurous young people who hitchhike across Europe or drive vans to India. He thought he'd take a flight to Bolivia or Paraguay or somewhere they couldn't extradite you. He'd have about fifteen hundred pounds left, and once he was there he'd contact some newspaper, *The News of the World* or *The Sunday People*, and sell them his story—for what? Five grand? Ten?

Twice more he had asked Joyce to take two thousand as the price of silence, and twice more she had refused. This time he went up to her with the gun levelled and watched her flinch and begin to put up her hands to her face. He wondered vaguely if she felt like he did as the result of their long fast, drugged as if with one of those substances that don't stupefy but make the head light and dizzy and change the vision and bend the mind. Certainly, she looked at him as if he were a ghost or a monster. He thought of shooting her there and then and keeping all the money for himself, but it was broad daylight and he could hear Bridey in the next room and, beyond the other wall, old Green's whistling kettle.

"What did you say it for if you didn't mean it? Why did you say you wouldn't talk?" Nigel pushed one of the bundles of money into her face. He rubbed it against her tears. "That's more than you could earn in a year. Would you rather lie here bleeding to death than have two grand for yourself? Would you?"

She pushed the money away and covered her face, but she didn't speak. Nigel sat down. Standing made him feel a bit faint. He was acutely aware that he was doing it all wrong. He shouldn't be pleading for favours but compelling by force, yet he began to plead and to cajole.

"Look, it doesn't have to be for two weeks, just long enough to let me get out of the country. You can go to a big hotel in the West End. And they'll never find out you've had the money because you can spend it. Don't you realise you can go to a jeweller's and spend the whole lot on a watch or a ring?"

Joyce got up and went to the door. She stood at the door, waiting wordlessly, until Nigel came over and listened and unlocked it. Joyce went into the lavatory. Behind her door Bridey was playing a transistor. Nigel waited tensely, won-

dering what was the point of a deaf man having a whistling
kettle. It was whistling again now. Nigel heard it stop and
thought about Mr. Green until a clear plan began to form in
his mind, and he wondered why he had never considered
Mr. Green from this aspect before. Nobody ever spoke to
him because they couldn't make themselves understood, no
matter how loud they shouted, and he hardly ever spoke because he knew the answers he might receive would be
meaningless to him. Of course the plan was only a tempo-
rary measure and it might not, in any case, work. But it was
the only one he could think of in which, if it didn't work,
there would be no harm done.

The idea of at last getting something to eat made him
hungry again. The saliva rushed, warm and faintly salty,
into his mouth. He could revive and perhaps bribe Joyce
with food. She came out of the lavatory and he hustled her
back into the room. Then he hunted in there and in the
kitchen for an envelope, but he had no more luck than Joyce
had had when she wanted to write her note, and he had to
settle as she had done for a paper bag or, in this case, for
part of the wrapping off Marty's cigarette carton. Nigel
wrote, "In bed with flu. Could you get me large white loaf?"
Of all the comestibles he could have had, he chose without
thinking man's traditional staff of life. He folded the paper
round a pound note. Joyce was lying on the sofa face-downwards, but only let him be out of sight for more than a couple of minutes, he thought, let him start down those stairs,
and she'd be off there raring to go as if she'd just got a plateful of roast beef inside her. The saliva washed round the
cavities and pockets of his mouth. He went out onto the
landing and pushed the note under Mr. Green's door, having
remembered to sign it: M. Foster.

Mr. Green went out most days. He had lived for years in
one room, so he went out even if he had nothing to buy and

although climbing back again up those stairs nearly killed him every time. The note, which suddenly appeared under his door when he was making himself his fifteenth cup of tea of the day, worried him intensely. This wasn't because he even considered not complying with the request in it. He was afraid of young people, especially young males, and he would have done far more than make a special journey to buy a loaf in order to avoid offending the tall fair one or the small dark one, whichever this Foster was. What worried him was not knowing whether his neighbour meant a cut or uncut loaf, and also being entrusted with a pound note, which still seemed to Mr. Green a large sum of money. But when he had drunk his tea he took his string bag and put on his overcoat and set off.

A young man in a blue jacket caught him up a little way down the road. Asking the way to somewhere, Mr. Green supposed. He did what he always did, shook his head and kept on walking, though the young man persisted and was quite hard to shake off. Because the cut loaf was more expensive than the uncut Mr. Green didn't buy it. He bought a large white loaf, crusty and warm, carefully wrapping it in tissue paper himself, and in the shop next door he bought *The Evening Standard*. This he paid for out of his own money. Then he went for a little walk in his own silence along the noisy Broadway, returning home by a different route and not taking too long about it because it would be wrong and inconsiderate to keep a sick man waiting.

Halfway up the stairs he had to stop and rest. Bridey Flynn, coming home from the Rose of Killarney, caught up with him and passed him, not speaking to him but reading out of curiosity the note which lay spread out on the flat top of the newel post. She disappeared round a bend in the stairs. Mr. Green placed the change from the pound note, a fifty-pence piece and two tens and a one, on the note and carefully wrapped the coins up in it. Then he laboriously climbed the rest of the stairs. At the top he put the folded newspaper on the floor outside Marty Foster's door, the loaf on top of the newspaper, and the little parcel of coins on top of the loaf. He tapped on the door, but he didn't wait.

Nigel didn't at once go to the door. He thought it was probably old Green who had knocked but he couldn't be positive and he had cause to be nervous. Between the time he had put the note under old Green's door and now, the doorbell had rung several times, in fact half a dozen times. The second time it rang Nigel pushed Joyce up into the corner of the sofa and stuck the barrel of the gun, safety catch off, hard into her chest. She went grey in the face, she didn't make a sound. But Nigel hardly knew how he had borne it, listening to that bell ringing, ringing, down there. He gritted his teeth and tensed all his muscles.

It was about half an hour after that that there was a tap at the door. Nigel was still, though less concentratedly, covering Joyce with the gun. At the knock he jammed it against her neck. When he heard the sound of Mr. Green's whistling kettle he went cautiously to the door. He opened it a crack with his left hand, keeping Joyce covered with the gun in his right. There was no one on the landing. Bridey was in the bathroom, he could see the shape of her through the frosted glass in the bathroom door.

The sight of the bread, and the smell of it through its flimsy wrapping, made him feel dizzy. He snatched it up with the newspaper and the package of change and kicked the door shut.

Joyce saw and smelt the bread and gave a sort of cry and came towards him with her hands out. He was still pointing the gun at her. She hardly seemed to notice it.

"Sit down," said Nigel. "You'll get your share."

He didn't bother to cut the loaf, he tore it. It was soft and very light and not quite cold. He gave a hunk to Joyce and sank his teeth into his own hunk. Funny, he had often read about people eating dry bread, people in ancient times mostly or at least a good while ago, and he had wondered how they could. Now he knew. It was starvation which made it palatable. He devoured nearly half the loaf, washing it down with a cup of water with whisky in it. Now his hunger was allayed, the next best thing to bread Mr. Green could have bought him was a newspaper. Before he had even finished eating, he was going through that paper page by page.

They had found the Escort in Dr. Bolton's garage. Not that they put it that way—"a shed in Epping Forest." They'd be onto him now, he thought, via the commune, via that furniture guy, that school friend of Marty's. He turned savagely to Joyce.

"Look, all I ask is you lie low for two goddamned days. That's a thousand quid a day. Just two days and then you can talk all you want." Inspiration came to Nigel. "You don't even need to keep the money. If you're that crazy, you can give it back to the bank."

Joyce didn't answer him. She hunched forward, then doubled up with pain. The new bread was having its effect on a stomach empty for five days. As bad as Marty, as bad as that little brain, thought Nigel, until he too was seized with pains like iron fingers gripping his intestines.

At least it stopped him wanting to eat up all the remaining bread. The worst of the pain passed off after about half an hour. Joyce was lying face-downwards on the mattress, apparently asleep. Nigel looked at her with hatred in which there was something of despair. He thought he would have to give her an ultimatum, she either took the money and promised to keep quiet for a day or he shot her. It was the only way. He couldn't remember, but still he was sure his fingerprints must be somewhere on that Ford Escort, and they'd match them with his prints in the commune, his parents' home, every surface of it, being wiped clean daily, he thought. John Something, the furniture guy, would link him with Marty Foster and then . . . How long had he got? Maybe they were already in Notting Hill now, matching prints. Had Marty ever been to the commune? That was another thing he couldn't remember.

If he was going to South America it wouldn't make much difference whether he shot Joyce or not. He would try to do it when the house was empty but for old Green. And he would like to do it, it would be a positive pleasure. Although he knew the view from the window by heart, could have drawn it accurately or made a plan of it, he nevertheless went to the window and looked out to check on certain aspects of the lie of the land. This house was joined to only one of its neighbours. Nigel eased the window up—the first time it had been opened since Marty's occupancy—and craned his neck out. Joyce didn't stir. He was seeking to confirm that, as he remembered from the time before all this happened and he was free to come and go and roam the streets, no curtains hung at the windows of the second-floor flat next door. This was in the adjoining house. It was as he had thought, the flat was empty and there would be no one on the other side of the kitchen wall to hear a shot. Very likely the people in the lower flats were out at work all day.

He had withdrawn his head and was closing the window when he noticed a man standing on the opposite pavement. Nigel closed the window and fastened the catch. There was something familiar about the man on the pavement, though Nigel couldn't recall where he had seen him before. The man was wearing jeans and a dark pullover and a kind of zipper jacket or anorak, and he had thickish fair-brown hair that wasn't very short but wasn't long either. He looked about thirty-five.

Nigel decided he had never seen him before, but that didn't make him feel any better. The man might have been waiting for someone, but if so it was a strange place to choose, outside a church in a turning off Chichele Road. He could be a policeman, a detective. It could be he who had kept on ringing the bell. Nigel told himself that the man's clothes looked new and his get-up somehow contrived, as if he wasn't used to wearing clothes like that and wasn't quite at ease in them. He made himself turn away and sit down and go through the paper once more.

Ten minutes later when he went back to the window, the man had gone. He heard Bridey's door close and her feet on the stairs as she went off to work.

22

Alan was almost sure he had got the wrong room. The young man with the fair hair, who just now had opened the window and leant out as if he meant to call to his watcher, must be the Green whose name was on the third bell. After the window had closed and the angry-looking face vanished, Alan had crossed the road and pressed that third bell several times, stood there for seconds with his thumb pressed against the push, but no one had come down to answer it.

He walked away and was in the corner shop buying a paper when he saw the girl called Flynn go by. He would talk to her just once more, he thought. The Rose of Killarney was due to open in ten minutes.

This was the second time since Monday that he had come to Cricklewood. He would have come on Wednesday and made it three times, only he couldn't do that to Una, couldn't keep on lying to her. Besides, he thought he had exhausted his powers of invention with Tuesday's inspiration, which was that he had to see his solicitor about Alison. Una accepted that without comment. She was busying herself with preparations for their departure on Friday, writing letters, taking Ambrose's best dinner jacket to the cleaners, ordering a newspaper delivery to begin again on Saturday. But Tuesday's sortie did him no good, he was no forrarder. Although he had spent most of the afternoon watching the house and walking the adjacent streets, he had seen no one, not even the Irish girl, come in or go out.

When he got back he had to tell Una he had been with the solicitor and what the man had said. It was easy for him to say that he would be giving up his share of his house to Alison because there was a good deal of truth in this, and he was rather surprised as well as moved when Una said this was right and generous of him, but how he must feel it, having worked for so many years to acquire it!

"You must think me very weak," he said.

"No, why? Because you're giving up your home to your wife without a struggle?"

Of course he hadn't meant that, but how could she know? He longed to tell her who he really was. But if he told her he would lose her. He had done too many things for which no one, not even Una, could forgive him: the theft, the betrayal of Joyce, the lies, the deceitfully contrived fabric of his past.

That evening they had gone out with Caesar and Annie, but on the Wednesday they spent the whole day and the evening alone together. They found a cinema which was showing *Dr. Zhivago* because Alan had never seen it, and then, appropriately, they had dinner in a Russian restaurant off the Old Brompton Road because Alan had never tasted Russian food. When they got home Ambrose phoned from Singapore, where it was nine o'clock in the morning.

"He was sweet," said Una. "He said of course he understands and he wants me to be happy, but we must promise to come back and see him for a weekend soon and I said we would."

Alan thought he would feel better about Joyce once he was in Devon and couldn't sneak out up to Cricklewood in the afternoons, for he knew he was going to sneak out again on Thursday. It was Una who put the idea into his head, who made it seem the only thing to do, when she said she'd buy their tickets and make reservations and then go on to the hairdresser. He could go out after she had gone and get back before she returned. He would definitely get hold of the Irish girl or of Green if Foster didn't answer his bell. It ought to be simple to find out what time Foster came home from work, and then catch him and, on some pretext, speak to him. With pretexts in mind, Alan picked up from the hall table in Montcalm Gardens a brown envelope with *The Occupier* written on it, and which contained electioneering literature for the County Council election in May. He put it into his pocket. After all, it would hardly matter if Foster opened it in his presence and saw that it was totally inappropriate for someone who lived in Brent rather than Kensington and Chelsea, for by then Alan would have heard his voice.

It was a cool grey day, of which there are more in England than any other kind, days when the sky is overcast with unbroken, unruffled vapour, and there is no gleam of sun or spot of rain. Alan was glad of his windcheater, though there was no wind to cheat, only a sharp nip in the air that lived up to its name and seemed actually to pinch his face.

He began by pressing Foster's bell several times. Then he walked a little before trying again. It was rather a shock to see an old man come out of the house, because he had somehow got it into his head by then that, in spite of the names on the bells, only the Irish girl and the fair-haired young man inhabited the place. The old man was deaf. Alan caught him up a little way down the road and tried to ask him about Foster, but it seemed cruel to persist, a kind of torment, and he felt embarrassed too, though there was no one else about to hear his shouts.

He tried the bell marked Flynn, and because there was no answer to that one either, went back to the Broadway and had a cup of tea in a cafe. He supposed he must have missed seeing the girl come home because he had been back to the

house and tried Green's bell in vain and was now buying his
paper when he caught sight of her turning into Chichele
Road, plainly on her way out, not her way home. There was
a paragraph on an inside page of the *Evening Standard* to
the effect that the car stolen in Capel St. Paul had been
found in Epping Forest. *Kidnap Car in Forest Hideaway.*
But the paper contained nothing else about the robbery, its
leads being *Man Shot in Casino* and 77 *Dead in Iran Earthquake.* He walked along the wide pavement, which had
trees growing out of it, until he came to the Rose of Killarney. When it got to five, the Flynn girl herself came out to
open the doors.

Bridey had been frightened of the man in the windcheater only for a very short space of time. This was in the
seconds which elapsed between her opening the front door
to him and her return of the five-pound note. She was no
longer afraid, but she wasn't very pleased to see him either.
She felt sure he was a policeman. He said good afternoon to
her which made her feel it was even earlier than it was and
reminded her of the great stretch of time between now and
eleven when they would close. Bridey made no answer beyond a nod and walked dispiritedly back behind the bar
where she asked him in neutral tones what he would have.

Alan didn't want anything but he asked for a half of bitter
just the same. Bridey accepted his offer of a drink and had a
gin and tonic. An idea was forming in her mind that, although she would never dream of calling the police or going
out of her way to shop anyone to the police, in this case the
police had come to her, which was a different matter. And
she would like to have revenge on Marty Foster for insulting
her and showing her up in front of the whole saloon bar. She
had never really believed that story of the five-pound note
being dropped by Marty as he left the Rose of Killarney.

More probably the man in the windcheater was after him for theft or even some kind of violence. Bridey wasn't going to ask what he was wanted for. She listened while the policeman or whatever talked about ringing bells and not getting answers, and about old Green and someone else he seemed to think was called Green—she couldn't follow half of it—and when he had finished she said:

"Marty Foster's got flu."

Alan said, half to himself, "That's why he doesn't answer the door," and to Bridey, "I suppose he's in bed." She made no answer. She lit a cigarette and looked at him, gently rocking the liquid in her glass up and down.

"If I come to see him tomorrow," he said, "would you let me in?"

"I don't want any trouble now."

"You've only to let me into the house. I don't mean into his place, I know you can't do that."

"Well, if I open the door and a fella pushes past me," said Bridey with a sigh, "and makes his way up the stairs, it's no blame to me, is it, and me standing no more than five foot two?"

Alan said, "I'll come in the afternoon. Around four?"

Bridey didn't tell him it was her day off, so she would be home all day and he could have come at ten or noon or in the evening if he'd wanted. She only nodded, thinking that that gave her a long time in which to change her mind, and got off her stool and went round the back out of his sight. Alan was sure she would only come back when more customers came in. He drank up his beer and went to catch the thirty-two bus.

Una was still out when he came back to Montcalm Gardens. It was nearly six. She walked in at five past with a bottle of wine, Monbazillac, which he and she both liked, for their supper. It was quite a long time, while they were eating that supper, in fact, before he realised that she must have been home in his absence. The skirt and jumper she had on were different from what she had worn to go to the station and the hairdresser. But she didn't ask him where he had been, and he volunteered no information. They went downstairs to say good-bye to Caesar, for they would be gone on the five-thirty out of Paddington before he came home on the following day.

"Send me a card," said Caesar. "I'll have one with Dartmoor Prison on it. I went and had a look at it once, poor devils working in the fields. D'you know what it says over the doors? *Parcere Subjectis.* Spare the captives."

That made Alan feel they were really going, that and the tickets Una had got. He wished now that he had arranged with the Irish girl to be let into the house in the morning instead of the afternoon, but it was too late to alter it now. And in a way the arrangement was the best possible he could have made, for it meant that he could make his phone call and immediately afterwards leave London. The police would trace the call to a London call box, but by then he would be on his way to Devon. That is, of course, if he made the call at all, if it didn't turn out to be a false trail and Marty Foster quite innocent.

Sitting in his room that night, he told Una that he didn't intend to divorce his wife. He told her because it was true. A dead man cannot divorce. He wanted no more lies, no more leading her into false beliefs.

"I'm still married to Stewart," she said.

"I shall never be able to divorce her, Una."

She didn't ask him why not. She said quaintly and very practically, as if she were talking of the relative merits of travelling, say, train or air, first-class or second-class, "It's just that if we had children, I should like to be married."

"You'd like to have children?" he said wonderingly, and

then at last, in so many words, she told him about Lucy. In doing so she gave him the ultimate of herself while he, he thought, had given her nothing.

The dream was the first he had had for several nights. He was in a train with two men and each of his hands was manacled to one of theirs. They were Dick Heysham and Ambrose Engstrand. Neither of them spoke to him and he didn't know where they were taking him, but the train dissolved and they were on a bleak and desolate moorland before stone pillars which supported gates, and over the gates was the inscription *Parcere Subjectis*. The gates opened and they led him in, and a woman came out to receive him. At first he couldn't see her face, but he sensed who she was as one does sense such things in dreams. She was Pam and Jillian and in a way she was Annie too. Until he saw her face. And when he did he saw that she was none of them. She was Joyce, and blood flowed down her body from an open wound in her head.

He struggled out of the dream to find Una gone from his side. He put out his hands, speaking her name, and woke fully to see her standing at the tallboy, opening and emptying the drawers.

It was a reflex to shout. He shouted at her without thinking.

"What are you doing? Why are you going through my things?"

The colour left her face.

"You mustn't touch those things. What are you doing?"

"I was packing for you," she faltered.

She hadn't reached the drawer where the money was. He sighed, closing his eyes, wondering how long he could keep the money concealed from her when they were living together and had all things in common. She had let the clothes fall from her hands and stood, lost and suffering. He went up to her, held her face, lifting it to his.

"I'm sorry. I was dreaming and I didn't know what I said."

She clung to him. "You've never been angry with me before."

"I'm not angry with you."

She came back into bed with him and he held her in his arms, knowing that she expected him to make love to her. But he felt restless and rather excited, though not sexually excited, more as if the deed he was set on accomplishing that day would set him free to love Una fully and on every level. And now he saw clearly that if he could show the two men to be the same and act on it, he would undo all the wrong he had done Joyce and himself on the day of the robbery. Ahead of him, once this hurdle was surmounted, seemed to stretch a life of total peace and joy with Una, in which such apparent obstacles as namelessness, joblessness, and fast decreasing capital were insignificant pinpricks.

Nigel and Joyce finished the loaf up on Friday morning. It was another grey day, but this time made gloomy by fog. Nigel wondered if he could get old Green to do more shopping for them—not more bread, certainly. Even a deaf old cretin like him would begin to have his doubts about a sick man on his own, a man with flu, eating a whole large white loaf in a day. He heard Mr. Green's kettle and then his footsteps crossing to the lavatory, but he didn't go to the door.

The first thing he had done on getting up was look out of the window for the watcher of the day before. But there was no one there. And Nigel told himself he was getting crazy, hysterical, imagining the police would act like that. The police wouldn't hang about outside, they'd come in. They would have firearms issued. They would evacuate the surrounding houses and call out to him on a loud hailer to throw down his gun and send Joyce out.

The street looked as if it could never be the backdrop to such a drama. Respectable, shabby, London-suburban, it was deserted but for a woman pushing a pram past the church. The man he had seen outside yesterday, Nigel decided, was no more likely to be the police than that woman. As for whoever kept ringing the bell, that could be the electricity meter man. The meter was probably due to be read. But, for all these reassurances, he knew he had to get out. There was no explaining away the evidence of the newspaper. Nigel thought how helpful his parents would be to the police once they'd been located via the Boltons. They'd shop him without thinking of anything but being what they called good citizens, rack their brains to think where he might be, sift their memories for the names of any friends he had ever had.

"Just keep quiet for twelve hours," he said to Joyce, "then you can phone the bank's head office and tell them all you want about me and this place, and hand over the money." He added, appalled at the thought of it, the waste, "Jesus!"

Joyce said nothing. She was thinking, as she had been thinking for most of the night, if she could do that with honour. Nigel thought she was being defiant again. Get some food inside her and all the old obstinacy came back.

"I can kill you, you know," he said. "Might be simpler when all's said and done. That way I get to like keep all the bread myself." He showed her the gun, holding it out on his left palm.

Joyce said wearily, "If I say yes, can we get out of here today?"

The hue and cry for Marty Foster had awakened memories in the mind of a policeman whose beat included Chichele Road. One foggy morning he had found a sick young man crouched on a wall and had helped him into Dr. Miskin's where, as he let go of his arm, the young man had whispered to the receptionist, "Name of Foster, M. Foster." All this came back to him on Friday and he passed it on to his superiors. Dr. Miskin directed them to the hospital in Willesden where Marty was in a ward along with a dozen or so other men.

Marty had been feeling a lot better. Apart from being confined within four walls, he rather liked it in hospital. The nurses were very good-looking jolly girls and Marty spent a good part of every day chatting them up. He missed his cigarettes, though, and he dreadfully missed his alcohol. They had told him he mustn't touch a drop for at least six months.

That he would have a choice about what he did in the next six months Marty was growing confident. He was glad Nigel hadn't come in. He didn't want to see Nigel or Joyce or, come to that, the money ever again. He felt he was well rid of it, and he felt cleansed of it too by removing himself in this way and voluntarily forgoing his share. Marty really felt he had done that, had done it all off his own bat to put the clock back, alter the past, and stay the moving finger.

So it was with sick dismay that after lunch on Friday, when they were all back in their beds for the afternoon rest, he raised his head from the pillow to see two undoubted policemen, though in plainclothes, come marching down the ward, preceded by pretty Sister, at whom only five minutes before he had been making sheeps' eyes. She now looked stern and aghast. Marty thought, though not in those words, how the days of wine and roses were over and the chatting up of the girls, and then they were beside his bed and drawing the screens round it.

The first thing he said to them was a lie. He gave them as his address the first one he had had in London, the squat in

Kilburn Park. Then he said he had been with his mother on 4 March, hadn't seen Nigel Thaxby for two months, and had never been to Childon in his life. After a while he recanted in part, gave another false address, and said that he had lent his flat to Nigel Thaxby, who he believed to have perpetrated the robbery and kidnapping in league with the missing bank manager.

Outside the screens the ward was agog, humming with speculation. Marty was put into a dressing gown and taken to a side room where the interrogation began afresh. He told so many lies then and later that neither the police nor his own counsel were ever quite to believe a word he said, and for this reason his counsel dissuaded him from going into the witness box at his trial.

That Friday afternoon he finally disclosed his true address but by then it had also been given to them by the Ministry of Social Security.

The few clothes Alan possessed went into the suitcase, but he didn't put the money in there. Suppose Una were to ask him at the last moment if he had room in his case for something of hers? Besides, how could he be sure of being alone when he unpacked it? What he should have done was buy a briefcase with a zip-up compartment. He could put the money in the compartment and books and writing paper, that sort of thing, in the main body of the case. For the time being he stuffed the bundles of notes into the pockets of his trousers and his windcheater. It bulged and crackled rather, and when Una, off up the road to fetch Ambrose's dinner jacket from the cleaners, came up to kiss him—they always kissed on meeting and parting—he didn't dare hold her close against him as he would have liked to do.

Her going out solved the problem of how to get out him-

self. It was almost three. He wrote a note: "Una, Something
has come up which I must see to. Meet you at Paddington at
5. Love, Paul." This he left on the hall table with the house
keys Una had given him three weeks before.

23

Joyce had given him the answer he wanted, but now that he
had it Nigel couldn't believe it. He couldn't trust her. He saw
himself at the airport going through the place where they
checked you for bombs, reaching the gate itself that led you
to the aircraft—and a man stepping out in front of him, another laying a hand on his shoulder. If Joyce was merely
going to surrender the money to the bank, there would be
no compulsion for her to respect her promise to him. She
would break it, he thought, as soon as he was out of sight.

He would kill her when the house was empty.

Nigel didn't know who lived on the ground floor, certainly
people who were out all day. The red-haired girl and her
"fella" were out a lot. Bridey didn't work every day, but she
always went out for some part of the day. Nigel thought it
possible that Joyce's body might lie there undiscovered for
weeks, but there was a good chance the police would arrive
that weekend and break the door down. By then he would
be far away, it hardly mattered, and it was good to think of
Marty getting the blame and taking the rap, if not for the
killing, then for a great deal else.

He listened for Bridey, who hadn't gone to work for the
eleven o'clock opening. At three she was still moving about
in her room, playing a transistor. Nigel packed his clothes
into Samantha's mother's rucksack. He put on his cleanest
jeans, the pair Marty had taken to the launderette, and his
jacket, into the pocket of which went his passport. In the

kitchen, over the sink, he removed with Marty's blunt razor the half inch of fuzzy yellow down which had sprouted on his chin and upper lip. Shaven and with his hair combed, he looked quite respectable, the doctor's son, a nice responsible young man, down from his university for the Easter holiday.

Joyce too had dressed herself for going out in as many warm clothes as she could muster, two tee-shirts and a blouse and skirt and pullover. She had put the two thousand pounds along with her knitting into the bag in which Marty had bought the wool for that knitting. She said to Nigel, in a voice and a manner nearer her old voice and manner than he had heard from her for weeks, that she didn't know what a hotel would think of her, arriving without a coat and with rubber flip-flops on her feet. Nigel didn't bother to reply. He knew she wasn't going to get near any hotel. He just wished Bridey would go out.

At three-thirty she did. Nigel heard her go downstairs, and from the window he watched her walk away towards Chichele Road. What about the red-haired girl? He was wondering if he dared take the risk without knowing for sure if the red-haired girl was out of the house, when the phone began to ring. Nigel hated to hear the phone ringing. He always thought it would be the police or his father or Marty to say he was coming home, by ambulance and borne up the stairs on a stretcher by two men.

The phone rang for a long time. No one came up from downstairs to answer it. Nigel felt relieved and free and private. The last peal of the phone bell died away, and as he listened, gratified, to the silence, it was broken by the ringing of the front doorbell.

At Marble Arch Alan had bought a briefcase into which he put the money, having deposited his suitcase in a left-luggage locker at Paddington Station. In the shop-window glass he looked with a certain amusement at his own reflection. He had put on his suit because it was easier to wear it than carry it, and his raincoat because it had begun to rain. With the briefcase in his hand, he looked exactly like a bank manager. For a second he felt apprehensive. It would be a fine thing to be recognised now at the eleventh hour. But he knew no one would recognise him. He looked so much younger, happier, more confident. I could be bounded in a nutshell, he quoted to himself, and think myself a king of infinite space, were it not that I have bad dreams. . . .

He was a little late getting to Cricklewood, and it was ten past four when he walked up to the house and rang the bell. He rang Marty Foster's bell first because there was a chance he might answer and he didn't want to bother the Flynn girl unnecessarily. However, there was no answer. He tried again and again and then he rang the Flynn girl's bell. Somehow it hadn't crossed his mind there might be no reply to that either, that she could have forgotten her promise or simply be indifferent to her promise and go out. She hadn't exactly promised, he thought with a sinking of the heart.

Of course a taxi could get him from here to Paddington in a quarter of an hour, there was nothing to worry about from that point of view. He stepped back and down and looked up at the windows, which looked back at him like so many wall eyes. Maybe the bells weren't working. He couldn't hear any sound of ringing from outside. But the Flynn bell had been working on Monday. . . .

Along the street the old deaf man was coming, a string bag in his hand containing some cans and a packet of tea. Alan nodded to him and smiled, and the old man nodded and smiled back in a way that was suspicious and ingratiating at the same time. Slowly he fumbled through layers of clothing to retrieve a key from a waistcoat pocket. He put the string bag down on the step and unlocked the front door.

Knowing it was useless to speak to him but feeling he must say something to excuse his behaviour, Alan muttered vaguely about people who didn't answer bells. He edged past the old man into the passage and, leaving him on the doorstep wiping his feet, began to climb the stairs.

Immediately when he heard the bell, the first time it rang, Nigel pointed the gun at Joyce and made her go into the kitchen. She understood this was because there was someone at the door he feared might be the police, but she didn't reason that therefore he wouldn't dare shoot her. There was something in his face, an animal panic, but the animal was a tiger rather than a rabbit, which made her think he would shoot her before he did anything else. He had taken off the safety catch.

He forced her into a chair and got behind her. Joyce slumped forward, the gun pressing against the nape of her neck. With his left hand Nigel felt about all over the draining board and the top of the bookcase and the drawer under the draining board for the rope. He found it in the drawer and wound it round Joyce as best he could, tying her arms to the back of the chair. When he had got the black stocking off his own bundle of notes, he put the gun down and managed to gag her. By then the doorbell had rung again and was now ringing in Bridey's room. Nigel shut the kitchen door on Joyce and went back into the living room to listen. From downstairs he heard the sound of the front door being softly closed. No more ringing, silence.

Then footsteps sounded on the stairs. Nigel told himself they must belong to old Green. He told himself that for about two seconds because after that he knew that they weren't the footsteps of a stout seventy-five-year-old but of a

man in the prime of life. They came on, on, up to the bathroom landing and then up the last flight to the top. There
they flagged and seemed to hesitate. Nigel went very softly
to the door and put his ear against it, listening to the silence
outside and wondering why the man didn't knock at his
door.

Alan hadn't knocked because he didn't know which was
the right door. There were three to choose from. He
knocked first at the door to the room on the side of the
house, the detached side. Then he tried the door that faced
it because the remaining door must be the one to the front
room, which was evidently occupied by Green. The old man
was coming slowly and heavily up the stairs. Alan stepped
aside and attempted some sort of dumb show to indicate
whom he wanted, but how do you indicate Foster in sign
language? The old man shook his head and unlocked the
door at which Alan had last knocked and went inside, closing the door behind him. Alan tried the door to the front
room. He waited, sure that he could hear on the other side
of it the sound of someone breathing very close by.

Nigel put the gun in its holster underneath his jacket, and
then he unlocked the mortice with the big iron key. There
was only one man out there. Very probably he knew the
room was occupied, so it might be less dangerous to let him
in than keep him out. Nigel opened the door.

The man outside was in a suit and raincoat and carrying a
briefcase, which Nigel somehow hadn't expected. The face
was vaguely familiar, but he immediately dismissed the idea
that this might be the man he had seen watching the house.
This was—he was convinced of it even before the brown envelope was produced—some canvasser or market researcher.

Alan said, "I'm looking for a Mr. Foster."

"He's not here."

"You mean he lives here? In there?"

A nod answered him. "I understood he was ill . . ." Alan was almost deterred by the look on the handsome young face. It expressed amazement initially, then a growing suspiciousness. But he went on firmly. "I understood he was at home with the flu."

At that the face cleared and the shoulders shrugged. Alan felt sure Marty Foster was somewhere in there. He hadn't come so far to give up now, on the threshold of Foster's home. The door was moving slowly, it was about to be shut in his face. Daring, amazed at himself, he set his foot in it like an importunate salesman, said, "I'd like to come in a minute, if you don't mind," and entered the room, pushing the other aside, though he was taller and younger than he.

The door closed after him. They looked at each other, Alan Groombridge and Nigel Thaxby, without recognition. Nigel thought, he's not a convasser, he's not from the hospital—who is he? Alan looked round the room at the tumbled mattress, the scattering of bread crumbs on the seat of a chair, a plastic bag with knitting needles sticking out of it. Foster might be in whatever room was on the other side of that door.

"I have to see him," he said. "It's very important."

"He's in hospital."

From behind the door there came a thumping sound, then a whole series of such sounds as of the legs of a chair or table bumping the floor. Alan looked at the door, said coldly:

"Which hospital?"

"I don't know, I can't tell you any more." Joyce was working herself free of the rope which tied her to the chair, as Nigel had guessed she would. He put himself between Alan and the kitchen door, his hand feeling the holster round the gun. "You'd better go now. I can't help you."

It was twenty minutes to five. He was meeting Una at

five, he was leaving London—hadn't he done enough? "I'm
going," Alan said. "Who's behind that door, then? Your girl
friend?"

"That's right."

Alan shrugged. He began to walk back to the door by
which he had entered as Nigel, striding to open it, called
back over his shoulder:

"O.K., doll, one moment and you can come out."

Alan froze. He had been pursuing one voice and had
found the other—"Let's see what's in the tills, doll. . . ." He
turned round slowly, the blood pounding in his head. Nigel
was opening the door to the landing. Alan was a yard away
from that door, perhaps only a hundred yards away from a
phone box. He stopped thinking, speculating, wondering.
He took half a dozen paces across that room and flung open
the other door.

Joyce had got her arms free and was taking the gag off
her mouth. He would hardly have known her, she was so
thin and haggard and hollow-eyed. But she knew him. She
had recognised the voice of the man she had supposed dead
from the moment he first spoke to Nigel. She threw the
black stocking onto the floor and came up to him, not speaking, her face all silent supplication.

"Where's the other one, Joyce?" said Alan.

She whispered, "He went away," and laid her hands on
his arms, her head on his chest.

"Let's go," he said, and put his arm round her, holding
her close, and walked her out the way he had come. Nigel
was waiting for them at the door with the gun in his hand.

"Leave go of her," he said. "Let go of her and get out,
she's nothing to do with you."

It was the way he said it and, more than that, the words
he used that made Alan laugh. Nothing to do with him,
Joyce whom his conscience had brought into a bond with

him closer than he had ever had with Pam, closer than he had with Una. . . . He gave a little dry laugh, looking incredulously at Nigel. Then he took a step forward, pulling Joyce even more tightly against him, sheltering her in the crook of his right arm, and as he heard the roar and her cry out, he flung up his left arm to shield her face and threw her to the ground.

The second bullet and the third struck him high up in the body with no more pain than from two blows of a fist.

24

Nigel grabbed the bundle of notes he had given to Joyce and stuffed it into the carrier with the other one. He had a last swift look round the room and saw the briefcase lying on the floor a little way from Joyce's right foot. He unzipped it a few inches, saw the wads of notes, and put the briefcase into his rucksack. Then he opened the door and stepped out.

The noise of the shooting had been tremendous, so loud as to fetch forth Mr. Green. Bridey, coming in when she thought the coast would be clear, heard it as she mounted the second flight. Neither of them made any attempt to hinder Nigel, who slammed the door behind him and swung down the stairs. In his progress through the vertical tunnel of the house, he passed the red-haired girl, who cried out to him:

"What's going on? What's happening?"

He didn't answer her. He ran down the last dozen steps, along the passage, and out into the street where, though only five, it was already growing dark from massed rain clouds.

The red-haired girl went upstairs. Bridey and Mr. Green looked at her without speaking.

"My God," said the red-haired girl, "what was all that carry-on like shots? That fella what's-his-name, that fair one, he's just gone down like a bat out of hell."

"Don't ask me," said Bridey. "Better ask that pig. He's his pal."

Mr. Green shuffled over to Marty's door. He banged on it with his fist, and then the red-haired girl banged too.

"I don't know what to do. I'd ask my fella only he's not back from work. I reckon I'd better give the fuzz a phone. Can't let it just go on, can we?"

"That's a very serious step to take, a very serious step," Bridey was saying, when Mr. Green looked down at the floor. From under the door, across the wood-grained linoleum, between his slippers, came a thin trickle of blood.

"My godfathers," said Mr. Green. "Oh, my godfathers."

The red-haired girl put her hand over her mouth and bolted down to the phone. Bridey shook her head and went off downstairs again. She had decided that discretion, or a busman's holiday in the Rose of Killarney, was the better part of social conscience.

In the room, on the other side of the door, Alan lay holding Joyce in his arms. He felt rather cold and tired and he wasn't finding breathing easy because Joyce's cheek was pressed against his mouth and nose. Nothing would have induced him to make any movement to disturb Joyce, who felt so comfortable and relaxed in her sleep. He was quite relaxed himself and very happy, though not sure exactly where he was. It seemed to him that they must be on a beach because he could taste saltiness on his lips and feel wetness with his hands. Yet the place, wherever it was, also had the feeling of being high up and lofty, a vaulted hall. His memory was very clear. He repeated to himself, Alas, said Queen Guinevere, now are we mischieved both. Madam, said Sir Lancelot, is there here any armour within your chamber that I might cover my poor body withal? And if there be any give it me, and I shall soon stint their malice, by the grace of God. Truly, said the queen, I have none armour, shield, sword, nor spear. . . .

He couldn't remember the rest. There was a lot of it but perhaps it wasn't very appropriate, anyway. Something about the queen wanting to be taken and killed in his stead, and Lancelot saying, God defend me from such shame. Alan smiled at the indignation in that, which he quite understood, and as he smiled his mouth seemed to fill with the saltiness and to overflow, and the pressure on his face and chest became so great that he knew he must try to shift Joyce. She was too heavy for him to move. He was too tired to lift his arms or move his head, too tired to think or remember or breathe. He whispered, "Let's go to sleep now, Una. . . ."

They started breaking the door down, but he didn't hear them. A sergeant and a constable had come over from Willesden Green, supposing at first they had been called out to a domestic disturbance because the red-haired girl had been inarticulate on the phone. The sight of the blood, flowing in three narrow separate streams now, altered that. One of the panels in the door had given way when up the stairs appeared two very top-brass-looking policemen in plainclothes and an officer in uniform. These last knew nothing of the events in the room and on the landing. They were there because Scotland Yard had discovered Marty Foster's address.

The door went down at the next heave. The couple from the ground floor had come up, and the red-haired girl was there, and when they saw what was inside, the women screamed. The sergeant from Willesden Green told them to go away and he jammed the door shut.

The two on the floor lay embraced in their own blood. Joyce's face and hair were covered in blood from a wound in her head, and at first it seemed as if all the blood had come from her and none from the man. The detective superintendent fell on his knees beside them. He was a perceptive

person whose job had not blunted his sensitivity, and he
looked in wonder at the contentment in the man's face, the
mouth that almost smiled. The next time I do fight I'll make
death love me, for I'll contend even with his pestilent
scythe. . . . He felt for a pulse in the girl's wrist. Gently he
lifted the man's arm and saw the wound in the upper chest
and the wound under the heart, and saw too that of the
streams of blood which had pumped out to meet them, two
had ceased.

But the pulse under his fingers was strong. Eyelids trembled, a muscle flickered.

"Thank God," he said, "for one of them."

There was no blood on Nigel. His heart was beating
roughly and his whole body was shaking, but that was only
because he had killed someone. He was glad he had killed
Joyce, and reflected that he should have done so before.
Bridey wouldn't take any notice, old Green didn't count,
and the red-haired girl would do no more than ask silly
questions of her neighbours. Now he must put all that behind him and get to the airport. By cab? He was quite safe,
he thought, but still he didn't want to expose himself to too
much scrutiny in Cricklewood Broadway.

On the other hand, it was to his advantage that this was
rush hour and there were lots of people about. Nigel felt
very nearly invisible among so many. He began to walk
south, keeping as far as he could to the streets which ran
parallel to Shoot-up Hill rather than to the main road itself.
But there was even less chance of getting a cab there. Once
in Kilburn, he emerged into the High Road. All the street-
lights were on now, it was half-past five, and a thin drizzle
had begun. Nigel felt in the carrier for the bunch of Ford
Escort keys. If that Marty, that little brain, could rip off a
car, so could he. He began to hunt along the side streets.

Nearly half an hour had gone by before he found a Ford
Escort that one of his keys would fit. It was a coppery-
bronze-coloured car, parked halfway down Brondesbury
Villas. Now he had only to get himself on the Harrow Road
or the Uxbridge Road for the airport signs to start coming
up. The rain was falling steadily, clearing the people off the
streets. At first he followed a bus route which he knew quite
well, down Kilburn High Road and off to the right past Kilburn Park Station. It was getting on for six-thirty but it
might have been midnight for all the people there were
about. The traffic was light too. Nigel thought he would get
the first flight available. It wouldn't matter where it was going—Amsterdam, Paris, Rome, from any of those places he
could get another to South America. His only worry was the
gun. They weren't going to let him on any aircraft with a
gun, not with all these hi-jackings. Did they have left-luggage places at Heathrow? If they did he'd put it in one, and
then, sometime, when it was safe and he was rich and had
all the guns he wanted, he'd come back and get it and keep
it as a souvenir, a memento of his first crime. But he
wouldn't go after Marty Foster with it, he wasn't worth the
hassle. Besides, thanks to his skiving off, hadn't he, Nigel,
pulled off the whole coup on his own and got all the loot for
himself?

When he got to the end of Cambridge Road, he wasn't
sure whether to go more or less straight on down Walterton
Road or to turn left into Shirland Road. Straight on, he
thought. So he turned right for the little bit preparatory to
taking Walterton and pulled up sharply behind a car stopped
suddenly on the amber light. Nigel had been sure the driver
was going to go on over and not stop, and the front bumper
of the Ford Escort was no more than an inch or two from
the rear bumper of the other car. Suppose he rolled back
when the lights went green?

There was nothing behind him. Nigel shoved the gear into reverse and stamped on the accelerator. The car shot forward with a surprisingly loud crash into the rear of the one in front, and Nigel gave a roar of rage. Once again he had got into the wrong gear by mistake.

In the other car, a lightweight Citroën Diane, were four people, all male and all staring at him out of the rear window and all mouthing things and shaking fists. The driver got out. He was a large heavily built black man of about Nigel's own age. This time Nigel got the gear successfully into reverse and backed fast. The man caught up with him and banged on the window, but Nigel started forward, nearly running him down, and screamed off in bottom gear across lights that had just turned red again, and straight off along Shirland Road into the hinterland of nowhere.

The Diane was following him. Nigel cursed and turned right and then left into a street of houses waiting to be demolished, their windows boarded up and their doors enclosed by sheets of corrugated iron. Why had he come down here? He must get back fast and try to find Kilburn Lane. The Diane was no longer behind him. He turned left again, and it was waiting for him, slung broadside across the narrow empty street where no one lived and only one lamp was lighted. The driver and the other three stood, making a kind of cordon across the street. Nigel stopped.

The driver came over to him, a white boy with him. Nigel wound down his window, there was nothing else for it.

"Look, man, you've caved my trunk in. How about that?"

"Yeah, how about that?" said the other. "What's with you, anyway, getting the hell out? You've dropped him right in it, you have. That's his old man's vehicle."

Nigel didn't say a word. He took the gun out of its holster and levelled it at them.

"Jesus," said the white man.

Nigel burst the car door open and came out at them, stalking them as they retreated. The other two were standing behind the Diane. One of them shouted something and began to run. Nigel panicked. He thought of the money and of help coming and his car trapped by that other car, and he raised the gun and squeezed the trigger. The shot missed the running man and struck the side of the Diane. He fired again, this time into one of the Diane's rear tyres, but now the trigger wouldn't move anymore. The jacket had gone back, leaving the barrel exposed, and the gun looked empty, must be empty. He stood, his arms spread, a choking feeling in his throat, and then he dropped the gun in the road and wheeled round back to the car.

The four men had all frozen at the sound of the shot and the splintering metal, even the running man. Now he came slowly back, looking at the useless weapon on the wet tarmac, while the others seemed to drop forward, their arms pendulous, like apes. Nigel pulled open the door of the Ford, but they were on him before he could get into it. The driver's white companion was the first to touch him. He swung his fist and got Nigel under the jaw. Nigel reeled back and slid down the dewed metal of the car, and two of them caught him by the arms.

They dragged him across the pavement and through a cavity in a broken wall where there had once been a gate. There they threw him against the brickwork front of the house and punched his face, and Nigel screamed, "Please!" and "Help me!" and lurched sideways across broken glass and corrugated iron. One of them had a heavy piece of metal in his fist, and Nigel felt it hammering his head as he sagged onto the wet grass and the others kicked his ribs. How long they went on he didn't know. Perhaps only until he stopped shouting and cursing them, twisting over and

over and trying to protect his bruised body in his hugging
arms. Perhaps only until he lost consciousness.

When he regained it he was lying up against the wall, and
he was one pain from head to foot. But there was another
and more dreadful all-conquering pain that made his head
and his neck red-hot. He moved a bruised cut hand to his
neck and felt there, embedded in his flesh, a long stiletto of
glass. He gave a whimper of horror.

By some gargantuan effort, he staggered to his feet. He
had been lying on a mass of splintered glass. His fingers
scrabbled at his neck and pulled out the long bloody sliver.
It was the sight of the blood all over him, seeping down his
jacket and through into his shirt, that felled him again. He
felt the blood pumping from the wound where the glass had
been, and he tried to cry out, but the sound came in a thin
strangled pipe.

Nigel had forgotten the car and the money and escape
and South America. He had forgotten the gun. Everything
had gone from his mind except the desire to live. He must
find the street and lights and help and someone to stop the
red stream leaking life out of his neck.

Round and round in feeble circles he crawled, ploughing
the earth with his hands. He found himself saying, mum-
bling, as Marty had said to him, "You wouldn't let me die,
you wouldn't let me die," and then, as Joyce had said,
"Please, please. . . ."

His progress, half on his hands and knees, half on his
belly, brought him onto concrete. The street. He was on the
pavement, he was going to make it. So he crawled on, looking for lights, on, on along the hard wet stone as the rain
came down.

The stone ended in grass. He tried to avoid the grass,
which shouldn't be in the street, which was wrong, a delu-
sion or a mirage of touch. His head blundered into a wooden

fence, at the foot of which soft cold things clustered. He lay there. The rain poured on him in cataracts, washing him clean.

Much later, in the small hours, a policeman on the beat found the abandoned car and the gun. Everything was still in the car as Nigel had left it, his rucksack and his carrier, his passport and the stolen money—six thousand, seven hundred and seventy-two pounds. The search for Nigel himself didn't last long, but he was dead before they reached him. He was lying in a back garden, and during that long wet night snails had crept along the strands of his wet golden hair.

25

When the train had gone and Paul hadn't come, Una went back to Montcalm Gardens. Whatever it was that had "come up" had detained him. They could go by a later train, though they would have no seat reservations. Una decided not to indulge in wild speculations. Ambrose said these were among the most destructive of fantasies, and that one should repeat to oneself when inclined to indulge in them, that most of the things one has worried about have never happened. Besides (he said) it was always fruitless to imagine things outside our own experience. One thing to visualise a car crash or some kind of assault if we have ourselves experienced such a thing, or if one of our friends has, quite another if such imaginings are drawn, as they usually are, from fictional accounts. Una had never known anyone who had been killed in a car crash or mugged or fallen under a train. Her experience of accidents was that her child had been burnt to death.

She made a cup of tea and washed the teacup and tidied the kitchen again. The phone rang, but it was a wrong number. At seven she read the note again. Paul's handwriting wasn't very clear and that five could be an eight. Suppose he had thought the train went at eight-thirty, not five-thirty? He had been so preoccupied and strange these past few days that he might have thought that. Una combed her hair and put on her raincoat, and this time she took a taxi, not a bus, to Paddington. Paul wasn't there.

Although there was a later train, she took her case out of the left-luggage locker where she had left it at five-thirty, because she felt that to do so was to yield to, not tempt, Providence. The curious ways of Providence were such that if you bought an umbrella you got a heat wave for a month, and if you lugged a load of luggage from a station to you home, you were bound to have to take it back again. This thought cheered her, and by the time the taxi was taking her back through the stair-rod rain in the Bayswater Road she had convinced herself that Paul would be waiting for her in Montcalm Gardens with a long story of some tiresome happening that had held him up.

Her first real fear came when she got in and he wasn't there. She went down into the basement and found the bottles he had left outside Caesar's door with a note to Caesar to have them. Caesar hadn't come home, he had gone straight to Annie's. Una poured herself some brandy. It nearly knocked her over because she hadn't eaten since one. They had planned to eat dinner on the train. She tried to obey Ambrose's injunction not to think of imaginary disasters, and told herself that no one gets mugged in the afternoon or falls under trains unless they want to or has a car crash if they don't have a car.

But then her own experience of life showed her what could have happened. Neo-Empiricism, applied by her, showed her what men sometimes did and where men sometimes went after they had left notes and gone out alone. She pushed the thought away. He would phone, and then he would come. She took a piece of cheese out of the fridge and cut a slice off the new loaf she had bought for Ambrose. She tried to eat and she succeeded, but it was like chewing sawdust and then chewing the cud.

At ten she was in his empty room, looking at the tallboy in which there had been papers or letters or photographs he hadn't wanted her to see. It frightened her now that he had left his keys, though what more natural than that he should leave them?

While she had been out that afternoon he must have had a phone call. She knew who would have phoned, perhaps the only person to whom he had given this number. Hadn't she phoned once before to make an appointment? Since that appointment, that visit, Paul had been a changed man. Una went upstairs and sat in the immaculate exquisite drawing room. She picked up the phone to see if it was out of order, but the dialling tone grated at her. Stewart's letter was up on the mantelpiece. She had left it there for Ambrose to read. Now she read it again herself, the bit about hoping she would be happy with her new man.

For a while she sat there, listening to the rain that beat steadily against the windows and thinking that it was a long time since it had rained like that, a month surely. A month ago she hadn't even known Paul. She got out the phone directory. His name on the page made her shiver. Browning, Paul R., 15 Exmoor Gardens, N.W.2. She looked hard at his name on the page and touched the phone and paced the length of the room and back again. Then, quickly, she dialled the number. It rang, three times, four times. Just as she thought no one was going to answer, the ringing stopped and a woman's voice said:

"Hallo. Alison Browning."

"Is Mr. Paul Browning there, please?"

"Who is that speaking?"

She had been told, hadn't she? It wouldn't be a revelation. And yet . . . "I'm a friend of his. Is he there?"

"My husband is in bed, asleep. Do you know what time it is?"

Una put the receiver back. For a while she lay on the floor. Then she went upstairs and got into bed in the room where she hadn't slept for three weeks. Three weeks was no time, nothing, a nice period for an adventure or an interlude. It is anxiety, not sorrow, which banishes sleep, and at last Una slept.

She had never had a newspaper delivered since Ambrose went. Not since Christmas had she heard the sound the thick wad of newsprint made, flopping through the letter box onto the mat. Any sound from the front door would last night have made hope spring, but no longer.

Una went downstairs and picked up the paper. The headlines said, *Joyce Alive* and *Bank Girl Recovers in Hospital*, and there was a big photograph of a girl on a stretcher. But it was the other photograph, of a man in a garden with a woman and an older man, which caught Una's eye because the man looked a little like Paul. But any man, she thought, with wistful eyes and a gentle mouth would remind her of Paul. It was bound to happen. She went into the drawing room and read the paper to pass the time.

. . . The nature of Alan Groombridge's wounds have made police believe he died protecting Joyce. She regained consciousness soon after being admitted to hospital. Her head injury is only superficial, says the doctor attending her, and her loss of memory is due to shock. She has no memory of the shooting or of events of the past month in which she and Mr. Groombridge were held prisoners in a second-floor rented room in North London. . . .

Una read the rest of it, turned the page, waiting for Ambrose to come.